LONGBRIDGE ADMINISTRATION PERSONNEL

THOMAS LONGBRIDGE
President of the United States and former Texas Governor

SETH HARRINGTON:
The President's closest unofficial advisor and longtime friend. Lifelong Christian evangelist and founder/chairman of Christians for a Moral America (CMA). Texas native. His special assistant and errand boy is Archibald "Arch" Leopold.

THOMAS STREETER:
U.S. Attorney General and head of U.S. Justice Department. Appointed on Seth Harrington's recommendation by President Longbridge. Texas native and Longbridge ally during his days as Governor.

TRAVIS CULPEPPER:
U.S. Secretary of State. Virginia native. The only cabinet member retained by President Longbridge from the prior administration and the only significant Longbridge appointment made against Harrington's insistent disapproval.

CHASE FALKINGHAM:
U.S. Supreme Court Justice

FEDERAL BUREAU OF INVESTIGATION PERSONNEL

LAWRENCE "LARRY" CHAPMAN:
FBI Director, appointed upon Harrington's recommendation by President Longbridge.

GUS SWANSON:
FBI Agent and chief renegade investigator of the conspiracy he suspects is taking place within the Longbridge administration.

BEN HARVEY:
Swanson's longtime friend and FBI Agent who joins in the investigation. Also Manhattan's Special Agent-in-Charge of apprehending and/or preventing Mayson Corelli from leaving New York.

PETE NICHOLS:
Swanson's and Harvey's Bureau adversary. Director Chapman's loyal protégé and Agent-in-Charge of the mission to apprehend and/or kill Corelli and Waddill.

Ed "Posterboy" Bilbro: Senior Partner

Tyler Waddill: Associate

Mayson Angelina Corelli: Associate

LIEBER ALLEN ATTORNEYS

GREGORY LAMP:
Managing Partner and nominee for Associate Justice of U.S. Supreme Court

MORRIS MENDELSOHN:
Senior Partner, murdered.

ED "POSTER BOY" BILBRO:
Senior Partner

TYLER WADDILL:
Associate

MAYSON ANGELINA CORELLI:
Associate

THE
LONGBRIDGE
DECISION

★

THE LONGBRIDGE DECISION

★

THE LONGBRIDGE DECISION

★

ROBERT M. BROWN, JR.

GREAT LITTLE BOOKS

Great Little Books, LLC.
Glen Rock, New Jersey

Any dialogue or behavior ascribed to the characters in this book is entirely fictitious.

2010 Great Little Books, LLC Hardcover Edition

Copyright @ 2010 by Robert M. Brown, Jr.

All rights reserved. No part of this book may be reproduced or transmitted in any form or by any means electronic or mechanical, including photocopying, recording, or by any information storage and retrieval system, without written permission from the publisher.

Jacket and book design by Dom Rodi

Published in the United States by Great Little Books, LLC

Distributed by Midpoint Trade Books, Inc.

Publisher's Cataloging-In-Publication Data
(Prepared by The Donohue Group, Inc.)

Brown, Robert M. (Robert Mason), 1951-

The Longbridge decision / Robert M. Brown, Jr.

p. ; cm.

ISBN: 978-0-9790661-5-3

1. Murder--Fiction. 2. Politics--United States--Fiction. 3. United States. Supreme Court--Fiction. 4. Religion and politics--United States--Fiction. 5. Mystery fiction. I. Title.

PS3602.R726 L66 2010
813/.6

Printed in China on acid-free paper

www.greatlittlebooksllc.com   www.thelongbridgedecision.com

★

I dedicate this book to our son, R. Mason Brown, III, whose courageous recovery from substance abuse and alcoholism, and his genuine commitment to a new life through his strong Christian faith, has not only made Anne and me both tremendously proud, but has served as an inspiration and stronger commitment of our own lives to our own faith.

ACKNOWLEDGMENTS

I wish to acknowledge and thank my loving, beautiful wife, Anne, and my wonderful son, Mason, for their patience, support and understanding during the long hours necessary to complete this challenging literary project -- hours that, under other circumstances, would have been devoted to them. Thanks, guys, for your tremendous sacrifices on my behalf.

I cannot say enough about my publisher, Great Little Books, LLC, for recognizing and appreciating my literary potential and then demonstrating the courage, commitment, and entrepreneurial savvy to invest its financial and human resources in my first novel's publication. Without GLB it would never have happened.

And to GLB's principals, Linda Dini Jenkins and Barbara Worton, two very classy ladies and enormously talented writers themselves: thank you for your infinite energy and the many hours you devoted to this novel's publication. Along the way, you educated me on the complex but fascinating process of book editing, printing, publication, distribution, promoting and marketing. To their respective spouses, Tim and Geoff, I also wish to express my appreciation: to Tim, for the most entertaining and educational tour of Manhattan I'm sure I'll ever experience; and to Geoff, for his wonderful sense of humor and faithful laughter at my often lame attempts to be funny.

Many thanks, of course, to Dom Rodi, for his artistic magic which graces the book's cover and his creative contribution to the book's title. Dom's talent is exceeded only by his soft spoken kindness and generosity.

Thanks also to Glenna Dowdy and Pat Collins, both good friends and former colleagues: to Glenna, for helping name "Mayson" and to Pat, whose assistance with the Italian vernacular truly made Mayson Corelli come to life. Gratitude is also due Deborah MacDonald and Pat Fielder, good friends whose encouragement and enthusiasm for my writing kept me going through those dark, gloomy days every writer experiences from time to time.

Finally I wish to acknowledge my deep indebtedness and undying gratitude to my good friend and Hilton Village Office pal, Jerry Fitz-Patrick, for introducing me to Linda Dini Jenkins and GLB. Thanks, Jerry, for opening that seemingly impenetrable first door to book publication.

CHAPTER ONE

★

Rumbling voices greeted Mayson Corelli as she entered the firm's library. Carefully averting her eyes, she drifted towards the back corner. That she ignored the others was hardly suspicious. They existed only as instruments necessary to her law practice. And she certainly never mingled in the groups milling around her now.

From her safe corner she watched them spill into the library; partners, associates, secretaries; everyone summoned to the emergency meeting. Yet who didn't already know? Isn't that what they were all whispering about? Lieber Allen, if not Wall Street's largest law firm, was without question its most prestigious. She'd been here two years and never once doubted that she'd also retire here, perhaps as Managing Partner like Greg Lamp, if she was lucky. There was no question about the will that had gotten her here, when to even dream such a thing had seemed foolish. Yet she'd defied the odds and at age twenty-seven had no intention of leaving, under any circumstances . . . even those she'd stumbled upon last night.

She felt so little emotion anymore. It hadn't always been that way, but now she wore masks in place of emotions, which was tolerable so long as she knew which one to wear. She didn't now. What was called for — shock, indignation, sadness? Shouldn't they all run through her? And yet not one of these scratched at her hardened heart. Just fear, like a chilling wind rattling in the darkness. And the cold voice that whispered: The one who threatened you is dead. Avoid the cloud of suspicion that may blow your way. Don't get trapped. Her eyes lifted as the crowd's rumble died. Greg Lamp entered the library, striding stiffly to the front podium, a distinct air about him.

"As you've no doubt heard," Lamp marched gravely into the silence. "Morris Mendelsohn was found in his Manhattan apartment last evening, the victim of an apparent homicide. NYPD detectives are pursuing leads and seem confident a suspect will be charged soon . . ."

How soon? Mayson's stomach knotted. How confident? And what leads? Was this a ruse or did the NYPD really have a suspect?

"These detectives are with us this morning," Lamp revealed. "They'll spend the day at the firm learning what they can about Morris's practice and talking with those of us who worked with him. Please give them your full cooperation."

As Lamp fielded the questions that came forward, Mayson wondered why they would start here at the firm. Is this where they expected to find their suspect? They'd most likely question her first. How would she hold up? Was she already a suspect? Did they know about her connection to The Lips? Her eyes collided suddenly with Tyler Waddill's.

"That's all we know at this point," Lamp said, concluding his briefing. "Just please give the detectives your full cooperation and hopefully Morris's murderer will be apprehended soon."

As he left, the crowd began drifting toward the doors.

"Excuse me. Do I know you?"

Mayson turned at the familiar irritation; Tyler Waddill, tall and handsome with his tangled, gold hair and eyes as deeply blue as the James River that spawned such snotty creatures. For Tyler life was a cocktail party, its infinite pleasures no farther away than the nearest buffet table.

"Forgive me, Mayson," he apologized. "For a moment, I had mistaken you for a human being."

"Why were you leering at me?" she snapped irritably.

"I wasn't."

"Don't pretend not to know what I'm talking about."

"There!" He nodded. "I definitely saw it that time."

"What?"

"Emotion. My God, Mayson, you're human after all."

She became conscious of the silence, realizing they were suddenly alone in the vast, quiet world of law books, mahogany tables and crystal chandeliers. "You want emotion, Tyler? Try hatred, contempt, disgust. The very sight of you can have me drowning in emotions!" With another icy glare she brushed past him.

"Mayson, what are you afraid of?" he asked.

Freezing, she glanced at Mrs. Nordfelt nose deep in her index cards, a pair of associates researching at a nearby table. "I need your opinion on something." He led her back into the bookshelves. Grabbing an ancient case reporter, he began flipping pages. "You're afraid. Why?"

"I'm not afraid," she whispered. "And I resent being dragged back here to explain myself. And who do you think you're fooling anyway? No one believes you read anything in here."

Shutting the book, he studied her intently. He'd never seen her like this. She was usually in control, but she wasn't now.

"Quit leering at me!" she snapped and again started away.

"Mayson, we need to talk."

Did he know something about the murder? No, it was a trick. "We have nothing to say to each other. Now leave me alone. I have to get back to work."

"Where?" he asked, returning the book to the shelf. "I mean, what are we supposed to do? Morris was our slave master but he's gone."

"You idiot," she huffed. "We're not slaves on your Tidewater plantation. This is Wall Street. And just because Morris is dead doesn't mean our assignments simply drift on down the Swanee River."

His expression didn't change with her ridicule. If she was angry, it had nothing to do with him. "Mayson, you must work hard at isolating yourself from the human race. You're quite good at it."

"Go to Hell!" She stormed off.

He caught her at the elevator. "I don't know who you think you're impressing with that shit."

Angrily she stabbed for the elevator, catching the solemn faces around her. They were in mourning, she remembered, groping for the appropriate mask.

With growing irritation, he watched the panel glow with each stop. Why did the Metropolitan, Wall Street's oldest building, also have its slowest elevators? Beside him, Mayson's eyes had become pained. "What's wrong?" he asked.

"It just really hit me that Morris is dead. We worked together for two years. He taught me so much. His poor sister in Connecticut

— what she must be going through."

This was an act, he realized, as the elevator arrived. She was covering her tracks.

"I admit Morris had his faults," she said, resuming her eulogy on the climb to Fifty-Eight. "But deep down, he was a decent, honest . . ."

"He was a prick, Mayson. You know that better than anyone. And although he didn't deserve to die, that doesn't mean we should bury ourselves in bullshit making him something he wasn't."

"And you think I'm emotionless?" she scowled. "How can you have so little sympathy for a man who was just murdered and discarded like trash in his ransacked apartment?"

"Ransacked? Who said anything about the condition of Morris's apartment?"

As the elevator opened she streaked off. "Damnit Mayson!" Catching her down the hall, he quickly pulled her into a supply room.

"Get your hands off me!"

"Tell me about Morris's ransacked apartment."

Ransacked. How could she have been so stupid?

"Now Mayson, how did you know about the apartment?"

"I . . . heard it on the news . . . this morning."

"What station?"

"I don't know . . . WNYC maybe."

"You were at Morris's apartment last night, weren't you?"

She gaped at him. Did he really expect her to admit it? "Let me go!"

He held her firmly. "You knew Morris's practice better than anyone. They'll question you first. Don't underestimate them, Mayson. These guys are pros."

As he released her, she opened the door and fled down the hall. Jill Allen met him as he slipped out. She'd been at Sylvia Lee's desk when first Mayson, then Tyler, streaked past. Following, she'd caught their agitated whispers behind the supply room door. "What's going on?" she asked.

"Beats the hell out of me." He started away, quietly anticipating her inevitable patter. Jill was his clinging vine; pretty with flowing, auburn hair and emerald eyes. They'd arrived at Lieber Allen the same Monday in May, shared the first harrowing weeks of Wall Street Law and, on several occasions, his bed. They'd helped each other through the first grueling, fourteen-hour days and together made a difficult adjustment tolerable. Then the relationship had ended — for him, but unfortunately, not her. He was sorry; he liked Jill. He liked a lot of people. Mayson Corelli wasn't one of them.

"Tyler, what's wrong with Mayson?" Jill asked.

"I guess she's upset. She was closer to Morris than anyone else."

"Which means she had more reason to hate him and did; only that hate will quickly evaporate when the cops question her. Morris will become her mentor. Maybe she'll even work herself into tears. Can you imagine that — Mayson Corelli crying?"

Not until this morning, he thought. But now he wasn't so sure.

"Do you have lunch plans?" Jill asked as he started off again. "The Deli at noon . . . ?"

Turning the corner at the end of the hall, Tyler reached Mayson's office and stopped. She stood over her desk, quietly studying a phone slip. Her large, dark eyes lifted to find him in the doorway. She had a delicate face, her skin creamy soft as if dipped in the oils of a pink rose before being spread over the exquisite angles and precise features. Lush, dark hair tumbled at her slender neck. With a smile she could've been My Fair Lady. "Your call upstairs?" he asked. As she nodded, he slipped inside and closed the door.

"You got back quickly," she said. "Squeal and peel — is that how it works?"

"What are you talking about?"

"Stool pigeons. If you've returned for a confession, you're wasting your time."

It was difficult to grasp the extent of her paranoia. "I'll state my piece, then leave. You're on your own after that."

"I've always been on my own. What's in this for you, Tyler — my job?"

"You're crazy, Mayson."

"Get out!" she snapped.

"Look, if you want to go to prison that's fine. Only before putting yourself under the microscope, you should realize those cops either know, or will soon, that you hated Morris's guts and had every reason to. The Lambrusco case was going to be your debut — and in the New York Supreme Court, of all places. An appeal that was sure to have an impact on commercial law and, in the process, become a featured article in every major bar journal. Winning would've brought you national recognition. In a year you would've made partner. Lambrusco's a golden opportunity and after busting your ass, you'd earned it."

He sighed. "Mayson, you're the best associate in this firm. Smart and hardworking, but also such a damned pain in the ass that no one cared when Morris took Lambrusco from you. But they will soon. I mean those cops upstairs, when they learn that the man they found last night with a bullet in his head is the same one who stripped you of your biggest case. . . And it gets worse, doesn't it? The prick didn't just take it away; he gave it to another far less deserving associate. Me, specifically. Morris gave me all your hard work on a silver platter."

Her glare frosted him. "Hasn't everything in your life been served on a silver platter?" she asked. "You'd hardly been here long enough to break a sweat. All you've done besides bedding every pretty face, a breach of firm policy no one seems to care about, is steal the fruits of my labor. Your career path has been shortened and mine lengthened, if it even still exists. But what's really ironic is that you don't even need this job. You must have millions socked away in some family trust fund. But here you are to rob me of the one thing I have in this world: my job, which means everything to me."

"And this obviously makes you very mad."

"Mad?" Her nostrils flared. "Morris ripped my heart out! Humiliated me! I could've . . .!"

He glanced at her clenched fists. "What? Killed him?"

The morning's second slip. Her fingers sprung to her lips. How many more would she commit with the cops upstairs? Her rage vented, she sighed with despair. "I worked so hard for him. He won cases on the arguments I crafted. I made him shine and not once did he acknowledge my work. He had no right to treat me that way."

He sensed her need to cry. Did she ever? What did it take to reduce cold Mayson Corelli to tears? "No," his eyes softened. "Morris had no right to treat you that way. And when I realized what he was doing, it made me sick."

Her eyes widened. "What did you realize?"

"Look, we don't have time to discuss it. You need to get upstairs. There's just one more thing. Morris called me last night, but I wasn't home. He left two messages: the first at eight, the second twenty minutes later. I discovered them when I got in around midnight."

Her heart pounded. She should've known these calls would be made, and what must certainly be coming next. Months ago her life, though empty, had at least been safe, charted. But almost overnight Morris's advances became more insistent, to the point where she was no longer able to brush them off.

Babe, you're doing so well. Don't screw it up.
You mean by screwing you?
I mean that I've been good to you. I gave you Lambrusco.
I earned Lambrusco.
I could give you bigger projects.
If I become your puttana?
Babe, you put words in my mouth I don't even understand.
It means whore. And here's another: gavonne. *I should tell Lamp what a gavonne I work for.*
That'd be stupid, Babe. You don't want to stake your credibility against a senior partner's.

No, she didn't. She'd wanted to practice law but Morris was making it impossible.

Babe, I could take away Lambrusco.
You wouldn't dare.
Try me.

She had and he did. Their arguments became more violent. *Screw you, you* gavonne!

Wrong words, Babe, if you expect me to dump Tyler.

She'd refused to give him the right ones and now suddenly he was dead. Yet nothing had changed. If one threat had been eliminated, another had taken its place. "Tyler, why tell me about these calls?"

"Because you can't dodge a bullet unless you know where it's coming from."

"And why should I expect a bullet?"

"In his first call, Morris said he had some emergency. He wanted me to pick him up at the Essex. But in the second call his agitation was gone. He said not to call back because he'd found someone else to pick him up, someone on the way at that moment. You, Mayson, you're the one he told me was coming. I assume you arrived before ten when the cops discovered his body and ransacked apartment?"

"He didn't call me! I wasn't . . ." Her eyes shot to the ringing phone then the opening door. Nicole Martin's suspicious glare shifted from her to Tyler. Heart in her throat, she snatched up the phone.

"Mayson, didn't you get my message?" an irritated Lamp asked. "We're waiting on you upstairs."

His secretary and Tyler in her office, the cops upstairs — who should she be more afraid of? Did it matter? Weren't they all on the same team; in a game played by their rules? Rule number one: A Corelli, no matter what the stakes, will always lose.

She was losing now.

CHAPTER TWO

★

A lump crept up Mayson's throat as the elevator rose.

At the sixty-fifth floor, she was expelled like a dazed alien on a foreign planet. She'd been here once before, but not like this. Power scented the air, heavy, gripping, close. It was eternally quiet here. Where power rested, loud voices were superfluous. This was the Inner Sanctum, where the Game of Law was played. The winners dwelled here. Morris had been on the team; until last night when he'd wandered into the wrong game. Now he was dead.

At the end of the hall, a stern-faced Nicole ushered her into the conference room. Greg Lamp, trim and elegant in his gray suit, sprung up as she entered. His silver hair was meticulous, his patrician face bronzed, his eyes azure; not Tyler's river-blue, but the blue of an overcast day. A half-moon scar cast the right eye in a perpetual smile, only he wasn't smiling now as he introduced the two detectives at the table.

"Lieutenant Duke," he indicated the fat, bald one, with the porcine face and beady eyes. "And Sergeant Santinez," the darker, thinner man.

Nodding coldly, she dropped into a chair across the table. Lamp took the one beside her. "Mayson, I've already explained that you were Morris's associate and therefore knew more than anyone else about his practice." He glanced at Duke. "Morris entrusted her with his most sensitive cases."

"Until recently anyway," she added.

"What happened?" Santinez asked.

She cringed. Ten seconds in the room and already she'd stuck her foot in her mouth. "Nothing really; associates are often shuffled between partners."

"Then you were recently 'shuffled' to another partner?"

Lamp's comforting hand settled on her shoulder, "About a month ago, Morris secured another young thoroughbred for his stable. He saw vast potential in Tyler Waddill, who'd just completed a Supreme Court clerkship before arriving in May. That's not to say Mayson doesn't possess tremendous potential herself. But Morris sometimes, well . . ."

"Sometimes what?" Santinez prodded.

"Made hasty judgments especially where people were concerned. Tyler was given Mayson's most important projects, a move I wasn't particularly happy about." Glancing at her, he asked, "Which appeal were you working on? The one scheduled for argument in a few weeks?"

"Lambrusco," she glared at him. Why all this detail? Santinez's question had hardly demanded it.

"Lambrusco yes," he nodded. "It presents a commercial law issue the Bar is following closely." He frowned. "Mayson was scheduled to argue it until its reassignment to Tyler. And she'd earned the opportunity with her hard work. I'm sure she considers it a setback but she'll recover. Her record suggests an uncommon resilience."

Santinez, detecting her irritation, wasn't so sure. "How about it, Miss Corelli? Were you mad at Mendelsohn over this appeal?"

"I wasn't happy about it, obviously."

"Did you two discuss the transfer?"

"I can't recall."

"But Mr. Lamp just said the decision was made last month. Even I can remember that far back."

She glanced now at Santinez's silent, pig-faced partner. Her instincts told her he was the one to fear. "We discussed the need for Tyler, which included Lambrusco, but the details I just don't recall." That was her first reconstruction of events. She'd blasted Morris repeatedly over Lambrusco and recalled every Italian curse she'd uttered. Their arguments had started calmly, ended violently. Finally an arctic silence had settled over their relationship, until he left on his Outer Banks vacation.

"You and Mendelsohn argued over Waddill?" Santinez asked.

"Discussed." Her eyes chilled. "Don't start putting words in my mouth."

He smiled at his taciturn partner. "I must remember we're interrogating lawyers . . . You're from Brooklyn, Miss Corelli?"

"Aren't all Italian girls?"

"Not all Italian girls look like you. *Bellissima,* I mean." Smiling at Lamp's confusion, he added, "*Bellissima* is Italian for very beautiful; a term that describes Miss Corelli better . . ."

"For Christ's sake, we're not voting for Homecoming Queen! We're looking for a murderer."

All eyes shot to Duke, who'd woken from his nap; quite irritably, too. Pudgy hands clasped, he leaned forward, "Miss Corelli, let's not waste any more time. I'll tell you what I think. You be just as candid and we'll get through this quickly . . . I think your relationship with Mendelsohn deteriorated the moment Waddill was assigned to your hard-earned projects. You were furious and in your shoes, I'd feel the same way. The question is how furious and what you might've done about it."

Clearly Duke was dangerous. Drop a heavy word like 'ransacked' and it'd be over soon. "As I said, we discussed the change. And because Morris was the boss, the decision stood. End of story."

"The end of your advancement at Lieber Allen, you mean?"

"Hardly," she smiled. "I'm uncommonly resilient. Just ask Mr. Lamp."

"You may be resilient, but losing Lambrusco was certainly a major setback. You'd worked too hard to let Mendelsohn snatch it away. You argued. He defended. Then what?"

"Nothing," she shrugged. "Having Tyler proved an advantage, allowing me to ease my pace. And although Lambrusco is an important case, there'll be others. I'll get one." And with Morris gone, the odds had definitely improved.

"Come on, Miss Corelli, you don't expect us to believe you were that accommodating?"

Her eyes fell as he flipped through his file. Morris had hardly been dead twelve hours. How had Duke accumulated so much paper? He now asked, "Why did Mendelsohn take Lambrusco and the other assignments from you?"

"I don't know."

"Your boss takes away two years of your hard work to benefit some guy who's been around six months and you don't know why?"

"He didn't give me his reason. What can I say?"

"Was he pressuring you for sexual favors?"

Not sexual favors, she thought. He wanted to fuck me. The word was disgusting, but so had been Morris's mistreatment. She was glad he was dead. "Morris never pressured me for sex. And the word is 'harassment' if you want to be legally correct." That was her second factual reconstruction.

Gravely, Duke glanced at Lamp. He didn't believe her. Scanning his file, he started down another path, "Did you know Mendelsohn had returned early from the Outer Banks?"

"No." Her third factual reconstruction.

"You didn't know that?"

"That's what I said, isn't it?"

"Are you sure?"

"Do you plan on asking every question three times now?"

He didn't answer, nor did he have to. He was the cop; she, the Corelli.

"Mendelsohn didn't call you when he returned?"

The question had Tyler written all over it. He'd told them about Morris's calls last night. Why else would Duke be starting down this road? "No, he didn't call. And why would he? We were furious, don't you remember?"

"I said you were furious. Then you didn't talk to him last night?"

"That's right."

"Nor were you at his apartment?"

"No, I wasn't."

"How about before last night?"

"No."

Duke smiled skeptically. "You worked together two years and never once visited his apartment?"

"That's right."

"Did he ever invite you?"

"I don't recall."

"Come on, Miss Corelli, if he'd invited you to his home, you'd remember."

"I don't." She was a suspect. That was painfully clear. Based on what — Lambrusco? Sexual favors? But they'd need more than motive to charge her.

"You've never been to the Essex to visit Mendelsohn or anyone else?" Duke asked.

"Never." Another factual reconstruction.

"Do you know where it is?"

"Ninety-Sixth?"

"Close," he smiled. "Ninety-Third."

What now? She studied him across the table. His eyes were like black gumdrops, deeply set in his fat face. They revealed nothing, yet absorbed everything.

"You didn't have a key to Mendelsohn's apartment?" he asked.

"No . . ." It remained in her purse, a detail she'd overlooked last night.

"What about the parking garage?"

Her eyes widened. "Morris's building has its own garage?"

"Yes Miss Corelli, you know it does."

Poor lighting and narrow ramps, too - a creepy place at night. Yes, she knew. "My building doesn't have a garage. I pay for the privilege of parking four blocks away."

"The Essex garage has eight levels including the basement. But you already knew that."

"How would I?" She used the basement, the same as Morris. It had a laundromat and adjoining lounge, TV-equipped, to catch the news while folding clothes.

"You've obviously forgotten our ground rules. We were going to be candid, remember?"

"I've never seen the Essex basement, its eight-level garage, lobby or anything else it might have. Nor have I seen Morris's apartment. And I certainly don't have a key. I can't be any more candid than that."

Duke's black eyes absorbed more details she couldn't see. He didn't believe her factual reconstructions, nor did Lamp, now watching her intently. Lamp knew associates did more for their partners than make them look good in court. They ran errands. So how in two years as Morris's Girl Friday had she avoided even one trip to his apartment?

Duke flipped through his file again. Where now, she wondered? Was she stumbling deeper into a trap she couldn't see? Santinez, at Duke's shoulder, nodded, "There."

Finally Duke looked up. "Essex residents have provided descriptions of people in the building last night. Several reported seeing a woman between 8:00 and 9:00; slender build, medium height, dark hair and eyes, mid-to-late twenties. Three had seen her before. All stated without prompting that she was uncommonly attractive. 'Bellissima.' And they're right, Miss Corelli. You're a very beautiful woman."

It was an indictment, not a compliment. Finally she knew where they were going. "It wasn't me, Lieutenant. As I've said, I wasn't at the Essex last night."

"Then where were you?"

"At home, like other law-abiding citizens."

"Can anyone corroborate this?"

"I live alone."

He didn't ask for the address. He either had it already or would soon. He'd assemble her life's details, like he did every murder suspect. He'd discover her connection to The Lips.

"If you were home last night, Miss Corelli, it wasn't between 8:00 and 9:00. During that period you were visiting Mendelsohn. The only question is whether he was still alive when you left."

Would she leave this room with her freedom or not? That the morning was slipping away no longer mattered. "The Essex must have many apartments, Lieutenant The woman you've described could've been visiting any one of them."

"Not any, Miss Corelli, just one. And she didn't use the building's lobby," Duke explained. "That's because the guard might've recognized her. He's good with faces. Certainly she knew this, which explains why she entered through the basement. There's a laundromat and adjoining lounge, with a TV, snack and soda machines and several storage rooms. And two elevators — one for residents, one for freight. Why she used the freight elevator is no great mystery. It's not programmed like the other to stop in the lobby. By using it, she was able to bypass the lobby and our eagle-eyed guard. It also means she knew the building well and could access something most residents can't."

Why? She wondered. A simple pass code was all it took. The custodian had shown her how to access the elevator one afternoon when she'd been burdened with two laundry baskets and a jug of detergent. He'd seen how flustered she was and felt sorry for her. Yet more than flustered, she'd been humiliated. A Columbia honors graduate, she'd passed the Bar, then landed an associate position with Lieber Allen — and for what? To wash Morris Mendelsohn's socks and shorts? She'd done far more than most associates, yet received not one ounce of gratitude; just humbling domestic servitude, as much as he could pile on. When she protested, his line was always the same: *I earned my keep the same way, Babe. Three years I put up with Saul Goldstein's crap; picking up his dry cleaning, shining his shoes. At least I don't make you do that.*

No, I wash your socks and shorts. And I bet Saul Goldstein never hounded you for sex.

Sex; what are you talking about? Hey, I'm redecorating my apartment. I want your opinion.

You just finished redecorating your apartment. I met the workmen every day for two weeks.

Don't complain, Babe. Being the partner's lackey is the initiation rite of every associate. Live with it. Then watch it pay off when you're a partner making six figures. So that opinion on my apartment — how about tonight?'

Go to Hell!

Listen Babe, these tantrums are getting old. You're wound too tight. Maybe the work's more than you can handle. I may add a new associate; taking Lambrusco and a few other cases off your shoulders.

Don't threaten me, Morris!

No threat, just a partner's prerogative. So how about tonight — Manhattan's finest veal cutlets?

Screw you! I could kill you!

I'm sure, Babe. The Lips must've taught you well. But that'd be stupid; and stupid you're not.

What would he say after last night? Hadn't she proven her stupidity in those terrible dark hours? Or would she somehow escape this predicament that seemed to worsen by the second?

Duke studied her in the deepening silence. This was a game he must enjoy immensely, where the puzzle's pieces were laid out and connected. When they were all in place the game was over, the case solved. Truth was irrelevant as long as the pieces fit. He said now, "The picture's quite clear, Miss Corelli, don't you agree?

Garage to basement; freight elevator to the fifth floor; down the hall to Mendelsohn's apartment; a quick escape along the same route. Two keys: one to enter the building, the other for the apartment. The pass code for the freight elevator. It was a good plan except for one thing. She forgot about the laundromat."

Not forgot, Lieutenant, just prayed it wasn't in use.

"Residents in the laundromat saw her enter and exit the same way; between eight and nine, as I said. The first patrol car arrived at ten to discover the body." He sighed, "Too bad those residents weren't as curious as Mrs. Carter. Otherwise they might've followed her out and seen the car she escaped in."

Mayson's hands trembled now, a gesture that didn't escape his sharp eyes. "Mrs. Carter?"

"Mendelsohn's neighbor. She heard someone in the hall around nine and assuming it was her niece, unlatched the door. Only it wasn't her niece but the young woman, whom she observed rush down to Mendelsohn's apartment, unlock the door and slip inside. She'd seen the very attractive, dark-haired, slender young woman there many times before. She'd seen you, Miss Corelli, don't we know that now?"

In frustration she sighed. "How many times must I say it? I've never been to the Essex or used its freight elevators, laundromats or garages. The residents, including Mrs. Carter, didn't see me last night or any other time. You've obviously confused me with one of the other fifty thousand dark-haired, dark-eyed, slender young women in Manhattan."

Santinez smiled, "In that fifty thousand, there couldn't be more than a handful as beautiful as you. Five residents; five very attractives."

"Which proves what?" she huffed. "Has it occurred to you that Morris's murderer, if a female, might have been a burglar? Certainly Manhattan has more than its share."

"Burglars don't usually have keys," Duke replied. "Or take time while lifting jewelry and silver to ransack the place."

'Ransack,' her word, now Duke's. Didn't this confirm Tyler was working for them?

"If valuables were taken, more were left behind," Duke explained. "A wallet with five hundred dollars, a slew of credit cards and two Rolex watches."

Only the gold-banded one was real; the other was a fifty-dollar-special Morris had gotten in a shop in Greenwich Village.

"No, the killer was looking for something specific," Duke said. "And with some secret value far greater than Rolex watches and silver sets. My guess is he didn't find it. What's your take, Miss Corelli?"

Another punctuating pause, one seized by Santinez. "The apartment was ripped to shreds, everything left where the hurricane dropped it. You should've seen the place."

"Oh, but she did," Duke nodded. "Didn't you, Miss Corelli?"

"Perhaps the killer was looking for a document," Lamp emerged, as if from under a rock. "Possibly one connected with Morris's law practice."

"We brought the recovered boxes of records in this morning," Santinez explained. "They should be inventoried just like his records here."

Lamp's hand settled again on Mayson's shoulder. "Frieda and Tyler are doing that now. They should be finished this afternoon. They'll need Mayson's help analyzing it. No one knew his practice like she did."

Which was why she, not Tyler, should be conducting the inventory. What would emerge that hadn't existed before last night? Was some document being manufactured that fingered her as Morris's killer? Fear shuddered her spine as Lamp added, "Morris's litigation involved large stakes. It's not difficult to imagine some desperate party stealing documents or even committing murder to save themselves."

Mayson glared at him, incredulous. Morris's world was inhabited by lawyers and business executives, not dangerous hoodlums who ripped up people's apartments.

"What about Morris's probate practice?" Lamp asked her. "Some of those will contests involve enormous estates and no doubt some intriguing family documents. Any desperate heirs come to mind?"

His face was braced with an anxiety she couldn't begin to fathom. One somehow connected to her predicament? "No sir. Maybe it'll hit me when we review the records."

"We must be patient," he nodded. "These things take time, as I'm sure our friends here can tell us."

Friends? She had none here or anywhere else. In her world there were only instruments and adversaries. Duke and Santinez were the latter. Was Lamp, too? "You're wrong about me," she glared coldly at Duke. "I didn't kill Morris."

"But you were at the Essex last night and enough times before that people recognized you," he replied. "You knew how to access the freight elevator. You had a key to the building, and also to Mendelsohn's apartment. Isn't it time you told us why?"

"Were you running errands for Morris?" Lamp asked.

Somehow she'd known he'd return to this. "Routine errands, that's all. Never to his apartment."

Lamp bent his head. No words could've burdened the moment more. Adversary - she reached her verdict.

"Were you and Mendelsohn romantically involved?" Duke pressed. "Is that why you had the key?"

"I never had a key. We were never romantically involved."

"Maybe you weren't, but he was, or wanted to be. How about those sexual favors - was I right?"

"No, Lieutenant. In fact, you've been right about nothing so far, yet your tireless questions keep tumbling out."

"Come on," Santinez sighed. "With your pretty face, Mendelsohn must've come on to you at some point, unless he was gay."

"He wasn't gay," Lamp scoffed. "Truth is, he was a notorious womanizer. Regrettably he'd been through three messy divorces and several scandals with married women. Perhaps he should've been asked to leave, but selfishly I must say, he was a tremendous asset to the firm. A brilliant litigator." He scowled. "Mayson, if Morris was harassing you, I must insist you tell me. Messy divorces are one thing; sexual harassment of firm employees is quite another."

"He wasn't, sir."

"I appreciate your loyalty, but covering up his misconduct serves no one's interests."

And its disclosure? She studied him with growing suspicion. How would this serve Lamp's interests? "I've told you the truth.

There was no harassment."

Duke pressed on. "A notorious womanizer works with a beautiful woman for two years and not once makes a sexual advance? How can that be explained?"

She turned sharply. "Besides asking him, Lieutenant, which we obviously can't do, I have no idea. Now please, can't we move on to a stupid question that hasn't already been asked a dozen times?"

Lamp sighed, "I suppose an investigation is in order."

She gaped at him. Investigation of what? There'd been no sexual harassment. Did he plan on investigating something that hadn't happened?

"We'd be interested in your findings," Duke said, turning at her snicker. "What is it, Miss Corelli?"

"I was just thinking how much sense it made — your interest in this investigation."

"And why's that?"

"Because it's a complete waste of time. No matter how thorough, it can't change the facts."

"Which are?"

"First, there was no sexual harassment. Second, I had no motive for killing Morris. Third, I wasn't at the Essex last night or any other time. And fourth, if you haven't yet guessed, I didn't kill Morris Mendelsohn!"

"Then prove it!" He smacked the table. "Prove it, so we can move on with our investigation! Give Mrs. Carter a chance to confirm that you aren't the young woman she saw last night."

Another terrible silence fell over the table. Wasn't she already guilty in their minds? Why provide a witness's identification to substantiate it? "I've answered your questions truthfully," she said. "I can't help it if you don't believe me."

"So what's there to lose by confronting Mrs. Carter?" Duke insisted. "It seems you'd have everything to gain."

"Not if she confuses me with the woman from last night."

Lamp, the new adversary said, "Mayson, I appreciate your concern over a misidentification, but that's a very remote possibility. And if you're innocent — something I'm not prepared to question — Mrs. Carter will eliminate you as a suspect. Then as

Lieutenant Duke says, we can move on and find the real killer. Consequently, I believe you should reconsider his request."

She glared at him stonily. "I have no intention of reconsidering the request. I know my rights."

"Let's make sure," Duke turned to his partner.

Crisply, Santinez marched through Miranda then offered a smile that defied its gravity. "First-year law school, right?"

Perhaps, but also an introduction to the criminal justice system that had knocked the breath out of her. "Does this mean . . . I'm being . . . arrested?"

Gravely, Duke glanced at Lamp. "Not yet."

"But I'm a suspect?"

"Yes. I'm certain we'll be talking again soon. I trust you'll be available?"

"Of course," Lamp nodded. "Any firm business conflicting with the investigation can be reassigned."

"Good," Duke nodded. "Then you're free to return to work."

As she rose, Lamp sprung up, too. "Take a break, gentlemen. I'll return in a moment."

Escorting her to the elevator, he muttered, "Damn hard bastards. I suppose they must be that way." His tone was conspiratorial yet she wasn't a fellow conspirator. "I was serious," he said. "If Morris was harassing you, I want to know."

He didn't have to convince her. She understood his dilemma perfectly. What evidence existed and what must be manufactured? Still she asked, "Why is it so important?"

"Isn't it obvious?"

"No sir, not at all."

"Then it should be. Sexual harassment is a reprehensible form of behavior this firm doesn't tolerate."

"I didn't think it tolerated romantic relationships between employees, either."

He studied her warily. "I suppose you're talking about Tyler. Yes I've heard the rumors, too."

"Rumors, sir? I'd say his exploits with a half-dozen females in this firm qualify him as a legend."

"I'll look into it," he replied. "Just as I'll look into Morris's misconduct."

"But there's been none. There's nothing to investigate. If I'm missing something, please tell me."

A shadow fell over him and she envisioned him ducking behind it. Something was there all right, but what? Pushing for the elevator, he muttered about the duties of Managing Partner, firm liability, hard-earned reputation - everything but the reason for investigating something that hadn't happened. "Mayson, I'd recommend you retain counsel. Duke's made it clear you're the prime suspect. I'll be happy to refer you to someone."

"That's kind of you, sir."

Oddly, she hadn't considered the matter of representation. She'd prayed the situation wouldn't reach that point. Now very quickly, it had. Was she prepared to entrust her fate to the criminal justice system? Certainly this was an odd question for a lawyer, but not a hard one. No, she wasn't. "Sir, you'll let me know when the inventory of Morris's records has been completed?"

He drew a blank. "Oh yes, the review. Certainly." Starting off, he then turned. "My mind's racing in a hundred directions this morning. Anyway, I received a call earlier about the Crenshaw case. I've gathered the files, but haven't had time to review them. Do you have any in your office?"

Crenshaw was one of Morris's will contests he'd referred to earlier. Desperate heirs. Desperate law partners, too? "No sir, I have none in my office."

"Then perhaps the library, or one of the research rooms? I want to keep them together."

Keep together; or did he mean search together? Did Crenshaw contain secret documents? "None that I know of, sir."

"Then what can you tell me about the case?" he asked.

Morris hadn't involved her very much in his budding probate practice. Consequently, she knew little about the cases, including Crenshaw. What she did know, she quickly rattled off.

Crenshaw, a retired Tennessee sheriff, had spent his golden years in Florida before dying with a ten-million-dollar estate and obvious questions over how it had been amassed. None, however, that had presented any problem for Morris, who had been retained by the disgruntled heirs to overturn the will which left the entire fortune to charity. The case was now mired in discovery. "I'm sure there's a wealth of detail in the files," she added as the elevator arrived. "Would you like me to review them?"

He shook his head. "You have enough on your mind."

Didn't think so. She got on, catching his eye as the door closed. Grave things, the life and death kind.

CHAPTER THREE

★

Mayson's world was crumbling. There'd been no one to help her build it, nor was there anyone now to help her save it. She'd spent her life making sure of that.

Shutting herself in her office, she slumped at the desk and gazed into a mountain of work. Movement, thought, any form of activity, seemed suddenly pointless. She was paralyzed by fear. All that mattered now was taking place in the conference room upstairs. When would she be called back? Would a warrant be waiting this time? Should she run or stay and find out? She wouldn't go to prison. Vinny had died there. Santa would remain there until he did, too.

Afternoon shadows lengthened and yet she didn't move, nor did the pile of work she'd once tackled with a feverish obsession. Why? It was difficult to recall. Her world was coming apart.

The autumn evening crept into the window and still she hadn't been summoned back upstairs or even to review the inventory of Morris's records. What review? Wasn't it a smokescreen? Did Lamp have a hidden agenda? Elusive ghosts swirled in her head: Morris's probate cases, secret documents. Crenshaw.

Finally rising, she went to the window. Night was falling over Manhattan's endless granite walls. Once the ramparts of a mighty fortress, they were now the infinite, gray blocks of a prison. And the city's myriad lights didn't illuminate the barracks of gallant centurions but the cells of lost, pathetic souls. This wasn't a City of Warriors like the Songbird had assured the little girl. It was a City of Prisoners; that's what life had taught the grown woman. Her gaze fell upon the building's last commuters trickling across the darkened square. Weren't they prisoners, too? Their suits, briefcases, and umbrellas didn't disguise them. Nor did their cars and train tickets provide a means of escape. No one escaped this prison. No one but the Songbird anyway. When would she finally accept it?

Night conquered the Manhattan sky. The conference room upstairs had been abandoned by now. Had Lamp's mysterious records review begun? And where was the golden boy, Tyler? He hadn't pestered her once since the morning. Closing her eyes she prayed, *Lord, should I run or wait for a miracle to sweep this disaster into the East River?* Faithfully she clung to the silence, but no answer came. Had it ever? She'd learned that faith was the flower of betrayal, blooming with promise only to wither and die. That behind every joy lurked a greater disappointment. That to invest the slightest bit of emotion guaranteed a return in pain only a fool would bargain for. And what had she invested instead? Sweat and labor — in schoolwork, Cellini's Market, endless night jobs. And her return; seventy-hour weeks at Lieber Allen and a West Side flat slightly larger than the one in Brooklyn. *Lord, please don't abandon me now!*

But had He ever been there? When the child waited by the silent door? Or now, as the woman poisoned by cynical parables waited by the office window? Was it more foolish to wait for a Songbird or the lifting of suspicion's shadow? Was the Lord telling her now that if she ran, she wouldn't be leaving much behind? No humanity, anyway. The Songbird had flown off with that long ago. And the woman, Mayson Corelli, was self made. Her hard work had paid the bills and financed her education. At Columbia she'd spent four years amassing credits and juggling jobs. Then catching her breath, she'd moved on to law school, passed the Bar and finally saw the sun's first glimmer: Lieber Allen. If only Rosa had lived to see it.

She'd left Brooklyn after Rosa's death, acquired her West Side apartment, shiny red BMW and lawyer suits. Finally she was on the fast track, too excited to care where she was going. She'd known only that nothing could stop her. But it had . . . last night, just as it had stopped Vinny. Foolishly, he'd trusted the system. She wouldn't make the same mistake.

Turning from the window, her gloomy eyes drifted over the cluttered office. Was this her farewell? She saw the work; there was nothing else here. No personal items or family pictures. A framed Rosa gleaming across the desk would've been too sad. Vinny, too painful, Santa, too shameful. Work in exchange for more work. She flicked off the light. Hadn't she expected a better return?

The Metropolitan, once known affectionately as Wall Street's Grand Old Dame, was now simply the Old Dame and Lieber Allen its oldest tenant. The black, haggard-faced janitor who mopped the floor never failed to reflect her own gloomy exhaustion after fourteen-hour days. But he had a smile that could be tugged out, as she'd discovered late one evening. As they'd crossed the lobby, Tyler Waddill, she discovered, possessed something no one else had ever acquired - the mopper's name. "Hey Amos!" he'd greeted. "Your Giants better be pumped for Sunday because my Redskins are coming to kick their ass!"

Amos had grinned deeply, shattering all of life's safe assumptions. "Don't be talking that trash now, Tyler. If there's any asskickin' to be done over at the Meadowlands, it'll be the Redskins who get it."

She'd left them to face a night much like this one - collar up, shoulders hunched against the chilling rain. Only this one hadn't been forecasted and like a fool she'd left her umbrella at home. Paying the price now, she hurried across the darkened square.

Minutes later she reached her bus, collapsing into the first seat, her clothes drenched, hair plastered to her face. The engine groaned, rain beading on the window as she slipped back into her gloom. Tyler Waddill: police informer, Virginia curse. Morris Mendelsohn: arrogant bully, despicable womanizer. If finding Tyler a convenient instrument of torture, Morris must've been tortured himself to discover that his young protégé need only smile to have all he coveted — a planet full of women.

She wasn't blind to what the others saw in Tyler: a young man, undeniably charming in a superficial way, yet able to convince a woman, whoever she might be, that she was the most special person on earth. It was a powerful force, yet simple in practice. He smiled. She melted. But if his charm was a talent, his physical beauty was a gift. Tall and lean-muscled, he moved with a commanding grace in his tailored suits. His thick, golden hair was naturally tangled as if swept by a sea breeze. It was the kind women loved to run their fingers through. His splendidly angled face included a fine chiseled jaw and the burnished glow of a summer beach. No man should be that handsome, but Tyler defied all the rules as he drifted through his charmed life.

The bus soon reached Mayson's stop and, bracing, she got off to confront the rain again. She hurried along the wet street, dodging puddles, still brooding over Tyler - the asterisk to every rule, the man born at the mountaintop others struggled a lifetime to reach. He was rich, she was poor. He didn't need a job and yet had hers. His image, like the bull's red flag, taunted her as the chilling rain sunk deeper into her bones.

"Where the hell have you been?" Like black magic he appeared, hands jammed into his drenched coat, gold hair dripping. "We need to talk, Mayson."

Waking to the weather's discomforts — numbed hands and chilled toes, crimping in her wet shoes – she snapped, "You just don't get it, Tyler. This isn't kindergarten and I don't want to be your friend!"

His hard glare held little patience. "You don't have any friends, Mayson, in case you haven't noticed. And don't worry, I'm no kamikaze, if you think I'm here to become the first."

Glancing at the warm lights glowing in her brownstone, she'd never longed more for her safe, dry apartment. "Your insult proves we have nothing to say to each other. Now unless you're here to arrest me, please leave."

"What do you mean arrest you?"

"You're a police informant. I thought perhaps they'd given you a badge by now."

"What the hell are you talking about?"

"Ransacked, you idiot!" she scanned the misty night. Were the others staked out in a nearby building? "How did you know I lived here?"

"This great new invention called the phone book. Now can we go inside? I'm chilled to the bone."

"Are you bugged?" Her eyes gleamed. "Yes, you are!"

He grabbed her before she could flee. "I'm not bugged!"

"Let me go!" she flailed. "I'll scream! I'll . . ."

"What?" he held her firmly. "Call the cops?"

"You stupid *gavonne*!" She squirmed furiously.

"Come on, Mayson, I hate it when you talk like that."

He turned just in time to avoid a savage blow to the family jewels. She snarled; he smirked. She snorted; he gloated. The more she squirmed, the deeper his grin. Finally grasping the futility of her struggle, she contented herself with watching the rain bead on his handsome face, trickle off his elegant nose. He was thoroughly soaked, and, she hoped, completely miserable. Finally he sighed, "Now may we please go inside?"

"I didn't ask you to come here and wait like a fool in the pouring rain!"

"Thanks for pointing that out. Now open the door!"

"Screw you!"

"Don't start that shit. I'm not in the mood for it. I've been waiting under the eave of that building for the last hour, getting wetter and colder by the minute. And because of that, I assure you, I'm not going anywhere until I say what I came to say — inside your apartment. Now open the goddamned door!"

"Don't curse me!" she shouted insolently.

"Why not? You're cursing me, aren't you? 'Screw you.' '*Gavonne*.' It's that same shit you slung at Morris every day."

Her eyes widened. "You heard that?"

"Hell, everybody did. You didn't think anything man-made like an oak door could drown out your Italian shock waves? When your mouth hits top gear, the Old Dame's walls tremble."

So they knew she'd hated Morris. "Let me go!" She flailed again.

"After I've had my say."

"Unless it's the Gettysburg Address, you could've said it a dozen times and been gone by now instead of keeping me out here in the rain."

"Mayson, you're just wasting time with all this blustering."

True, she was forced to concede. He wouldn't leave without first having his say. And she wasn't about to scream for the cops. "All right, say what you've come to say and then leave. Deal?"

"Deal." He released her.

Digging out her key, she let them inside the empty lobby. A TV droned in the back office. They rode the rattling elevator upstairs, and scowling, she led him down the hall to her apartment.

It was small, cold and gloomy, like her - precisely what he

would've expected, had he expected anything. He searched in vain for a plant, hanging basket, needlepoint pillow . . . anything bright, cheerful, feminine. Even the walls were barren, except for a few cheap pastels. The furniture was stiff and uninviting. An ancient TV sat in a corner, black-and-white no doubt, like everything else in the apartment. How could she live in such a dreary place, where hard, colorless objects filled up space, yet added neither warmth to the air nor food to the senses? Why was she so cold, miserable, and angry, when she was so intelligent, strong-willed and beautiful? What he'd never pondered before he did now intensely, in this strange moment of introduction to her world.

"Get a good look," she said. "It's the only one you'll have."

Her coat drenched and hair sopping, she leaned against the counter separating the living room from the kitchen. Even dripping wet she was gorgeous, yet from a world he couldn't begin to understand. "A good look at what?" he replied. "I mean, I don't see anything. It's almost like . . ." He shook his head. "It doesn't matter."

"What?" she snapped. "If you must insult my home, at least have the courtesy to finish the job." Teeth chattering, chilled to the bone, she simmered with contempt.

"I was just going to say there's no warmth or color, as if no one actually lived here."

"Certainly that doesn't surprise you. Everyone at the firm thinks I'm cold and dead inside, anyway."

He'd hurt the feelings he now realized she had. "I am curious to know why a person with such obviously sharp senses would live in a place that offers them no gratification."

She'd underestimated him. He wasn't the empty-headed playboy she'd assumed. He was perceptive enough to make her very uncomfortable suddenly. Lamp, Duke, or whoever was behind this visit wouldn't have sent him unless they were convinced he could satisfy their objective. "Now that we've dispensed with your opinion of my home, state your piece and leave."

"All right," he nodded. "I came to warn you this murder investigation is moving quickly. Now that Duke has his suspect, meaning you, it's all downhill in his mind. He and Santinez had planned on spending the day at the firm yet were gone by one. After returning to their precinct, they left again - this time for the Essex, where they spent the afternoon. They then returned to the precinct, jubilant I'm sure, and got their grunts busy with some computer checks. What they're looking for exactly, I don't know."

The Lips, her stomach knotted, that's who they were looking for!

"Anyway," he continued, "with the NYPD computers cooking, they returned to the firm for a confidential meeting with Lamp. They were still behind closed doors when I left at seven."

"What they were talking about?" she asked.

"For starters, I'd say the evidence they obtained in their afternoon chats with Ruby Carter and the other Essex residents who saw you last night."

"They didn't see me!" Her heart pounded. "I wasn't there!"

"Of course you were, Mayson."

Her eyes narrowed as he peered through the blinds. "How do you know so much about all this?"

"Don't worry about that." He scanned the dark street.

"You've accounted for everyone's activities this afternoon except yours. Where were you?"

"Don't worry about it."

"Stop saying that! I wouldn't be asking these questions if I wasn't worried!"

"Honestly Mayson, there's no law requiring you to be such a goddamned pain in the ass all the time."

"Why wasn't I asked to help with the review of Morris's office records?"

"Because there was no review." His restless eyes searched the street again.

"But I thought you and Frieda were preparing an inventory?"

"We did," he nodded. "Lamp took it and nothing else was said."

She frowned. "Lamp thinks I killed Morris, too."

"No shit, Mayson. Everyone does, except me, of course. I wouldn't be here otherwise. You may be the world's biggest pain in the ass," he squinted out the blinds again. "But you're no murderer."

"How can you be so sure?" she challenged him. "Unless you killed Morris yourself?"

He smiled, "I have one of those air-tight alibis. I was at McDougal's last night when Morris left those messages I told you about. Only a hundred or so regulars saw me. Have you been there?" he asked. "McDougal's, I mean. It's just a few blocks from here."

No, but she'd walked past it dozens of times and peered through the windows at the mahogany and brass bar with its sparkling glass racks and cozy dining area. She'd wanted to go in but hadn't. There'd been many places like that.

"McDougal's is like an oasis in the desert," he said. "Which I guess tells you what I think of Manhattan. Anyway, that's where I hang out."

Usually with a woman, she felt certain. "Did you have a date last evening?"

"I had dinner. Prime rib, the best anywhere."

"I didn't ask about dinner. I asked if you had a date."

"I said there were a hundred familiar faces. Does it really matter whose they were?"

"You can assume it does since I asked."

"All right yes, I had a date."

"With whom?"

"I'm certain that doesn't matter."

Her eyes narrowed, "Someone from the firm, wasn't it? Jill Allen, your hall fairy, or Sibyl Harrison?"

"Meg Wilkinson," he confessed.

She scowled. "You had a date with Curtis Samuels's secretary! The firm's Vice Chairman! You know the firm's rule against dating employees."

"Let's not go ballistic here, Mayson, it was just dinner. And that stupid rule should be abolished."

"Stupid or not, you just confessed to breaking it, something Lamp will be most interested in."

"Probably," he nodded. "If Lamp didn't already know. He was present this morning when Duke asked about my evening. Obviously he wasn't thrilled I'd been out with Samuels's secretary, but I had the distinct impression he was more interested in

Morris's murder."

She watched him peer out the blinds as he'd done several times already. Her eyes hardened suddenly. Duke, Santinez - they were probably staked outside her building! Nostrils flaring, she charged him, the blinds rattling as they crashed against the window. "You filthy *gavonne!*" She clawed at his coat. "I knew it!" Struggling, he managed finally to latch onto her hands. Still she wrestled furiously. "It won't work! It's there! I'll prove it!" Again she lunged, clawed at his coat. Again he struggled to subdue her.

"What the hell are you looking for?" He dodged a vicious kick.

"The bug!" Grabbing his coat collar, she shrieked, "Screw you, Duke! Screw you, Santinez! You'll never trick me into a confession!"

Gazing at her in disbelief, he opened his coat. "Look, goddamnit! No bug! No recorder! Nothing but your goddamned paranoia!" She withered against his indignation like a sheepish child. "Here!" He ripped a pen from his jacket. "It might contain a micro bug. I sometimes forget to remove them when my 007 missions are over. Check it out. You can never be too sure about these things."

But she didn't dare. His point made, he slipped the pen back in his jacket. "Why would I want to trick you into a confession when I've just said I believe you're innocent?"

His anger was incomprehensible to her. In her world, actions were explained by self-interest, not moral codes. If the action resulted in gain there was nothing else to consider. "You'd entrap me, Tyler, because it would mean my arrest and dismissal from the firm; at least after my conviction for Morris's murder, which my confession would guarantee."

"I see," he nodded. "And I guess it's equally clear why I'd want this?"

"Don't pretend you're so stupid!" she snapped angrily. "You know exactly why - to get my job."

He shrugged. "I thought I already had it - Lambrusco and the other stuff."

"They're just assignments. To get my job, you must push me out, meaning that in six months you could have what's taken me two years to earn. Specifically, Senior Associate."

"You're sure?" he squinted. "All this I can have just by putting you in prison for a crime you didn't commit? I had no idea."

As he started away she followed, her eyes gleaming angrily. "No one can trick me into a confession for something I didn't do! Never, do you hear me?"

"Yes," he nodded. "And it was stupid to try. I'll tell Duke we need another approach, or on second thought, that I've had enough of this case." He turned at the door. "Mayson, I hope you're not offended, but your job just isn't worth the hassle. In fact if it's not too much to ask, maybe you could tell Duke for me."

Hopelessly confused, she watched him leave. Did he work for the NYPD or not? Dashing to the window, she scanned the street below. They were out there . . . weren't they? Clenching her fists, she raced from the apartment. He turned in the hall as she approached. "Are these elevators always so slow?"

"Tyler, don't go!"

"Why not?" he asked.

"Because . . . I mean, we were . . ."

"You're going to tell Duke I'm off the case and went to McDougal's for a beer. I may have forgotten to tell you that part. And I think now I'll have a steak, too. Tell him a T-bone . . . No a Rib-eye; and a baked potato. Can you remember all that?" The elevator opened and an elderly woman peered at them curiously. "Sorry," he smiled.

As they returned to her apartment, she asked, "If not Duke, who were you looking for?"

Lifting the blinds, he scanned the dark street again. "Who said I wasn't looking for him?"

"What!" she snapped. "Why I ought . . .!"

"What you ought to do," he quickly cut her off, "is stuff a sock in your mouth and let me explain." The miracle unfolded; she became quiet. "Now I'm looking for Duke because I don't want him to see me, something that could easily happen if your apartment is under surveillance. Which is a clear possibility, since you're the prime suspect in a murder case. And if I'm spotted they'll think one of two things: I'm sympathetic to you or else insane, a diagnosis I'm beginning to fear may have some validity. Furthermore, if I'm under suspicion I'll lose the flexibility and resources needed to help you. That's why I didn't pester you this afternoon, waiting instead in the pouring rain to tell you what you must know."

Absorbing this explanation, she quietly came around the counter. "I don't have beer, but there's wine or coffee if you want."

He studied her warily. Had a peace been negotiated? "Thanks, but it's late." If he was lucky, he could still catch Marilyn Warren before she left McDougal's.

Mayson stopped her forage in the cabinets. "You must be anxious to escape this colorless place. I can't blame you for that."

Yet he remained, unable to escape the struggle in her eyes. She needed help but refused to admit it. She wanted him to stay and hated herself for it. The conflict was much too deep to grasp, yet there was hope at least for a cease-fire. "The only time I've spoken with Duke and Santinez was in the conference room today. That's the truth, Mayson."

"Did you tell them about Morris's calls last night?"

"They didn't ask about that."

"Not if you didn't disclose them. But they certainly asked when you last spoke with Morris."

"And I told them the Friday before he left on vacation."

"Then you lied. You spoke with him last night."

"No, he spoke with me or rather with my machine. I just listened to his recorded voice. That's not speaking with him — a technical distinction maybe, but a material one."

"And one Duke could give a damn about! Honestly, Tyler, do you expect me to believe you'd obstruct justice to spare me?"

"They also asked if I knew Morris had returned from his vacation," he continued. "I said I found out this morning like everyone else."

"That's certainly a lie."

He shook his head, "I didn't discover Morris's messages until midnight, which was this morning."

Arms folded, she glared at him. He was a paradox she could never hope to understand. "I thought you had to leave."

Marilyn, he remembered now. "May I use your cell?" As he grabbed it off the counter, their eyes met. Hers weren't hard like he'd believed, but soft and vulnerable. More frightened than hostile, like a fawn lost in the woods . . . and deep. How deep? Did he really want to know?

She watched him drop the phone without dialing. "Backing out on your date? Missing tonight will probably snap a streak or something. Maybe end your quest for the *Guinness Book of World Records*. 'Most Consecutive Dates: Tyler Waddill, Virginia *Gavonne*.' Do you sleep with them all?"

"I'm sure that's none of your business."

"Have I become the next notch to add to your prodigious belt? It's either sex or my job. I have nothing else you could want." She watched him start for the door. "What, not even one token denial?"

"What's the point?" he swung around. "You've already found me guilty. And besides, you're so blinded by paranoia you couldn't see the truth anyway."

"Then try me!" she snapped angrily.

"All right, I don't want sex or your job; I just want to help you. And the reason's obvious but unfortunately one you can't grasp. The idea of you going to prison for someone else's crime offends me."

"Tyler, people don't lie to the police in a murder investigation just because they're offended!'"

"Believe what you want, Mayson, I don't care anymore."

Again he started for the door. "Why don't you want sex?" she asked. "I'm not pretty enough?"

"I never said you weren't pretty." Returning inside now, he quickly shifted the conversation to safer ground. "I don't understand Lamp's attitude. It's bad enough a firm partner has been murdered, but why make it worse by assuming his associate did it? When I told Duke your relationship with Morris had seemed fine to me, Lamp said it was only natural I wouldn't want to cast you in a bad light after just taking your most important assignments. 'The gracious victor,' he called me while insisting that Lambrusco must have caused bad blood between you two."

Then she hadn't been imagining Lamp's strange behavior. "What did you say?"

"That if you'd been upset initially, you got over it when you learned the reason for the reassignment."

"The reason?" she asked, puzzled.

"The state court's practice of inviting a Supreme Court Justice to join the panel when significant constitutional issues are involved," he explained. "For Lambrusco, that would be Chief Justice Falkingham. That's why Morris picked me to argue the case. I spent my first eighteen months out of law school as Falkingham's clerk. I did such a great job in fact, he recommended me to his close friend, Lamp. That's how I ended up here . . . And for the record, you're not pretty. You're beautiful."

She stared at him, incredulous. "You told Lamp the reason Morris . . . why he . . . ? Did you really mean that?"

"Of course," he nodded. "Morris assumed that with Falkingham . . ."

"Not that, you idiot! The 'beautiful' part."

"I wouldn't have said it otherwise."

"How could you possibly think Lamp would believe that?"

"Mayson, everyone thinks you're beautiful. Just like they think . . ."

"Not that! Your stupid lie of why Morris gave you Lambrusco. Can't you keep anything straight?"

He had until this conversation. Now however, his head was spinning without a clue where it might be jerked next. "What's so hard to believe? I learned enough at the Supreme Court to know a lawyer's strategy is more than evidence and case precedents. If there's a political advantage, like having a wise old mentor hear his apprentice's first case, it's exploited."

"But it wasn't here and Lamp knows it. He's convinced Morris was pressuring me for sex."

Tyler frowned. "Then he was?"

"No. The point is Lamp believes it, but not your political advantage theory. If the firm needed such an advantage he'd argue Lambrusco himself. All you've done is draw suspicion on yourself."

Possibly, but if Lamp was suspicious, he was more suspicious of the Managing Partner.

"I repeatedly denied Duke's sexual favors angle," Mayson said. "Still, Lamp plans to investigate."

"Goddamnit, I knew it!" he growled. "Morris was harassing

you!"

"No he wasn't! Now stop."

Yes he was . . . or had been. The horny prick was now a dead prick, murdered not for sexual blackmail but for something else. What? Was there even one clue? "Do you know what Morris kept in the firm's vault?" he asked. "Lamp was in there several times today."

"Let me guess," she said. "Meg Wilkinson told you?"

"She's the vault custodian, Mayson."

"I have no idea what Morris kept in the vault. But what's so strange about Lamp being in there?"

"Several times in one day, specifically the day after Morris's murder? Maybe it's nothing."

But clearly he wanted it to be something, she realized. He wanted to link Lamp's vault visits to Morris's death, specifically to help her. "Tyler, why are you doing this?"

He gazed at her vacantly. Besides outrage over the injustice he saw unfolding, what did he feel? Guilt, possibly, for having served as Morris's instrument in sexual blackmail, and for not having been home that night to take his call? Had he been home, he, not Mayson, would've gone to the Essex that night.

"If you're not working for Duke, how do you know what he was doing all afternoon?" she asked now. "You must be his informant. There's no other explanation."

Why was she so distrustful? Did the answer lie hidden in her large, dark eyes? If he discovered their depth, would he also learn their secrets? "Mayson, I can't help unless you tell me the truth. I know you were at Morris's last night. He called and you went. His message proves it, as do the residents' descriptions. You used the freight elevator, then your apartment key. Why did you have the key?"

"I didn't, Tyler. And I wasn't there last night."

"You said the apartment was ransacked."

"No," she insisted. "The radio did."

"Did something in the apartment frighten you? Is that why you ran instead of calling the cops?"

"I did neither. And I wasn't frightened." She sighed, "This is all so pointless."

More than pointless, the evening had been wet, irritating and completely wasted. Glancing at his watch, he started out. She followed, right on cue. "I always win."

"You've turned away a friend, Mayson. That's not winning."

"You're no friend." Again on this roller coaster night, she stopped him as he opened the door. "Tyler, did you really mean what you said earlier?"

"About what?" he asked.

Her eyes dropped, her hands twisting nervously. "You know . . . the part about me?"

"Yes Mayson," he smiled. "You're very beautiful . . . a beautiful pain in the ass. But this *gavonne* you keep calling me . . . what does it mean?"

"Redneck," she said closing the door.

CHAPTER FOUR

★

Her career at Lieber Allen was over. Another Corelli was going to prison . . . if they could catch her. Should she run this morning? The question had echoed through the darkness and into the dawn, through the shower, hair dryer, radio and the groaning bus downtown. A voice whispered, "Hang on" as the gray buildings rushed past. But for how long? How could she know when the warrant might be served and the handcuffs clicked around her wrists? Closing her eyes, she prayed for the answer.

Reaching Wall Street, she hurried across the bustling square. The Old Dame had never loomed larger than on this gray morning and likely never would again. Oddly, the question struck her for the first time on the elevator. Who'd done this to Morris, to her, and why? Would she languish in the eternal darkness of an Attica prison cell without ever learning the answer? Emerging on fifty-eight, clad in her gray tweed suit, hair coifed, nervous eyes darting, she hurried for her office. Shutting herself inside, she gazed at the serried Manhattan skyline, the dull East River and finally sank into her chair. Inevitably, her eyes drifted to the phone. When would it ring? Would Duke return this morning? Why ask these stupid questions, a voice whispered. Run while there's still time! Grabbing her purse, she dashed out.

Her heart pounded as she rushed down the hall. What if she encountered Nicole or another Inner Sanctum secretary? Lamp or . . . She stopped suddenly outside Tyler's office. His door, always open, was now closed. Without knocking, she quickly slipped inside. Startled, he looked up from his phone call at the slender, bristling maniac looming over him. Cupping the phone, he whispered, "Go back to your office and wait."

"I will not!" she snapped. "Who are you talking to?"

Anger hardened his face as he resumed his conversation. "Nothing, just the usual office pest. So based on what you've said, you'll know more, later this morning. Then I'll expect your call . . .

Listen, I have to go." Hanging up, he rose angrily. "Didn't I tell you to stay away?"

"You don't give orders around here!" she snapped. "Now who was that on the phone?"

His anger quickly faded. The situation was much too grave, time too critical to waste on recriminations. "That was Lauren Belli, the only person I know with access to confidential murder investigations. And she wasn't exactly thrilled to exploit it on my behalf. Nevertheless, she's proven quite helpful in getting developments. So now you know my source. And since you're here, I might as well give you the latest."

The image of a striking blond, with baby-doll blue eyes and long, strutting legs taunted her now. Lauren Belli, from the Women's Bar Luncheons. "Lauren Belli's an assistant DA who prosecutes murder cases; no doubt she'll be prosecuting mine. While you . . . you'll be sleeping with her!"

"Goddamnit, Mayson, you don't understand."

"I understand perfectly. You don't work for Duke. You work for his boss, Lauren Belli. That's why you wanted me to stay away, not to help but to put me in jail!"

Spinning, she stormed out before he could respond and raced for the elevator.

In a fog, she left the Old Dame and hurried across the square. Catching the first bus, she rode for endless blocks until finally snapping awake in Brooklyn. Memories, like cobwebs, fluttered in her mind as the bus rumbled over the streets of her old neighborhood. Wistfully, her eyes settled finally on a shabby corner tenement - the Corelli's first home looking just as it had then, except for the ground-floor pizza shop now replaced by a pool hall with plate glass windows.

Mayson, why do you sit by that door? The Songbird isn't coming back. I tell you that every day. Now go play.

No Mama, he's coming back . . . you'll see.

Days passed. She cried her last tears and then went, not to play but to work at Cellini's Market.

Mr. Cellini asks why I don't have a good Italian name like Maria or Rosa like yours, Mama.

You tell Sal Cellini to mind his own business. Angelina — that's not

Italian?

He means the one everyone calls me.

I named you after Mayson Summers, my favorite movie star.

But she has blond hair, Mama. Mine's brown, like his wife's mink stole, Mr. Cellini says.

So what if your hair's like an expensive fur instead of platinum like Mayson Summers? You're just as beautiful, the paesani *say.*

Stephen says I look like My Fair Lady.

Audrey Hepburn. And he's right. You look more like her every day — and just as beautiful.

But she didn't feel beautiful. All she saw were large, sad eyes that no longer shed tears. It was terrible being unable to cry. She hated the Songbird and missed him even more. As the years passed, the *paesani* raved even more about her beauty. Again she looked in the mirror and only saw herself slipping further away. *Mayson, you have no friends, Rosa complained. You don't play.*

I have Stephen. And I work. And go to school.

Stephen's a grown man. You're a young girl.

He's nice, Mama. And he makes me feel better.

He may be nice but he's no prince. You deserve a rich, handsome prince.

She'd settled for Stephen, who made the Songbird's absence easier and later Santa's, who'd let them down terribly. Santino Corelli, 'Santa' to his kid sister who idolized him, had been big, strong and handsome. He was the leader of his gang, which meant no one batted an eye when she tagged along to the empty lot where the football games were held. As the boys played, she guarded their coats and valuables, then ran to Cellini's for the halftime refreshments. Santa had been the star and she, the mascot. For hours she'd watch their games and never get bored. Santa explained the intricate details later on the way home. She'd learned quickly, developing a passion for the game that exceeded most men's. On Sundays, she and Santa would watch the Giants games on TV and the lessons continued. This became their special time, the Giants, their team. She still loved the Giants and football, and would do so until her dying breath.

Santa had been everything — and then nothing. Worse than nothing. They'd given him a name - The Lips. Rosa's heart broke.

Just look at what your oldest brother has become!

He makes so much money, Mama. And yet we don't see a nickel.

Blood money! You want blood on your hands?

Rosa cried. Mayson saw Santa's cherished image shattered and slipped further away.

Stephen had been there to ease her pain. *Santino's so handsome, he'd said. He must have many girlfriends. That's why they call him The Lips.*

No it's not! And he's no longer my brother. I only have one now.

And then she'd had none.

If Santa was handsome, Vinny had been beautiful. If Santa had become mean and rotten, Vinny died as he'd always been - sweet and childlike. There'd been no way for him to survive in prison. And just months into a fifteen-year sentence, he died for a crime he hadn't committed. Again Rosa cried. Mayson had wanted to but couldn't. Stephen, her salvation, had been there to hold and comfort her. She'd learned long ago that handsome princes existed only in fairy tales. In this cold, brutal world, if you had a lifeline you were fortunate. You grabbed it and held on tightly.

Stephen had been her lifeline from the moment they'd met at Cellini's Market. She'd barely reached her teens and he was already a grown man. But age had been no obstacle to their friendship, one that had deepened with each passing year. Stephen had proven he could be counted on, trusted. And when she finally believed it, he proved he could not. Rosa cried. And Mayson slipped still farther away.

If only the Songbird hadn't flown away, how different things would've been! Its ghost remained unspoken between them until Rosa died. Now its lyrical presence haunted her dreams, reinforcing the harsh lessons of its flight: *Little girls' hopes are foolish. Grown women sink or swim by their own wits and hard work. When help is needed they rely on themselves.* And so she had. She'd followed the rules religiously, worked hard, gone so far and yet nowhere at all. She remained in Brooklyn even now as the last bus dropped her off near the Lyons. If she was going anywhere, wasn't it to prison? Brooklyn or Attica - there seemed no place in between for a Corelli.

Breathless, she reached her apartment. How much time had she wasted playing musical buses from Wall Street to Brooklyn to the Lyons? Dashing for the window, she scanned Seventy-Fourth. Were they already watching? Hadn't Tyler suggested the possibility last night? And wasn't he sleeping with the woman who'd prosecute her? Quickly she packed. Duke must've received the forensic reports by now. And he already had the statements of the Essex residents and those at the firm portraying her as a cold, crazy bitch who hated Morris enough to kill him. What else did Duke need to go rushing off to a magistrate?

So you think this little Italian girl put a bullet in the schmuck's head, the magistrate would say.

Who cares? Duke would snort. All the pieces fit — enough anyway that no one can say they don't. And besides she's a Corelli. Now issue the goddamned warrant!

Her suitcase on the bed, she ripped out drawers and grabbing clothes, crammed them into it. Precious minutes were slipping away. Would they arrive before she escaped? Shutting the suitcase, she lugged it down the hall, her eyes brushing over the cold, sterile apartment; two years and not one memory to pack. She'd brought no joy and would take none away. She couldn't even take her car. An APB would be issued the instant she became a fugitive. She'd be captured before she crossed the East River.

Leaving the suitcase, she grabbed her purse and rushed out. First Manhattan's closest branch was four blocks away. She'd withdraw her savings, call a cab and with any luck be at La Guardia within the hour. Quickly she vanished into the crowd on Seventy-Fourth. What if her accounts had already been frozen? Wouldn't Duke anticipate her need for money?

Heart pounding, she hurried along, alert for patrol cars, suspicious sedans, trench coats, angled hats. Seventy-Third, Seventy-Second and Seventy-First were covered. If only she hadn't . . . A horn shrieked suddenly. As she spun around, others shrieked, sparking a chain reaction. Then she spotted the problem - an idling black Porsche blocking the curb lane. What an inconsiderate idiot! Suddenly recognizing the driver, she stormed off, the Porsche following, oblivious to the shrieking horns. She refused to acknowledge him or even break her stride. "Goddamnit, come back here!" he shouted.

"No!" she spun furiously. "Leave me alone!"

Curious pedestrians stopped, their eyes darting between the black Porsche and the wild young woman. "Get in the car!" he snapped again.

"No! Now leave me alone!" Would he follow her all the way to the bank? In desperation, she watched the crowd grow around them. Peering through the window, she spotted his phone. Had Duke been summoned to the scene? As she started off again, he yelled, "Goddamnit Sally, I said I was sorry!"

Slowly she turned and now detected the urgency in his hardening face, his nod at the patrol cars in the next block, across from her bank. They were waiting for her! To clattering applause, she now climbed into his car. Squealing off, he ducked into the traffic flowing north on Amsterdam. "That was quite a performance," he said. "What do you do for an encore?"

Incredulous, she stared at Tyler in his tailored suit, Oxford shirt, silk tie and the most handsome face on the planet. Sunglasses rested in his gold, windswept hair. He put them on and his face hardened. "You're one huge pain in the ass, you know that."

"Then let me out!"

"Don't tempt me." Alertly, he caught the police procession headed for the Lyons. "Get on the floor."

"Why?"

"Because I said so!"

"No!"

He screeched to the curb as heads turned along Amsterdam. "Listen Mayson, this isn't a game. Ten seconds from now, Duke will arrive at the Lyons to arrest you. If you want to be there just say so and I'll drop you off. Otherwise get on the damned floor!"

Glaring defiantly, she nevertheless dropped to the floor. "So you intend to hand me over to your *puttana* personally, is that it?"

"My what?" He squealed off again.

"Your whore, Lauren Belli!"

"Lauren's no whore. And she just saved your ungrateful ass. I wouldn't have gotten here in time without her tip."

"Tyler, how stupid can you be?" She squirmed in her tight quarters. "To think I believe an assistant DA just rescued me from her own prosecution?"

Stopping for the light at Seventy-Seventh, he pushed the glasses back up his nose. "She doesn't know that part yet . . . The cops were staking out First Manhattan. Is that your bank?"

"I wasn't going to the bank."

"Oh," he nodded. "An idle stroll, or maybe a little shopping for prison? Never know what you might need, right?" A patrol car crept into the mirror at the next light. "Don't jump up suddenly. We have company." The unit remained on his bumper as he crept again. "If you'd hung around this morning, I would've told you what to expect. Where'd you go? I tried your apartment a dozen times."

"I was out."

"Look Mayson, you better start trusting me. I'm all you have at this point."

"Trust a snake?" she snapped.

"Why not, I'm helping one!"

Muttering incomprehensible Italian, she yanked her skirt down. Finally the unit turned, his eyes slipping from the mirror to her face. "Duke must be cursing into his radio about now. In a few minutes, every cop in Manhattan will be looking for you."

And they'd know she hadn't gone far. She envisioned her packed suitcase at the door, her BMW in the Columbus Avenue lot. Why had she made such a stupid scene?

At the next light he studied her, cramped and sullen-faced on the floor. "Even with motive and opportunity, I still thought there was a chance you might duck a warrant. No matter how strong Duke's suspicions, without weapon or confession he really didn't have a case. So what if Ballistics confirmed the bullet in Morris's head came from a .38? How could it be traced to you? Easy, I learned this morning."

"I don't own a gun."

"It's registered to you, Mayson."

"I . . . don't have it anymore. I sold it . . . to a gun dealer. He must've forgotten to change the registration."

"Then how could he resell it?"

"How should I know?" Cautiously she raised her head as they stopped at the light on Ninety-Fourth. "Where are you taking me?"

"Get down!" he hissed. "Now why did you take the gun to Morris's Sunday night?"

"I don't know what you're talking about."

"Hopefully you put it some place Duke can't find."

She certainly had, unless Pig Face planned on dredging the East River.

He turned east toward Central Park. "I found out why Lamp spent so much time in the vault yesterday. Morris's papers; specifically, that damned memo."

"What memo?"

The sunglasses shielded Tyler's eyes as he studied her intently. "That's what I was about to ask you."

"I have no idea what you're talking about." She tugged again at her skirt. "And quit leering at me."

Lifting the shades, he studied what he hadn't before - her tightly folded legs. They were slender and well formed. He turned again sharply, her skirt sliding back up her thighs. "You did that on purpose!" she shouted.

"The memo, Mayson. Did Morris really write it?"

"How should I know? I don't even know what memo you're talking about." No factual reconstruction; she really had no clue. "What does it say?"

"That Morris recently discovered certain financial improprieties which he confronted you with and you denied, leading naturally to the heated exchanges we all heard. Those Italian shock waves, remember?" She was speechless suddenly, a rare thing, and in this case a good sign. "Supposedly Morris drafted the memo, intending to file charges with the Management Committee when he returned from vacation. Naturally we're to assume you were sweating bullets and formulating a plan for his murder."

"What kind of improprieties?" she asked.

"Little things like embezzling from the firm, selling confidential client information, submitting phony expense vouchers — nothing that could earn you more than disbarment and twenty-to-forty in Attica."

"Tyler, it's a lie. All of it!"

"I know," he nodded. "But it creates one helluva murder motive and also a reason to submit to Morris's sexual blackmail.

Then you never saw it?"

She shook her head. "Memos weren't Morris's style. If one was required, I did it."

"You wouldn't have done this one."

"Neither did he."

"How can you be so certain?"

"Because if he had dirt like you've described, I would've known long before he drafted a memo or brought charges. Morris was confrontational. He couldn't keep quiet about anything. Believe me, our arguments weren't over financial improprieties."

"I know what they were over." His jaw quivered angrily. "And if I'd known then, I would've killed him myself."

"Tyler, the point is that neither the financial improprieties nor the memo documenting them existed before Sunday. They've obviously been manufactured."

"Lamp supposedly discovered the memo while cleaning out the vault yesterday," he explained. "Meg said he was in there three times - twice alone, the third with Samuels to retrieve Morris's papers for his sister, who's settling the estate."

Anticipating his next turn, she caught her sliding skirt. The trees rimming Central Park loomed above. Already they were shedding their colorful autumn feathers. By Thanksgiving their limbs would be bare, dark, crooked veins in the gray sky.

"If we're right about Lamp," Tyler asked, "why would he want Morris dead?"

She thought again of Lamp's mysterious interest in the Crenshaw case.

He continued, "When Duke and Santinez returned to the Essex yesterday, they were armed with your PR photo courtesy of Lamp. On this basis, Mrs. Carter and the other residents were able to identify you as the woman they saw in the building Sunday night."

The photo had been taken shortly after her arrival at the firm. She recalled her pride upon finding it among the *Times* professional announcements, wanting Rosa to be alive so badly that Sunday morning to see what her daughter had accomplished. Mayson Corelli, Lieber Allen associate . . . Mayson Corelli, Inmate #99999, kid sister of The Lips. Catching her skirt with another sharp turn, she gazed up at the Upper East Side's swanky apartment buildings. "Is this Madison?"

"Park," he replied.

Park Avenue. As a child she'd envisioned it with royal palaces, the street paved in gold. As they stopped for the light at 105th, she caught him staring, his shades again nestled in his golden locks, his blue eyes awe-struck. "What?" she asked.

"Your brother, a Mob assassin, that's amazing. Lauren says Lucky was the most feared mobster on the West Side before he went to prison. Did he give you the .38?"

It wasn't enough that she sat humbly knotted on the floor of his expensive sports car. She must be doused in family shame, too. "It isn't Lucky, you idiot, it's The Lips, a name he acquired by kissing his smoking gun after killing *paesani* on the orders of Don Bertolucci. Fortunately he's now in Attica where he belongs. And I can't help it if he's my brother, so don't mention him again unless you want your tongue ripped out."

"What about your other brother?"

"Vinny. He died in Attica. Don't mention him either."

"What did Vinny do to land in Attica?" he asked.

"I just said not to talk about him." Her heart thumped suddenly as they zipped into the garage of a large apartment building. Snaking up the ramps, they glided finally into the darkened corner of an upper level. "Where are we?" She crawled up now.

"Home." He snapped off the engine.

Her eyes narrowed. "Not my home. I'm not staying here." As he crisply restarted the engine, she asked, "Now where?"

"Wherever you say," he replied.

"How am I supposed to know that?"

"But you just said . . ."

"I know what I said. And don't pretend you're clever by spitting it back at me."

He waited; she glared. The engine idled. She stewed, folding her arms fretfully. Smiling, he slumped back. He was quickly learning her moods, this particular one being an obvious pout. "So where to? Quickly now, I need to get back to the firm."

"Why?" she snapped. "You don't do any work there."

Her pout faded and the vulnerability returned to her eyes. She was helpless and too stubborn to admit it. "You're staying." He offered the lifeline he knew she wanted.

Yet it was met by renewed suspicion. "What do you want from me, Tyler?"

"The truth about Sunday night."

"I've told you the truth."

"No Mayson, you haven't even come close."

"So? Why should I risk . . ."

"Risk?" he snapped. "Who's taking the risk here? In the last twenty-four hours, I've stolen classified information in a murder case, using it to rescue the key suspect from certain arrest and am now offering her sanctuary in my home. I've risked my life for you, Mayson, and am asking for nothing in return but the truth."

"Hah!" she snorted. "No one wants just the truth. The catch, that's what they're interested in. I won't sleep with you, Tyler."

"That's right," he nodded. "My body's not part of the deal."

Her fists clenched. "Stop confusing me this way!" How could he expect her to believe he'd actually put his life on the line for someone he called a pain in the ass? "You say you don't want sex now but once we're inside your apartment it'll be a different story."

"Mayson, if I slept with half the women you think why go to so much trouble for one more?"

"Because I'm the only one left and your ego can't stand it."

"I'm not like that, Mayson."

No he wasn't, his eyes confirmed. Their sparkle was pure and honest, like pennies at the bottom of a pool . . . Well if not sex, then what? "You'll have to reveal your conditions at some point."

"The truth, Mayson, that's my condition. Except I'll add a second one now: That you start being a little nicer." He gave her his apartment key and security card. "The card accesses the building. Take the first elevator you come to."

She studied the key to Apartment 805. It had a spectacular view, no doubt, of the East River, Central Park or both. Certainly there was another way to elude a city's police force without money, transportation or change of clothes. "I can't do this."

His eyes hardened. "This paranoia, Mayson, get over it. We have more important matters to deal with, like who killed Morris?

And how can we prove it?"

"And how do we do that, Tyler? Do you have the first clue?"

He hadn't meant to get into this now. He must return to the firm before attention shifted from her disappearance to his absence. If a connection was made, their mission would end quickly. "There've been other developments I haven't told you about."

Her eyes widened. "What developments?"

"Morris didn't return to New York from the Outer Banks. He flew instead to St. Paul, Minnesota on Thursday, leased a car and headed north. He returned on Saturday and caught a flight home, then changed his mind somewhere between St. Paul and Chicago, got off at O'Hare and flew back to Minnesota - Duluth, this time. He returned to New York the next day to get himself killed. The cops have no clue why he went to Minnesota or what he did there. They're checking, but I doubt they'll strain themselves. And why should they, with their prime suspect right here? Catching her will be their biggest concern now."

Why Minnesota, she wondered. What could it hold to pull Morris away from his cherished fishing trip? The two weeks he spent on the Outer Banks weren't a vacation, but a religious experience.

"Another thing," Tyler said. "When returning on Sunday, Morris booked another flight for that same evening - San Francisco this time. Now we know why he was in such a hurry." His eyes fell to the apartment key in her hand. "A ride to the airport. Isn't that what Morris wanted?"

"I didn't talk to him." Her eyes fled to the window.

"Why was he going to San Francisco?"

"Tyler, you're wasting your time."

"Why not take his own car to the airport? Was he being followed?" He frowned at her stubborn silence. "Then you'll force me to solve this mystery alone?"

"No one's forcing you to do anything!" she retorted.

"Mayson, you still don't get it. This isn't about your job, sex or anything but saving your goddamn ass. Now if you won't help, just get the hell out!"

She'd never seen him this angry. Again she studied the key. If there was another choice, she couldn't see it. "I'll stay until this evening, decide on a plan and then leave."

In the mirror, he watched a silver Cadillac cross the garage and park nearby. Both the car and the well-dressed couple alighting from it were familiar. "Hurry up, Mayson, get out."

"Didn't you hear me, Tyler? I'm leaving tonight."

"Yes. Now get out."

"Then you really don't care if I leave or stay?"

"Goddamnit, get out!"

"Don't curse me! You know, I might've stayed longer . . ." Tires squealed suddenly as he spun the Porsche around, throwing her against the door. "*Madonna mia*, what are you doing?"

"I thought I'd made that clear." Clutching her purse, she exploded from the car.

CHAPTER FIVE

★

Mayson's anger evaporated once she was inside Tyler's apartment. But the fear returned, and with it came a suffocating isolation as she gazed out at a world from which she'd been cut off - sprawling Central Park, the crisp autumn breeze, Fifth Avenue's hustle and bustle and the East River sparkling on the horizon. She couldn't go to the Lincoln Center or Bloomingdale's, nor drive her shiny red BMW or even return to the Lyons for a change of clothes.

Fretfully, she turned from the window to study her new surroundings. The elegant trappings were gold, silver and brass, and the furniture strong and handsome. Persian rugs tastefully adorned the hardwood floors and the video equipment was naturally top of the line. This was Park Avenue, where all the apartments were the same - enormous, luxurious and where Corellis didn't belong. She felt imprisoned here just as if she were in jail. So what if the toilets had seats and the windows were bar-less? She still couldn't do what she wanted.

Time crawled. The afternoon sun faded and a reddish glow crept into the sky, followed by a golden hue so sweet she could taste it. A hot-air balloon glided over Central Park in a billowing descent. Who was there to greet it? Someone who'd been to the Bloomingdale's sale? Did they have exciting plans for the evening — Broadway, Lincoln Center? She was cut off from it all.

Miserably, she wandered through the apartment. For all its princely space, there was only one bedroom. And why would Tyler need another? Didn't his overnight guests, all female, share his king-size, satin-sheeted bed? Did rich, stupid *gavonnes* sleep on anything else?

Returning to the study, she dropped into the cozy window chair, again drawn to the strange souvenir posters adorning the walls. He'd made his Park Avenue apartment not an art gallery but a childhood museum. The posters were ancient and yellowed, creased yet clearly treasured as their expensive brass frames and glass cases proved. Two announced Barnum and Bailey's arrival in Norfolk, Virginia over consecutive summers. He'd been nine and ten, she calculated; she'd been the same age in Brooklyn. She'd never been to the Barnum and Bailey, but if she had, would she have memorialized the event with expensively framed posters?

Her gaze drifted next to the two stadium posters announcing clashes between the Washington Redskins and Dallas Cowboys. He'd been twelve, then thirteen; she was the same age - twelve before the Songbird's departure and thirteen after. Two different lives, two different worlds. Examining the posters more closely, she noticed the ticket stubs and game programs inside the glass, as if he'd been intent on remembering every detail of the experience. Why had they been so important to him?

Two more posters featured Redskin Super Bowls, one in Pasadena, the other Tampa. They'd been fifteen for the first, eighteen for the second: he in the stadium, she in a Brooklyn tenement watching the games on her fuzzy, black-and-white TV. She recalled how superb the Skins had been during Joe Gibbs' glory years, with the Hogs blocking, John Riggins running and the Posse receiving. She'd also seen her beloved Giants win two Super Bowls, wishing to be in the stadium like Tyler, to meet the players afterwards as he had. She studied their autographs scrawled on box corners, whatever had been handy at the time.

With time to kill, she drifted out to inspect the other posters. Where the study's theme had been the circus and football, the hall was devoted to the silver screen with classic movie posters: *The Good, the Bad, and the Ugly, Butch Cassidy and the Sundance Kid, Bullitt;* fast cars and thrilling action that dazzled a little boy's eyes. The next posters puzzled her: *The Sound of Music, Mary Poppins, My Fair Lady*. It was hard to imagine Tyler sitting through these movies, much less their leaving a lasting impression. Why had they been included in his museum?

Aimlessly, she drifted into the bedroom to examine the posters of Disney World and its neighbor, Sea World. Her eyes glowed wistfully. Places she'd dreamed of, places he'd been. The others memorialized events she knew nothing about: the Annual Oyster Roast sponsored by the James River Country Club, some snobby social event, no doubt, invented by empty-headed Southern Belles;

and the last three announcing, of all things, piano recitals - two at the Tidewater Academy of Arts, one at the Dorothy Hamilton Cultural Center. Tyler devoting his Saturday afternoons to piano recitals was impossible to imagine. She returned to the study. Dropping into her cozy chair, the claws of fear scratched at her again. Outside the reds and golds had faded from the sky, a purplish pall now blanketing Manhattan with a chill she could almost feel. Soon the night sky glittered with myriad lights. People were dressing for elegant dinner parties at expensive restaurants and Broadway plays. So many things were happening in a world to which she no longer belonged and maybe never had.

The sight of Tyler suddenly in the doorway made her skin crawl. The evening breeze had fluffed his golden hair, enhancing his face's glow. He'd spent the last hours at the firm and yet escaped without a wrinkle in his tailored suit. He was the most elegant, handsome man in Manhattan and why shouldn't his river-blue eyes glow with the same confidence that carried his tall, athletic body?

"Dinner." He held out a bag. "Pizza, with extra cheese; no anchovies, though. Not everyone shares my passion. Do you like them? Anchovies, I mean?"

"I don't even like pizza, you stupid *gavonne*."

"Why not?" he asked.

"Because I'm Italian you assume I was born with a craving for pizza? Anything with tomato sauce, pasta and sausage - just throw it in a pot and whatever comes out is certain to light up the eyes of a Corelli."

"I didn't expect miracles," he frowned. "I just thought everyone liked pizza. I guess you don't like Chianti either." He took a bottle from the bag. "I can't blame you for that. Molson - now that's what you drink with pizza."

Three movies now came out, two of which she'd meant to see. How did he know? Putting the movies on the shelf, he left her in a wake of conscience. Pizza, Chianti, movies and she'd offered no gratitude, just insults. Rising, she followed him into the living room where he gazed at the glittering skyline. Until yesterday he'd been a one-dimensional "trust fund baby" blessed with material things she didn't have, but she was beginning to realize he was much deeper. He did more than smile, joke and slap people on the back. He also brooded and fell victim to deep reflection. "I'm sorry for calling you a *'gavonne.'* You're not, of course."

"No." He turned from the window. "I'm much worse. I'm an idiot."

"For helping me?"

"Then you finally believe that's what I'm doing?"

She shrugged. "If not, you would've turned me in by now. Yes I believe you're helping me, but I still don't know what you expect in return."

"The truth, Mayson, that's all."

She shook her head. "No man risks his life to save a murder suspect, hide her in his home, and bring her pizza, wine and movies, while suffering her ungrateful bitchiness and expecting nothing but the truth in return."

"Well I hate to disappoint you, but this one doesn't."

"Yes he does. He just doesn't want to tell me."

His face hardened. "I thought you were leaving."

The tone of his voice stung her. "I am, right now."

"Where are you going?"

Where? All these hours and did she have the first clue? "As far by bus as my money will take me."

"Mayson, don't you realize every bus station in New York is being watched? The airport and train stations, too. You think you can just walk up and buy a ticket, then sit in some crowded waiting room until the bus leaves? Every cop in the city is looking for you." He sighed. "Didn't you watch TV this afternoon? Your disappearance is all over the news. By six, all the networks were airing your story on their evening programs. Duke's outraged; and the NYPD is embarrassed."

Did he want her to leave or not? "And Lamp?" she asked.

"He summoned me to the Inner Sanctum the moment I returned — not a real good sign. He wanted to know where I'd been all afternoon. Fortunately it was ideal for jogging. I said I got carried away and forgot the time. I'm sure he bought it. Then, on the pretext of planning the transition of Morris's practice, we danced around my relationship with you and where you might be hiding. It got real hot for a while."

"Then he suspects your involvement in my disappearance?"

"I'd say the question's crossed his mind."

"How did you convince him you weren't?"

"By reminding him you hated my guts because of Lambrusco and that we never talked outside work. I'm sure he didn't find that hard to believe. By the way, Nicole told him about finding us in your office Monday morning."

"How did you explain it?" she asked.

"I said that even if we hated each other, there were certain things we couldn't avoid discussing: joint projects, our boss's murder..."

"Did he buy it?"

"There's no reason he shouldn't." He studied her intently. "Mayson, the killer used your gun Sunday night, which means it was at Morris's apartment. Why did he have it?"

"He didn't. I sold my gun to a dealer, remember?"

"You must have arrived within minutes of the murder. You found the apartment trashed, then Morris's body, then the gun. The violent arguments at the firm must've flashed through your mind and how everyone knew you hated him. And there you were, standing over his fresh corpse, the murder weapon registered in your name." He sighed, "No wonder you ran. Anyone would."

"I have to leave now."

"You can't, Mayson. Cops are everywhere. Five minutes on the street, and you'd be picked up."

"I'll take my chances."

"There are no chances. That's what I'm telling you."

"Well, it's obvious you don't want me here," she shrugged. "And I'm not your responsibility."

"Neither is solving this goddamned murder case."

Her eyes flickered angrily. She grabbed her things, and found him sipping a beer in the kitchen. "I'm glad, at least, not to have disrupted your routine. You'll want to check your messages. Your *puttanas* really scorched the line this afternoon. It must be quite a challenge keeping them all straight."

He noted her disheveled appearance, her jacket and skirt badly wrinkled from her long roost in the study, no doubt the same place she'd acquired the run in her hose. "I assume you didn't answer the phone?"

"That's why you have messages." Clenching her purse, she snapped, "Ciao, *gavonne*!"

He listened as her shoes clicked down the hall then returned. As she reappeared, he smiled. "Ciao."

"Your key and security card!" She smacked them on the counter.

Again she hesitated. He sipped, waited, then finally asked, "Anything else?"

"I suppose I should also thank you for rescuing me this afternoon, whatever the reason."

"Then are you?"

"Am I what?" she frowned.

"Going to thank me? You said you should, so I . . . "

"Stop it, Tyler! I hate you! So much that I'm leaving, even with the heavy odds against me. But I'll gladly take jail to another second with you . . ."

"Then I'd suggest buttoning up." He nodded at her jacket. "It's awfully cold out. And you'll need gloves. I have an extra pair."

As he started toward the closet, she yelled, "I don't want your stupid gloves!"

"Fine." He continued down the hall. Reaching the bedroom door, he turned. "One other thing. If it were me, I'd leave through the garage. It's less conspicuous."

She stayed in the hall until he emerged later, freshly showered and clad in navy blazer, white turtleneck and gray flannels. His spicy after-shave scented the air.

"Where are you going?" she asked suspiciously.

"Since you're leaving, I thought I'd have dinner at McDougal's," he explained, stopping at the mirror to comb his hair. "By any chance, was Kelly Murphy among this afternoon's line-scorchers?"

"You expect me to remember their names?" she asked as he headed for the study. "Kelly's the one who called twice." Confused, she watched him turn for the front door. "Aren't you going to call her?"

"Who?"

"Kelly Murphy, you idiot."

"No. Now come on, I'll drive you to the bus station. There's one just a few blocks from here." She didn't budge, her fawnish eyes clutching him with a fear she'd never admit. "You need money; is that it?"

She shook her head. "I told you, I have plenty. Ninety dollars, remember?"

"Yes," he nodded. "You can probably get to Connecticut on that."

"You said I'd get caught before getting on the bus."

"You will. I was speaking hypothetically."

"Tyler, don't try to stop me."

"I wouldn't think of it," he replied. "Your mind's obviously made up, so let's go." But still she didn't move. "For Christ's sake, Mayson, what is it?"

"I was just thinking," she shrugged. "You took a shower, and well . . . if it's not an imposition . . ."

"Jeez, Mayson, take a shower! The towels are in the bathroom cabinet. And grab a few sweaters from my bureau. You'll be glad to have them later. And if you really don't like pizza, take some food from the refrigerator. On ninety bucks, meals will be like showers — it might be a while until the next one."

"Thank you," she said, surprising even herself.

McDougal's was buzzing, as usual. As Tyler nursed a Molson's, Mark Ryan, who moonlighted as bartender, reminded him of his law school graduation in the spring. "Tyler, you tell the powers that be I'd make a fine addition to Lieber Allen."

He smiled. "As a first-year associate, I hardly have any influence over the firm's recruiting decisions."

"Don't worry, Mark, he'll get you in." Bud Berryman slapped Tyler's shoulder. "No doubt he's taken over Lieber Allen, just like he has McDougal's."

Ruffling his hair, Maddy Moran offered her two cents: "If a female does the hiring and Tyler puts in a good word, I'd say you're in like Flynn."

A special TV news bulletin diverted their attention. Tyler

cringed at Mayson's picture as the anchorman reported, "Mayson Corelli, the young Wall Street attorney charged in the murder of prominent Lieber Allen partner, Morris Mendelsohn, vanished today before authorities could arrest her. Although the motive for the murder hasn't been disclosed, it's known that Corelli and Mendelsohn worked together at the Wall Street firm." Glancing at his report, he added, "Police are convinced at this hour that Corelli, whose brother is reputed Mob assassin, Santino 'The Lips' Corelli, remains in Manhattan, although regional authorities have been alerted. Further sources have confirmed that the FBI will be joining . . ."

FBI! Tyler cringed again. What interest did the Feds have in a local homicide case? As coverage of the Knicks game resumed, he was besieged by questions. "You know her?" Berryman asked.

"A real pain in the ass," he nodded, gulping his beer.

"A beautiful pain in the ass." Mark wiped the bar.

"If she's a pain in the ass," Maddy cracked, "I'm sure Tyler can tame her."

Wanna bet? He'd have better odds with a rattlesnake.

"Why's the FBI getting involved?" Mark asked.

Damn good question. "No idea."

"She must've been tipped off," Berryman said. "How else would she have known to skip? Unless the cops called to say they were on the way."

Not the cops, the assistant DA - one who must be spitting bullets about now. He must deal with Lauren soon, he thought as Kelly Murphy, her auburn ponytail bouncing, now made her way over. All Spandex beneath her coat, her pretty face glowed from a workout. "Wonderful! You got my message."

"Aerobics?" he hugged her.

"Bodybuilding."

"Why lift weights when you already have the most beautiful muscles in Manhattan?"

"What a sexist thing to say!" She swatted him.

"Take the compliment," Maddy sighed. "You won't be getting one from a better-looking man."

He led Kelly over to his favorite table as the mocking New Yorkers chorused, "See y'all!"

He was soon cutting into a T-bone as she picked at an antipasto salad across from him. "Honestly, Tyler, how do you stay so trim on a diet of beer and red meat?"

"Simple. I jog a mile for every Molson." And to think he'd been prepared to eat anchovy-less pizza with a neurotic Italian shrew — neurotic enough to venture out into the cold night where a city of cops waited? Hadn't his leaving given her the time and space she needed . . .

"Tyler!" Kelly's piercing voice scattered his reflections like rats making for the closest hole.

"Sorry, my mind's still at the firm. There's a lot going on."

"So I heard. Do you know her, this Corelli girl?"

"Not well. She's a very disagreeable person."

"A bitch, you mean. I saw her picture on TV. With those big brown eyes and mink stole hair, she reminds me of an actress I can't seem to place. So you really haven't been out with her?"

"Get serious," he stabbed another slice of steak.

"It's just hard to imagine you overlooking someone that gorgeous, right there in your firm."

"The firm has two hundred lawyers. And besides, there's a rule against dating . . ."

"There, you're doing it again!" She snapped at his drifting eyes. "Please pay attention. Now how do you think Corelli got away so quickly? An accomplice?"

"How's the antipasto tonight?" he asked.

"Her brother was in the Mafia." She shivered. "Doesn't that give you the creeps? Maybe the Mafia rescued her. If not, someone did, don't you agree?"

"The T-bone's great." He deposited a juicy sliver in her bowl. "Go ahead. One bite won't hurt."

"Maybe it was a mob hit." Her emerald eyes glowed with intrigue. "Did you know Mendelsohn?"

"Not well. Now may we please change the subject?"

"Tyler, why are you always so restless? Your eyes never stop drifting, as if you're searching for something you've lost." Curiously she watched them dim now. "Have you ever been in love?"

"Once," he nodded.

"What happened?"

"It was a long time ago."

"Then why can't you tell me?"

It hurt enough just to think about it. Talking about it was unimaginable. "Where does a woman go to buy clothes at night? Say you need a dress and it's late at night. Where do you go?"

Her eyes widened. "Why are you asking me this?"

"They say you can do or buy anything day or night in New York. That must include women's fashions."

"Tyler, are you a transvestite?"

An hour later, he breezed into Loehmann's, a women's clothing store at West 73rd and Broadway, and quickly proceeded to sift through the racks, browse over the display tables and peer studiously at the mannequins. Hunter Leigh was a ten, Stafford, an eight. A smaller Mayson must therefore be . . . a six? He began grabbing.

Fifteen minutes later he left with three bags full of sweaters, slacks, skirts, lingerie and, rolling the dice, a pair of size seven topsiders. Reaching the apartment just after midnight, he set his bags down and called out, "I'm home!"

He quickly found her, a suspicious lump in the big recliner by the study window. She was curled up asleep, the half-consumed Chianti bottle and empty pizza box on the floor. This was the dangerous fugitive all of Manhattan was looking for, he smiled? Scooping her up, he carried her down to his room and laid her gently across the bed. Then, covering her with a blanket, he left, closing the door behind him.

Damned if this wasn't a first.

CHAPTER SIX

★

"Pssst, Tyler! Are you asleep?"

His eyes opened slowly to the slender silhouette looming in the moonlight. "What the hell kind of question is that?"

"It's almost five."

"Thanks for the bulletin."

"Are you always this grumpy in the morning?"

"I don't know. I'm never up this early."

"Monday night at the Lyons, I called you a clown. And you said, 'Thanks, I love clowns.'"

He yawned. "So what?"

"You love them so much you framed circus posters and hung them on the wall. Why?"

"You woke me just to ask that?"

"Of course not. I was frightened to wake up in a strange bed."

"Where did you expect to wake up? On a bus for Cleveland?"

"You knew I wouldn't leave last night, didn't you?"

"I hoped you wouldn't."

"Hoped nothing. You invested a fortune in women's clothes . . . They are for me, aren't they?"

"Yes, Mayson, they're for you."

"Then thank you. And don't worry, I'll repay you."

"They're a gift."

"You don't know me well enough to be making gifts."

"Then how about discounts? Give me your ninety bucks and we'll call it even."

"Those clothes are worth ten times that. And besides, I'll need the money for my bus ticket."

Dawn crept into the window, exposing her disheveled clothes and hair. "You're not going anywhere, Mayson."

"Tyler, I stayed last night but I can't again. I'm leaving this morning."

"That's smart," he sat up now. "Leaving in broad daylight will will make it much easier for Duke to spot you. Maybe your thoughtfulness will persuade him to knock a few months off your life sentence."

"You're not clever, Tyler."

"Clever or not, you're not leaving. That's final."

"I'm not one of your possessions!" she barked. "I'll go when and where I please. And further, I'm not very happy that you carried me into your bedroom last night."

"You were asleep. Half a bottle of Chianti — how do you drink that stuff?"

"Don't change the subject."

"All right, I'll close it. You're not leaving."

Jumping up angrily, she stormed out.

He rose too, peering out at an endless, granite hell that not even the morning sun could brighten. On the streets below, a city's police force searched for a murder suspect hiding in his apartment. Would the FBI join them today? What had Mayson stumbled upon at Morris's apartment Sunday night? It was much too dangerous to stay and find out. They'd have to leave soon. Turning at a sudden rustle, he found her in the doorway. "Now what's wrong?"

"You're in your underwear."

He glanced at his plaid boxers. "So what? I have swim trunks shorter. Pretend we're at the beach."

"I'll pretend no such thing. And I'm not one of your *puttanas*. Now put your pants on."

"See? There you go again . . ."

"Tyler . . ."

"All right, goddamnit." Grabbing his slacks from the closet, he quickly pulled them on.

"And while we're on the subject of underwear," she said. "I noticed you bought me such intimate articles last night."

"A kind you don't like, obviously. And the bras — too large, I bet?"

"Stop. You're embarrassing me."

"You needed underwear," he shrugged. "I got it. What's wrong with that? I'm gonna make coffee." He started for the kitchen.

She followed him. "Do you really think my breasts are too small?"

"Underwear we can't discuss." He opened the cabinet. "But women's breasts; now there's a safe topic."

"Not 'women's' breasts," she blushed. "My breasts. Well, are they too small or not?"

"They're fine." He glanced now, pulling the mugs down. "You take yours with one sugar, right?"

She nodded as he started the microwave. First movies, now preferred condiments. He'd really noticed her this past month. "Your museum includes piano recitals. Do you play?"

"No."

Was he embarrassed to admit it? "There's nothing wrong with playing the piano, you know."

"No, there's not." As the microwave beeped, he pulled the mugs out, adding sugar to hers.

Sipping her coffee, she studied him in his gray flannels. Shirtless, shoeless, tangled gold hair in his eyes, he needed only a straw hat and corncob pipe, with perhaps a dangling weed in his teeth to make an elegant Huck Finn. "What's wrong?" She became conscious of his staring.

"Your face," he nodded.

Yes, she felt it now - her cheeks' pleasant warmth. She was smiling. "Tyler, what's going on? Why are we sipping coffee in your kitchen, me smiling, you, half-dressed?"

"Because you need help. Beyond that, I haven't a clue."

She studied her elegant Huck Finn again, with his broad shoulders and chest, and his lean-muscled arms. *Madonna mia*, his flat stomach even had ripples. "You're very hard to understand."

"And you're not?"

Taking her coffee into the study, she drew her hair back to look at herself in the mirror. As he drifted in, she asked, "I don't suppose you'd have time to buy me some makeup?"

"Write down what you want."

She turned from the mirror. "Shouldn't you be getting to the firm?"

Work. He'd forgotten. "I'd better take a shower."

He'd almost finished dressing when she slipped quietly into the bedroom. "What's wrong?" He caught her solemn face in the mirror.

"Nothing." She idly studied his dark suit and white Oxford shirt. The garnet-and-gold striped tie went well with the suit, she decided, following his loops, tucks, and slashes that ended finally with a perfect Windsor knot. "How can you remember all those steps?" she marveled.

"I do this every morning," he smiled. "For a small fee, I'll be glad to teach you the process."

She gazed at their reflections. Her head barely reached his shoulder. "How tall are you?"

"Six-three. Why, are you writing a book?"

Six-three, her guess to the inch. "Do you really like that movie, *My Fair Lady*? It's one of your museum pieces."

He noted her restlessness. "I've seen it about twenty times."

"I didn't ask how many times you'd seen it." She flicked at lint on his suit. "I asked if you liked it."

"Why else would I sit through it so many times?"

"Why must you be so difficult?" Slipping into the bathroom, she returned with a damp tissue. "Now hold still." She dabbed his jaw. "You clumsy *gavonne*, you nicked yourself shaving. Well, did you like it or not?"

My Fair Lady, he remembered. "Yes, I did."

"Why?" she asked.

"Why what?"

"Why did you like it, you idiot! Certainly there was something worth remembering, or else you wouldn't have included it in your museum."

He studied their reflections. They were sniping at each other in the mirror and she was driving him crazy. "I don't know why I liked it, I just did."

"After twenty times, nothing stands out in your mind?"

He looked at her expectant face. Of course. "The actress; you look like her."

"You think I look like Audrey Hepburn?"

"Isn't that the reason for this drill? You look just like her. Everyone must tell you that."

A shadow fell over him. "Tyler, what's wrong?"

"Nothing." He squirmed into his jacket, checking his watch. "Did you jot down the makeup you wanted?"

"The pad on the hall table. Then you won't tell me?"

"Nothing's wrong, goddamnit!"

His sharp tone revealed the opposite. Something was wrong. He just had no intention of revealing it. There was something, however, she must reveal. The time had come. "Tyler, you were right. I was at Morris's apartment Sunday night. I found him dead."

Slowly he turned. "The .38 was yours?" When she nodded, he asked, "Where is it now?"

"At the bottom of the East River."

"Morris had it before that night?"

Again she nodded. "Long before our relationship deteriorated. So long, I'd forgotten about it."

"How do you forget a snub-nose .38?"

"Because I no longer needed it. After moving into the Lyons, I stored it in an old chest, where it remained until I lent it to him." She sighed over his obvious confusion. "Tyler, I come from a world you can't begin to understand. While you were struggling with table manners and ballroom etiquette, I was learning how to protect myself on the Brooklyn streets. When you were returning from oyster roasts, I was locking up Cellini's Market and contemplating the six treacherous blocks home. The odds of being mugged weren't much different than getting picked off by a sniper in Vietnam. So I bought a gun for protection.

"Fortunately I never had to use it." She dropped on the bed. "But the peace of mind was worth the pennies I scraped together to buy it. Only after quitting Cellini's and moving to the Lyons did my fear finally disappear. I bought the BMW and no longer had to walk the dangerous streets at night. The .38 was stored and forgotten."

"Why did Morris borrow it?" He dropped beside her.

"The same reason I bought it: protection."

"But if you felt safe at the Lyons, why wouldn't he in his maximum-security apartment on the Upper East Side?"

"I guess we found out it wasn't so secure after all," she replied.

"But Morris was skittish - obsessed with his mortality. He said there'd been some recent muggings in his neighborhood, one just that week in the Essex garage. That was enough for him. Despite his fear of guns, he was convinced he needed one. So I lent him mine."

"Why not just sell it to him?"

"Tyler, it's perfectly legal to own a gun. How was I to know it'd become the weapon in a murder case? Every time I asked him about it, he promised to buy his own and return mine. But he never did, and after a while, I just forgot about it - until Sunday night, anyway."

"Tell me about that night, Mayson, beginning to end."

"End?" she frowned. "It hasn't yet. The scene inside his apartment is still so horribly fresh, like . . ." She glanced at his hand, suddenly over hers. The sensation was much too sweet to be safe. Discreetly, she slipped her hand away.

Yet she couldn't escape his eyes, insistent but gentle. He wanted to help and she wanted to know why. He meant to calm and yet frightened her, as much as the police, she was beginning to realize. "When Morris called that night, he sounded desperate, failing to mention he'd tried you first. But I should've assumed it. Anyway as he began groveling, I quickly saw an advantage to accommodating him. I had nothing to lose. He'd made it clear he was out to get me. I knew my days at Lieber Allen were numbered. He didn't explain his predicament, but the desperation in his voice was real as he begged me to drive him out to La Guardia. There was no time to waste. *Everything, Babe, depends on me making that flight.*

"My antennae went up. What did he mean? When I asked why he didn't take his car, he said it was in the shop.

So what about a cab? I asked. Look, Babe, he snapped. I don't have time for this. Now come get me!

Why should I? I asked. You want to destroy me and I'm supposed to drop what I'm doing, and rush you out to the airport? You'll have to do better than that.

"He must've wanted to break my neck," she sighed. "But he was in such a hurry."

Look Babe, I've been a putz, all right? You want an apology, you got it. *And I said, I want more than an apology, you arrogant sonofabitch! I want Lambrusco and my other assignments back. And I want Senior Associate. Now do you still want a ride?*

"For cab fare," Tyler smiled. "You were negotiating me right out of the picture. What did he say?"

"That we'd talk on the way. And I said, 'Talk's cheap, Morris.' To which he sighed, 'All right, Babe, we'll see.' "

"Then you went for the jugular, right?"

"No." Her eyes dimmed. "That's when I realized something was wrong. That he wasn't rushing to meet a deadline, but to avoid one. My suspicions grew on the drive over to his building. Why had he cut his vacation short? Why leave again so soon? And why consider giving me not only what he'd stolen but more?

"I got there around nine and parked in the basement. His BMW was down there, too, in the usual corner spot. Why had he lied about it being in the shop? Why not take it to the airport? Why Senior Associate? A zillion questions swirled in my mind as I rushed up to his apartment. I knew something was wrong and yet . . ." She shook her head.

"What, Mayson?"

"Don't you see? I knew something was wrong and yet it was only my welfare I was concerned about. If Morris was in trouble, why stick my nose into it? Didn't I have enough problems of my own?"

"But you did stick your nose into it. You went upstairs using the freight elevator. Why, is it quicker?"

She nodded. "I began using it when I did his laundry. That's why I had the key, and to meet repairmen and decorators. I was his Girl Friday. Didn't you know?"

He shook his head. "Why didn't you go to Lamp?"

"What would he have done, assign me to someone else? I would've been branded a complainer."

"Not if you'd gone to him with the real rub, not this Girl Friday bullshit - Morris's sexual extortion."

Meeting his insistent eyes, she no longer saw a reason to protect her terrible secret. "It was harmless at first, the kind you swat with an insult or curse. But six months ago it got ugly. Words, what you call my Italian shock waves, became useless."

"The same time I arrived," he sighed. "A grievance, lawsuit . . . you could've done something, Mayson, and yet you didn't. Why?"

"If I'd started making noise, even with cause, I would've lost any hope of advancing at the firm. And a lawsuit? So what if you win damages after five years and a dozen appeals? I wanted to practice law. Become a partner. I figured if I kept my mouth shut and worked hard, I'd be rid of Morris sooner or later. I just didn't realize it'd be Sunday night."

"Since the Essex records don't reflect a visitor that night, how would the killer have gotten up to Morris's apartment unless he had a key?" Tyler asked. "Who besides you had one?"

"Just Morris's sister in Connecticut, that I know of."

"What about Lamp?"

"He or anyone else at the firm could've gotten one if they wanted. All they'd have to do is steal the key long enough to make a copy at that little shop in the square. Everyone knew Morris took his jacket off the instant he arrived in the morning. He'd wrap it over his chair and there it'd remain until he left in the evening, unless he had a client meeting."

Tyler glanced at his watch. It was almost nine but he had to hear the rest. "Tell me about the apartment."

She gazed at her knotted hands. She'd prayed for that night to go away. But it hadn't, its threatening shadow growing until now, when she was forced to confront it and to trust the last person on earth she could ever have imagined. "By the time I reached his apartment, I was so frightened, I wasn't thinking clearly. I didn't see Mrs. Carter or bother knocking. I just groped for my key, unlocked the door and went inside." She shook her head as the horrible scene was replayed in her mind. "You wouldn't believe it, Tyler, unless you'd seen it with your own eyes. Not a piece of furniture was left standing. Bookshelves, cabinets, drawers — everything had been ripped out and tossed on the floor.

"Wading through it, I recall thinking just one word: desperation. Whoever ransacked the apartment had been desperate to find something. Had they? Or was it still buried somewhere in the rubble?" She sighed. "Poor Morris. All this destruction had taken place in the hour since our call. Then I realized he must be buried in the rubble, too; maybe if I hadn't kept him on the line all that time, he wouldn't be."

"Mayson, you couldn't have saved him, with, or without those minutes."

His hand was over hers again and it frightened her. The more she wanted it there, the more she knew she shouldn't. She slipped her hand away again. "The bedroom was a wreck like the rest of the place. I finally found him sprawled in the bathtub, his eyes open, lifeless. He'd been shot in the head, blood dripping into the basin. For an eternity, I just stood there gaping at this bloody corpse, trying to comprehend that just an hour ago it had been the loud, obnoxious, brilliant lawyer I'd worked for. This was Morris Mendelsohn? How could it be? Finally the fog lifted and I heard the terrible quiet, wondering if possibly the killer was still in the apartment watching me. I looked back in the tub . . ."

"That's when you found the gun?" he asked.

She nodded. "I grabbed it just before the spreading blood reached it. My first thought was, What if he hadn't called, if I hadn't arrived in time to snatch it?"

"You never considered his death a suicide?"

She shrugged, "Who rips up his own apartment before putting a gun to his head? Morris had been desperate, but to save his life, not end it."

"So you decided to split rather than hang around and try to explain the circumstances?"

"I saw no other choice. It wasn't just my gun I'd have to explain, but why I was there. And how long would it take them to discover our hatred of each other? They'd hardly have to open a file to put the pieces together: motive, opportunity and physical evidence."

"The old couple who lived below made the call," he said. "They claimed to be hard of hearing, but I guess some things you just don't miss, like furniture being tossed around . . . gun shots." Checking his watch again, he said, "So you fled — observed in the process, we know. What then? You tossed the gun?"

"Not immediately," she replied. "At first I just drove around, up one busy street, down the next, realizing a time bomb was ticking in my purse. I had to get rid of it. Like a maniac, I raced for the East River, stopped below the Queensboro Bridge, and tossed it. When I heard the splash, I ran away."

"You went home then?" he asked.

"To a horrible, sleepless night," she nodded. "Hours crept by as I sat at the bedroom window, questions circling in my head. Had anyone seen me at the Essex? Who knew about the gun or my feud with Morris? Had any of my neighbors seen me come or go that night? Would my family's past cloud the investigation? Certainly the NYPD archives had at least one room dedicated to Santa's murders." She sighed. "I'd wrestle with one question then confront another. It went on like that until suddenly, the gray morning was in the window and I realized that wrestling with the questions might not be nearly as bad as learning the answers. Should I wait to see or skip town? And you know the rest of the story." Looking up now, she said, "It's late. You'd better get to the firm."

As he rose, she followed him out. "So what do you think?"

"That we have our work cut out for us." Reaching the door, he withdrew a file from his briefcase. "Your first assignment," he explained. "The records inventory Frieda and I prepared. It's all there — cases, clients, adversaries. Assuming Morris knew his killer, he may exist somewhere in the records."

Her eyes lifted with a budding admiration. "If I've ever called you lazy, you're sure not when you don't want to be. And I'm grateful for what you're doing. But more than grateful, I'm desperate to understand why. I've given you no cause to feel anything towards me but contempt; but instead of celebrating my downfall with everyone else, you've joined me in it. So again I'm forced to ask: why?"

He studied her impassively. "I've told you: I don't know. But if it comes to me, you'll be the first to know. Now," he shut his briefcase. "I must . . ."

"Wait!" Rushing off, she returned quickly with her purse over her shoulder, orange juice in one hand, muffin in the other.

"What's this?" he asked.

"Breakfast, you dope."

Setting his briefcase down, he bit into the muffin. "Delicious. Can you do Eggs Benedict?"

She gave him a scrap of paper from her purse. "I found this while wading through the rubbish in Morris's apartment. It probably means nothing."

"Robert Hunter. 343 6217," he read. "A client's phone number?"

"Not one I recognize. Do you think it's important? If so, why didn't the murderer take it?"

"Maybe he didn't see it. Why not disguise your voice and call the number with each Manhattan area code. If Robert Hunter answers, hang up and we'll decide our next move tonight. Only don't tie up the line. If I need to reach you, I'll ring twice, hang up and call back thirty seconds later. You'll know it's safe to answer then. Only disguise your voice just to be sure."

"And if I need to call you?"

"If it's an emergency, ring twice, then hang up. I'll call back. And another thing: stay away from the windows. If you go into the study, draw the drapes."

"Tyler, we're eight stories up."

"So what? They have these things now called telescopes. And thanks for breakfast." Kissing her head, he slipped out.

CHAPTER SEVEN

★

A thousand things swirled in Tyler's mind as he emerged from the elevator. Shutting himself in his office, he thumbed through his messages. Lamp had called twice. As he grabbed the phone, Jill Allen, wearing a gray suit and the scent of conspiracy, slipped inside. "Tyler, what's going on? You're out half the afternoon yesterday and most of this morning. Lamp's looking all over for you."

Grimly, he studied the missed phone slip. Lauren Belli. Certainly she'd want to know the same thing. "I strained my knee jogging. I saw a doctor this morning."

She now eased into the topic of the week. "Isn't this thing with Mayson wild? Where could she be hiding? Certainly no one here would help. Tyler, why is the FBI joining the case?"

Good question. "Jill, I have to return Lamp's call."

"Okay, okay. But Harborside's having a lunch special. Fresh shrimp, all you can eat. I'll buy."

He'd declined a dozen such invitations in recent weeks, yet she still asked. Sex had been a mistake they were both paying for now. "The offer's tempting, but my doctor's appointment has put me way behind. And Lamp's pushing hard with the transition of Morris's practice."

"Another time then," she said, hope draining from her face as she left.

He called Lamp's office and Nicole summoned him upstairs. She was waiting as the elevator arrived to escort him down to the partner's spacious, corner office. "We've been worried about you." Lamp waved him into his usual chair. "Some morning emergency?"

"I strained my knee jogging yesterday. Fortunately an orthopedic friend was able to squeeze me into his morning schedule, but I'm sorry to be so late getting in. Any word on Mayson?"

"No, but there should be soon. The City's transit stations have been sealed off; the airports are, too, now that the FBI and Special Services have joined the operation. Duke assures me that if she hasn't already left, there's no way out now."

First the FBI. Now Special Services, a sophisticated law enforcement arm of the Justice Department. All this high-tech police power in Manhattan for the sole purpose of capturing one beautiful pain in the ass named Mayson Corelli. "Any idea what the Feds' interest is?" he asked.

Lamp studied him intently. "Not really. With everything going on, I'm afraid I didn't think to ask."

But he knew. No matter how busy, it was an obvious question to ask. "Sir, as I said yesterday, I'll do all I can to make the transition easier."

Lamp weighed this commitment without expression. "What's important is Mayson's capture and the removal of this nightmare from the front page. Every day it's there just tarnishes the firm's image that much more. At least with the Feds, we now have the resources to find Mayson and end the operation quickly. She must also be advised of this morning's developments. I'm sure they would affect her decision to continue this dangerous game she's playing with the police."

"What developments, sir?" he asked.

"The ones Duke and I discussed earlier. Despite Morris's memo charging her with financial improprieties, I told Duke I still believed sexual harassment played a role in this murder. Given Morris's reputation as a womanizer, it seems quite plausible; it certainly would've affected her state of mind. Duke agreed sexual harassment clouded the case and promised leniency if Mayson turned herself in."

"Leniency, sir?"

"If Mayson surrenders, Duke said the murder charge would be reduced to voluntary manslaughter, meaning she'd be out of prison in ten years." He frowned. "It's a shame we can't let her know."

Don't worry, Tyler thought, she'll hear the proposal and be ecstatic - ten years for a crime she didn't commit. "It's a shame, all right. But given the manhunt's scope, I doubt she'll be a fugitive much longer."

Lamp's chin rested in his fingers as he studied Tyler again. "Do you think she's still in Manhattan?"

"Hard to say, sir. But if she's been cut off from the transportation lines, her car and bank accounts, how could she get out?"

Lamp turned the heat up a notch. "Can't we assume she has a friend?

"I wasn't aware she had any, sir."

"To the contrary; she could easily have one we're not aware of. A man, perhaps. With the firm's rule against dating, it would've been natural to keep the relationship secret."

"That's possible, sir. But I'd think more about someone outside the firm."

"Perhaps," Lamp nodded. "But clearly someone helped her slip away. She was here one minute, gone the next, without money or a car. Even her packed suitcase was left behind. Now, twenty-four hours later, she remains at large without resources or even a change of clothes."

"Has Duke checked her family's background?"

Lamp nodded. "Most he already had from past investigations of her brother." He sighed. "A sad ending to a sad tale. Mayson overcame so much adversity to reach Wall Street. Now so quickly, she's thrown it all away."

"What kind of adversity?" Tyler asked.

Lamp's gaze sharpened at his curiosity. "She comes from a poor, crime-ridden Brooklyn neighborhood. Her two brothers ended up in prison. Her mother died shortly before she joined the firm."

"What about her father?"

"He's not reflected in her file; she didn't discuss him any more than the rest of her family. Mayson's a very private person, as we all know. Duke was amazed, after talking to so many people, that virtually nothing was known about her, except that for the past two years, she's been the first to arrive in the morning and the last to leave at night. In between, she's kept to herself, worked harder than anyone else, and when the men got too close, bit their heads off. Frankly," he sighed, "if anyone could reach Mayson, my guess is it'd be you, Tyler. Don't think we've missed the rumors about your breaches of the firm's rule against dating employees.

We're not that isolated up here."

"I've never dated Mayson, I assure you."

"But you don't deny she's beautiful?"

"No sir, she's very beautiful, but even more disagreeable, and she hates my guts."

"She hated Morris more. She killed him. Still, I see your point. You represented all that had been stripped from her."

"Peaceful co-existence," Tyler said. "That's all I ever hoped for."

"I don't suppose in this peaceful co-existence, she ever revealed the name of a friend to whom she might turn for help, say in avoiding a murder charge?"

"She's much too smart for that, sir."

Lamp's gaze now drifted out the window where afternoon shadows had lengthened over Manhattan. The day was slipping away and yet he seemed quite content to spend it with his lowly associate. Grabbing his favorite toy, the handsome oak gavel awarded for his service as National Bar President, he turned back. "Mayson's more than smart; 'brilliant' is the word. Seven years at Columbia and no grade less than A. Imagine that." He rolled the gavel in his fingers. "Not seven years of academic excellence, but perfection - an amazing feat. But try doing it while holding down two or three jobs, not just to pay your tuition but your invalid mother's support. That's a study in self-discipline few can duplicate." He smiled at Tyler's bewilderment. "Mayson comes from a world we'll never understand, where privileges we take for granted don't exist - where a person works for everything she gets. It toughens her and in Mayson's case, leaves her cold and mistrusting."

Tyler was sorry not to have known this, but if he needed a reason to help Mayson, Lamp had just provided it.

The partner's gavel rolled again with his reflections. "What's ironic is that the toughness that got Mayson to Wall Street is the same toughness that couldn't tolerate Morris's threats to drive her away. She did what she had to. She killed him. Still," he sighed. "Who could've expected it? She seemed the ideal candidate for our associate program. Anyone who'd accomplished what she had could handle our seventy-hour weeks without breaking a sweat. What else did we need to know, in her case and also yours."

"Not my work ethic," Tyler smiled.

"Hell no," Lamp's eyes sparkled. "Because the Chief Justice of the U.S. Supreme Court recommended you, not because he's Chief Justice, but because I trust his judgment unconditionally. If Chase says it's a six iron to the green when you'd swear it's a four, you damn well better take his advice. The same applies when he says, 'There's a boy you need at Lieber Allen.' He's right on the money every time."

Tyler had served his Supreme Court clerkship right out of Harvard Law. When it ended, Chief Justice Falkingham had passed him along to his good friend on Wall Street. The move had proven a huge mistake. He hated New York's madness, its cold, unfriendly people who bumped into each other on frantic flights to nowhere.

"How do you like New York?" Lamp asked now.

"I love it, sir. I'm grateful to the Chief Justice for recommending it."

Lamp smiled, "There's no denying you've brought a breath of fresh air to this place. I'm sure that blind girl who runs the lobby's newsstand would agree. I've seen you talking to her."

"Cathy Walters."

"There, you see. I've been buying my morning paper from her for years and never knew her name. You're here six months and already know it."

Precisely why he hated New York. And he'd known "the blind girl's" name the first day. "Cathy's read *War and Peace* in Braille. And *Gone with the Wind*, twice."

"Amazing!" Lamp exclaimed as he studied his gavel's gold-plated inscription.

And in this instant, Tyler studied the scarring around the partner's eye - a half moon that made it smile even if the owner wasn't. How had the scarring occurred? If anyone knew, it wasn't discussed.

"I must say this investigation has been filled with revelations," Lamp drifted from his silence. "Your ignorance of the animosity between Mayson and Morris, for example."

They'd covered this ground yesterday. Why trudge through it again? "I'd heard about their feud, sir, but as I've explained, it was all hearsay."

"I wonder how much Mayson knew of Morris's activities between Thursday and Sunday?"

More plowed ground. "Why assume she knew anything?"

"Because feud or not, they'd worked together for two years. She must've known why he flew to Minnesota on Thursday and why he was zooming off again to San Francisco on Sunday."

Did Lamp know? Tyler now wondered. Was he desperate to discover who else might've known? So desperate he'd ripped up Morris's apartment, killing him in the process? Did some document exist, which held the answer - one explaining the reason for Morris's Minnesota trip? Had Lamp believed it could be found in Morris's apartment, and had it been found or not?

"Tyler . . . ?" Lamp frowned at his associate's distracted gaze.

"I was just thinking. There's really no basis for assuming Mayson knew anything about Morris's activities."

"But he confided in her."

"Before the feud, yes. But the Minnesota trip occurred afterwards, when Morris was on vacation. It's doubtful he would've discussed it with Mayson then."

Again Lamp studied him intently. "You're right, of course. I just can't help wondering what she knows about all this."

Yes, Tyler could see that and it was scaring the hell out of him. "Sir, have you made a decision on the case reassignments?"

The question jolted Lamp from his reflections. "Yes, of course. That's why I summoned you up here. Ed Bilbro is assuming Morris's cases. Brief him on your projects as soon as possible."

Tyler rose now, remembering to wince. "I'll meet with Ed this afternoon."

Nodding absently, Lamp turned back to the window, the gavel once again rolling in his fingers.

Where had this latest inquisition left him, Tyler wondered, beyond suspicion or somewhere in its shadow? One thing was certain; the shadow wasn't going away. As the search continued, everyone who knew Mayson would be put under the microscope.

Back in his office, he called Ed Bilbro to arrange a six p.m.

meeting. The instant he hung up, the phone rang twice. A half-minute later as it rang again, he quickly grabbed it.

"You kissed me," Mayson snapped. "Don't do it again. Where have you been?"

"With Lamp," he replied.

"For two hours? Lauren Belli called. She's not very happy with you."

He cupped the phone as Jill Allen suddenly loomed in the doorway. "Jill, this may take a while." Then into the phone, he said, "Not tonight, Kate, I'm sorry."

"Someone's in your office. Your Hall Fairy, Jill Allen? You forgot my list of makeup items."

Was there a bigger pain in the ass anywhere? Across the desk, Jill gleamed curiously as he spoke to New York's most wanted fugitive. "Make it quick," he grabbed a pen, jotting the items down.

"Tyler, I bet you'd like to wring my neck about now."

"Very much, in fact."

"Is Drooling Jill still there?"

"See you later," he hung up.

"At least I'm not the only one being rejected today," Jill said. "Tyler, you seem very edgy."

He squinted at his own scrawl. Was that 'Lorin' or . . . He snatched up the ringing phone.

The instant he hung up, Jill pounced again. "Kate?"

"Bilbro's secretary. Our meeting to discuss Morris's practice has been pushed back."

She watched him squint again at his list. "For heaven's sake, what is it, a recipe or something? Tyler, are you in love with Kate?"

"Who?" He grabbed the quiet phone and started dialing. Sometimes it worked, sometimes it didn't. "Kate? Oh no, we're just friends. Look Jill, I don't want to seem rude . . ."

"Okay, okay." She glanced at the phone in his hand, then recalled her question. "Yesterday, when Mayson burst from your office, she was very upset. Did she say where she was going?"

"Of course not," he said. "She was much too busy bitching over Lambrusco and . . ." Gazing at the phone, it suddenly hit him. Shit! Grabbing his jacket, he started out. "I'm late for an appointment."

Outside the phone booth, the afternoon sun was fading over the square. Soon the commuters would begin herding past on their way to the nearby station. Hanging up, he waited then redialed.

"Heee-lll-ooohhh."

"Bette Davis?" he asked.

"Scarlet O'Hara, you idiot!"

"Then it's pathetic. Mayson, don't call me at the firm anymore. My phone might be bugged."

"Where are you now?" she asked.

"A phone booth in the square."

"Why would you be under suspicion?"

"Because you make such a goddamned scene everywhere you go. Jill saw you storm out of my office yesterday. Just now, she asked if you'd asked for my help. How much longer until someone on Seventy-First yesterday connects you with the picture on TV? And Lamp scares the hell out of me. I'm not sure where he's coming from." His restless gaze now picked up the first commuters crossing the square. "Then there's Lauren; one phone call from her . . ." He sighed. "Mayson, we need to leave. It's just too dangerous to stay."

"Tyler, we can't leave New York."

"Why not?" he asked.

"Because you can't just leave your home, job, everything to go running around the country with me. I can't ask that."

"You're not asking. And New York isn't my home. I hate this goddamned place . . . Look," he sighed. "Just don't call the firm anymore. We'll discuss our plans tonight."

"Not if they include leaving New York," she insisted. "Tyler, I'm not your responsibility. And besides, I'm quite capable . . ."

"Capable shit! You're in a goddamned mess you can't get out of. You need my help and . . ."

"Don't tell me what I'm going to do!"

The commuter traffic had thickened in the square. Carefully he searched the faces. Firm secretaries would soon be among them, curious over what he was doing. Did he know himself? "You still don't trust me, Mayson, that's the bottom line. The rest, this heroic Joan of Arc crap — its bullshit. I've staked my life on your innocence and yet when the chips are down, you can't do the same for me. What's next; a polygraph test, a stack of Bibles? 'I swear I don't want Mayson's job or her virtue.' "

"Then what?" she demanded. "Only an idiot would risk his life without expecting something in return. And despite acting like one sometimes, you're not an idiot. So I repeat: What do you want?"

"Nothing!" Slamming the phone down, he stormed across the crowded square. Let her go to prison! She and Lucky could have a swell reunion . . . Only she wasn't like him. She might be paranoid, contentious, spiteful, but she wasn't a murderer. So could he allow her to be punished like one? She wouldn't do well in prison. She was delicate, yet ferocious — a bad combination for prison survival. Should he care? Digging his hands into his coat, he stopped to gaze up at the Old Dame: ancient, gray, magnificent. It didn't matter if he should care. The point was he did. Which said what about his sanity?

How long had it been since he'd talked to himself this way? He'd been dead inside for so long, until now, as he stood quietly gazing at the Old Dame, as voices again whispered inside his head and warm blood flowed through his veins. Returning to the booth, he placed the first call, then after hanging up, the second.

"Rhee-ttt darling?" she answered.

"It's still pathetic."

"Tyler, I'm so sorry. I didn't mean those things."

"So are you prepared to leave New York?"

"How? Every news program says we're sealed off. Why is the Attorney General looking for me?"

"Good question. I wish I knew. I think Lamp does."

"Why?" she asked.

"Because he wasn't curious enough to ask the question."

"Do you think he killed Morris?"

"I'd say he's definitely in the running."

"What about your family?"

"They had no reason to kill Morris."

"No, I mean . . ."

"I know what you meant and I'll deal with them."

"Well do it soon. I'd hate for them to learn on the evening news that their son is on the FBI's Most Wanted List. Your father doesn't have a heart condition, does he?"

"I said I'd deal with it."

"Deal with Lauren Belli, too. She left another nasty message."

"Have you started reviewing the office inventory?" he asked.

"I've finished. In fact, there's something . . . Wait a minute." Dropping the phone, she retrieved the inventory to confirm she hadn't been mistaken. "Tyler, one of Morris's probate cases is missing. 'Crenshaw.' All the others are listed."

"Mayson, that inventory's complete. Frieda and I picked up everything on the computer. We even manually flipped through the office files. If there was any record of Crenshaw, it'd be reflected."

"Tyler, we're talking about a will contest over a ten-million-dollar estate. The files took up an entire drawer, not the new tan cabinets but the gray one behind his desk. Did you check it?"

"We checked them all," he confirmed.

"Then Lamp has the files. He quizzed me about Crenshaw Monday morning. Someone had called about its status and he had to get back to them."

He looked up now as the square traffic peaked, commuters jostling each other as they passed. Lamp had also been interested in what she knew about Morris's Minnesota activities. Was his trip somehow connected to Crenshaw? "Mayson, it's not just the files. The case has vanished from the firm's database."

"That's it, isn't it?" Her spine tingled. "Crenshaw is the link between Lamp and Morris."

"It looks that way. A drawer full of records doesn't just . . ." He froze at the face glaring at him through the glass. Quickly the woman vanished into the crowd. "Mayson, I have to go."

"What's wrong?" she asked.

"Nicole just spotted me on her way to the train station."

Lauren had called again, he discovered on his return to the office, her message instructing him to call ASAP. Taking the elevator up to Ed Bilbro's office, the partner looked up from a thick deposition as Tyler entered. A square-faced man with solemn eyes, crew cut and sturdy body, Bilbro would've been the perfect poster boy for a Marine recruiting ad.

They discussed Morris's practice, a subject he'd intellectually abandoned, and then set timetables for projects he'd never begin. While Bilbro rambled, Tyler focused on the dangerous plan that had begun spinning in his head. On his way out, he ventured upon the treacherous ground he'd been contemplating. "Crenshaw?" Bilbro said. "If it's one of Morris's cases, it hasn't been assigned to me."

And most likely never will be, Tyler thought.

A cold drizzle greeted him as he headed for his car. But it was lurking ghosts, not the rain, that quickened his pace as his eyes darted over the dark, wet streets, absorbing everything, touching nothing. Had Nicole told Lamp about seeing him in the phone booth? Had Lamp gone to Duke with his suspicions and Lauren to the DA with hers? Or would she wait until talking to him?

The rain strengthened as he reached the garage. Exiting minutes later, he snapped on his wipers for the drive uptown. A dark sedan quickly loomed in his mirror, remaining there as the next wet blocks were covered. Finally the rain weakened enough for him to study the car's occupants: two men, sitting motionless, without conversation. He moved again. The sedan moved with him, through Gramercy Park, Murray Hill, Midtown. The Queensboro Bridge came, vanished and still the sedan kissed his tail. He proceeded north on Park. The sedan did, too. Did they suspect him of hiding Mayson? Why else would they be tailing him? Should he stick to his regular route?

The sedan remained in his mirror at Eighty-Ninth, then Ninety-Second. His building soon loomed in the mist. Ninety-Third, Ninety-Fourth, and Ninety-Fifth were covered in quick succession. Heart pounding, he watched his building fade into the misty sky. Reaching East Harlem, the sedan remained. The rain had stopped and he could now see the solemn-faced men clearly as he drifted up to the light. His sweaty palms clenched the wheel as he moved again. He was accomplishing nothing by clipping off blocks and burning gas. Without warning, he suddenly whipped into a dark side street. The sedan's horn blasted, its high beams flashing as it blew past. Slumping over the wheel, he sighed and recalling his errand, started off again.

He returned to the apartment later, a Bocelli number drifting from the study. As he put his bags in the kitchen, the door opened down the hall and soft footsteps pattered on the carpet. Breezing around the corner, Mayson's eyes glowed expectantly. Her lush hair was waved, her smooth, arched cheeks glowing like her eyes. The white cashmere sweater accentuated her slender neck, the snug jeans serving up delicate angles he'd never seen before.

"Tyler, what's wrong?" she asked.

"Nothing." He pulled groceries out, most of which they didn't need now. "I'm sorry to be so late."

"You forgot my makeup — is that it?"

"No." He started on the second bag. "I met with Ed Bilbro. He's taking over Morris's cases."

"What a terrible choice," she answered. "He has the personality of a drill sergeant."

"He also knows nothing about Crenshaw."

"Wasn't it dangerous to ask?"

"Probably, but without the files we have to start somewhere." He paused, "Is that L'Air Du Temps?"

Before she could reply, he ducked into the living room, his gaze settling on Manhattan's glittering skyline. Whatever it did for others, it didn't do for him. He'd been planning to leave for weeks, serving notice on Lamp and his landlord, then hitting the road. Where it would take him, he hadn't been sure. Castlewood? Hadn't he left it, too? Or was he still leaving? Castlewood wasn't a place like Manhattan, but home, a state of mind. Everything . . . or it had been. Now it was gone.

"Why don't you like L'Air Du Temps?" she suddenly asked behind him.

"It's fine."

"No Tyler, it's not. Your tone, body language, the fact that you won't turn and look at me says that it's anything but fine. I won't wear it again if it bothers you."

"Don't be ridiculous."

"Then turn around. I want your opinion on my new clothes."

As he switched on the lamp, she twirled gracefully. "The jeans fit well, don't you think?"

"They're too tight but I can live with it." He nodded at her new topsiders. "Do they fit?"

"They'll be fine once I get used to looking like a 'prep.' Want to see the study?"

"You haven't redecorated already?" Following her into the study, he found the coffee table dressed with his expensive linen and finest china, candles glowing in the brass holders. Now he understood the Bocelli. "Romantic."

"Well that certainly wasn't my intent. I just wanted to thank you for what you've done and, with limited options, I chose a nice, quiet dinner."

"So what are we having?" he asked.

"T-bones, unless you bought something better. Steaks and Molson; is that all you keep in stock?"

"I'm a man of simple tastes." He opened the drapes.

"A man of 'excessive' tastes, you mean, at least with women. Why did you open the drapes?"

"It doesn't look natural with them all closed. You'll just have to stay away from the windows."

"And how am I supposed to get around - crawl on my belly like a snake?"

"Maybe you'd rather spend the next forty years at Attica with your brother, Lucky."

"The Lips, you idiot. Why can't you get that straight?"

His gaze stopped now on the walnut shelves. "Keep the TV down. And for music, use my iPod."

She scowled. He certainly was bossy all of a sudden. "I called that number finally - four area codes. No Robert Hunter at any. And by the way, tonight's telephone Lotto includes five women, Lauren Belli excluded, who sounds more upset each time she calls."

He couldn't put Lauren off much longer and wouldn't have to. The plan was coming together.

"It's disgusting the way those women pant after you," she said. "Stafford was the most pathetic of all. She even has your dripping-with-molasses drawl. 'Tiles, deaaahhh.' She must be one hot babe."

"You'll have to ask my brother-in-law, Parker, about that. Stafford's my sister." Pausing to enjoy her foot in the mouth cringe, he said, "Branch out tomorrow with the Robert Hunter number. Connect it with every area code in the country, if necessary. Only scrap the Scarlet voice for one more in your range - a Harlem rap queen maybe."

"And what happens, Rhett Butler, if Robert Hunter answers?"

"Hang up and we'll figure it out later."

She huffed, "Men always say that when they don't know what to do."

"And what do women say?"

"They say . . . How do you like your steak?"

"Medium rare," he smiled.

"Then go change while I finish up."

She returned to the kitchen to put the groceries away. Standing over the counter, she smiled at the makeup items in the last bag. Hadn't she known he'd screw it up? Revlon, not L'Oreal. But he tried, that's what counted. And hadn't he gotten everything she'd asked for, just the wrong brand?

She reached for the remaining items: Jordan Almonds, her beloved 'Jams' and to her teeth's dismay a bag of jawbreakers, her 'JBs.' They'd gotten her through seven years at Columbia and the dawn-to-twilight days at Lieber Allen. Her one addiction and Tyler had learned it in their brief time together. Alone in his apartment, gripped by fear and boredom, she'd been craving a fix but not so terribly she'd thought to ask for them. Yet he'd remembered. She removed the last item, a paperback novel titled *Robes of Vengeance*, a legal thriller she'd been dying to read. Just weeks ago she'd been thumbing through a copy in the library when Tyler passed by on one of his restless jaunts.

"Read it?" he'd asked. To which she'd retorted, "If I had one-tenth the leisure time you do, I'm certain I would have by now." Despite her rudeness that afternoon, he'd bought her the book. Tomorrow's long, empty hours would now be filled by *Robes of Vengeance*, JB's and Jams. All because . . . Oh Tyler, please don't do this! Her eyes shut tightly. I'm from a place where people like you don't exist. Don't tease me with your kindness when I know it can't last.

He found her minutes later, head bent over the cluttered counter. "Mayson, what's wrong?" he asked. When she didn't answer, he gently lifted her face. Her eyes were swollen with tears. Breaking away, she fled down the hall. The bedroom door slammed. Following, he knocked on the door and found it locked. "Damnit Mayson, what the hell's going on? Open up."

"No! Leave me alone!"

"Did I do something wrong?"

"Yes . . . I mean, no. It's just . . ."

"Just what?" He tried the knob again. "Mayson, open the goddamned door."

How could she have known with her pipes bone dry for so long that tears would suddenly come? It was wonderful to cry again but so confusing and terrifying. She needed to be alone to sort all this out. Only he wouldn't let her. Streaking into the bathroom, she locked the door.

When she came out twenty minutes later, he was gone.

CHAPTER EIGHT

★

The November night had brought a chilling rain and dense fog that blanketed the huddled blocks of Georgetown. Impatiently the man at the window glanced at his watch. Didn't they know better than to keep him waiting?

He was tall and husky, with silver hair that crested his forehead. He had a florid face, broader than he would've preferred, his blue eyes aglow with a religious zeal he wasn't ashamed to admit, even to the godless journalists who ridiculed him. Let them joke. Hadn't he built the most powerful religious coalition in the western world? Wasn't he the envy of every evangelist claiming to serve the Lord? Who among them could deny that he'd been chosen above the others to lead the country into the next glorious era? And were they not on the eve of that era now? The foundation was in place or would be Friday, with the President's announcement. Later in a CMA broadcast carried to millions, he'd express both surprise and joy at the announcement, one that would complete the mission's team and assure their glorious destiny. Praise the Lord and His servant, Seth Harrington, who'd planted the man's name in the President's ear as he had the first two, then carefully tended the seed until it yielded the divine fruit that would soon be served to a nation that had become barren and desolate with the chilling winds of a government without soul, conscience or the backbone of Christian principles. As the sirens of its godless insanity had screeched across the forsaken land, the Lord's voice had been lost.

Was it any wonder then that in this dying world sin was celebrated rather than punished? Abortions performed daily in the nation's clinics? Pornography sold on every street corner? That the nation's children were praised not for possessing Bibles but government-issued condoms? And why should anyone be surprised that they came home with dangerous drugs that polluted their bodies, while their teachers polluted their minds with irresponsible liberal propaganda? That the law didn't ban sexual perversions but protected them; the more vile they were, the more openly they were embraced. Homosexuals weren't pariahs but champions, and family values were the chains of bondage they'd escaped. Only in a modern-day Babylon was this insanity possible - here in America, which he'd become convinced must be saved before it was too late.

The Lord hadn't just revealed the nation's plight, but also the means to its salvation. He'd led Seth to the Galveston church of Reverend Luke Haynesworth to deliver a special sermon that hot, July Sunday. There, he'd met a parishioner named Thomas Longbridge, the young Galveston prosecutor intent on becoming the next Texas Governor. He'd seen a news clip of the tall, awkward Longbridge, dark eyes gleaming as he boasted to a shopping mall crowd that he'd unseat incumbent Jess Morton in the fall election. But not without polish and poise, and he'd need more than a lesson or two in political rhetoric. Still, Longbridge possessed the fire of a righteous soul, the courage of a holy warrior, and most importantly a life's view in harmony with the CMA. Weren't these the raw ingredients necessary to win the election?

As they discussed the campaign that first Sunday, he began envisioning the possibilities with the fervor of a Dr. Frankenstein: a modulation of Longbridge's strident voice, a pitch adjustment to heighten the urgency of his message, facial expressions and hand gestures to punctuate his words. Timing was the key, and so was the long, hard practice necessary to master the techniques. New suits, with less shiny fabrics and more subdued colors were needed and the bushy hair must be trimmed. It was a major overhaul but no less achievable than the one he'd prescribed for a young tent revivalist working the hot, dusty back roads of southern Texas. Hadn't that young man soon found himself commanding larger audiences with more generous hearts and deeper pockets? Enough to finance his own ministry and expand his influence to broader horizons. Hadn't he become Chairman of the world's largest Christian coalition? Praise the Lord and the Christians for a Moral America. Praise its Chairman, Seth Harrington.

The church hall chat that morning had led to a luncheon at Longbridge's ranch. By evening, he'd been persuaded to spend the night and attend a morning meeting in Galveston with

Longbridge's top campaign advisers. By Monday afternoon the alliance had been formed. In exchange for incorporating the CMA's doctrines into his campaign platform, Longbridge would receive its support in his bid for Governor, plus lessons in image and oratory from the CMA Chairman himself. Harrington had then returned to Houston to begin assembling his forces and marshalling the resources necessary to unseat the pompous agnostic, Morton. By week's end, the CMA juggernaut was rolling forward on its new mission — the election of Thomas Longbridge as Texas Governor.

As his CMA disciples raised money and spread campaign literature, Harrington went on the air to blister Morton's godless policies that had undermined Texas. Morton, he charged, had been corrupted by power, seduced by the Left's Anti-American atheism. Young Tom Longbridge brought fresh idealism in which God, family and decency were championed, not scorned. When not preaching from his TV pulpit, Harrington could be found on talk shows, addressing business groups and community leaders, and spreading his urgent message to anyone who'd listen. Texas needed Longbridge's vigor, fresh intelligence and uncompromising Christian values, not Morton and his godless assault on everything Texan and American. Austin, Houston, Dallas, Fort Worth, San Antonio - the CMA canvassed every city and border town. Longbridge quickly became a household name. But who was he? Behind the scenes a tireless Harrington was getting him ready, coaching him in style, image and oratory. Long, patient hours were committed until finally with just weeks remaining until Election Day, Harrington was prepared to unveil his creation.

Hair trimmed, his wardrobe now consisting of tailored suits, silk ties and Oxford shirts, Longbridge hit the campaign trail with his new mentor. Stepping up to the podium in packed convention halls, he was astounded by the massive support he'd garnered in such a short time. And moved by his gratitude, he delivered address after address with poise and polish, bringing the crowds to their feet and a gleam to his mentor's eyes. Still, the election was close; but with the last vote counted, the margin was immaterial. The lanky Galveston prosecutor had become Texas Governor, a miracle that lifted Harrington's eyes to the Heavens. Wasn't it now clear that his bond with Longbridge had been divinely ordained?

Texas prospered over Longbridge's two terms and his bond with Harrington deepened. He came to rely almost exclusively on the CMA Chairman's advice, making no significant move without his endorsement. Harrington's choices for key political positions and judgeships became Longbridge appointments. At the same time, a tide of political conservatism deeply rooted in Christian values was sweeping across the country. Longbridge, at the height of his popularity, became its rallying symbol. As his second term ended, he was besieged with offers to run for President. If he could bring honest, effective government to Texas, why not the entire country? America needed him. And with the party's nomination assured, he responded. Once again, he and Harrington joined forces to unseat an incumbent politician, this time, the President of the United States. The battle was much larger than before, but so were the resources to fight it. By now the CMA claimed forty million members and financial assets in the billions. By summer's end, the incumbent's lead was overcome with a momentum that never faded. By Election Day, there was no question who'd win. By midnight it was over. Longbridge had become President.

Again Harrington's eyes lifted to the Heavens. Praise the Lord, and His faithful servant, Seth Harrington, in whose hands the divine mission had been entrusted.

Longbridge consulted him on all appointments and, with one exception, adopted his choices. Three years later that exception remained an insult Harrington couldn't forgive. Still his hand-picked men occupied positions critical to the mission's success, the last man's identity to be revealed on Friday. Then they could begin the march into the new era, one he'd named with the Lord's blessing, "The Great Christian Renaissance." How fitting that the greatest nation on earth should be saved in the moment of its deepest suffering - that he, who'd devoted his life to this purpose should be chosen as the instrument of salvation.

Yet there'd still been the uncertainty of how to use his abundant resources, until the Charleston aristocrat had appeared in his Houston office one morning after Longbridge's inauguration. A chain-smoking cynic, he'd seemed an unlikely candidate, but within minutes Harrington became convinced the Lord had sent him. The aristocrat's appointment had been essential, but Longbridge was protected from the circumstances that spawned it. Hadn't there also been circumstances of the deliverance Moses had been unable to share with the others? How could a mission be controlled without its confidentiality protected? The aristocrat, like the others, had been made to understand that if Longbridge had put him in power, it was Harrington to whom he was accountable. The Lord had understood this strategy and blessed its implementation.

The aristocrat's friend had since joined him in power and with Friday's announcement a second would, too, meaning he'd delivered on his promises. It would then be up to them to deliver on theirs. And with the information he possessed, there was little doubt they would.

Things had fallen into place just in time. The spring term, with its glorious opportunities, would soon be upon them. And if all went well by term's end the first steps would've been taken on the road to salvation. Children would again be free to carry their Bibles to school and to pray in their classrooms. Debate would end on whether abortion was a family planning option or clinical murder, homosexuality an alternative lifestyle or criminal perversion. No longer would citizens argue over whether pornography was a protected form of expression or an intolerable pollution of man's soul. Laws enforcing moral decency would be added to, not removed from, the statute books. And this was only the beginning. There was so much work to be done.

His attention was now drawn to the limo gliding up the dark, misty street. Again he checked his watch. Thirty minutes they'd kept him waiting. He wouldn't even be here on this cold, miserable night were it not for their betrayal: an ancient skeleton that had slipped from the closet this past Sunday to threaten the mission. It sickened him to realize the enormous price they'd been forced to pay to put it back. And yet how were they to know the threat didn't still exist?

The limo door opened and the men emerged in their raincoats. Scanning the street, they hurried up to the brick townhouse. "You're late," he said as he met them and the limo vanished into the night.

"Sorry." The Charleston aristocrat wrestled out of his coat, hanging it with those of his companions in the foyer closet.

"I'm to blame," the new man replied. "The fog delayed my flight."

Harrington studied him carefully now. He had the New Yorker's worldly polish, his handsome face thin and meticulous like his body, his eyes solemn, even if the one with its half-moon scar suggested a smile. Had the scar existed before that dreadful night forty years ago? He was certain he didn't want to know.

The third man was neither handsome nor tall like his friends, but toad-like: short, round and balding. Only he looked his sixty-six years, their common age as former classmates, friends and now extremely powerful colleagues. "We'll meet in the study," Harrington said, and he led them down the hall.

He was a guest himself in the elegant home of Ashton Lakeland, his wealthy CMA benefactor. One of the nation's leading industrialists, Lakeland owned homes all over the world and devoted an inordinate amount of time to traveling between them. He was rarely in Georgetown except to visit friends or lobby for a cause. Consequently, he'd left his home at Harrington's disposal, who had far more need for it. Taking his favorite chair at the coffee table, he glanced at the new man. "Close the door. The housekeeper has retired, but I don't want her coming downstairs for cocoa and catching a whiff of our conversation."

When they were settled around him, he began. "I hope you appreciate how close your treachery has come to destroying our mission. Not to mention the heinous crime that sent an innocent man to the electric chair. Good Lord! Can you imagine if this abomination was ever exposed? It would make a mockery not just of the noble institution you serve, but also of me, the CMA, and the President of the United States. In one blow, you would've destroyed everything we've worked so hard to accomplish." He paused as the aristocrat slouched across the table, lit a familiar Dunhill and vanished inside a smoke cloud. "What will it take to make you appreciate the gravity of this situation?" He glowered at the man he'd elevated to national prominence with but a whisper in the President's ear.

The aristocrat replied, "I'm sure I speak for everyone when saying I fully appreciate that this is a crisis. Now let's get to the meeting's real objective, which is bringing it to a swift conclusion."

Bristling, Harrington now turned to the pair on the sofa. Unlike the insolent aristocrat, they were properly anxious. "We can't bring anything to a swift conclusion until we grasp all the facts. Didn't they teach your friend that in law school? Or have those imported cigarettes finally rotted his brain?"

The New Yorker sighed. "We should've informed you of this threat in June. We knew it was real and that it wasn't going away. Otherwise our families wouldn't have met Crenshaw's demands all these years. He assured us the crime's proof would remain safely buried and that only two things could dig it up: our families not meeting his demands or his death, which of course occurred in June."

His toad-like friend added, "The questions keep grinding in my head. When will the evidence surface? Who has it? And can they be bought off like the sheriff?"

"We've all been tortured by these questions," the New Yorker echoed. "Yet there was no choice but to wait."

"You're wrong," Harrington countered. "You could've informed me of the threat."

The aristocrat, puffing greedily, already sensed a full pack meeting. Most meetings with the pompous, long-winded Harrington were. "And what would you've done, Seth, had you known of the threat in June?"

Harrington answered, "First, let me tell you what I would've done had I known three years ago; I wouldn't have foolishly recommended a lying murderer for the important position you now hold. Likewise for your friends here, who carry the same shameful baggage! It's a mistake that threatens to destroy the fruits of my lifelong labor and tragically it's one I can't correct! I must live with it and pray the disaster it threatens never comes to pass."

"Then the plan hasn't changed?" the New Yorker asked.

"Of course not, you fool! What would you have me do? Go to the President on the eve of your nomination and say I've just learned that you and your two friends are cowardly murderers who stood by while an innocent man was electrocuted for your crime? Certainly not - instead it's our grave challenge to insure that neither Longbridge, nor anyone else ever learns of your horrible past." He turned to the aristocrat, whose discarded butts, with their distinctive black-and-gold ringed filters, were already accumulating in the ashtray. "And to answer your question, had I known of the threat in June, I would've used the same strategy: define it, locate its source and then eliminate it - something that would've been much easier when the Jew lawyer was alive. Now we've lost that advantage." He frowned at the New Yorker. "Why did you quietly sit by when the Jew became involved in the sheriff's estate? Wasn't it obvious he'd stumble upon this mess sooner or later?"

"He'd already filed the probate suit when I discovered his involvement," the New Yorker replied. "It was too late by then to pressure him into withdrawal without creating suspicion. And I didn't 'quietly sit by.' I monitored his activities closely. His involvement didn't necessarily mean he'd discover the old murder case, even if it was the primary source of the estate the heirs were fighting over. His concern was getting the fortune for his clients, nothing else."

"Are you still convinced his discovery of the murder case occurred while he was on vacation?"

The New Yorker nodded. "It's the reason he flew to Minnesota. Had he known before, I would've been approached with his extortion scheme. Morris never dallied when money was involved, especially the kind here."

"So what do we assume about Corelli?" Harrington asked.

"I'm certain she knows very little; and Morris wouldn't have shared his Minnesota discovery because it would mean giving her a cut - something not in his makeup. Besides, they weren't even speaking when he left on vacation. Their feud was well known, but not its cause. My fabricated memo regarding Corelli's alleged financial improprieties not only addresses this, but also provides her motive for the murder."

The Toad asked, "Has the probate files' disappearance created any suspicion?"

He shook his head. "Had anyone missed them it would've been Corelli, and I kept her distanced from Monday's inventory."

"How can you be sure Tyler didn't miss the files?" the Aristocrat asked.

"Because he'd just gotten involved in the practice and wasn't familiar with the probate work."

"Then can you assure us the case has been purged from the firm's records?" Harrington asked.

He nodded. "As far as anyone knows, it never existed."

"And you're sure the Jew didn't reveal his Minnesota discovery to Corelli?" the Toad asked.

"Yes," he insisted. "And Morris was in too much of a hurry to discuss anything but fleeing New York. Fortunately Leopold arrived in time to prevent that."

At least there was something to say grace over, Harrington thought. Leopold had been just a shuttle away when disaster struck Sunday. Rushing to New York, he'd rescued them from the hot cauldron and was now in Minnesota, posing as a Lieber Allen partner. As if reading his mind, the Toad asked, "What has Leopold learned in Minnesota?"

"So far, just that the Markhams gave Mendelsohn the chest on Thursday. They have no idea where he took it or most importantly what it contained. Apparently it remained in that Snow Peak bank vault for forty years, without the seal being broken. According to Dale Markham, the Jew privately examined it in one of the bank offices and then left without sharing his discovery. On this basis, we can assume no one else knows of its contents, at least if our New York friend is right about the Jew not confiding in Corelli. Still, recovering the chest will take time. Mendelsohn's apartment, car, bank box and vault space at Lieber Allen have all been searched, which I suppose turns us back to Minnesota."

"What about an airport locker?" the Toad asked. "Has La Guardia been checked?"

"Not just La Guardia, but Kennedy, Newark, St. Paul and Duluth," Harrington replied. "Whatever the Jew did with the chest, he didn't store it in an airport locker."

The Aristocrat crushed out one Dunhill then quickly lit another. "I bet Chapman and Streeter had those airports scoured by Monday afternoon. That's a lotta leg to go with Leopold's muscle.

"Strange, isn't it?" he smiled. "Leopold with his littered past teamed with the Bureau and Justice."

"Let's just be thankful we're so rich in resources," Harrington said as he turned back to the New Yorker. "Chapman and Streeter agree with your homicide detective that Corelli's trapped in Manhattan. They also believe she has an ally. Have you picked up any scuttlebutt at your firm?"

"I've been mildly suspicious of Tyler Waddill," he replied. "However, after quizzing him extensively, there seems to be nothing there. Still I've had my secretary keep tabs on him. She last reported his odd purchase of women's cosmetics."

"Hell, there's nothing suspicious about that," the Aristocrat laughed. "Tyler has more girlfriends than he knows what to do with. Why risk his life for one more?"

"Corelli's a beautiful young woman," the New Yorker rejoined.

"Even so," Harrington said, "as our Charleston friend says, Waddill must have dozens. Why risk prison for this particular one? Is there anything else on Corelli?"

"No," the New Yorker replied.

"Well, there should be soon. If your homicide detective doesn't nab her, the Feds will. I'm more concerned now with recovering that chest."

"What if Corelli reaches it before we do?" the Toad asked.

"She doesn't know about it," the New Yorker replied. "And besides, she has far too much else to worry about."

"The first sign she knows anything that can hurt us, she'll be eliminated," Harrington said.

"And if that's after she's in custody?" the Toad asked. "Leopold can't just waltz into a New York jail and put a bullet in her head."

"Trust me, her disposition won't be a problem. Now," Harrington studied them gravely. "The Jew left St. Paul on Saturday, switched planes in Chicago and returned to Duluth. I assume his change in plans was related to the chest; since it wasn't assigned a baggage claim, he must've had it with him. If so, where did it end up — Chicago, Duluth or New York? So far, we know only that upon arriving in Duluth, he leased a car and headed east, possibly as far as Lake Superior. Granted there's a lot of ground in between, but Leopold's convinced the chest will be found somewhere north of Chicago. And based on the places already eliminated, it seems unlikely the Jew had the chest on his return to New York on Sunday. Put your thinking caps on, gentlemen. Is there anything we've overlooked?"

"Knowing Morris," the New Yorker said, "I can't believe he'd return home without the chest. He knew its value and that he'd have to prove possession before receiving any extortion money. When he called Sunday, he seemed quite confident of both."

"But he didn't admit having the chest with him," Harrington said.

"Certainly it was implied."

"Maybe you just read it that way," the Aristocrat suggested. "Why assume Mendelsohn was any less shrewd than the 'Sheriff of Briarpatch' who bled our families all those years? If he could figure out on a sixth grade education that the more distance between him and the chest, the safer he was, why couldn't Mendelsohn? I believe Seth's right. We'll find that chest somewhere between Chicago and Lake Superior."

"Then the Outer Banks cottage has been eliminated?" the Toad asked.

"Yes," Harrington confirmed. Clearly, their analysis had reached a dead end. Hopefully the morning would bring fresh developments, either from Leopold in Minnesota, or Chapman and Streeter's men in New York. "The bottom line, gentlemen, is that proof of your forty-year-old crime still exists in the form of that chest which, until found, will remain a threat. Nevertheless, we must operate on the assumption it'll be recovered. Longbridge will make his announcement on Friday as planned. Our new friend here will then be thrown to the lions in the Senate. But like you," he nodded at the Aristocrat and Toad, "he'll emerge victorious — by Christmas, if all goes well.

"The three, murderous school chums together again," he smiled coldly. "What a happy reunion you must have planned. Just don't lose sight of the Court's critical spring term now almost upon us; it's a term like no other in the Supreme Court's history - one crammed with opportunities to virtually reshape America's constitutional landscape for decades to come. And you'll seize these opportunities for all they're worth!" He shook his fist.

"You'll honor your oaths of allegiance not to some anachronistic bunch called 'The Framers' but to me, the President and God Almighty. You'll act, think, speak, write and, in the end, decide precisely as you've been ordered. There'll be no surprises. In return for your powerful positions, you'll deliver word-for-word, line-by-line, page-by-page, the Renaissance's first victories. And gentlemen," he told them gravely, "I pray for your sake that you don't let us down."

CHAPTER NINE

★

The man parked down the street began snapping pictures as the trio emerged from the dark mansion and quickly ducked inside the waiting limo. As the limo vanished into the mist, he recorded the time, location and subjects. This wasn't an official investigation, although he'd tried to make it one. Getting one lame excuse after another on his climb up the FBI's chain of command, he'd finally reached the Office of Bureau Director Chapman, a Texan recently appointed by another Texan, President Longbridge. Upon hearing his request, Chapman, unlike the others, had offered no lame excuses, just an icy threat that if he didn't back off, he could kiss his Bureau career and generous retirement benefits good-bye.

He'd discussed the matter with his wife, Jean, that same evening. "Gus, suppose you're wrong?" she asked.

"I'm not wrong. I'm certain the evidence exists."

"So certain you're willing to stake your family's security on it? Billy starts college in the fall and Sarah next year. If this fantastic conspiracy really exists, why are you the only one who believes it? Everyone at the Bureau has told you to drop it. Please, Gus, for your family's sake, listen to them!"

And to the world, he had. Never again had he voiced his suspicions to anyone but his best friend, Agent Ben Harvey. He'd sunk back into his daily activities as if Chapman's threat and Jean's pleas had been just the wakeup calls he needed. But they hadn't been, he brooded now, closing his notebook and returning the camera to its case. He'd been wrapped too tightly to abandon his search for the conspiracy he knew existed. And yet, after two years of investigation, how much more did he really know?

Leaving, he passed the Lakeland home, its front windows blackened where the CMA's bulky, silver-haired Chairman typically waited for his guests. Tonight's guests had included the new guy, almost certainly the nominee Longbridge would unveil Friday. Last night's guests had been the pair of Texans: U.S.

Attorney General, Thomas Streeter, and his own boss, FBI Director Chapman, whose frequent presence at the Lakeland home explained why he hadn't wanted an investigation.

Gus was spinning one mysterious meeting after another into a deepening web of conspiracy he couldn't yet fathom. He knew only that it existed and that its scope was frightening. What other conclusion could he reach when enormously powerful men, whose connections to each other weren't publicly known, met under clandestine circumstances in the dead of night? Men who were somehow connected to another visitor to the Lakeland home - the dark giant with the grotesque face and lame leg, the visitor who frightened Gus the most.

Arch Leopold had been a sadistic killer long before Gus had sent him to Leavenworth. Just six months into his long prison term, Leopold had been savagely beaten by another inmate, an Irish giant named Red Murphy, who'd matched him in both brawn and nasty temper. Murphy had left Leopold a bloody, shattered mess the prison guards had been forced to scoop off the concrete and carry to the hospital.

His injuries had been grisly, Gus recalled as he exited the I-95 ramp. A fractured jaw, ruptured eye, shattered septum, broken teeth and a leg so badly crushed by Murphy's club it had hardly been worth saving. After months in the hospital, Leopold had been released with a glass eye, new dentures, leg pin and a nose that even with reconstruction looked like salami. He would never forget his shock the morning Leopold limped grotesquely into the courtroom to hear the judge rule him unfit even with his new parts to be safely returned to prison. Having paid a terrible price, he left the courtroom almost a free man in his paroled status.

Unofficially, he'd also remained under Gus's surveillance, who refused to believe Leopold's rehabilitation extended beyond his physical injuries. When his parole ended, Leopold moved into his sister's Houston home, getting janitorial work in the new Tower of Faith, the national headquarters of the Christians for a Moral America. Gus had received the news in a cryptic note from his Houston contact: "Here's one for the record books. Leopold 'The Butcher' has become the CMA's 'Born Again Janitor.'"

Another note from his contact months later was less cynical:

"Leopold now works directly for Seth Harrington, the CMA Chairman. Who would've believed it?" Gus would, and had; until Vermont two years ago, when he'd learned with the rest of the nation that the body of Chief Justice Wilson Rogers had been discovered in Lake Witteoka, his abandoned fishing boat nearby. Rogers had been vacationing at the quiet Vermont resort, his cottage just a quarter-mile from the cove where he'd been found. An autopsy performed by the Vermont medical examiner concluded death was caused by accidental drowning. Rogers, the report stated, had either slipped or experienced a seizure while fishing. Hitting his head, he'd tumbled, dazed or unconscious, into the water and drowned.

This report raised more questions than it answered. Why would the seventy-two-year-old Rogers, with no history of seizures, suddenly have one while fishing at night in an isolated cove? And if he did, why hadn't the autopsy revealed a vascular accident? Without witnesses or hard evidence, these questions had cast an ominous shadow over Rogers's death. But there'd been a much larger one, Gus now recalled as he covered Alexandria's familiar streets.

Chief Justice Rogers had been the Court's last pure liberal, an avowed atheist and ideological leader, who'd sanctioned the godless liberalism the new, arch-conservative President and his friend, Harrington, were intent on destroying. Committed to massive legal reforms mirroring their vision of a Christian America, Rogers had represented a major obstacle. And who'd believed their prospects would improve? Hadn't Rogers, exceptionally fit for his age, just completed his last marathon? Wouldn't he outlast even a two-term Longbridge Presidency? But now, so suddenly, Rogers was gone, the victim of a mysterious drowning. What greater miracle could Longbridge and Harrington have prayed for? Had fate capriciously blessed them, or had they taken it into their own hands? Unfortunately, the Vermont investigation hadn't answered this question to the satisfaction of a growing number of Americans. Pressure mounted for a federal investigation into Rogers's death. And faced with his first political crisis, Longbridge relented.

Chapman, the new FBI Director, swiftly dispatched a Bureau

team to Vermont, one that included Agent Gus Swanson. Rogers's autopsy was reviewed by the nation's foremost forensic experts and the factual evidence thoroughly developed by experienced Bureau agents. Progress reports were faxed daily to Chapman, who didn't respond. Why, Gus had wondered, as the silence lengthened and a concerned nation waited? Wasn't Chapman curious about their progress? Or was he simply overwhelmed by the investigation's critical nature and the intense national interest it had garnered? Whatever the case, Gus's distress deepened until the investigation finally ended. By then he and several others were convinced Rogers had been murdered. A more thorough analysis of the forensic evidence had conclusively eliminated a vascular accident as the cause of Rogers's death. The splintering of his skull was far more consistent with a blow from a hard object than a fall against the boat's hull.

Caleb Wyndham, a lake resident, had provided a statement in which he recalled hearing a boat leave the cove on the night of the murder, clearly suggesting that Rogers hadn't been alone. Records of the Lake Vista Inn further confirmed the presence of three men in the resort community during this same period. Marina records documented their rental of a small cruiser. Bills at both places had been paid in cash and the men's names, after failed traces, were found to be fictitious. Nevertheless, their presence had been quite real, as proven by detailed witness descriptions — two men in their mid-thirties, medium height and build; one dark in hair and complexion, the other light; both 'ordinary-looking.' Gus had shuddered at the third man's description - a dark giant, with salami nose, glass eye and grotesque limp. Goliath, they'd called the man who went by the name of David. Yet he'd been neither. He'd been, was and could be just one man.

Arch Leopold had been at Lake Witteoka the night of Rogers's death. He was the errand boy of Seth Harrington, who'd blistered Rogers from the pulpit, calling repeatedly for his impeachment. And Longbridge - hadn't he moved swiftly to replace Rogers with Falkingham, the obscure Charleston aristocrat? Had Longbridge masterminded the murder or been the beneficiary of others' bloodied hands? However the questions were answered, the nation was entitled to the truth. And as he left Vermont that final afternoon,

Gus had been convinced they'd receive it. Having established Rogers's death as a homicide now meant finding the killers. And the investigation, far from being over, was just beginning.

Or so he'd thought. Two days after returning, he received his copy of the final report and discovered that all he'd understood had been lost somewhere between Vermont and D.C., the team's findings either altered or deleted entirely by Special Agent Nicholas. Medical opinions that had ruled out a stroke were now inconclusive, as was the skull fracture. A hard object or boat hull — who could say? And Caleb Wyndham's claim to have heard a boat on the night of Rogers's death? Boats were in that cove every night, according to other lake residents. Who could say the elderly Wyndham had the right time if he was suffering from Alzheimer's, as these other unidentified residents suspected? Having changed the team's findings, Nicholas now changed its conclusion: no basis existed for reversing Vermont's finding of accidental drowning.

A stunned Gus had reread the report, trying to grasp how a month-long investigation could vanish with nothing more than a word processor and a corrupt Special Agent. Didn't Nicholas know the Bureau didn't tolerate scams like this? They were exposed and the plotters were punished, unless the plotters were larger than the Bureau. So who were they? He took this alarming question to his teammates, who believed, like him, that Rogers had been murdered. Together they'd go to Chapman and explain the report's gross inaccuracies. Only he now learned they agreed with Nicholas. "We were wrong," they shrugged. "That's clear after further reflection."

And what else, his furious glare accused them. Bribes? Threats? "Forty-eight hours ago we agreed Leopold was the Goliath at Lake Witteoka."

"Agreed, Gus? What does that mean? We can't prove it. Give it up. It's over."

His eyes gleamed with a dawning obsession as he started up the chain of command.

"Do you realize what you're suggesting?" his superiors asked. "If by some remote chance you could connect Leopold to Rogers's death, you're not actually prepared to claim he was acting on orders of the most respected religious leader in the country, are you?"

"How can I know until an investigation is done?"

"It was done, Swanson, and it's over."

Mired in reflection, he turned into his prosperous Alexandria subdivision. If only he had access to the Bureau's sophisticated surveillance systems to record the secret Georgetown meetings, especially with things heating up again. There'd been little activity when Agent Orville's call had come that Sunday afternoon. Orville hadn't known of Gus's secret operation, but he did recall his interest in Leopold. At Dulles on his own assignment, he'd just spotted Leopold rushing to catch a flight to La Guardia. "Limping like a mad giant, Gus. Had two flunkies with him, both medium height and build, ordinary-looking."

'Ordinary-looking.' He'd immediately called Ben Harvey in Long Island.

"So you want me to drag my ass out to La Guardia and meet the plane?" Harvey grumbled.

"The fresh air will do you good, Ben. I assume you just saw the Rams clobber the Giants?" Watching pro football on Sundays had been akin to a religious ritual during their years together in Atlanta. "Ben, this could be the big break we've been waiting for."

"You say that, Gus, every time Leopold flies up here. But all he does is check into that same Fifty-Second Street hotel then take a cab to some Manhattan office I can't get into. Not that it matters. I know what he's doing— squeezing blood out of poor saps for Harrington, like he used to for other scumbags. Hell, who knows?" Ben sighed. "Maybe we'll get lucky this time."

Harvey didn't call back until almost midnight. "Gus, I'm at La Guardia. Leopold and his pals just returned to Dulles. I'd say it was another waste of time except . . ."

"What Ben?"

"Hell, it may be nothing. They checked into that same hotel then left again for this fancy apartment building on the Upper East Side. The Essex. It was a new stop but they obviously knew their way around, and had access to the building. Leopold and one guy went inside while the driver waited in the garage."

"Do you know who they went to see?" Gus asked.

"Not at the time. I still don't really, but . . . Gus, I just caught the the news. Some Wall Street lawyer was found shot to death in his apartment about an hour ago. Name's Mendelsohn. He lived in the Essex."

Gus's heart pounded. "How long were Leopold and his flunkey in there?"

"A good forty-five minutes. Then they squealed off for the airport. I figured something was up, but had no idea what until now."

This was no coincidence, but why a Wall Street lawyer? "Ben, find out what you can about Mendelsohn — his firm, the type of law he practiced, everything."

"No problem, Gus. Forty-five minutes — that's a long time for a hit. I'd say they were looking for something. So besides collecting Mendelsohn's bio, how do we handle it?"

He thought quickly. If Harvey reported his surveillance of Leopold, they'd risk exposing the operation. Chapman would interpret it as a deliberate violation of his orders. They'd lose their jobs and also further opportunity to gather evidence. "We'll let the NYPD do its job alone for now. Otherwise we'll be on the street tomorrow."

"Or under it," Harvey sighed. "Gus, these guys scare the shit out of me. They're cocky enough to blow off a Supreme Court Justice and now a Wall Street lawyer, all with the Bureau's blessing."

Gus smiled. His friend, it seemed, was in with both feet now. "Then you believe me about Rogers?"

"You think I'd be risking my ass otherwise? All right, I agree we can't risk exposing the operation just for Mendelsohn."

Monday crept by without a word from New York. Then Tuesday brought a startling development. The NYPD charged Mendelsohn's associate at Lieber Allen with the murder, only to have her vanish before arrest. Harvey called that afternoon. "This young lawyer is the kid sister of Santino 'The Lips' Corelli, once the Bertoluccis' big muscle on the West Side. A cocky bastard: big bankroll, big gun and big mouth. He's doing life in Attica. Imagine that, a Corelli being hunted for a murder she didn't commit."

The line dripped suddenly with conscience. How could they

keep quiet now? Certainly Corelli was frightened and desperate as she ran from a crime they knew, or at least suspected, she hadn't committed. Which duty was greater: the one to Mayson Corelli or to their country, whose national security was threatened by a conspiracy possibly extending into the White House? Coming forward now assured them of never getting closer to it. "We're doing everyone more good in the shadows than we would in the spotlight," Gus said finally. "And even if you reported Leopold's visit to the Essex Sunday night, that alone wouldn't save Corelli. But exposing the conspiracy will."

Harvey called Wednesday with further developments. "Here's one for you, Gus. I've been assigned to the Corelli manhunt. And guess who's coming up from D.C. to head the operation?"

"Pete Nicholas?"

"Bingo. The arrogant bastard's obviously deep in Chapman's pocket."

"What's the latest on Corelli?" Gus asked.

"Word is she's trapped in Manhattan. The City's sealed off tight."

Yet since that call, the hours had become days and still she remained at large.

Arriving home, he parked behind Jean's Explorer and entered the kitchen, where he was met by Max, their German Shepherd. Quietly, he slipped back to the dark bedroom to undress. What would he tell Jean this time? Another stakeout? Or that nasty paperwork he couldn't get to during the day?

As he joined her in bed, she stirred. Then he told her about the new stakeout.

CHAPTER TEN

★

"Pssst, Tyler! Are you awake?"

He'd had this dream before.

"Tyler . . .!"

It was no dream. She sat over him on the study's foldout, her delicate frame swallowed by his flannel shirt. Had a new intimacy crept into their relationship? "You look like a clown in that shirt."

"Thank you," she replied.

"For what?"

"You love clowns so I assumed it was a compliment; I'm sorry for my behavior last night."

"Why were you so upset?"

"The JBs and Jams." She tugged nervously at an errant shirt thread. "And *Robes of Vengeance*."

"What the hell are JBs and Jams?"

"Jawbreakers and Jordan Almonds," she replied.

"Let me get this straight." He sat up against the pillows. "You were upset because I bought your favorite candy and the novel you've been dying to read? I'm afraid I don't understand."

She studied him wistfully. "Maybe you will one day."

And he wanted to. But now there were more compelling matters to address. "Where was the Crenshaw suit filed?"

"Naples, Florida. Why?"

"Because we need to get our hands on the case records."

"And how do you propose doing that?"

"Well, since Lamp isn't likely to turn them over, I guess we'll have to go to Naples and get them ourselves. Tell me what you know about the case."

"That shouldn't take long." She folded her arms. "Crenshaw was the redneck sheriff of some Tennessee county who, after turning in his badge, moved with his fortune into a cozy Naples retirement. Then I assume after buying a fancy condo, he spent his golden years watching Gulf Coast sunrises, as he plotted how to keep his no-good kids from inheriting his ten-million-dollar estate. See, that didn't take long."

"Ten million dollars," he marveled. "That's a lot of speeding tickets."

"Obviously he didn't amass his fortune from traffic fines."

"Extortion," he mused. "The kind Morris was playing with Lamp, maybe with the same deck of cards. If so, where did Morris stumble upon it — Minnesota?"

"Something lured him up there," she nodded. "And huge for him to cut his vacation short. Money, obviously; it's what lured him into probate work in the first place. The larger the estate, the larger his fee."

"Let's assume the Minnesota trip was related to Crenshaw. And instead of completing his vacation, Morris returned to New York to cash in on his discovery, using the same blackmail scheme that had made Crenshaw a multimillionaire. Let's also say Lamp was the target. Morris would've contacted him the moment he returned Sunday, or for that matter may have already been talking to him from Minnesota."

"The phone records would prove it," she said. "Let's assume they do and that Morris demanded money. Did Lamp pay?"

"He certainly had the resources. And his payment would explain Morris's urgency to catch the first flight to Margaritaville. Still," he paused. "Before financing Morris's exile, he must've considered the alternatives, one being how much cheaper it would be to just eliminate the pest from the planet. Certainly Morris was aware of this and after coming to his senses, realized he'd gotten in over his head."

"And that possibly he was being watched," she added. "That's why he couldn't drive or take a cab to the airport. He was afraid of detection."

"So he called me, then you when I wasn't home. No one would recognize our cars. We'd slip into the garage, pick him up then leave again right under their noses."

"But Lamp might recognize our cars," she pointed out.

"Lamp wouldn't be the one watching." He sprung up to stretch his long body. Out the window the sun had begun its rise over the East River. "He'd pay someone else to snoop then kill Morris;

someone like your brother, Lucky."

"The Lips," she sighed. "Why can't you get that straight?"

"What was he like growing up?"

"Kind, trustworthy. I loved him very much."

"And?"

"He grew up. And I learned that neither he, nor anyone else, could be trusted."

"What about your father?"

Glancing at her knotted hands, she turned away. "I don't want to discuss this."

Would the time come when she would? "Mayson, if you ever want to talk, I'm here to listen."

Slowly her eyes lifted. Yes, she'd remember; the day would come. She wanted it to. As she glanced at his boxers, he smiled sheepishly. "It's your home," she said. "Dress as you want."

He studied her now, sitting perfectly content on the foldout, her legs bare below the flannel shirt. New ground had been broken. "I should've bought you a gown to sleep in."

"The shirt's fine. And you can have your bed back tonight. I'll be perfectly comfortable in here."

"We may not be here tonight," he said ominously.

Alarm widened her eyes. "We'll need more than a day to plan our escape."

"Who says we have it?"

Anxiously she watched him leave.

He found her later in the kitchen, spatula in hand, sleeves rolled up as she labored over the stove. She looked up at him, all dressed for Wall Street. "I hope you don't like your eggs sunny side up. It may be too late for that. How do you like them?"

"Scrambled." He inspected the frying eggs.

"You would," she sighed. Transforming the spatula into an instrument of destruction, she shredded the eggs to his specifications. "There," she said. "Scrambled."

Sitting at the table, he noticed the lone place setting. "You're not eating?"

"I'm not hungry."

"Because you're nervous?"

"Of course I'm nervous." She deposited the sausage and eggs on his plate. Grabbing the muffins, she joined him at the table. "If you weren't such a dope, you'd be nervous, too."

"Dope? What happened to idiot and *gavonne*?"

"They're too mean for you."

He watched her swat her hair again - a mussed, but lustrous mane that regrettably would have to go. Tonight, if the arrangements could be made. "Who says I'm not nervous?"

"You just aren't. Why, Tyler?"

Sipping his juice, he dug into the breakfast, a luxury rarely bothered with. "So you really can cook."

"Then you won't answer me?"

"Hell yes, I'm nervous. If not as much as you, maybe it's because I don't care about what I'm leaving behind. I don't belong in New York. I never have."

"Then where do you belong?"

Once he could've answered this without thinking. Now he had no clue. "Castlewood, my family's home, I guess . . ."

As he said this, she noticed his saddened eyes. Was his life painful, empty and colorless like hers? Did something haunt him, too? "Tyler, even if we get out of New York you'll have abandoned your life and everything in it. And if I have no family, you do - one that will worry itself sick. I can't ask you to do this."

"You're not, Mayson. I'm helping because I want to."

"Well if you insist on throwing your life away, at least tell me why. Otherwise I have no intention of going anywhere with you."

"I'd better get downtown." He got up.

"Tyler, you can't just walk away from this." She followed him. But he already had; he was leaving her with so many questions unanswered, so many lonely hours to face once the door closed behind him. She was so confused. She cared, but didn't want to. She didn't want him to throw away his life, yet no longer had the strength to face hers alone. She didn't want to be responsible for his family's grief, but even that seemed beyond her control. "Tyler, you have to answer me sooner or later. The question won't go away, I assure you." She watched him open the door. "Was there a girl at McDougal's last night, one of yesterday's 'panters'?"

"No 'panters,' just the Molson's." And Rebecca, the Bellevue resident - refreshingly Virginian and beautiful. He'd declined an invitation to her place on the grounds of morning depositions when insanity was the proper plea. He'd been too worried about Mayson to enjoy himself. "Don't forget to call the remaining area codes for Robert Hunter." She nodded sullenly, her toes digging into the carpet. "Something's on your mind, obviously. Do you plan on telling me or not?"

Slowly her eyes lifted. "I cried last night because emotions I'd thought dead ambushed me. I didn't know how to deal with them and so, well," she shrugged. "I just cried."

Glancing at her drooping shirt cuffs, he imagined her hands knotted inside. "Good or bad emotions?"

She studied her toes like busy worms in the carpet. They were alive; she was alive, and it terrified her. "Tyler, can you imagine what it's like to be dead inside, to feel nothing at all? To hear only the terrible silence when voices, laughter, music, once filled your ears? Can you possibly understand that?"

"Perfectly," he nodded.

She'd been right, his solemn eyes confirmed. He was or had been in pain. Was he still? Should she help? Did he want her to? Is that what this was all about? "Tyler, if the time comes when I want to talk about my life, I mean, I've never done it before. I've been much more interested in forgetting than remembering. But I'm beginning to sense . . ." Her throat tightened suddenly. She brushed at fresh tears. "If that day comes . . . if I asked . . ."

"You don't have to ask, Mayson, I've already said that. When you're ready, just start talking and I'll be there. Is that plain enough?" When she nodded, he kissed her hair and then slipped out.

His world had never seemed more threatening than on the drive downtown. Every shrieking horn in the thick traffic, every car that crept into his mirror sent a shiver up his spine. NYPD units were everywhere, and so were the ubiquitous Feds, who'd recently hit the streets. In their dark suits and glasses, their faces expressionless, they were easily identified clones as they huddled on street corners and climbed in and out of dark sedans. Why were they here? Did they know who'd killed Morris?

It was almost nine when he reached his office. Closing the door, he quickly checked his messages. Lauren had called twice, Bilbro three times. Poster Boy would be a nuisance right down to the wire; that was clear. On his way out, he grabbed the ringing phone.

"I told you not to kiss me," Mayson snapped. "Don't do it again."

Didn't she realize someone might be listening to this asinine conversation?

"Lauren just left a message," she explained. "If you don't call by noon, she's going to the DA."

As the line clicked, he checked his watch. Lauren was the key. If she didn't agree to the plan, they were doomed. Taking the elevator to sixty-four, he hurried down the hall. An intense Frieda looked up from her PC. She was assigned to Bilbro now and if Poster Boy played his cards right, he would also soon have Morris's prestigious corner office. "I see Ed has you slaving away already," he said.

"He'll take some getting used to," she muttered.

"Don't worry," he smiled. "After Morris, GI Joe should be a piece of cake."

"You overestimate my abilities." She offered a toothy grin.

If only her parents had put braces on her teeth, she'd be pretty or close enough. "Have you gotten Ralph's birthday present?"

Nodding, she reached under the desk for a jewelry box. Inside was a sparkling gold watch and chain. "Do you think Ralph will like it?" she asked hopefully.

"He'll love it," he nodded emphatically. "Wasserman's, huh?"

She beamed. "You might get one yourself?"

"I'll definitely look." And if he'd planned to be around, maybe he would. "So where's dinner?"

"Lutece. Saturday night."

"I'll see that Ed gives you plenty of overtime. You'll need it after this weekend."

"Ralph's worth every penny."

"The man's lucky as hell."

"Tyler, stop!"

Not if it made her grin like that. He slipped into Morris's office, with its prestigious glass walls and handsome furnishings. Once galvanized by the partner's frantic, gesticulating presence, it was now a cold, sterile mausoleum - dead, like him. His personal possessions had been meticulously removed; with a few boxes and can of air freshener, the senior partner had been effectively erased. All that remained were his files, the only stuff that mattered in the world of Wall Street Law.

He began his search with little expectations. Still, they weren't in a position to leave any stone unturned. Whoever had purged the office could've gotten sloppy.

Finding no scrap of Crenshaw in the desk, he moved on to the file cabinets. He'd been through them before when preparing the inventory, but then he hadn't been looking for Crenshaw. He'd almost gotten through the last cabinet when the floor creaked behind him.

"There you are. Didn't you get my messages?"

Closing the drawer, he looked up at an impatient Bilbro. "I haven't been to my office yet."

"What time do you normally get in?"

"Seven-thirty," he rose now.

"Then you were late this morning."

"I had a doctor's appointment. I strained my knee jogging."

"It looked okay when you were kneeling over that drawer just now." His eyes dropped to the cabinet, "You're not still looking for that Crenshaw case you mentioned last night, are you? I planned to ask Lamp about it this morning."

Tyler froze. "Then you haven't?"

"No, he's in D.C. through the weekend," Bilbro explained. "Anyway, I need some motions prepared for a Boston prelim tomorrow in the Breckinridge suit. I didn't know about it until sorting through some stale correspondence. Now I must postpone the Garrison depositions and fly up to Boston in the morning."

"Can't you get the prelim continued?" Tyler asked.

"Morris had continued it twice already. Judge McCarthy said two continuances were enough."

Was this the opportunity he needed? "I could fly to Boston and cover for you."

"You know the firm's policy: no unsupervised court appearances for first-year associates."

Yes, he knew. He'd graduated from Harvard, passed the Bar and clerked for the U.S. Supreme Court, only to arrive at Lieber Allen and discover he had the equivalent of a learner's permit. "Ed, that stupid rule is broken every day."

"Yeah? Well I know another rule you're not particularly fond of either, the one about dating firm employees. Now come on, let's get down to my office so I can brief you on those motions."

It was almost eleven when he returned to his office. Head spinning, he shut the door and dropped behind his desk. They had to get away. He had to avoid the slightest wrinkle or rumble of suspicion and then when heads were turned, magically disappear. Meanwhile, time was slipping away. How could he squeeze the Breckinridge motions into what was left? All these obstacles . . . He grabbed the ringing phone.

"Honestly Tiles, why have voice mail if you don't check your messages?"

'Tiles.' Must his sister continue calling him that? "I'm sorry, Stafford, there's a lot going on."

"So we've heard. Do you know this Mayson Corelli and the lawyer she murdered?"

"I knew them both but not well. And Mayson didn't murder Mendelsohn."

"How do you know that?" Stafford asked.

"Just a hunch." He checked his watch. He couldn't push Lauren past her noon deadline. "Stafford, things are really hectic . . ."

Childish squeals pierced the line suddenly. "Anne Randolph, give your brother his ball!" Stafford scolded. Then she explained, "The academy's closed for a teachers' conference. Remember how we loved those days? Well I dread them now."

"Stafford, I'm late for a meeting."

"Okay, but don't forget Schuyler's birthday Saturday."

He'd sent a package last week with instructions not to open it until this Saturday. It was a hunting jacket his father would love, almost as much as having his son at Gobblepatch when he wore it.

"Tiles, you never forget Schuyler's birthday," she confessed now. "You know why I called."

Of course he did.

"Do you still hate New York?" she asked.

"More every day."

"To the point you'll quit and come home?"

"I'll give it a while longer." Hours they were now talking about.

"You don't plan to miss another Castlewood Thanksgiving?"

Missing was the problem. At Castlewood he missed everything. Not from a distance but up close, where the memories gripped him so tightly that he could see, hear and feel everything that had been, and never would be again. "I'll try to make it this year."

"Just do all right?" She sighed. "Imagine what it would mean to Schuyler if you joined him in Gobblepatch for the hunt Thanksgiving morning."

A lump crept up his throat. He might never see his sister again. "I love you, Stafford. You've . . ."

She gasped at his faltering voice. "Tiles, it's worse this year, I can tell. Please come home. I . . . have to . . ." Her tears flooded the line as she hung up.

Eyes misting, he checked his watch. Four minutes to noon. Nothing like cutting it close. He called the Manhattan DA's office. "Lauren Belli, please."

"Miss Belli's in with the DA. May I take a message?"

She wouldn't . . . not without talking to him first.

"Lauren Belli," a breathless voice now responded.

"She said you were with the DA."

The line instantly chilled. "You sonofabitch!"

"I have an explanation."

"Don't all you Virginia boys, with your charming drawls, manners and thoughtfulness. What bullshit! I see she relayed my noon deadline, which proves she's at your apartment."

"Let's have lunch. I'll explain everything."

"I'm too disgusted to think of food. This explanation - you have thirty seconds before I return to the DA's office."

"Goddamnit Lauren, I can't explain it in thirty seconds and you know it. Come on - Guido's in the Square, your favorite pasta and my explanation." The line's silence deepened. "Come on, if . . ."

"Twenty minutes, Tyler. Don't be late."

Hanging up, he slumped at his desk. The day from hell, and it was only noon. Eight Breckinridge motions. Stafford. Lauren. The Italian tempest in his apartment. Reaching for his personal stationery, he scrawled the note he was certain to forget later:

Hunter Leigh, Schuyler,

I'm sane - I think - although I have no idea why I'm doing this. Leaving at least was in the cards before. I'd planned on giving my notice this week. Now I think I'll just slip off quietly. I hate Wall Street. I don't belong here and the truth is I'm not sure where I belong. I haven't since — well, we all know when.

I just got off the phone with Stafford. Please make sure she knows how much I love her. I'm afraid I'll miss another Thanksgiving but hope that in a minute you'll understand why. I also hope you can read this. My mind's blazing, my fingers barely limping after it.

Mayson didn't kill Morris Mendelsohn no matter what you've heard, and I plan to help her prove it, although at the moment I don't know how. She doesn't have anyone else and spending five minutes with her, you'd understand why. But I suspect there's a reason, just like there's a reason for the way I am. I hope she'll open up soon.

Anyway, I know you're going to worry and I'm sorry for that. Just believe in me as you always have. Mom, Dad, I know it sounds crazy, but suddenly I have a destination and it feels good. I'll explain it all when I return. And Schuyler, Happy Birthday. And good hunting! Your loving son, Tyler.'

Slipping the note into an envelope, he added a stamp and address and, tucking it in his jacket, left. Minutes later, he dropped it off in the box outside the building and hurried for Guido's across the square. Not spotting Lauren, he grabbed a window table to wait. The waitress soon appeared to take his order. "Two pasta specials, a coke and . . . iced tea, unsweetened."

She offered a gum-popping grin. "I'm sure the lady will be impressed you remembered."

"Let's hope so."

Lauren, a statuesque blond, entered and finding him, briskly strode over. Heads turned at the busy counter, eyes following her long, shapely legs. Her gray suit was professional, the skirt too short as usual, the heels, high. Lauren on display - she was gorgeous and knew it. Rising, he greeted her with a smile, which she coldly brushed off.

"I'll get your iced tea," the waitress winked. "Unsweetened."

As she left, Lauren snapped, "That down-home charm snows them all, I see."

"You're one to talk." He dropped back across the table. "I've already ordered. I'm sure neither of us has time to burn."

"Oh, you'll burn all right. Count on it." The waitress brought their drinks then left again. "You said your interest in the case stemmed from your close relationship with Mendelsohn. As he was your mentor, you felt a special duty to bring his killer to justice. 'Lauren,' you pleaded, 'just tell me if a suspect turns up at the firm.' When I said one had, Mayson specifically, you said you'd suspected her, too, and that if she was the killer, you couldn't let her escape prosecution."

She paused to study him, quiet and expressionless - polite, deferential to the lady talking. If he was interfering in the investigation, he'd first resolved the moral issues, convincing himself it was justified. What hurt the most was that his justification involved another woman. Mayson Corelli. "You're good, Tyler, I'll give you that. I took the bait - hook, line, and sinker. I actually thought I was recruiting you to watch Mayson in exchange for my classified information. I could've had Duke tail her, but you were right there, ready, willing and able. And you certainly were — to help that cold Sicilian bitch, not the law, as I learned to my humiliation Tuesday afternoon."

He studied her intently. "Even cold Sicilian bitches don't deserve prison for crimes they didn't commit. Whatever you or I think of Mayson, she didn't kill Morris Mendelsohn."

"Oh? And how do you know? Let me guess; she told you?"

"Why would Mendelsohn call her for help Sunday night if he thought she wanted to kill him?"

Lauren replied, "If victims knew these things in advance, Mr. Contracts Lawyer, there'd be a helluva lot less murders."

The waitress appeared with their pasta specials. "More Coke?" she asked him. "It's extra, but I can make an exception."

"This is Wall Street," Lauren's eyes shot up irritably. "Don't you recognize a millionaire when you see one? You don't make exceptions for them; you charge double. Didn't they tell you that when you got off the bus?"

The waitress's chin ducked into indignant wrinkles as she huffed off. "What the hell's wrong with you?" Tyler snapped. "That was way out of line."

"So was your conduct in this murder investigation," she whispered harshly.

Digging into his pasta, he became aware of the curious eyes at the counter. "Morris's Minnesota trip is connected to the murder. I'm surprised neither you nor Duke picked up on that."

Unable to force her fork into the pasta, she set it down. "I'm surprised you didn't pick up on the fact that Mayson owns a .38 - the one that killed Mendelsohn. Or did her big eyes make you forget that part?"

"Morris borrowed the gun from her several months ago for protection against muggers."

She scoffed, "And naturally you believe this explanation."

He was establishing himself as a material witness, but he needed to rehabilitate himself in her eyes. And besides, he had nothing to lose. He'd either gain her confidence or go to jail. "Lauren, she went to Morris's in response to his call for help. Don't you see? She wouldn't have been there if I'd been home to take his call. And she arrived after the murder. After his apartment was trashed."

"If she's innocent," Lauren asked, "why slip off like a guilty rat instead of reporting the crime?"

"Because it was her gun in his apartment and his fresh corpse at her feet as sirens shrieked outside. Everyone knew she hated his guts. What would you have done in her place?"

She pulled away from his intense eyes. She wasn't required to put herself in Mayson's shoes or ask what she would've done. That wasn't the issue . . . it was . . . was it possible Tyler was right about that night?

"I know what I would've done," he said. "The same as you if you weren't too stubborn to admit it: slipped off and hoped nobody saw me. Which, as we know in Mayson's case, they did."

"Even so, Tyler, it was wrong."

"I know that. But only the most naive person in the world

would believe they could explain away circumstances like those."

"Her brother's a killer. Why couldn't she be, too?"

"That's a cheap shot, Lauren. Lucky was a Mob assassin. Mayson climbed the ladder the hard way, the honest way. And because of that she wasn't about to throw it all away by murdering a loudmouth prick like Morris Mendelsohn."

"Her brother is The Lips," she replied. "And Morris the Prick? Then you're saying he wasn't really your mentor? And you said you hated Mayson. Obviously that was bullshit, too."

"My feelings for Mayson have nothing to do with this."

"Now who's being naive?" she laughed.

"Lauren, why is the FBI involved in this?" he asked. "And Special Services? What kind of jurisdiction does the Justice Department claim in a Manhattan homicide?"

Good question. And he wasn't the only one asking. The official line, she explained, was that Mendelsohn's murder was linked to Mayson's activities within the Bertolucci family; however, because of the threat to Federal agents involved in the undercover operation, the details couldn't be disclosed.

"And you believe that?" he asked.

"It's not my job to question the legitimacy of FBI operations. Enforce the laws of New York. That's what I'm paid to do."

"In other words, you think it's bullshit, too," he said.

"What if I do? That doesn't change anything. The Feds want Mayson, the same as the DA."

"So what are you saying? You don't believe Mayson's innocent or you just don't give a shit?"

The growing desperation in his eyes was difficult to confront. Yet he and that Sicilian bitch were the villains, not her. So why did she suddenly feel like the bad guy?

He sighed. "At least now I know how you feel."

"Like hell!" she shouted. "You have no idea." As the nosy waitress stopped wiping a nearby table, she whispered, "Tyler, why can't you understand that what I feel or think isn't the issue? She's wanted for murder. Nothing I say or do will change that. Furthermore, when the smoke clears, the fact remains that you lied to me. You used me, you sonofabitch."

Reaching for his wallet, he rose. "I think we could use some air." Leaving the waitress a generous tip, he paid the cashier then escorted Lauren out to the square where the lunch crowd had thinned. "Walk with me a minute. There's something I'd like to say."

A minute? He'd crushed her and yet she'd give him a lifetime of minutes if he'd only ask. They'd met two months ago at McDougal's the evening after the Boris Clansky murder trial. Victorious but exhausted, she'd been on her way out when their eyes connected. For her it had been love at first sight. She'd slept with him that same night, something she'd never done before. Certainly there'd been other women in his life, but he'd treated her as if she was the only one, and it had been so easy to believe. They'd spent other nights together when she could track him down. Quickly she'd discovered his pathological restlessness. He and his eyes were in constant motion.

He gave yet wanted nothing in return. Even with sex, all the moves were for her. But she'd also wanted to please him. She loved him and thought in spite of everything, he'd come to love her, too — until Tuesday afternoon. She'd been ready to castrate him. Now suddenly it was Thursday and she was here in the square, ready to give him minutes and so much more.

The November air chilled them as they strolled, the gusting wind sweeping the lunch crowd's litter across the empty square. She hated Mayson Corelli. She envied her. Finally he turned to her with the full burden of his emotions. "Lauren, I'm sorry for using you. It was wrong, I know that."

Choking back her feelings, she replied, "You can't imagine how stupid I felt to learn that I, an assistant DA, had unwittingly conspired to help a murder suspect escape the same law I'd sworn to enforce. You ripped my heart out, Tyler. And yet rather than going to the DA, I returned to you praying I was wrong, that you'd reassure me you had nothing to do with Mayson's escape." She smiled sadly. "You knew I was bluffing; I'd never turn you in. You knew the way I felt . . . feel . . ."

He held her as she began to cry. He cared about her but she cared more about him. It was the same sad story, over and over again, a futile attempt to recreate the love he'd felt just once in his life - one whose promise had been infinite and so, too, he'd discovered, had its pain. Desperate and clawing for options, he'd seen Lauren not as a person but a resource to exploit. The realization sickened him. "Lauren, I never meant to hurt you. I'm so sorry." Reaching for his handkerchief, he dabbed her eyes. "But I couldn't let her go to prison for a crime she didn't commit."

"But why is she your responsibility?"

Mayson had asked the same question. He still had no answer. "I picture her sitting alone in a jail cell, no family or friends, facing a murder charge for which she's innocent but without the means to prove it. I see her forced to appreciate the career she's worked so hard for is suddenly gone and she's helpless to prevent it. I imagine her spending the rest of her life behind bars - not the years but the hours, days, weeks. I imagine her pain until it hurts too much to think about; I have to do something."

She was drawn again by his eyes' intense glow. He was convinced of Mayson's innocence and prepared to take on the world to prove it. That it was a hopeless cause didn't matter. Simply for her vindication, he was prepared to throw his own life away. He had the world and it wasn't enough. He must have Mayson, too. But he wasn't greedy or stupid. He wouldn't sacrifice himself for a murderer. Yes, Mayson was innocent, she conceded now. As a prosecutor, she knew mistakes were made, and somehow one had been made in this case.

"For Mayson," he said, "it's always been her against the world, and right now she's not doing so well. Still, she's having trouble admitting she needs help. But she must trust someone or she doesn't stand a chance. And that someone, I guess, is me. I don't see any other volunteers around." He smiled as a maintenance man pushed by with his broom. "You must think I'm the craziest fool in the world."

"No," she smiled ruefully. "Just in love."

"My personal feelings for Mayson have nothing to do with this."

"You're in love with her, Tyler, admit it. You're acting crazy even if you aren't. You've acted selfishly but you're not that, either. You've hurt me, when in your right mind you wouldn't hurt anyone. If that isn't love, what is?"

He frowned. "It's heaven one minute and hell for the eternity that follows. It's like an addiction. One minute you're soaring, the next you're on your knees with a burning obsession to return to the sky. But you never do. And because I've been there I have no intention of returning, for Mayson Corelli or anyone else."

"But can't you see, Tyler, you already have. You love her. If you don't realize it yet, you will later."

"No, Lauren," he shook his head firmly. "I control my own feelings."

"Yes, we've just been through that, haven't we? The 'you hurt me but didn't mean to' line." Her eyes narrowed suddenly, "She's in your apartment at this very minute, isn't she?"

"She had nowhere else to go," he nodded. "But it's no longer safe. We have to leave New York."

Lauren watched his restless eyes scale the Old Dame. "Tyler, don't press your luck."

He studied her intently. No, he wouldn't do that. "Thanks for coming, Lauren. Whatever you decide, I'll understand."

As he started away, she called, "Wait! You can't leave without explaining your proposition."

He turned, "But you just said . . ."

"I know what I said. And I'll enjoy rejecting your proposal, whatever it is. Now tell me."

His eyes hardened with deliberation as he led her into the afternoon shadows, stopping behind a large planter. "There's something much larger than Morris Mendelsohn and Mayson Corelli going on here. Something so vast it scares the hell out of me. And whatever it is, Mayson and I are caught in the middle. Think about it," he said. "Mayson's been a fugitive for all of forty-eight hours and already the two largest law enforcement agencies in the country are looking for her. By the size and intensity of this manhunt, you'd think she's Public Enemy Number One. Why is that, Lauren? Why is an army of cops turning Manhattan upside down for one frightened woman named Mayson Corelli?"

"I can't explain it," she sighed. "You know that."

"I'm beginning to. Morris stumbled upon something huge. And whoever killed him ripped up his apartment looking for it." He explained, "The files of one of his Florida probate cases have been missing since the murder. Greg Lamp asked Mayson about them Monday morning after her questioning. When I inventoried Morris's office later, they were gone. I mean, every reference. It's like they never existed."

"Maybe they didn't," she said. "But if they did, you think they explain Mendelsohn's murder? A document perhaps that someone would kill for, but not Greg Lamp: the National Bar President, director of a half-dozen Fortune 500 companies, the Dean of Wall Street Law, Lieber Allen's Managing Partner. Need I go on?"

"You see his achievements. I see a big reputation to protect."

"Come on, Tyler. Lamp murdering his law partner? That's a huge one to swallow."

"The truth is sometimes." He did his best to convince her. "Lamp's choreographed this investigation from the start, even providing the murder motive. The memo that conveniently surfaced . . . shit, if Morris had had dirt like that he wouldn't have put it in a memo, stuffed it away and then gone fishing. He'd have used it to blackmail Mayson for sex. That was his game. Only the memo never existed. Lamp manufactured it to frame Mayson . . . Look," he sighed. "If you can't accept my murder theory, at least give me the chance to prove I'm right. Justice, Lauren, what we lawyers swear to serve. Now unless Morris's murderer found what he was looking for, it's still out there. Maybe Mayson and I can find it."

"And maybe you can get yourself killed," she said.

"Lauren, we've got to get out of New York."

"And how do you propose doing that when the city's been sealed off? Radio the Starship Enterprise and have Scotty beam you up?"

"I had another idea."

"Ah," she nodded. "This is where I come in, right? Now that I've helped Mayson avoid arrest, you expect me to help you two get out of New York."

"I have no expectations," he said. "I'm up to my ass in suspicions at the moment."

"Are you asking for my help or not?"

"No . . . I mean I was. But after the way I've treated you, I can't. We'll just have to find another way. There's one thing I will ask, however. That you not turn us in, especially since we don't know what the Feds are up to."

"Why should I turn you in? You said Mayson's innocent."

His eyes widened. "Then you believe me?"

She nodded. "You're not stupid enough to fall in love with a murderer. No, I won't turn you in."

"Thank you," he sighed. If he couldn't get what he'd hoped for, at least he could eliminate a threat. "I guess that's it, then."

Her conscience began whispering furiously as he started off. Mayson was innocent. He was left to prove it. What if he was killed? What if Mayson was killed and he spent the rest of his life in prison? She couldn't allow it. She hated Mayson but loved Tyler more. "Wait!" She hurried after him. "What is it you want me to do?"

He turned back. She'd help. But could he really ask? "Lauren, I have no right."

"You're damn right you don't. Now tell me."

Again his eyes scaled the Old Dame. Poster Boy must be going nuts over an absence ticking now into its third hour. "Come on." He led her away, explaining the plan as they walked. Refusing to downplay the risks, he emphasized them instead. When he finished, they stood at the corner of William and Pearl.

"I make a reservation tomorrow morning for a departing friend or relative," she summarized. "The flight is to Naples, Florida; the fewer connections, the better."

Buying a paper, he looked at the front-page headline, MAN-HUNT CONTINUES. "Then what?"

Wistfully, her eyes slipped over the congested intersection, the air gray and stale, like the endless granite. What was so crazy about wanting to leave? Sometimes she wished she'd never left Iowa. "Then I make a one-week reservation for my friend or relative in a Naples hotel, preferably a common chain. Both it, and the flight, will be charged to my credit card, which fortunately has a squeaky clean balance." As the light changed, he led her across the busy street. She resumed. "Tomorrow morning I drive to a certain Park Avenue apartment building, where my friend or relative will be waiting for me to transport her to La Guardia. There, shielded by my well known prosecutorial presence, she'll slip undetected through the police checkpoints and safely board her flight." She looked up, "That's it, I think."

He smiled. "It's all I've told you so far."

Reaching the First South Bank, he headed for the closest ATM and completing his transaction, ushered her out again. As they started back, he pressed a wad of cash into her palm. "This should make your card squeaky clean again."

"How much is it?" She slipped the bills into her purse.

"With this last of a dozen ATM withdrawals over the past week, six thousand dollars."

"What?" she gasped. "That's three times what the reservations will cost."

"If you do this, you'll have earned far more than the difference between six grand and the costs."

"Tyler, I'm not doing this for money."

Stopping, he pulled her under the eave of a building. "I know why you're doing it, just like I know that all the money in the world can't buy a friend like you. Still," he smiled. "If you're rich, it's a nice way to show your appreciation." As they started off again, his conscience grew heavy. "Lauren, if the plan fails, you'll be in as much trouble as I am."

"It won't. Who'll suspect an assistant DA of escorting a murder fugitive to the airport? Isn't that why you asked me? Just make sure she's well disguised."

What a difference a few tumultuous hours made. "You wouldn't happen to have a friend or relative living in Florida, would you?"

"No, but my cousin, Deborah, lives in Atlanta. She visited last summer while her husband was on a golfing trip with his buddies."

"Does she look like you?" he asked.

"To some extent, only her hair's shorter. Bobbed, I guess you'd say. And she wears granny glasses. I've told her to get contacts but she won't listen."

"Is she your size?"

"Smaller, and thinner."

So was Mayson: five-four, a hundred pounds of Italian fire. "Then let's use an Atlanta connection in case someone questions your companion's identity. That is, if Deborah will lie for you."

Lauren hunched against the chilling wind, her hair swirling in her face. "Deborah won't be a problem. But what about you? Will you drive or fly?

"Fly. They'd have my car pegged before I left Manhattan."

She smiled. "After all the build up, I won't get a ride."

"Sure you will. Just ask Duke for the keys after he's seized it."

"At least you're going some place warm." She shivered against another icy gust. She'd never felt this way before and wasn't sure she wanted to again. "Tyler, please take care of yourself."

An idea grabbed him suddenly. "That Iowa horse farm you're always talking about . . . are you serious about it?"

"It's been my dream since I was eight. Maybe when I'm sixty, I'll be able to afford it."

"With the land, you'd need stables, storage buildings, a home and of course some exquisite Virginia thoroughbreds. What kind of money are we talking about?"

"A half-million dollars. Why, for heaven's sake?"

"Because I don't want you to wait until you're sixty to have your dream. I want you to have it now."

She gaped at him, speechless.

"My assets will be frozen this time tomorrow," he explained. "But this mess won't last long. Days, weeks, whatever; it'll end. Successfully, thanks to you. And when it does, you'll have your horse farm."

"Tyler, I can't! I mean, it's because . . ."

He embraced her as her face crumpled with tears. Yes 'because.' Nothing else needed to be said.

Seconds passed before her misty eyes lifted. "Tyler, I said a half-million, but the farm could easily cost more."

He lifted her chin firmly. "Not so much that buying it will present a problem. I'll enjoy picturing you on horseback as the morning sun creeps over some lush Iowa meadow."

"Then you'll have to be alive."

"I will." He kissed her now, sweetly, honestly, without promise or expectation. A postscript, she thought. 'Fondly yours, Tyler.'

Starting across the square, he turned back suddenly, "Your hair — what color is it?"

She laughed. "Blonde, Bozo, what else?"

"I mean the shade — if I was to look for it in a store?"

"Ash, I guess." She now remembered the question she'd meant to ask before. "Tyler, the one time you were in love, it ended badly. That's obvious. Did she hurt you?"

The wind gusted, the leaves swirling across the cold, empty, square as a deep sadness crept into his eyes.

"She didn't mean to," he replied, then turned and left the square.

CHAPTER ELEVEN

★

"Mr. Bilbro's looking for you," the receptionist announced as he got off the elevator. "And someone keeps calling and hanging up on the second ring. Is that a code or something?"

"No," he started down the hall. Was she crazy? The code had been a terrible . . .

"Tyler, wait!" Jill Allen rushed up. "Bilbro's looking for you. And he didn't seem very happy. Are you dating Lauren Belli? I saw you two in the square during lunch."

"We're just friends."

"Does she have the latest on our star fugitive?"

"I didn't ask." He started off, then quickly stopped again with her next tug.

"That car," she asked. "A Lamborghini, I think you said. Did you ever get it?"

"No, I didn't."

Reaching his office finally, he frowned at Poster Boy's messages, then quickly called.

"Where the fuck have you been?" Bilbro growled. "Do you know what time it is?"

Almost four - he checked his watch. "I got tied up on some Bar committee activities."

"Get your ass up here . . . Now!"

The instant he dropped the phone, it rang twice. As he dashed out, it rang again. Damnit Mayson, not now. Taking the elevator up to sixty, he hurried down to Bilbro's office. Poster Boy munched on a sandwich at his desk, his sleeves rolled up, coffee thermos on the credenza. 'Ed Bilbro, Wall Street's Blue Collar Lawyer,' among his other claims to fame. "Late for lunch, isn't it?" He dropped into the chair.

"Yeah?" Bilbro munched. "Late lunches, late associates. It's been that kind of day." Gulping coffee, he ripped open a bag of Fritos. "May he rest in peace, Morris picked a helluva time to get murdered. End-of-the-year is always crunch-time around here, like a vice on your nuts - especially when you have to waste time chasing associates all over the place."

Not much longer, Poster Boy. "I'll have those motions done before leaving tonight."

"You should already have a draft for me to review. Bar committee activities, bullshit. You probably wasted the afternoon on some cozy lunch with a babe. Let me find out she works here and I'll break your ass." Munching Fritos, he said, "I couldn't get the Garrison depositions continued. The witnesses are medical experts. Opposing counsel, some young prick at Anthony and Bartlett said it was too late to juggle things around since the good doctors had already set tomorrow aside out of their busy surgery schedules."

In other words, Tyler glowed with fresh hope, you're shit out of luck - and exhausted. He studied Poster Boy slumped in the chair. The fourteen-hour days and nut vices had taken their toll. "Let me handle the Breckinridge prelim and your problem's solved."

Bilbro studied him. "It's tempting, I admit."

"And also a piece of cake," Tyler said. "I'll simply submit the motions and using Morris's strategy, stipulate nothing for the record. You can stay here and depose your high-priced surgeons."

"Lamp would break my ass if he found out."

"But he won't. He's in Washington through the weekend."

"I don't know," Bilbro shrugged. "Aronson could handle the depositions. I just wish he was more familiar with the case."

"Doesn't sound too efficient to me," Tyler sighed. "Wasting a day on a prelim when you could be here chewing on those surgeons' expensive asses."

"Hell, just do it!" Bilbro buckled finally. "Insist on liberal filing deadlines, and don't stipulate a goddamned thing."

He was glad later that Poster Boy hadn't insisted on seeing the motions. What came off the PC that evening was essentially what had gone in, cosmetically brushed-up to fit the Breckinridge facts. The motions could be overhauled later. Federal litigation never ended; it just faded away when the clients could no longer pay the attorneys' fees. By eight, the copies had been made and his briefcase was packed. He'd reached Lauren to confirm Mayson's reservations had been made. If all went well, she'd be at the Naples Holiday Inn by noon tomorrow. "The room's registered in the name of Mr. and Mrs. Ralph Butts," Lauren had cheerfully explained.

"You got twin beds, I hope?"

"One king-size; the Butts like to snuggle. And Ralph, have her packed and ready at 6:20 sharp."

His own flight to Logan was at 6:45 a.m. He'd be in Boston before Mayson left New York, if she left. He'd made no contingency plans. Everything depended on them reaching Naples, concern gripping him now as he left Frieda's workstation with his loaded briefcase.

The Inner Sanctum was dark and quiet as he emerged from the elevator and hurried down the hall. Quickly he searched Nicole's tidy workstation and then slipped into Lamp's office. Snapping on the light, he dropped at the desk to call Mayson. With the second ring, he cut the line and redialed. One ring rolled into the next. Where the hell was she?

Dropping the phone, he turned his attention to Lamp's desk. The top drawer was locked. Wasting no time to search for a key or risk breaking it open, he groped through the other drawers - a forage that rewarded him with paper clips, pens, rubber bands, calling cards . . . bullshit! He searched the credenza, then the file cabinets, tables and shelves, quickly reaching the end of a fruitless effort. Hadn't he known this would be a waste of time? If Crenshaw held a clue to Morris's murder, Lamp certainly wouldn't be stupid enough to store the records in his office.

Scanning the shelves, his eyes stopped at a corner picture he'd never noticed before. Picking it up, he studied the familiar subjects, their faces tanned and relaxed as they posed on the tee of a sun-splashed golf course. The toadish Mann was dwarfed between the tall gateposts of his friends, Lamp and Falkingham. Three golfing buddies, three lions of the law: two on the Supreme Court, the other the Dean of Wall Street. How long had they been friends? Did Mann or Falkingham know how Lamp had acquired the smiling scar around his eye? Replacing the picture, he recalled Falkingham's first mention of his ill-fated career choice. "Greg

Lamp could use a well-bred Virginia boy like you. And New York judges would find your manners right refreshing."

He'd gazed at the ashtray full of Dunhill butts and longed simply for a smoke-free office. "New York's crowded, sir. I'm not sure I'd fit in."

"Nonsense," Falkingham had lit another Dunhill, stretching his long legs across the desk. "If you build ships, you do it in your Daddy's docks on the James. But if law's your game, you play it on Wall Street. Next to D.C., it's the most powerful legal arena in the world."

"I'll think about it, sir."

"What's there to think about? I'll call Greg." And so the grave mistake had been made.

A cynical Charleston aristocrat, Falkingham preferred to ridicule the law over his Jack Daniels rather than interpret it in the courtroom. A broad shouldered six-six, he was an imposing presence in his black robe and took great pleasure in browbeating lawyers. His piercing eyes could drop one with a scornful glance. In private chambers, he'd wrestle out of his robe and immediately light a Dunhill. "Those goddamned feeble-minded, liver-lipped lawyers get so tongue-tied in precedents they forget the law is ninety-nine percent common sense. Don't they know their precedents don't mean diddly squat to the Supreme Court? We create the only ones that matter."

"We" meant the Court's conservative bloc, specifically the four who voted together on major constitutional issues and who with one recruit, would become a majority capable of rewriting the law as it damn well pleased. And they'd soon have it. Longbridge's nomination to replace retiring Justice Sampson was due any day. Certainly the nominee would be someone of the same conservative cloth as his first two, Falkingham and Mann. With Rixell and DeJarno, their voting bloc would become a majority with frightening power. What would they do, create some kind of Christian Utopia in . . . His eyes shot to the ringing phone. As Lamp's recorded voice requested a message, the caller came on the line.

"This is Lieutenant Duke. An elderly couple stopped by the precinct earlier this evening. Apparently they've seen Corelli on the news enough times that it finally registered. They claim to have seen her get into a fancy black sports car on Seventy-First, Tuesday afternoon. Unfortunately, they didn't get a good look at the driver. And they're not sure of the car's make but the man swears it's a foreign job; Porsche, Lamborghini, who the hell knows? At least it's a start. Does anyone at Lieber Allen drive a black sports car? Check it out, will you? I'll call back in the morning. Thanks."

As the recorder switched off, he quickly erased the message. How many at the firm knew about his new 911? Were he and Mayson safe in Manhattan for even one more night? Calling her again, he cut the line, counted and redialed. A dozen anxious rings later, he hung up. Why had she made that goddamned scene on the street Tuesday? Hadn't she known it'd come back to haunt them? Shutting off the light, he grabbed his briefcase and left.

The apartment was black as he entered a short while later. How many cops would spend the night checking DMV records for every fancy black sports car on the East Coast? He'd driven his for the last time. Dropping his things, he turned on the light. "I'm home!" he announced.

Checking the study, he hurried down the hall to the bedroom and knocked on the door. When she didn't answer, he entered, putting on the light. The bed was made, the room neat and orderly. Had she simply panicked and left, he wondered as entered the bathroom, flipping on the light. She was gone. Something had happened and . . . he froze at the soft scrape. Jerking back the shower curtain, he now found her huddled in the tub, her eyes swollen from crying. "What happened?" he reached to help her up.

"No!" she turned to the wall. "Leave me alone!"

"I'm sorry to be so late, but there were arrangements to make," he dropped down to the tub. She'd cried wolf too many times. How was he to know this had been a real emergency? He turned her gently towards him. Her eyes brimmed with fresh tears. He gave her some tissue. "Now, what happened?"

Snatching the tissues from him, she blew her nose. "I hate you, Tyler. I really mean it this time."

"No, you don't. You're frightened and a little mad . . ."

"A little mad! I called you a zillion times and you ignored me. They could've found me and taken me away in handcuffs. Put me in a cell with some lesbian maniac with hairy arms and tattoos."

"Someone was here?" he asked.

"That's what I said, isn't it?"

Giving her more tissues, he waited as she blew her nose again. "Now, who was here?"

"How am I supposed to know?" She crumpled the tissue, missing the toilet with her shot.

"What did they do?" he asked.

"Which time?"

His eyes broadened. "They were here more than once?"

"Twice!" She stuck two fingers in his face. "The first time I knew it wasn't you because you make such a dope of yourself blurting like *Father Knows Best*, 'I'm home!' And being in the study, all I could do was dive in the closet and wait an eternity, five minutes at least, as they thumped around the hall."

He had a sudden suspicion. "During this eternity of five minutes, did you hear any humming?"

"Humming? What kind of question is that? I just recall being frightened out of my wits until they left and I crawled out to call you for the first of a zillion times. But you didn't care I was in danger."

"I care, Mayson, you know that."

"Then why didn't you answer your phone?"

"Because I was making arrangements to get us out of here."

"A lot of good that would've done if they'd carted me off to jail while you were making them."

"But they didn't." It hit him now that she was wearing his William and Mary football jersey. All the new clothes and she'd been forced to scrounge through his footlocker for something to wear. "Tell me about the second visit."

"Are you sure you have time? I hate to bother you with my problems."

"I've been up to my ears in your problems all day. One more won't make any difference."

Her eyes gleamed insolently. "It was much later. I'd just gotten out of the shower when the front door opened again and they thumped down the hall. I barely had time to slip on your stupid shirt and duck in here."

"In the tub, you mean?" he asked calmly.

"Of course in the tub!" she snapped impatiently.

"But if you'd just showered, it would've still been wet."

Her glare scorched him. "I hate it when you do this. The tub was wet. My bony butt, too. But I would've sat in cow urine if it meant saving my life."

"The person had a key, you realize," he said now.

She frowned. "How do you know that?"

"Never mind; go ahead."

"Anyway, they rummaged through the hall closet again."

"That's where the vacuum cleaner's stored. No humming this time either?"

"Why do you keep asking that? How can I recall if they were humming? I was in mortal danger. Anyway, after rummaging through the closet, they thumped around the apartment again until finally the bedroom door opened, then quickly the bathroom door. I was so frightened. Sitting deadly still, I waited for the curtain to open, but it didn't. Instead, the intruder just stood there, humming some stupid, ethnic melody. Spanish, I think." Her eyes slit angrily now. "You know who it was. I hate you, Tyler! I really, really do!"

"Come on." He pulled her up. "Another blow would be good." He grabbed more tissue.

Blowing her nose, she crumpled the tissue then missed the can again with another toss. "Why are you gawking at me?"

"My football jersey," he nodded.

She glanced at it sagging on her shoulders. The hem cut just above her knees, the same as her skirts. "It's soft and warm. Do you mind me wearing it?"

"Of course not."

"You obviously played a lot of football in it." She picked at one of its many tears. "Did all the boys have one? I mean with the same colors and stripes?"

"What the hell are you talking about?"

"The sporting goods store where you got it; did they have enough for everyone to look the same?"

"Mayson, this was my team jersey at William and Mary."

She knew that, of course. She'd found the jersey in her idle rummaging and been unable to resist the temptation to slip it on. This was something, however, she had no intention of telling him. "Tyler, how stupid do you think I am? William and Mary doesn't have a football team."

"They most certainly do," he answered. "A damn good one when I was there."

"And who did you play? The Radcliffe Pussycats? The Mary Washington Muffins? Or . . . no, the Columbia girls played field hockey."

"You shouldn't ridicule a sport you obviously know nothing about."

"I know enough to appreciate how stupid, dirty and violent it is - to the degree, in fact, that I can't imagine you playing. Scraped knees and elbows? Soiled pants? That's not you, Tyler."

As he left, she quickly followed. "Then you really did play?"

"It doesn't matter." All-Conference Quarterback twice didn't matter?

"What position did you play — shortstop?"

Entering the study, he turned on the recorder. "It's no wonder you don't like football. Who does in New York? The Jets are horrible. And the Giants . . ."

"Tyler, hi," the first message clicked on. "It's Rebecca, from McDougal's last night." The new Bellevue resident. Her sweet Virginia drawl brought an ache to his heart. "Tyler, I'd love to get together tonight. I'll be back from the hospital at nine. Call me. Bye."

"What about the Giants?" Mayson asked now.

"I was just going to say . . ."

"Tyler, it's Meg," the second message started. "Why won't you return my calls? You're not getting jittery over the firm's rule against dating, are you? I assume we're still on for tomorrow night. Eight's good for me. See you."

"The Giants are *what*?" Mayson asked again.

He frowned. What was she so hot about, Meg and the firm rule? "The Giants suck. That's all I ...

"That's a lie. You just . . ."

"Tyler, hi, it's Melanie," the third message began. "How does a cozy weekend at Martha's Vineyard grab you? I have my folks' cottage through Sunday. Call me. Bye."

"This is so disgusting," Mayson said. "A pathetic parade of hormonal females. And the Giants *don't* suck. You . . ."

"Tyler, it's Mom," the fourth message clicked on. "Dad and I wanted to make sure you're all right. Today is . . . well, we all know what today is. Stafford said you sounded a little bluer than usual. You don't have to call back. Just please make it home for Thanksgiving. We love you, sweetheart."

Mayson watched his eyes dim as he turned to the window.

"Tyler, it's Maria," the fifth message played. "You'll never guess what happened. Yes," she laughed. "Mrs. Dandridge's dinosaur broke again. I think she's finally ready to bite the bullet and buy a new Kirby like yours. Anyway, I just wanted to let you know I borrowed yours again. Say, when do the renovations begin? Can they get the work done in the next two weeks? Let me know. Bye."

So Maria had been the intruder. First to get the Kirby, then return it and snoop at some fictitious renovation he'd made up to keep her away. "It wasn't your fault." Her eyes lifted to him at the window.

"I should've warned you about Mrs. Dandridge's vacuum cleaner. A millionaire living on Park Avenue, who can't part with a few bucks for a decent Kirby. I'm sorry for what you went through this afternoon."

"Then tell me what 'today' is."

"Our last in Manhattan."

"I mean your mother's call. She said we all know what today is. But she's wrong. We don't."

"It doesn't matter."

"Yes Tyler, it does; so much that your mother and sister called to make sure you were all right." She watched as he slipped out then quickly returned with a shopping bag. Now she recalled the other thing that had been nagging at her. "Maria's second visit was at five. The last scare occurred at seven. The NYPD. They identified themselves, knocked a half-dozen times, then left. When I couldn't reach you, I hid in the tub convinced they'd return."

He wasn't surprised. With a thousand Feds providing reinforcement, checking every home in Manhattan suddenly seemed a feasible plan. "Did they know it was my apartment?"

She shook her head. "I guess it was a random check. But the next one might not be."

He told her about Duke's call. "They'll soon learn about my 911. Let's hope it's after we're gone."

Her eyes filled with remorse. "Tyler, I'm sorry I made such a fool of myself Tuesday afternoon."

"You were just frightened."

"I was a pain in the ass."

"You still are," he said, pulling the accessories from the bag: clippers, thinning shears, hair coloring, and a pair of wire-rimmed glasses.

"Yuk!" She frowned at the glasses.

"They're pretty awful," he smiled. "But you'll get used to them."

The surgery began minutes later. Sitting cross-legged on the study floor, she cringed with the first snip, then watched her dark locks flutter to the towel. "I don't see why I have to look so ugly!"

"I doubt we'll be able to accomplish that." He wielded the clippers behind her.

Fretfully she reached for her wine on the table.

"Damnit, sit still!" Gulping his Molson, he then grabbed two chunks of cheddar, giving her one.

"Don't I get a cracker?" she complained.

He dumped several in her hand. "Now shut up and sit still."

"I don't take orders from stupid *gavonnes*!"

"Listen goddamnit, I have clippers here."

As her shoulders slumped he snipped again, quickly falling into a rhythm. "Oh!" She glanced at the hair accumulating on the towel. "I hate this."

"I guess you'd rather spend the next fifty years in Attica with Lucky."

"The Lips! Why can't you get that straight?"

He paused to inspect his work. "What does a bob look like?" Her head dropped as she muttered in Italian. "Very short, I guess." After another minute of furious clipping he stopped, the length now gone.

"Are you going to tell me the plan?" she asked. "Or am I supposed to guess it?"

Reaching again for the shears, he explained it in between snips. "Doesn't Lauren have a cousin without bobbed hair and granny glasses?" she fretted.

"Just be thankful she has one."

"Can she be trusted?"

"Yes, Mayson, she can."

"Because she's in love with you?"

"I didn't ask her motive."

"Tyler, do you think Lauren's beautiful?"

"Not as beautiful as you —at least when you had hair."

"Ooohhh!" Grabbing a fistful of hair, she broke into another Italian staccato. Ending the butchery finally, he plopped a grape in her mouth and sat back to inspect the damage.

"You're cringing, Tyler. Is it really that bad?"

"Worse actually." Smiling, he sipped his beer. "I'm joking; you'll do fine tomorrow, don't worry."

She replied, "I won't do anything but worry until you walk through that hotel room door." After years of avoidance, at last there was another door to face. "Tyler, you need a good meal before we start this odyssey. How about a steak?"

"Thanks, but it's time to dye your hair."

Springing up to the mirror, she absorbed the stranger's reflection. An inch remained maybe. She plucked at the short, cropped hair. *Madonna mia,* she had sideburns!

Rising too, he studied her closely. The bobbed hair drew attention to her thickly lashed eyes, enhancing their fawnish innocence and her cheekbones' high arch. By removing the distraction of hair he was forced to appreciate just how beautiful she really was.

"It's awful, isn't it?" she asked.

"It's fine." He began gathering the clumps of hair.

"Tyler, what's wrong? You're so quiet suddenly."

"I'm not quiet," he answered. "I'm busy."

"Will you tell me what 'today' is?"

"No." Dumping the accessories and hair in the bag, he tossed her the tube of hair coloring. "Now get started. It's late."

A dark shadow had fallen over him suddenly. "Tyler I wish you'd talk to me."

"And I wish you'd get in the goddamned shower."

"I want to know what 'today' is," she insisted.

"The day we leave New York; now get in the shower or I may get a hankering to put you in myself!"

"Hankering? What's 'hankering?' " As he started towards her, she fled down the hall.

Setting his bag by the front door, he grabbed a fresh Molson and returned to the study. Sipping pensively, he gazed at his cherished posters. More than memories, they were pieces of him - too real, too close to discard. But he was leaving them just as he was leaving his expensive Porsche, which he coveted far less.

Minutes crept as he drifted from one reflection into the next. Clowns cackled, lion tamers' whips snapped, the organ resonated. The grandstands trembled, first in the circus tent then the Pasadena Coliseum. The crowd roared as the Redskins streaked onto the field, the Super Bowl blimp floating across the crystal sky. The vivid images now sprung to life as her warm fingers slipped through his, her soft lyrical voice in his ears - in the Coliseum, the circus tent, the dark movie theater. Everywhere they'd been . . . Looking up he now found Mayson in the doorway. She'd slipped back into his jersey but not the jeans, her slender legs bared, velvet soft, like her face.

"You were lost in your posters." She toweled her hair. "The football games or the circus?"

"I was just thinking." He sipped absently.

"About leaving them? I'm sorry for that."

Wearily he watched her wrap the towel turban-like around her head, then drop down beside him. "Since this is autumn, can I assume you were entranced by the football posters?" she asked.

"Assume anything you want," he said.

"Tyler, what's wrong? Please tell me. I never realized you weren't always the happy-go-lucky guy you seemed at the firm. But you're not. You brood like the rest of us and get grouchy. And you . . ."

"I get the point!" he snapped.

"And something else. Your eyes . . ."

"What, Mayson? It's too late to start being mysterious. What about my eyes?"

"They're always so restless, except like now when we're sitting here. The hall posters." She glowed with fresh intrigue. "Are they related to 'today?'"

"If I say yes, will you stop?"

"No."

"Then no; now let's look at your hair."

She swished off the towel. Like magic the blond nubs sprung from her head; a shade darker than Lauren's. "You'll need to color it again in the morning." He settled the glasses on her delicate nose.

"Well?" she asked anxiously.

They masked her large, dark eyes even with a careful study. For the first time, he felt confident. "They're good. See for yourself."

Rising she peeked cautiously in the mirror, then stomped her foot. "Yuk! Am I the Beverly Hillbillies' Granny or Little Boy Blue?"

"Neither." He unfolded the sofa bed. "You're Deborah; then at the Naples Holiday Inn, Mrs. Ralph Butts. Damn Lauren." He grabbed pillows and sheets from the closet. "I can't believe she did that."

She ventured another peek. "Tyler, I hate this."

"Damnit Mayson, quit griping and go to bed."

She glared as he stretched out comfortably on the foldout. "I said I'd sleep out here tonight."

"I make the rules in my house. And in this case, guests sleep in the bedroom. Now go to sleep."

"If I don't, I suppose you'll hanker again?"

"If I must."

"You don't scare me." Her eyes drifted over his fully dressed body. "I said underwear was all right."

Rising obediently to undress, he hung his clothes in the closet. As she left, he dropped back on the cot and snapped out the light. He was out in seconds, but then jerked back and was kicked.

"Move your big butt, Mr. Butts!"

Switching on the light, he found her looming in his jersey — a clownish mascot, hugging two pillows under her chin. "You can't sleep out here," he said. "It's not proper."

She said, "Since when did proper ever stop you?"

"You mean with my *puttanas*? That's different."

"You're damn right it is. Don't even think of putting your philandering paws on me. Now scoot over." She kicked him again. "I said I'd sleep out here tonight and I meant it."

"Honestly." He rolled over. "Must you be such a pain in the ass every second of the day?" He watched her drop primly on the foldout. "Anything else before I turn the light out?"

Fluffing the pillows, she slipped under the covers. "Go ahead; only no hands, feet or snoring."

Blackness swallowed the room. Again he was out in seconds, then . . . "Goddamnit, what now?"

"Am I really that different from the others?" she asked.

"Very different," he sighed.

"Oh . . ." The sheets rustled as she turned away.

He'd hurt her feelings. "Mayson?"

"Yes Tyler?"

"A good different, I meant."

CHAPTER TWELVE

★

It seemed just seconds before the gray dawn was in the window. Beside her, Tyler solemnly inventoried his posters, a reluctant curator bidding farewell to his precious museum.

"Tyler, please tell me about your museum."

"We don't have time," he replied.

"Yes we do. You just won't tell me."

"Please Mayson, don't start." He rose. "I'll shower first." Glancing at his watch, he dashed out.

She rose to the window, catching the sun's first glimmer over the East River. It would be a sparkling autumn day, one that would end where – a Naples hotel or a Manhattan jail? Her eyes dropped to the street below where an army of cops waited, and fervently she prayed it would not be the latter.

Wistfully her gaze settled on the Disney World poster. She'd never been except in her dreams, vividly painted by Cellini's customers. She'd been scraping pennies together for college while they'd been throwing away thousands for a week at Disney World. Bagging their groceries, she'd listened wondrously to their tales, each adding fresh detail and color to her vision. She'd wanted so badly . . . The ringing phone shattered her reflections.

Tyler's recorded greeting was followed by the voice of an agitated Lauren Belli. "More witnesses to the scene Mayson made Tuesday have come forward. Last night's black sports car, as of fifteen minutes ago, has become a black 911. Duke now has every cop in Manhattan looking for it. Tyler, get out as fast as you can. And have Mayson ready. I'll be there in fifteen minutes." As the line clicked off, Mayson flew down the hall, bursting into the bedroom. "Lauren just called! They have the make of your car!"

"Shit!" Tyler furiously snapped the last shirt buttons as Mayson dashed into the bathroom, cranked on the shower and got in. Quickly her hand poked out of the curtain. "Tyler . . . ?"

He gave her the hair coloring tube and then quickly retrieved her traveling outfit: cream sweater, navy slacks and topsiders.

Minutes later, she emerged fully dressed and found him pacing by the front door.

"You're ready." He nodded at the suitcase and purse, then studied her damp hair. "At least it's lighter." Placing the glasses on her nose, he helped her into the ski jacket. "You won't need this very long."

"We hope, anyway." Her heart pounded. How many cops would they encounter on the way to La Guardia? It'd take just one to recognize her. What if she was caught? If he didn't . . . if she . . .

"Hey." He caught her fluttering hand. "You'll do fine. Feast on JBs and Jams, start *Robes of Vengeance* and the next thing you know, I'll be there." He reached for the note. "Didn't I tell you I'd forget? It's all there — flight times, boarding gates and hotel reservations, including that pain-in-the-ass name."

"Not ass," she smiled. "Butts. And my brother is The Lips. You're so horrible with names."

"No argument there," he nodded. "Lauren should be here any minute, as will my cab."

Her eyes watered. "Tyler, please be careful."

"I will." He grabbed his things. "Now, I have to go."

Yes, he did. He was flying to Boston; she in the opposite direction. It'd be long hours until she saw him again — if she did. She'd count the seconds, minutes, hours as she waited by the hotel door. She was good at that. She'd done it before. "Tyler, please . . ."

Glancing at her fingernails pressed into his arm, he smiled. "Have the Molson on ice. I'll see you on the Gulf Coast by six." Planting a kiss in her new blond hair, he left.

Minutes later a knock came at the door. She opened it to tall, blond Lauren Belli, all legs in her navy suit. She looked very Nordic with her rosy cheeks, wide blue eyes and braided hair. "Tyler just left."

"Good," Lauren did her best to smile as she inventoried the new Mayson. Even with bobbed blond hair and granny glasses, she was much too beautiful to be Deborah but at least she'd made herself unrecognizable. She grabbed the suitcase. "It'll be more convincing if I'm carrying something."

Slipping her purse over her shoulder, Mayson locked the door and followed Lauren down the hall.

"You won't have any trouble." Lauren pushed for the elevator. "I can't even recognize you. It's fortunate you don't practice criminal law. There isn't a cop on the force who couldn't spot me in a crowd, no matter what I was wearing."

"Lauren, I'm deeply grateful for what you're doing," Mayson said as the elevator started down.

"Forget it." She dismissed the gratitude as neither necessary nor wanted. As they reached the garage, she followed Mayson out. "I always park on the third level." She nodded at her blue Volvo. Putting the suitcase in back, she slipped behind the wheel as Mayson got in. Glancing in the mirror, she drove off.

Mayson's stomach knotted as they snaked down the ramp. Quickly reaching the end of the tunnel, they plunged into the threatening light. Concealed only by Park Avenue's thick morning traffic, she felt naked suddenly, anxiously scanning the busy streets as they crept between lights. Patrol cars were on every block. At Eighty-Sixth one finally loomed in the mirror.

"Lewis and Alvarez." Lauren waved to the officers. "They're on their morning bagel run." A second unit crept up behind them on Seventy-Ninth. "Delwood and Jordan." She named its occupants then caught two dark-suited men suddenly emerge from a building on their right. "Those guys, I don't have a clue about, except they're much scarier than the NYPD."

Mayson's eyes followed them up the street, where they met two other men. All wore the same dark suits, glasses and creepy expressions. "FBI?" she asked.

"Either that or Special Services. They all look the same, breathe the same. They run on batteries, I'm told." Lauren sighed. "Get used to it. They'll be on every corner between here and La Guardia."

As the light changed they crept again. "Why are they looking for me?" Mayson asked.

"I thought that's why you and Tyler were going to Florida; to find out." As another unit crept up beside them, Lauren waved to the officers. "Breedlove and some new guy."

"Lauren, I didn't kill Morris Mendelsohn."

"That's what Tyler said."

"Do you believe him?"

She surveyed the traffic with growing frustration. "Mayson, I wouldn't be helping unless I believed him. Unfortunately, my opinion doesn't mean squat since the rest of the world thinks you're guilty as hell."

"Your opinion's important to me. I wish we'd gotten to be friends through the Bar functions."

"Friends?" Lauren repeated. "Come on, Mayson, you made it obvious at those bar functions that you considered yourself better than everyone else. You didn't want friends."

"I don't think I'm better than anyone else," Mayson replied. "I just didn't . . ." Belong. The others had been warm and secure, she cold and secure only in her mistrust of everyone and everything. Only now Tyler would have her make one big, handsome exception, and it frightened her to think she might.

"Save it Mayson," Lauren snapped. "What I'm doing is based solely on my feelings for Tyler, nothing else." The light changed again but the traffic didn't move. Horns shrieked around them. "Damn!" She smacked the wheel. "We'll miss the flight at this rate!"

Mayson's stomach knotted. Would she be able to get another flight? Was Tyler . . . ? A cop in the unit beside her suddenly signaled for her to roll the window down.

"Let me handle this," Lauren whispered.

As Mayson rolled the window down, the young cop, clean cut and darkly handsome, smiled at Lauren. "Some mess, huh, counselor? Want me to radio downtown and advise them you'll be late for court?"

"That won't be necessary," Lauren replied. "However, there's something you can do, Loukanis, if you really want to help."

"Yeah?" His dark eyes narrowed. "What's that?"

"Give us an escort to La Guardia. Otherwise my cousin will miss her flight."

Loukanis studied Mayson with a growing interest. "I don't know, counselor. They frown on that stuff at the precinct."

Bullshit, Lauren thought. The hot-blooded Greek was just negotiating. "The escort would be well-received, I assure you."

"You've turned down my last two dinner invitations. You saying a third might be charmed?"

"I never eat a salad without feta cheese and Greek olives, if that tells you anything."

In awe, Mayson watched Loukanis turn to his partner to discuss the proposition. To help Tyler in a desperate venture offering her nothing, Lauren was prepared to date this cop. Loukanis turned back now. "Which airline?"

"American."

"Let's go, then. And stay close, Counselor, I'd hate to lose you."

The unit's lights flashed, the siren shrieked and yet there was nowhere to go in the clogged street. Finally the traffic parted and Lauren followed Loukanis through the narrow seam. Ignoring traffic lights, they were soon sailing across Manhattan, La Guardia once again reachable. "Can you believe this?" Lauren smiled over the irony. "A murder fugitive being escorted to the airport by an assistant DA and the NYPD. Make sure you tell Tyler. He'll get a real kick out of this."

Mayson braced as they skidded into a turn behind the streaking unit. "You'll accept his next invitation, won't you?"

"Why not? He's great looking, don't you think . . . Hold on." She skidded into another turn, her tires squealing. Coming out of it, she hit the gas hard. "That'd make the guys at Indy proud!" She grinned at her frightened passenger. "Don't wet your pants, Mayson. There's no time for a change."

The sun was rising as they streaked across the Triborough Bridge. La Guardia loomed ahead. Turning off his siren and lights Loukanis whipped into the service road, Lauren on his bumper. "Whatever you think of me," Mayson said, "I respect your feelings for Tyler and the risk you've taken to help him."

"Look," Lauren sighed. "I'm sorry for what I said back there. I get that way when I'm flustered."

"Me too," Mayson smiled. A real pain in the ass, Tyler would say.

Reaching American's flight lanes, Loukanis took the one closest to the terminal. Flashing his lights and starting the siren again, he coaxed the traffic forward. "Bully," Lauren laughed, creeping behind him.

At the terminal entrance, he parked in an emergency zone,

leaving space for Lauren to squeeze in behind him. Mayson tensed as he and his partner climbed out. "Jerome Crawford," Lauren identified the older, heavier officer. "Close to retirement, a bushel of grandkids; a real pussycat. Just stay calm."

How? Mayson anxiously searched the faces along the walkway. A beaming Loukanis helped Lauren out of the car. "How's that for service, huh?"

"I'm impressed. How about you, Deborah?"

"Wonderful," Mayson groped for enthusiasm in a pit of nerves.

Grabbing her suitcase, Crawford helped her out. His ruddy face was thick like his body, his moustache, salt-and-pepper frizz. "And where might you be off to so early this morning, Deborah?"

"Atlanta." She realized now he was absorbing her face. Did he recognize her from one of her many excursions to Manhattan's courthouses?

"Nice place, Atlanta," he nodded. "And sure warmer than New York this time of year."

"That's a strange accent for Atlanta," Loukanis said.

"Deborah grew up in Flatbush," Lauren quickly explained. "Only Jeff Burns came along to make a carpetbagger out of her."

"That must explain why she looks so familiar," Crawford nodded. "I pulled some years over at the Flatbush precinct. It's the eyes; I've seen them, only without the glasses."

"I've worn them since fifth grade," Mayson replied. "You must be thinking of someone else."

"Jerry's a genius with mugs," said Loukanis. "Especially pretty ones. If he says he remembers you, I'd bet a month's pay, he's right."

Mayson's eyes flashed at Lauren. Taking the cue, she grabbed the suitcase. "Call me, Loukanis. We have to run now."

"This afternoon," he grinned. "Count on it."

Crawford stopped Mayson before they could get away. "Your maiden name wasn't Corell, was it?"

She glanced at a frozen Lauren. "Stanley," she groped. "That was my maiden name."

"Johnny Corell had a garage over in Flatbush," he explained. "Did all the precinct's repairs. His daughter looked just like you."

"We'll watch your car," Loukanis said as they started off. "Just don't be too long. We get a call, we gotta go."

Mayson froze as she caught the Feds posted at the terminal entrance. Lauren smiled. "Don't act suspicious or you will be. Did I tell you? Your last name is Burns."

"I'm a carpetbagger and my husband's Jeff."

"Right, and he'll be furious if you miss your flight. Now come on, cuz." She nudged Mayson towards the entrance where the Feds solemnly studied the traffic flowing through the glass doors. Holding her breath, Mayson slipped under their noses and followed Lauren over to the ticket counter.

Checking the suitcase in, Lauren answered the attendant's questions which he briskly fed into his computer as Mayson's eyes bounced between the counter and the Feds. Her stomach tightened as her eyes' next bounce was into a Fed's threatening dark glasses. Quickly she turned back to the counter. As Lauren finally led her away, the Fed's shades followed them into the busy concourse. "He was watching me," Mayson whispered.

"How could you tell with those shades on?" Lauren hurried along. "He could've been admiring my fantastic legs."

They reached the screening station manned by a cluster of NYPD Blues, State Grays and dark-suited Feds. "I can't do this." Mayson froze.

"Yes, you can," Lauren ordered. "We can't have Tyler arrive in Naples only to find you've chickened out. Now if bullshit's required, let me handle it. It's my specialty."

They drew increasing attention as the line shortened, the officers' alert eyes missing nothing as subjects passed through the metal detector. As the woman ahead of Mayson stepped through the detector, a dozen pair of eyes meticulously disrobed her. One pair, dark and piercing, drifted back to Mayson – those of the diminutive State Gray, who now whispered to the Fed beside him. Was he . . . ? *Madonna mia*, he was — the process server who delivered suit papers to the firm! Dropping her purse onto the belt, she started for the detector as Lauren found an acquaintance. "Bennie Devlin! Where have you been keeping yourself?"

"I got a promotion," the young NYPD Blue grinned.

"Promotion?" Lauren tossed her purse onto the belt as Mayson grabbed hers on the other side. "You mean they have something better than DA Liaison?"

"Runner," Devlin laughed. "I just got my own beat. We're pulling time on the Corelli manhunt."

Stepping through the detector, Lauren snatched up her purse. "Congratulations, Bennie, it's . . ."

"Miss, hold it right there."

Lauren's eyes shot to Mayson, who'd frozen down the hall as a Gray and two Feds converged. "She's my cousin, Deborah Burns." She hurried over. "I'm getting her on a flight which leaves . . . Oh Lord!" she glanced at her watch. "In nine minutes. Deborah, we should run."

One of the Feds smiled coldly. "We still need to establish her identity."

Lauren cringed as the crowd grew around them. "Look, she's my cousin who's been visiting and is on her way home. Her husband and baby will be expecting her at the Atlanta airport in two hours. Please don't make us late."

"ID," the Fed repeated. "Plastic stuff with Deborah Burns on it. That should take ten seconds."

"They're just stalling," the Gray said. "This woman's Mayson Corelli. I've seen her at Lieber Allen a hundred times."

"You're sure?" the Fed asked.

He nodded. "I wouldn't have stopped her if I wasn't."

"This is insane!" Lauren fumed. "Don't you think I know my own cousin? I'm an assistant DA, for Christ's sake! Do you think I'd escort a murder fugitive to the airport?"

The Fed's hard glare found Mayson. "Let's have the purse, ma'am. If you're who your loudmouth friend says . . ."

"Watch who you're calling loudmouth!" Lauren snapped.

With an arrogant cackle, he reached for Mayson's purse. "No!" she clutched it tightly. "I've done nothing wrong."

Nodding at his associate, the two Feds now converged on the small, feisty woman. "Lauren, you're the prosecutor." She wrestled furiously. "Tell them I have rights!"

Finally she was stripped of the purse. One Fed was about to dig inside when his associate warned, "Better wait for Agent Big-Shot."

The crowd's attention shifted to the dark-suited, dark-shaded clone approaching rapidly. Distinguished by his silver-streaked hair, he nevertheless moved with the same swiftness as the younger Feds; he was a handsome man, and one with apparent rank. The others moved back as he reached the scene. "What do we have, Agent Salzburg?" he asked his subordinate holding the purse.

Salzburg nodded at the Gray. "Daniels claims the subject here is Mayson Corelli. When she resisted our efforts to confirm her identity, we were forced to restrain her."

"That's her purse?"

"Yes sir."

He removed his dark glasses to study her more closely. "Who does she claim to be?"

"I don't claim to be anyone," she retorted furiously. "My name is Deborah Burns and I've been visiting my cousin, Lauren Belli, who prosecutes criminals, not helps them escape — something these stupid brutes can't get through their thick heads. And their gross incompetence has probably caused me to miss my flight to Atlanta, where my husband and baby are waiting."

"Thank you," he nodded. "I believe that answers my question." He glanced at the others. "A feisty one you've hooked here. Your accent, Mrs. Burns, strikes me as a little further north of Atlanta."

"I'm from Flatbush. We moved to Atlanta three years ago."

"Would you remove your glasses?" As she obeyed, he asked Daniels, "What do you think now?"

"It's Corelli, all right," he nodded.

"Well we can confirm it quickly enough," he said, grabbing her purse from Agent Salzburg.

She glanced at a horrified Lauren as he opened her purse and began flipping through the plastic cards -.VISA, Exxon, ATM, New York Bar card, and driver's license, with the glossy picture, issued to Mayson Angelina Corelli - they all flashed across her mind. She'd been so proud of her identity, of all she'd accomplished. Yet now it was sending her to prison. The rules never changed; she was, after all, a Corelli.

"Sir, is it her or not?" Salzburg grew impatient.

Finally Chief Fed returned the purse. "I'm sorry, Mrs. Burns, we're just doing our jobs. Unfortunately, we make mistakes. I hope you can still catch your flight." Behind him the others groaned with disappointment and confusion. Mayson glanced at an equally stunned Lauren.

"Sir, this must be some clever alias," Daniels insisted. "This woman is Mayson Corelli."

"Her Georgia driver's license is the real McCoy," Chief Fed replied. "I had one myself once."

But Daniels wasn't ready to concede the point. "That's Mayson Corelli. I'll swear it in an affidavit."

"The lady has a valid ID," Salzberg replied. "There's nothing we can do."

"We can take her in," Daniels persisted.

"That'll be enough!" Chief Fed barked, then turned to Salzburg. "Check on Mrs. Burns' flight. If it hasn't left, hold it. If it has, get her on the next one out."

Salzburg's glare frosted her as he hurried off. Chief Fed now scribbled on his business card and gave it to her. "I noticed your Diners Club Card. A friend of mine has the best seafood restaurant in Atlanta; the First Mate. Maybe you've been there. If not, take your husband and tell the owner, Joe Wright, I sent you. He'll fix you up with the best broiled seafood you've ever tasted." He nodded. "The address is on the card."

She caught the urgency in his eyes. It was hardly restaurant information he was providing, and she didn't have a Diners Club card. Who was he, this man who'd read "Deborah Burns" when her ID plainly stated "Mayson Angelina Corelli"? She slipped the card into her purse as Salzburg returned. "Her flight's waiting, sir."

"You'd better hurry," Chief Fed now smiled. "You don't want to keep that baby waiting."

"No sir. And thank you for straightening this mess out; thank you very much." Winking at a speechless Lauren, she hurried off to catch her flight.

CHAPTER THIRTEEN

★

The eyes of Judge McCarthy's secretary snapped to attention as the handsome young lawyer breezed in. He was tall, with crystal blue eyes and wavy gold hair. "Tyler Waddill?" When he nodded, she handed him the message. "You can use the library phone."

Lugging his briefcase into the library, Tyler closed the door and placed his call. Mayson was certainly in the air by now. There'd been no news flashes. Bilbro's secretary now answered. "Heather," he said. "I'm returning Ed's call."

"He's in a meeting, Tyler. Can he call you back?"

"This message says he wanted to catch me before the prelim. You'd better see if he needs to tell me something."

"I'm not sure that's a good idea. Hold on . . ."

An undefined fear crept into the drifting silence. Had Duke's suspicion over the black 911 already trickled down to Poster Boy? Bilbro now came on the line. "All set for the prelim? I'm sure you'll do fine."

His tone was much too casual. He was hiding something. "Your call wasn't about Breckinridge?"

"No," Bilbro replied. "There's some Back Bay litigation I've just gotten involved in. I wanted you to pick up a copy of the case record at the state courthouse."

It was just around the corner. He'd seen it on the ride in from Logan. "What's the case name?"

"Ah, just forget it," Bilbro now dismissed the project. "I'll have Heather arrange for a copy to be shipped. You don't want to lug a heavy box of records back to New York."

No, but since when did Poster Boy, or any other partner, give a shit about the traveling convenience of a first year associate? Did he need the records or not?

"Say Tyler, I guess you put your flight on your personal credit card, huh? Damn, I wish I'd thought to lend you my firm card. Give me your account number and I'll have Heather transfer the expense."

Was someone eavesdropping? Duke, maybe? Had they been discussing his 911? Without hesitation, he provided the number of an account he didn't have with American Express.

"Heather said to get your other accounts, too, in case this happens again," Bilbro added.

It won't, Poster Boy, don't worry. He relayed the names of three banks he'd never done business with.

"Tyler, which airline are you flying - for the expense adjustment? American?"

Bingo. "Atlantic Coastal. Listen, McCarthy's secretary is calling me into the conference."

"Okay. Just call before you leave, all right?"

Count on it, dickhead, he thought, and hung up.

"Wow!" McCarthy's secretary grinned in the doorway. "How did you know I was calling you?"

"ESP," he smiled. "Is the Judge ready?"

"He's winding up a call now."

As she left, he gazed at his briefcase, then quietly slipped out the side door. A man rushing down the hall stopped just in time to avoid a collision. "My fault," Tyler smiled at the balding man in the expensive dark suit. A lawyer, obviously. There were so many in the world, especially courthouses.

The man stopped him before he could get away. "Are you here for the Breckinridge prelim?"

"No, I'm not." He caught two more men approaching. Ducking out the hall door, he flew down the stairs, and slipping out of the courthouse, grabbed the first taxi.

Minutes later, he was dropped off at Copley Square and hurried towards the Prudential Center. He'd used a bank there once to pay for an expensive sailing weekend with Betsy Fairgate, who now practiced law in her father's Boston firm - here in Copley Square, for all he knew. Using the bank's ATM, he made his last cash withdrawal of the many made this past week; the accumulated sum would most likely have to last for a very long time. By noon his accounts would be frozen.

He checked his watch. By now, his vanishing act had been reported to Bilbro in New York, which meant he was officially a fugitive. Loosening his tie, he grabbed a cab back to Logan.

He hurried through the crowded airport, his eyes bouncing from the flight monitors to the TV screens. He'd yet to see a news flash, which hopefully meant Mayson was in Atlanta, waiting for her Naples connection. If lucky, they'd be watching a Gulf Coast sunset a few hours from now. He bought a paper and started down the American concourse. The monitor indicated his flight was boarding at Gate 12J. Quickening his pace, he saw a Fed suddenly emerge from the men's room and start in the opposite direction. They were here! Just in this concourse or others?

Reaching his gate, he quickly joined the boarding line. In a few minutes he'd be in the friendly southern skies. By evening . . . He froze as a Fed stepped from behind a column. Scanning the crowd, the man's eyes quickly found him. The paper slipped from his fingers as the Fed whispered sharply into his wireless. Nope, he wouldn't be flying today. Spinning, he streaked out of the concourse.

"Stop that man!" the Fed barked over the crowd's rumble.

Alertly, he caught the next Fed as he reached the mouth of the concourse. Spotting him at the same time, the Fed reached for his gun and gave chase. Turning suddenly, Tyler charged, slamming him against the upper level railing. The gun slipped from the Fed's hand as he crumpled to the floor. Gunfire shattered glass overhead. Diving to the floor, Tyler quickly crawled for the escalator as the first Fed, joined by several airport guards, exploded into the terminal. As the guards checked on his associate, the Fed caught Tyler's head rise above the railing. "The escalator!" he shouted as Tyler flew down the steps. Now spotting two associates racing for the landing below, he yelled, "Olsen, he's coming down now!"

The Feds rushed to cut Tyler off as the guards filed onto the escalator above. He was trapped — or was he? As the Feds reached the landing, he suddenly dove, his powerful body crashing into them. Like their associate before, they too crumpled to the floor, their guns sliding away.

Jumping up, Tyler caught two more Feds racing towards him, followed by several airport guards. Above, the escalator thundered with pursuers. He had but one option now, and ducking against more gunfire, he took it, exploding through the plate glass.

Heads snapped around as shards sprayed the pavement. Women screamed at the madman with desperate blue eyes and sparkling glass in his hair.

Surveying the chaos of people, cars, baggage and dollies, he plunged decisively into it as his pursuers rushed out. "Stop that man!" they shrieked as he dashed across the congested traffic lanes. Shots were fired into the air; people screamed all around him. The bedlam soon faded as he reached the last lane. There he spotted a party of nuns leaving their cab and dashed for it. "Get me out of here!" he yelled as he dove into the back seat.

The black cabbie studied him gasping on the floor, then saw the quick, hard glances of his pursuers working through the crowd. "Sneakin' off without paying your fare, huh? Well if you ride with ole' Jake here, you payin'. Otherwise we're sittin.'"

"I'll pay! Now get me the fuck outta here!"

"Ummm, ummm," Jake glanced in the mirror at his passenger, brushing glass from his hair. "I'm glad them ladies I just let off can't hear the filth that's coming from your mouth." Scooting into the traffic now, he asked, "So where to?"

Breathing easier, he slumped back to study the thick traffic flowing from Logan. "The bus station."

"Which one?"

He glared at the cabbie strangely. "The closest."

"That'd be South Station."

"Fine. Just hurry."

"We're almost there," Jake nodded, taking the next exit, which deposited them in a district of ancient gray buildings huddled along shabby streets. "So what'd you do?"

"Not a goddamned thing - nothing illegal, anyway. Stupid maybe, but not illegal."

"Right," Jake smiled. Turning onto Atlantic Avenue, he pulled in front of South Station, two blocks later. "I hope things work out. But if not, don't worry about me." He grinned as Tyler greased his palm with two crisp hundred-dollar bills. "No sir, a crowbar couldn't pry these lips apart."

As the cab slipped back into the traffic, Tyler entered the dingy station, empty except for an old couple huddled in a corner with their shabby suitcases and a businessman browsing at the magazine rack. He glanced at the clock. His plane was now well into the southern skies and he was a fugitive who counted his freedom by the seconds, ones he must stretch into minutes, then hours, until reaching the frightened young woman a thousand miles away.

Smiling, he approached the clerk behind the counter. "I'd like a ticket on your next bus south."

"South where?" she asked. Her teased red hair, helmet-shaped, framed a sharp, suspicious face.

"Anything south will do." He reached for his wallet.

Annoyed by his vagueness, she keyed into her computer. "The sixty-seven to St. Louis leaves in ten minutes."

"Too far west."

"You just said south." She keyed back into the computer. "The eighty-six to Atlanta leaves in twenty minutes."

"Perfect," he smiled. Paying for his ticket, he ducked into the waiting room crammed with travelers, their baggage and restless children clogging the aisles. A TV blared overhead. Avoiding the chaos, he drifted out to the boarding area. The St. Louis southbound soon left, taking a large chunk of the waiting room crowd. Through the glass he watched it fill again. How long until the Feds arrived?

Finally a patrol car drifted into the terminal. Turning towards the glass, he watched the two cops get out and talk with attendants. Were they looking for him or some local hood? One cop went inside to question the ticket clerk, returning a few minutes later to huddle with his partner. Then quickly they left.

The minutes crawled. Twenty were piled up and then added to. The waiting room overflowed again, the TV airing an ancient *Leave it to Beaver*. How long until a special news flash interrupted it? *Tyler Waddill, Fugitive*, complete with firm photo. His family would be horrified.

The eighty-six finally rumbled into the terminal. Passengers trickled off; their replacements scooped up baggage and straggled outside. Climbing aboard, he grabbed a window seat in back. Another ancient rerun played inside the empty waiting room. A wistful smile settled over his face as Sheriff Andy debated one of life's infinite dilemmas with Deputy Barney, his homespun grin a classic contrast to Barney's agitated strutting. There was something

something safe and warm about Mayberry — and Castlewood. Home, that place which had slipped away so long ago, leaving him lost and drifting like a tumbleweed. Would he ever find his way back? He ached so badly for it now as the noisy terminal melted away . . .

Tyler, it's time!
Lavinny's baking project, he remembered now.
Come on, Tyler! Missing the beginning spoils the rest.
She meant their show, *Andy Griffith.*
Just remember it from last time.
It's not the same. She jumped up, quickly disappearing down the tree house ladder.

She met him with a broad, Opie Taylor grin as he descended seconds later. *Race ya?* She nodded at the distant mansion.

She'd been there from the beginning, like the massive oak, the fading autumn sun, the mighty James River that sparkled in the east, like Castlewood looming before them. *Come on, Tyler. Are ya chicken?*

Her lilted voice had been there, too, skipping over the river breeze. He'd assumed it would always be there. *'Course not. One . . . two . . . three. Go!*

She won as always. But the margin was getting thinner. "Soon you'll be flying past me," she consoled him.

The race was forgotten as he remembered their mission. *Come on!* Dashing across the terrace, they burst through the French doors. The sweetly delicious scent greeted them as they flew down the broad hall and skidded finally into the kitchen. Lavinia, the Queen of Castlewood's kitchen, was just pulling her cookies from the oven. Setting them on the counter, she glanced at their eager faces. *Figgered you two'd be showin' up about now. I guess you'll be wantin' to sample a few cookies 'fore supper?*

Just a dozen. He reached for the pan.

Dozen shucks! She swatted his hand. *That many'd spoil your appetite and then your Mama would give me the dickens.*

Then half a dozen. Please Lavinny! You're the best damn cook in the world!

Damn nothing! She shook her finger at him. *Where'd you be pickin' up a word like that? Has Davis been 'a cussin' around you?*

No, Lavinny . . . Schuyler. He says it all the time.

Don't be callin' your pappy 'Schuyler.' It's disrespectful.

Like calling Mama Hunter Leigh?

Same thing, she nodded. *It ain't right.*

He turned to his blond, blue-eyed companion. *Lavinny is the best cook in the world, isn't she, Kara?*

The little girl nodded, *The very, very, very . . . very best cook in the world!*

Lavinny shook her head, *You chilluns' ain't known no cook 'cept me and Fannie Johnson over at the Randolph's place. And Fannie tells me, Miss Kara, that when you two's over there, you be tellin' her the same fib every time she pulls one of her pecan pies out of the oven: Gosh, Fannie, you're the best cook in the whole world!* Her eyes narrowed, *Only Master Tyler better not be sayin' that cuss word over at your place.*

Oh no, Lavinny, Kara shook her head. *Never.*

And I'm supposed to believe that? You two'd lie for each other on a stack of Bibles, high as Castlewood itself. A couple of hellions I been stuck with, while your mammies are playin' Bridge over at that fancy club. Don't hardly seem fair . . . Her hands dropped to her hips as a smile spread across her broad black face. Then came the rumble, next the quake, until finally her entire body shook with laughter. Lavinny was the fattest, jolliest, blackest woman he'd ever seen.

Still giggling, she waddled to the cupboard. *You two chilluns! Your mammies brought you into this world the same weekend and you ain't been pried apart since. You might as well be Siamese twins.* Pouring milk into two glasses, she piled a plate high with cookies. *I 'spect one day you'll get married and have your own chilluns; wouldn't surprise no one, least of all me. Now shoo!* She waved them out with their snack.

They ducked into the study where Davis, the King of Castlewood's grounds, had started a fire to cut the autumn chill. Grabbing sofa pillows, they curled up on the carpet to watch *Andy Griffith.*

Do you think Lavinny's right? Kara sipped her milk. *About us getting married, I mean?*

Heck, I don't know. If keeping her around meant marrying her, he guessed he'd do it when the time came. After all this wasn't his world. They'd discovered it together — Randolph Estates, the James, and Castlewood with its tree house, where they shared their most intimate thoughts.

Mary Glenn and Sally Hylton said that having a boyfriend is stupid, Kara confessed one day, her feet laced in new tennis shoes dangling next to his out the tree house door. He said, *that's because they're pains in the asses.* He'd heard the expression in a recent movie and felt it described irritating people better than any other he'd found. *They're just jealous because you can throw the football farther.*

Tyler, they don't care about that stuff.

He shrugged. *Then what?*

Dolls and things. Girl stuff.

You have dolls, he nodded at the pine chest.

No! They mean I should take my dolls to their houses and play dress-up.

Is that what you want? he asked.

No, silly, I just hate them being so snotty.

Weeks later, he confessed that John Giles and Mark Harrison had been disgusted to learn she could throw the football farther. *Don't worry,* she consoled him. *Remember when I said you'd soon win the race from the tree house? You win all the time now. The same thing will happen with football.*

The low point of the second grade came when he bloodied Tommy Bradshaw's nose and was sent home. He hadn't told anyone the reason for his outburst, nor did it seem he'd tell her. *Please, Tyler,* she demanded again as they sat, legs dangling out the tree house door. *Why did you hit Tommy?*

Scowling, he ripped another acorn across the knoll. *Because he's a pain in the ass, that's why!*

The new spring leaves shivered as he crawled recklessly out onto the limb. *Tyler, you're scaring me,* she shouted. *What if you fell and died? Then what would I do?*

As she began crying he quickly shimmied back across the limb. *Kara, I'm sorry. I won't do it again, I swear.*

You also swore you'd never keep a secret. You broke that promise, too, by not telling me why you hit Tommy.

He returned inside the tree house. She joined him at the window, where they quietly surveyed their empire of forests, meadows and the sparkling James. Finally he turned: *Tommy said a guy would never have a girl as his best friend unless she was a whore. He meant you, so I punched him.*

She asked, *What's a whore?*

I'm not sure. But the way Tommy said it, it must be bad.

This crisis had passed along with the others and they grew stronger, like trees in the forest, their vines weaving ever more securely around each other. Third grade slipped by; fourth came and then was gone, too. Summer rain beat again on the tree house roof as Kara spread her growing collection of colored glass across the floor. It had doubled with the recent finds at Nags Head, York and the James. And the Disney World trip still remained. Florida was full of beaches. Orlando must have a dozen, they'd decided.

He inspected the new glass, all sizes and shapes, their edges worn smooth from the sea's gentle erosion. They'd drifted for years, he guessed, until the capricious tide had finally washed them ashore for Kara to find. Reds, greens, yellows, browns and the sparkling blues she prized most. *We'll get some off Hawaii's beaches one day,* he predicted. *I bet they have the bluest glass in the world.*

And Bermuda, she said as the rain pelted overhead. *Only I bet the glass there is emerald-green, like the water.* There'd been so many places to go and time was flying by. Fifth grade was added to the scrapbook, then the second Disney World trip. There'd been no beaches but so many other things it hadn't mattered. *Tyler,* she said again. *You bring those posters back from everywhere we go. Instead of stuffing them in that old footlocker, why not put them in nice frames and hang them on the wall?*

Another year passed. The summer rain pelted the tree house roof again. *I guess Lavinny was right,* he said, watching her lay the new glass out. *We'll get married, only no kids. I'd like a golden retriever, though.*

We'll discuss children later. She'd always said that when she disagreed. And he could count on the subject slipping into a future conversation.

Seventh grade arrived and, as usual, she was right. Now he could throw the football farther, and run faster than anyone in their academy class. *Told you so,* she grinned with her new braces.

Kara, I have a new dream.

Don't tell me until we reach the tree house. It'll break the spell otherwise. Climbing the ladder, she dropped to the floor. *Now let's hear it.*

I want to be a college quarterback like Uncle Frank.

Then you need to practice like him, too. You just remember the glory from his Thanksgiving stories. I remember the hard work.

Will you help me, Kara?

She hadn't heard her, mind already fixed on how she would.

Eighth grade arrived. *Tyler, I want to take piano lessons. Do you think that's stupid?*

He had until now, when he saw how much she wanted to. *Of course not. Some of the smartest people in the world play the piano. And look,* he held her hands up. *You have great fingers. Only you'll need more than talent and fingers. Hard work, I mean. Have Blair call Mrs. Harwood for the lessons. And tell her not to worry about you sticking to them. I'll take care of that myself.*

Tyler. Her eyes teared. *I . . .*

Yeah, he grinned. *Me too.*

Eighth, then ninth grade, were added to the scrapbook. *Tyler, you really should hang those posters. I want people to see them. They're pictures of our life together.*

Tenth, eleventh and twelfth grades whizzed by in quick succession. He became a record-setting quarterback whose worst butterflies were on the nights of Kara's piano recitals. She became an accomplished Tidewater pianist, who read music almost as well as the academy's offensive game plans.

At some point in these hectic years, puberty quietly arrived to add yet another sweet dimension to their world. They'd been best friends, soul mates and on one moonlit Saturday night, finally lovers. Kara had been his first; the only one he'd ever wanted. Graduation arrived and they said good-bye to the academy without fanfare. There'd been no time to waste on misty-eyed reflection. College loomed next on the horizon — William and Mary. *Tyler, should I try out for cheerleader?*

Cheerleader, Hell. I need you focusing on the game.

But you'll have coaches in the booth to follow the plays. This isn't the academy. It's the big-time.

Big-time or not, all those coaches together don't have your eye for weaknesses in zone coverage.

He became the starting quarterback his sophomore year. Kara slipped away from their families to meet him as the team emerged from the locker room that first Saturday afternoon. *We did it!* Her eyes glowed proudly.

Thank you, he smiled back through his helmet bars.

Are you nervous? She asked.

Almost as much as that night you packed 500 people into the James River Art Center. You didn't miss a note.

I missed several, she laughed. *And I only packed 200. Tyler, watch the Blue Hens' corners. They looked quick in warm ups. And number forty-one reads the play action very well.*

Got it, he nodded. But not well enough, it turned out. Forty-one picked off his first pass that afternoon, a play action, and returned it for a touchdown. He'd done well, however, after that shaky start, finishing the year as the Conference's second leading passer. William and Mary's rebuilding year had proven a winning one that exceeded everyone's expectations. They'd toasted it with champagne in their tree house, where the dream had been born. In all the years the spell had never been broken. There was no reason to believe it ever would be.

Life was sailing along like the James on a breezy day. *Are we certain it's law?* she asked one summer afternoon at Castlewood. With two years of college behind him, it was time to choose a career.

Definitely he said, although it was anything but. He knew only that he didn't want to work for his family's shipbuilding company. People would look at him as royalty. He didn't want that.

We have the summer to decide, she said.

I thought we just did. Law.

It'll take hard work.

He smiled. *You mean like piano and football?*

They strolled along the riverbank as the sun faded in the crystal sky. This was their world, and this afternoon, the sweetest slice it had to offer. They couldn't walk fifty feet without kissing or laughing. She chased him, then he chased her. Finally their shoes came off and the sandy shore snuck up, like cool marble, between their toes. Memories, their most special ones, spilled into the gentle breeze, her voice skipping beside him as always. *Tyler, I'm so happy I could cuss! You've made my life one big, happy summer day . . .*

How could they've known that midnight was almost upon them?

We'll be married in Bruton Parish. She danced along with plans made years ago in the tree house, where dreams were born and spells never broken. *The first June Saturday after graduation, Colonial Williamsburg will glitter in evening. The Church bells will ring for us as they did for Blair and Austin. Schuyler and Hunter Leigh. Our marriage will bond the Waddills and Randolphs for an eternity . . . And,* she tugged him along, *you agreed to children, don't forget.*

Lavinny's prophecy, yes. *Two,* I said.

We'll discuss it later.

You want more than two?

Ending the discussion with a kiss, she dashed down to wriggle her toes in the surf. Joining her, he caught the sun's dying glow in her eyes. He'd never seen her more at peace, her smile so content as she gazed at the river. *I'm envisioning you in a courtroom one day,* she said.

How do I look?

Brilliant; handsome. Honey, are you sure you don't want the shipyard position with Schuyler?

I'm sure.

Me too, she grinned. *I just want you to be happy with the decision and never look back with regret.*

Life's too interesting to look back.

And fast, she added.

He first noticed the black mole on her back one August afternoon when they were out on the river in their Sunfish. At Castlewood later, he'd shown it to her in the mirror. *It's probably nothing, but I'd see Dr. Thomas just to make sure.*

He left for football training camp the next day; she went to her dermatologist. The lab report came back Friday. *It's malignant melanoma.* She called him with the terrible news. *Dr. Thomas is putting me in the hospital . . .* The line cracked with her tears. *Tyler, he thinks it might've spread!*

He left camp that night and stayed with her until Tuesday, when the test results came back. The cancer had spread. Kara was going to die.

I'll quit school.

You will not! she ordered. *Tyler, you'll make All-Conference this year. I won't hear another word.*

So he played the best damn football of his life — for her. She attended the games as long as she could. Looking back for the first time in his life, he remembered. It was worse than hell, something that couldn't be described as he drove the dark, desolate road between Williamsburg and Randolph Estates, a thousand times, in a thousand tearful storms.

Do you remember when you bloodied Tommy Bradshaw's nose? She looked so frail lying on the porch lounge. She'd come home to spend her final days. The autumn afternoon was crisp, the sun wickedly bright. *You crawled out on that limb rather than tell me why you hit him. It scared me so bad, I cried. I said if you ever left me . . .*

You never finished that thought.

I will now. She gazed deeply into his eyes. *I'd find the strength, no matter how difficult, to go on. I'd do it, because I'd know you wanted me to.*

It was a lie and they both knew it. A lazy smile settled over her face now. *I'll never forget our first Barnum and Bailey circus. The instant we went into the arena, your eyes popped out of your head. The lights, the elephants, and of course the clowns.* She squeezed his hand with fading strength. *You always loved them best — except that first time. Do you remember?*

Her hair was like golden silk in his fingers. Of course he remembered. He was drowning in memories. *Those pain-in-the-ass clowns,* he smiled. *They sprayed everyone with seltzer and tripped over their big, floppy shoes. But I never expected their guns to make such a hellacious noise.*

She laughed. *You dove under the bleachers, your fingers jammed in your ears. A tow truck couldn't have pulled you out.*

But I loved them the next year.

And every one after that. You loved the clowns best, Tyler, you always did.

No, he loved Kara best. *Remember the first Redskins game at RFK?*

We were twelve, she smiled. *And the first Super Bowl? Pasadena, the blimp, the balloons?*

And a Redskins championship. He sighed. *You knew the name, number, and bio of every player. You loved football more than any girl alive. You loved everything I did.*

I loved you. She squeezed his hand. *The rest was a piece of cake.*

I never thought I'd like the piano, he smiled. *But I did — every time you played.*

The week before she died, he carried her up Castlewood's tree house ladder for the last time. It was another sparkling afternoon, the sun's glow stretching over miles of meadows, forest and the timeless James. Standing quietly at the window, arms folded, she gazed at it all for the last time. The sunlight transformed her hair into flowing honey. It always did. *Our empire,* she exclaimed. *It was a joyous reign. I leave it now in your capable . . .* Turning at his sudden outburst, she rushed to embrace him.

Kara, I can't imagine one minute without you! He cried. *How can I face an hour, a day . . .*

Tyler, promise me you'll find the strength to go on, that you'll be happy again and never, ever, look back. Night was finally falling over their happy summer day. He buried his face in her perfume-scented hair. L'Air Du Temps. He'd never want to smell it again.

Tyler, if I'm to leave this world, and it seems that I am very soon, then I have to know that the part of me remaining behind will try to be happy. Now please, promise me.

He did, knowing it would be impossible.

Days later, at the hospital, she faded away in his arms. Her mother, Blair, gave him the note she'd written the night before. It was crisp, sweet, like Kara:

Tyler,

Just remember we were great together and that I always loved you. No matter where I am, please remember that. And your promise, too . . . Oh, and if the Redskins ever win another Super Bowl, drink a toast for me. I'll be watching. All my love, Honey. Your Kara, Forever.

Not his Kara, but his world. And she died November 12th, six years ago, yesterday. He'd died the same day, his soul left behind in her hospital room. The man who'd walked out may have looked and talked the same, but he was an imposter. Then how did he explain the new thoughts clanking in his head, this fresh trickle of feeling? Why did he care suddenly if the next minute came, and even more, what it might hold? But he did, as the bus's engine now roared to life. Glancing back through the glass, he froze at the special news flash, not the one expected but another. Its ominous specter gripped him as the bus crept away: President Thomas Longbridge, with his new Supreme Court nominee, a beaming Greg Lamp.

He was left with hours on the road to consider the announcement's implications. Lamp would join Mann and Falkingham on the nation's highest court, after weathering the storm of a bitter Senate confirmation. And it would be bitter; the liberals would see to that. But Lamp's friends' confirmations had been bitter, too, and they'd survived. There was no reason to believe he wouldn't as well.

He'd be on the Court in time for the spring's explosive cases. Never had so many critical issues been presented in one term. The Court could literally rewrite the Constitution. It was all there: abortion, church and state, gun control, censorship, the death penalty. The Bill of Rights from A to Z. What could conceivably emerge were the blueprints of a new Christian State. A document once hailed as revolutionary in its championing of liberty could quickly become a manual for the good Christian soldier. Longbridge wanted it as did his alter ego, Harrington, and the millions of people and dollars backing the CMA. And with Lamp creating the majority it needed, the Court could deliver. Wasn't that the plan? If so, what had it cost? And what had threatened it — Morris Mendelsohn? Had his death eliminated the threat? Or would someone else have to be eliminated?

He stopped before asking the next question. He'd much rather watch the Connecticut countryside slip by. The motion was satisfying, the sense of direction. Each mile carried him closer to Mayson. Hartford, New Haven, Bridgeport all passed and suddenly he was back in New York, where the day from hell had begun. His stomach lurched. Boston had been a camp; New York was headquarters.

A small battalion of Blues and Dark Suits was waiting when the bus arrived at the Manhattan station. He spotted them in the crowd, their hard glares focused on the departing passengers, the arrivals ignored. No fugitive returned to the place he escaped from. How about passing through?

Grabbing their bags, passengers shuffled off the bus. Others soon herded up the aisle to replace them, throwing baggage into overhead compartments and filling the vacated seats. Finally the bus continued its journey south. The Holland Tunnel was passed before he realized he'd never been to Brooklyn. Never seen it, except as part of an infinite gray skyline. He wasn't much on sights, unless they were connected with people. And Mayson had grown up there. Castlewood, Brooklyn - two different worlds. But how different?

The bus reached I-95. Newark loomed. And then . . . "This lawyer's nomination was a real shocker, huh?" The voice belonged to the burly man in front of him, as did the neck pimples and pocked oily skin. It wasn't a pretty inventory.

"Not being a judge may be the best thing going for him," his blond, fair-skinned companion mused, his nose in the *Times*. "Lamp knows his way around the legal world, though. National Bar President. Lieber Allen partner."

Despite their contrasting appearances, the pair wore matching red windbreakers and crisp new Yankees caps. Vacationers, he decided.

"Lieber Allen," Pimple nodded. "Isn't that the Jew lawyer's firm? You know, the one murdered by the pretty WOP girl? I'm sure it's the same. She's still on the run."

"So is another young lawyer in the firm." The blond flipped the page. "I caught the report while you were getting your Snickers. He disappeared in Boston this morning."

"No kidding? Another WOP, I bet."

"Not this one. A big blond kid, and rich, they said."

"What's the kid rich from?" Pimple asked.

"Shipbuilding, they said."

"Lotta money in shipbuilding. Damn Cawthorn, you got one head for details."

Tyler watched Cawthorn's eyes lift to the window. How good

was he with faces? He'd find out the first time the man turned around.

"Longbridge shut those reporters up when they asked Lamp about the murder case," Cawthorn said.

"Yeah?" Pimple munched on his second Snickers. "Well, he won't be able to shut up those bleeding heart Senators."

"Lamp's certainly one of those card-carrying CMA freaks. Longbridge wouldn't have appointed him otherwise."

"Harrington, that self-righteous prick," Pimple announced. "He's got Longbridge by the balls.'"

They soon reached the Baltimore station, the pair's stop. His eyes dropped as they rose, chattering about their Chesapeake Bay fishing trip. Pimple grabbed his suitcase from the overhead; Cawthorn stretched, then grabbed his bag too as they joined the straggling exodus. He counted a dozen seconds before looking up, right into Cawthorn's eyes. The blond froze, then grabbing his forgotten *Times*, hurried down the aisle.

Tyler spotted the pair seconds later in the boarding area as Cawthorn pointed at the bus's rear windows. He'd made the connection. Pimple's dismissing paw explained that he hadn't. Scowling, Cawthorn started through the crowd. Was he safe or not, Tyler wondered, as the bus crept from the station?

Washington, then Richmond were eclipsed on I-95's fast track. The North Carolina border slipped by with his thoughts still in Virginia, at Castlewood, where his family had learned the shocking news and were floundering in a darkness his note would do little to illuminate. Six o'clock arrived and he envisioned Mayson beginning to wonder if the only person she trusted had let her down. Intending to call first in Raleigh, then Charlotte, he found both stations crawling with police and didn't dare use his cell phone.

At ten, the bus rumbled finally into the Columbia, South Carolina station which looked like all the others, except for the absence of cops. Leaving the bus, he went inside, first to the restroom, then the coffee shop where he bought a sandwich and coke. Returning to the boarding area, he spotted a phone booth and quickly slipped inside.

"Tyler Waddill, for the third time! New York issued a fugitive warrant for him this afternoon. The reason you haven't heard is because you've been driving all day."

Glancing across the platform, Tyler found the trooper on the Atlanta southbound's steps, a second pacing the aisle inside. At the wheel the driver muttered something to which the trooper replied, "This is the Eighty-six, right? And you just said you stopped in Boston this morning where Waddill disappeared. What time did you arrive?" As the driver offered another inaudible reply, the trooper accommodated with a translation. "Eleven? Then that means Waddill had time to board your bus, the same ridden by Cawthorn and his companion. Cawthorn identified Waddill as the passenger sitting behind them." Again the driver shrugged, muttered. To which the trooper snapped, "The report didn't say what they were wearing, but being from New York it's not surprising they'd have on Yankees caps. Then you *do* remember them?"

Frowning, Tyler put the phone back as the trooper's voice sharpened, "Yes ladies, then you're sure? And you, sir?" He caught something now being passed up the aisle: a picture. Had he just been identified?

The second trooper got off the bus and quickly started across the crowded platform. "Steve, make it a dozen units!" his partner shouted. "If Waddill *did* get off, he couldn't have gotten far, but I'd sure hate to screw this one up."

Watching the trooper enter the terminal, Tyler grabbed his dinner and slipped from the booth. Drifting along the crowd's edge, he quickly vanished into the shadows. Patrol cars streaked past on the dark street, then minutes later, the Atlanta southbound, minus one passenger. Midnight and he was stranded in Columbia, South Carolina, closer to . . . No, Naples was closer. No place was further away than Castlewood now.

CHAPTER FOURTEEN

★

The Chairman finished his special morning broadcast and went upstairs. The CMA owned and occupied the entire downtown building. The Tower of Faith; his name, his vision, the Lord's guiding hand. From here the final campaign against evil would be waged and the world prepared for the Lord's Kingdom.

For months he'd cried into the TV cameras, opened his heart and soul to millions of viewers. "The Lord has decreed the building because if the world is under Satan's siege, there must be a Holy Fortress where the righteous may prepare for the battle ahead. A fortress, brothers and sisters, where the Lord's soldiers shall be armed with the weapons of righteousness, and begin their march to victory over Satan and all his evil! The 'Tower of Faith,' the Lord has whispered the name unto me, to be built here in Houston, where His good work is already being done. He needs it. America needs it, and so too, the very world!"

The CMA's phone lines had lit up instantly. The donations poured in. And so it had been built.

At seventy stories, the Tower was Houston's tallest building, an inspiration born not of vanity but necessity. Doing the Lord's work required sufficient space and equipment. First there was the TV network, then the radio station, the publishing operation that disseminated the CMA's literature across the globe, the library and archives, facilities for the missionary programs, and the financial division that managed the CMA's enormous investment capital. There were staff offices and residential quarters. The list went on and on.

Rarely, however, was it necessary to mention the Tower's penthouse, although everyone knew its occupant: the Captain responsible for navigating this Holy Ship through the treacherous waters of a world not yet ready for the Lord's return. Praise the Lord, and His servant, Seth Harrington.

His secretary, Rose, caught him as he emerged from the elevator. "The President just called to express his approval of this morning's program. He seemed genuinely inspired."

"Praise the Lord." This morning's program addressing the Lamp nomination had drained him. It had been critical to garner support, without sounding too political in the process. He'd succeeded with this delicate task but another remained — a certain police investigation now into its fifth bumbling day.

"Mr. Leopold is waiting," Rose explained as he started for his office. She was a good secretary who didn't ask too many questions or express an unwholesome interest in matters that didn't concern her. Like why Leopold, an untitled project coordinator, was granted the privilege of waiting in his private office when the CMA's Vice Chairman, Earl Resenstadt, was not.

As he entered, Leopold's heavy-lidded eye followed him over to the desk, the sightless glass one unmoving. It was a hideous face the Irish brute had left him with: an eye that didn't see; a nose that drained yet barely absorbed a thimbleful of air; a mouthful of dentures that infected his gums; and a rubber leg that dipped his shoulder with each step. Yet Leopold was infinitely resourceful, a precious CMA asset. Despite his grotesque appearance, a Brooks Brothers' suit and handsome leather briefcase were the only tools needed to impersonate affluent businessmen or a Wall Street lawyer on his recent Minnesota assignment. Whatever the task, he handled it competently and without unnecessary questions.

"This morning's program was wonderful, sir," Leopold said now. "I also heard Rose say the President called. I'm sure your eloquent words added comfort to his decision yesterday."

"I hope I didn't sound too political in my endorsement of Lamp. Our mission is Godly, not worldly."

"It rang with the Lord's inspiration, sir, nothing else."

Harrington's gaze drifted to the closed door, his heart quickening with his true feelings: anger and frustration, which were taking a greater toll on his aging body. Since his sixty-fourth birthday, he'd begun thinking more about his grueling pace. Hadn't a massive coronary taken his father's life at the same age?

"Arch, the President's announcement yesterday should've been momentously joyous. It should've left us with the sweet taste of victory, yet it's the bitterness of Satan's apple that sours my tongue now, and there it'll remain until this new serpent is slain and its vile carcass swept from our path. Just when we have our Court in place to rewrite the nation's laws as the Lord has instructed, a dark cloud has arisen that may bring the same rain of destruction that befell Moses . . . I won't allow it!" His eyes flamed with indignation. "The CMA will not disappoint the Lord or bring Him the disgrace of Moses. And I will not swim in the seas of hell with a pack of miserable Jews!"

"Praise the Lord!" Leopold refrained.

"Praise Him, indeed." He struggled to calm down. However great his anger, a cool head was needed to safely navigate them out of this dark storm. "Arch, our mission's survival depends upon a well-conceived and flawlessly executed plan. Everyone must be committed and possess a clear understanding of the consequences if we fail."

"They understand, sir." Leopold had met with them in Georgetown last night: Mann, Falkingham, Chapman, Streeter and their new teammate, Lamp. They'd known he carried the Chairman's authority and the reason he'd remained in Houston. Because of his close ties with Longbridge, Harrington was careful to distance himself from the White House when major appointments were made.

"So tell me about last night's meeting," Harrington said.

He began with the positive of a negative report. "Lieber Allen has withdrawn from the Naples probate case. Lamp confirmed with the Crenshaw family what I explained earlier: that will contests were the Jew's specialty and that with his death, the firm has no one experienced in Florida probate law. Consequently, they've retained a Naples firm to continue the suit."

"That's heartening, at least," Harrington sighed. "Now what about Corelli and this new nemesis, Waddill? Does Lamp have any idea what they know about Crenshaw?"

"I'm afraid so." He frowned with his first negative news. "After Waddill's disappearance in Boston yesterday, Lamp learned from firm sources that he'd been asking about the Crenshaw records. Lamp assumes Corelli tipped him off. He'd just started working for the Jew and wouldn't have known about the case otherwise. Based on this, we must assume the two of them are sniffing after Crenshaw. What they know is anyone's guess."

"Do we also assume Waddill's rejoined Corelli?"

He nodded. "No other scenario is indicated. We know that after escaping the Feds at Logan, he caught a southbound bus. He was identified by another passenger between New York and Baltimore. Later reports place him as far south as Columbia. Assuming he's on the scent of Crenshaw, his logical destination would be one of three places — Pine County, Tennessee; Snow Peak, Minnesota; or Naples, Florida."

Harrington grimaced. "Minnesota is a thousand miles north of Columbia."

"And Tennessee is a healthy distance west," Leopold added. "I don't believe I mentioned that Waddill's ticket covered the bus's last stop in Atlanta. Only he wasn't aboard when it arrived."

Harrington smiled, "You're getting him ever closer to Naples with these suppositions, Arch. If that's his destination, is Corelli already there?" He'd been sickened to learn the catastrophic news that Corelli, just minutes from capture, had somehow slipped away. "Twenty-four hours ago she was trapped in Manhattan, and through Chapman and Streeter's incompetence she's vanished like a puff of Italian smoke."

Leopold scowled over a disaster that had cost them a tremendous advantage. Once confined to Manhattan, the operation had suddenly expanded to the entire East Coast. Further, Corelli was now joined by someone with potential resources, yet to be identified.

He reported his next piece of bad news, one that at least could be fixed. "Last night, as I waited at the Lakeland's window for the others to arrive, I detected a Fed car down the street. I can spot them a mile away. Before finding the Lord, I was a popular subject of their surveillance."

"Arch, the Lord has forgiven your past mistakes. Hold your head high for the courage shown in finding Him."

"Praise the Lord, sir."

"Praise Him indeed, for providing the finest instrument I possess to do His work. Now tell me about this car."

"It was there on an obvious stakeout," he explained. "I waited until after the meeting to have Frankie and George tail him to his Alexandria home. They got the number of his Bureau plates and his name and address off the mailbox. I only needed the name to remember the pain of the savage beating that left me this way. Every time I look in the mirror, I remember him, just as I do the agent who sent me to prison where this terrible thing happened."

A deep compassion moved Harrington as his valued lieutenant bordered on tears. Who wouldn't cry to own such a grotesque face? "Swanson. The same knuckle-head Chapman was forced to muzzle after the Rogers investigation. Then you're saying our stubborn friend didn't get the message?"

"It seems that way, sir. But I doubt he's learned much."

"Don't fool yourself, Arch. We've had many meetings in Georgetown. And it didn't take much for him to place you at Lake Witteoka, the weekend the Antichrist Rogers drowned."

"But he couldn't sway anyone else with his suspicions."

"That we know of. There may be others we simply haven't discovered. But if they exist, we'll find them. Swanson's left us no choice."

Leopold studied him gravely. "You're thinking what I am?"

"If that Swanson may try to contact Corelli and Waddill, I am indeed."

"We're assuming he's smart enough to connect Rogers with the Jew lawyer."

"Smart?" Harrington scoffed. "I'd say making that connection is pretty stupid, just as it was to disregard Chapman's warning two years ago. How much clearer could it have been? Accept Rogers's death as accidental or forfeit your career." He sighed. "Your stubborn friend doesn't listen very well, does he?"

"He never did, sir."

"Then a second warning would be a waste of time. And besides, it's too late for that now."

"What about Corelli and Waddill?" Leopold asked.

"Are they any less of a threat than Swanson?" He paused. "I wish there was another way, Arch. I don't relish making sacrificial lambs of people. It burdens my conscience deeply. But the Lord's mission must be fulfilled at any cost."

"Should I consult with Chapman and Streeter?"

"They need to be involved. This is a police operation, after all. Just don't let them get in your way. And handle Swanson as you wish. Unless there's a problem, I'd rather not hear anymore about him."

The mammoth tractor-trailer rumbled down I-85's Naples exit, pulling over for the young man to hop out. "Hey, if it's a boy, name him after me!" the driver called down to his companion of these last two hundred miles.

"You got it!" The man slung his rumpled jacket over his shoulder. Not even noon and already it was eighty degrees. "Say Jess, once the furniture's dropped off in Miami, grab a six pack and hit the beach. And drink that first one for me."

Jess laughed. "I thought I was supposed to light a cigar."

Waving as the monster truck clanked back up the ramp, the man squinted against the bright sun and started off.

Naples's granite and glass towers shimmered in the horizon. Soon the Gulf emerged like a glittering emerald carpet. Naples was a retirement haven for the rich: capitalists, doctors, lawyers, corrupt county sheriffs. The traffic breezed past, oblivious to his hitching thumb. Turning finally, he lengthened his strides along the steamy pavement. A gray patrol car glided by as he approached downtown. Stopping at a service station, he bought a Coke then slipped into the phone booth to place his call. The line clicked but stayed silent. "Mrs. Butts?" he asked.

"Where are you?" she demanded angrily.

"Naples, of course."

"Where have you been?"

He sighed. "It's a long story."

"It's been a longer wait."

"I tried calling."

"What do you mean 'tried?'"

"Are you gonna give me directions or not?" he asked impatiently.

"I'm not sure."

He wiped his grimy brow as a second patrol car passed. Naples was either hosting a police convention or this was his welcoming committee. "Listen, I'll explain it all when I get there."

She gave him directions: four more steamy blocks west, two south. "Room 434." The line clicked sharply.

He reached the white granite Holiday Inn minutes later and, passing the palm tree-shaded courtyard, quickly climbed the stairs to the fourth floor. Room 434 was halfway down the hall. "Alice!" He knocked, waited patiently then knocked again. "It's Ralph, open up!" But it was apparent she had no such intention. "Alice, I'm not late on purpose!" His anger rose as the stubborn silence deepened. "Alice, open the goddamned door!" His fist now rattled the hinges.

Finally it opened and bobbed, blond Mayson appeared. "I'm sorry it took so long. I was memorizing the Naples TV channels. I didn't realize there were so many."

Brushing past, he tossed his dirty jacket over a chair then turned back. "Where are your glasses? You need to keep them on."

"Sitting in the room by myself?"

"Can't you do one thing I ask without griping?"

Her eyes burned angrily. "Ten seconds in the room and already you're giving orders! Don't think you can sashay in here a day late and start bossing me around."

His gaze fell to the crystal pool below, where children splashed and squealed with delight. Coated in grime, his joints aching from bumpy truck rides, he'd sell his soul for a quick plunge into the cool water. "I'm gonna take a shower."

"First tell me why you changed your mind and decided to come."

Exasperated, he glared at her. He was hot, tired and grungy, but before granted the simple privilege of a shower, he must defend himself against another paranoid inquisition. Hell no, he didn't!

Shutting himself in the bathroom, he splashed his face with cold water. Her toilet items were neatly arranged on the counter. So she'd ventured out after all. He'd underestimated her. Reaching for a towel, he spotted a bottle in the trash and returned it to the counter. Another discovery waited in the bathtub — a six pack of his beloved Molson in a cooler of water that last night had been ice. Smiling, he lifted it out.

The shower revived him. Emerging in fresh jeans and a navy polo, he found her at the window. She turned, a deep vulnerability widening her eyes. "Please tell me why you changed your mind and came?"

"I didn't change my mind about anything." He toweled his hair. "Except my travel plans, of course, over which I had no control. Thanks for the beer. I'm sorry I wasn't here to drink it." He now told her about his desperate escape from Logan and the near disaster in Columbia. "Didn't you watch TV yesterday?"

"Not enough, obviously, to pick up *The Great Escape*."

He nodded at *Robes of Vengeance* on the table. "How is it?"

"I wouldn't have survived the last twenty-four hours without it. It was great, thank you."

"I've been worried about you those same twenty-four hours, Mayson, you know that."

Yes she knew. But she'd also been terribly frightened, one eye on the book, the other on the door. She hated doors, and after all this time avoiding them, there was yet another. It wasn't fair.

"There I was," he sighed. "Stranded in Columbia, South Carolina at midnight, my bus leaving one way, patrol cars shrieking by the other way."

"What did you do?" she asked.

"I took a cab out to the I-95 truck stop then hit the first driver coming out with a song and dance about my wife in Naples ready to spit one out. Only I couldn't be there because my clunker had clunked out - a predicament I blamed on my boss, who'd sent me on an ill-fated sales trip. Anyway, the bullshit was good enough to get me on Bert Thompson's Macon hardware delivery, then Jess Harley's Miami furniture run. Jess wants us to name the baby after him, if it's a boy. I said we would."

She held him with a begrudging admiration. "I guess I owe you an apology. You did well to get here at all."

They watched a mother scoop her irate toddler from the pool below. Like a hooked fish, the little boy squirmed furiously. Finally Tyler's eyes returned to her and gratefully relaxed. "So how about you? Were there any hitches at the airport?"

"A real heart-stopper." She described the police escort and Crawford's fixation over her resemblance to the Flatbush mechanic's daughter.

"Lauren, I guess, talked you out of the situation?"

"She's clever with bullshit, and quite proud of it."

"So that was the big hitch?"

"Hardly." She now explained her identification by the state process server and the potential disaster it had set in motion. "Lauren's BS was superb but the cops weren't about to sink their shoes in it. When I refused to turn over my purse, two Feds ripped it away and were about to peek, when Chief Fed arrived. Grabbing it, he started firing questions as he flipped through my cards. I knew it was over then."

He gawked at her. "You're telling me this Fed flipped through all those cards and let you go?"

She nodded. "He returned my purse and told the others that I was Deborah Burns of Atlanta, just as I claimed. He even sent his flustered subordinate off to hold my flight."

Leaving him to wrestle with this astonishing development, she retrieved the Agent's card. Studying it carefully, he jumped up to grab the phone. "What are you doing?" She watched him dial.

"Following Agent Harvey's instructions. By the way, Lamp's been nominated to fill the vacancy on the Supreme Court."

"What!" she gasped. "Tyler, are you serious?"

"As a heart attack . . ." A man came on the line now, identifying himself as Harvey. "The lady at La Guardia," Tyler began delicately. "Do you remember her?"

The silence deepened. Then, "The one from Atlanta, sure. I gave her a tip. What was it now?"

He cupped the phone. "Harvey gave you a tip."

"An Atlanta seafood restaurant his friend owns," she quickly replied.

Tyler relayed the answer then waited through another long silence. Finally, Harvey said, "Let me call you back. What's your number?"

"No way," Tyler replied. "I'll call you."

"Fine kid, we'll do it your way." He relayed the new number. "Give me fifteen minutes."

The phone was ringing as Harvey reached the booth across the street. Breathless, he grabbed it. "Perfect timing," he announced. Beyond the glass the Hotel Kensington's guests strolled the promenade, the expensive shops bustling as usual. "This is Waddill, right? And since you passed my pop quiz, I assume Corelli's with you."

"And I assume by your rescue, you want to make it a threesome?"

"A foursome if it's all the same to you, kid. It's easier to get a tee-off time that way."

"Who's the fourth?"

"The first actually. Gus Swanson, an agent like me. Say, where are you two anyway — Atlanta?"

"Where are you?" Tyler retorted.

"The Hotel Kensington. It's across the street from the Bureau's office. Listen kid, let's cut the crap, okay? If I couldn't be trusted, Corelli would be in the slammer now. So how about it – you tell me where you are and maybe I'll consider helping you two again."

"Why would you want to do that?"

"Good question. I'll answer it, then you tell me where you are." He turned as the promenade swelled with a noisy convention crowd that had just adjourned in a nearby ballroom. "You remember Chief Justice Rogers's death two years ago? Gus Swanson was on the Bureau team sent to Vermont to investigate it. He claims the team's accidental drowning report was a sham and that Rogers was murdered."

"Didn't he take the matter to his superiors?" Tyler asked.

"Sure kid, all the way to the top. Only Director Chapman wasn't interested. He warned Gus that if he pursued this nonsense about Rogers being murdered, he'd fire him. Chapman's done everything in his power to silence suspicion. And not just him; his buddy, Attorney General Streeter, is up to his ears in this mess, too. And as Longbridge appointments, don't we assume the White House is involved as well? Kid, we may have stumbled upon the conspiracy of the century here."

"What proof does Swanson have that Rogers was murdered?"

Harvey explained the basis for Gus's theory that Leopold had murdered Rogers. "If you saw this big, ugly monster, you'd realize there's no way to confuse him with anyone else on the planet. And although no one saw him the night Rogers drowned, you can bet your ass he was on that boat the old man heard leaving the cove. No question: Leopold knocked Rogers off. There's also no question about who gave the order - the man he works for and who benefited most from Rogers's death. Seth Harrington, I'm talking about.

"We've been tracking Leopold ever since. He bounces between New York and D.C. but obviously goes a lot of other places, too. Where and why, we have no resources to determine. Gus has also documented numerous Georgetown meetings, hosted by Harrington. The guest list typically includes Falkingham, Mann, Chapman, Streeter and starting this week, your boss, Lamp. He has pictures, dates, times, participants — everything except what the fly on the wall knows which, of course, makes the other stuff worthless.

"To be honest," he sighed, "we'd run out of leads, and without resources to penetrate the conspiracy things looked pretty hopeless. Mendelsohn's murder Sunday night changed that." He paused now to catch the pretty, auburn-haired manager of Mimi's Fashions watching him across the promenade. "Listen kid, I have to move this along. Anyway, that same Sunday afternoon, Gus got a tip that Leopold and two flunkies were en route to La Guardia. I rushed out there to establish a tail, which took me to the Essex. Leopold and one bozo went inside, while the driver waited in the garage. They returned forty-five minutes later and squealed away. The time fits perfectly with Mendelsohn's murder."

Tyler glanced at Mayson. "Why didn't you report it?"

"First, I had no proof Leopold went to Mendelsohn's apartment. Second there's nothing connecting him to the lawyer, anyway. Third, this obnoxious detective, Duke, had Corelli pegged and nothing I said was going to change his mind. Fourth, all it would've done is expose our investigation. Not that we had much, but things looked a lot more promising after Sunday night. And fifth, for what it's worth, we could've kissed both our careers and asses good-bye. Still, we wouldn't have let Corelli join her brother in Attica. You know about him?"

"Lucky? Yeah," Tyler replied.

"The Lips," he laughed. "Anyway, we know Leopold killed Mendelsohn. But what's his connection to Rogers? We assumed the answer lay inside your law firm and Lamp's nomination seems to confirm it. Like the first two, it must've been in the cards all along. Only Mendelsohn got in the way, stumbling upon something big enough to get himself killed. Any idea what it was?"

Mayson's eyes held Tyler impatiently as she waited for this bounty of information he was receiving. But did she really want it? If Harvey was right, the odds against them couldn't be more overwhelming. "We have a theory," he revealed. "Who knows if it'll lead to anything."

Mimi's manager still watched Harvey through the glass. They'd been on the line a half-hour now, in which he'd shared what sparse fruit their investigation had yielded. It was time to get something in return. "Listen, you kids are obviously smart but you're in way over your heads. We either join forces or we're all going down. So how about it?"

"We're at a Holiday Inn in Naples, Florida," Tyler now revealed, providing their room and phone number. "We're registered as Mr. and Mrs. Ralph Butts."

"Clever. Who'd purposely choose a name like that, right?"

"Lauren Belli deserves all the credit."

"The long-legged blond prosecutor at the airport?"

"That's the impression she usually leaves, yeah."

"I won't ask why she got herself mixed up in this mess."

"Thanks." He revealed their suspicions about Crenshaw and the need to examine the court records.

The news was a shot in the arm for Harvey. "Sounds like you're on the right track. Lamp's strange behavior, the missing files and his court nomination must be more than coincidence. Do you need help getting the records?"

"I can't think of a way that wouldn't risk exposure."

"My guess is, kid, they already know you're there."

He thought again of the patrol cars spotted on the way into town. Weren't they what he'd feared — a welcoming committee?

"I gotta run," Harvey said now. "Some store manager's giving me the hairy eyeball. Oh, and don't use that number I gave Corelli unless it's an emergency. Just wait for my call."

"When will that be?"

"After I've talked to Gus. Meanwhile be thinking of how we can help with the Crenshaw angle."

As he hung up, Mayson's eyes caught Tyler's anxiously. "It's really bad, isn't it?"

He nodded grimly. Harvey had confirmed their worst suspicions, which he now detailed, starting with the circumstances surrounding Chief Justice Rogers's death, and ending with Lamp's Court nomination.

Sitting cross-legged on the bed, she absorbed his account, her intensity quickly replaced by shock. "There's no way out is there, Tyler?"

"Of course there is," he insisted with a confidence hardly felt. "If the enemy's been identified, so have our allies - ones with resources we didn't have before."

"Wonderful," she sighed. "You, me, Harvey and Swanson against the entire world." Still, it could be worse. She could be alone, but she wasn't. He was with her. Why exactly seemed less important with each passing hour. He'd turned her world upside down, the same as this terrifying web of conspiracy. He and these circumstances were forcing her to redefine that world. Life had taught her not to trust, yet each minute with him strengthened her belief that he could be trusted. For years, she'd invested in an emotionless, uninhabited future that suddenly could no longer be envisioned. All that remained was a new, undefined hope and a yearning for something unidentifiable.

Because of him, she'd lost control of her life, even her body's motion she realized as her hand crept boldly over his. This gesture, like her gentle smile, was offered to relieve the pain she saw in his eyes. "It's not enough that you rescue me from a murder charge. Now you have to save America from Seth Harrington, three corrupt Supreme Court Justices, the Attorney General, the FBI Director, and some dangerous monster named Leopold."

He studied the strange sight of their hands joined on the bed. "Don't forget the President."

"Tyler, you should let your family know you're safe, at least for the moment."

"I sent them a letter explaining my plans."

"A call would still be nice. You're so pale. You need to eat. And take a nice, long nap."

He sighed. "Please don't start acting like my mother."

"Did you only send one letter? Or is there some Tidewater debutante you correspond with? I assume you're obliged to marry some eighth cousin, according to the customs of your plantation society."

He glared at her. "You've been watching too many movies."

"Of all the women you date, you mean there isn't one you're serious about?"

"No, sorry."

"But there was?" His eyes dimmed as he turned to the window. "Then you won't tell me?"

"That's right."

Her natural impulse was to pout, but his love life was none of her business. She must remember that and never grow accustomed to his presence. When the danger was gone, so would he — if they survived it.

Slipping into the bathroom, she quickly returned with a perfume bottle. "What's this?"

"L'Air Du Temps."

"I know that, Tyler."

"Then why did you ask?"

"Because I threw it away. Why did you put it back on the counter? I thought you didn't like it."

"I never said that. And I don't have the right to tell you what perfume to wear." Grabbing another beer, he returned to the window. How long until the cops began searching the hotels along the coast?

"Tyler, you want me to wear the L'Air Du Temps," she said. "Why?"

He watched the sun sink slowly over the Gulf. It wasn't as spectacular as he'd imagined. "Wear whatever perfume you want. We have more important things to think about."

He dropped onto the bed. His sour disposition was nothing more than exhaustion. "You need a nap."

"And how would you know?"

"Because you're acting like an insolent child."

He gulped his beer. "I don't need a nap."

Seconds later, she covered him with a blanket and, being careful not to wake him, slipped his shoes off.

Dinner waited on the bed-stand when he woke: a toasted BLT and an ice cold Molson. She stood at the window, the Gulf Coast glittering against the night sky. "I guess I really was tired," he sighed. Gratefully he bit into the BLT. "I love these."

"You ordered them whenever we ate in Morris's office."

"Aren't you eating?" he asked.

"I had a sandwich earlier. There's a dark, quiet pub across the courtyard. It's safe, don't worry."

"What else have you been doing?"

"Thinking about our predicament mostly," she replied.

"And?" he sipped his beer.

"I didn't come up with a brilliant plan, if that's what you mean."

"Maybe it'll come to you while we wait for the courthouse to open. Meanwhile, cops are pouring into the city. By Monday morning they'll have Naples sealed off."

"Getting those records will be difficult, if not impossible." She sat on the bed beside him. "And if we do get them, what then? I'll go to the courthouse," she said. "I'm disguised, at least."

"We'll leave the moment we get the records," he added. "That'll mean a car. Any ideas on how Harvey can help?"

"New IDs would be nice, in case we get stopped. Assuming he can swing it, where do we go?"

"Tennessee."

"Why not Minnesota?" she asked.

"Tennessee's closer."

"Gee, that's brilliant." She returned to the bathroom for her purse and got another Molson for him.

"You're learning," he smiled.

"What, that *gavonnes* like beer? I've known it for years." Sitting back down on the bed, she dug out her Jams. It was the start of a feeding frenzy that would last until the box was empty.

He watched her eyes gleam suddenly. "What?"

"The coincidence of five cases, each with enormous potential for creating new law, coming up in the same spring term. What a rare opportunity for the court to rewrite the Constitution." She shook her head. "I mean it's all there, isn't it? The dream agenda for a fanatic like Harrington, obsessed with transforming America into a theological state, based on his own moral precepts."

"Then you believe that Longbridge is Harrington's Puppet President?"

"Don't you?" she asked.

"I'd rather not. If Longbridge is part of this, there's no one left to save us. Even armed with the truth, our situation would be hopeless. If everybody in power is corrupt, the truth becomes meaningless."

She replied, "The truth is nothing more than what the game's players say it is. They make it up as they go along. 'Reconstructing facts,' I call it."

"I call it lying," he said.

"Then you're a dope."

"I'd rather be a dope than a liar."

He was neither, but what he was exactly, she lacked the courage to discover. "What I don't understand is why Harrington would choose Lamp, Mann, and Falkingham to help create his religious state. How could he insure their vote on critical issues? Lamp, at least, has no track record of extremist right wing views or sympathy for religious causes."

"Neither do Mann or Falkingham."

"Maybe they approached him," she mused. "Judicial obedience in exchange for the power he could deliver."

"That sounds like Falkingham — an opportunist if ever there was one. But let's assume the deal was struck, and with Rogers's death, then the two retirements, the path was cleared. If Lamp's confirmed, Harrington will have placed his trio on the bench in time for this auspicious spring term."

"So what went wrong?" she wondered. "What did Morris find out, and why did he have to be killed?"

"Let's hope Crenshaw tells us."

"Tyler, are we going to die?"

Her fawnish eyes, once empty, now glowed warmly with a passion to live. "Everyone dies, Mayson. Our predicament doesn't change that. We just need to focus on smaller units of time: minutes instead of years. And live each one with the hope of getting to the next."

"Wow! I think you've just conceived a new philosophy for

people in our shoes." Yawning, her enthusiasm waned as she glanced at the clock. "I wonder when Harvey will call?"

He shrugged, "Unless there've been developments, there's no urgency."

Stretching across the bed, her sudden movement sweetly stirred the air with L'Air Du Temps. In seconds she was asleep. Slipping off her shoes, he gently covered her with the same blanket she'd used to cover him. By midnight, it covered them both.

The ringing phone shattered the darkness. Tyler grabbed it.

"We've got big trouble." Harvey's agitation edged the line. "Our cover was blown last night. Gus has taken steps to preserve the evidence: volumes that don't say much now, but might if they're connected with Crenshaw. I say if because it's doubtful we'll ever dig up another scrap. Those bastards must be scrambling like rats for cover."

Tyler squinted at the clock as Mayson stirred beside him. "What the hell happened?"

"There was another Georgetown meeting. Gus was on the scene, as usual. Apparently Leopold spotted him and put on a tail, which means that Chapman, who was there, now knows about the investigation. Who knows when and how they'll strike? Gus sent his family to the country but he should've gone, too - only not 'to' the country but out of it. But he doesn't listen; he never has, the stubborn bastard."

Swanson was doomed unless he ran. Delay could mean the difference between life and death. "Harvey, you have to reason with him," Tyler said. "He's no good to us dead."

"I will, but I wanted to bring you up to date. With our cover blown things'll get hotter for sure."

How much hotter could they get? Beside him, Mayson had fallen into a pouting silence after his stonewalling of her persistent *'What did he say?'* Drawing her against him, he was surprised when her head settled on his shoulder.

"Have you thought of anything you need?" Harvey asked.

"New identities," Tyler quickly replied. "Naples will soon be sealed off like Manhattan. We won't have a prayer of getting out without them."

"Does Corelli plan on keeping those short blond curls?"

"I'm afraid so," he glanced at her resting head.

"How about money?" Harvey asked.

"We have plenty for the time being."

"Good. I'll get the IDs to you by Monday morning. Just sit tight until you hear back from me."

"That shouldn't be tough with cops pouring into Naples," Tyler said.

"The guy you need to worry about won't be wearing a uniform," Harvey warned. "But he also won't be difficult to spot. Leopold, I mean. The first sign of a six-six, three hundred pound ape with a glass eye, run like hell. You don't want any part of him, trust me."

As he hung up, Mayson renewed her assault. "Swanson's in danger? How does it affect us?"

Patiently he addressed each question. At the end, she shook her head. "I'm so afraid for Swanson."

He'd been warned, and Harvey would implore reason with another call. After that it was up to Gus.

Settling back in the darkness, their thoughts raced. Sleep proved elusive. L'Air Du Temps scented the air as she rolled towards him. He waited expectantly, but she said nothing. He'd learned his cue. "What's the matter?"

"I never gave you permission to put your arm around me," she replied.

"I keep forgetting that idle gestures require a license," he sighed. "You must be more patient. And I also don't recall granting you a permit to rest your head on my shoulder either, but I didn't cite you for it."

"Well it certainly won't happen again." She rolled away now, ripping the covers from him.

"That wasn't nice, Mayson. Why are you acting like this?"

"Because I hate you."

"You don't hate me."

"Well then, I'm very close."

He drew her into his arms now, the moonlight exposing her glistening eyes. "Mayson, I know you're frightened. But we'll survive this and celebrate the day those pricks are carted off to prison."

"And how will we manage all this?"

"I'll need time to fill in the details." He stroked her neck. A shiver of pleasure startled him and his fingers retreated.

She sighed. "I hope you understand I'm only allowing this intimacy because I'm frightened and much too exhausted to protest. So don't get this close again, okay?"

He smiled in the darkness.

"I'm wearing L'Air Du Temps. Is that why you're lying so close to me?"

"No, because you were upset."

"Why didn't the L'Air Du Temps make you want to?"

"That's immaterial now since you just explained I wouldn't be allowed to anymore."

"But my question just now made it material again."

"Go to sleep, Mayson."

CHAPTER FIFTEEN

★

Gus Swanson couldn't recall a more stressful time in his twenty-five years with the Bureau. The fireworks had started with Harvey's call from La Guardia Friday morning. Then Lamp's Supreme Court nomination had been announced, and in its wake, the revelation that another Lieber Allen associate had disappeared. "What did you do?" Harvey toasted their good fortune. "Rub Aladdin's lamp?"

"Lamp," he gloated. "Has a nice ring, doesn't it? He connects Rogers and Mendelsohn. Now we must wait for Corelli's call, and it'll come. We're all she's got."

"Not anymore. Another Lieber Allen associate vanished at Logan this morning. Name's Waddill. We can assume if he's lucky enough to get out of Boston, he'll meet her down south."

That afternoon, Gus had gotten a tip about another Georgetown meeting, then dedicated the evening to its usual documentation. On the way home he'd been so absorbed with the day's developments, he failed to pick up the headlights in his mirror until reaching his driveway. He'd hurried inside to catch a car glide down to his mailbox then quietly slip away. He'd been seen at the Lakeland home! Sick with fear, he'd crawled into bed which he knew held no sleep. Was the investigation lost, or could swift damage control save it? What steps should he take? He took the first when talking to Jean later that morning. "Why don't you and the kids leave for the farm this weekend? I'll join you for Thanksgiving."

"But they have school through Wednesday," she said. "Gus, is something wrong?"

"No, I just think it'd be nice for you to have some extra time with your family. Billy loves to help your dad around the farm. And Sally can ride the chestnut filly with her cousins."

"I guess it wouldn't hurt the children to miss a few days from school," she nodded finally.

By two, the plans had been made and the car packed. "You'll

make it by Tuesday?" she asked.

"Yes." He waved to the kids. "Give your folks my best, and don't forget to call when you arrive."

Standing in the driveway until the Explorer disappeared around the bend, Gus wondered if he'd ever see them again.

Unable to reach Harvey, he plunged ahead with plans that had crystallized in the last few hours. He removed his precious records from the basement cabinet and lugged them out to his car. The thought of their destruction sent chills up his spine, yet he'd never taken the time to copy them. That time had come. He dropped behind the wheel and hurried away.

Paranoia crept over him. Was he being watched? Anxiously his eyes roved the busy streets, jumped to the mirror at every intersection. By the time he reached the mall, he was sweating profusely. Lugging the first box inside, he hurried down to Quick Stop Copy, claiming a corner machine. With one eye on the crowded promenade, he copied, collated and stacked. Finishing, he lugged the box back to the car and returned with the second box. If anyone was watching, he'd know soon enough. They'd never let him leave with his copied records.

He'd almost finished the second box when the copier broke down. Forced to wait for another, he dug out his cell phone and again tried Harvey without success. Was something wrong? Had last night's disaster rumbled as far north as New York? Grabbing the next open copier, he finished the second box and headed out for the last. Finishing it quickly, he returned to the car. It was getting dark as he locked the trunk and left. He stopped next at Atlantic Express, arranging for overnight shipment of the copied records to Harvey. Finally he relaxed. If he was being watched, they'd never have let him ship his records. Perhaps they didn't consider him a threat. And why should they? Who would listen? Then again, how did he even know that last night's tail had begun at the Lakeland home? He hadn't picked it up until reaching his driveway. It wasn't unusual for agents to be tailed by paranoid criminal elements who were investigation-shy.

Turning into Jack Rabbit Storage, he leased a unit in one of the rear buildings, then dumped his records and left. He arrived home at ten and after dinner tried Harvey. Where the hell was he? He must be alerted to last night's disaster and the records' shipment. And there was a new strategy to conceive. They couldn't throw in the towel now, not with potential allies and the connection between Mendelsohn and Rogers established.

He'd just dropped in front of the TV when Harvey called. "Ben, where the hell have you been?"

"I could ask the same question," Harvey sighed. "Between my visitation with Jimmy and a stop by the office, I've spent most of the day trying to reach you. Finally Medfield called and asked me to meet him out at Kennedy. He was about to crap in his pants over the arrival of some of the Salendez's purest powder. Only his great tip turned out to be a hoax, which didn't surprise anyone but him. I just got back and figured I'd try you again. Gus, I've got great news."

"I have terrible news." He now revealed his exposure and the precautionary steps taken, including the records' shipment to the dummy P.O. Box in Queens.

"The only thing you've done so far that makes any sense," Harvey snapped, "is getting your family out. Now pick them up and catch the first flight out of the country, preferably to some South Pacific island."

"Ben, I can't do that. The investigation . . ."

"Screw the investigation! We're talking about your life!"

"But how do we even know it was Leopold's tail last night? Remember when that Atlanta drug ring shadowed Roger Austin?"

"Come on, Gus, who are you fooling? These guys are serious!"

"I'll get away, Tuesday at the latest."

"Tuesday hell! We'll be planning your funeral by then."

"Ben, I'm safe as long as I have the records."

"Those records don't say shit!"

"They don't know that."

"They know everything, Gus. Don't you realize that yet?"

"Ben, pick up those records first thing in the morning. Don't forget. Now what's your great news?"

"The kids called me today from a Naples, Florida hotel."

This was great news. "Why Naples? They have a lead?"

Harvey told him about the promising Crenshaw case. "Don't you see, Gus? With our focus shifting to Florida there's no reason to stay in Alexandria. There won't be anymore leads to follow with your cover blown."

Left unspoken was the reality that his Bureau career was over. "It sounds like the kids are on the right track, but I doubt it ends in Naples. Likely the real dirt exists in Tennessee or Minnesota, if Mendelsohn's activities there are related. Maybe . . ."

"Forget it, Gus. The minute you show your head in Tennessee, they'll shoot it off. If anyone goes, it'll be me."

"Ben, you can't go running off to Tennessee. We can't have your cover blown, too." Already his mind was moving forward. He could leave tonight. He just had to pack, and then have Jean sit tight until his return. "What county was Crenshaw 'lord and master' over? Did the kids say?"

"Forget it, Gus."

It could be easily traced through the government archives in Nashville. "Ben, we need to discuss strategy."

"The only strategy I'll discuss is getting you out of Alexandria."

"Okay, I'll leave. But don't forget those records."

The instant he hung up, the phone rang again. "This is Don Prillaman at Atlantic Express. You're the Swanson who shipped those three boxes this evening, right?"

An undefined alarm crept over him as he glanced at the clock. The shipment should be well on its way to New York by now. "Yeah, that was me. Is there a problem?"

"You could say that," Prillaman replied. "Federal agents were waiting with a search warrant when my driver pulled into the Queens station. They not only seized your boxes but took him in for questioning. Then just now, I got a call saying that agents are on the way over to question me about how the boxes got on our truck. You better know I plan to tell them. And listen, buddy, while I have you on the line, I don't appreciate being used as an instrument in your criminal enterprise!"

Shattered, Gus hung up. They'd been watching the whole time. They'd seen him copy the records, ship the reproduced set, and then they intercepted it in Queens! A cold sweat sprouted on his forehead. If they had the copies that meant — Oh God! In a panic, he dashed out to the car and streaked off. The tables had suddenly turned — ghosts he'd been chasing for so long were now chasing him.

In a fog, he covered the dark streets, racing against time he might not have, against enemies he couldn't see. Skidding into the Jack Rabbit, he burst down the alley to his compartment. Jumping from the car, he opened the compartment and jerked a flashlight from one dark, empty corner to the next. The records were gone. Two years of carefully documented investigation, the long nights parked outside the Lakeland home, the lies he'd been forced to tell Jean. It had all been for nothing.

He returned home, exhausted. Reaching the drive, he gazed desperately at the dark house. What should he do? Go to Tennessee in search of fresh hope, or flee to Rockbridge?

It hit him as he crawled from the car. Something had been missing at Jack Rabbit when he'd grabbed the flashlight. In a panic, he jerked open the glove compartment. His .45 was gone! As he hurried inside, the phone was ringing. The recorder switched on and his own, crisp voice drifted down the hall. An anxious Harvey then came on the line. "Gus, where the hell, are you? Call me the second you get in!"

Harvey had talked to the kids again. Was good or bad news responsible for his agitation? "Max?" he said, drifting down the hall. "Where are you, boy?" Flipping on the den light, he gasped.

"Don't worry about the shepherd." Leopold looked up from the desk typewriter. "He's enjoying a nice, medicated sleep in the basement, but he'll be fine. That's more than I can say for you, I'm afraid."

A second intruder emerged from the shadows: sandy-haired, medium-size and build. "Ordinary looking," as in Leopold's ordinary blond companion at Lake Witteoka. "Gus, you remember Frankie." Leopold introduced the man. "You put him in Leavenworth. But that's ancient history, right Frankie?"

"Sure, Arch," the gum-popping stooge grinned. "Let bygones be bygones."

The hall creaked as a third intruder now appeared, his eyes cold and emotionless, the revolver steady in his hand; it was the "ordinary" dark companion at Lake Witteoka. "George George," Leopold nodded. "Can you believe anyone would name their kid that? George hasn't smiled much since San Quentin. Doesn't say much either, but he's awfully good with that piece in his hand."

"Did he kill Mendelsohn?" Gus asked. "Or was that your work?"

"I think you're confused, Gus. Corelli murdered the Jew lawyer. The cops are pursuing her and Waddill hot and heavy, as I understand."

"Cops? Don't you mean Harrington's God Squad?"

Frankie snickered, an insolent lapse that drew Leopold's scowl. "Gus, where you're going, now isn't the time to desecrate holy men. Instead, why not tell us what has Harvey so agitated? I hope he's not waiting on your record shipment."

"Harvey's not involved in this. He's upset over some personal things happening in his life."

"Gus, those records were intended for someone. If not Harvey, who?" When he didn't answer, Leopold nodded, "We'll find out one way or the other. The important thing is they don't have the records." Proofreading his letter, he then passed it across the desk to Gus. "Your suicide note - a real tearjerker."

Gus sensed he wouldn't leave this room alive or ever see again the family smiling in the desk pictures. The letter, addressed to Jean, read:

I know what I've done is wrong, but the money was just too great to resist. I wanted things, not so much for myself, but for you and the children — things we couldn't afford on my salary. At the time, it seemed easy to give those Bureau records to the criminal elements willing to pay so much. How could I get caught? But I did, this very weekend, when agents seized the records I had shipped to Queens and also the originals stored at the Jack Rabbit. They have me, Jean, and as I sit at the typewriter, I see only this black void that once held our future. Both my Bureau career and our life together are over. Prison looms, a prospect I can't face anymore than the pain I've brought you and the children. Please, Jean, forgive my crimes, and also this last desperate act. Love always, Gus.

His eyes lifted. "You expect me to sign this?"

Leopold nodded. "Unless you can improve it."

"I'm not very good at embellishing lies, I'm afraid."

"What lies, Gus? Your disregard of Chapman's warning to

back off the Rogers investigation was tantamount to suicide. And weren't you caught today in the unauthorized dissemination of Bureau records?"

"The letter also references a big payoff," Gus pointed out.

Leopold shrugged. "If you cracked the case, you would've appeared on *Oprah* and *Larry King Live* to boast about it. And there would've been a book, of course. You'd have become rich and famous. Don't tell me you weren't thinking about that."

"Prison." Gus glared at him icily. "A savage beating. Religion. Nothing works with you, does it, Leopold? You're still scum and always will be."

Frankie and George gaped at Leopold as if expecting a bomb to go off. Leopold limped around to snatch the letter. "That prison beating, Gus, robbed me of an eye and shattered my teeth. It also left me with a steel cord in my jaw, a rubber leg, and this grotesque face that guarantees me work as a freak in some circus sideshow. Not a minute passes that I don't feel either pain or humiliation. But I no longer harbor ill feelings for those responsible for my suffering. As a Christian, I'm required to forgive you and Murphy, just as the Lord forgives you."

"Praise the Lord!" Frankie refrained.

"Yes, praise Him for cleansing my wicked soul."

Soul? Gus peered into Leopold's eye. None existed that he could see. Just a moron inside a huge body that had been perverted to suit the evil purposes of Seth Harrington.

"Gus, if your death is necessary, it brings me no personal satisfaction," Leopold said now. "If anything, I feel grief that you won't take part in the Great Christian Renaissance that is almost upon us."

"Praise the Lord!" Frankie popped his gum.

"What Lord?" Gus scoffed. "And why praise Him for transforming his followers into cold-blooded killers?"

Leopold nodded patiently. "It's regrettable that lives must be sacrificed in the struggle between good and evil. Doesn't the Bible bear grim testament, documenting the countless slain - both the wicked and the righteous? No one said that service of the Lord is easy. The road to salvation is fraught with obstacles, unpleasant tasks and regrettable tragedy. But the journey must be completed and the world prepared for the Lord's return. That means the eradication of the godless behavior now celebrated in a world run by atheistic liberals. And if lives must be sacrificed, those in the Lord's service must be equal to the task."

"So far, those sacrificed are Chief Justice Rogers and Morris Mendelsohn," Gus said. "How many more are required? Or does it matter?"

"What matters, Gus, is that no one undermines the Lord's mission. Not the two you mentioned, those foolish young lawyers, and, as I'm afraid you must learn, not even you. Now please sit down and let's get this over with."

Gus found his .45 next to the typewriter. Was it possible that in seconds an exploding shell would spill his brains out on his grandfather's cherry desk? "And if I refuse to participate in this travesty?"

Leopold sighed. "Even if you've shown a disregard for the Lord's mission, at least you've demonstrated a Christian love for your family. Don't screw that up now."

"Then you'd actually murder my family?"

"No Gus, you would, by disobeying the Lord."

"Rockbridge is just a few hours away," Frankie said. "We can finish business and still catch that noon flight out of Dulles. Man, I can't wait to hit that Naples beach!"

"You'll be too busy to waste time on the beach," Leopold scowled. "And that Rockbridge detour won't be necessary ... will it, Gus?"

Harvey had been right. They *did* know everything. "Just tell me this — does the conspiracy reach into the Oval Office?"

Leopold glanced at Frankie, then the taciturn George.

"Come on, you want me to sign this trash. At least tell me if Longbridge knows who killed Rogers and Mendelsohn."

Leopold sighed again. "Gus, you're hardly in a position to negotiate."

"What's the harm? It's not like I'll be telling anyone."

"Gus ..."

"All right." He dropped at the desk. Grabbing the pen, he quickly signed the letter. Jean would know this wasn't suicide, that he couldn't be bribed, that these weren't his words.

"Now pick up the gun," Leopold ordered. "Once the trigger's squeezed, you won't feel a thing."

He looked up, astonished. Did they actually expect him to put the bullet in his own brain? "The secret Mendelsohn was killed to protect — would its exposure have kept Lamp off the Court?"

Leopold frowned. "That secret, Gus, if it got out would do far more than keep Lamp off the court. It would destroy the CMA, the Longbridge administration and the Lord's mission. Now please . . ."

"The administration," Gus persisted. "Then Longbridge is involved?"

Wrapping his handkerchief around the gun, Leopold lifted it carefully. "Take it Gus, and squeeze the trigger - quick, simple, painless."

Gazing at the gun, his eyes slowly lifted. Would they laugh if he dropped to his knees and begged for his life? "The secret . . ."

"No Gus, the gun."

"Mendelsohn knew it before he died. Am I not entitled to the same privilege?"

"The greedy Jew took it to hell with him. Let's pray you're going somewhere else."

"What if I swore to forget all I know?"

"Gus, we both know it's too late for that. Now you can handle this yourself or be a coward and have us do it. But then you'd be taking your family, too, and no one wants that."

No, he wouldn't take his family. His eyes fell now as urine flowed uncontrollably, soaking his pants and socks. Humiliated over the mess he'd made, Gus began to cry.

Frankie snickered at the puddle spreading across the floor. "Look Arch, he's pissing all over himself!"

"Take the gun." Leopold grew impatient. "What follows couldn't be any worse than sitting in your own piss."

"He ain't gonna do it," Frankie whined. "You might . . ." He stopped as the condemned man put the gun to his temple.

Offering a final prayer that his family wouldn't discover his splattered brains on the desk, Gus clamped his teeth and pulled the trigger.

CHAPTER SIXTEEN

★

Kara stood beside him at the Bruton Parish altar in the gown he'd always envisioned. Eyes shining, veil in her golden hair, she recited vows that seemed superfluous echoes to a love spoken with each breath of her life. His vows came next, then the ceremonial kiss and they were presented as man and wife. But the minister's words were drowned by a sudden rumble as the church collapsed and water rushed in. First Kara, then he, was swept away - not by water, but soft, warm sliding fingers emerging from the haze with Mayson shouting, "Tyler! Tyler!" Rain smacked the window. The wind howled. The nightmare hadn't been Kara's death but her return.

Crawling from the bed, he saw the pounding storm. The courtyard's palm trees swayed against the fierce wind; pool furniture scuttled across the grounds. Streets were already flooded, and the lights of stranded cars shimmered through the thick curtain of rain.

"I've never seen anything like it," Mayson said. She sat anxiously on the bed, her slender legs silky below his shirt, her toes crimped in the carpet.

"You mean they don't have storms like this in Brooklyn?"

"They do in Virginia?"

"Sometimes," he smiled. "Without the palm trees, of course."

Her pensive gaze returned to the window. "Tyler, who is Kara?"

"No one." As he slipped into the bathroom, she followed. "Is she a girlfriend?"

"No," he inspected the stubble on his chin.

"Was she ever?"

Splashing his face, he smeared on shaving cream. "Was she ever what?"

"Your girlfriend!" she snapped. "Why can't you ever pay attention?"

"Yes, she was." Grabbing the razor, he began shaving, conscious of her inquisitive eyes in the mirror.

"But not now?"

"No, Mayson, she's not."

"Then you never see her anymore?"

The razor froze on the ridge of his jaw. Had a minute passed in the last six years when he hadn't seen Kara, her soft voice refraining his every thought? "I'm gonna shower." He turned on the water.

She was gone when he came out, her note on the bed stand. Still, he worried until she returned. "Don't do that again."

"Didn't you see my note?" Setting her bag on the table, she removed sandwiches and steaming coffee. "The pub was packed, because of the storm, I guess."

"No one looked at you suspiciously?"

She shook her head. "That rowdy bunch had nothing on its mind but the football game. They're hoping the Bucs can beat the Steelers up in Three Rivers. Fat chance . . ." She stopped at his odd stare, remembering her charade. "That's what the girl at the bar said, anyway."

They ate at the window as the storm thrashed the coast outside. "Tyler, what if the courthouse is closed tomorrow? People in the pub said that with the flooding, a lot of businesses could be closed."

"We'll stay until we get the records or have no choice but to leave."

"How will we know there's no choice — except when there isn't?"

It was a good question, and one he couldn't answer. Turning on the TV, he zipped through the channels. "You can watch the Bucs game if you want," she said. "It won't bother me."

He paused for a storm update – weakening, heading north. Frowning at the rain-riddled window, he zipped on. "If you don't want to watch the Bucs game, I'm sure there's another one on," she said. "Go ahead, Tyler, I know you like football. Watch your game, I really don't mind."

"I'm more interested in other things at the moment."

He stopped for a GNN news update. As usual, the manhunt

was the hour's top story, their pictures appearing as the anchorman reported the latest developments. "FBI sources believe the pair has reunited since Waddill's daring escape from Logan Friday and are hiding somewhere along the Gulf Coast . . . And to repeat this morning's development," he added, as an 800 number appeared at the bottom of the screen, "Lieber Allen, the Wall Street firm which employed the fugitives, has offered up to $100,000 for information leading to their capture."

Moving on to the next story, the anchorman reported, "The body of an Alexandria, Virginia man found in his home this morning . . ."

Tyler cut the volume as Mayson grabbed the ringing phone. It was the office advising that their package had arrived. Slipping on her shoes, she relayed the message. "I'll be right back."

He cringed suddenly. She'd been walking around the last day with Harvard Law boldly printed on her chest. "Let's chuck my shirt."

"Madonna mia!" Grabbing a sweater, she rushed into the bathroom to change. Then leaving, she returned a minute later with their package.

"What's the matter?" He detected her fear.

"Two Feds are in the lobby scanning the hotel's registration records. I walked right past them."

"Thank God you weren't wearing my shirt."

"Then you're not worried?" she asked.

"Of course I am." He dropped on the bed to open the package. "And I'll be more worried when they return. I just hope we're gone by then."

"What do you mean?" She sat beside him.

"That last report still has you with long, dark hair. But sooner or later, the computer will change your picture to reflect the bobbed blond hair and granny glasses. That's when we're in trouble."

"What about the hotel's guest records?"

He dumped the package's contents on the bed. "I doubt anyone will get too excited over a couple of jerks named Mr. and Mrs. Ralph Butts.'"

She looked at the plastic cards on the bed. "Who are we now?"

"Jonathan and Marcia Cartwright." He handed her the Florida driver's licenses. "The pictures are pretty convincing."

They were indeed; she studied them. Marcia's hair was bobbed like hers, a shade lighter, an inch or two longer. And her glasses were just as hideous. Jonathan also resembled Tyler, although not as handsome. But who was? "Oh look, we have children!" She reached for the wallet-size pictures.

"It's all here," he nodded. "Credit cards, social security numbers, driver's licenses, family pictures."

She read Harvey's note. " 'This is the best I could do on such short notice, but with luck it'll get you out of Naples. The credit cards look genuine but don't use them. The accounts are phony. I'll call soon.' " "What's soon?" she worried. "It's been twelve hours since his last call."

He was beginning to worry, too. "With Swanson exposed, something must've happened by now."

She smiled at her driver's license. "We're from Orlando."

"So what?"

"Nothing, as long as I'm not asked about Disney World. Someone might find it odd that Marcia Cartwright lives next door to the world's most popular theme park but has never been."

Grabbing the remote, he zipped to GNN for another news update. "We can live with those odds. And there's no time to educate you now. We'll save Disney World for our next trip."

Her eyes widened. "You'd actually take me to Disney World?"

He nodded. "Since you've never been, it'll take a week to get everything in."

Stuffing the new IDs in their wallets, they spent the remainder of the afternoon formulating a plan. Meanwhile, they grew frustrated with their inability to reach Harvey. "He's probably home watching football like every other American male," said Mayson, as she watched Tyler pace restlessly.

He glared at her sitting cross-legged on the bed, remote in hand, as she watched the second game of an NFC doubleheader. "You're supposed to be checking for news updates. We've missed the last three."

"Four," she corrected.

"Well then leave it on GNN. There could be all kinds of shit happening we don't know about."

"Don't yell at me. You're just mad because you can't reach Harvey. If you had any sense, you'd try him at home where I told you he'd be."

He paused his restless pacing. "I don't know where he lives and I'm not gonna risk a bunch of phone calls finding out." He watched her eyes grow larger as the Bears' safety intercepted a pass. "What the hell are you doing, Mayson? You don't even know what's going on. Why watch?"

"To make you mad. How am I doing?"

"I'd hoped it was obvious."

"Tyler, you love football. You have framed posters and a torn jersey to prove it. So why aren't you watching?"

"Because I'm . . ." He stopped as the Bears' quarterback drilled a pass into the middle. Receiver and defender collided, the ball squirting away. The shaken-up defender had to be helped off the field.

"Is that what happened to you?" She watched the trainer hold up three fingers for the dazed man to count. "You lost your brains like that poor quarterback?"

"Cornerback," he corrected. "Not quarterback."

Should she abandon her charade by pointing out that the quarterback had missed his wide-open primary receiver?

"The Bears should try that play again." He sat beside her. "The primary receiver was wide-open."

"Oh . . ."

He was still watching later when the Bears scored with the same play. Not until the game ended did he try Harvey again. After a dozen rings, he dropped the phone. "Something's happened. Something we'd know about if it wasn't for that goddamned game."

"Tyler, calm down." She watched him storm to the window.

Outside the ravaged coast languished in the dying storm. Screaming sirens haunted the night. With the lifting clouds, the Coast Guard cutters could now be seen in the Gulf. Were they here for the storm's emergencies or to seal the fugitives off from a desperate escape? "What if the law firms are closed tomorrow?" he asked, as he pounced on another concern. Grabbing the phone book, he studied the circled listing, its bold advertisement reeking of exploitable greed. But only if the firm was open. "What if this ambulance chaser is out signing up clients in the morning? Who knows how many tragedies this storm has produced?"

"Tyler, we've been over this," she sighed. "There are half a dozen firms in the same building." She grabbed her list off the bed stand. "I should get my shopping done. What would you like for dinner?"

"Whatever." He still brooded over the phone book.

"Is that with mustard and onions?"

"Yeah . . ."

"Great." She breezed out.

She returned an hour later, disappointed and drenched. Ashen-faced, he met her at the door. "Swanson's dead. I just caught the news report."

"*Madonna mia!*" she gasped. "How?"

"The Alexandria police got an anonymous tip. They found him at home this morning. A gunshot wound to the head. They say it's suicide, based on his note confessing to corruption, which naturally the Bureau was quick to confirm, along with its aborted plan to arrest him."

In shock, she set her bag down and followed him to the window. "What kind of corruption?"

"The Bureau claims he'd been selling investigative records to unnamed criminal organizations, some of which were intercepted in Queens this morning."

"Records intended for Harvey," she mused. "Not of a Bureau investigation but an investigation of the Bureau."

Their eyes locked with the question that followed: Had Harvey "committed suicide" too? "Maybe he saw what was coming and got away," said Tyler as he studied her drenched clothes and hair. There was a lone bag on the table. "You couldn't get the supplies?"

"The storm's closed everything. The streets are a mess - debris, stranded cars, wreckers."

"And patrol cars?" he asked.

"Everywhere. But there's so much confusion, I couldn't have

been safer."

As he put dinner out, she slipped into the bathroom to shed her wet clothes, emerging minutes later in his football jersey. "Can I admit it's my favorite gown of all time?"

"If you must," he nodded.

They ate at the window as distant sirens addressed the storm's emergencies. The moored Coast Guard cutters' lights shimmered in the darkness. Sipping a second beer, he nodded at her half-eaten sandwich. "I can eat BLTs until hell freezes over, but that doesn't mean you have to."

"They're better than I thought."

"Meaning?"

"That my taste buds are in a state of adjustment."

"Bullshit."

"Must you be so vulgar?" she asked.

"It helps sometimes."

Their world was collapsing, yet the next minutes spent sparring over her struggle to finish one measly sandwich were the easiest for him of the past six years. She was, in these minutes, a miracle unfolding as she laughed and teased. She was beginning to like herself and learning how to be happy. If they died tonight, this was something that couldn't be taken away.

Fear returned to the darkness as they retired, reminded that four was now three. Or was it two? Where was Harvey? The tense silence was broken only by screaming sirens and rustling sheets. Sleep was impossible in the clutches of such a terrible uncertainty. Finally Mayson voiced the terrifying implication of Swanson's death. "Their power is so great, they can kill a man in his own home, make it look like suicide and then invent a crime to explain it. Tyler, I'm so frightened."

"Do you want to talk about it?" he asked.

"I mean 'frightened' like last night." As he drew her into his arms, her eyes closed gratefully. "Will you tell me about Disney World?"

He described everything he could remember: the rides, shows, every sight and sound. She lost herself in it completely. "I can't wait. A whole week, really?"

"At least. Now tell me about Cellini's Market."

She reciprocated with an account much like his: factual, but impersonal. "I see the stocked shelves," he said. "The busy counter where neighborhood gossip is exchanged, the warehouse — stifling in summer, freezing in winter. But where are you?"

"Where were you during the Disney World tour?"

"Mayson, I can't understand unless you open up."

"And this is something you want?" she asked.

"I wouldn't be much of a friend if I didn't."

"So is this friendship a bilateral arrangement – meaning you'll tell me about Castlewood?"

"Later . . . maybe."

The pain in his voice ran deep. Was it a crazy impulse that made her suddenly desperate to share it? "When later comes, will you also tell me about the posters?"

"We'll see . . ."

Her head rested comfortably against his shoulder. She could easily sleep but didn't want to. "I remember the first night we met. It was the firm's spring reception welcoming the new associates."

"I remember, too," he smiled. "You were the most beautiful woman I'd seen in my first week, and for a moment, I actually felt something besides contempt for New York."

"And after this magical moment?"

"I realized that although you were beautiful, you were also followed by a dark shadow and dismissed both you and New York as hopeless causes."

"Is it my turn?" she asked.

"After what I've confessed, it's fine if you'd rather pass."

She reflected on that night. "Despite the feminine raves, I wasn't prepared for that moment you breezed into the Club."

"Will I like this or not?"

"The first part anyway, which is that you were the most handsome man I'd ever seen. Wealth, breeding — you had it all. And I imagined how happy and secure you must be waltzing through life with a zillion options. I envied you and when you took away my one option, I hated you."

"And how many do I have now?"

"You gave them all up for me, a sacrifice I still can't comprehend. But the reason seems less important all the time." The gray morning was suddenly in the window. She was so relaxed it was almost possible to block out the threatening world. "We still have time to sleep. Are you okay?"

"Hell no," he sighed. "Are you?"

"I could be worse. There's one thing though; could you rub my neck like you did last night?"

CHAPTER SEVENTEEN

★

It seemed her eyes had just closed when the phone jerked her awake. Tyler, already up watching the news, grabbed it. "I guess you've heard the latest," Harvey sighed, his voice ragged with grief.

"I'm sorry," Tyler offered their condolences. "So you couldn't persuade him to leave?"

"I thought I had. Still, I called back to confirm he was taking the necessary steps. After getting his voice mail a half-dozen times, I figured something was up."

"Did you give the cops that anonymous tip?"

"Yeah, that was me."

"What about Swanson's family?"

"I tried reaching Jean at her family's farm but she'd already left. Then I called Gus's sister to explain that his death was no suicide and the truth would come out eventually; when it's safe I'll call Jean again."

"How do you think it happened?"

"Leopold. He was likely at Gus's home when I left those messages. I've tried like hell to recall what I said, but who can remember every word they use on the phone? Anyway I'm sure Leopold or whoever is thoroughly scrubbing those recordings. So how's the weather this morning?"

"The courthouse is open. That's the main thing."

"Did you get my package?"

"Yesterday. The pictures are a good match."

"Listen, Corelli's either been unveiled or will be soon. They must know the Queens shipment was for me. And I ruffled more than a few feathers by letting her board that plane Friday. That little State prick who recognized her is still blowing smoke over the blond Georgian, with the Brooklyn accent. Chapman's surely gotten wind of the incident by now."

"There's been nothing so far about a change in Mayson's description," Tyler said.

"So what? How long does it take to alter a picture with computer graphics — five minutes, maybe?"

"But they can't be on to you. You're still on the planet."

"Not anymore. I've been underground now for eighteen hours. Let me give you my new number."

He took it down as Mayson grabbed her purse. "Where is this?" He squinted at the area code.

"Trust me, kid, you don't want to know. Now tell me your plans."

Tyler explained what they'd come up with. "We'll be moving within the hour." As Mayson gave him the scrawled note found at Morris's apartment, he relayed the information.

Harvey quickly jotted it down. "Any idea who Robert Hunter is?"

"No clue. We've called every area code in the country. Maybe it's not even a phone number."

"You want me to nose around and see what I come up with?"

"That's the idea — unless you have something better to do."

"Being cooped up is making you cranky," Harvey laughed. "Get used to it; the alternative's not so great."

"Listen, we have to move. We'll call when we can." As he hung up, Mayson looked up from the phone book. "Based on this area code, Harvey's in western Pennsylvania. And how do you know the courthouse is open — did you call?"

He nodded, "Our ambulance chaser's office is, too."

The next hour passed quickly as showers were taken, the suitcase packed and the room scoured for traces of their presence. "You'll need a great performance this morning," he said. "I'm afraid there won't be a second show."

She sighed. "I wish we knew the volume of court records. What if it's more than I can carry?"

"I'll pick you up as close to the office as possible."

"But I won't even know what kind of car you're driving."

He smiled. "Just look for the dickhead with the cap and shades. That'll be me."

"If you're trying to calm me, it's not working," she fretted. "And you're not a dickhead. Just a thickhead with a face, unfortunately, that's anything but common." Reaching up, she fluffed his thick, golden locks. "At the very moment our lives depend upon blending, you would have to be the most handsome man in town." What if he was caught? Killed? What if she never saw him again?

As her eyes now filled with tears, he embraced her. "Hey, there's no need for that."

"Tyler, what if something happens to you?"

"It won't."

"Don't say things you have no way of knowing."

"Mayson, it's a good plan. And it'll work, but only if you believe in it. Can you do that?"

She nodded slowly. If it meant saving his life, she imagined she could do just about anything.

"Good. Now wash your face and let's get out of here."

Seconds later, they slipped down the stairs and out to the parking lot. Debris left by the storm littered the hotel grounds. "You're sure you know the way?" he asked.

She nodded. Three blocks south, two, east.

"After getting the car, I'll return for the suitcase, then get as close to the courthouse as possible," he recited the plan. "If you don't see me right away, don't panic. Just start back to the hotel. I'll find you."

With an anxious glance, she started off and he hurried away in the opposite direction. Covering two blocks, he entered a convenience store, empty except for the clerk slouched against the register. Her curious gaze followed him back to the cooler, where he grabbed a jug of water then a pair of dark glasses off a corner rack. Putting on the shades he moved quickly up and down the aisles, grabbing items off the shelves. Reaching the last, he asked, "Do you have fishing caps?"

"The large barrel over by the glass." She pointed.

He found it just as a patrol car rolled up. Donning a navy cap, he headed for the counter as the two troopers entered. A cigarette dangling from the clerk's lips, she rang up his purchases: water, flashlight, map, pens, Jordan Almonds and those items he was wearing. "Need bait?" she asked.

He looked puzzled. "What?"

"You said you were going fishing. We have crawlers in back if you need 'em."

"No thanks." He reached for his wallet as the troopers approached. He sensed their attention behind him as she bagged his merchandise. Were they studying the gold hair beneath his cap? Agonizing seconds passed until she finally gave him his change. Grabbing the bag, he started out.

"Hey, wait a minute."

He turned slowly.

"The cap," the trooper nodded. "Take it off."

Reluctantly, he obeyed, his thick hair spilling out. Grabbing the cap, the trooper sliced the price tag off and returned it. "You'd look awful silly walking around all day with that in your hair."

"Thanks," he smiled. Relieved, he put the cap back on and left. Four blocks and a half-dozen patrol cars later, his heart still pounded. Was his pace too fast, his stride too jerky? Were the glancing troopers curious about his bag? As he reached the Gulf Shores Agency, a passing unit made a sudden U-turn and streaked back towards the courthouse, lights flashing. Had Mayson been caught?

As he entered the Agency, a young man popped up from behind the counter. "Yes, sir. What can I do for you?"

"My wife and I are leaving on a skiing trip this morning, but our car was damaged by the flooding. My cousin Jerry's a mechanic but he can't have the car ready until Wednesday."

"The storm's victimized a lot of people," the man nodded geekishly. "A real doozie. So where do you ski?"

"Snowshoe. We have one of those time-sharing deals."

"Are you carrying skis?"

He glanced at the game show on the counter TV. "We're renting them up there. So can you help us out?"

"Sure, sure. You want a four-wheel drive?"

They needed a trunk more. "What else do you have?"

"A Honda Prelude - fully equipped, in excellent condition."

"Sounds like a winner." He reached for his wallet.

The man whipped out an application. "I'll need a valid driver's license and major credit card."

Laying the required ID on the counter, Tyler quickly filled out the application. "Orlando, huh?" The man studied the cards.

"Where'd you go to school, Mr. Cartwright?"

"Shreveport. My company just transferred me to Orlando. Nice town."

"Yeah, I grew up there." As Tyler slipped the application back across the counter, the man studied it carefully. "You live on Bridlewood. That's south Orlando, right? Near the new mall?"

"Just a few blocks from there," he nodded.

The man returned his ID. "Four twenty-five will cover a week and deposit, plus the tank of gas."

As he retrieved his wallet, the TV game show ended, followed by an update on the Naples manhunt. Grabbing the Prelude's keys, the man glanced at the screen flashing Tyler's picture. "You been following this manhunt?"

"The pair from New York? Yeah it's something, huh?"

"What would draw them to Naples, of all places? Not that I'm an expert, but it seems even if they'd been here, they'd be gone by now. What fugitive in his right mind hangs around a city crawling with cops?"

"Beats the hell out of me." Tyler scooped up the keys.

"I'd say they headed north, maybe to the mountains, like you. What do you think?"

Me? I'm just glad to be wearing this cap and shades, Tyler thought as he grabbed his bag. "The mountains, like you said." Smiling, he started out, "The next time you're in Orlando, look us up. The Cartwrights. Bridlewood Lane."

Leopold squirmed irritably in the Escort's bucket seat. Had large men been completely forgotten in this age of compacts? Why couldn't you find a decent Cadillac or Town Car to lease anymore? Just these cramped little boxes on wheels. There'd been nothing but complications since leaving D.C. yesterday. First, they'd arrived in Atlanta to learn a tropical storm had cancelled their Naples connection. Six hours they'd waited for the weather to clear and another available flight. Then a screw-up at the Naples airport had landed them in this sardine can. And if that weren't enough, flooded streets had turned a ten-minute drive to the hotel into an hour of detours and traffic jams.

Now after a restless night at the Gulf Sands, his leg was cramping in a bucket seat designed for midgets. And Frankie, slouched behind the wheel, was popping gum in his ear. An hour across from the courthouse, and already his dim-witted associate had gone through a pack of Juicy Fruit. How much more could he take? "Cut the gum-popping before I go nuts," he growled.

"Come on, Arch," Frankie whined. "Don't you remember the old days? You smacked it louder than anybody."

"That's when I had teeth. Now either chew quietly or spit it out." They needed to put these kids away quickly. It wasn't helping anyone's nerves to have them running around. Who knew what they might stumble on? And what about Harvey, who'd quickly vanished after Swanson's suicide? They'd missed him by minutes, Chapman had said. Minutes, hours, days; what difference did it make? A miss was a miss. The prudent course would've been to eliminate Swanson two years ago, when he'd first made noise over the Rogers investigation. Now they were being haunted by a tactical error that never should've happened.

"Come on!" Frankie rapped the wheel impatiently. "You kids ain't gonna make us sit here all day, are you?"

He checked his watch as activity increased across the street. Briefcase-toting lawyers trickled into the courthouse; cops clustered on the granite steps with their coffee and tall tales. All the metered spaces along the curb were filled. Carefully he scanned the block again: the Florida American Bank on the distant corner, then moving south, the parking garage, courthouse, and on the near corner, a professional office building.

The courthouse had three entrances: the front they now monitored, and the side and rear, inconspicuously watched by Feds in casual beach attire. George was posted in the Clerk's office where record requests were made. His identity, like Crenshaw, was known only by the handful of agents on Chapman's payroll. The others knew only that a reliable lead placed the kids in Naples, the courthouse their suspected destination.

The Florida troopers were present to seal off the city and satisfy the manpower needed to search the hotels along the coast. If the kids delayed their courthouse trip long enough, they'd be nabbed. Still, the massive convoy of patrol cars was a concern.

Waddill and Corelli, if they were here, knew their presence was no secret. What if the gray units had scared them off or were keeping them away now? Only time would tell.

"You think maybe they skipped out?" Frankie echoed Leopold's fear. "Or with the heat, went to Tennessee first?"

Leopold winced with another painful shift of his leg. Damn compact cars! "They're here, Frankie. Just be patient for once in your life. And throw that gum out."

"You said chew quietly. I'm chewing quietly."

"Get rid of the gum!"

End of discussion. Frankie knew that tone all right. Rolling the window down, he spit the gum out as another patrol car drifted by. "Arch, do you really think those kids are dumb enough to come down here with the entire Florida police force circling the place?"

"They're not circling, stupid. They're patrolling."

"Circling, patrolling," he shrugged. "What difference does it make? The kids know we're here and... Wow!" His eyes snagged on the slender blond, striding down the street. "Would you look at that cute little tail!"

Leopold watched her pass the courthouse and enter the corner office building. She was a beauty, all right. But why cut her hair so short and wear those awful glasses? "Probably a secretary to some big shot lawyer in that fancy building."

An edge returned to the silence as the morning dragged on. Finally, Leopold squeezed from the car to stretch his cramping leg. Overhead, the sun burned off the last storm clouds. Soon the courthouse would bake in the afternoon heat. Would they have the kids by then? As he returned to the car, Frankie said, "Assuming they are here, who's to say they'll come to the courthouse together?"

It was a good point. "That's possible. But have you seen anyone remotely resembling either?"

Frankie sighed. "I haven't seen anyone remotely interesting except that gorgeous blond. Hey, you don't . . ." He watched Leopold grab the beeping phone, nod gravely then hang up. "What's up, Arch?"

"That was Nicholas. One of his agents, who worked with

Harvey at La Guardia this past Friday, claims he stopped some pretty blond that a State guy swears was Corelli. Only Harvey, after checking her ID, said she was some simple Atlanta housewife and let her go."

"A pretty blond?"

"No doubt with a nice butt and granny glasses. Ring a bell?"

"Arch, that was her — the one who went in the building!"

Probably. But was she still there? The phone beeped again. He was drawn into another quick, agitated conversation. Frankie watched him hang up. "Now what?"

"Reardon, the Naples Agent-in-Charge, has located the kids' room at a Holiday Inn five blocks from here. He's sealing off the area between the hotel and courthouse."

"Arch, we've got'em! Praise the Lord!"

Wincing, Leopold again crawled from the car. "Frankie, wait in the lobby of that office building until either Walters or McCormack joins you. If Corelli's still there, I want her."

Bernie Deveraux had just slumped back with his morning coffee when his secretary buzzed him. "What is it, Janice?"

He had a major hangover after the half-dozen martinis at Tribello's last night. He didn't go there usually, but with the storm it had been the only decent bar open on Gulf Shore Drive.

"There's a woman out here," Janice explained. "She doesn't have an appointment but says it's urgent she speak with you."

The grounded stewardess from Tribello's? They'd ended up at his condo. Sheila . . . or was it Sherry? Oh God, he hadn't promised her anything, had he? "Auburn hair?" He cringed. "Green eyes?"

"No, Bernie. Can you see her or not?"

Relief settled over him now. "Show her in."

Dropping the phone, he stood at the window to wait. Maybe it was the first storm victim. There should be many promising walk-ins if today was like others that followed disasters. Specifically, that plane crash in the Gulf two summers ago: a settlement bonanza that had fallen in his lap, simply by being in his office the next morning. Isn't that why he was here now, instead of home in bed nursing this awful hangover? His gaze followed another patrol car down the street. Were the Tallahassee Boys here for the storm or the two fugitives supposedly in town? The glum-faced men in the Escort parked across from the courthouse looked as if they could give a shit either way. His sentiments exactly. He turned now as a beautiful young woman appeared. "Mrs. Marcia Cartwright," Janice introduced her.

"How about some coffee, Mrs. Cartwright?" He sprung around to seat her.

"No, thank you," she declined as Janice left. "I'm in a hurry and I'm sure you're busy."

"How were you referred to me?" He sat behind the desk. This was always his first question. Lawyers were no different from salesmen. They needed to know which marketing strategies were working best.

"I caught your TV commercial over the weekend," she explained. "And I must say, Mr. Deveraux, the message certainly hit home. A catastrophic injury really does tumble a person into a bewildering nightmare of hospitals, doctors, pushy insurance people and endless forms filled with incomprehensible medical and legal jargon - a 'Jungle of Jibberish that won't victimize those smart enough to hire Bernard Devereaux and Associates, the Lions of Jungle Law.' *Madonna mia*, what a compelling message!"

"What was that — 'Madonna' something? Is that Italian?"

A stupid slip, she scolded herself. "My girlfriend uses that expression all the time. I guess I've picked it up. But to be honest, I'm not sure what it means."

Nor did it matter. So then the new commercial really was a hit, maybe even worth the hefty bill Channel Three had stuck him with. "I hope your family survived the storm without serious injury or property damage."

"Oh yes," she nodded, marveling at how quickly two simple words could flatten a smile. "We survived quite well."

"Then this isn't . . . I mean, it has nothing to do with yesterday's storm?"

"Oh no; but wasn't it frightening? Barbara, my cousin we've been visiting, says it's the worst she's ever seen."

"Then you're not from Naples?"

"Orlando." Taking her purse out, she showed him the Cartwright family picture, including their three children.

"That's your husband?" Bernie pointed.

"Before the accident," she nodded.

"Accident?" he snagged on the key word.

"Jonathan was in a car accident three weeks ago, while returning from our store. You know, groceries, fishing supplies, boat accessories. We even have a lunch counter. Our little store rakes in a bundle. A real cash cow, Barbara calls it. Until . . ."

As her delicate hand fluttered, her face crinkling, a kaleidoscope of impressions flashed across his mind — beautiful, sweet, fragile. What an impact she'd have on an Orlando jury! "Please go on." He passed her a box of tissues. "The store was a cash cow until what — Jonathan's accident?"

The crumpled tissue over her eyes, she nodded. "As I said, Jonathan was on his way home. It was late, dark, that time when we're most vulnerable to those monsters."

"What monsters?" he asked.

"Drunk drivers, like the one who ran the red light and plowed into Jonathan. Not only was he drunk, he was speeding — according to the witnesses, anyway."

His eyes widened. "There were witnesses?"

"A preacher and his family," she nodded. "They were on their front porch, eating ice cream. They saw the whole thing."

Bernie was salivating now as he absorbed this stunning scenario. *Drunk driver plows into family man on his way home from work - the witnesses, a preacher and his ice cream-eating family.* Had he died and gone to Heaven? "Is Jonathan . . . ?"

"Dead? No, but his injuries are permanent. He'll never be able to . . ."

His heart quaked as she collapsed again. She was so fragile, so huggable. "Never be able to what? Run the store?"

"Run the store? He won't even be able to feed himself. He'll need nurses and expensive medical equipment for the rest of his life."

Bernie tingled as the damages mounted in his head. They were talking about millions!

"We'll lose the store," she sighed. "Jonathan ran it by himself.

I don't have his head for numbers. And there are the children to care for and the house, which I guess we'll lose along with the store."

"Have you consulted any lawyers in Orlando?" he asked.

"Oh no, I never even considered that."

"Why not?"

"Because they can't be trusted."

"I don't understand," he said.

"Well you would if you knew who the drunk driver was." Her eyes gleamed viciously. "Jason Spillwood, the richest, most despicable man in Orlando. He, no doubt, has every lawyer there in his hip pocket."

Spillwood? He drew a blank on that one. "And how did he acquire his wealth?"

"By cheating people stupid enough to buy his cars - those expensive foreign jobs, like the Lamborghini he was driving the night he hit Jonathan. He smashed it to pieces but why should he care? He has a lot full of them and millions of dollars in the bank." Her eyes hardened.

Bernie nodded solemnly, already thinking two or possibly three million for the Cartwrights and one for himself. "I'm quite confident I can help you." He slid a retainer agreement across the desk.

Scanning it, she took the offered pen and signed. "These last weeks have been so difficult. It's such a relief to turn this mess over to you, Mr. Deveraux."

"It should be." His smile dripped with compassion. "You've just retained the Lion of Jungle Law."

"And your fee will come out of the settlement?"

He nodded. "You'll just be responsible for my expenses. I require two hundred dollars to begin."

She promptly withdrew the amount and laid it on the desk. "Now," he reached for a legal pad. "Let's review the facts. I'll need . . . What's wrong?" He watched her frown.

"I just remembered what Barbara asked me to do."

"What's that?"

"Get a copy of the estate records for the old man she cared for. Barbara's a nurse. Isn't that the courthouse next door?"

He nodded. "Why does she want the probate records?"

"Probate. Yes, that's the word she used. She said the rich old codger left her a bequest, but it's tied up in probate. She needs the records because she's thinking about hiring a lawyer. Say, Mr. Deveraux, do you handle probate cases, too?"

"Yes, as a matter of fact I do," he said. But he was thinking, Lady, if money's involved, I handle it.

"Great." She rose. "I'll make sure Barbara knows. Now, I really must get to the courthouse. She wants a complete copy of the records. And who knows how thick . . . Oh no." She glanced at her watch. "I've got to hurry. After dropping the records off, I have to pick up the kids and get back to Orlando for a meeting with Jonathan's doctors."

He gaped at the sweet, fragile thing. She was trying to be brave, but there was just too much to cope with. "Please." He coaxed her back into the chair. "I'll get the records. We can review the case until they're ready. Then you can leave."

"But it may cost a lot to copy them." She watched him grab the phone.

"Don't worry," he winked. "There's a young clerk who'll not only put a rush on our order, but won't charge either. Now what's the name of that estate?"

Tyler grabbed a parking space near the courthouse as another patrol car drifted past. They were everywhere, unlike Mayson, who'd yet to appear on the dangerous streets.

Meter-hopping was the only way to dodge the troopers' endless parade. Park, wait, then move, again. At least this space offered a clear view of the office building. Was Mayson still inside? Had the shyster agreed to get the records? Had there been a delay, or had he simply missed her on the street? Another gray unit drifted south. Pulling out, he headed north, back to the hotel. He'd covered these blocks so many times that by now, everything was familiar. Had Mayson been forced to take another route? Was she possibly trapped in an alley somewhere?

He covered the five blocks, then the adjacent streets before parking again, a block north of the courthouse this time. Almost instantly, another gray unit drifted by, and again he pulled out, heading in the opposite direction.

As he passed the courthouse, a huge man squeezed from a tiny car and limped off. The giant's face was hideous. Leopold! He fit Harvey's description perfectly.

As he continued south, another unit loomed in his mirror. Instantly its lights flashed. As he pulled over, it streaked past, then fishtailed into the Holiday Inn.

He saw the fleet of gray units converge at the hotel office. Clerks, in their navy jackets, mingled with troopers and Feds, fingers pointed, eyes gazing in the same direction: to their fourth floor room.

He cringed as several Feds dashed for the stairwell. Was Mayson up there? Starting back towards the courthouse, his desperate eyes scraped up every face along the familiar streets.

Stopping for the last light, he again inventoried the scene: Deveraux's building, the courthouse, garage, bank, and Leopold's still-parked Escort.

As the light changed, he moved again, eyes darting. Reaching the courthouse, the Escort's doors suddenly flew open and the driver, a medium-sized man with blond hair, dashed for Deveraux's building. Leopold hesitated, then without warning, limped into the street.

As he hit the brakes, the giant swung around. Did he see anything more than an annoying schmuck with cap and shades behind the Prelude's wheel? The suspense ended as he spun and limped furiously into the courthouse.

Finding McCormack, Leopold sent him to join Frankie. "Search the entire building. And don't leave until you have Corelli, or can swear on your mother's life she's not there."

As he limped to the Clerk's office, George sprung up from his seat near the counter. "Get Walters," he ordered.

George quickly returned with the agent. Confirming that they hadn't seen anyone fitting the fugitives' descriptions, Leopold asked, "The front counter here is where a person comes to inspect the probate records?"

Walters nodded. "The case name is given to the clerk, who then either brings the records out, or puts the person in one of the viewing rooms. There's a copier back there, too. You want to see the area?"

He nodded. "George, keep an eye on things out here."

As he followed McCormack down the hall, two agents looked up from an open office. It was dangerous to get this close to the Fed's operation. Only a handful, like Walters, McCormack, and Reardon, knew his identity. Hopefully, this morning's exception wouldn't have to be repeated.

"Don't worry about Dillon and Casey," Walters said. "If they ask, I've been told to say you're a private eye retained by Lieber Allen. And you sure don't need to worry about him," he nodded at the cadaverous, old man snoozing in the corner office. "Chief Clerk Courtney, two weeks from retirement."

They found Courtney's senior deputy, a bright, competent redhead, who escorted them into one of the record rooms. "Probate cases are maintained in here," she explained. "Is there one you'd like to see?"

"The Jasper Crenshaw Estate," Walters replied.

Rummaging through the cabinet's top drawer, she quickly nodded. "Yep, that's the one."

He glanced at an equally concerned Leopold. "The one?"

"Follow me," she led them down to another office. "Crenshaw," she pointed at the files stacked on the desk.

"Why are they in here?" Walters asked.

"Because Susan Peebles, one of my junior deputies, pulled them this morning. Tied up the copier for an hour. Obviously, she also failed to re-file them. She's done this before, but I assure you it won't happen again. Two warnings are enough. She'll be placed on corrective discussion this time."

Corrective discussion. He cringed at Leopold's angry face. What would he get for letting this happen? Castration?

"Where is Ms. Peebles now?" Leopold asked.

"She took an early lunch, then had a doctor's appointment."

"Do you know who she made the copies for?"

"No, I'm sorry." Grabbing the phone, she buzzed another deputy, a thin, solemn-faced woman who quickly appeared. "Ramona, did Susan say anything before leaving?"

"Not much. She was in a hurry to drop those records off."

"Do you know where?" Leopold asked.
"Sure. Bernie Deveraux's office next door."

Leopold's urgency haunted Tyler as he searched for Mayson on streets growing more dangerous by the minute. What had sent the giant limping into the courthouse, his companion dashing into the building next door? Did they know about Mayson's altered appearance and her visit to Deveraux's office? Finding the hotel still jammed with gray units, he started back to the courthouse. Two blocks later, he finally spotted Mayson hurrying along the sidewalk. A blue bandana covered her head, shades having replaced the grannies. She lugged what appeared to be a box of blankets but her grimace suggested much heavier baggage.

Pulling over, he rolled the window down, "I see you've finished your shopping." Like a frightened squirrel, she froze, her head turning in his direction. "Let's go home, Marcia, what do you say?"

Her slender arms screaming from her burden, she peered through the window. His cap and shades were commonplace; the feathered gold hair and magnificent jaw were uniquely Tyler. She wanted to pummel and hug him at the same time as she hurried over. "I couldn't have carried it another ten feet." She dropped the box in back then joined him up front.

"Bullshit," he grinned. "You could've carried it to Georgia, if you had to."

"Where have you been?" she demanded.

"Where the hell do you think?" Whipping around, he started north. "You got them all?"

"Every page."

"Nice bandana," he nodded. "The shades, too. You couldn't have timed them any better. They've updated your description."

"Don't you think I know that?"

He sighed. "I'm sorry it took so long to find you. You must've been scared shitless."

"It wasn't your fault," she shrugged. "And I'm sure it was no picnic for you either, out on these shark-infested streets."

They soon confronted a roadblock. "They've sealed us off. Now what?"

"Look for a crack in the seal," he said, turning sharply.

They found the east road blocked, too. Certainly the south and west were, as well. Moving into the operation's next phase, he ducked into the closest alley. She'd hated this part from the beginning. "Tyler, it's ninety degrees. And it'll be a hundred-and-ninety in the trunk. You might suffocate."

"I'll be fine."

"Don't say things you can't possibly predict!"

"Look, Mayson, in their minds we're a pair. That means one draws less suspicion. One disguised draws even less."

"But you're as much disguised as me now. So, it doesn't matter who rides in the trunk, except that I'm smaller, which means I'll fit more comfortably."

"That wasn't part of the plan." He glanced down the alley. It'd take just one curious unit to end the show.

"Tyler, I won't have you die from heat stroke because of some stupid plan."

Climbing out, he scowled as she stayed in her seat. "Come on, quit screwing around!"

Stubbornly, she folded her arms.

"Maybe you're right," he sighed. "Maybe we should just turn ourselves in. That way, no one will have to ride in the trunk."

She glared at him through the window. "How many times do I have to say it? You're not clever."

"That's right, I'm mad. Now get your ass out of the goddamned car."

"Don't talk to me like that!"

"Talk, hell! I'm ready to take you across my knee!"

"You'd love that, wouldn't you?"

"You're damn right. Now get out of the car."

"Tyler... No!" Jerking the door open, he scooped her up as she squealed, flailed and clutching his neck, surrendering finally to tears.

"Now, the map's in the glove compartment." His anger quickly faded. "The course is charted, but just stick to I-75 for now, all right?" When she nodded, he set her down. "There's still plenty of gas, enough to reach the Georgia line, anyway."

"That's where I'll stop to bury you," she fretted. "You'll be dead by then."

God knows, she never quit, just paused long enough to catch her breath. The man she loved one day — a miracle he could now envision — would be the luckiest bastard alive. More than a beautiful mate, he'd have the most fiercely loyal ally alive.

"Tyler, if you die, I'll haunt your grave."

"I've no doubt." He grabbed the records and, stuffing them in the trunk, crawled in with the water jug.

"I suppose you think this stupid prank makes you noble or something," she worried, as she loomed over him.

"Just shut up and close the trunk, all right?"

"This redneck gallantry doesn't impress me at all."

"Close the goddamned trunk!"

She did him one better and slammed it viciously. Storming around the car, she quickly returned. "Tyler, I hate you for making me do this . . . Are you all right in there?"

"Drive the goddamned car!"

Slipping behind the wheel, her eyes brushed over the equipment. Taking a deep breath, she started off, joining the traffic north along the route to I-75. Short blocks later she confronted a roadblock. She crept over the baked pavement, imagining Tyler sweating like a pig in the trunk. What if he ran out of water or lost consciousness? Finally, she spotted the cluster of gray units ahead. Stern-faced troopers ducked into cars and snapped up IDs, their gestures crisp as one car was dismissed and the next waved forward. Anxiously, she studied her bandana-covered head and the shades that hid her eyes. She was still Mayson Corelli. Wouldn't they know?

She crept forward again. Four cars remained between her and the checkpoint. Why was the trunk so quiet behind her? If she could just hear a bump, anything to confirm he was all right. The jeep in front of her finally reached the checkpoint, the trooper taking up the blond boy's license. Others threw open the doors. Quickly the inspection was completed and the boy waved on. Her heart in her throat, she drove forward. "Good day," the trooper greeted. "May I please see some identification?"

As she grabbed her purse, the doors flew open. Hands pounded cushions, swept under seats, sifted through the glove compartment. Struggling to free her license from the plastic, she finally passed it out the window. The trooper studied the photo, then her face. "Would you please remove your glasses?"

The search stopped now, solemn eyes watching her as she removed the glasses. Apparently satisfied, the trooper asked, "You have a registration for this vehicle?"

"Here," the trooper beside her grabbed it from the glove compartment and passed it out the window.

The trooper at the window studied it, then the car lease. "Jonathan Cartwright is your husband?"

She nodded. "We've been visiting family here in Naples. Jonathan leased the car this morning so I could return to Orlando on business."

"Orlando's south," the trooper beside her said. "This map charts a northerly route . . ." Radio staccato intruded suddenly, then another trooper loped up. "We just got a report that Corelli was in Bernie Deveraux's office this morning."

"That confirms she's inside our little quadrangle," the trooper at the window said. The one inside the car added, "We know the fugitives planned to visit the courthouse and that their next move would likely be north. This map charts a northern route."

"It came with the car," she shrugged. "I'm not going anywhere but to my job in Orlando – assuming I still have it when I get back."

The trooper at the window studied the lengthening traffic, then her license again. "This is a genuine Florida permit. God knows, I've seen enough of them." He peered inside at his companion. "Anything else in the glove compartment, Doug?"

"It's clean, Leo. But maybe we should check the trunk." A fourth trooper approached, quickly spotting him. "Reynolds wants to see you at HQ, Doug. He says it's urgent."

"Everything is with him." Doug climbed out.

The trooper at the window returned her license. "That DMV photo hardly does you justice, Mrs. Cartwright. But they rarely do. I-75 is two blocks east. You're sure you're not taking it?" When she firmly shook her head, he backed away from the car. "Then proceed. And my apologies for the delay."

She was floating suddenly, disconnected from her waving

hand and her shrill voice that cried, "Happy Thanksgiving!"

She coasted past the cluster of patrol cars, then two blocks later the I-75 ramp. Behind her the trunk remained quiet, yet Tyler must know they'd dodged another bullet. Why wasn't he shouting, knocking, something? The gray units thinned as she reached the outskirts of Naples. Ducking into a car wash, she grabbed the last bay and hurried back to open the trunk. Tyler was curled around the water jug, his face flushed and glistening from the intense heat. "Look at you! You're soaking wet!"

"I'm fine." He squinted against the harsh light.

"Boiling like beef in a pot isn't fine. Now get out."

"You handled those troopers brilliantly." He lolled in the cool draft.

"Tyler, you'll have heat stroke, then suffocate and die, all because you're a pigheaded *gavonne!*"

"Goddamnit, will you listen . . ."

The spraying water died suddenly in the adjoining bay. Holding the hose, a man appeared. "Need some help, lady? You sounded a little upset muttering that way."

Peering at him over the trunk, she smiled sheepishly. "I get like that when I'm in a hurry. No, thank you, I'm just getting my soap and rags out." Her eyes closed as the water sprayed once again in the next bay.

"I-75 is out," Tyler whispered. "All the primary roads north will be smothered. And they'll soon realize they screwed up by letting this Prelude slip through. I didn't chart an alternate course but at least considered one. Which way have you been traveling?"

"East," she replied.

"Then we must be close to Route 953. Take it north to . . . 82, I think. Then 31. You'll run into them sooner or later. If not, just pull over and we'll check it out."

"But how am I supposed to . . ." Quickly she slipped around the bay corner to find the man wiping his brown Taurus. "Could you tell me how to get to Route 953?"

He pointed out the bay. "Three blocks east, turn left and you're on it."

"Thank you." She slipped back around the corner.

"Let's go," Tyler urged.

Were they looking yet for a leased Prelude? One appeared in the mirror beyond Graball, hugging her bumper as miles were eclipsed along dark, desolate Route 14. Her eyes bounced from the speedometer to the mirror, as she imagined the trooper gushing over the radio, *Got a make on that blue Prelude, JP. Yeah boy, I'm gonna pull her over right now.* Anxious minutes later, the unit turned off at a truck stop near Edwin, and into the deepening night she sailed on. But she was tired now, her vision blurred from endless stretches of pavement, swaying yellow lines, headlamps like shimmering blobs that jumped out from the darkness. How much longer could she go on?

She pondered this on the desolate stretch between Comer and Spring Hill, then Rutherford, Hurstboro and Uchee, of all places; each eclipsed in the night's thickening fog. Beyond Marvyn, she stopped again to check on Tyler. He stretched, visited the trees and then studied the map. "You're doing great," he nodded. "We've covered half of Alabama. But you must be tired. I'll take over."

She could do cartwheels at the very suggestion. But she'd gone this far; surely she could go a little farther. "Thanks, but I'm fine."

"I know. But if it's all right, I want to drive awhile. My ass is getting numb like you said it would. Besides . . . What are you smiling about?"

He was giving her an easy out. "Be my guest." She handed him the keys.

As he took the wheel, she slumped gratefully beside him. "It's such a shame."

"What?"

"That you missed all the beautiful scenery in Graball, Comer, Marvyn, Uchee . . ." She was asleep in seconds.

She woke later in the parking lot of a pizzeria. "Where are we?" She rubbed her eyes.

"Hollis Crossroads," he replied.

"Why did I even ask?" She squinted at the thoroughly foreign intersection.

"How does a large pizza with extra cheese grab you?"

hand and her shrill voice that cried, "Happy Thanksgiving!"

She coasted past the cluster of patrol cars, then two blocks later the I-75 ramp. Behind her the trunk remained quiet, yet Tyler must know they'd dodged another bullet. Why wasn't he shouting, knocking, something? The gray units thinned as she reached the outskirts of Naples. Ducking into a car wash, she grabbed the last bay and hurried back to open the trunk. Tyler was curled around the water jug, his face flushed and glistening from the intense heat. "Look at you! You're soaking wet!"

"I'm fine." He squinted against the harsh light.

"Boiling like beef in a pot isn't fine. Now get out."

"You handled those troopers brilliantly." He lolled in the cool draft.

"Tyler, you'll have heat stroke, then suffocate and die, all because you're a pigheaded *gavonne!*"

"Goddamnit, will you listen . . ."

The spraying water died suddenly in the adjoining bay. Holding the hose, a man appeared. "Need some help, lady? You sounded a little upset muttering that way."

Peering at him over the trunk, she smiled sheepishly. "I get like that when I'm in a hurry. No, thank you, I'm just getting my soap and rags out." Her eyes closed as the water sprayed once again in the next bay.

"I-75 is out," Tyler whispered. "All the primary roads north will be smothered. And they'll soon realize they screwed up by letting this Prelude slip through. I didn't chart an alternate course but at least considered one. Which way have you been traveling?"

"East," she replied.

"Then we must be close to Route 953. Take it north to . . . 82, I think. Then 31. You'll run into them sooner or later. If not, just pull over and we'll check it out."

"But how am I supposed to . . ." Quickly she slipped around the bay corner to find the man wiping his brown Taurus. "Could you tell me how to get to Route 953?"

He pointed out the bay. "Three blocks east, turn left and you're on it."

"Thank you." She slipped back around the corner.

"Let's go," Tyler urged.

"I'll stop every twenty-five miles to check on you."
"Seventy-five," he impatiently countered. "Now let's go."
"Twenty-five!" She slammed the trunk.

CHAPTER EIGHTEEN

★

She reached Route 953 and then with only one wrong turn, covered the connecting roads to Route 31. North of Lehigh Acres, she stopped to mail her secret letter; a few miles later she pulled into a deserted construction site to check on Tyler.

"Why did you stop back there?" he asked.

"To get my bearings."

"Well now that you have them, let's get some distance between us and the law."

She soon discovered the advantage of country roads as she inched her way north. Except for the route numbers, they were identical, each with convenient side roads to check on Tyler, who grew testier with each stop. "Tyler, you'll cramp. Don't you want to stretch your legs?"

"'No, for the hundredth time! Now close the trunk!" he growled as the afternoon slipped away.

Route numbers spun in her head as she crossed the Alabama line, and just north of Fadette she stopped to check on him again. It was almost dark as he finally crawled from the trunk, grabbed the map and turned on the flashlight to study it. "What are you doing?" she asked.

"Stretching my legs; isn't that what you've asked me to do for the last three hundred miles?"

"I mean what are you looking for?"

"I dug into the records long enough to discover the good sheriff's fiefdom. Pine County, Tennessee. Mountain country, it appears." Folding the map, he started into the woods.

"Now where are you going?" she asked, then blushed at his impatient glance. "Oh . . ." All the water consumed, the miles covered and —phenomenally — this was the first time.

A chill crept into the night as they breezed along the banks of the Choctawhatchee River. The patrol cars, once Florida gray, were now Alabama white. She held her breath as each one passed.

Were they looking yet for a leased Prelude? One appeared in the mirror beyond Graball, hugging her bumper as miles were eclipsed along dark, desolate Route 14. Her eyes bounced from the speedometer to the mirror, as she imagined the trooper gushing over the radio, *Got a make on that blue Prelude, JP. Yeah boy, I'm gonna pull her over right now.* Anxious minutes later, the unit turned off at a truck stop near Edwin, and into the deepening night she sailed on. But she was tired now, her vision blurred from endless stretches of pavement, swaying yellow lines, headlamps like shimmering blobs that jumped out from the darkness. How much longer could she go on?

She pondered this on the desolate stretch between Comer and Spring Hill, then Rutherford, Hurstboro and Uchee, of all places; each eclipsed in the night's thickening fog. Beyond Marvyn, she stopped again to check on Tyler. He stretched, visited the trees and then studied the map. "You're doing great," he nodded. "We've covered half of Alabama. But you must be tired. I'll take over."

She could do cartwheels at the very suggestion. But she'd gone this far; surely she could go a little farther. "Thanks, but I'm fine."

"I know. But if it's all right, I want to drive awhile. My ass is getting numb like you said it would. Besides . . . What are you smiling about?"

He was giving her an easy out. "Be my guest." She handed him the keys.

As he took the wheel, she slumped gratefully beside him. "It's such a shame."

"What?"

"That you missed all the beautiful scenery in Graball, Comer, Marvyn, Uchee . . ." She was asleep in seconds.

She woke later in the parking lot of a pizzeria. "Where are we?" She rubbed her eyes.

"Hollis Crossroads," he replied.

"Why did I even ask?" She squinted at the thoroughly foreign intersection.

"How does a large pizza with extra cheese grab you?"

She spotted the McDonalds across the street. "Wouldn't you rather have a Big Mac and fries?"

"No, a pizza with extra cheese."

"You're just saying that because I'm Italian and like pizza."

"No, because I'm a Virginian and a very hungry one at the moment."

"Tyler, why are you being so nice? No one's this considerate. It's just not possible."

"Please Mayson, it's too late to start this. Now what do you want to drink?"

"When she didn't answer, he said, "A coke it is then," and climbed out.

The pizza was gone by Piedmont Springs; by Pine Grove, she was asleep again. Then came Caloma, Leesburg, and after picking up Route 11, Portersville and Collbran. By Fort Payne, he'd encountered three Alabama whites, a figure that doubled by Valley Head and forced him to leave 11 for a less crowded 117.

They were now deep in the mountains with enough darkness, by his calculations, to reach Pine County. But then what? Wouldn't the Feds be waiting, just as in Naples? Shouldn't he find a sleepy little inn where they could take their time figuring out a plan?

"*Madonna mia*, it's so cold!" she said as she woke.

He glanced at her hunched against the chill. "The mountains get that way in November."

As his arm wrapped around her, she snuggled against him gratefully. "So where are we — and please don't say Alabama?"

"Fifty miles southwest of Chattanooga, Tennessee. How's that?"

"Yeah, doggies!"

He squinted. "Yeah, doggies?"

"Isn't that what the Beverly Hillbillies say?"

"Are they from Tennessee?"

"How should I know? Are we getting close?"

"A couple hundred miles." He now shared his dilemma — go to Pine County or not?

"We'd be safer somewhere else," she said. "But how much?

And even if we don't know what we're looking for, it must be in Pine. Hopefully the records will tell us more. If not, Naples was a complete waste of time."

"Not entirely," he smiled. "You experienced your first tropical storm. So what are you saying?"

"That sooner or later we must go to Pine. Why put it off? Whenever we go, the Feds'll be waiting."

She was right. There was nothing to gain by delaying the confrontation. Stopping in Hindon for gas, he charted their northeastern course. She slept again as he negotiated an intricate network of highways around Chattanooga. By four, they reached Waterville and the first Pine County posting. "Hallelujah!" He kissed her head. "Thirty miles to go!"

"Great." She burrowed into his neck. "You need a shave." As they rounded the next bend, a cluster of lights suddenly jumped out from the darkness. Hitting the brakes, he quickly shut off his lights. "Turn around!" she shrieked. Instead he crept forward until spotting a side road on the right. The moonlight vanished as he ducked into it.

Creeping through the darkness, he was guided only by the grinding pavement beneath him. When he finally turned on the lights again, he discovered what he already knew; they were on a back road that snaked into the Tennessee woods. "I wonder where it goes?" Mayson asked the question of the minute, one remaining unanswered miles later as they crossed the same twisting creek three times on a steady climb up the mountain. "Are we at least heading towards Pine?"

He shook his head. "It's thirty miles north of that roadblock. We're heading east . . . and up."

An abandoned pickup soon appeared on the right; Tyler nodded at the logs in back. "Paul Bunyan, maybe?"

A mile later they came upon a large woman in boots and bulky coat, hiking up the shoulder. Turning, she squinted into the approaching headlights. "Mrs. Bunyan?" Mayson mused.

Tyler stopped and climbed out. "Is that your pickup back there?"

"Sure is, sonny. You wouldn't happen to have a jack, would you? I got a spare but no jack. That's 'cuz Earl never puts it back.

I'm gonna give him the dickens, too, only it won't do no good. He's deaf as a door. Dumb as one, too, since he can't remember to put the jack back in the truck. So you got a jack or not?"

Tyler was totally absorbed by the large mountain woman with the square face and feisty tongue who spoke to him on this dark road as if she'd known him a lifetime. Her scarf and coat were badly tattered, her boots large enough to fit his own feet. "A jack? I don't know . . ."

"What you mean you don't know? Everybody knows if'n they have a jack or not."

He hadn't checked but certainly they had one. Opening the trunk, he quickly discovered both jack and lug wrench.

"So you have a flat?" Mayson asked the woman.

"Course, gal. You don't think I'd leave my truck back yonder if'n I didn't?"

"Well, you shouldn't be on this road alone at night."

"And what road you figger I should be on? This here's the only one that runs down to Mill Creek."

"I meant you shouldn't be on any road. Anything could happen; things far worse than a flat tire."

"If'n I wasn't to use a road," she glared at a much smaller Mayson, "how else was I supposed to get to Sara Jackson's place? I ain't got wings, you know."

"You don't need wings, just the sense to visit Sara Jackson during the day."

"My sense ain't got nuthin' to do with it. Sara's water done decided when I'd be going."

"Her water?" Mayson asked.

"It done broke. And when Sara called, there weren't no dad-blamed choice but to go."

"You're a midwife?"

"When I ain't cookin' and cleanin.' Say, do I know you two?"

"No ma'am," Tyler replied. "We're the . . . Comptons. I'm Bob and this is my wife . . . Lucy. We're . . ."

"On our honeymoon," Mayson picked up the tale. "We just got married in . . . Dothan. We're on our way to . . ."

"The Great Smokies," he added. "We're real nature lovers."

"If'n that ain't a crock!" she huffed. "The only nature you

two'd be lovin' is each other's. Name's Bessie Lou Adkins." She extended her hand. "Just call me Lou. Everyone else does . . . So Bob, you got that jack or not?"

They returned down the road to her truck. Inspecting the flat right front tire, Tyler dropped in the gravel with his tools. "Bob, I can do that," Lou protested. "I ain't no invalid, you know."

"I don't mind. Just keep Lucy company and I'll be through in a minute."

"He's a sweet one," she nodded as he began working. "Goodlookin' too. And you ain't so bad yourself, Lucy, 'cept you could use some fat on them bones."

Removing the flat, Tyler reached for the spare. "Maybe we'll fix that on the honeymoon."

"That'd do it," she nodded. "Did for Clara Bradley, anyhow. She came back from her honeymoon carrying a young'un. Delivered it myself."

"I'm not quite ready for young'uns," Mayson said.

Lou squinted. "That's a funny accent you got, Lucy. What part of 'Bama you from? Dothan?"

The blood rushed to her cheeks as Tyler explained, "We were married in Dothan but we're actually from Shreveport." Grabbing the wrench, he fastened the spare. "You know us Louisiana Creoles, Lou. We all talk funny. Wrestle gators and eat crawfish, too." He deftly twirled the wrench.

"If'n you ain't a mess!" she giggled like a schoolgirl. "How does Lucy put up with you?"

Charming Tyler had won over another, Mayson realized. As a neutral observer, she'd seen his effect on women many times, but she wasn't neutral any longer. Genuine feelings flowed through her now - feelings she should ignore and that certainly could never be fulfilled. If her heart didn't know it, her head surely did. It recalled life's lessons well: the world is filled with doors that don't open and songbirds that fly off in the night.

"Bob, you better get Lucy to bed," Lou said now. "The skinny little thing's so tired, she's crying. You know our camp's just sittin' there, empty and all. Will be 'til spring when Colonel Masters returns with them rich Nashville kids — bus loads, just itching for mischief after being cooped up all winter in them fancy boardin' schools.

"Babysittin,'" she snorted. "That's all Masters and his counselors do on this dadblamed mountain from May to August. Babysit a bunch of spoiled kids whose parents don't want'em around, or else they wouldn't have sent'em off to boardin' school in the first place. By August they're gone. Then it's just Earl and me to look after the place. There's the lake and cabins - ours here and a few others for the counselors nice enough to make you forget about them Smokies. Big, soft beds, full baths, color TVs. You and Lucy can stay as long as you like. Nobody'll bother you."

He looked up hopefully. "What do you think, Lucy?"

"Could we, darling?"

Everyone attended the Monday night meeting in Georgetown. Nine days into the crisis, there were no assurances that it would end any time soon.

Harrington studied the solemn group huddled around the coffee table: Thomas Streeter, the lanky, silver-haired Attorney General; Larry Chapman, the balding, bland-faced FBI Director; Supreme Court justices Mann and Falkingham; and the recent nominee, Lamp. Despite their powerful positions, or rather because of them, these men owed him an allegiance that transcended all others. Perhaps it was wise, as he began the meeting, to remind them of this. "Each of you I have blessed with the highest position in your respective disciplines. I've elevated you to the pinnacle of power, fame, and influence. And yet look at how you repay me." He shook his head miserably.

"This crisis has exposed your woeful inadequacies." He glared at Mann, Lamp, and Falkingham. "And your abject professional incompetence," as he turned to Streeter and Chapman. "It should never have happened and yet it drags on, deepening every day as we sit helplessly by, a shameful reality that leads me to wonder whether you've forgotten your loyalties and what's at stake here."

Falkingham spoke for the sad lot. "Our presence here tonight would seem to confirm both our loyalties and our appreciation of the stakes involved. So let's not waste more time with preambles and move on to the meat of this conference. It's late as it is."

"It's late all right." Harrington bristled at his impertinence.

"Let's just hope not terminally late, if my meaning's clear. Now what's the latest on the fugitives? Are we to assume they've slipped out of Naples with those court records?"

Streeter nodded. "After checking the rental agencies, we learned that one Jonathan Cartwright, matching Waddill's description, leased a blue Prelude this morning. Unfortunately, by then that same Prelude, driven by one Marcia Cartwright, had slipped through our checkpoints. A DMV search quickly established her license as a fake, albeit an excellent one that fooled the Florida troopers who let her —meaning Corelli — pass through. We assume Waddill was either stowed in the trunk or else waiting to be picked up and that they're now headed for Tennessee. All primary roads north have been blanketed and roadblocks set up on every artery leading into Pine County."

Chapman added, "Agent Nicholas has established a command post in Pine and will soon begin a reconnaissance of the region. Authorities not only in Tennessee but Alabama and Georgia as well, have been briefed, although it's taking longer than expected to get word out in the more remote jurisdictions."

Falkingham flicked a long ash. "There are a lot of those remote jurisdictions in the Deep South, Larry. And back roads, too. Do you plan on covering them all?"

"As many as possible," he confirmed. "At this hour, most if not all law enforcement officers below the Mason-Dixon Line are on the lookout for two subjects in a leased Honda Prelude, traveling under the identities of Jonathan and Marcia Cartwright of Orlando, Florida. We can assume the identities were provided by ex-Bureau Agent Harvey. How else could Corelli have obtained a Florida driver's license so genuine-looking it fooled state troopers?"

"The Naples hotel records confirm several contacts with Harvey over the weekend," Streeter added. "Certainly the IDs were arranged during these calls."

"While we're making all these assumptions," Falkingham said, "are we sure Harvey's aware of the Crenshaw Estate and is acting in concert with the kids to try and connect it to Mendelsohn and Rogers?"

"Of course he is!" Harrington barked. "The question is what to do about it?"

"As we've said," Streeter replied, "roadblocks have been established. There's no way these young hotshots can penetrate Pine County."

"Haven't we learned not to say no way?" Harrington scowled. "The lessons of New York and now Naples?"

"What's Leopold's role in this?" Falkingham asked.

"He's compiling a list of people who recall the 1954 murder," Streeter explained. "Hopefully there are very few left. Those who do, he'll talk with to determine if they remember enough to be a threat, and if so, put them under surveillance in case the fugitives approach them."

"What about Waddill's family?" Harrington asked.

"Thus far, there's no indication they know where he is."

"How do we know Harvey or the kids aren't on their way to Minnesota?" Mann asked.

Chapman replied, "If a subject resembling any of the three sets foot within a fifty-mile radius of Snow Peak, we'll know immediately."

"We should also keep the White House insulated from this mess," Lamp reminded them.

Harrington nodded. "I assure you, neither Longbridge nor anyone on his staff has the slightest suspicion of what these three are up to. The sooner we stop them, the better our chances of keeping it that way."

"It's not just Longbridge." Falkingham snuffed out another Dunhill. "Don't forget the Senate investigation that's just begun. As we speak, those who oppose Greg's nomination are putting a microscope to every detail of his life. The media's doing the same."

Harrington grimaced. "We must never allow a connection to be made between the fugitives and our mission. The first hint may create a snowball effect we'll be unable to stop."

"Nevertheless, we'll be prepared," Streeter replied. "Should it become necessary, we're formulating a response to charges of a connection between the Longbridge Administration and the crisis we've been addressing these last nine days - one implicating Mendelsohn, Harvey and the fugitives in an elaborate criminal conspiracy, the details of which are being manufactured now. Actually, it's the same one used to explain Swanson's suicide. We're just expanding it to connect the others."

Harrington offered a rare smile. "Thomas, it's refreshing to see you thinking ahead for a change. If the public accepted the explanation once, it should again, with the proper embellishments. Let's just pray we don't have to use it."

"But we will, Chairman, once Harvey's found," Streeter replied.

"Not necessarily. The response you and Larry are working on is very promising, but also dangerous. If, when the time comes, a safer one will work as well, we'll use it."

"What's the situation with Harvey, anyway?" Mann asked.

"He's vanished without a trace," Chapman replied. "There's been no contact with any known associates, friends or family, all of whom have been questioned. Neither have his office or Long Island home turned up any leads. But the investigation's less than forty-eight hours old. Clues will surface."

"What about his bank accounts?" Lamp asked.

"He cleaned them out; close to eighty grand, we estimate."

Falkingham laughed. "That kind of money could make him hard to find for a while. He's a shrewd SOB. I'll give him that."

"Why applaud a man whose resourcefulness could bury you?" Harrington asked. "Anyone else want to praise the foresight of our slippery adversary?" He studied their grim faces. "I didn't think so. Sorry Chase, you're a one-man peanut gallery as usual."

The day had begun with Corelli and Waddill trapped in Naples. Exuberant, he'd waited for news of their capture, but instead learned to his horror that they'd escaped. An hour later, he'd been on a plane to Dulles. The long day was now ending with this Georgetown meeting. Grimly summarizing their dilemma, he asked, "Am I the only one to see the irony?"

"What irony?" Streeter asked.

"That while our vast resources permit us to chase these three albatrosses across the country, watch their families, blanket the roads and seal off states, there's one point we can't seal off."

"What point, Chairman?"

"The one where lies a ticking bomb with enough explosive power to destroy us all. Crenshaw's blessed chest. We can't seal it off because we don't know where it is!"

"We'll find it, Chairman, we will."

"If not," he sighed, "we may all very likely burn in hell."

CHAPTER NINETEEN

★

"Tyler, who is Kara? Please tell me."
The sheen of his nightmare dried and his breath misted the arctic air as he found the cabin's pine walls, bureaus, counters and chairs. Everything in this strange world seemed made of pine. "This must be the coldest goddamned place on earth."

Her head rested on the pillow as she studied him. "One of the highest anyway. Was she a lover?"

"Let's discuss you instead." He turned to acknowledge her inquisitive eyes. "I've been patient to wait this long."

"I've been patient, you mean! Now who is she?"

He sighed. It didn't take her long to rekindle the embers of exasperation. "A girl."

"*Madonna mia*, what a revelation!" She jerked the covers around her neck. "She must've dumped you."

"She didn't dump me." He yanked the covers back over his chilled body.

"Yes, she did. That's why you won't discuss her."

"Let's go back to sleep," he sighed.

"No." Folding her arms corpselike, she glared holes in the pine ceiling.

"Mayson, I'm cold."

"Who cares?"

Drawing her back in his arms, they slept again.

Kara didn't chase him from the darkness this time. He woke instead to the lengthening shadows on the cabin walls, the arctic air. He pulled on his jeans and reached for his football jersey, only to recall it was now hers. Throwing on his gray sweater instead, he went to the window as she still slept in the bed behind him. Four o'clock and night was already falling over the mountains, the bare trees rattling in a chilling breeze. Lou might call this place Rocky Peak. He called it Arctic Hell. But they couldn't be more isolated and therefore, safe for the time being. Iron Ridge, the closest town, was eight miles down the mountain. And this was Flavin County, not Pine, which bordered it to the west.

He turned as she stirred. "Hungry?"

Rubbing the fuzz from her eyes, she nodded.

"Get dressed and we'll pay our respects to Ma and Pa Kettle. Maybe wangle a dinner invitation."

Minutes later they started across the deserted camp, a hodgepodge of cabins, stables, lodge and clearing for games and ceremonies. The Adkins cabin was at the opposite end, leading into the camp. The couple waited at the front window as they approached. "Look very satisfied," he whispered.

"What?"

"We're on our honeymoon. How else would my wife look?"

Before she could swat back, Lou opened the door. "Where the dickens are your coats? Don't you know its fifteen degrees out there?"

"And I can feel each one," he nodded. "Lucy?"

"Exhilarating, dear."

Stoop-shouldered Earl appeared in his faded overalls. His glasses were bottle-bottom thick, his bushy hair, snow white. "Bob, why ain't you got your coat on? Don't you know it's cold outside?"

"Told you he don't hear nuthin,'" Lou sighed. "Don't remember nuthin' either, like that tar jack. Can y'all stay for supper?"

"Great," he nodded. "If you're sure you have enough."

They soon sat over a meal of smoked ham, black-eyed peas, steamed cabbage and corn bread. Mayson had never seen such food, but ate everything, as did Tyler, she noted with satisfaction. He'd lost weight with their ordeal, his ribs more pronounced, his face thinner. A pleasant warmth settled over her as he shouted his stories into Earl's ear, then winked at Lou when forced to repeat something. By meal's end, both host and hostess were huddled around him. Poor Lou was obviously smitten as she giggled and blushed profusely. "Bob Compton, ain't you a darn mess! How do you come up with such nonsense?"

His nonsense was nothing more than current events, enriched by his wonderful sense of humor. Like his beloved circus clowns, Mayson thought, he reveled in others' laughter. But was his glow genuine or did it mask a deep, inner sadness? Yes, she sensed now, as she had that morning in his apartment, and again wondered how it was possible that he, with so much to live for, had risked his life to save a cold, ungrateful shrew? But was she that shrew any longer? Wasn't she beginning to feel good about herself?

Her reflections were shattered by Tyler shouting, "Earl, how do you get news up here?"

"Mews?" the old man squinted. "We ain't got no mews - doves and sparrows mostly. A few owls at night and them damn pigeons. 'Cept you don't want to put them in mews. Just shoot the ornery..."

"He said 'news,' you old fool!" Lou yelled.

"Oh, news," he shrugged. "Well now, we get the Knoxville paper. And there's the Sunbeam radio Lou's cousin, Wally, give us last Christmas. And that confounded machine." He nodded at the ancient TV. "At least when it has a hankerin' to work."

"We don't miss nuthin' up here," Lou added. "Jimmy Dale tells us all we need to know. He's the mail carrier for these parts. He was here this mornin' same as every other. But I reckon y'all was too busy to notice his jeep." She winked.

"Anything interesting going on?" Tyler asked.

"Nuthin' but them doin's over in Pine County. Jimmy says the place is crawling with John Laws looking for them two New York outlaws. Don't know why they'd be hiding in Pine, of all places."

Mayson's eyes connected with his. "Lou, did you tell Jimmy Dale about us?"

"Course, Lucy. I told him how Bob here fixed my tar and how nice you two was to be foolin' with an old woman, just after gettin' hitched."

"How about us staying here?"

"Sure did. But that's all. I figgered you wanted your privacy. Ain't none of his business nohow."

"And we'd like to keep it that way," Tyler winked.

"You devil!" she giggled, then remembered her baking pie.

Over coffee and dessert, they received their standing invitation to the Adkins' table. "Colonel Masters overstocks the mess hall every year," Lou explained. "It's more'n enough to feed us plumb through spring." She gave them each a Camp Eagle's Nest sweatshirt. "I noticed you ain't used the farplace yet. There ain't no heat in the cabin, so don't be bashful about startin' a far tonight. Otherwise you'll freeze your fannies off." Hugging them, she remained at the door as they disappeared into the trees.

Back in the cabin, Tyler started a fire. "I thought it would create suspicion. Not having one creates more, I guess we just learned."

Shivering, she put the camp sweatshirt on over her sweater. "You'll get no argument from me. Do you think Lou will keep her word and not tell that mail carrier any more about us?"

"I think we're safe as long as they don't get too curious about the 'doings' over in Pine County."

After a while the fire blazed and they roasted themselves with quiet satisfaction. "I was really proud of you tonight," he said. "You were gracious and friendly. And don't think I missed your smile."

"I hope not," her eyes lifted. "You were its inspiration."

He studied her as the warmth rose. After scores of forgettable women, here was one finally with a face and lips that made him hunger again for life's sweetness. Yet she couldn't replace Kara . . . or was he afraid she could? The question was more than unsettling; it was dangerous. Their survival depended on many things, clear thinking being one. "We'll stay as long as circumstances permit. But we need to be prepared to leave when the time comes."

"And how do we prepare?"

"Tomorrow I'll ask Lou to drive me into Iron Ridge to do some shopping. Be thinking about what we need. In the meantime," he sighed. "I guess we should dig into those records we risked our asses to get."

There were several thousand pages of petitions, orders, exhibits, depositions and briefs, which measured by their sheer volume should - if there was any justice - contain at least one clue to Morris's murder. The review proved a tedious exercise, with documents scoured and notes jotted. Taking breaks to call Harvey, he hung up, grumbling each time, and then to Mayson's increasing irritation, paced restlessly by the fire. "Why is some chirpy woman answering Harvey's phone? He never mentioned a girlfriend."

"*Madonna mia*, why don't you just leave a message?"

"Shit, what if he gave us the wrong number?"

"And what if you took it down wrong? If you'd left a message, we'd have an explanation by now, instead of wasting precious time with your stupid suppositions!"

"Goddamnit." He paced. "It must be the right . . ."

"Stop! Either get over here and help or take your mad rambling outside and share it with the trees."

Grumbling, he crawled back beside her with a fresh stack of records. "That's my boy." She reached for his hand.

Another hour passed. Despairingly, Tyler gazed at the remaining records, then at Mayson beside him, a statue of intensity as she absorbed an endless stream of documents. "I guess that's how you made straight A's at Columbia."

Her large, dark eyes lifted. "How did you know that?"

"Lamp; he thinks you're pretty awesome. Me, I just can't believe you're human. How can you sit so still, digesting one document after another? You haven't been off that bed in three hours."

"You do what you have to," she shrugged.

"No, Mayson, *you* do what lesser creatures can't."

"Then you're saying I'm special?"

"I guess that's exactly what I'm saying."

Her eyes fell to the deposition in her lap. "I never wanted to be special, just happy."

"And you were. But something happened. What?"

"Why do you want to know?" she asked.

"Because I care about you, Mayson."

"I . . . care about you, too." She knew what this meant for her, no clue for him. "You're not happy either, Tyler, I know that."

"Then make me happy. Share your past. Is it really that difficult to discuss?"

"It's far more difficult to escape."

"Are you afraid I won't understand?"

Not *understand*. She was afraid he'd leave and she'd have to wait anxiously by another door. The realization was terrifying. "Please Tyler, I'm just not ready. Now let's review what we have." She scanned her notes. "Jasper Crenshaw served as Pine County Sheriff for forty-two years. Widowed, he then retired to Naples, where he died four years later."

"Interesting," he sighed. "And totally unimportant."

"Be patient. His estate was valued at ten million dollars. That's certainly important."

"And something we already know."

"We didn't know his executor, Phillip Rothenberg, was given the power to designate the charitable institution to receive his large estate."

"So Crenshaw hated his kids," he said. "Maybe they were deadbeats, or didn't visit him on Christmas. Or perhaps it was something really earth-shaking like not taking out the trash."

"Will you be serious?" She returned to her notes. "Now, Rothenberg wasted no time in designating the Hope Mountain School in Pine County to receive the estate. Certainly this had been prearranged, although Rothenberg denies it in his deposition. Why the secrecy?" she wondered. "If Crenshaw wanted to benefit this school, why not just leave the estate outright, instead of hiding his intentions behind Rothenberg? Tell me that's not an important question, one I'm sure Morris could answer, if he was alive."

"Answering it most likely is what got him killed."

"Then are we crazy to be attempting the same thing?"

"Hardly," he sighed. "If answering that question can kill us, it may also be the only thing that keeps us alive. So what do we know about the Hope Mountain School?"

She scanned her notes again. "It's an institution for mentally disabled children, founded thirty-four years ago by a woman named Lativia Norris. Until Crenshaw's bequest, the school existed on private endowments and special grants from the state of Tennessee. By virtue of the bequest, it's now guaranteed a perpetual existence."

He considered the other implications. "It also means Crenshaw's kids must work for a living unless they overturn the will. And assuming none are mentally disabled, what is Norris's connection to all this?"

She dug back into her notes. "Mrs. Norris is a sixty-eight-year-old widow with a mentally disabled child, Edgar Jr., who's now forty-nine and a self-employed carpenter."

"Living proof of the success of his mother's school," he nodded. "But what's her connection to Crenshaw?"

"I haven't found it yet."

With a renewed interest, he reached for more records. She smiled. "May I have some too, please?"

By midnight they'd finished, pages of fresh notes accumulated in the process. "At least we now know Lativia's connection to Crenshaw," Tyler said as he slumped back wearily.

The will contest Morris had filed on the children's behalf alleged that Lativia Norris had exerted undue influence over Crenshaw in his last months, a period in which declining health made him particularly vulnerable. It was her relentless pressure, the suit charged, that had resulted in his execution of a new will just weeks before his death. There were voluminous exhibits to support the charge, including Lativia's raging epistles in which she blamed Crenshaw for her husband's execution for a crime he hadn't committed, something Crenshaw had known when testifying at the trial forty years before. The trial concerned the rape and murder of a female student at Tennessee State University, where Edgar Norris had been employed as a maintenance man. She'd been white, Norris black, not an auspicious circumstance, considering the trial's setting: predominantly white backwoods Tennessee in the early sixties.

But had the all-white jury sent the wrong man to the electric chair, as his widow claimed? If so, who had committed the crime? Crenshaw had been the chief prosecution witness in the circumstantial case, a credible one, given the guilty verdict. But had he known Norris was innocent? Why else leave his estate to a school founded by the man's widow? Years of appeals had followed, until finally Norris had been strapped into the electric chair and the switch flipped.

Lativia's correspondence war had endured the next four decades, intensifying sharply in the months preceding Crenshaw's death. Her last letters were filled with biblical prophecies to prove Crenshaw would burn in hell for his sins. Certainly her assault had taken a toll on the cancer-ravaged man, as he crept closer to the grave. *Sheriff, you lied on that witness stand!* She charged. *If you don't recall your palm on that courtroom Bible, God does! He remembers everything . . . People must pay for the pain they cause, if not under Tennessee law then under God's. And you'll pay soon, you wicked monster, He'll see to it!*

"Crenshaw's bequest to Lativia's School is an admission of guilt," Tyler said. "Unfortunately, her assault may also provide the undue influence necessary to throw the will out."

"So are we thinking the same thing?" Mayson asked.

"If you're wondering who, other than Norris, might have committed that murder forty years ago."

"A fellow student?" she mused. "Or three? If my math is right, they'd be in their mid-sixties now."

"Mann and Falkingham are sixty-six."

"So is Lamp. They could've been graduate students. TSU has a law school."

"Falkingham's degrees are from South Carolina. Mann went to Purdue, Northwestern for law."

"Lamp's Bachelor's is from Bucknell, his law degree, NYU." Mayson gazed at the fire's dying embers. "So when and where did their paths cross?"

"It could've been anywhere," Tyler sighed. "A bar convention, wedding, funeral, the airport . . ."

"TSU." Her spine shivered. "We can't be sure they weren't there. One thing we do know: they're good friends and have been for a long time."

"We also know something else. Crenshaw's cover-up, if that's the case, didn't come cheaply. The real murderer, or murderers, must've been forced to pay some serious money."

"Ten million is definitely serious," she nodded.

"So is this new theory we're building. Making Crenshaw a millionaire would've been easy for our trio's wealthy families."

"So what's next?" she asked.

"Have Harvey find out if we're on the right track." Trying the agent again, Tyler quickly dropped the phone in frustration.

"Don't say it!"

"What, that you should've left a message?"

"Why do I bother asking? I should know by now you do what you please."

Her glare followed him across the cabin. "I hate it when you get this way."

"Then don't get me this way."

"Don't blame your grouchy moods on me!" she shouted.

Stuffing the records back in the box, he shoved it under the bed. "Did it ever occur to you that this Madelyn Stump might be a Fed herself? For all we know, they've found Harvey and expropriated his number, just hoping we'd be stupid enough to call and leave a message: 'Hi, this is Tyler and Mayson. We're on some God-forsaken Tennessee mountaintop!'"

His ridicule bruised her, yet he seemed indifferent to it as he wrestled out of his sweater and slung it on the chair. "I thought you cared about me, Tyler," she said.

"I do care." He finished undressing.

"If you did, you wouldn't treat me this way. I guess you just didn't mean it."

His eyes hardened. "I don't say things I don't mean."

"Of course you do. All men do."

Striding into the bathroom, he quickly swung back out, toothbrush pointed. "I won't be drawn into another tantrum, so just save the theatrical posturing."

She became conscious now of her stiffly folded arms and pouting lips. "You also didn't mean it when you said I was beautiful!"

"It won't work." He swung back out again. "And I mean everything I say."

"Tyler, why aren't you attracted to me?"

"Did you say something?" he asked as he gargled mouthwash.

"I said: Why aren't you attracted to me?"

Again he swung out, jangling a piece of dental floss. "This is precisely the way you do it."

"What — floss your teeth?"

"Suck me into your tantrums. You ask a question based on a false assumption: why am I not attracted to you? But who said I wasn't?"

"Tyler, we've been sleeping in the same bed for a week and not once have you tried to kiss me."

"Yes I have and been censured twice."

"Those weren't kisses! A kiss is on the lips."

The bathroom glass clinked on the counter. "What difference does its location make?"

"In this case, that you're not attracted to me. Otherwise you would've tried to kiss me like you have every other woman on the planet." She sighed. "I'm afraid your nefarious reputation explains far more than your words just how you feel."

Her arrogance now drew him from the bathroom. "I said you were beautiful and I meant it."

"Stop saying things you don't mean."

"Goddamnit, read my lips: You're beautiful."

"Then why don't you want to kiss me?"

With an exasperation only she could ignite, he swept her up and kissed her with a fierce satisfaction.

CHAPTER TWENTY

★

Mayson woke to the gray morning, the fire's soft popping, the crisp scent of burning wood . . . and the sweet memory of last night's kiss. How had Stephen, given complete authority over her, tapped but a thimbleful of passion when Tyler, with just a kiss, had opened the floodgates of paradise? It was the kiss she hadn't dreamed possible. And when it ended, he'd looked her squarely in the eyes. "Let the record reflect that you've been officially kissed."

They'd gone to bed then; him to sleep, her to spend the next hours trying to grasp what had happened. It was something wonderful, yet dangerous; something sweet, yet probably disappointing. Turning, she found his abandoned pillow and a note which read: *I've gone for a walk by the lake.* So she'd know where he was. *I won't be long.* So she wouldn't worry. *I started a fire.* So the cabin would be warm when she woke. She put the note down and closed her eyes.

He returned from his hike, invigorated. The cabin was toasty, the shower running. Reaching for the phone, he froze at the strange sounds coming from the bathroom. She emerged to find him gazing out the window. "I didn't know you were back," she said.

Turning, his eyes fell to her slender legs, bared to the panties' lace where they molded into exquisitely rounded hips. Her delicate shape did more than stimulate his senses. It seemed to solve their mystery, touching chords deep inside him.

"Thanks for starting the fire," she blushed. "How was the lake?"

"Deep."

"Don't tell me you took a swim?"

"Let's say it *looks* deep."

"Maybe we can we take another walk later." She pulled on her slacks, then brushed her damp hair. "Tyler, you're being so quiet. Something's on your mind."

"You were singing in the shower."

"Oh . . . And do I have a good voice?"

"It moves me," he replied. "But what does that prove?"

That nothing else matters, she thought.

"That song," he said. "I've never heard it before."

"That's because it's old — and very Italian. A Dean Martin classic." She offered another verse. "Non dimenticar means don't forget you are my darling . . ."

"Go on," he insisted, until she'd rendered every verse.

"You really like it, don't you?" she marveled.

"Enough to imagine buying a Dean Martin CD."

She laughed. "It was our song. We used to sing . . ."

"Who is 'we'? A boyfriend?"

"It doesn't matter," she shrugged.

"The fact that you won't tell me proves it matters a great deal."

"I don't want to talk about it. And I don't owe you an explanation anyway," she yelled as she dashed out.

"Damnit Mayson, come back here!" He followed her down to the lake. Gazing over the water, she refused to acknowledge him as his arms wrapped around her waist, his chin dropping in her hair. Quiet seconds drifted as they enjoyed the beauty of their strange, new world: the silvery lake, the crisp air so still they could hear the wind sigh, the trees creak, and every rustle and crawl of life. They could hear their own thoughts, and for an instant, imagine the towering mountains sealed them off from the threatening world.

He followed an eagle's glide across the gray sky - Eagles Nest, the camp's name. "You're going to tell me. Why not now?"

"Because I'm not ready," she replied.

"When will you be?"

She turned sharply. "When will you?"

"And what do you assume I have to say?"

Her eyes gleamed impatiently. "Tyler, don't you think I know that behind your quick smile and easy manner is a deep sadness? One that draws you to the window, pains your eyes, and expresses itself in everything you say or do. *Madonna mia*, it's even driven you to create a museum of souvenir posters!"

He'd been foolish to allow her so close, he realized now as she scratched on the private chamber holding Kara. Releasing her, his eyes drifted away.

"Then you're not ready either, I see."

"I guess not." He started back up the slope.

Following, she reached him at the top. "I'm surprised you haven't mentioned last night. I guess you'll want to kiss me again, now that I've stupidly set the precedent."

He smiled. "Would you mind?"

"You're not supposed to ask."

As he kissed her, her arms slid up around his neck, her mouth eagerly meeting his. Like the first, this kiss was a fresh discovery, his warmth flowing sweetly through her, melting the world away. Breaking it first, he left her mouth still hungering, her eyes smoldering. "I guess we've missed breakfast," he sighed. "Let's go see about leftovers."

Retrieving his cap and shades from their cabin, he rejoined her for the hike across the camp. "Since you haven't provided a shopping list, I'll improvise. That is, if Lou will take me to Iron Ridge."

Thinking quickly, she rattled off items as they descended the knoll: "Shampoo, toothpaste and hand cream. This cold weather is drying out my skin. And some nail polish — any dark red will do. And I guess you've already thought of gloves. And don't forget you need a coat. Maybe some thermal . . ."

"Wait a minute!" He spun sharply. "I can't remember all that!"

"I'll write it down at the Adkins. What's your excuse for not driving the Prelude?"

They froze suddenly at the sight of Lou talking with a man in front of her cabin. His Jeep left no doubt about his identity. "Jimmy Dale!" Mayson gasped.

As they watched, Lou's suspicious gaze drifted up to their cabin. Soon Earl ambled out to join them. A ridiculous pantomime then followed — Earl's cupped ear, Dale's shout, Earl's shrug, Dale's shout, Lou's scowl and flapping arms. Finally Dale returned to his Jeep and left. Tyler nodded at Earl's blank expression. "I still don't think he got it."

"Got *what* is the question," Mayson said.

"I suppose there's no choice but to find out." He continued down the knoll.

As Earl met them at the cabin door minutes later, Mayson asked, "Was that your mail carrier, Jimmy Dale?"

"Mail?" He squinted. "Jimmy Dale just brung it. You two expectin' something?"

Lou appeared, her eyes and hands restless. "Figgerin' on some breakfast, I reckon?"

"Earl was just telling us Jimmy Dale brought the mail," Tyler said. "Anything new from Bayou country?"

"Nuthin' like that, Bob. Sit down and I'll warm you up some leftovers." She shuffled off to the kitchen. As Earl drifted back out, they exchanged grave glances. She knew. But what had she told Dale? She soon returned with their plates, joining them at the table.

"Lou, you're spoiling us." Tyler beamed at the fluffy biscuits and gravy. "And grits? They're Lucy's favorite," he explained, as Mayson studied the creamy puddle on her plate.

"There's a heap more if your skinny bride can finish that pile on her plate."

As Mayson turned her first shade of green, Tyler stated his request. "I reckon I can do that," Lou nodded. "We need some things at Callahan's Hardware anyway."

As she went to get ready, he said, "She's either taking me shopping or to jail. We'll know which pretty soon."

"Tyler, don't go."

"If we've reached the end of the road, going to Iron Ridge won't make a difference."

"It will to me. I might never see you again."

"Why are you so upset?" He smiled at her plate. "I got you out of that second pile of grits."

Lou returned wearing a floppy hat and tattered coat. On the way out, Mayson stopped to study the pictures cluttering the shelves. Some were of a little boy, a larger boy and finally a young man, his features blunted, his eyes dull. "Earl, Jr.," Lou explained.

"So . . . I mean where . . . "

"He's dead, Lucy, if that's what's got you so tongue-tied. A drunk driver kilt him back in '75."

"Oh Lou, I'm so sorry!" she exclaimed.

"You were living here at the camp?" Tyler asked.

She nodded, "Fore that we lived over in Pine County."

"How old was Earl, Jr. when he died?" Mayson asked.

"Nineteen," she frowned. "Damn near kilt Earl and me, too. Almost lost him at birth. Fool doctors didn't know what they was doing. That's when I started midwifin'. Figgered I could spare other women what I went through."

"So he was injured at birth?" Mayson asked.

"Can't prove how it happened. All I know is he never was like them others. He weren't no retard or nuthin, just slow in the head. But not enough he didn't know he was diffrn't. He had no confidence in hisself. We could hardly get him out of the house. That special school changed all that. We boarded him when he was twelve. Shoulda' done it sooner, only Earl was too stubborn to admit his boy was diffrn't. Earl, Jr. done real good at that school. Them teachers learn't him what no one else could; to believe in hisself. When he left at eighteen, he was full growed in every sense of the word; even had a girlfriend.

"Just a week 'fore he was kilt, he got a job pumping gas at Bernie Larkin's station down in Iron Ridge. He was real excited. Me and Earl was just thankful for that school and the wonderful lady who runs it — Lativia Norris, a saintly woman. I don't give a darn what color she is."

Mayson glanced at Tyler. "Would that be the Hope Mountain School, the one that just received the huge private endowment?"

"If that means a big mess of money, it is sure 'nuff. Folks like Earl and me think it was long overdue, too."

"Why is that?" Mayson asked.

" 'Cuz Jasper Crenshaw owed it to Lativia. The old coot never was no good in my book, even if the rest of Pine County kissed his feet. That sheriff's badge made him the Big Daddy and he didn't let nobody forget it. He bullied people, 'specially when he was drinkin'. Jasper was a big drinker; gambler, too. Only he didn't let nobody else do it unless he was invited. He was crooked as hell. How else you figger he piled up all that money? Only decent thing he ever done was leaving it to Lativia instead of his no-count kids."

"Why did he owe Lativia Norris so much money?" Tyler asked.

She studied him carefully now. "That's real important to you, is it? Well I reckon there ain't no reason not to tell you what folks in these parts already know. Those who weren't on that Pine County jury forty years ago, anyway. Most think Lativia's husband, Edgar, didn't kill that white girl they executed him for. Just 'cuz he did maintenance work over at that university and talked to her on occasion don't mean he's the one who kilt her. But Crenshaw and that county attorney he carried around in his hip pocket tried to twist everythin' into somethin' it wasn't. If you ask me," she said, "it was one of them sex-crazed boys. Most were spoiled brats who thought all their rich daddies had to do was write a check to bail 'em out of trouble. And I reckon maybe that's what happened in this case."

"The university you're talking about is TSU?" Mayson asked.

Lou nodded. "Fanciest school I ever heard of. They say if you want to be a lawyer or judge, there ain't no better place to go. Don't know why they put it in Pine County, but personally I'd just as soon they'd put it somewhere's else. Them college kids think they're better than other folks. Call us townies, as if we should be ashamed of ourselves."

As she left to tell Earl good-bye, Mayson followed Tyler out to the truck. He looked like a handsome redneck in his cap, gold hair tumbling over his ears, the shades hiding his magnificent blue eyes. As he slipped behind the wheel, she gripped his arm, "Tyler, please be careful."

"I will, darlin'." He grinned as a huffing Lou hopped in beside him. "You ready?"

"Ready as I ever will be, I reckon."

Lou clammed up again as they rattled down the mountain, her eyes glued to the window. They'd almost reached Iron Ridge when a patrol car passed in the opposite direction. Instinctively Tyler clenched the wheel. "Them John Laws scare you, do they?" she asked now. "You want to tell me somethin, Bob? Or's that your real name?"

He smiled. "What else would it be?"

"Oh, maybe one that'd snap them John Laws' heads over in Pine." She nodded at his cap and glasses. "You figger that disguise will keep 'em from recognizing you? And that Jap car? Hunnerd-to-one says it starts just fine."

"Come on Lou, you don't . . ." His eyes fell to the pistol in her hand.

"Don't what, Bob? Believe you and Lucy's the pair them John Laws are looking for? Jimmy Dale says you're dangerous, but knowin' you somehow makes that hard to believe."

They reached the town limits. Heading where, some Mayberry-like jail? He must make her understand. "Now Lou, I don't know what Dale said, but trust your sharp senses that told you I wasn't dangerous. And I bet they're also telling you I'm not a crook. So how . . ." His eyes widened on the mirror as a patrol car now closed in.

"Pull over," she ordered. "You've got some explainin' to do and there ain't no better time."

The crisp mountain air soon relieved Mayson's anxiety. As she strolled by the lake, resounding fear became the calm voice of reason, then finally the whisper of reflection. Stopping at the spot where Tyler had kissed her that morning, she closed her eyes to indulge another playback of the moment. How easy to push away the world's clutter in a place like this, where there was no sound but the occasional dapple of a fish, a chirping bird, the wind's gentle brush over the mountains. Not disruptions to her thoughts, but pleasant refrains. How she'd changed! And in the quiet refrain, her heart echoed, *I know*.

She returned to the cabin later with pinkened cheeks, misting breath and an exuberance she'd never known. Starting a fresh fire, her eyes drifted restlessly. How empty the world had become without him. How dreadfully quiet. He was returning, wasn't he? Her gaze stopped on the door. If she believed in him, she must also have faith in this new door and know that if she waited long enough, he'd come through it. If it was within his power - if he wasn't dead. Fear glistened in her eyes.

The trip down the mountain, the shopping, the return trip; how long should it all take? Three hours? They'd been gone for four. She wanted to cry but called Harvey instead. Madelyn Stump's recorded voice greeted her. Taking a deep breath, she said, "This is Deborah from the airport. I just wanted to let you know the scallops at your friend's restaurant . . ."

"Don't give me that bull." A man came on. As the line's silence deepened, he said, "It's me, kid, don't worry. Where the hell have you two been? I thought I would've heard from you by now."

"We've tried," Mayson replied. "Only Tyler wouldn't leave a message."

"But you figured it was worth the risk," Harvey laughed. "So'd you make it to Tennessee like the world assumes?"

"Flavin County. It borders Pine, although I can't recall on which side."

"It wouldn't mean crap to me anyway. You're close to the target, that's what matters."

"Who's Madelyn Stump?" she asked.

"An old friend, only that's not her real name. Anyway, that's another story. Listen kid, in case you're not following the news, the Feds and their John Law sidekicks have canvassed your Redneck Paradise. The clock's ticking. Get what you can and get out."

" 'John Laws' — that's what Lou calls them."

"Who the hell is Lou?"

She explained the circumstances that had brought them to Eagles Nest. "It was safe until this morning, when we think the mail carrier put a bug in Lou's ear. Tyler's in town with her now getting supplies."

Harvey sighed. "Let's just pray the carrier's bug didn't include the one hundred grand reward. I assume you got your hands on those probate records?"

"A boxful," she confirmed, now summarizing its contents: the Norris murder case, Lativia's letter campaign and Crenshaw's bequest to the Hope Mountain School.

"You're hoping one, or possibly all three jurists, attended TSU at the time of the girl's murder?"

"Their ages fit chronologically. And their families were wealthy enough to buy Crenshaw's silence. That is, if you can imagine them raping and murdering a defenseless young woman."

"We're talking forty years ago," he replied. "A man's hormones don't incite him at sixty like they do at twenty. They could've gotten drunk, done something stupid and then killed her to cover it up."

Restlessly, her eyes drifted to the window. How long could it take to buy supplies in a small town like Iron Ridge? Certainly they should've been back by now. "If our theory's valid, the trio's attendance at TSU would've likely ended with the girl's murder."

"And the records destroyed," he added. "So thoroughly they didn't surface in either Falkingham's or Mann's confirmations."

"So far, no one's had a reason to ask about TSU."

"It's no problem to check out. I have a few contacts left."

Her gaze returned to the window. Had Lou turned Tyler in? Had someone else spotted him? She asked, "Can you get us new identities?"

Harvey laughed. "Real flashes in the pan, those Cartwrights. They're suddenly liabilities just like Corelli and Waddill. The IDs won't be a problem," he confirmed. "How's the money holding out?"

"Tyler's loaded." Her eyes were glued to the empty lane. But was he coming back?

"Don't worry." Harvey sensed her fear. "He'll be back. Now give me your new mailing address." Jotting it down, he grabbed his notes. "So you wanna hear what I've got?"

"Of course." Her eyes watched the lane with growing fear.

"I got access to the NYPD's files through a remaining contact. Duke's one thorough sonofabitch, thank God. Anyway, let's start with the Outer Banks call Mendelsohn received from Crenshaw's nephew, Dale Markham. He lives in Snow Peak, a little Minnesota ice-hole. We can assume their conversation was serious, given that hours later Mendelsohn was on a flight to St. Paul. He took a rental car to Snow Peak, checking into the Norsemen's Lodge, where he stayed two nights. On Saturday he returned to St. Paul, boarded a flight to La Guardia but got off instead at O'Hare and returned to Minnesota. Duluth this time. He returned to New York the next morning."

"What did he do in Snow Peak and Duluth?" she asked.

"Spent a lot of time with Markham and his cousin, Ford Crenshaw, one of the Sheriff's shafted kids, who flew in from California at the same time. Something big was up, no question."

"But do we know what they did, where they went?

Anything?"

"Duke asked the same questions but got nowhere. Crenshaw and Markham claimed their discussions were protected by the attorney-client privilege. Any idea where they got that line?"

"Lamp, no doubt," she replied.

"Probably, but also the firm partner who flew to Snow Peak after Mendelsohn's murder. A guy named Demetrius Colonna."

"There's no partner by that name."

"No kidding. And you'd remember this big, ugly sonofabitch. Six-six, glass eye and Igor limp?"

"Leopold was in Snow Peak!" she gasped.

"Telling Crenshaw and Markham to keep their mouths shut, no doubt. Coming from a guy like him, I'm sure they took the advice to heart."

"Duke didn't press the issue?"

"Why should he? Minnesota wasn't important when he had you right there in Manhattan." Scanning his notes, he added, "I've also got phone records documenting Mendelsohn's and Lamp's calls through the weekend. Lamp explains these as 'pressing firm business.' The last nuggets don't come from Duke's files, but my own. Specifically the phone records from Lamp's Westchester home, which reflect numerous calls that Sunday — to Mendelsohn's apartment, Harrington's Houston office, and a certain Manhattan hotel Leopold uses. I guess it takes a lot of hot air to arrange a murder. So what do you think, kid?"

"That our next stop is Snow Peak, Minnesota."

"An army will be waiting," he warned. "You won't be able to get anywhere near . . ."

Lou's battered truck suddenly rattled up the lane. "Tyler's back!" Mayson shouted as she dropped the phone, burst from the cabin, and flew down the knoll. As she approached the Adkins cabin, Lou squirmed out of the truck with her bags. Rushing towards her, Mayson quickly froze, then ducked behind the closest tree as a patrol car glided up the lane. Where was Tyler? Horrified, she watched Lou greet the trooper, their solemn gazes soon drifting up to the fugitives' cabin. He started towards it. Lou's laughter stopped him. He shrugged and retraced his steps. Playfully smacking his arm, Lou started into a long-winded tale.

Mayson remained pressed to the tree until the trooper returned to his car and left. Then she rushed forward again.

"Well, I'll be darn!" Lou spun around. "I thought you'd locked yourself in the cabin. Wouldn't done no good though, if you seen what just happened. Clark darn near talked hisself into believin' you two was up there. It took some fast jawin' to convince him you weren't."

"Where's Tyler?" Mayson asked.

"You mean Bob, don't you? Why he's . . ."

They turned as an ancient VW Beetle suddenly rattled up the lane. Jumping out, Tyler's grin quickly vanished as Mayson charged him. "You scared me!" she thrashed viciously, a tearful spasm ending with her arms wrapped tightly around his neck.

"I didn't mean to." He held her. "You know that."

"Why should I? Give me one good reason."

"There," he nodded proudly at the Beetle. "It's for you."

She scowled at the dent-riddled car. "And what am I supposed to do with this German jalopy?"

"Drive it, you darn fool." Lou answered.

"I've never driven a stick shift."

"I'll teach you," he said. "It's not hard, is it Lou?"

"Shucks no." She marveled at them in a lazy embrace. "I declare, if you two really ain't married, you should be the way you carry on."

"No, we shouldn't," Mayson fretted. "No husband would scare his wife like Tyler just did to me, and then apologize by giving her a German jalopy she doesn't even know how to drive." She realized now that their names had changed. "Lou, then you really won't turn us in?"

"I'd be a liar if I said I wasn't figgerin' to do just that when Darrell Pamplin stopped in his Big Blue Top. Only that's when Tyler here done some mighty fast jawin' at the end of my pistol." She laughed. "And they say I can flap my jaws. You shoulda' heard this charmer's silver tongue. It was a skippin' and a dancin' like you wouldn't believe as he swore y'all didn't kill nobody, same as Edgar Norris didn't kill that girl, which he said was why you was in Tennessee - to help Lativia prove it. And hell, Lucy, or Mayson, I reckon it is. I couldn't argue with that. Which led to my next question, 'cept I couldn't get it out 'fore he was a tapshoin' again about who really done the murderin' - them big Washington judges, when they was rich kids at the University.

"He said y'all was sure they done it but that knowin' and provin' was two diffrn't things. And hell, I couldn't argue with that point, no more'n the next. That the provin' wouldn't get done if you two was sittin' in jail, or worse, gettin' yourself kilt, which he said would happen if I turned him over to Darrell Pamplin, whose big nose was pressin' against the window by then. So you're I-talian, are you?" She squinted at Mayson now. "Never seen one with blond hair. Anyway, my gut feelin', which ain't too far off most times, told me he was shootin' straight even if his story was crooked. Ain't no lie's ever been told anymore twisted than the one he managed in under a minute."

"With a gun in my ribs, too," Tyler added.

"I done told her that part. Anyway, as the window come down, I figgered Tyler might just as well be my sister's boy, Grover. Darrell didn't know no diffrn't. Didn't ask for his license or nuthin.' Just told us about the Thanksgivin' sale at Callahans and then waved us off."

"Darrell was the trooper just here?" Mayson asked.

"Shucks no. That was Lem Cain's boy, Clark. He come by 'cuz he thought you two mighta' strayed up here. Scared the dickens out of me when he started towards your cabin."

"What did you say to stop him?"

Lou shrugged. "Just that there weren't nuthin' on that knoll 'cept black bears, like the one I seen snoopin' around this mornin'."

"Black bears?" Tyler asked.

"Clark's scared of 'em; has been since one chased him off from Jackson's Pond as a boy. He was fishin' when he shoulda' been school learnin.' Gretchen, his Ma, said he never played hooky again. Didn't take no more'n the mention of them big hairy critters for Clark to plumb forget you two."

"Lou, you're a genius!" Tyler cried as he hugged her.

"If you ain't a mess!" She blushed. "So now that I saved you from jail, can you really clear Edgar?"

"If not, we'll spend our lives running from John Laws."

"You'll figger it out. Then you'll get hitched like you was supposed to be in the first place."

"He doesn't want to marry me," Mayson frowned. "He thinks I'm a pain in the ass."

"You are a pain in the ass," answered Tyler.

"And you're a big *gavonne*! How much did you pay for that German jalopy, anyway?"

"A thousand."

"Then you're not just a big *gavonne* but a stupid one!"

"Harley Bogins swore it was a sweet deal," Lou said. "And them Bogins been sellin' cars darn near fifty years."

"And it's in excellent condition," he added.

"How would you know?" Mayson huffed. "Let me guess — you changed the oil once on your Porsche? No, I've got it. You put gas in the country club's golf carts one summer?"

"See?" He glanced at Lou. "There's no bigger pain in the ass on the planet."

But Lou only saw a mess of energy flowin' between the two that wasn't the anger or frustration they pretended, but a fierce passion that made folks want to kiss one minute and spit the next.

"So you think I'm a sucker for every two-bit car dealer who comes along?" he asked.

"Think?" Mayson came back. "How much more proof do I need than this ton of dilapidated metal here?" She cringed as his eyes fell away. She'd hurt his feelings. *Madonna mia*, so she'd learn to drive the car. "It's not so bad actually," she said as she studied it again. "With a paint job, it might even be cute. And I don't think you're a stupid *gavonne*. I practically let you kiss me at will."

Watching his smile return, Lou started off. "There'll be supper if you want. If not we'll expect you for Thanksgivin' at noon. And don't be late. Earl don't wait for nuthin'; cuts the turkey right on the dot."

A chilling dusk settled over the mountains as they returned to the cabin. He started a fire as Mayson unpacked the bags. Rejoining at the hearth, they kissed soothingly. "There's no law forbidding a second," she said, her eyes lifting hopefully.

"Are you sure?" he smiled. "This is Tennessee."

"Of course there's none requiring it, either."

"Do you want a second kiss or not?"

"I told you: You're not supposed to ask."

As their lips touched she quivered, daring to imagine them joined completely, his warm, sweet passion flowing through her, rippling into every nerve. Again he left her breathless. "Did I mention thirds are permitted, too? In fact, I now recall Tennessee allows an unlimited number."

He smiled. "I won't take advantage of your generosity just because the law allows it."

"Only because you don't want to," she pouted. "Tyler, don't lie just to spare my feelings. The truth is you find a third kiss intolerable."

He glared at her with fresh irritation. "What difference does it make how many kisses I want? The first two were fine. If there was a third, you'd ask why not a fourth. And if a fourth..."

"I get your stupid point." Zillions of women, and she must be the first to repulse him. "No matter what you say, you don't want the third kiss because I sicken you."

"Mayson, you don't have the first clue what I want."

"Then tell me."

"When I'm ready."

"One thing. You can't even tell me one thing."

"All right," he relented. "I miss your hair."

"Then why did you cut it off?"

"You're raving, Mayson. You should know it's not very becoming."

"And *you* should know you'll never kiss me again." She suddenly remembered something. "I reached Harvey this afternoon. I was right; Madelyn's recording is a cover."

He gaped at her, incredulous. "You made contact with the only person on the planet who can help us, and yet we've wasted all this time counting kisses before you can remember to tell me!"

"At least I had the thimbleful of sense necessary to get him on the phone."

"You're unbelievable." He stormed to the window.

"Do you want to hear about the call or not?" She summarized all they discussed, including the calls gleaned from Lamp's phone records.

"It's unfolding just like we thought." He gazed at the moonlit sky. "Morris was drawn to Minnesota by something related to Crenshaw which, once acquired, was taken to Lamp."

"The negotiations got hot and heavy," she mused. "Beginning in Minnesota and ending with Morris's death in New York - a death we assume resulted from Lamp's cry for help and Harrington's response in the form of a big ugly *gavonne* named Leopold."

He extended their supposition. "Hours after the murder, Leopold was in Minnesota posing as a firm partner to sweep up Morris's litter."

"He must be in Pine County now to finish the job," she said. "Or two-thirds, anyway. Once they kill us, then Harvey, it's over."

"There's an *if* in there, Mayson."

"A *when*, you mean. With an army of cops surrounding us and a professional killer lurking in the shadows, how could it not?"

"Because you're overlooking one important factor."

"What's that?" she asked.

"The forty-year-old secret that made Crenshaw rich and has the conspirators sweating now. We're being pursued so heavily not because of what we know, but what we might find - the secret they were unable to bury with Morris."

His optimism glowed much too brightly for the dark storm facing them. "That's wonderful, but where's the proof of this secret: Florida, Minnesota, Tennessee or New York? And what form does it take?"

"If it's not here, we'll go to Minnesota," he said.

That was much easier said than done; she recalled Harvey's warning about the welcoming party that'd be waiting. "Then you're not mad at me anymore?"

"Over five minutes now." He glanced at his watch. "A new record. What else did Harvey say?"

"He's sending new IDs."

"Did you tell him what we've learned from the records?"

"Yes, and I recruited his help in uncovering what two Senate confirmations couldn't." She watched his eyes gleam. "I don't know why you're smiling. The reason quite possibly is because it doesn't exist."

"Then again it might. Come on," he nodded. "Let's go see what's for supper."

The phone was ringing when they returned later. He reached it first. "So does that old mountain woman know the score?" Harvey asked, then quickly received an account of the afternoon's close call.

"Have you checked on our three jurists?" Tyler asked.

"No TSU, kid, but the holes are definitely in the right places. You'll see what I mean when you get my research. If you have a pen, I'll tell you . . ."

Tyler scrawled three pages of notes, which Mayson quickly swiped up. Harvey added, "I think your suspicions are valid. We just need to fill in the gaps. Corelli says you may be heading north soon. Like I told her, icy roads will be the least of your problems. The trail will be hot wherever you go."

"Thanks for the warning – and the research." Hanging up, he nodded at the notes in Mayson's lap. "What do you think?"

"There's definitely an unexplained gap between their bachelor and law degrees. It took them four years to earn JDs, when the Western world knows it takes just three."

"Four if you hang around for tax certification."

"They didn't."

"Are the four-year periods the same?"

"Identical," she nodded.

"Why didn't this gap year come out in the previous confirmations?" he asked.

"Why should it? There was too much else for those predatorial senators to sink their teeth into — abortion, family values, public decency laws and the death penalty. That gap year was certainly the last thing on their minds."

True, he thought, too exhausted suddenly to debate it any further. "Are you ready for bed?"

His eyes opened to the crackling fire and Mayson standing pensively over it. More than the icy cabin and a midnight restlessness had inspired the fire. It was a ghost she was chasing away.

"Is it time for our talk?" he asked.

"What if it is?"

"Then I'm here, like I said I would be."

"And when you're not?" she asked.

"I wasn't aware I was going anywhere."

"I meant: How long will you be here?"

"As long as you need me. Now get back in bed," he insisted.

Shrugging, she slipped back under the warm covers. One fragile glance was enough for him to draw her into his arms and wait patiently for the story lived but never told.

"He was the largest presence in my life," she began. "He made the world safe, warm, happy; the wonderful place of fairy tales. When I woke to find payment for a lost tooth under my pillow, he'd double the amount. *The Tooth Fairy can be a little chintzy because she has so many kids to pay*, he said. And I believed him. I believed everything he said."

"Who are we talking about?" Tyler asked.

"Anthony Corelli, my father, my reference source for everything. He made the most complex things seem simple, wrapping his explanation in some colorful tale as he twirled dough in Corelli's Pizza Shop. It was tiny and our apartment above it was cramped, but it was my world - a full, happy one. And noisy," she laughed. "Italians are loud, passionate people. I never knew the difference between a friend and customer. The people who came to our shop were the same ones who visited the apartment, gave me Christmas presents and sat in St. Mary's pews on Sunday. Their children were my friends and schoolmates.

"In the evenings, Mama would shuffle between the shop's cash register and tables in a floating conversation, until Papa emerged from the kitchen. Then they'd sit with our friends and the *vino* flowed," she remembered dreamily. "The air grew thick with smoke and the tales grew taller."

"And the bullshit deeper?"

"Of course." She squeezed his hand with a deepening intimacy. "While Santa and Vinny took over the shop's duties, I sat in Papa's lap, trying to follow the twists of a conversation that shifted between English and Italian."

"You loved both your parents, but your father more," Tyler

mused.

"Not more, just in a different way. Mama was the quintessential Italian wife: submissive, loyal, and quiet. She took her cue from Papa. When he was in the room, she blended. There were things I could only discuss with her. But she doted on Santa and Vinny, while I was clearly Papa's pet. In the afternoons, he'd leave the shop in Mama's care and take me on his forages for supplies.

"For me, the shopping trip was a very special moment. I was small and my tall, handsome Papa was the king of my world, which included the noisy Italian market, where zillions of *paesani* dashed about in a zillion directions — like a carnival, each street with its own attractions. Try to imagine these same Italians crammed into these narrow streets, absorbed in their bartering and tall tales."

"I get the picture," he smiled.

"Papa would greet the proprietor at every sidewalk stand and then nod at me on his broad shoulders, *Hey Gino, Sal: you met my little girl here?* And they'd answer, *Hey Tony, can't you see I'm busy here?* But always they'd stop what they were doing to shake my hand as if for the first time. *My Mayson Angelina!* Papa would boast. *She's bellissima, huh? Go on, tell me she's not bellissima!*

Bellissima, Tony! They'd shout back. *I tell you this every day! Why you not listen, huh?*

Give her a cookie, Tozani, Papa would say. *One of those freshly baked ones. Or Gino, give her a soda, huh?* At the next stop it'd be a stick of gum or whatever the *paesano* had, and off we'd go again.

"Later we'd return to the shop, and I'd curl up on the kitchen counter as Papa tied his apron on and began slicing vegetables and cooking the sausages that would dress the pizzas that evening. Soon the oven glowed as he twirled the dough in his skillful fingers. We'd sing, laugh and chatter away the time until Mama came back to announce the Gentilinis; then the Taravanos and Silecchios. By six the shop would be buzzing, Papa singing louder with each pizza pulled from the oven. He had a deep, beautiful baritone that carried out to the tables and brought Mama back to scold, *Stop now, Papa! No one can hear themselves think!*

"Think? He'd shrug. *This is Corelli's Pizza Shop. Paesani pay to eat, drink and be merry. They want to think, you tell'em to go to the library!* Grabbing her, they'd soon be dancing around as old Mr. Pilenzo slinked back. *Vincent Pilenzo!* Papa would grin. *Is my sweet Rosa bellissima or what?*

"*Bellissima! Bellissima!* He'd growl. *Now bring me my dinner!* It was like that every night," she laughed.

"The shop's kitchen was my personal classroom, where Papa taught me about the world. He cooked and rambled. I listened and learned. Then as the steam rose, pepperoni spicing the air, we sang. Some afternoons he'd say, *Mayson Angelina, let's go shopping, huh? Maybe there'll be a fresh cookie at Tozani's bakery.* Lifting me to his shoulders, off we'd go singing, always singing."

Tyler cradled her as she cried softly, envisioning a sunny afternoon, she and her father serenading each other along the narrow streets of their Italian market. *Non dimenticar means don't forget you are my darling . . .* He'd learn it, every verse. And then sing it with her.

"I remember the day I learned what to call our joy," she resumed. "We'd shopped that afternoon, then returned to prepare for the evening crowd. As Papa sliced vegetables, twirled the dough, then finally turned the oven on, we moved from one song into the next. When my lungs gave out, he marched on alone.

"*Papa,* I asked. *Why do you sing so much?*

"*Mayson Angelina!* He gaped at me. *How is it that the wonderful truth has escaped you this long?*

"*What truth?* I shrugged.

"*That your Papa is a songbird, of course.*

"*A songbird?* I asked, confused.

"*Why not? Am I any different from the birds that sing in the trees? Don't you know why they sing?*

"*Why Papa?*

"*Because they're happy, Mayson Angelina.*

"*But Papa, how can a songbird know it's happy? Its brain isn't big enough.*

"*What brain?* He scoffed. *Happiness flows from the heart.*

"After that, whenever I was sad, I'd go to him and beg, *Please songbird, sing away my sorrow!* And each time he'd take me into his lap and say, *Mayson Angelina, sing along and together we'll chase your sadness away.* And without fail it fled, until finally one night, so did the songbird."

"What happened?" Tyler's fingers slipped down her neck.

"I woke one morning and Papa was gone, without explanation. Mama called the police and sent my brothers out looking for him. We could only imagine him mugged, lying dead in some alley. Our friends were wonderful, visiting the apartment in shifts so we'd never be alone, bringing food and hounding the police for reports. Poor Mama was shattered. She just sat by the window in shock, while my brothers struggled to keep the shop going. They tried to hide their fear but I knew when they'd been crying."

"And you?" he lifted her chin.

"My world rested on Papa's strong shoulders," she confessed. "Without him, I was suspended in a terrible darkness. For days I waited by the apartment door, my ears desperate for his cheerful voice in the street, his heavy feet on the steps. Many times I imagined these sounds, only to return to the terrible silence. I cried, prayed, even sang, hoping somehow he could hear me. But I never left that door, even at night, when I'd dream of him bursting inside, singing and lifting me from the floor. Finally I woke to the reality that he wasn't coming back."

She sighed. "It never occurred to us that he'd just walked away. At least not until that morning Mama tried to withdraw some funds to pay for shop repairs. Imagine her shock upon discovering that our entire savings had vanished the same day as Papa. He was never again mentioned in our home.

"But his ghost remained. It could be heard in the deep quiet of night, in the walls that echoed with his singing, in Mama's sobbing behind the bedroom door and in the questions that ripped at my sleepless soul."

"What questions?" Tyler asked.

"How Papa could be the rock of our family one day and tumbleweed the next? Had I made him mad? Disappointed him? Or had Santa and Vinny, by not helping more around the shop? Or was it Mama's fault? Had she not loved him enough? For years I asked myself these questions until I was finally forced to confront the truth. Papa was to blame; no one else."

"Did you ever hear from him again?"

"Not *from* but *about* him. It was years later, after we'd sold the shop and moved into another neighborhood - one of those small-world coincidences. Mama's cousin from Newark, Carlo Metzanno, was in San Francisco visiting an old army buddy when he stumbled upon Papa." Her eyes gleamed with a bitter irony. "You'll never guess what he was doing."

"Twirling pizza?"

She nodded. "In one of those fancy waterfront pizzerias. He was remarried to a young Italian girl, and had . . ."

"Had what?"

"Two little girls." Biting her lip, she resumed. "Anyway, having found him, Mama now sued for her share of the savings and any support she could get. Papa's new wife worked for one of San Francisco's most prominent judges, something we didn't discover until it was too late to appeal the ruling that despite his desertion, Papa had a new family to support and most critically, a California one. With only so many pennies to go around, the court held the New York Corelli family must take its place in line. Suffice it to say, we never collected a cent."

Having been blessed with so much, Tyler now struggled to comprehend this injustice. "How did you get by?"

"After selling the shop, we moved into an older neighborhood, a euphemism for more rundown. But it wasn't so bad. We had three large rooms, running water, electricity most of the time - and only a few mice," she smiled.

"I hate to think of you living with mice," he frowned.

"I said a few." She stroked his elegant nose. "But we weren't the only ones in Brooklyn who shared living space with little, fuzzy creatures."

His pained eyes disturbed her, as did the dark shadow that had settled over him. Her private reflections had deeply affected him. And if their release had freed her to a degree, they'd shackled him in an equal amount. This meant he cared. And that she chose now to end her confessional, when she wanted desperately to continue, meant she cared as well. "A chapter in my troubled life," she smiled.

"Then let's begin the next. This is good for you."

"To snooze in your arms is even better." She settled back in her safe, warm nest.

A soothing silence crept into the darkness. The fire's shadows danced on the cabin walls. "Mayson, there aren't any doors in our friendship," he said finally. "I just wanted you to know that."

A serene smile crept over her face as she drifted off.

CHAPTER TWENTY-ONE

★

Jimmy Dale woke at dawn every weekday. Only this wasn't every weekday. It was Thanksgiving, which meant no mail to deliver. Beside him, his sweet Nell was a precious lump, her silvery curls gracing the pillow as they had for thirty years now. It was immensely reassuring to find her in these first seconds of dawn. Rising, he clutched his back. Age had crept into his joints and retirement was looking better every year. Just six more; he could make it until then.

Throwing on his robe, he crept down to the kitchen. By eight, Nell would shoo him out to begin her Thanksgivin' cookin.' By noon, it'd all be warming on the table when the tribe arrived: daughter Sally, her husband Jerry and their three young'uns; Jimmy, Jr., his pale wife Lucille, who ate like a sparrow, and their son, Trip, his favorite of the whole flock, with whom he shared a love of hunting, fishing and football - which they'd sure get a stomach-full of today.

Switching on the TV, he sat back with his coffee to watch the morning news. The manhunt remained the top story, authorities still convinced the pair was hiding out near Pine County. Yet why would a couple of New York lawyers be holed up around here? If the Feds knew they sure weren't saying. Again the fugitives' pictures flashed on the screen, with the 800 number to call with information. He sure could use that hunnerd grand to fix the place up like Nell wanted. Grabbing the notepad, he wrote the number down.

"This just in," the Knoxville anchorman's tone sharpened. Listening carefully, he nodded with a fresh understanding. If not knowing why the fugitives were here, at least he now knew why the Feds were. Murder was a local crime, but selling FBI records to the Mafia something else.

He thought again of the fugitives' car - a Prelude. But it wasn't the make that kept flashing before his eyes like a stuck slide projector. It was the color – metallic blue . . . He froze as another detail emerged: a metallic blue frame. Shrouded by a dense web of what . . . vines, branches? As the anchorman moved on to the next story, the light flashed again. Lou Adkins' flapping tongue. Only it hadn't been flapping yesterday. Her lips had been puckered as if she'd just gulped a bottle of Castor Oil. So how was she connected to the vine-webbed, metallic blue frame?

He looked up as Nell shuffled in, in her frizzball slippers and tattered, pink robe.

"Jimmy darlin', take your coffee and run along. I have a mess of work 'fore them young'uns arrive. Go figger out the games you and Trip'll be watchin.' I declare you love that boy more'n your own son."

Escaping the Thanksgiving chaos, Harley Bogins ventured out to the lawn with his third Bloody Mary. Myrna had just scorched his ear with another fire and brimstone sermon about drinking too much again. *That's your third vodka and I ain't even served dinner! Pastor Ford says drinkin liquor's the same as invitin' the devil into your soul. Is that what you want?* She'd been screaming in one ear, the other withering against the noisy herd of young'uns that had taken over his house for the afternoon.

Breathing the crisp air, he gazed at the majestic green mountains. Iron Ridge's gray rooftops were just below, a tiny cluster of civilization nestled in a mountainside rich in ore. A redneck town maybe, but one that had always belonged to his family. *Boginsville*, the jealous whispered. And wasn't it the truth?

He'd built his stone mansion here for no other reason than its magnificent view. The steep mortgage was a challenge each month, causing him to drink more, only Myrna couldn't understand that or anything else but those ridiculous "laws-a-livin'" the High and Mighty Neville Ford imposed on his flock. Only who was he to be giving advice? What did he know about running a car dealership and making fat mortgage payments? Now Ford had hooked up with that greedy egomaniac Harrington. It seemed all the country's churches were joining his powerful CMA, adding bucks to the coffers and votes for that President he carried around in his hip pocket. It hardly seemed fair for Harrington to have all those millions, when he had to bust his ass just to make his mortgage.

Gulping his drink, he reluctantly returned to the mansion.

He shut himself in the study, poured another drink and put the TV on. Flipping through the channels, he stopped finally on the fugitives' pictures. Were they really hiding in this neck of the wood like the John Laws believed? If so, why? These tiresome news reports never . . . Goddarn, he snagged on the anchorman's last words! No wonder the Feds were chasin' 'em so hard. Murder was one thing; selling FBI records to the Mafia was another - and making a goddarned bundle in the process.

He studied the pictures again as the 800 number appeared on the screen. Iron Ridge was buzzing over the hundred grand that had been staked on their capture. And damn if he couldn't use a healthy chunk himself to get the bank off his ass. With her angel's face and doe-like eyes, the girl was pretty enough to pass for that actress Myrna liked so much. Sophia Loren — or was it Audrey Hepburn? Waddill had a pretty face, too, with that chiseled jaw and tangled, gold hair. He looked more like a surfer than a killer, and . . . He studied Waddill more closely. Why did he look so familiar?

Unconsciously he etched a cap in Waddill's wavy hair, then shades over his clear blue eyes. Lou Adkins' nephew? The dumb bastard had given him a grand for that broken down Beetle, then left the lot grinning as if he'd struck the deal of the century. That moron couldn't be . . . The door flew open suddenly and a furious Myrna gleamed at him in his recliner. "Number four," he said as he raised his glass defiantly. "So sue me, all right?"

"Sue you!" she snapped. "Why, I'll strip you clean down to them soiled shorts!"

"For drinkin' four Bloody Marys?"

"No! For screwin' Maggie Springer!"

The glass slipped from his hand, shattering on the floor. "Now Myrna . . ."

"Don't Myrna me, you cheatin' devil! All them Wednesday nights I thought you was at the Pine County car shows you weren't no place but the Hillside Inn, rubbing hot bodies with Maggie Springer! Betty Sue says there's a dozen witnesses!"

Vodka gurgled in his gut. If someone had to find out, why Betty Sue Kellers, the biggest snoop in Flavin County? "Now

Myrna, you don't know . . ."

" 'Course I know! And I'll tell you what else! In ten minutes, your two-timin' butt'll be out of here for good!"

"Just a goddarned minute!" he growled. "This here's my house!"

"Not anymore; it's mine! Same as them bank accounts and car lot where you swindle people out of their hard-earned money. And if there's any doubt, I'll have Lawyer Murdock explain it, just as soon as I can get him on the phone. I hope Maggie's worth it," she snarled. " 'Cuz she done broke you good this time, Harley Bogins. Now start packin' and get out of my house!"

Deputy Sheriff Darrell Pamplin finished his charitable service at the Iron Ridge Community Center and left for Valley Springs. Cheerfully he saluted his brethren in other units, their numbers growing as he approached the Pine County line. This was the largest force ever assembled in these parts. If those two were here, they'd be found soon.

Passing the final checkpoint, he turned at the Valley Spring Junction and climbed the ridge to Bobbi Jo's folks' place. The whole crew was waiting as he swung into the drive and climbed out. "How'd everything go at the Center?" Bobbi Jo asked as she pecked his cheek.

Nodding at his in-laws, he fluffed Timmy's chestnut curls and Darlene's honey waves. "We fed two hunnerd. And there was another hunnerd on the second shift." He'd been servin' Thanksgiving dinner to Flavin's indigent for eight years now. As a deputy sheriff, protecting meant providing, at least in his book. The only thing was, after serving so much turkey it was hard to look at another with much appetite. As they entered the house, Bobbi Jo pointed at the festive table. "Didn't Ma do a great job with the turkey?"

"Looks wonderful as always." He managed a smile. Smiling, even when you didn't feel like it, was something required of every Christian, according to Pastor Michaels and Chairman Harrington, who now controlled Lantern Forge Trinity. It seemed most churches were hooking up with Harrington these days. And it made good sense, he reckoned. If anyone could return Christian values to government, it was Harrington, who everyone said had the President in his pocket.

His appetite soon returned and he found himself nursing a full belly as they crowded around to watch football. A halftime report updated the fugitive operation. "Darrell, what's all that mean?" Bobbi Jo frowned.

"That them kids did more'n murder that Jewish lawyer. They sold FBI documents to the Mafia."

"But that ain't as bad as murderin' is it?" she asked.

As the family's law enforcement expert, all eyes now turned on him. "Depends on how you look at it. The Mafia has folks kilt. And if you help a murderer, you're just as guilty in the eyes of the law. And stealin' from the FBI threatens national security. Ain't no crime worse than that." He studied Waddill's picture again. Why did the man look so familiar?

"Darrell, you look like you seen a ghost," Bobbi Jo said.

"I've seen Waddill. I just can't remember where."

"Well don't fret," she exhorted. "If you seen him afore, it'll come to you. It always does."

Leopold would always remember this miserable Thanksgiving, when in his dreary Pine County motel room, he'd slipped back into the clutches of a filthy habit. *Dear Lord, forgive my weakness*, he prayed, crushing one burning Marlboro and quickly lighting another. They'd been holed up at the Mountain Ambassador since Monday, braced for the fugitives' arrival. Pine County and the adjacent counties — Flavin, Harrison and Boone — were sealed tight, every road and motel within the cordoned area under close surveillance. An intense news blitz also had the natives on full alert. Waiting was the hard part. He limped to the window. It drove him crazy. Damn kids! Where were they?

Seconds passed as he gazed at the TSU campus across the street, now a checkerboard of lights against the dark mountain wilderness. He'd spent the past three days limping across it. Administration, Records, the new library. He inventoried his stops again: the Sanford Arts Center, Student Union, Law School, and maintenance facilities. Diplomatic inquiries as the noted historian, Dr. William Cassevetes, researching his latest book, *University*

Education in the Fifties, had gotten him a private research room in the Archives, where he'd spent the first day reviewing student records - applications, grade reports, club membership rolls, school papers, yearbooks, even the Pine County *Gazette*. In sum, every source that might hold a remnant of the three law students who'd quietly vanished before spring exams forty years ago. Bottom line? The records had been purged for the critical year. To the world, the Three Stooges had never been here, their rich families having gotten their money's worth in stiff bribes.

Thanking Dr. Jenkins, the Dean of Records, he'd moved on to the Treasurer's Office to examine the financial records. Dr. Cassevetes's new book would include a chapter on the cost of university education in the fifties. Again the records had proven clean.

The TSU staff whose careers spanned the last forty years had presented the next challenge. Completing a list from the extensive employment records, he'd spent another day tracking down these dinosaurs. Fortunately there hadn't been many, just a handful of administrative types and doddering professors, and one self-important maintenance man he'd finally caught up with in a smoky campus tavern Wednesday night. Feeding the desiccated little man his line about the richness of university life in the fifties, he'd then nudged him down Memory Lane.

"Guess you heard about the spring of '54," Wally Vernon said as he sipped his beer.

"That girl's murder, sure," Leopold answered across the booth.

Vernon's glassy eyes had hardened. "Edgar Norris didn't do it. I know that for a fact."

"How?" he asked.

"Cuz I worked with him. He was as good as any white feller I knew. Sure he liked the girl. Who didn't? She was a sweet, pretty thing, not stuck-up like them others. She and Edgar became friends, a dangerous thing for them times - uneducated nigger and pretty white girl. Raised a lot of eyebrows and made it easier for that bastard, Crenshaw, to point the finger when she was raped and kilt. But their relationship was innocent. Don't let nobody tell you differn't. Edgar loved his wife and besides, he'd never hurt nobody. One of the gentlest men I ever knew."

"Then who do you think killed the girl?"

Vernon studied him thoughtfully. "Them three law students, the ones who hung out right here." His crooked finger stabbed the table. "Only it wasn't called the Mountaineer in them days, just Luke's Tavern - plain and simple. Luke Smallwood owned it. He's dead now - has been for twenty years, I reckon."

"Tell me about the law students."

As Vernon gazed into his empty mug, Leopold snapped his fingers for fresh beers. Soon Vernon sipped again. "Them three weren't no diffrn't from the rest - rich and snotty, I mean. They'd come into Lukes wearin' their navy blazers, acting like they owned the place. Two were tall, the other squatty. Don't remember their names. Maybe never knew 'em. But I do recall they didn't return after that spring term of '54. Made me wonder if it weren't for a reason, say to avoid being fingered for the girl's murder."

"What makes you think they did it?"

Vernon's weary expression didn't change as he sprinkled salt in his beer. "I seen 'em leave with the girl that night - leave Luke's, I mean. She worked as a waitress in the evenings to help pay for her schoolin,' I reckon. And them three was drunker 'n hell. Don't know when they studied or if they did. They was in here practically every night, drinkin' imported beer. One even smoked a fancy, imported cigarette with black and gold-ringed filters. Can't recall the brand.

"Anyway, they gave the girl a ride that night back to campus, she musta' thought. Only she never made it. No one seen her again 'til three days later when Bones – that's the old hound who hung around the maintenance shed — sniffed something back in the trees. Tom Berry, our foreman, finally got curious and went out there. Tom's dead now, too, like so many of 'em." Draining his beer, he glanced at Leopold, who snapped his fingers again for another. "Mighty nice of you, Mr . . ."

"Cassevetes."

He laughed. "I'd never remember that in a million years. You I-talian or somethin'?"

"The Cassevetes are Greeks now living in New York."

"Big place, New York." He sipped. "Where was I?"

"Your foreman found Bones digging in the woods."

"Oh yeah," he nodded. "Well, by then the damn hound had dug up the foulest stench you can imagine. Naturally, Tom was suspicious because of the missin' girl. He had me and Ned Samples bring our shovels out to finish the job Bones had started. Likely Edgar would've been with us 'cept he'd gotten sick the day before - some facial infection Doc Maxwell said was caused by the girl's claws as she tried to fight him off.

"Anyway, we found her about four feet down, wearing the same dress she'd had on that night at Luke's. Only it was torn and bloodied, her panties balled up in the dirt nearby. Her eyes was the worst thing - big, pretty blue ones, just like I remembered, still open after three days in the ground." He sighed. "You could almost see them horrible last minutes right through 'em. We didn't move her and I'm glad, 'cuz we learned later the side of her skull restin' in the dirt had been shattered by a shovel. Edgar's shovel."

At least Crenshaw had been thorough. "What happened after you discovered the body?"

"Tom had me run inside and call Crenshaw. The pompous bastard was out there in minutes with his sidekick, Barney. Bernie Edwards was his real name, but Barney fit better. Dumb as dirt and the most fidgety person you ever seen . . . Anyway, the first thing Crenshaw does is order us the hell away. And 'course we did what he said. Even if you hated his guts, you knew better than to give him any lip. We returned to the shed and watched out the window as Doc Maxwell arrived, then an ambulance and another patrol car. Pretty soon them woods was crawlin' with County folk."

"Maxwell was the County Coroner?" Leopold asked.

He nodded. "Crenshaw had him in his pocket, same as the others. Wasn't more'n a week 'fore Edgar was arrested."

"Did you tell Crenshaw what you knew?"

"'Course; same as George Elroy. He's dead now, too. Forty years is a long time."

But long enough? Leopold wondered as he offered a grateful prayer for Vernon's difficulty with names, if not an otherwise astonishing memory for details. "Elroy knew as much as you?"

"More, since he lived on Gray's Ridge. That's where we figgered the murderin' took place."

"I don't understand," Leopold said.

"That's 'cuz you ain't heard it told. But this here's the gospel you won't get nowhere else." He stabbed the table emphatically. "George was with me that night the girl left with them boys. When we left later, he went one way, me another."

"He went to Gray's Ridge?"

"Exactly." Vernon's eyes twinkled. "Now every college has its own make-out spot and this 'n here's Gray's Ridge. So it wasn't unusual George spotted them on his way home that night, parked in that yellow Studebaker them three catted around in. He didn't think no more about it 'til later when the girl was missin.' Still, he didn't say nuthin' until she'd been dug up and then only to Crenshaw - the same time I told the crooked bastard what I knew. After givin' him our statements, we didn't think no more about it, just figgerin' that he'd soon get enough evidence to arrest them three.

"Only it didn't happen that way," he sighed. "Instead, it was Edgar who got arrested. Crenshaw never questioned us again - just pushed our story right out of his head, for a price, of course. He could always be bought for the right price. Say, you mind if I have another beer? All this talkin' is makin' my throat dry."

Leopold called for another draft. "Did George think Crenshaw was being bribed, too?"

Vernon's eyes gleamed with an old bitterness. "He confessed as much. Even said he was gonna confront the bastard. I reckon that's exactly what he done. It sure 'nuff explains a lot."

"What do you mean?"

"Why a few days later, George's memory vanished. The next thing I know, he's quit his job at the University cafeteria. Got a better one at the Pine County Lumber Mill. George didn't know nuthin' about lumberin' but I reckon it hardly mattered. It's what he knew but forgot that counted. I'm speakin' about that night, of course."

"Crenshaw owned the mill?"

"His brother, Dennis." Vernon guzzled his fresh beer. "And you can figger it was a successful one, too. Most are when you ain't got no competition. And Jasper made sure no other mill operators ever got a business license. He ran this County, Mister. Ain't no two ways about it."

"You think the boys' families paid him off?" Leopold asked.

"Think, shit! I know it, even if I can't prove it."

"But no one saw the boys do anything to the girl," Leopold pointed out. "It's all circumstantial."

"It is, huh?" Vernon scanned the smoky tavern. "Well I'll tell you somethin' I ain't never told a soul, not that I didn't want to. But I was scared - somethin' I ain't proud of, but it's true nonetheless."

"What's that?" he asked.

"Cigarette butts. Maybe a half-dozen scattered in the dirt where we dug that afternoon. The fancy, imported kind the tallest feller smoked. Only they was gone when I returned the next morning. Crenshaw scooped 'em up. He must've."

Leopold had no difficulty envisioning Falkingham, the arrogant university student, stamping out his Dunhills as Lamp and Mann buried the girl, leaving behind critical evidence as they sweated to conceal the rest. "So what did they have on Norris, besides the shovel and interracial relationship?"

"I'll tell you what they didn't have," Vernon grunted. "That fancy DNA testing. Otherwise Edgar'd still be alive today. When Doc Maxwell said it was his facial tissue under the girl's fingernails, there weren't no way for his lawyer to prove it wasn't. And it didn't help that Edgar had a facial infection at the time. That white jury wasn't about to buy no coincidences for a nigger, even a good one."

Leopold watched him guzzle his beer. Was the old drunk a threat or not? He didn't remember their names and couldn't connect their current national personas with the ancient murder case. But for the Dunhill cigarettes, they were simply vague shadows of the past.

"Say Mister," Vernon said. "I have a question for you. If Crenshaw didn't send Edgar to the chair for them boys' crime, why'd he leave his estate to the Widow Norris's school?"

The answer was painfully obvious yet also circumstantial, praise the Lord. What wasn't circumstantial however, was the missing chest that contained hard evidence of both the crime and the identity of the three guilty parties. In the wrong hands, it could destroy the CMA, the Longbridge Administration and the greatest Christian Renaissance of all time.

"Can't think of no reason, huh?" Vernon grinned. "Well there ain't but one. Crenshaw left his fortune to the Widow Norris 'cuz he was afraid of burnin' in hell for what he done. He was hopin,' I reckon, to set the record straight 'fore reaching St. Peter and the Judgement Gate. I guess we'll never know if the gesture done him any good."

Rewarding Vernon with a final beer, Leopold left and called Harrington with his report: TSU was clean but for one harmless germ named Vernon, who for all the clutter in his beer-soddened brain, possessed no names, faces or anything else connecting their trio to the ancient murder.

"Praise the Lord," Harrington had sighed. "Then he shall be spared."

His reflections were broken by the ringing phone. It was Harrington again. "Good news, Arch. Our slippery Agent Harvey has been found."

"Praise the Lord, sir! Where?"

"Mountain Creek, a small town in western Pennsylvania. When a bank account with the Social Security number of one of Harvey's girlfriends didn't match the owner's name, sirens went off. The owner, one Myrtle Johnson, is an alias for his longtime acquaintance, Anne Foxworth. No one at the Mountain Creek bank, however, could identify her picture. Fortunately tonight, a local hairdresser could. Foxworth is a client, one Madelyn Stump, who rents a farmhouse outside Mountain Creek."

"How did Harvey get the cover set up so quickly?" he asked.

Harrington replied, "A few years ago, Foxworth had trouble shaking a stubborn ex-husband. Harvey helped her disappear. That's what made her a suspect. Anyway, we've confirmed the pair is occupying the farmhouse. Agents are on the scene."

"Praise the Lord, sir! When will the Feds move in?"

"The moment you arrive."

"What about the operation here?" Leopold asked.

"Once you've completed the disposition, you can return

immediately. How soon can you leave?"

"Tonight, sir. And Miss Foxworth?"

"The situation's far too critical to leave anything to chance, Arch. Having said that, I'll leave the matter in your capable hands."

When would the killings end, or would they? Crumpling the empty Marlboro pack, Leopold hurled it at the wall in frustration.

"Arch, did you catch this afternoon's story?"

"Yes sir, although the fugitives' involvement in that Mafia conspiracy was hardly surprising."

"The news was certainly timely," Harrington noted, "especially after Longbridge's announcement yesterday. We'll be meeting here in Georgetown shortly if you need to reach me."

"I'm on my way to Pennsylvania, sir."

Pulled from their Thanksgiving festivities, the men gathered in the Lakeland study and waited for Harrington to begin the meeting. This latest crisis had begun with Longbridge's call the previous morning, summoning Streeter and Chapman to the Oval Office to discuss an urgent matter - one he hadn't disclosed, but hadn't needed to. Everyone was painfully aware of the criticism now being vented over the administration's handling of the fugitive operation.

Why, the national media asked, had the FBI and Justice, both under the leadership of obscure Texas bureaucrats, committed such enormous resources to the capture of two baby-faced lawyers, whose crimes, as reprehensible as they might be, were the subject of local jurisdiction? Hadn't it been the conservative Longbridge, who'd reminded the nation ad nauseum that the federal government far too often intervened in matters that didn't concern it? Had chasing Mayson Corelli out of New York transformed a local homicide into a national security threat? And even more disturbing, why hadn't the fugitives been caught? How much was this operation costing the taxpayers? Wasn't it time the administration explained its puzzling stance in the Corelli-Waddill affair?

"You're damn right!" Longbridge had growled at his Attorney General and FBI Director. "If the nation wants an explanation, it'll get one!"

Harrington appreciated the challenge facing them now. "Thomas or Larry, why don't we start with a report of your meeting yesterday with the President?"

"As you know," Streeter replied, "the President decided rather precipitously yesterday to respond to the media's attack on our handling of the operation. After briefing him on its status, Larry and I helped craft his response, which was delivered at the press conference yesterday afternoon. This response included revelation of the fugitives' involvement in a conspiracy to sell confidential Bureau records to certain New York crime families - the same conspiracy which caused Agent Swanson to take his own life. The families and the conspiracy's scope hadn't been previously revealed because disclosure would hamper our efforts to obtain indictments against the key suspects."

"What was the President's reaction?" Lamp asked.

"He accepted our explanation, including the decision not to involve him until the operation became a political issue which, of course, it has now."

"His comments yesterday reflected our recommendations verbatim," Chapman added.

Harrington asked Streeter, "You were the last to speak with him. How is his mood this evening?"

"Good; public reaction has been favorable but we can expect a flurry of questions in the days ahead."

Lamp, sitting between his friends, expressed their mutual sympathies. "I must say Thomas and Larry have handled this crisis brilliantly. They've not only justified the operation's massive federal involvement, but at the same time kept Longbridge at bay."

"That may be," Harrington frowned, "but for how long? All we've done is explain the federal government's interest in the fugitives. Now that the proverbial can of worms has been opened, we must address the questions it raises, which can only sink us deeper into the sludge of our prevarication. This isn't country club gossip we've propagated. Yesterday we informed the President of the United States, and this morning, the nation he governs of an elaborate criminal conspiracy that doesn't exist. But having been postulated, it must now be kept afloat. If it sinks we all go down."

Lamp voiced another concern. "Lieutenant Duke has been trying to reach me since the conspiracy's disclosure. I'm sure he wants to know why he wasn't informed of it before."

"Tell him you were apprised of it several months ago," Chapman said. "That we requested your help in exposing the fugitives as the link between the Bureau and the New York families."

"But he'll obviously ask which families, and also how two young lawyers managed to position themselves between those families and the FBI."

"Maybe Larry didn't volunteer all this detailed information," Mann said.

"You're overlooking my extensive collaboration with Duke and his associate. We spent hours discussing the murder. Assuming I've known about the conspiracy yet remained silent, don't I owe him more than, 'Larry didn't disclose all the details?' "

"But Mendelsohn's sexual harassment had been well developed by then," Chapman reminded them. "It was perfectly reasonable for you to assume this was Corelli's motive for the murder."

"So where does this leave the murder case?" Mann asked.

"With the fugitives gone, there'll be no one to prosecute," Chapman explained, then turned back to Lamp. "Tell Duke that when informed of your associates' suspected criminal activities, you agreed to cooperate, recruiting Mendelsohn, who as the partner for whom they worked, was in the best position to snoop without arousing suspicion. Unfortunately, that's exactly what happened. Upon discovering his snooping, they decided he must be eliminated, which Corelli took care of that Sunday night. When a warrant was later issued, Waddill rescued her and together they planned an escape."

Streeter added, "Today's disclosure, which we've blamed on the media's interference, has sent the New York crime families running for cover, cutting off further avenues of investigation. Consequently, we have no alternative but to close our files and bring a swift end to this nightmare."

"Hardly," Harrington snorted. "It can never end until that chest is recovered. And public scrutiny won't stop with the investigation. Suspicion will likely peak then, producing the toughest questions."

"Which we'll be prepared to answer," Streeter replied. "And if necessary prove a criminal conspiracy consisting of Swanson and Harvey inside the Bureau, Corelli and Waddill as intermediaries, and Bertolucci family members with known connections to Corelli's brother. The crime's being manufactured now, complete with phony investigative records we'll be able to prove flowed through this pipeline into the Bertoluccis' hands. One can only guess how the family might retaliate. Perhaps a media war, even legal action, but I doubt they'd resort to violence. Why should they? There'll be no threats of prosecution."

"How can we be assured of your agents' cooperation once the fugitives are captured?" Lamp asked.

"Because they've been thoroughly briefed and possess the competence needed to execute the plan."

"Still, the fugitives' handling is fraught with risk," Lamp pointed out. "It's easy to imagine the potential complications. Suppose they're captured by the state authorities and carted off before our plan can be executed? Regaining the necessary access may be impossible. Or suppose they're wounded in pursuit and hospitalized? Who knows how their capture will play out? We must address these contingencies."

"This plan does," Chapman confirmed.

Mann raised another concern. "What about Pennsylvania?"

"Leopold's en route now. Our on-site team will take no action until he arrives."

"How will Harvey be explained?" Mann asked.

"Any number of things could happen. The New York families implicated in the conspiracy could decide he's enough of a liability to order a hit. I also understand burglaries are quite common in the Mountain Creek area."

"So what's left?" Lamp asked.

"The fugitives' capture," Harrington replied. "I'm certain none of us will sleep well until that occurs." He turned now to the man who, uncharacteristically, hadn't uttered a word the entire meeting. "So Chase, certainly you must have something to share."

"If I did," Falkingham puffed insolently, "you'd have heard it

by now."
"Perhaps there's something we haven't considered?"
"Not 'considered,' overlooked completely."
"Oh," he frowned, "and what's that?"
"Travis Culpepper."

CHAPTER TWENTY-TWO

★

Mayson woke to the crackling fire and Tyler looming over it. "Are you all right?" she asked him.

Appreciation warmed his eyes as he turned. "I couldn't let Thanksgiving pass without calling my family. They received your letter. Hunter Leigh said it was like a boulder being lifted from their shoulders."

"Are they being watched?" She sat up.

He nodded. "Between the cops and the media they haven't had a minute's peace since Friday."

"What if their phones are tapped?"

"I didn't mention where we were. Besides, we'll be leaving tomorrow if those new IDs arrive." He grimaced. "They want us to surrender. Schuyler envisions retaining the world's best defense lawyer. He doesn't understand it'll take more than Perry Mason to bail us out. I saw no point in shattering his illusion."

He called his mother Hunter Leigh; his father, Schuyler. She inferred from this a close relationship. "I promised Lou I'd help with dinner," she said as she rose. "Just relax and I'll be back later."

She returned later to take her shower. Tyler's boisterous singing in the bathroom told her she'd have to wait her turn. She knocked crisply.

"I'll be out in a minute!" he shouted over the shower.

Smiling, she intruded just the same. "You should see the turkey. It's bigger than you! And Lou showed me how to snap beans. I did the whole pot!"

He whistled. "And I thought a perfect GPA at Columbia was something."

"I peeled the potatoes, too." Her twinkling eyes fell to the sink. Quickly filling the cup with icy water, she slung it over the curtain.

"I can't believe you did that!" he growled. As his hand shot around the curtain, she squealed, dodged, then burst out the door, giggling. Finally the shower shut off and she detected the soft rustle of his dressing. Why? He always shaved first, then primped in his boxers.

"Are you all right in there?" she asked.

"Go to hell."

"Lou told me about Dale Markham. His mother, Doreen, is Crenshaw's older sister, who left Pine County fifty years ago to marry a Minnesota man she met during World War II - an army recruiter at the Draft Board where she worked. The last Lou heard, she was still living in Snow Peak near her family."

He emerged, dressed. "Snow Peak is where Morris discovered his 'get rich quick' scheme, and also where Leopold went after putting a bullet in his head. The Markhams must know something. We'll just have to go find out what it is."

"I see. Just drive up in our new car? Or should I make airline reservations?"

"I get your point."

"Then explain how we can get off this mountain, much less reach Snow Peak a thousand miles away." She sighed. "I'm the one charged with murder. You're just an accessory. Maybe your father's lawyer can get you off with a light sentence."

He glared at her strangely. "Mayson, we're not going to prison. Haven't you grasped that yet?"

Of course, she was just resisting it. "Look, if you want to go to Minnesota, fine. Now get down to the Adkins while I shower. Lou needs you to pop the champagne." Watching him grab the keys, she cautioned, "Those are to the Prelude. We're using the Beetle now."

"I know. I just need to check something."

When he returned, she was already singing cheerfully in the shower. Slipping into the bathroom, he filled the Prelude's jug with icy water, then slung it over the curtain. "You big *gavonne!*" she screeched at the shock. "I'll get you!" But the door had already slammed, his laughter fading as hers rose.

The Adkins table was dressed with their best linen and china. "Straight from that fancy Nashville store," Lou beamed. "Has its own catalogue and everythin.' " The holiday bird, roasted to a golden brown and festively trimmed with cinnamon apples, sat in a silver tray. Earl, looming over it in his shiny blue suit and wide burgundy tie, grumbled impatiently, "Don't see why you got to dress so dadblamed fancy just to eat dinner in your own house. And where'd that girl run off to? Don't she know we're waitin'?"

"Don't be rushin' everybody!" Lou scolded. "It ain't like you got a train to catch or nuthin.'"

Tyler winked at her in her peach dress, her silver curls wearing the wild flower he'd picked on the way over. "So Earl, that should be some game down in Dallas, huh?"

"Halas coached the Bears," he snorted. "It's them damn Cowboys and Redskins playing today."

"He said Dallas!" Lou yelled. "Can't you hear nuthin'?"

Mayson breezed through the door. "Sorry I'm late," she smiled meekly.

"Don't matter," Lou said. "Nobody's in a rush 'cept that cranky old fool I'm married to." She studied Mayson closely. "I declare, if you ain't the most beautiful young woman to ever grace these mountains. What you say, Charmer?" she glanced at Tyler.

The return of her lustrous, mink-colored hair had stunned him. She wore the purchased gray flannel skirt, white turtleneck and navy sweater. A garnet silk scarf and gold earrings enhanced her delicate beauty, which he suddenly found unsettling. Unrequited seconds crept by as he struggled, speechless. Did words exist to describe her supreme beauty, and if so, should he find them? Finally he asked, "Shall I pour the champagne?"

"Reckon so," Lou nodded. "Ain't no one else coming I know of."

Filling four goblets, he gave them each one and then toasted the festive occasion. Lou gawked at him in awe. "How do you make them words come out so orderly and pretty-like?"

Just seconds before, he'd been at a loss for even one. "Practice," he smiled.

As they sat at the table, Earl offered the blessing and then the plates were filled with helpings from Lou's extravagant spread. The conversation flowed beyond reach of Earl's deadened ears, but he didn't seem to mind as he cleaned his plate and helped himself to seconds. Tyler nodded at Mayson's plate. "You don't like the white meat?"

"I like the dark better," she replied.

So had Kara. She'd squirreled away drumsticks from Castlewood's table, for later when they curled up for the last game. She'd nibble, gnaw, pick and then with the game's first miscue, point the drumstick at the TV and yell, *Tyler, if you ever called a stupid play like that, I'd be humiliated!*

"Don't you want more turkey?" Mayson drew him back.

"No thanks." He then recalled her contribution to the meal. "More of those great snap beans, though. Earl, how about you?"

After dinner, they gathered around the TV with their pie and coffee. The game seemed much farther away than Texas Stadium on the tiny black-and-white screen. "Earl!" Tyler shouted. "Are you a Skins fan?"

" 'Course!'" he growled. "Ain't no other team to root for in these parts."

"Ain't gonna root for them Cowboys," Lou huffed. "They may be America's team, but by darn, they ain't Tennessee's. Ain't that right, Earl . . . Earl!"

"The pie's good, I done already said!"

"Damn fool!" she sighed. "I might as well be talkin' to the wall."

Shreds of precious history were gathered as the afternoon drifted. "Ain't nobody in these mountains who don't remember that college girl's murder," Lou said. "And there's been a lot of speculatin' over who done it, but that's the first I heard tell of them boys. And I ain't sayin' they didn't do it, but if so, it's a mighty well-kept secret, which means Jasper Crenshaw done what he promised them rich families." She sighed, "Them college kids was all the same. Folks would see 'em in town, just like them weird Halos, all just faces, one no differn't from the next. Too high and mighty to associate with regular folks." She crossed her thick arms. "Wouldn't surprise me none if it was them judges who kilt the girl. Judges ain't no better'n sheriffs in my book."

"Who are the Halos?" Mayson asked.

"Not what you'd think by their name. Sure, they wear them plain black clothes like the Dunkards, the menfolk sportin' beards, the women, those silly caps, but they ain't the same."

"How are they different?"

"I'll tell you how," she said as she rocked in her chair. "You ain't never seen no Dunkards treat their women like the Halos treat theirs. Orderin' them around like they was slaves or somethin.' And makin 'em carry the heavy shopping bags. Ain't no tellin' what they do to 'em back in the mountains. Beat 'em with whips most likely, if they raise their voices or put supper on the table a minute late. They're weird all right, and what's more, they're mean . . . Huh," she grunted at the game now. "It'd be a darn miracle if the Skins beat the Cowboys in their own house. Can't call it a backyard no more when they play inside. Did you play, Charmer? You're sure big enough."

"Quarterback," he nodded.

"That figgers. Seems the quarterbacks are always the good-lookin' fellers." She looked at Earl, who'd nodded off, his chin in his chest. "Old fool will soon be snoring loud enough to wake up the whole mountain - everyone but him, anyway."

"What else do you know about the Halos?" Mayson asked.

"Ain't much more to tell. Folks don't know much, which suits them just fine, I reckon. They don't associate with nobody less they have to. Like buyin' things in town they can't make or grow theirselves. They live deeper in the mountains than other folks care to go, which I reckon's why they picked it. They mistrust anyone who ain't a Halo - and the government, too. Don't matter which kind, they hate 'em all."

Mayson watched the Redskins celebrate their second touchdown. Tyler was grinning, and so was she. Seeing him happy made her happy.

"So what's a Halo?" he asked. "An acronym, I assume."

"An acro what?" She stopped rocking to squint. "Don't think we use them big words even if we have to put up with that fancy university. But if you're askin' what Halo stands for, it's Holy Army of the Last Order. Them weird birds figger they're God's soldiers, 'cept I doubt He'd claim 'em, if you could ask. Jimmy Dale says they're a paramilitary group, which the best I can figger makes them enemies of the government . . . See," She grunted at Earl's snoring. "Ain't that the most obnoxious noise you ever heard?"

They followed her back into the kitchen as she put the coffee on. Tyler asked, "I don't suppose Crenshaw was very close to his sister, since she lived in Minnesota?"

"Big sisters usually dote over their baby brothers," she replied. "And Doreen weren't no differn't. But you're right. She didn't come home too often after gettin' hitched to that Army feller."

"Were they close enough that Crenshaw might've confessed some of his shady dealings?" Mayson asked.

"If he'd tell anyone, it'd be Doreen," Lou said as she poured the coffee. "She was far enough away not to be gossipin.' Not that Doreen did much anyway. She was as quiet as Clara was a chatterbox. Clara was Jasper's wife and Pine County's biggest busybody. If he shared any secrets with her, he'd been crazier'n hell."

Tyler sipped his coffee. "Do you know anyone still around who'd remember much about TSU in the early fifties?"

"Well, I reckon I did know some folks who worked over there, 'cept it's been forty years, you know. Let's see," she rubbed her chin. "There was Maxine Gates. She worked in the dining hall. Cancer took her the same as Clara Crenshaw. And the Welton boys did somethin' but I can't recall what. Don't matter, though; they's dead, too." She watched his mind working now. "You ain't figgerin on doing somethin' stupid like going over there? They'd grab you sure as shootin.' "

He shook his head. "Assuming our judges were there, the records would've been purged long ago. What we need is someone who remembers."

"Let me think on it." She studied Mayson leaning cozily against him. "He might not 'a said nuthin' Sugar, but you done my scarf and earrings real proud. Keep'em, they look a sight better on you than me."

"Lou, I couldn't."

"Hush now. I ain't gonna hear another word." Astonished, Tyler watched Mayson embrace her.

As they returned to the living room with their coffee, Mayson groaned, "Wonderful! Just in time for the halftime news."

Their pictures above the anchorman's shoulder, he reported the manhunt's startling new developments. "The President's revelation that the fugitives, former Wall Street attorneys, are suspects in a conspiracy to disseminate classified FBI records to major New York crime families has for now quieted criticism of his administration's handling of the operation. Further, the recent murder of Morris Mendelsohn, a law partner of Supreme Court nominee, Lamp, is also believed to have been a desperate attempt to prevent the conspiracy's exposure."

They looked at each other in shock as he continued, "One prominent figure, a well-known supporter of the President, had this to say . . ."

The scene shifted to Seth Harrington inside a busy airport terminal, his silver pompadour meticulously coifed, his blue eyes glowing with a self-righteous obsession. "Quite honestly, I haven't paid much attention to this affair. Like most taxpayers, I leave such matters to the professionals. However, the media — and I hope you don't take this personally, Mr. Michaels — doesn't hesitate to interfere in matters that doesn't concern it. Nevertheless, the President has now come forward to explain his administration's actions and quite persuasively, I believe.

"Let's just hope the media's curiosity has been satisfied, and that these fugitives are apprehended soon, so we can get this behind us. There's so much more than FBI operations to occupy us in this exciting time, one being the Lamp nomination. Let's pray he's quickly confirmed."

As the report ended, Mayson shook her head. "Classified FBI records, Mafia investigations — how can they get away with this?"

"Because they're the FBI." Tyler's jaw quivered angrily. "The Justice Department, Supreme Court, Christians for a Moral America." . . . And the President? The silence echoed. Did they want to know or not?

"So what you figger to do?" Lou asked.

"Run like hell," he replied.

"Why not stay here? Them John Laws ain't comin' back."

"They'll be back, all right, just as soon as they've eliminated the rest of the county."

"Then how you can prove them judges kilt the girl, if you're runnin' all over the place?"

"By people providing the critical facts," Mayson said. "Lou, isn't there anyone you can remember who was connected with

TSU in the early fifties?"

As she rubbed her chin thoughtfully, Tyler asked, "Did Norris have an alibi for the night of the murder?"

She remembered that part, at least. "He told the jury he was fishin' over at Maynard's Pond. Working days at the University, I reckon he didn't have no other time to fish, 'cept at night."

"There wasn't anyone to corroborate this?"

"No one but them catfish and croakers. And if they could talk, that lily-white jury would've been more likely to believe them than a nigger." She sighed. "Things was differn't in them days. Black folks was niggers, which meant to prejudiced busybodies like Dottie Smith and Ellen Jackson, they was lower'n dirt, who, even if you could understand 'em, you couldn't believe half they said.

"Dottie and Ellen was on the jury that sent Edgar to the chair. And it didn't matter to them, anymore'n the others, that he swore he weren't nowhere near the white girl that night. I heard him the same as everybody else, 'cuz I was in the courtroom that day. But they weren't about to believe him. They had nuthin' on their minds but puttin' him on the road to Knoxville. And sure' nuff, that's what they done."

"Norris's friends in campus maintenance didn't testify?" Tyler asked.

"What could they say?"

"For starters, that others had access to the shovel used to bury the girl, his habit of night fishing, the innocent nature of his relationship with the girl, and his good character."

She beamed in admiration. "I reckon he'd been better off if you'd been born to defend him, instead of that little weasel, Jake Nevers. Jake had no backbone. And if you'd seen him slink around that . . ." Her eyes flashed suddenly.

"What?" Mayson asked.

"Somethin' Charmer just said — about how them boys on Edgar's crew coulda' helped. There was this one feller — the craggy-faced drunk from Luke's. Earl and I'd see him there after Thursday night bowlin', always drunk, his tongue a-flappin.' One night, I remember him talkin' about how he wished there'd been somethin' he coulda' done, like tellin' the jury what a fine man Edgar was. Only it was after the trial, with Edgar already countin' time in the death house.

"I remember thinkin': 'Ain't it a little late to be worryin' about such things?' And why in tarnations hadn't he put a bug in Jake Nevers's ear, if the weasel couldn't figger for hisself that Edgar's crewmates might be able to say somethin' on his behalf?"

"Do you recall the man's name?" Mayson asked.

" 'Course. Wally Vernon's the craggy-faced varmint. Don't shut up longer'n it takes to suck down a cold draft. I ain't seen him in years, although I ain't heard he died, neither. You two figgerin' on talkin' to him?"

Tyler shook his head. "If he worked with Norris, I'm sure our powerful friends have already gotten to him. They may even be watching, in hopes we do the same thing."

"Then you want me to talk to him?"

He glanced at Mayson. They couldn't ask her to do that, even if she was willing. "Thanks, but it's too dangerous."

"More dangerous than harboring you two?"

She had a point, but not good enough to justify putting her in more danger than she already was.

She scoffed, "So then you figger just to run off, and ignore the fact that Wally might know somethin' that can help?"

"You know," Mayson said now, "if Vernon has been contacted, he'd assume others had, too. And if one — like Lou here — happened to approach him to compare notes, I doubt for a second he'd be suspicious."

Lou winked at Tyler. "You got yourself a real smart one, Charmer. Sweet as pie, too."

"A sweet pain in the ass." He drew her against him.

Lou watched Mayson's eyes instantly glow. If the love bug hadn't bit her, she reckoned like Earl swore, the critter didn't exist. Charmer, she wasn't as sure about. He was 'fectionate enough now, but had been acting strange all afternoon. Like his mind was some place he wasn't.

"Lou, I was just thinking out loud," Mayson said. "I didn't really mean for you to consider contacting Vernon."

"Don't have to," she grunted. "I done made up my mind while you two was moonin' over each other."

Tyler watched her grab the phone book. "Damnit, Lou . . ."

"Don't you be damnin' me, young feller. You're a big'un all right, but not so big I can't take a switch to you." Licking her thumb, she flipped pages until she found the number.

"Shouldn't you talk to Earl first?" Mayson glanced at her snoozing husband.

"What for? The darn fool ain't ever stopped me from doin' what I set my mind to. And the odds ain't no better he could this time neither." She squinted as someone now came on the line. "Billy's that you? Sure, I remember them tall tales of yours. Now get Wally on the . . . Oh, he is, huh? Well tell him to call me when he gets back. If he's at Toot Hinker's, more'n likely he's drunk, but I want to jaw with him anyhow. Now take down my number."

As she barked it out, Tyler nuzzled Mayson's neck. "Billy must be deaf, too."

"That was Billy Springer. Him and Wally rent a place near the campus. He says Wally's eating turkey at Toot Hinker's. If he ain't too drunk, he'll call when he returns. If he is, I'll call him. What kinda' stuff you reckon I ought to ask?"

"First, if he's been questioned," Tyler replied. "Second, what they asked, and what he told them. Third, no matter how he answers one and two — find out what he knows that you haven't already told us. Only don't get too specific. Dance around some to disguise your intentions. Otherwise, we might find an army of Feds up here within the hour."

"Ain't nuthin'," she grunted. "I'll pick Wally clean 'fore the ole buzzard knows what . . ."

"I'll be damned!" Tyler burst as the game's score flashed. "The Skins are gonna beat Dallas!" It was a quiet, sullen crowd watching the final minutes in Texas Stadium. "Schuyler's putting a fresh log on about now," he smiled. "And pouring another Scotch." . . . And Kara would be dancing around the Castlewood study, drumstick in hand. She made him promise that if the Redskins won another Super Bowl, to drink a toast for her. She said she'd be watching. Had she, when they'd won four years ago? He'd toasted just in case.

"Schuyler's his father," Mayson explained.

"A boy callin' his daddy by his given name," Lou scolded. "I ain't never heard of such a thing."

"He calls his mother . . ." Mayson stopped as Tyler left the room. He'd been distant all afternoon, and she had no clue why.

At the kitchen window, he studied the moon glowing over the dark mountain ridge. Eight years ago they'd been in Pasadena as the Redskins clawed their way to a Super Bowl championship. As the horn sounded, Kara had sprung from her seat and said, "If football's played in Heaven, it must be just like this!" He wondered.

"I'm leaving."

He turned to Mayson, her arms stiffly folded. "All right."

"Does that mean you're coming, too?"

He nodded, very tired suddenly. Yet when he reached the living room, Lou's frown explained that she'd already left. "Didn't say it, but her feelings were bruised a bit."

"Then I better get up there. Thanks for having us, Lou."

"Say, where'd Macon run off to?" Earl glanced around now.

"It's Mayson, you darn fool!" Lou shouted.

"Ain't that what I just said!"

They'd go on like this until one died, Tyler realized. Then the other would hear the cabin's silence, and remember. He knew, and wished so badly that he didn't.

"It's a heavy ghost weighin' on you," Lou said. "Holidays are good and bad like everythin' else. Bad, 'cuz them ghosts can play hell then. That's what your eyes are tellin' me now. But what makes it worse, and I ain't tellin' you somethin' you don't already know, is that Mayson's feelin' your pain, too, 'cuz her heart's done hooked itself up with yours. 'Cept she don't know what you two is hurtin' over, unless you told her, and I ain't bettin' a dime on that."

Gazing at his hand on the door, he smiled, "Lou, you must be the smartest woman in these mountains."

He embraced her and then started across the dark camp. Passing the Beetle, he grabbed his bag from the glove compartment as he'd meant to that morning.

The cabin's deep chill soon greeted him, as did her soft crying behind the bathroom door. Nervous, he went over to knock. "I didn't tell you before, but you really blew me away when you breezed in this afternoon. I had no idea you were changing your hair back. I love your hair, you know." If he enjoyed occasional moments of eloquence, this definitely wasn't one. "Mayson, you looked beautiful. I mean, you are beautiful. The most beautiful woman I know."

The sobbing stopped now, but the bathroom silence deepened.

When she emerged minutes later, he was gone, a bag resting on her pillow. Inside were her Jams, JBs and a card. Smiling, she studied the card's touching scene: a little boy and girl, hands clasped, as they gazed up at the moon. Behind them was a festive table, with turkey and all the trimmings. *What would Thanksgiving be without a best friend?* the card read. It was inscribed, *To Mayson, my best friend. Tyler.*

Quietly, she slipped it back into the envelope.

The cabin was black, the TV on, when he returned. A fire blazed in the hearth, a wool quilt covered the bed and Mayson, like a cozy cat, was curled up watching football. "What's that?" she nodded at his bag.

"I ran into Earl. Lou had sent him up with our supper." He sighed. "As if we can eat after that spread this afternoon."

"Thanks for the JBs and Jams and the card. I didn't . . . I mean if I'd known . . ."

"If you're trying to say they don't give Thanksgiving presents in Brooklyn, it's all right."

Her large, dark eyes held him solemnly. "Tyler, am I really your best friend?"

"I wouldn't have given you the card otherwise."

"Oh . . ."

He could almost see her fragile emotions grappling over the meaning of her new status. Yet how could he clarify it? He knew only what his heart had labeled this fresh feeling — one felt just once before.

"There must be something else on." He grabbed the remote and flipped to an Eastwood western. Wrestling out of his jacket, he dropped on the bed to unlace his boots. As she switched back to the football game, he turned and asked, "Why'd you do that?"

"Because I was watching it."

"Right," he grunted. "And who's playing?"

"The Dolphins and Patriots, who happen to be tied for first in the AFC East."

He slashed his laces, unimpressed. "Have they said how Joe Montana's doing?"

"No, but I wouldn't expect them to."

"And why's that?"

"Because I'm certain their viewers are more interested in active quarterbacks than retired ones. Specifically, a rookie named Jake Fielder, who because the Dolphin vet is out with a torn ACL, is getting his first start. And so far, he's lived up to his billing as a first round draft pick."

As he turned to gape at her, she continued, "Coming from UCLA, with its pro style offense, everyone knew Fielder had a strong arm, quick release and excellent scrambling ability. But how many college QBs, even with his credentials, have what it takes to make it in the pros?

"So far, he does. He's shown tremendous poise against the Patriots' pass rush, but he hasn't confronted a safety blitz yet. I expect he will, however, if the Patriots' front four keeps giving him all day to pick up his secondary receivers . . .Tyler, did you face many safety blitzes at William and Mary?"

A revelation far more startling than Jake Fielder's pro potential now rippled over him. "I, ah . . . not that many . . . Why the hell didn't you tell me this?"

"About Fielder? I thought . . ."

"No! About football — how you know so much."

"I didn't think it was important."

Her eyes held a fresh intelligence that hadn't existed a few moments before. How could this not be important?

"Tyler, you loved football. But now it makes you sad. Did a cheerleader break your heart? Was Kara a cheerleader?"

"Please Mayson, don't."

"Sad to mad," she frowned. "You move from one emotion to the next, and I'm not allowed to ask why. That doesn't seem fair."

"What is?" he shrugged.

This was the inner darkness she'd suspected. And if she was ignorant of its cause, she at least knew its effect on him. One she refused to accept, as her lips now touched his.

One kiss drifted into the next: warm, sweet and for him, soothing, she hoped. For her, it was crippling, leaving her a rag doll as their lips parted.

Laying her back, he marveled again over her new hair. "It's growing," she rolled a lock in her finger. "How long do you want it? The same as before?"

"You be the judge of that."

Pouring coffee from the thermos, he stretched out beside her. "Who are we for?"

"Does it matter?"

"Only when the Skins are playing."

She sipped her coffee. "Then we're diehard fans, right?"

Gazing at her nestled inside his arm, he recalled her reaction to his comment on New York football. "And when they play the Giants?"

"We're Skins fans, even then."

"Mayson, best friends don't ask each other to give up their favorite football team."

"Nor put their lives on the line. When one needs help, the other is just there, like you were for me. Besides," she said as she stroked his nose, "it's hardly a sacrifice converting to Redskinism. Since you're among its faithful, my commitment flows naturally."

Or, like a piece of cake. That's what Kara would say.

The game flew by as they sipped coffee and snuggled inside the warm quilt. Her sharp commentary returned the game's richness and color that had been missing for so long. She knew football as well as Kara had, with the same fiery passion. "You're right," he nodded as Fielder led the Dolphins to victory, with a last-minute touchdown drive. "The rookie has a hell of an arm."

"So did you," she quickly added. "You couldn't have piled up seven-thousand yards and sixty touchdowns otherwise."

As the game ended, she settled back inside his arm. Grabbing the remote, he channel-surfed over anything smelling of news. The threat was constant. Their odyssey could end any moment with a siren-shrieking procession. They didn't need a news flash to remind them they were living on the edge.

Soon, they slipped into the safe harbor of Gilligan's Island.

Then the cozy warmth of the Petries' New Rochelle home. The zany, yet unthreatening world of Lucy and Ricky Ricardo. Had the past really been better, or did it just seem that way?

He drifted into a place where memories were sweet and discovery was exhilarating. A place where the old and new merged.

She knew only that he'd slipped away. Where, she had no clue. Nor did she ask. Certainly he wouldn't tell her. And she wasn't so sure she wanted to know.

They stumbled next into Mayberry. "Do you remember this one?" she asked. "Barney gets everyone over at Andy's because he thinks Andy's getting married."

"I remember . . ." Lavinny's cookies, a warm fire on a crisp autumn afternoon at Castlewood. Ozzie and Harriet came next. "Do you think a family like the Nelsons ever existed?" Mayson asked. "Their world is so calm and orderly. When something goes wrong, they're so unflappable: 'Gee, Harriet. Darn Dad. Golly, Ozzie.'" Her chin settled in his chest. "Don't you think they ever wanted to say 'shit?'"

His fingers dabbled in her hair, as he smiled. "Can't you imagine Ozzie coming home from work, being handed Ricky's report card and shouting, 'You stupid goddamned sonofabitch! I'm gonna break your ass!'"

"TV screens would go black all across America," she laughed. "Believe it or not, I'm hungry."

Jumping up, she lifted two turkey sandwiches from the bag, then two drumsticks. "Wasn't Lou thoughtful to . . ." She suddenly recalled his question at the table. Her answer? Dark meat. Earl's bag had contained two sandwiches, but not two drumsticks. Tyler had returned to the Adkins with a special request.

He caught her pensive glow. "What's the matter?"

"Nothing," she shrugged. "Let's eat."

Later, she slipped into the bathroom to prepare for bed. He smiled when she emerged looking like a delicate scarecrow in his football jersey. "For some reason, it fits better this evening."

"Because I'm a gridiron wizard?" Impulsively she dove, attacking him with relentless tickles. When he squirmed, she tickled harder. When he cussed, she giggled louder. Furious minutes passed until she finally straddled him. "I win!"

His eyes found her delicate, apple-like breasts inside the loose jersey. "How do you define 'winning?' "

"Because you can't get up. You do admit you can't?"

"Like hell."

"Then try!" Her eyes gleamed.

"When I'm ready."

"Now! Let's see you!"

"It wouldn't be very nice of me to embarrass you during your victory celebration."

"Embarrass me? How?"

"By swatting you off like a gnat."

"In your dreams. Now come on, try."

He sighed, "Just remember you asked for it." Like a panther, he slipped from her grasp and slung her, kicking and squealing, over his shoulder.

"Put me down!" She pounded, as he strutted about the cabin. "I hope you realize this doesn't count."

"And why's that?"

"Because you started before the three count. Now we have to do it all over again."

"Like hell." He stopped at the window. The Adkins cabin still glowed in the darkness. "I wonder what's for breakfast?"

"Tyler, put me down before I really get mad."

He carried her into the bathroom instead. "Just close your eyes," he stood over the toilet. "This won't take long."

"You wouldn't . . ."

"I most certainly would."

"Wait! Maybe we can negotiate."

"Negotiate, hell. I won."

"We'll call it a draw . . . No, a timeout. Then we can decide who won later."

Later. Kara's strategy, until the day it no longer existed. Putting her down, he shut himself inside the bathroom.

"Tyler?" She knocked instantly. "You're not mad about the timeout, are you?"

"Of course not." His eyes closed over the sink. Did any of this make sense? What was he doing here?

"Tyler, come quick!" she shouted. "*Bullitt!* A poster movie — Steve McQueen. Fast cars. Chases. Hurry!"

He emerged to find her perched on the quilt, as she pointed at Steve McQueen crawling into his hot Mustang. "You won't like it." He dropped beside her.

"A poster movie? How could I not?"

They were soon absorbed in the movie. With her close, the world suddenly became safe and comfortable. But also transient. Kara was eternity. She hadn't died, just moved into the next life, where they'd one day rejoin. It terrified him to imagine anything else.

When the movie ended, he turned off the TV; she, the lamp. As they embraced in the darkness, her slender leg slipped inside his. "Tyler, we may not survive this odyssey. Any minute, sirens could shriek over the mountains."

"I'm well aware of that."

"Suppose you knew you'd die an hour from now, and could spend it any way you wanted — how would you?"

He realized he was being set up. "I don't know. How about you?"

"I asked first."

"Yes, Mayson, but it's your question, and I believe you deserve the first crack."

"Tyler, I hate it when you do this . . . How many women have you slept with?"

"Counting you?"

"Not sleep. Sleep!"

"You mean sex — and it's none of your business."

"Dozens?"

"Even if there were, no honorable man would answer a question like that."

"You mean no honorable man would sleep with so many women."

"I admit I'm not proud of everything I've done in life," he sighed.

"Then it is dozens! Maybe a hundred. Tyler, have you slept with a hundred women?"

"I'm going to sleep now."

As he rolled away, she crept over his shoulder. "Is it a hundred? A simple yes or no will do."

Nothing was simple with her. If he'd learned anything, it was that. "How the hell should I know how many? I don't keep records or collect notches in my belt. What kind of egotistical bastard do you think I am? Now go to sleep."

"That means you have. A hundred women!"

"If it was, no doubt you'd throw it in my face every chance you got."

"I would not. Then it is a hundred?"

"I just said I've never counted."

"Approximately, then?"

Would he be insane to exchange a few hours sleep for an eternity of persecution? "Maybe. Now go to sleep."

"A hundred. Tyler . . .!"

"Goddamnit, Mayson, go to sleep."

The darkness became quiet . . . and sharp. Razor sharp. He knew his cue. "Are you all right?"

"Of course not."

"Then do you plan on discussing it, or should I prepare to spend the night chasing these absurd notions that sweep through your mind at the drop of a hat? Just tell me which."

"Not if you insist on being hateful."

"Fine." He smacked his pillow. "I asked. I can't do anymore than that." Closing his eyes, he counted.

"Tyler?"

Twenty-two seconds. "What?"

"If you've slept with a hundred women, why haven't you tried with me? Am I that undesirable?"

"There you go again, baiting me with another false assumption. I've never said you were undesirable. I've said you're beautiful. Furthermore, I've kissed you a dozen times, which proves it."

"But you don't want sex, which proves I'm undesirable."

Didn't his astonishing tolerance count for anything? His keen grasp of her cue cards, like the one flashing now?

Drawing her into his arms, he gathered his thoughts. More than desirable, she was shadowed by something vast, undefined.

And until it was defined, there could be no sex. Then what could he say that wouldn't confuse or hurt her? The truth, which came easily, as it usually did. "Mayson, if there've been a hundred . . . none has brought me the satisfaction of just holding you like I am now." Excluding the first, who neither time, nor circumstance, could disturb.

She trembled softly in the darkness. And when he finally slept, she whispered, "Tyler, you're my best friend, too."

CHAPTER TWENTY-THREE

★

On Friday morning, Nicole Vermilion relieved the Columbia Law student hired to answer the special 800 number at night. "No calls," he smiled wearily, grabbing his coat.

As he left, she slipped into Mr. Lamp's office to start the coffee. Would their D.C. offices be as nice as those here in the Old Dame? Certainly they would. U.S. Supreme Court Justice: how much more prestigious could you get? She'd agreed without hesitation to join him. They'd been a team ever since he'd grabbed her from the firm's typing pool twenty years ago. And with her mother's recent death, there was nothing keeping her in New York.

She had an irresistible urge to start packing. But how could she? They wouldn't know they were going for sure until after the Senate hearings that began Monday. The Longbridge administration was pressing for swift confirmation so Mr. Lamp could be on the Court for the spring's critical cases. The only glitch to confirmation, besides his conservative views, was the Corelli-Waddill affair, which was gaining momentum daily. How much would the Senate liberals make of it? Would they claim this messy affair wouldn't have happened if he'd run a tighter ship at Lieber Allen?

She'd never liked Mayson Corelli who, with her beautiful face, model's figure and Columbia honors degree, considered herself better than everyone else. Who cared if she looked like Audrey Hepburn? Didn't Tyler Waddill, with his family wealth, have far more reason to be snooty? Yet he wasn't. When her own mother had died, Tyler, just weeks at the firm, had sent her a large flower basket and to her shock, appeared at the Long Island funeral home to offer his condolences. He'd shown her more compassion than people she'd known a lifetime. How could he throw his own life away on a murderer like Mayson?

After checking Mr. Lamp's messages, she took her coffee back to her desk. Oddly, Carl hadn't received any calls. He rarely received many, but always a few, which meant someone had to man the phones, even if the calls were being simultaneously transmitted to the FBI's Washington office. There were scripted questions to ask and details about the reward to provide. And who could say when a person's information might be acquired? When they might accidentally spot the fugitives? It could be anywhere, any time.

She inspected the recorder now to insure Carl hadn't missed any calls while snoozing over his books. The dial didn't move. Still, she listened to a minute of silence until satisfied. Perhaps Thanksgiving explained the quiet night. The vast majority of callers were kooks with wild fugitive sightings anywhere from L.A. to Timbuktu. Only a handful had proven legitimate, like the guy on the bus from New York to Baltimore.

The first call came at 8:00 as morning news programs concluded on the East Coast. "Is this the number to call about them fugitives?"

"Yes, sir," she replied. "Where are you calling from?"

"Flavin County. I don't reckon you know where that's at?"

She hadn't until this week. Now, however, like everyone else, she knew there were enough police concentrated in the region to wage a full-scale war - certainly enough to find the fugitives. Did this man know where they were? "You're referring to Flavin County, Tennessee. Yes, I know where it is. Do you have information on the fugitives?"

"I reckon you could say that."

It took just a minute of Tennessee-twanged explanation to make her a believer. This was the call they'd been waiting for. Crisply, she answered his questions about the reward.

"You reckon I'll see one darn penny?" he grumbled. "I could use that money today."

"You'll be contacted the moment a decision's made." She quickly scanned the script. Oops, she'd forgotten the most basic question of all. "Your name, please?"

"Harley Bogins."

She took it down, along with the address and phone number of an Iron Ridge car dealership. "Make sure you put confidential on any mailing," he added. "And don't speak to nobody 'cept me when you call."

Spine tingling, she hung up. Mr. Lamp would be so excited.

She started to call him in D.C. where he was preparing for the confirmation hearings, when the phone rang again. It was another Flavin County resident. "Name's Jimmy Dale. I'm a carrier for the U.S. Postal Service," he said. Quickly, he confirmed the information provided by Harley Bogins.

Jotting it down, Nicole answered his questions about the reward. "Thank you, Mr. Dale. We'll be in touch soon."

She'd just hung up, when yet a third Flavin County resident called: Deputy Sheriff Darrell Pamplin, whose information corroborated the first two. Answering his questions about the reward, she hung up and quickly called Mr. Lamp.

Upon hearing the news, Lamp contacted Harrington, who'd just received the same report from Chapman. "The Lord has responded," Harrington offered a divine interpretation. "Thomas and Larry are en route now to Iron Ridge, Tennessee to establish a command post and supervise the operation's final phase."

"Is there anything I can do?" Lamp asked.

"Pray for another miracle on this prophetic day."

"What miracle?"

"That no ghosts emerge from the millions viewing your televised confirmation next week."

Hanging up, he began preparation of Streeter's briefing of Longbridge when the fugitives were caught later that day. He was still working on it when the phone rang again. "We just landed in Knoxville," Leopold reported. "We'll be back in Pine by noon to grab a little sack time."

"I doubt you'll want to sleep after hearing my news."

"They caught the kids?" Leopold asked.

"Three tips place them at a boys' camp in Flavin County. Chapman and Streeter are en route now." He sighed, "It should be over soon."

"Praise the Lord!"

"Yes, Arch, praise Him indeed."

"I haven't seen the news, sir. Anything interesting?"

"There is, as a matter of fact. GNN reported a burglary in Mountain Creek, Pennsylvania last night. I'm not sure why it made national news, except that the homeowner killed when discovering the intruders was an ex-FBI agent. Benjamin Harvey.

His girlfriend was killed, too."

"A shame, sir. I happened to be in the same vicinity last night. I didn't realize it was such a dangerous place."

"Was it also a revealing one?"

"Our visit couldn't have been better timed. The residence turned up research indicating Harvey and the kids were on the right track. The place was clean, otherwise."

"You've done well," Harrington sighed. "Now return to your hotel for some well deserved rest."

The jet carrying the Attorney General and FBI Director landed at a remote Federal compound fifty miles west of Knoxville. Quickly they were escorted to a waiting chopper, and in seconds were clipping over the mountains for Flavin County.

By noon, they'd established their command post atop the Iron Ridge courthouse, a brick monstrosity with white pillars and portico. Surrounded by their lieutenants, Flavin Sheriff Lucas Breeden, and a handful of his deputies and Tennessee troopers, they studied a map of the Eagle's Nest Camp. Local participation, or at least its perception, would be important later when the questions started flying. The more involved the locals were, the easier it'd be to blame them for the grievous tragedy.

Chapman turned to the potbellied, pock-faced Breeden. "Are we certain no word of the operation has been leaked?"

Breeden nodded. "Bogins and Dale are in my office downstairs and they ain't goin' nowhere, until it's over. And 'course Darrell ain't told nobody." He nodded at his solemn-faced deputy.

"How about security at the camp?" Streeter asked.

Breeden gripped his gun belt. "Dodson's unit is posted at the camp road. Your boys, Morris and Garth, are with him. Two units are also stationed a quarter-mile east and west of the junction. No one's been reported on the road since surveillance began, 'cept that parcel carrier this mornin'."

"We're certain there's no other road into the camp?"

"Just the one," he nodded, "and it's sealed off. Them fugitives ain't goin' nowhere without us knowin'."

"Unless perhaps on foot," Chapman qualified.

"I wouldn't worry about that. There's nuthin' beyond that camp 'cept miles of steep mountain. How far you reckon a couple city slickers can get on foot?"

"Let's not find out." He gauged the anxious faces around him. "All right. The units assembled outside will leave the courthouse and proceed north to the camp. The Attorney General and I will ride in the lead unit with Sheriff Breeden. Pete Nicholas, the agent-in-charge, will occupy the second unit, along with Conrad. At least one Federal agent will occupy each of the remaining units. Upon reaching the camp, Nicholas's agents will form the front line of attack. That's no reflection on you Tennessee gentlemen. It's just that we're confronted with an extremely dangerous situation, and if lives must be placed at risk, they should be those of Federal agents. The fugitives, after all, are wanted for Federal crimes. They're also desperate and heavily armed.

"Now," he said as he pointed at the map, "Nicholas's force will move quickly to seal off the camp, securing the cabins and other buildings. A second contingent of troopers and deputies under Sheriff Breeden's command will form an outer ring and assist in the fugitives' capture, as circumstances require. The remaining force will secure the road and front grounds here," he stabbed with his pencil. "Are there any questions?"

"Givin' how dangerous them two are," Breeden asked, "you figger there'll be a shootout?"

"That's certainly a possibility and the reason our agents will lead the assault."

"If you do take them alive," Breeden said, "we got plenty of cell space here."

"That won't be necessary, but thanks anyway," Streeter replied. "Now unless there's anything else, let's get moving."

A shuffling exodus ensued as Nicholas, Conrad, Butterfield and Bingham remained behind. Nicholas, a swarthy-skinned New Yorker with cold black eyes, closed the door. Chapman's tone now became conspiratorial. "If by some chance we can't avoid taking the fugitives alive, and that Huckleberry Sheriff or any of his deputy huckleberries ask where we're taking them, explain politely that it's none of their goddamned business. Personally, I've found 'confidential' works wonders in these situations."

The room trickled with laughter. "The explanation to other agents is that the fugitives will be temporarily housed at the Green

River Compound in Kentucky," Streeter added.

"What if they ask why so far north?" Butterfield asked. "Knoxville is our closest facility."

Chapman replied, "It's not equipped to handle dangerous prisoners like Corelli and Waddill."

"Dangerous how?" Conrad asked.

Nicholas turned to his subordinate. "Have you forgotten Corelli's Mob connections that make her the point person in this records conspiracy? Who knows how the New York families will react to her capture? They could send a few battalions down to break the fugitives out. Or else execute them, if they think their confessions might bring indictments against key family figures. Because of this, and myriad other possibilities, we need a tighter facility than Knoxville."

"Most within the Bureau don't know Green River has reopened," Butterfield said. "What do we say about it?"

"Just that its detention facilities have been reopened for those classified as presenting a 'special danger' to national security or else are themselves threatened by a special danger. Because of their Mob connections, these fugitives, if taken alive, will be eligible under the latter of these guidelines."

Bingham raised another concern. "There's been rumbling about whether Harvey, because of his friendship with Swanson, was possibly involved in the Bureau conspiracy. How should we address this?"

"Explain confidentially it appears that way," Chapman replied. "There's no point in publicizing the corruption of a deceased agent. I believe everyone will understand that."

"Assuming the fugitives end up at Green River," Conrad asked. "How difficult will it be to explain their suicides?"

"Not difficult at all," Nicholas replied. "When faced with life in prison or possible Mob execution, suicide must seem an attractive alternative. Didn't the Nazis also resort to cyanide ingestion after the Nuremberg Trials?"

"Precisely," Chapman agreed. "And their captors couldn't prevent its ingestion anymore than we'll be able to."

"The media will scream negligence just the same," Butterfield predicted. "They'll say it was brought on by the fugitives' detention in a maximum security facility, where things like that aren't supposed to happen."

"But they do," Nicholas replied. "Don't you think Nuremberg was the world's most heavily secured prison at the time?"

"We can deal with a negligence claim," Streeter added. "It's the alternative I'm not so sure about."

"There'll be questions just the same," Butterfield insisted. "Ones that will carry over into next week's confirmation hearings."

"If we dispose of the fugitives at the camp as planned, we won't have to worry about Green River," Chapman reminded them. "I assume we have the untraceable .38s?"

Nicholas nodded. "They'll be found near the bodies if the fugitives don't have their own."

"Containing a half-round each and freshly fired," Butterfield added.

Streeter repeated another critical instruction. "The fugitives aren't to be interrogated under any circumstances. If taken alive, they'll be transported to Green River. Let's pray that won't be necessary."

Chapman and Streeter remained as the others left to prepare for departure. Quietly they studied the frantic scene outside. Patrol cars lined Main Street, the front units curled like a cane handle into Town Square, where a curious crowd had gathered. Sheriff Breeden, standing beneath the bronze statue of a founding father, barked orders, his arms waving furiously. "I dare say this is better than the County Christmas Parade," Streeter smiled.

Chapman nodded. "I assume you caught this morning's news?"

"Travis Culpepper, you mean? Yes, I caught the report. But I'm not worried. He can't hurt us, despite what Falkingham, that other pompous ass, thinks."

"But he has the President's ear," Chapman pointed out. "Especially now."

"Maybe so, but Harrington has his soul. That's much better. Come on." Streeter slapped his friend's shoulder. "Let's not keep the troops waiting."

CHAPTER TWENTY-FOUR

★

Tyler woke to the morning sun filtering through the cabin window. Mayson was awake beside him, her eyes fixed on the mountain wilderness outside. Drawing her into his arms, he kissed her with a startling hunger. He was beginning to crave her delicate body's quiver, her soft sigh, knowing precisely where her lips would wander: over his nose, and into his hair. He knew then to stroke her neck and when his fingers slipped down her spine, her legs would curl and with another sigh, her lips would return to his.

With a determined effort, he tugged the reins on his passion, breaking their last kiss. Rising, she peered fretfully out the window. "I just don't understand. I'm the one who warms your bed, yet she's the one you cry out for in your sleep."

"I hurt your feelings," he said as he recalled the dream.

"Why should they concern you?" she pouted. "You love Kara."

"Kara has nothing to do with this."

She didn't respond, which meant her entire being was responding. Lying back, he counted the seconds. Finally she shouted, "I know Kara has nothing to do with this! Don't you think I know that? I hate her, Tyler. She broke your heart and yet you still can't let her go."

Rising, he began to dress. "I don't want to discuss this."

"Because Kara's some sort of sacred ground; yes, I know that well."

"Then why do you keep bringing it up?" He threw on his sweater.

"Because I'm jealous."

"You're not jealous."

"Stop telling me how I feel." She watched him lace his boots. "So where is your dream woman now? Did she marry someone else? Move to China? Or vanish in the Bermuda Triangle? She wasn't on the space shuttle. I would've heard about that."

As he grabbed his jacket and started out, she yelled, "Tyler, you can't keep running away!"

He swung around, his jaw quivering. "You just don't know when to quit."

Confused not by his anger, but the deep pain in his eyes, she watched him vanish.

When she emerged from the bathroom later, she found him brooding at the window. There were so many questions she wanted to ask and yet so few he'd answer. "We're leaving today?"

"It's too dangerous to sit still."

"What if Harvey's package doesn't arrive? And you haven't plotted a course on the map. What roads can we take that aren't sealed off?"

"There's only the one, north. We'll get through with our new car and IDs."

He was much too confident. How could they possibly pull off the miracle of Naples? "Even if we get off the mountain, they'll be waiting wherever we go."

"Listen Mayson, I don't make the goddamned rules, okay?"

"Why can't we just stay here?" she asked.

About to reply, he stopped at the door's sudden rapping. As he opened it, Lou entered in her tattered coat and boots, a scarf covering her head. "I reckon you've been waitin' on this," she said, and stuck a package in his chest. "Feller drove it up in his fancy jeep; a lot newer'n Jimmy's." She studied Mayson. "A little sleep brought that rosy glow back to your cheeks. I reckon you'll be wantin' breakfast. There's plenty when you're ready to come down."

Tyler emptied the package on the counter: new ID cards, family pictures and the promised biographical research. "Well I'll be darn," Lou marveled. "Just like that, you're somebody differn't." Her eyes narrowed. "Enough to get you off the mountain, you figger?"

"We were taking a vote when you came in," Mayson said.

Lou now recalled the other reason for her visit. "I reckon y'all need to know somethin' and I hope it ain't as bad as I think."

"What?" Mayson's eyes widened.

"Well, you know Earl and me don't watch much TV, 'cept since Wednesday, we've been followin' the news pretty regular, seein' as you two is the stars and all. Anyway, this mornin' the news feller was talkin' about a burglary last night. And them burglars, whoever they was, were pretty darn mean to break into those folks home on Thanksgivin'. Noisy as hell too, seein' as they woke 'em in the process, then kilt 'em both."

"Who are you talking about?" Tyler asked.

"Them folks in Mountain Creek, Pennsylvania." She nodded at the package. "I damn near jumped outta my skin when that news feller said Madelyn Stump, 'cuz I was lookin' right at her name just as I was her address there."

They gaped at each other in shock. Harvey dead? It couldn't be. Tyler quickly turned the TV on to GNN as a Wall Street report ended. The hourly news was next. "What do we do now?" Mayson shrieked.

Pray. Run like hell, Tyler thought. His heart pounded as the news update began. The manhunt remained the lead story; the pair were still believed to be hiding in the eastern Tennessee mountains, and were still wanted for a murder they hadn't committed and a records conspiracy that didn't exist.

The anchorman moved on to the next story. "After two weeks in the Orient, Secretary Culpepper is returning home with a new trade agreement..." The vision of oriental prints and vases in the Culpepper York County mansion gripped Tyler suddenly. Betsy had enjoyed the trip more than Travis.

"Just tell us about Harvey!" Mayson insisted as Tyler slipped off with his treasured reflections...

They flew down the lush slope as Matt Culpepper and Kelly Carlisle prepared the sleek cruiser for launch. Kara lugged the picnic basket. He juggled the heavy cooler. Sixteen years old, they moved with a child's energy, yet appreciated the joys of adulthood. And on that brilliant summer morning, anything had seemed possible.

"They'd never leave us," Kara said. "We have the food."

"And the beer," he added, although uncertain it mattered. "Matt wants to be alone with..."

"Hurry!" Kelly shouted above the engine.

"She sounds desperate," Kara said. *"Come on!"*

They reached the dock before Matt could get away, Kelly taking their provisions as they jumped aboard. Starting off now, the day breezed by as they cruised the river, sunned on the bow and sucked down the new contraband acquired only with careful planning: ice cold beer. Anchoring finally in their special cove, they swam, ate lunch, and played on the beach. Kara scooped up another piece of glass, dazzled as always. *"Where did it start?"* *she asked.* *"How long has it drifted?"* *She watched Matt pull Kelly into the trees.* *"Maybe the beer wasn't such a good idea."* *"Do you know what Betsy and Travis would do if they knew we had it out here on the cruiser?"*

"I know what Travis would do," he smiled. *"Send Matt to military school like he's always threatening."*

"How much beer does it take to get drunk?" she asked.

"Six, I think."

"Then you'd better take the helm on the return trip. Matt's way past six."

The York mansion had glittered for the evening barbecue, the terrace crawling with guests. Filling their plates, he and Kara ducked into the magnolias as the sun slipped over the river. Her perfumed hair scented the evening breeze. *"What is it again?"* *he asked.*

"L' Air Du Temps. And I'll expect a bottle for my birthday."

He now asked the question that had been on his mind recently. *"Kara, are we going steady?"*

"I don't really know what that means," *she shrugged.* *"But if it's like Matt and Kelly, we moved past that long ago. I can't even define my life without you. When I look back, you're in every memory. When I look forward, you're in every dream. Beginning to end. What we have, Tyler, will sustain us the rest of our lives. We're 'best friends,' that's what I'm . . ."*

"It's true!" Mayson's yelling jerked Tyler from his reflections. "Harvey's dead!"

The anchorman now stated, "Authorities believe this is the latest in a recent series of burglaries to plague Mountain Creek, having found no evidence linking Harvey's murder to the conspiracy involving his late friend, Swanson, and the fugitives, Corelli and Waddill."

"This doesn't change our plans," Tyler said. "Lou, have you talked with Vernon yet?"

"This mornin', " she nodded.

"Did they question him?"

"Some feller with a foreign name Wally couldn't pronounce too good; he bought Wally beer as long as he kept talking. Drinkin' and talkin.' Wally ain't never had trouble with either. He said the feller was real interested in the Norris case and claimed to be a history writer doin' research. Real big feller with a bad limp."

"Leopold!" Mayson exclaimed. "What did Wally tell him?"

"That he remembered the girl leavin' Luke's with them boys the night she disappeared. He couldn't recall their names but said one was real tall. Smoked a fancy cigarette, with black-and-gold ringed filters. Them same butts littered the girl's grave when they dug her up."

"Falkingham," Tyler nodded. "He must've been smoking Dunhills even back then."

Lou asked, "Them hearin's the news feller was talkin' about. They'll be on TV next week?"

"That's right," Mayson confirmed.

"Well, now I know forty years adds more 'n a few wrinkles to a person's face, but supposin' Wally was to watch them TV hearin's real close and finger the new judge as one of them boys? It's a long shot, but there don't seem no harm in findin' out if he can do it."

"Just make sure he keeps his mouth shut," Tyler said.

"Wally ain't too good at that as I said, 'cept he did manage to keep real quiet about the girl's murder forty years ago, lettin 'em put the juice to Edgar when he know'd he was innocent. Made Wally madder 'n hell when I pointed that out; he damn near broke my eardrum sayin' he and George put their John Hancocks to statements for Crenshaw, all official-like, the same day the girl's body was dug up."

"Who's George?" Tyler asked.

"George Elroy. He was with Wally at Luke's the night the girl left with them boys, only George seen more 'n Wally - enough to get hisself a job at Dennis Crenshaw's lumber mill. Dennis was Jasper's brother. And he's dead now, too, 'fore you go askin,' same as George. Anyway, George seen them boys with the girl later that night on Gray's Ridge. That's where the college kids did their neckin' in them days."

"So Vernon and Elroy gave statements to Crenshaw, who then saw more than three suspects - dollar signs, specifically," Mayson mused.

"And after getting the statements, Crenshaw must've then scooped up the Dunhill butts," Tyler continued. "Evidence gathered for blackmail, not prosecution."

"As long as the evidence existed, he knew he was safe," she added. "They wouldn't kill him for fear it would come out. Instead, they met his demands, hoping to buy time until the incriminating evidence could be acquired."

"But it never was," he said. "It ended up in Morris's hands, who was killed to keep the secret safe."

"But it's not," she said. "We have to assume the evidence — Vernon and Elroy's statements and the Dunhill butts, at the very least — wasn't recovered. Likely it's in a safe somewhere just waiting to be found. Maybe Crenshaw entrusted it to his sister's Minnesota family, who then turned it over to Morris." Thoughtful for a minute, she then asked, "Did they know its contents?"

"If so, they'd be dead now," he replied. "Assuming they didn't, Morris wouldn't have shared the discovery or left the safe behind. He'd have taken it back to New York."

"And hide it where?" she asked. "A rented locker at La Guardia?"

"If so, it'd be gone by now."

"How about another storage facility?" she asked. "The Post Office, maybe?"

"Don't you think those pricks have already checked those places? If Morris drove from Snow Peak to St. Paul to catch his Saturday flight, he could've dropped the safe off anywhere along the way."

"Then why return to Duluth later that day?" she asked. "If it was to hide the safe, he would've certainly had it on the plane."

"So what you figger to do?" Lou asked.

He shrugged. "Find the safe, if it exists. There's no other way to prove who murdered the girl."

"Well, when the time comes, I can guarantee Wally'll tell them John Laws all he knows. Won't take no more 'n a keg of premium draft. And in the meantime, I reckon you've got a lot of figgerin' to do and I'll just get in the way. When you're done, there'll be omelets and spoon bread waitin.' Done threw the grits out, though. Not that it bothers Mayson. She don't like 'em, no matter how much she pretends."

As she left, Tyler said, "I'm sorry about Harvey. I can't imagine where we'd be without his help."

"I can," she smiled mournfully. "It's an hour from now I'm not so sure about."

As he retrieved the map from the car and began plotting a northern course, she rearranged their wallets, replacing the old IDs with the new ones. "I'm Blanche Berry this time."

"That'll be hard to forget," he said as he studied the map. "Harder to say with a straight face. Who am I?"

"Clement Alvin Berry."

"Nice . . . I've just gotten us to St. Louis."

"If only it was that easy," she sighed. "What should I do with the old IDs?"

"We'll dump them in the lake before leaving." He folded the map. "Are you ready?"

Her stomach lurched. They were leaving after breakfast. Would it be their last?

Grabbing the records under the bed, he followed her out. "I'm still trying to grasp how you carried this damn box halfway across Naples."

"The same way I carried the boxes from Cellini's warehouse to the store shelves. You do what you have to."

They looked up as a black chopper glided south across the mountains. "FBI," he said. "One just like it dropped Falkingham off at a party on the Potomac once. He'd gotten shit-faced playing golf that afternoon, so rather than going home to change he arranged for a chopper-hop to the party. Can you believe the arrogant bastard? He landed on the hosts' lawn in his seersucker pants and alpaca sweater, his nose glowing like a cherry, a Dunhill dangling from his lips."

"You were there?" she asked.

"Oh, yeah. I watched him make a complete ass of himself that night. But why should he care? He's only Chief Justice of the Supreme Court."

"And crony of the FBI Director in the conspiracy of the century," she replied. "No doubt everyone in the Longbridge administration is."

"Except Travis Culpepper." Tyler grabbed the box again and followed her down the knoll.

"Why not him?" she asked.

"He just isn't." He'd explain later. The box was like lead in his arms. "That chopper means something's up."

"Do you think Director Chapman was on it?"

He shook his head. "I doubt he'll show up until . . ."

She caught the sudden flash of alarm in his eyes. "Until what — he knows where we are?"

"Tell Lou I'll be there in a minute." He started off.

"Answer me, Tyler. Is that what you were going to say?"

"Yes, Goddamnit."

Putting the box in the car, he returned to find Mayson and Lou sitting gloomily at the table. "Earl's in the shed messin' with his lawnmower," Lou said. "It needed fixin' last summer when the grass was growin,' but he waits 'til we ain't got none to do somethin' about it. The man's always done things backwards." She nodded. "Sit yourself down. You best be goin'."

He glanced at Mayson's untouched plate. When would they eat again? Or would they?

Setting his plate out, Lou watched him eat quickly. "I ain't gonna' ask where you're goin.' It's best I don't know, 'cuz them John Laws will be callin' again, sure 'nuff."

"Come on, Blanche Berry," Tyler said as he rose. "It's time to hit the road."

Lou gave them warm hugs. "When you're fixed to go, honk that Beetle if'n Harley Bogins left it with a horn. I'm gonna fix you up a dinner bag for the road."

Back in the cabin, Mayson slipped on Tyler's charcoal sweater. It'd be cold driving down the mountain. And was there any reason to assume their new rattletrap had a competent heater? When they finished packing, Tyler grabbed the suitcases. "Why don't you toss the old IDs while I pack the car?" he said.

As he left she scanned the cabin again, her eyes snagging on a scrap beneath the counter, where she'd rearranged their wallets. Robert Hunter's number. Or was it a phone number at all? By calling every area code in the country, hadn't she proven it wasn't? Still, she retrieved the scrap and hurried down to the lake.

After packing the car, he returned to the Adkins cabin. "Coffee's brewin'," Lou said as she met him at the door. "Go get your woman. I'll have the thermos filled when you get back."

Shrugging, he returned across the camp. Why did every woman feel it her life's mission to make a man wait? His only spats with Kara had been over this same irritating subject, one that . . . He turned suddenly at the groaning air. A strange noise was rising above the trees. He scanned the peaceful mountains, the sleepy cabins, the empty lane, the . . . A terrible thunder suddenly shattered the sky.

Instinctively, he scrambled up the knoll and quickly cresting it, turned - to see the dust rising and the patrol cars streaming, bumper-to-bumper, into the camp. Lou burst from the cabin as Earl hobbled from the shed. Cars doors flew open and an army spilled over the campgrounds. "Give'em hell!" he thought to himself as he watched Lou's arms wave furiously.

Bursting into the empty cabin, he then quickly dashed down to the lake. Mayson spun as he swooped like a madman from the shivering trees. "They're here!" he told her breathlessly. "Hundreds!"

"Where?" she cried in alarm.

Desperately, Tyler scanned the towering mountains; yesterday they were a protective barrier, but today they were a prison. Did direction matter? "Let's go!" he shouted.

Quickly they fled north across the jagged shoreline, swatting brush, trudging through marshes, and stumbling over rocks. Finally reaching the mountain's base, they paused to catch their breath. "Corelli! Waddill!" boomed a voice over the water. "Give it up! There's no way out!" The first Feds trickled down to the shore, half heading north, half south.

"They're trying to outflank us," Tyler said.

Again the air vibrated. "This is Special Agent Nicholas. Our forces are surrounding you. Surrender now."

Oddly he watched Mayson's eyes shut tightly. "What the hell are you doing?" he asked her.

"Praying," she replied.

"Well, do it on the climb." Grabbing her arm, he plunged into the dark mountain wilderness. The brush thickened, daylight reduced to thin cracks in the canopy. At times it disappeared entirely, leaving them to grope blindly on their treacherous ascent.

"Corelli! Waddill!" Nicholas's command reverberated over their jagged breathing. "Give it up!"

The slope steepened and slippery rocks dominated the higher elevations. Mayson moved slower and grunted louder as she pulled herself up, root by cold, wet root. Clearly she was running out of gas. Tyler began stopping every twenty feet to allow her to catch up, then every ten. With each shiver of brush, each rattling stone on the slope, his heart stopped until she finally crawled, huffing, over the rocks. If there was a woman who could beat this damned mountain, it was Mayson Corelli.

"What are you grinning at?" she asked.

"One hundred pounds of Italian grit." He studied her flushed face. "You're tired. Let's rest."

"I'm fine."

"Just five minutes."

"I said I'm fine."

"Well, I'm not." Dropping wearily on the rocks, he gazed at the endless mountains as he pondered their situation. Her foot soon tapped impatiently. "Do you plan on sitting here all day?"

"Just wait a goddamned minute. There's no bus to catch. I'm considering our options."

"Which are?" she asked.

He was about to explain when he spotted a gray trickle approaching on the lower ridge. "There," he pointed. "Those troopers are cutting off the north and, given their numbers, plan to seal off the summit as well. That means our only option is south." He reached for her handbag, crisscrossed over her shoulders. "Let me have it."

"I can carry it, thank you."

"Suit yourself." He started off on the new route. Moving laterally proved even more dangerous than vertically. Like snails, they molded themselves against the slope-less granite and inched their way over infinite space. With less brush, they were exposed for minutes at a time. How long until the first gunshots cracked the air?

Reaching one rocky parapet, they caught their breath and then moved on to the next. An hour passed, along with a quarter-mile of mountain ridge. Soon the slope angled enough for them to walk again over the rocks. The barking returned from above, which meant the troopers had crossed the ridge. "The dogs will pick up our scent," Mayson warned.

"So what am I supposed to do about it?" he growled.

"Try being a little nicer."

"You plan on giving me hell up to the last minute, don't you?" As he reached for her hand, she jerked it away. "Damnit, quit doing that."

"Then stop grabbing me every five minutes."

The hounds' barking faded as an eerie silence settled over the wilderness. Afternoon shadows lengthened on the ridge as they reached another tree cover. With both the mountain's peak and base likely sealed off, where would they be when night fell and the temperature plummeted?

They leapfrogged across another quarter-mile of rocks as the hounds bayed again overhead. Then without warning, he jumped into a thicket. "No!" Mayson said as she swatted at his offered hand. "You've treated me like an invalid ever since we started. Now stop." Stubbornly she jumped, her legs collapsing as she tumbled forward at his feet. "Shit! Shit! Shit!"

Tyler examined her scraped palms. The left was bleeding. Wrapping it with his handkerchief, he pointed at her ripped slacks. "Maybe you won't be so hardheaded next time."

Her nose wrinkled. "What's that awful smell?"

"Stink weed. It may mask our scent from the dogs."

"We jumped into this brush because of stink weed?"

"You have a better idea, Miss Brooklyn Trail Guide?"

"Of course, only . . ." He yanked her into the trees as the air suddenly thundered. Branches rattled overhead and dust swirled at their feet. As if shot from the sky, a chopper hovered above the thicket. Frozen, they waited until its vibrations finally faded. "Now what?" she wondered aloud as it vanished over the ridge.

Before he could reply, two more choppers appeared; one climbing the slope, the other descending. Like the first, they, too, vanished into the eastern sky. He pulled her from the thicket. They continued south until they reached a deep gorge.

"I had no idea the Black Hole of Calcutta was in Tennessee," she gasped. "How do we cross it?"

He studied the dark, bottomless abyss. "Very slowly, I'd say. Come on." Foot by ginger foot, root by root, they crossed the deep gorge; a tedious hour passed until they finally reached the other side. Again he picked up the hounds' barking. "They're below us now."

"No doubt on the trail of some stink weed," she mocked him.

The sun slipped over the ridge and with the temperature plummeting, they continued on safer ground. Their sweaters would offer little comfort when the night chill settled in, he realized. Without food, water or destination, their situation couldn't seem more hopeless as the choppers now returned. Diving for the closest thicket, they watched them break rank; one climbing the slope, another descending, the third approaching on a lateral course. Pressed to a tree, they waited as the first, then second vanished over the ridge; reaching their thicket, the third hovered just feet above, its vibrations deafening as dust swirled in their eyes. Would it land? Open fire? When they were certain of both, it suddenly streaked away. Lifting Mayson's chin, Tyler found her eyes filled with terror. "Hey, come on. Have you forgotten the old saying, 'It ain't over 'til the fat lady sings?' "

"But hasn't she, Tyler?"

"Hell no," he smiled. "The only singing I've heard has been that damn Brooklyn songbird: *'Non dimenticar means don't forget you are my darling . . .'* " Soon her soft soprano took over. He'd come to appreciate her voice's subtle qualities; its happy lilt, its razor-sharp anger and the gentle glide in between.

Her fear ebbed as she finished the song. "Tyler, when you say I'm your best friend; what does that mean?"

"That we're like songbirds, I guess, the kind that don't fly off, but are always there for each other — at least until we can't be any longer."

"When is that?" she asked.

"When we die."

"For me, it means we're there to remind each other the sun is always shining. That no matter how black the sky may appear, at least one ray of happiness can be found, one spark of hope. Even if we die in the next minute, I have hope in this one because I'm spending it with my best friend." Her solemn eyes demanded a kiss; as the sun slipped over the ridge, he tenderly obliged. As it ended, she shivered, "How much colder can it get?"

"A lot, I'm afraid." He studied the darkening sky. "We need to start moving. We'll stay warm that way." They didn't stop again until they reached the next thicket an hour later. By then, the hounds' barking had returned to the wilderness. But he now caught a new threat on the ridge below: a detachment of Feds and troopers snaking towards them. "We've got to turn around," he urged.

Light was fading as they returned across the treacherous terrain, soon reaching the deep gorge it had taken an hour to cross. They'd have to dedicate another to its re-crossing, clearly a more dangerous proposition. "We'll have to move slower this time," Tyler said. He studied the darkening sky, then the steep shelf that curled, horseshoe-like around the gorge. "Do you remember the drill?"

"Grab the root, get a foothold in the rocks, then take the next step. And of course, don't look down," she answered. "As if I'd do something so stupid." Still grumbling, she followed him onto the steep slope. Then, like timid monkeys, they started across the rocks, clutching with one hand, grabbing with the other. Progress was slow but steady as they rounded the horseshoe-shaped gorge. Reaching the bend, they rested, then resumed their tedious journey.

The mindless drill soon echoed her thoughts and she grew tired. Grab the root, plant the foot, take the next step. This was hell, an eternal journey, where thoughts never transcended the body's idiot-like motions. Grab the root, plant . . . Suddenly the earth collapsed. "Tyler . . .!" she screamed.

He turned to find her clinging to a root, feet kicking wildly as she tried to regain a foothold in the rocks. "Wait!" he shouted, crawling back to lift her safely onto the rocks. "You're damn lucky that root didn't snap," he sighed. "I know you're tired, but you've got to concentrate on what you're doing. We don't have much further." She was terrified and exhausted, but he couldn't let her lose control. Taking a few moments to calm down, they resumed their creep across the rocks. "You're doing fine," he encouraged her. "We're almost there."

How could he tell, she wondered? Just feet ahead, he was barely visible in the gathering darkness. Grabbing the next root, she extended herself. When her foot wouldn't reach the ledge, she grunted, then tried again. "Shit!" she cursed.

He turned, smiling. "Your purse is caught on the root behind you. Just ease it off."

But with one frustrating tug after another, she remained captive. The root had many knots and her purse had managed to coil around each one. Again she jerked it helplessly.

"Don't put so much stress on the roots!" he warned. "Calm down and don't forget where you are!"

"Forget where I am?" she panted. "I couldn't forget even if I wanted to." Finally she managed to free herself and once again, her weight shifted easily as she grabbed the next root. Her heart shuddered as the dark ledge now merged with the dark sky. Her foot slipped, spewing rubble into the gorge.

Again he found her swinging helplessly and crawled back to the rescue. She kicked and clawed in a desperate attempt to regain a foothold in the rocks. "Grab my hand!" he said as he extended himself.

The root started to give way. "Tyler, help me!" she screamed, dangling wildly.

He lunged a split-second too late as the root snapped. Horrified, he watched her fall screaming into the gorge. "Mayson!" he shrieked, quickly beginning a reckless, spider-like descent of the treacherous slope, reaching the bottom minutes later with his hands raw and his joints burning. Surveying the dense woods, his eyes lifted to the rocks from which she'd fallen. Did he dare hope she was still alive?

Shouting her name, he started across the gorge, swatting vines, crunching brush, and stumbling over rocks. Chopper thunder rattled the trees and then faded as he plunged deeper into the gorge. An eerie silence returned to the darkness, closing around him as he finally reached the point of her fall. Slowly his gaze drifted up to the rocks glowing in the moonlight. Wasn't he looking for a body? Certainly there . . . He froze at her sudden moans. Plunging through the vines, he found her sprawled on the ground, broken branches scattered all around her. One leg restlessly scraped the earth, the other lay motionless. She grabbed his arm as he knelt to examine her injuries. "I'm . . . all right," she told him.

Gently he rotated her head in the moonlight. Blood glistened along the scalp. Lifting her clotted hair, he found a deep gash in her temple. He slid the purse off her arm and wedged it beneath her head. Then he pulled his sweater off. "Tyler, no . . ." she protested.

"Hush!" He ripped the sweater, transforming it into a bandage which he applied to her scalp wound. "You have a concussion. We'll rest and then move again before dawn."

"You . . . don't understand," she whispered painfully.

"Lie still! Save your strength."

As he examined her more closely, she stroked his nose and strong jaw, finding comfort in their familiar lines. How much she wanted a lifetime of this. But it wasn't meant to be. "Tyler, I . . . can't go."

"Why? It's just a concussion."

"No, *amore mio*," she whispered with a new intimacy. "It's not just . . . a concussion."

She'd never appeared more beautiful as the moonlight enhanced her face's exquisite angles and deepened the glow of her fawnish eyes. She smiled serenely despite the pain, as one who'd come to grips with her fate. "Mayson, what is it?" Tyler asked.

"I can't move . . . my leg."

Inspecting it, he cringed. Twisted grotesquely, blood trickled down a calf swollen twice its normal size from a compound fracture. Very soon the shock would fade and a terrible pain would take its place.

"Tyler . . . you'd better go."

"I'm not going anywhere."

"Don't be . . . so stubborn."

"Listen to yourself, the one who gives new meaning to the word."

"That's right," she swallowed hard. "I *am* stubborn. And I insist you go . . . while it's still . . . dark."

He smiled. "You never shut up, do you? You fall halfway down a mountain, shred that poor tree and still your mouth is running."

"And my heart; do you know . . . what it's doing?"

"Tell me," he stroked her cheek. It was like ice; shock — nature's remedy for pain.

"It's singing. You performed a . . . miracle. Didn't you know?"

"I perform so many. Which one are you referring to?"

"The one where you turn the shrew . . . into a songbird."

"Mayson, you were a songbird long before meeting me."

"I was nothing . . . before you." Her temple burned now, her leg's throb deepening by the minute. "Tyler . . . there's not much time."

"Hush." He pressed his finger to her lips. "Just once, stop talking long enough to listen. I'm not going anywhere, so don't waste another breath."

"But you'll . . . die!"

"No one's gonna . . ." His eyes shot up as searchlights suddenly scanned the night sky. Were teams approaching the gorge? "Mayson, we need to get you to a hospital."

"No." her eyes shone defiantly. "They'll kill you." The searchlights now crisscrossed the trees overhead. The hounds' barking grew louder. Her face twisted with pain. "My leg . . .!"

Inexplicably, the searchlights faded from the darkness, as did the hounds' barking. The stupid bastards were leaving. "Tyler, go." She writhed as if agony was a condition that could be crawled out of.

Grabbing a twig, he placed it between her teeth. "Bite on this. They say it helps." Lifting her gently over his shoulder, he scooped up her purse and started off. Mercifully her screams faded and she soon slept. The wilderness silence echoed with his thrashing, a warning to all within earshot. Soon the mountain shelf rose in the moonlight. Whoever waited, he prayed they would be wearing Tennessee gray and not . . . A spine-tingling squeal pierced the darkness. Had a hound just fallen from the rocks as Mayson had? Moving on, he froze again at the sound of metal clicking. Once, twice . . . he counted a dozen sharp echoes.

As he crept closer, the moonlight exposed the gleaming rifles above. Dark-suits, Tennessee Grays or both? Did it matter any longer? He continued towards the rocks.

"Stop!" a gruff voice ordered.

Squinting, he made out the silhouetted figures on the ledge above. The order had come from the center: the tall man, with the tall hat – a trooper? Again the man barked gruffly, "Waddill?"

Unable to suppress a wry smile, he shook his head. After weeks of running, their odyssey was now ending with the most witless one-word question ever asked. "Waddill? Hell no, I'm Jack the fucking Ripper!"

CHAPTER TWENTY-FIVE

★

The Presidential limo glided up the stately drive of 1600 Pennsylvania Avenue, where a cluster of Secret Service agents waited. Buttoning jackets and straightening ties, they quickly converged to greet the returning Secretary of State. A tall, rangy man, with silver hair and commanding blue eyes, he emerged to shake hands and nod politely before being ushered inside for his Presidential briefing. There was much on his mind, far more than the trade agreement he'd just negotiated.

Minutes later, he was escorted into the Oval Office, where an anxious Longbridge warmly embraced him and said, "Welcome home, Travis!"

"It's good to be back, sir," he said, dropping into his customary chair as Longbridge returned behind the desk. Arnold Westbrook had disdained such formality. His successor insisted upon it.

"No one thought Tokyo would budge," Longbridge marveled. "Seoul, either. So how did you manage it?"

"It's no great mystery," he modestly explained. "Negotiation is the same whether you're working a real estate deal, foreign trade pact or buying a car. You just probe for the weakness."

"In this case, cheaper raw materials?"

"Steel and textiles," he nodded.

"So we not only get our trade pact but new markets for our surplus raw materials," Longbridge gloated. "If I played poker, Travis, it certainly wouldn't be with you. But how do we position ourselves for the European trade summit next spring? We've ruffled more than a few feathers over there lately."

"We'll find vulnerability in Europe just as in the Far East," he predicted. "The rules never change. No matter how strong an adversary appears, there'll always be a weakness to exploit."

"I'd say you've proven that splendidly."

Yet would he be forced to again? He studied his boss. With his gaunt face and dark, solemn eyes, Longbridge looked like a burdened Moses, a most appealing effect for a nation that hungered more for a religious leader than another self-interested politician. He and his Rasputin-like mentor, Harrington, were riding the wave of a massive, Neo-Christian resurgence. America was born again and Longbridge was its Preacher President. His popularity was enormous, brilliantly choreographed by Harrington, a public relations genius. "I see a lot has happened in my absence," he said quietly.

"The Corelli-Waddill affair, you mean."

"Betsy and I have been deeply disturbed over it, naturally. And the Waddills are suffering terribly."

"I'm sure of that," Longbridge nodded. "To have an ungrateful son like Waddill is inexcusable."

"And even more incomprehensible," Travis replied.

"I understand your skepticism, Travis, but I'm afraid I can't share it. There's obviously good reason to believe Waddill is a criminal. Otherwise the Bureau and Justice wouldn't be hunting him so intensely. Larry and Thomas are good men - law enforcement professionals. I wouldn't have brought them to Washington unless they were fully qualified for their positions."

Qualified? Travis scoffed to himself. They were utter fools. They'd demonstrated it numerous times in this very office. The only question was whether they were corrupt fools. Would Longbridge grant him the opportunity to find out? Hadn't he earned that much, not by negotiating trade agreements but by offering valuable insight the others seemed incapable of?

"I need a devil's advocate," Longbridge had confided in the first weeks of his administration. "You're courageous enough to speak your mind, Travis, even if it happens to diverge from mine. The others are sycophants." Indeed. But also corrupt sycophants?

Longbridge now asked, "So what, besides this great friendship, leads you to believe Waddill isn't involved in this conspiracy? You have my ear for the moment. Take advantage of it."

He fully intended to. "Schuyler Waddill, Blane Randolph and I grew up together. We were classmates at the Tidewater Academy, then college. We married girls in the same crowd and raised our families together. I was at the hospital the morning Tyler Waddill was born and then again a few hours later when Blair Randolph gave birth to her daughter, Kara. A beautiful girl," he sighed. "She and Tyler left the hospital together and never really parted, at least not until her death from cancer twenty years later. Her death shattered him."

"He and Kara were in love?" Longbridge asked.

"I guess that's what you'd call it. Betsy and I used to say they were soul mates. Born under the same moon, in the same delivery room, just hours apart. We laugh at astrology but having seen those two together, it makes you wonder if there isn't something to it. We had a party for Matt's sixth birthday at our York estate," he said. "The middle of August; hot as the dickens that afternoon. All Matt's friends were there, either rolling in the surf or tumbling on the lawn. Everyone except Kara and Tyler. She was scooping colored glass off the beach, and he was right behind with that damn bucket of his. 'Don't you ever leave her shadow?' I asked him. He just squinted at me like I'd lost my marbles.

"Betsy and I were at Castlewood one Saturday night, shortly after Kara died. We'd been at the William and Mary football game that day. Tyler was a helluva quarterback. He'd rallied the Indians with a pair of touchdown passes in the final minutes. It was a sensational victory, one he should've been celebrating. Yet instead, he was there at Castlewood. After dinner I found him behind the mansion, gazing up at the dark tree house where he and Kara had played as children. When I gripped his shoulder, he turned, his eyes filled with tears. 'Uncle Travis,' he said. 'Do you remember Matt's birthday party when you asked if I'd ever been outside Kara's shadow? Well, I am now.' He hasn't been the same since. His parents have expressed great concern over his indiscretions with women. He's done well in law but I can't help wondering if he isn't just drifting through it, like he does women."

Longbridge rose to the window. "That's a tragic story. But how does it address his criminal propensities? If anything, doesn't his emotional instability perhaps explains his involvement in this conspiracy?"

"If Tyler's emotionally unstable," Travis joined him now, "then nothing I've said places his character at issue. He's honorable to a fault – a Waddill. I don't need to know anything else to appreciate that he didn't commit these crimes."

"Unfortunately I do," Longbridge frowned. "Isn't there something beyond your personal allegiance to support his innocence?"

"Well for one thing, Tyler doesn't need money. His family's wealth is well known."

Longbridge nodded. "We pay Waddill Shipbuilding millions each year in Navy contracts. He stands to inherit this fortune?"

"He and his sister, Stafford, will split it. And they already enjoy income from the family's trust funds. My point being, why with all this wealth would he risk prison, and possibly his life, for money he doesn't need?"

Longbridge gazed pensively out the window. He'd asked himself this same question. But didn't people often become criminals for illogical reasons?

"I suspect Tyler's been framed for these crimes and I want to know who's responsible," Travis finally revealed.

"If that's true, then the FBI and Justice must either be involved or else qualify as fools of the century."

But which? Travis needed to know. Still, as an experienced negotiator, he never bit off more than he could chew. Weaken resistance, then advance slowly. Never get reckless. "Sir, I don't make accusations beyond what I'm convinced is fact. And I won't compromise my principles based solely on my personal feelings. Nevertheless, I have certain suspicions which beg scrutiny."

"Get it out, Travis. What do you want from me?"

"Proof of Tyler's participation in this crime. Certainly that's not an unreasonable request, and an easy one to satisfy."

"You're asking me to interfere in a confidential Bureau investigation?"

"Sir, you are the President of the United States."

"I know damn well who I am! I also appreciate my responsibilities, without you or anyone else reminding me."

"Then you're refusing my request. I'm sorry to have burdened you with it. I won't again."

"Travis, you're asking too much."

"I can see that. Enjoy your triumph today." He started out. "I'm honored to have been the one to bring it to you."

"Damnit, Travis." Longbridge grabbed the phone. "You'll get your proof — just as soon as I get it myself."

"Thank you, sir." He smiled graciously, then slipped out.

Within minutes, sirens were shrieking at the Bureau and Justice. An urgent call was placed to Georgetown. "Culpepper," Streeter groaned inside the Flavin Courthouse war room. "Why else would Longbridge demand another briefing?"

The blood of frustration rose in Harrington's cheeks. Would this crisis ever end? "How soon does he want it?"

"Larry and I are supposed to return for a meeting tonight."

"Have there been any developments since your bloodhound report?"

Chapman had earlier reported the discovery of an unconscious tracking dog in a mountain gorge, where it was assumed the fugitives had spent the night. "That gorge has been scoured," Streeter said. "But for suspicious limb damage, it was clean."

"Suspicious limb damage?"

"Possibly the fugitives used the tree as a lookout. Or fell from it. Either way they're gone now."

"How could two people climb from a gorge under the nose of six hundred police officers?" he growled. "Thomas, I want them found! They are still on that mountain, aren't they?"

"Of course, sir; it's sealed tight."

"Then have Nicholas grab them while you and Larry return to Washington."

Harrington watched the afternoon press conference as a beaming Longbridge announced his new Far Eastern Trade Agreement. The mere sight of Culpepper — the large, silver-haired Secretary of State at his side — brought an angry gleam to Harrington's eyes.

Switching off the TV, he called Leopold to discuss Lamp's confirmation and the tactics to be employed. "Arch, I want you to digest Chapman's dossiers on those liberal Senators, just like you have in the past — and their key aides as well, this time. If they have skeletons in their closets, we'll find them. Chapman's also composed a list of potential informants in each Senator's camp, but be careful whom you approach." He revealed the latest threat.

Leopold sighed. "Not everyone's happy with that new trade deal Culpepper negotiated with the Japs. Some Detroit autoworkers may soon be without jobs. And you know how riled up those labor unions get. Enough maybe to seek revenge against the man responsible."

"Let's pray it doesn't come to that, Arch."

Chapman and Streeter arrived later that afternoon.

"Two days is a long time without food and water while dodging men, dogs and choppers," Harrington said. "Don't you think if the fugitives were still on that mountain, someone would've spotted them by now?"

"The mountain's sealed tight," Streeter insisted.

"And it's enormous," Chapman added. "It takes time to cover that much ground."

He was sick of their excuses. The operation was taking much too long. "All right, let's have your story for tonight. And it better be good. If Longbridge doesn't buy it, we're all going down."

Chapman presented their joint briefing. "Swanson and Harvey establish the Bureau connection. It's the easiest piece, since they're not here to dispute it. Next, the Bertolucci connection, thanks to Corelli's brother, Santino The Lips. When he was arrested for knocking off Manny Lugosa, The Lips was the most feared Bertolucci *capo* on New York's West Side. Personally, I think he deserved a medal instead of life for knocking Manny off. It was a real public service.

"Manny worked for the powerful Servose brothers, who were moving in on the Bertolucci drug trade. After his murder, however, the Servoses backed off. And for The Lips' faithful service, especially his willingness to take the rap for the hit, the family considers itself deeply indebted. Despite his life sentence, a strong bond remains."

"One that extends to his sister?" Harrington asked.

"It's what makes her the point person between the family and the Bureau."

"But how was the connection between Corelli and the Bureau established? Did she go to them?"

"She would've known how to approach them, either through her law practice or the family."

Streeter added, "We have memos covering critical family meetings in which the conspiracy was discussed - dates, times, locations, participants." He smiled. "The beauty is that we were investigating the Bertoluccis anyway. All we had to do was doctor a few files. Our key family witness is Louie Venecchio, who'll sing to whatever we say. Louie was under our thumb before this mess. If needed to testify, we'll grant him immunity then stick him in the Witness Protection Program."

"How does Waddill fit into all this?" Harrington asked.

"It's a big job. Corelli needed a partner."

The story was both consistent and credible: provable if necessary. Streeter assured him it wouldn't be. "Don't worry, they can't get off that mountain."

"They couldn't get out of Naples or the Eagle's Nest Camp, either. So far they've made complete fools of us. If they're still on that mountain, get them. If not, find them. Otherwise, prepare to prosecute the most fantastic, make-believe crime of the century."

Chapman and Streeter met with Longbridge that evening. No details were spared as they unveiled the manufactured conspiracy and brought him up to date on the operation. At the end he asked, "Then you're satisfied the evidence is sufficient to indict both Corelli and Waddill?"

"Yes sir," they chorused.

"This informant in the Bertolucci family . . ."

"Louie Venecchio," Chapman replied. "He establishes the conspiracy and connects the principal players. His identity must be protected to preserve both the evidence and his life."

"I understand. And this Special Agent Nicholas will testify about his discovery of the conspiracy?"

Streeter glanced at Chapman, his veins pulsating with dangerous excitement. They were lying to the President of the United States and pulling it off. "As we've said, Nicholas uncovered the conspiracy quite by accident, during his audit of the Bertolucci investigation. You're welcome to examine the records and talk to the witnesses, of course."

"That's not necessary," Longbridge replied. "Nicholas reported the conspiracy to you, Larry. That's when Lamp was recruited to help expose the conspirators inside his law firm?"

"Correct. Lamp then recruited Mendelsohn and we all know what happened after that."

"Those seized records prove the fugitives' receipt of money for the stolen Bureau documents?"

Chapman nodded. "They contain confidential bank accounts traced directly to them."

"How much did they receive?" Longbridge asked.

They looked at each other blankly. This question hadn't been anticipated. "A hundred thousand each," Streeter replied.

"Waddill is a multimillionaire. Why would he take such a risk for one hundred thousand dollars?"

"Because he expected to receive much more."

"These payments were merely initial installments," Chapman quickly echoed. "And Thomas's estimate is a bit low anyway. Actually, they received closer to a hundred-fifty thousand each."

"Even so," Longbridge wrestled with this fresh detail. "Have you considered that it wasn't money, but perhaps an attraction for Corelli, that drew Waddill into this conspiracy?"

"The romantic angle," Streeter nodded. "That's certainly a possibility."

"And Corelli's a beautiful young woman," Chapman added.

"Well, whatever his motive, I expect you, gentlemen, to prove it when the time comes. How close are they to capture?"

"We expect a report any moment," Streeter replied.

"I've heard that for days. Just get them soon — and alive. I want them brought to trial so this mess is explained to the satisfaction of the American people."

"We'll do our best," Streeter assured him. "But you must realize, sir, the fugitives are extremely desperate. We can't risk the lives of our men."

"I understand." He frowned over another concern. "How will Lamp be perceived? The timing couldn't be more sensitive, with his confirmation starting Monday."

"As a hero," Chapman predicted. "An ordinary citizen rising gallantly to the service of justice."

"Greg Lamp is no ordinary citizen."

"No sir," they agreed.

Streeter's midnight call bolstered Harrington's fading confidence. If the shrewd ex-prosecutor, Longbridge, had bought the fabricated records conspiracy, certainly the nation would, too. Now if they could just catch the fugitives. Hopefully the news would arrive by morning.

Chapman's call at dawn confirmed that it wouldn't. "How can they possibly still be on that mountain?" he demanded.

"Because it's been sealed off, sir."

"Then find them!" He slammed the phone down.

The President's limo soon arrived to carry him to the White House for a private worship service, a practice frequently followed when business brought him to D.C. Strategically, it was important to meet with Longbridge now. Lamp's confirmation began in the morning and thanks to Travis Culpepper, his interest in the fugitive operation had peaked once again.

The service was well received by Longbridge and his dour-faced First Lady. Revelations had always been the President's favorite biblical book, its symbolism especially satisfying to his intellectual tastes, and its urgent message the perfect inspiration for his zealous spirit. And on this Sunday, it couldn't have been more appropriate to remind them of what was at stake. "If Greg is confirmed and proves all we hope," Longbridge ruminated over a lunch of New England clam chowder, "then I'd say we're on the eve of this Great Christian Renaissance you've promised, Seth."

"I have no doubt Greg will be confirmed. And I assure you, Tom, he's all we've hoped for."

"I'm not worried." Longbridge sipped his tea. "Greg's credentials are impeccable, his character beyond question. Once again, Seth, I find myself in your debt for delivering a candidate perfectly suited for a position I have to fill."

"Then you're not worried about Senator Adamley and his liberal pack?"

"Adamley's an atheist," Marge Longbridge snapped.

"Agnostic, dear," her husband gently corrected.

"But they have identical views on abortion, pornography, school prayer," she insisted. "And both question the very existence of Almighty God."

Had Eve been as homely as Marge Longbridge, Harrington often marveled, most likely there wouldn't have been a human race to save. How had his friend suffered her colorless, desiccated face all these years; her shapeless figure? What greater testament to his piety than his devotion to this aging wallflower? "Adamley and his bunch will spar with Greg as they did the others. And he'll handle himself just as well."

The First Lady dipped her spoon daintily into the chowder. "What's important is that the three men share our views on the critical spring cases. Their solidarity is vital."

"They're cut from the same cloth, Marge, I assure you."

A zealous gleam brightened Longbridge's eyes now. "Our new court will deliver us from the clutches of godless politicians like Adamley, who will no longer have grounds to debate the disturbing issues that so bitterly divide us. And if it's not ready to abolish the separation between Church and State, perhaps our court will give its constitutional blessing to an agency dedicated to Christian values. Candidly Seth, I don't believe there's anyone more qualified than you to head that agency. You're the spiritual leader for millions of Americans. Would you consider joining my administration as the spiritual architect of a new Christian America?"

"I'd be deeply honored," he nodded. "And of course pleased to dedicate myself to the noble mission you've described."

The First Lady sighed rapturously. "After so much wickedness, to at last be on the threshold of the Lord's Kingdom! We've been truly blessed!"

"Praise the Lord!" Longbridge refrained. "Now we must prepare for His arrival."

"And provide the leadership necessary to govern His Kingdom," Harrington added.

The First Lady excused herself as the two men ventured out to the balcony to enjoy the crisp autumn air and a view of the world's most powerful city: one that for the moment was under their control. Only Harrington knew how precarious that control was. "Our court will provide the legal means to do the Lord's work, Tom, but without our leadership secure and unencumbered by time constraints, how can we be assured it'll get done? Aren't we forced to ask the court to lift those constraints and allow us the time necessary?"

Longbridge studied him solemnly. They'd had this discussion before, only then its relevance had seemed so remote, almost academic. Despite their political strength, it had been too dangerous to attempt a repeal of the amendment standing in their way. However, repeal seemed unnecessary now that they had, or soon would have, a sympathetic Court majority capable of finding a legal precedent for removing the amendment restricting a President to two terms and allowing him a lifetime, if necessary, to fulfill the nation's destiny. "We'll need a case to get the issue before the Court."

"Are there any with suitable potential?" Harrington asked.

"One should reach the Court next summer," he nodded. "At the moment, however, I'm more concerned with this fugitive operation. The longer it drags on, the sharper public criticism becomes."

"What will you do?"

"What can I do? Other than carefully monitor the situation and pray it's soon resolved?"

"Perhaps, in desperation, the fugitives will choose another way out. One never knows. The Lord works in such mysterious ways sometimes."

"Granted, only in this case I want the fugitives captured. The country wants justice, Seth. And we can't have it until the truth comes out —all of it."

Lord help us if that should ever happen, Harrington prayed.

CHAPTER TWENTY-SIX

★

Longbridge found himself procrastinating over his next encounter with Travis Culpepper. By Tuesday morning however, he could no longer put it off and summoned Travis to the Oval Office.

"Have you had an opportunity to review the case against Tyler Waddill?" Travis asked.

"Quite thoroughly." Longbridge related as much of the last briefing as he could without breaching the operation's confidentiality. "I'm sorry, Travis, but despite the stock you hold in the young man, it appears he's gotten himself into a predicament for which he must suffer the consequences."

"Your summary didn't address the possibility of manufactured evidence."

"That's because there is none," he crisply replied.

"Because Chapman and Streeter are in charge of it?"

"Be careful, Travis. We don't want to make reckless accusations that have no factual foundation."

"I've made no accusations, sir; I just asked questions - deeply troubling ones that remain unanswered."

"Questions!" Longbridge snapped. "Well let me ask you one: why would the FBI Director and Attorney General want to manufacture Federal crimes against Tyler Waddill?"

"I have no idea, sir."

"Nor do I, which must, to some degree, prove my point."

"Sir, if the crimes have been manufactured, the fugitives won't live long enough to be tried."

"That supposition is irrelevant, of course, since the evidence wasn't manufactured. Further, I've ordered that the fugitives be taken alive, so that justice may be dispensed."

As Travis rose to leave, Longbridge held him warily. "Don't interfere, Travis. That's an order. Do you understand?"

"Perfectly, sir."

"Then you intend to obey it?"

"Certainly, if my conscience tells me it's the proper course."

Anxiously, Harrington tuned into GNN's coverage of the hearings Tuesday morning. The first day had gone well, but today promised a tougher test. Although Leopold had assured him Adamley's camp had no dirt, no one could be certain what might stumble out when the questions started flying. Adamley's chief ally on the committee, Senator Banyon of California, had just begun the morning assault when Streeter called. "Two abandoned mining shafts have been discovered on the mountain's northeast sector. We should know very soon if the fugitives are hiding in one."

He wasn't impressed. "It's been four days. They couldn't possibly remain on that mountain."

On TV, Lamp offered his first evasion on abortion. Banyon tried another angle. Again he skillfully dodged. Keep it up, Greg, he smiled.

"The fugitives are on that mountain," Streeter insisted.

"Then find them! And don't bother me again until you do."

Gil Aikman watched through the glass of Mabry's Waffle Shop as the tall young man crawled from his Pinto and crossed Main Street. A cap rested in his wavy gold hair, sunglasses concealing his eyes. Aikman sipped his second cup of Virgie's coffee. The only detail out of place was him.

The tall, handsome stranger shadowed the small town, not blending nearly as much as he seemed to be trying in his mud-caked boots, tattered jeans and Army jacket. And a man with his imposing presence didn't drive a Pinto unless trying to be somebody he wasn't. "Who the devil's that?" Virgie's eyes popped behind him, a pencil poking her permed red hair.

Aikman watched the man slip a letter into the mailbox, then return to his car. "A damn weird duck. At least if he come all the way to Truitville just to mail that skinny letter."

A smitten Virgie watched him crank the Pinto's engine. "Best lookin' man I ever seen. Gil, you reckon he's one of them country and western singers travelin' incognito?"

"Beats me." He watched the Pinto make a hasty U-turn and

squeal away.

"What you reckon's got him all upset?" she asked.

He caught Sheriff Wilson's car in front of the Farmers' Exchange Bank. "I reckon the law done scared him off, Virgie. He's runnin' from it. Ain't no question about that."

Behind her, the TV droned. What was it — this connection she was suddenly trying to make? Something the Knoxville newsman had said.

Sitting before the TV, Harrington munched on Sonja's tuna salad sandwich as Adamley asked his first question. Lamp had begun his answer when Chapman called with a report. "Where in God's name is Truitville?" Harrington frowned.

"Fifty miles northwest of Knoxville," Chapman replied. "The Tennessee police received the call this morning. A waitress in a breakfast shop there saw a man matching Waddill's description drive up in a battered Pinto, mail a letter and then squeal off. Chopper and ground patrols are blanketing all road systems north of Truitville now."

"That's marvelous, Larry! Was Corelli with him?"

"He was alone, according to the waitress. However, we can assume he's meeting her somewhere."

"Any ideas about this letter he mailed?"

"His family, possibly. We've alerted our Virginia surveillance team to be on the lookout for suspicious activity."

"He could also be corresponding with Culpepper."

"We'll check it out."

"Yes Larry, you do that." Harrington dropped the phone.

His spirits rose as the hearing's second day ended. Lamp was holding up splendidly. Soon he'd be on the court and work could begin to bring moral order to a country in chaos. Chapman called again later that evening. "The Pinto's been found abandoned in Mitchellsville, Illinois. Our forces are moving into the area now and all road systems north to Snow Peak are blanketed."

"Make sure to check all the car dealerships," he replied. "We know from that Iron Ridge redneck that Waddill isn't beyond buying the first piece of junk that catches his eye. Any idea where Corelli is?"

"She's most likely rejoined him. We'll know soon."

"Anything else?" Harrington asked.

"Blood stains were found on the Pinto's back seat. We're getting samples now . . . Hold on." He returned quickly. "We just got a report that explains a lot that's happened since Friday."

Harrington's fingers clenched the phone. "And what is that?"

"The identity of the Pinto's owner."

This latest revelation warranted yet another crisis meeting, which he arranged before calling Leopold.

"Arch, we've traced Waddill to Mitchellsville, Illinois. All primary roads north have been blanketed. However, given their travel habits, Waddill's inclined to take the back roads. Consequently, you and your men should establish positions along the most remote systems between Mitchellsville and Snow Peak so as to be close . . ." A terrible chest pain jolted him suddenly. With the second, his eyes shut and he envisioned his father sprawled in the garden, eyes open and vacant, shirt ripped open in the last desperate seconds of life.

"Chairman?" Leopold snapped with alarm.

The pain faded as quickly as it had come. Perhaps it wasn't his heart. Surely the Lord wouldn't take him before the mission was completed. "Arch, Sonja's spicy casseroles have given me a nasty case of indigestion," he said. "I have to talk to her about that. Now, once you and your men are situated, begin searches within your respective areas. But also keep your cell phones nearby for Nicholas's call that will certainly come. When can you leave?"

"We're on our way, sir."

"Bless you, Arch. That's straight from the Lord's lips."

They convened at ten that evening in the Lakeland study. Chapman began with a crisp briefing. "The Pinto that Waddill abandoned near Mitchellsville is registered to one Brother General Isaiah of Flavin County — or as we knew him before he founded his religious sect, Jerome Warren Basham.

"Basham was a Baptist minister in Jackson, Mississippi, an outspoken critic of the Vietnam War. His protests became violent when his son, Nathaniel, stepped on a mine in some godforsaken Mekong Delta rice paddy. After Nathaniel's death, his sermons became hate-filled harangues against the American government in which he openly advocated rebellion. He was dismissed finally, and outraged over the rebuke, severed all ties with the Baptist Church. He then left Mississippi with his family and a handful of friends.

"Over the next decade they drifted across the southeast, living on odd jobs and tent revivals, where Basham railed against the injustices of worldly government, while his people worked the crowd for donations. It was during this period that he attracted the Bureau's attention. Preaching rebellion to captive audiences in these superstitious backwoods communities made him a legitimate threat to national security.

"In the early eighties, he took his flock into eastern Tennessee to establish a retreat on some land inherited by one of his followers. It was then that he began having his visions and private communions with God.

"According to Basham, all earthly government is evil, the instrument of Satan, which has as its purpose the corruption of man and the destruction of the world. Anyone who supports such a government becomes an agent of Satan. To be good, according to Basham, is to remove oneself from the reaches of government and when that becomes impossible, to resist it."

"That's no religion," Falkingham grunted. "It's anarchism — and dangerous, since it advocates rebellion. This maniac should've been locked up long ago."

Chapman replied, "That would've been difficult, since he's never actually taken up arms against the government, or intended to. At least not until the Great War."

"The Great War?" Mann asked.

"Basham's version of Armageddon, in which the righteous must unite for the ultimate confrontation between good and evil that will determine the world's fate.

"His sect has grown steadily over the years. At last count, there were 8,000 followers, located primarily in the southeastern United States. They typically live a Draconian communal existence in wilderness isolation. Each man is called brother, each woman, sister. The middle name connotes rank or status in the sect. The last is of biblical origin, usually from the Old Testament. Take

Basham's name, for example. Brother connotes male. General, the sect's military commander. And Isaiah, the religious prophet, to whom God will confide when the Great War is at hand."

An incredulous Falkingham asked, "You had all this dope on Basham's sect, but prepared no plan to address a possible encounter?"

Chapman's face reddened. "We only knew Basham was in the general area. Those mountains cover half a dozen counties. And even as crazy as he is, we couldn't have anticipated his interference with a Federal investigation of this magnitude."

"And if you'd caught the fugitives in Florida," Falkingham reminded him, "we wouldn't be sitting here now, worrying about maniacs like Basham or juggling a conspiracy that doesn't exist!"

"And if you trio of idiots hadn't committed the crime of the century," Harrington bristled, "we wouldn't be embroiled in this mess now. So what's your point, Chase? Or is this more whining? If so, stuff a sock in it so we can determine how to extricate ourselves from the dilemma your stupidity has created. Now," he said to Chapman, "please brief us on the strategy to be followed in light of today's developments."

Chapman nodded. "What we're planning could eliminate most, if not all our problems. Our choppers have located Basham's camp, three miles east of the gorge where we assume the fugitives were rescued. The sect remains unaware of our surveillance as we prepare for a raid that will snare Basham and other unnamed John Does. Once captured, they'll be taken to Green River to determine if they've been infected by the fugitives' virus."

"And if they have?" Lamp asked.

"Either way, they'll be disposed of."

"This is getting way out of control," Falkingham said. "We can't just keep killing people."

"And aren't we risking another Waco with this strategy?" Mann asked.

"We're much better prepared than at Waco," Chapman replied. "There'll be no victimized women and children, no real aggression on our part at all. The cyanide will be smuggled in."

"But how can you control who might've been exposed to the fugitives' claims?" Falkingham asked.

"You don't understand, Chase. Basham's harboring of the fugitives is just the tip of the iceberg. What we'll discover on that mountain, is the arsenal of a dangerous paramilitary group intent on overthrowing the United States government. We've suspected this for a long time. Tonight Bureau choppers will simply confirm our suspicions."

Falkingham crushed out another Dunhill. "Don't you realize what a media circus this'll create? And Waco or not, there'll be Congressional hearings. Count on it."

"We're prepared," Streeter assured him. "And don't forget we're part of a very popular President's administration and our enemies are a handful of religious fanatics intent on overthrowing our government."

Mann asked, "What if someone in Basham's sect screams about the Norris case?"

"It's Basham who conceived the lie," Streeter replied. "Living in eastern Tennessee, it's only natural he would know about the case. Many inhabitants still question the jury verdict that sent Norris to the chair. And if you're among them, you naturally ask: if he didn't commit the murder, who did? For Basham, that raises all kinds of interesting possibilities."

"Or opportunities," Chapman added. "Here, it's the propagation of a malicious lie contained in a one-page flyer accusing you three gentlemen of the girl's murder. And while causing emotional distress, it also damages the integrity of the institution you serve. It's quite forcefully written. In fact we're printing it now. Don't you see? Your participation in this murder is nothing but Basham's malicious nonsense."

"And also prosecutable sedition," Streeter added. "Because of that we'll print 10,000 flyers."

"An incredible coincidence, isn't it?" Chapman mused. "Discovering this seditious trash while raiding Basham's camp. Weapons we'd expected to find, but not this."

"I assume these maniacs have some pompous-ass name?" Falkingham asked.

"The Holy Army of the Last Order, or as they're popularly known, the Halos."

CHAPTER TWENTY-SEVEN

★

Harrington was eating breakfast when Chapman called. "The plan was executed at dawn. Basham and his top men were arrested. They're on their way to Green River now."

"There was no resistance?" he asked.

"None. The raid was carried off so well the Halos hardly had time to react. In addition to the arrests, Nicholas's team planted and then seized a small arsenal of automatic weapons and explosives."

"All to be employed in this Great War, I assume."

"Sure. Yet the Halos seemed as surprised as anyone to discover the arsenal's existence."

"Are you and Thomas prepared for the next step?" he asked.

"We're meeting with Longbridge within the hour. Assuming all goes well, we'll alert the media and then proceed directly to Justice. Stay tuned, sir."

"Oh, I will, Larry. Rest assured of it."

After breakfast, he tuned into the third day's coverage of the confirmation hearings. His interest peaked as Adamley began a morning assault on Lamp's credentials. To the packed chamber's delight, Lamp skillfully dodged the vicious hooks and jabs. Undaunted, Adamley next quizzed him on his Law Review article endorsing restrictions on morally offensive behavior. "You're saying, Mr. Lamp, the government has the power to legislate morality?"

"Doesn't most legislation to a degree, Senator?"

"Then you condone it?"

"No sir, two hundred years of American jurisprudence condones it."

Applause rippled through the chamber as a persistent Adamley marched on. "Mr. Lamp, isn't the morality you would legislate based upon Judeo-Christian doctrine?"

Smiling, Lamp leaned into the mike. "I dare say, Senator, our Constitution and the society which spawned it, are both deeply rooted in Judeo-Christian doctrine. The framers were devout believers in God, to whom I'm sure they credited the faculties necessary to conceive what is without question, the greatest legal achievement of the modern world."

Amidst thundering applause, Adamley read a passage from Lamp's article. "Are these not your dangerous words, sir, which threaten the freedom of every American?"

"I'm not nearly that eloquent," Lamp smiled. "But if you check the footnotes," he said as he nodded at the article in Adamley's hand, "you'll see I've credited the Honorable Francis Banbury with these 'dangerous' words. Banbury is perhaps the greatest constitutional jurist of our time - from Massachusetts, Senator, your home state."

The chamber exploded with laughter. Watching on TV, Harrington beamed; this was much too easy.

GNN's coverage was soon interrupted by a special news bulletin, the broadcast shifting to the crowded Justice Briefing Room, where Chapman and Streeter stood at the podium. As the noise died, Streeter began. "Early this morning, Federal agents acting upon a magistrate's warrant raided the Flavin County, Tennessee camp of a religious sect led by one Jerome Warren Basham. The sect, known as the Holy Army of the Last Order, has been the subject of an extensive Federal investigation, based upon its subversive activities, which we believe pose a threat to national security.

"As well, we learned yesterday that Basham's sect, whose central mission is the overthrow of the United States government, aided and abetted fugitives Mayson Corelli and Tyler Waddill in their continued efforts to elude Federal authorities. Specifically, the Halos, as they're called, supplied the fugitives with food, shelter, medical treatment and a car, which was found abandoned in southern Illinois.

"Discovering that the car, a Ford Pinto, was registered to Basham, we investigated further and obtained warrants for him and the other Halo conspirators."

As he stopped, a solemn Chapman stepped up to the mike. "At six-thirty this morning, Bureau agents apprehended Basham and four other Halo suspects at their Flavin County camp. The five are now in custody, pending arraignment on the federal charges and will be afforded due process of law. We don't anticipate any other arrests at this time." His eyes lifted over the crowded briefing room. "We'll now take a few questions."

They quickly shot forward. "What, specifically, are the charges?" the AP woman asked.

Streeter replied, "In addition to aiding and abetting the fugitives, the charges include unlawful possession of firearms and explosives, which we believe have been stockpiled for armed rebellion against the United States government."

Chapman added, "A primitive printing press was also confiscated, along with 10,000 copies of a pamphlet containing libelous charges against key figures in the Federal government. Based on this hate propaganda, other charges are being considered."

"Can you describe this hate propaganda?" the GNN correspondent asked.

"Not at this time, Mr. Warren, I'm sorry. Next?"

"Where are the Halos being held?" the UPI man asked.

"A maximum security prison which shall remain confidential for reasons of national security and the prisoners' safety," Streeter replied. "Thank you, ladies and gentlemen."

Before they could get away, the *Times* reporter asked, "Have there been any developments in the fugitive operation since your tracking of Waddill to southern Illinois?"

He smiled. "I'm sorry, but we can't answer that question at this time. Good day," he said, following Chapman out.

"You handled the press conference brilliantly," Harrington praised them in a call later. "I may have misjudged you two."

"This latest report from Green River shouldn't change your opinion," Chapman said. "After some intense questioning, it appears the Halos haven't been infected by the fugitives' virus. This doesn't alter our plan, but the next development certainly makes it easier to explain.

"Katrina Evans, a nurse for a Flavin County orthopedic surgeon, called after watching the press conference. The national security implications frightened her enough that she was ready to spill her guts."

"She knows about the Halos?"

"Better than that. She works for one. A Dr. Wayne Stanley

who, six years ago, battled the IRS over back taxes due from his medical practice. After losing in court, he paid the full amount, plus a small fortune in penalties, interest and legal fees. Suffice it to say, the doctor wasn't a happy camper, which I guess made it easier for Basham to convince him of the evils of earthly government. Mrs. Evans says he's been stockpiling medical supplies for the Great . . ."

Harrington shuddered with a sudden jolt. Sweat beaded his brow as the second, then third jolt arrived. He braced for the fourth, but it didn't come. Instead, the chest pain faded quickly, as before.

"Sir, are you all right?"

"Yes . . . I'm fine." His breath returned. "Now, what's Stanley's role in all this?"

Chapman explained. "Despite his eccentricities, Stanley appears to be an excellent surgeon. Do you remember the gorge with the limb damage? That tree apparently broke Corelli's fall, no doubt saving her life, although she sustained a compound leg fracture, which Stanley repaired. She'll need frequent medical evaluation, which should help us track her movements."

"Does Evans know anything about the fugitives' plans?"

"They didn't tell her anything. Nor did she ask. Then Tuesday, when Corelli was well enough to travel, they left." He explained how Stanley fit into their promising new plan.

Sonja's casserole mellowed Harrington as he watched GNN's recap of the day's hearing. The sight of Adamley over his mike, lips snarling as Lamp outwitted him, merely deepened his glow.

Leopold soon called. "We're settled in, sir. Aurora. Stevens Point. La Crosse. Ames and Mankato. Not exactly household names, but strategically positioned, at least."

He laughed. "And which remote point do you occupy?"

"I'm at the Mankato Lodge. Actually, the accommodations aren't bad. And with Nicholas's men pouring into Minnesota, I can't imagine one of us won't be close when something breaks."

Harrington revealed Stanley's capture, and how this unexpected development would be exploited. "This crazy Halo doctor has apparently played right into our hands."

"Praise the Lord, sir. The hearings also went well again today."

"Yes, Arch, I'd say ol' Liver Lips is clearly reeling."

"Things are finally going our way, sir."

"The Lord delivers all He promises, and soon that'll include the fugitives."

George St. Martin sorted the mail Thursday morning, as usual. Five months on Senator Adamley's staff, and so far he'd been entrusted with nothing more critical than a letter opener. He was a glorified office grunt. Actually, not so glorified. He studied his tiny cube in the bowels of the Senate Office Building. Didn't an Amherst honors graduate deserve better?

The long epistles from Adamley's constituents soon piled up — as if the Senator had time to personally respond. He'd never known Massachusetts had so many kooks.

His irritation found another target as he moved on. Lloyd Tamrack specifically — Adamley's aide who, at this very moment, was attending the Lamp confirmation across the street. Tamrack was sleazy, hardly someone to be entrusted with important Senate business.

Completing the batch, he then sorted it into three categories: Senate business, party matters, and fund raising. Personal mail was discreetly returned to the envelope, to be given to Adamley's secretary.

As he shuffled the mail into the proper trays, one letter suddenly caught his eye. When had they last received mail from Tennessee? And where the hell was Truitville? Intrigued, he read the handwritten two-pager. The writer was articulate, the tone, confidential. By the end, he understood why.

Lamp, a rapist and murderer! And the two Longbridge justices already on the court? The anonymous writer was clearly insane. Or else an enemy attempting some sort of trick. There couldn't be any truth to these accusations . . . could there?

He reread the letter. The charges were wild, but also earth-shaking. And if it was not his place to determine the writer's credibility, someone had to. Springing up, he hurried out.

He was waiting upstairs when Tamrack returned during a hearing recess. "What is it?" the aide asked, breezing into his office. "I have to get right back."

"You need to see this," St. Martin said, giving him the letter.

Tamrack's expression didn't change as he read it. "Thanks for bringing this to my attention. I'll see it's properly handled."

He'd expected more of a reaction from the flamboyant aide. "I know this person might be crazy, but what if the charges are true? Isn't this precisely the political dynamite needed to blow Lamp out of the water?"

Tamrack stuffed the letter in his jacket. "He's probably some maniac making a little noise, but you never know."

Puzzled, St. Martin now followed him out. Why wasn't he more excited?

At the hall window seconds later, he watched Tamrack dash — not for the Capitol, but for the open parking lot across the street. Slipping into his red BMW, the aide placed a call, and then read the letter over the phone. Hanging up, he drove away.

The hearing's afternoon coverage was interrupted by another special bulletin. Harrington watched the scene shift to the same Justice Briefing Room. As before, Chapman and Streeter stood solemn-faced at the podium.

As the noise faded, Streeter began. "Last night, Federal agents, acting upon information received, obtained a warrant for the arrest of Dr. Wayne Carter Stanley, a Flavin County physician, and also a well- known member of the Halo sect. The warrant charged Stanley with participation in the Halo conspiracy to aid fugitives Corelli and Waddill. Specifically, for receiving them at his Flavin County clinic, performing surgery on Corelli, who broke her leg in a fall, and harboring them until this past Tuesday, when they left in Basham's Pinto." Streeter turned to Chapman. "The Director will explain the tragedy reported within the last hour."

A dramatically pained Chapman approached the mike. "Upon his arrest, Dr. Stanley was taken to our Green River facility where — it may now be revealed — the other Halos were being held. Upon arrival, he was processed under the same security procedures, and scheduled for a medical evaluation this morning.

"Before that, however, under circumstances now being investigated, he managed to slip cyanide tablets to his companions, which were quickly ingested, despite the presence of security guards and sophisticated monitors. When this became apparent, medical personnel administered emergency lifesaving procedures, which proved too late to be of any value. Regrettably," he gazed into the cameras, "all six Halos have been pronounced dead from self-induced cyanide poisoning."

A question quickly rose above the rumble. "How was Stanley able to smuggle cyanide into the Green River compound?"

Streeter returned to the mike. "The tablets were concealed inside his hearing aid, which was examined upon arrival but, because there was no probable cause, it was not disassembled."

The GNN correspondent asked, "Did you have reason to suspect a mass suicide might be attempted?"

"Suicide is always a consideration," Chapman replied. "But we can only take the steps necessary to prevent them as was done here."

"What's the President's reaction?" the UPI man asked.

"Precisely as you'd imagine. As a religious man, he receives any tragedy with deep sadness. He has expressed sympathy for the men's families and requested a full report as soon as possible." Masking a victorious grin, Chapman studied the somber crowd. They'd bought it. The crisis was over. Or would be the moment the fugitives were captured. "Good day, ladies and gentlemen."

"Something's going on, sir."

Longbridge gazed at Travis Culpepper across the desk. "How do you mean?"

"The Halos rescued the fugitives from that Tennessee mountain. Days later they're arrested, carted off to a remote Federal compound and within hours, dead from cyanide poisoning. That's a bit fantastic, don't you agree?"

"Stranger things have happened," Longbridge shrugged.

"Sir, the Halos either knew or were suspected of knowing something."

"Like what?"

"Whatever's made the fugitives the focus of this manhunt."

Restlessly, Longbridge rose to the window. "You're talking in riddles, Travis. Give me something tangible."

"All right, let's start with Green River. It's been closed since

December, except for use as a chopper maintenance station. A victim of budget cuts."

"Travis, don't you have enough to do at State without checking up on FBI chopper bases?"

Joining Longbridge at the window, he studied the dense fog that had settled over D.C. The season's first snow was expected by morning. "Sir, three weeks ago Green River was inexplicably reopened to house Federal prisoners. Oddly enough, that's also when this fugitive operation began."

"The point?" Longbridge frowned. "I assume you have one."

"The point, sir, is that Green River is isolated, staffed by Chapman's agents and until recently, too expensive to maintain. Now within hours of arrival, these Halos we've been told, have committed suicide. Surely you find these circumstances a little suspicious."

Longbridge offered his own challenge. "If not suicide, how would you explain their deaths? Forced cyanide ingestion ordered by Chapman and Streeter? Travis, you're not seriously asking me to believe these men to whom I've entrusted enforcement of our nation's laws, plotted the murder of a half-dozen men to prevent exposure of some secret, the existence and nature of which you haven't the first clue?"

"I'm not asking you to believe anything, sir; just to investigate these clearly suspicious developments." Quietly he started out. He'd stated his concerns. Longbridge needed time to ponder them and hopefully emerge with a fresh perspective. "Oh," he turned at the door. "There's something else you should consider."

"What's that?"

"Where the fugitives will be taken when captured; if it's Green River, the odds are that they'll meet the same fate as their Halo rescuers. Thank you for your time, sir."

"Adamley's office received a very sensitive letter," Leopold reported from Mankato that evening. "Fortunately, it got into the hands of his aide, Tamrack, who's on our payroll."

Harrington, in robe and slippers, dropped on the bed. "Who's the letter from?"

"The writer remained anonymous, but we can assume it's

Waddill. It was mailed from Truitville on Tuesday." He sighed, "The letter confirms they know the story, sir."

Harrington shuddered with a sudden chest pain. A second bolt quickly followed. Clutching the bedpost, he braced for the next, but it didn't come.

"Sir, are you still there?" Leopold asked.

"Arch, I've been having chest pains," he confessed. "It's the stress of this crisis. I plan to see a doctor this week. But I'm sure I'm fine." And he believed that. Hadn't there been fewer bolts this time? "This aide, Tamrack. You're sure he didn't make copies of the letter to blackmail us with?"

"He's too smart for that, sir. He knows that if we pay well, we also pay just once."

"Then what should we anticipate? If Waddill wrote one letter, won't he write a second and third, until someone finally listens?"

"Possibly. But without proof, no one will. Empty charges can't hurt us, sir. Evidence like that chest, however, can bury us. We know that. They know that. The key is finding them before they find it."

"Then we'd better do that, Arch. Now."

CHAPTER TWENTY-EIGHT

★

Streeter called Friday morning to advise that he and Chapman had been summoned back to the Oval Office. "Culpepper has obviously been buzzing again at Longbridge's ear," Harrington said, then revealed the alarming letter that had been intercepted.

Streeter sighed. "It's disturbing, if for no other reason than it represents the fugitives' first publication of the story. We're now convinced they didn't share it with the Halos or the old couple at the Flavin camp."

"Have you decided what to do with those two?" he asked.

"The old man's deaf, and the woman doesn't stop talking long enough to hear what anyone else has to say. Prosecuting her would be far more trouble than it's worth."

"Report back after your meeting with Longbridge. And be careful what you say. Who knows to what extent Culpepper has poisoned him."

Longbridge studied the two men across his desk. Was it his imagination, or did they seem unduly anxious? "I assume there's no word on the fugitives?"

"They're reportedly heading north, somewhere between Illinois and Minnesota," Chapman replied.

"Minnesota's usually covered with snow this time of year; that would be an obstacle for someone on crutches like Corelli. Any idea why they're going there?"

"Not yet, sir."

"If they're captured, where do you plan on taking them?"

"Green River," Chapman replied.

"Why transport them to Kentucky when there are a half-dozen closer facilities?"

"Green River was my decision," Streeter explained. "It's our most secure facility."

"That's very lamentable, Thomas, given the tragedy that's just taken place."

"Tragic, sir, but also unavoidable. I thought we agreed on the need to isolate the fugitives."

Longbridge held him thoughtfully. "Why was Green River reopened? I assume not just to accommodate Corelli and Waddill?"

"Of course not, although I admit its reopening has proven timely. We determined months ago that its reopening on a limited basis wouldn't significantly increase its current expense as a chopper base."

"Don't take the fugitives to Green River," Longbridge now ordered. "Take them to New York, which has jurisdiction over their cases."

"With all due respect, sir, this constitutes . . ."

"Interference?" he snapped. "Yes, I suppose it does. But right or wrong, responsibility for this operation rests on my shoulders. I'm the one the people elected and the one they'll inevitably judge. Now, if you'll excuse me." He rose stiffly. "The Senate hearings concern another man I'm responsible for. He's on the hot seat, too, hopefully for the last day."

Harrington still brooded over Longbridge's order when a dazzled Streeter called back. "It's amazing how you can go days without a lead, then in minutes receive an earful."

He cut the TV volume. "Go on?"

"First, a service station owner in Aurora reports that a young couple matching the fugitives' description sputtered into his station Tuesday. Finding their heap beyond repair, he drove them to a Chicago hospital, where the woman's mother was dying. Not until he saw their pictures on this morning's news did he make the connection."

"Why Chicago?" Harrington asked.

"Probably because they were tired and figured a large city was safer to hide in. By the way, the station owner wants a reward. We've decided two grand is fair."

"For what?" Harrington scowled. "Three-day old information telling us the fugitives might be in a city with eight million people? You and Larry certainly drive a hard bargain."

"You haven't heard my earful yet."

"Then get on with it. What do you have?"
"Corelli and Waddill. Any minute now."

Leopold headed east on Route 59, his map beside him. After a day spent checking the motels, restaurants, convenience stores and service stations around Mankato, he remained without a lead on the fugitives' location. Maybe he'd have better luck heading south to Albert Lea in the morning.

He grabbed the beeping phone. "Arch, we have them!" Harrington gushed.

He quickly pulled into a mini-mart. "Where, sir?"

"This morning a woman named Sprinkle boarded a Boorstin bus in Chicago. Corelli boarded at the same time, taking the seat beside her. Waddill then boarded at the next station, and they began sneaking glances at each other. Sprinkle quickly made the connection, having seen their pictures on TV.

"She got off at the Madison station and promptly called the police. However, by the time they arrived, the bus was gone — with the fugitives still aboard. Agents are tailing it now to insure there are no unscheduled stops before Eau Claire."

"Frankie's in Eau Claire."

"That's fine, Arch, but with Green River no longer an option, the disposition must be immediate, and I want you there to handle it."

He gazed at the empty highway. He'd have to burn rubber to reach Eau Claire in time. "I'll have Frankie meet the bus. If the fugitives get off, the Feds should hold them until I arrive. If they don't, the Feds should continue their tail. Frankie and I'll catch up. What's the next stop after Eau Claire?"

"Duluth is the last. That's all I know. Nicholas can brief you on the details."

"I'm on my way, sir.," he said, returning to the highway.

Frankie was waiting when Boorstin #37 rolled into the Eau Claire station.

He watched a pair of Feds emerge from the shadows to position themselves at either end of the bus. Did they really think they blended, wearing identical black coats, shoes and hats? The same hard expressions, as if they needed to crap? To him, all Feds looked homesick for a john.

His eyes sharpened as the first passengers trickled off the bus. Come on, Corelli, show that cute little tail, banged up and . . . His gum-smacking stopped as a tall man with wavy, gold hair got off, blue eyes darting over the station. The Feds also spotted, then quickly dismissed, him. Not Waddill. He read their faces. And they were right. The guy wasn't pretty enough.

As the last passengers emerged, his gaze returned to the remaining heads in the windows. He wanted the fugitives off here, not Duluth, another hundred miles north.

"Hey Dumbo, did the circus arrive without our clowns?"

He turned to find Leopold looming. "They must still be on board, Arch."

"You didn't miss them, did you?"

"No Arch, I swear."

Leopold nodded at the Feds, who returned to their car as #37's driver approached. A small, gray-haired man, with pencil-thin moustache. He squinted. "I'll bet I can save you guys some time."

"How's that?" Leopold asked.

"Well now," he said, tugging at his belt. "I knew something was strange ever since them big, dark sedans started tailing us just beyond Madison. My point being that if you're looking for those two, you won't find 'em on my bus."

"Where'd they get off?" Leopold frowned.

"Madison. Not at the station, but a few blocks later. That's when the girl hobbled up on crutches to ask where the next stop was. When I said Eau Claire, she started crying.

"Next thing I knew, the guy was on his feet asking about her problem. She said she'd been traveling for two days to see her mother, who was dying in a Madison hospital. Only she was so upset, and her leg hurt so badly, she'd missed her stop. Anyway," He tugged at his belt again. "Here we are at the light, the hospital out the window, and the man starts begging me to let 'em off. We're not supposed to do that. But if he was willing to take responsibility, I figured, what's the harm? So I did."

"Do you know who they are?" Leopold growled.

He nodded. "I began tossing the question around about the

same time them big, black sedans popped up in my mirror. I said to myself, Benjamin, ol' boy, you may've really done it this time. And I guess you're telling me I did. They were Corelli and Waddill? Is that . . . ?" He stopped as the furious giant limped off, his gum-popping companion on his heels.

Adamley glanced down the dais as Senator Fulton, the granite-built Texan, announced the afternoon recess. At counsel table, the slippery adversary rose to shake hands with a crowd of supporters. Unlike his interrogators, Lamp appeared as fresh as he had Monday morning. A week of grilling on his conservative views and dull corporate law practice hadn't shaken him in the least. His confidence remained intact; his smile, just as unctuous.

It was a sight Adamley could no longer bear as his eyes connected with Banyon's. His closest ally on the committee, Banyon was a big, handsome blond who, at fifty-three, still looked more the Stanford fullback than three-term Senator. Grumbling, Banyon followed him out into the hall. "If that slippery sonofabitch has a skeleton in his closet, I'll be goddamned if I can find it."

"Anyone who rises to Lamp's level of Wall Street prominence has one. We've just overlooked it."

"Have you seen the latest poll? Thanks to these televised hearings, Lamp's popularity has tripled."

Yes, he'd seen the poll. And also the swelling ranks of Lamp supporters that now packed the committee hearing room.

"Lamp's just a clone of the other two Longbridge appointments," Banyon sighed. "Why can't people see it?"

"They can," he smiled mournfully. "It's what they want. Or they wouldn't have put Longbridge in the White House."

"If we don't stop these religious fanatics, we'll soon see the court striking down every piece of social legislation put in place since the New Deal."

"And replacing them with moral decency laws," he predicted. "I'm talking a moratorium on civil liberties and every vestige of compassionate government." He placed his hand on Banyon's shoulder. "I can see it now, Phil. The halls of Congress resounding with Onward Christian Soldiers as we joyfully surrender our freedom to the Preacher President, and his Rasputin, Harrington.

You want a prophecy? There's one. And it's coming, just as sure as I'm standing here."

They looked up as a young, flaxen-haired page approached. Trim and professional in her gray suit, her wide, blue eyes latched onto Adamley. "Senator, you just had a call. The man said he'd try again before the hearing resumed."

He didn't have time to be taking calls. "Just take a message."

"I tried, sir, but he wouldn't leave his name."

"Well I hate to disappoint him, but I'm in hearings right now that profoundly affect the national interest. If it's important, he'll call back."

"But Senator," She became flustered. "He said it's urgent he speak with you before the hearings end."

"Perhaps you should take his call," Banyon said. "I can handle things until you return."

Reluctantly, he followed the page down to the conference room. "The switchboard will put the call through," she explained. "It shouldn't take but a minute."

As she left, his eyes drifted impatiently to the table phone. Who could be calling at such a critical time? He looked up as Banyon reappeared. "Dan Pentforth just caught me," Banyon beamed. "Great news. Ways and Means has wrapped up in the House. I think we have our bill."

This was great news — the kind that could salvage a rotten week. If it passed, 10,000 civil service jobs would be spared, many in their home states. Glowing with fresh energy, he led his friend out. "You can fill me in as . . ." He stopped at the ringing phone then caught his aide, Tamrack, rushing down the hall. "Lloyd, please take that call and then report back to me in chambers."

As Tamrack grabbed the phone, they started off again.

That night, Leopold brooded over the latest debacle in an operation that seemed far more cursed than blessed. He studied the cramped motel room. Where was he, anyway? The rooms all looked the same. Naples, Pine, Mankato . . . Eau Claire. Yes, he remembered. Rather than return to Mankato, he'd sent Frankie to assume his old location.

Crushing out one smoldering Marlboro, he quickly lit another. Three weeks and what did they have to show? A dead Jew, two FBI agents, a girlfriend and six poisoned wackos. Yet the yuppy-puppy lawyers remained at large. How much longer could they defy the odds?

The news he just received about the committee's vote to confirm Lamp was hardly enough to lift his dampened spirits, even if a full Senate vote was expected next week. No one questioned anymore that Lamp would be on the court for the critical spring term. But would he? Until the fugitives and the chest were recovered, it was impossible to say.

Smoke thickly wafted through the darkness as he brooded again over the operation. Logistically, they'd covered their bases since the debacle at the Eau Claire station. Madison had been sealed off, and an extensive search was conducted. Police in Wisconsin, Iowa, and Minnesota had blanketed the road systems, as Nicholas's forces scoured the tri-state region. And his own men maintained their positions in Stevens Point, La Crosse, Ames, Mankato, and Eau Claire. So what had been overlooked? Would the elusive details sneak up and bite them on the ass like they had this afternoon?

The Eau Claire disaster had been avoidable, the Feds' tail being established within minutes after Bus #37 left the Madison station. The only problem was that the fugitives had slipped off in those same critical minutes, having obviously picked up on Sprinkle's suspicion.

So what were they looking for now — another bus? A Chevy Cavalier or Ford Pinto? VW Beetle or Honda Prelude? Whatever, they'd know soon. All transit stations between Madison and Snow Peak had been notified and every car dealership and rental agency alerted.

CHAPTER TWENTY-NINE

★

Concerned over Harrington's health, Leopold called again Saturday morning. "Thanks, Arch, I'm feeling much better," he answered. "Any news from the Midwest?"

"No sir. How about D.C.?"

"Longbridge has invited me to a White House celebration next Saturday for Lamp. He wants me to set the spiritual tone for the new court. With friendly journalists on hand, we should get some favorable press for a change."

"Longbridge seems confident about the confirmation vote."

"As he should, Arch. Senator Fulton's private poll indicates a 73-27 majority in Lamp's favor. I doubt next week's floor debate will change those numbers significantly."

"And your heart, sir; have you made that doctor's appointment?"

"No, but I intend to this afternoon."

After checking in with Nicholas, Leopold headed north on Route 49. With the primary routes blocked, the fugitives were most likely traveling this desolate stretch of 49 or else 51. He called George, who was scouting the latter. "Ain't seen nothing, Arch, and I've been out since nine."

"Then start hitting the road at eight like the rest of us. Where are you?"

"Between Wausau and Merrill."

"Maybe the fugitives were, too —at eight." The line suddenly crackled. "What's that?"

"A monster truck. They blow by every five minutes or so."

"I'm getting them, too. Those big Duluth shipping operations must be responsible." He pulled off at a convenience store. "George, you better be checking everything on the road."

"Arch, there ain't much to check. Since Wausau there's been a half-dozen shanties, a feed store and a mini-mart . . . Ah, make that two. Catch you later."

Hanging up, Leopold limped into the store. The proprietor, a a bald, stocky man, eyed him intently as he approached the counter. "You a ballplayer?"

"No, why?" he asked.

"Because you're so big. We get 'em in here a lot; Packers, Vikings; some with bad knees like yours."

He scanned the store. The midday traffic was considerable. "I'll have some coffee," he said as he nodded at the pot. "And a pack of Marlboros."

"My brand, too," said an old woman who set her carton on the counter. "You play for the Packers?" Her eyes scaled the dark giant. "If so, go easy on them things. They cut your wind . . . What do I owe you, Jerry?"

He rang up her merchandise. "Reese, are you stocked for the blizzard?"

"Have been since Thanksgiving. Let it fly." She grabbed her bag and walked out.

"They're calling for snow?" Leopold asked.

"Say it's gonna be a doozie, too." Jerry rang up a young couple's merchandise. "The store fills up quickly when snow's coming. It'll be like this all day."

Others soon came up with their merchandise, but nobody claimed the Jordan Almonds and Jawbreakers resting on the counter. The almonds suddenly scratched at Leopold's brain. Idly, he scanned the store. "Is there a truck stop nearby?"

"Callahan's," Jerry nodded. "Just north at the 107 junction. So if you don't play football, Mr. . . . ."

"Navros." He handed Jerry the pictures. "I'm an attorney with Lieber Allen, a New York law firm."

Nearby, a young man suddenly froze as he studied the giant's reflection in the cooler glass. A stocking cap covered his gold hair, shades concealing his blue eyes. But nothing hid his evenly featured face. Anxiously he glanced at his cart full of groceries.

"These are the fugitives?" Jerry studied the pictures. "I've seen 'em on the news a hundred times."

"Anywhere else?" Leopold asked. "Like here in your store?"

He shook his head. "If they're around here, I haven't seen 'em. Lieber Allen, sure." He made the connection. "That's the firm . . . Hey!" he yelled at a young man suddenly streaking out. "Don't you want . . . guess not." He glanced at the candy. Smiling, he watched the young man quickly pull away in an old Nova. He'd had one just like it thirty years ago.

Leopold wrote down his phone number and gave it to him. "If you see or hear anything about the fugitives call me. There'll be a fat reward."

"Sure thing." he said as Navros left.

"Jerry!" A heavily bundled woman approached. "Some guy just left a full cart back there."

"Probably the same one who left the candy. Cap and glasses?"

"That's him," she replied.

They turned as an agitated Navros limped back into the store. "You seen a '63 blue Chevy Nova?"

"One just left," Jerry answered. "The boy driving was in such a hurry he forgot his candy there."

Leopold's looked at the unclaimed Jordan Almonds. Now he remembered the box from the Naples hotel room. The one flimsy clue in an otherwise spotless room, and he'd forgotten it. Waddill had just been here; the realization sickened him.

Jerry had figured it out, too. "That was . . .?" He stopped as a furious Navros limped out, the door rattling behind him.

Phone in hand, Leopold sped north.

"Arch, they've picked up Waddill's trail again," Harrington reported. "A Madison car dealer . . ."

"Johnson Motor Sales. I know, sir. Waddill's latest heap is a '63 Nova." Reaching the 107 junction, he passed Callahan's with a morose glance. The fugitives no longer needed a truck stop. They had a new car. "Sir, Waddill was in Eau Claire, just minutes ago."

"How do you know?"

"I was in the store at the same time."

A pained silence gripped the line. "That was before you knew about the Nova?"

"Yes, sir."

"Then you couldn't have made a connection."

"At least we're closing the gap, sir. I plan to move my men north, and establish new positions closer to Snow Peak, while Nicholas seals off Wisconsin and Minnesota. Don't worry." He pulled into the next service station. "We'll nab them soon."

The new northern positions were established over the afternoon, effectively cutting the fugitives off from the east at Manitowoc, from the south at Eau Claire, and from the west at Ortonville. Heavily blanketed 149, at its Snow Peak junction, became the new point, north.

With everything in place, Nicholas left Bingham in St. Paul and Cooley in Madison to coordinate with local authorities as he established his new command post in Snow Peak. Leopold, meanwhile, relocated to Duluth, moving men north to Benidi and Rhinelander, while keeping George in Stevens Point and Frankie in Mankato. Now they had only to wait — again.

The first lead came as the storm's first snow fluttered from the evening sky. A roving chopper spotted the abandoned Nova behind Callahan's Truck Stop. Within minutes, a dozen Wisconsin units were on the scene to inspect the car, and question people inside Callahan's. None had seen the fugitives.

They could be looking for any of a hundred trucks now . . . And factoring in the last fugitive sighting, six hours earlier with travel time on a tractor-trailer quickly doubled the cordoned-off search area.

The operation's response was predictable — and for Leopold, agonizing. Hold your ground, and wait. Again.

The storm buried the Midwest in two feet of snow before ending late Sunday. A bone-chilling cold settled in. No one needed to hear that another storm was on the way.

The storm in the nation's capital proved much milder, depositing but a modest, silky-white dressing on the Potomac's banks and the nearby District. That Sunday afternoon, Senator Adamley received an unexpected caller at his Georgetown home. He knew the young man's face as that of a recently hired staff member.

"George St. Martin," the visitor identified himself. "I'm sorry to bother you on the weekend, Senator, but there's an urgent matter to discuss, if you have the time."

Curious, Adamley showed his visitor into the study, where they were soon drinking his wife's freshly perked coffee while St. Martin offered his account of the anonymous Truitville letter.

Adamley looked dumbfounded.

"Then Lloyd never showed you the letter, sir?"

"No." He remembered the mysterious call during Friday's recess. Tamrack had taken it, then returned to the hearing to explain: a real crackpot. The guy swears Lamp is an intergalactic alien sent here to destroy our justice system. Had that caller also been the anonymous Truitville letter writer, attempting to publicize his fantastic charges? Not about intergalactic aliens, but an ancient Tennessee murder?

"I saw Lloyd on his car phone minutes after giving him the letter," St. Martin added. "He read it over the line."

Adamley envisioned Tamrack's shiny BMW, tailored suits, and ritzy Georgetown condo. "I suspect he was handsomely paid for that information by a Lamp sympathizer. Do you think the letter has any merit?"

"That's hard to say. But I have a good idea who sent it."

"Who?" Adamley's brows arched.

"Tyler Waddill. Reportedly, he mailed a letter from Truitville on Tuesday. I doubt seriously that's a coincidence."

He agreed. "Waddill must hate Lamp for helping the FBI expose his actions."

"But he had no reason to hate the other two. The Chief Justice gave him his first job."

Adamley was impressed. "You've obviously done your homework." Springing up, he grabbed the phone.

"Who are you calling, sir?"

"Senator Banyon." Pausing, he studied the bright-eyed messenger responsible for his new vigor. "You better run along now, St. Martin. You have a lot to do, especially with your new job."

"My new job, sir?"

"As my chief legislative aide. Take Tamrack's office; I'll have his things moved out in the morning."

At the opposite end of Georgetown, an elegant, silver-haired woman gazed out her study window at the falling snow. The fine homes were dressed in white, their lanterns aglow, chimneys smoking. Two storms in as many days, she marveled. But they were mere dustings compared to the several feet dumped on the

Midwest. How was the young man she worried about managing under such extreme conditions? And his female companion on crutches, for heaven's sake! Shouldn't they surrender and let the legal system straighten this mess out? They were lawyers. Didn't they know this better than anyone?

Worry surrendered to reflection as she envisioned the children sledding down their York estate's snowy slope, the adults roasting weenies by the fire. They'd had a wonderful time, including the young man she worried about now, and his girlfriend, who'd clung to him as they raced down the hill. Snowstorms had been rare events in Tidewater. And their last white Christmas? Yes, she remembered. It had been spent at Castlewood — such a noisy, cheerful place, especially at Christmas. But not that year. The girl on the sled had just died. And Castlewood had become a tomb.

"Betsy Culpepper." Her husband's comforting hand settled on her shoulder. "You've worked yourself into one of those moods, haven't you?"

Smiling, she slipped her fingers through his. "I was just thinking about our last white Christmas. Six years ago. Can you believe it's been that long?"

Travis gazed at the confetti-like snow littering the sky. Four inches on the ground, and several more expected. "It was snowing like this on that Christmas Eve at Castlewood. Only it was much colder. The coldest night I ever remember."

"Travis, what would you think about asking Matt and Harrison to bring their families to York this Christmas?"

"I don't suppose this came up in your earlier conversation with Hunter Leigh, did it?"

"Well, I confess it came up. But I didn't make any promises." She sighed. "Hunter Leigh seems more despondent each time we talk. She says Schuyler just sits by the phone. Yet he won't turn the TV on. He's frightened to death of the news. And poor Stafford's taking it just as hard. Dr. Brannigan has them all on tranquilizers. Honestly Travis, it's like they're trapped in a nightmare, unable to do anything but wait."

"Unfortunately, it's been that way for the last six years," he said. "Tell you what — let's call the kids, and see what they think about a York Christmas."

"I'll tell Hunter Leigh we're coming. And good heavens, we need to make plans quickly. Maybe Tyler will even be home by then."

"I wouldn't count on it."

"Why won't that imbecile in the White House listen to you? How can he possibly believe Tyler committed those terrible crimes?"

"Because he doesn't know him like we do."

"He knows you, Travis. And if he was as holy as he pretended, he could recognize another principled man besides himself."

"He must think I'm principled to some degree. You'll recall, I'm the only one from Arnold Westbrook's . . ." He stopped at the ringing phone.

"That's probably Harrison," she said as hurried after it. "Jordan's leaving for a medical convention in Tampa tonight."

He turned back to the window, when she suddenly shouted, "Good heavens! Where are you?"

Turning, he found her anxiously clenching the phone. "What in Sam Hill is wrong?"

Her eyes glistened as she handed him the phone. "Tyler wants to speak with you."

CHAPTER THIRTY

★

Harrington gazed at the blanket of snow left by the storm. The morning sun had returned to the sky, and if the temperature got anywhere near the forecasted sixty degrees, the snow would melt quickly.

His friends in Minnesota, however, weren't so lucky, enduring their second major storm in two days. Businesses were closed and road systems shut down. Still, the fugitives remained one step ahead of their weary pursuers. Last spotted at a St. Cloud truck stop, they'd vanished again before the Minnesota police could reach the scene. They learned that four tractor-trailers had also left the truck stop in the same critical minutes — one reaching Minneapolis with its cargo, two becoming stranded by the storm.

The fourth was believed heading northwest on either 10 or I-94, although radio contact hadn't yet been established. That truck would almost certainly hold the fugitives. If not, they were trapped somewhere on the road, destined either for capture or a hypothermic death. How far could they get in the deep snow, Corelli on crutches, the wind chill at zero? Brutal conditions, surely ordained by the Lord.

Closing his eyes, he prayed for another divine blessing — that this morning's critical meeting, once and for all, would remove the threatening shadow of this ancient ghost.

How swiftly the meeting's dark specter had arisen, leaving them little time to seek shelter. Longbridge's call to Streeter had come just last night. "One way or the other, Thomas, I intend to resolve this mess. You better understand that right now."

At midnight, they'd gathered in the Lakeland study for yet another emergency meeting. After adopting a strategy, they'd adjourned and, unable to sleep, he'd conferred again with the Lord. His prayer was simple and direct: that if Satan's chest couldn't be found, that the fugitives who'd dare use it against them, would be very soon now, because he couldn't take the stress much longer.

Longbridge had replaced the rectangular table with a round one, because he needed to see the men who advised him. Did their eyes express confidence or timidity? Did they glow with insight, or were they clouded by myopia? The nation's fate often rested upon this answer.

This morning's meeting was different only in that its participants included not just advisers, but outspoken adversaries, and still others whose loyalties weren't yet known. This last group concerned him the most, and made him appreciate how dangerous this confrontation was.

Solemnly, his gaze passed over those present, moving around the table: Attorney General Streeter; FBI Director Chapman; Justices Falkingham, Mann, and the nominee, Lamp; Secretary Culpepper, and Senators Banyon of California and Adamley of Massachusetts. "I've spoken with each of you since last evening," he began. "Therefore, I won't waste time on a lengthy recitation of the facts.

"Simply put, Senators Adamley and Banyon plan to reopen their hearings and postpone a vote on Greg's nomination. In response, I've thanked them for bringing this to my attention before going to the media, and also agreeing to meet so that we might get to the heart of this grave situation."

He turned to Travis. "Following my conversation with Senator Adamley last evening, I received a call from Secretary Culpepper, who shared yet another startling revelation about this ancient murder case, which simply refuses to go away.

"Now," he continued as he studied them again. "We're going to exhume both Mary Sandover, the TSU student murdered in 1954, and Edgar Norris, the man executed for the crime, then retry the case, and mercifully return them to their graves. Who would like to testify first?"

Travis was never one to be shy. "As you all know, Tyler Waddill contacted me last night. From where, I have no idea. He didn't say, and I didn't ask.

"His greatest concern is for his companion, Miss Corelli, whose condition is precarious. Besides the injuries sustained in her mountain fall, he reports her suffering from extreme exhaustion. Her deteriorating condition, and the need for medical attention, make it imperative that the crisis end as soon as possible. That's why he first wrote to Senator Adamley, and then tried to reach him by phone Friday afternoon.

"Tyler hopes that by going public, he may draw enough attention to support an investigation, while at the same time, create a more hospitable climate for surrender. He'd do it now, if he wasn't convinced that Federal agents would murder him and Corelli, just like they have the others."

"That's preposterous!" Streeter snapped.

"Granted," Longbridge agreed, "but if they're willing to surrender, I assume we're prepared to guarantee their safety."

"Of course," Chapman confirmed.

"And the investigation?" Travis asked.

"Investigating this absurd fantasy will only stamp it with credibility," Lamp protested. "The national attention alone will convince people that we committed this horrible crime. Meanwhile, what happens to my nomination?"

"It'll have to be delayed until the investigation is completed," Adamley replied.

"But that could take months!"

"Then perhaps, Mr. Lamp, your withdrawal is the only realistic alternative."

"Hold on," Streeter rejoined. "The investigation can be completed much quicker than you gentlemen realize. Certainly before the spring term."

"I've obviously misled you," Travis smiled apologetically. "Tyler insists that the investigation be conducted by a special prosecutor, with no ties to this administration."

Streeter glared at him. "You don't trust us to conduct an impartial investigation?"

"These are Tyler's terms, and I think they're quite reasonable."

"Perhaps a Senate probe might satisfy everyone," Banyon suggested.

"Please gentlemen," Longbridge held up his hand. "We're getting way ahead of ourselves. Senate investigations, special prosecutors . . . on what basis? A fugitive's desperation call? His letter, dredging up an ancient crime, heard by a jury and for which a man was executed? Where is the evidence?"

"Why shouldn't the forum for Waddill's charges be the District Court where he will be tried?" Chapman asked.

"If the fugitives surrender," Travis said, "they'll have abandoned their own search for the evidence they're convinced will exonerate them. Consequently, they must insist on an independent investigation, conducted by a prosecutor with the freedom and resources to get at the truth."

Falkingham turned to Longbridge. "With all due respect, sir, isn't it obvious what's taking place? The fugitives aren't just grasping at straws. *Revenge* is their motive, pure and simple. They hate Greg for blowing the whistle on their lucrative records conspiracy."

"If that's true," Adamley asked, "then why does their charge include you and Justice Mann? What have you done to deserve Waddill's wrath? Didn't you give him his first job?"

Lamp mused, "Perhaps in his muddled thinking, Tyler assumed the more sensational the charge, the more attention it'd draw."

"And then again," Adamley responded, "maybe it just happens to be the truth."

"Now just a minute!" Mann joined the fray. "If we can't keep you and your gang from believing every wild lie that happens to suit your liberal cause, we can certainly keep you from propagating it. There's a definite line between legislative immunity and libel, Senator, so I'd watch my step."

"There's also a definite line between libel and truth," Travis said. "And the requested investigation would seem the perfect way to determine which this charge is."

Longbridge sighed. "I suppose you can argue that every factual dispute warrants an investigation. Yet isn't this meeting just that? If truth is to be found, why not here, in this conference room? Let's at least make a valiant effort before resorting to a costly investigation."

"If truth was as easy to find as you suggest," Travis replied, "I suppose we could eliminate Thomas's Department, Larry's Bureau, and the Court these gentlemen serve on."

"This matter is much too grave for cynicism, Travis."

"I agree, sir." It was clear there'd be no investigation. Further discussion was pointless. He turned now to the anxious trio – Mann, Lamp, and the world's greatest cynic, Falkingham. "It's easy to understand how you gentlemen became such good friends. You have so much in common."

"Oh?" Lamp asked. "And how's that?"

"Your ardent interest in the law. Your wealthy families, even though you're from different parts of the country. Rich is rich, wherever you're from."

"Like Virginia, for example," Mann retorted.

"True enough," he assented. "My family's wealth is hardly a secret. And I've enjoyed all the privileges that come with it. A university education, graduate school — not law like you, but business. UVA. And Chase? You're South Carolina, if I'm not mistaken. Greg? NYU. And Thomas — Northwestern, right?"

"Very impressive," Falkingham laughed. "It must've taken five minutes to gather that well-worn information."

"What's not well-worn, Chase, is that you each skipped a year between your undergraduate studies and law school — the same year, in fact. 1954. The year Miss Sandover was murdered. But you needn't explain. I'm quite confident I already know where you spent that year."

"TSU, I suppose," Mann huffed.

"I don't believe there's any question."

"You have records, of course, to support this claim?" Lamp asked coldly.

"Come on, Greg," he smiled. "You were law students for heaven's sake. Much too smart to leave records lying around."

"Witnesses, then? Certainly someone must remember if we were there."

"No witnesses either, as you must know."

"The reason being quite simple: we weren't there."

"Nor did we know each other in 1954," Mann added. "And I'm sorry you find our accounts of that sabbatical year unnecessary, because we have quite credible ones. We met for the first time at a National Bar conference in Hawaii, thirty years ago."

"I have pictures if you care to see them," Falkingham smiled smugly. "There's a great shot of Diamondhead."

Streeter watched Longbridge's eyes harden with resolve. The

battle had been won. And with the next revelation, so had the war. "I believe it's time to end this regrettable situation," he said, retrieving a thin folder from his briefcase.

"What do you have there?" Longbridge asked.

"The origin of this malicious charge. We'd hoped to avoid its disclosure, but I'm afraid that was wishful thinking."

Opening the folder, he lay the pamphlet before them. The paper was coarse and gray, the black print bold yet uneven, some letters too light, others too dark. All of which he now explained. "You'll notice the pamphlet's obvious flaws —not just the irregular print and ink consistency, but the spacing and punctuation errors, as well. The message is forceful, yet equally incompetent in its lithography and diction."

Longbridge asked, "This is the Halo pamphlet which you're now saying is related to Miss Sandover's murder?"

"Not just that, sir. It mirrors, precisely, the fugitives' explanation of the murder, including the government figures targeted: Chase, Thomas, and Greg. The printed material is much too detailed to be a coincidence."

Longbridge explained, "I previously advised Thomas that I wasn't interested in the pamphlet's contents, unless he was persuaded it was something more than hate propaganda. Otherwise, I saw no reason to further our enemies' cause by participating in its dissemination. Consequently, I ordered that its contents remain confidential, until such time as it became material to a government inquiry."

As Longbridge read the pamphlet, Streeter explained, "Ten thousand of these were seized in the Halo raid, all produced by the same confiscated printing press. It's safe to say there's no one living in Pine, Flavin, and the adjacent counties, who isn't familiar with this murder case. This includes the Halos, of course."

Longbridge passed the pamphlet on. Pausing, Streeter took note of the others' expected shock. "The case's intrigue naturally flows from the issue of Norris's guilt and the all-white jury that convicted him — an intrigue his widow's publicized protests has kept alive. Obviously, it was Basham's fascination with the case that inspired this hate propaganda against our three jurists."

As the pamphlet reached Travis, he tossed it, like rubbish, into the center of the table.

"Please read it," Longbridge implored.

"For what purpose, sir? I already know its contents, and the motives of the men who manufactured it."

"You'll recall, Travis, that I was convinced of the operation's proper handling, yet out of respect for your concerns, I looked into the matter with an open mind. Can't you do the same for me now?"

He wouldn't be broken. If travesty were to reign, he wouldn't swear an ounce of pretense to it, even at the request of a man he'd once respected.

"Travis, why is it so difficult to believe the Halos conceived this tale?" Streeter asked. "Isn't it logical that they'd appreciate the Norris case's potential for inciting the masses, and in an effort to engender hatred for the Federal government, create their own explanation of the murder?

"And was there any doubt, that when the fugitives heard the story, they'd be receptive, and participate in its propagation to further their own cause?"

Travis glanced at a resolute Longbridge, who'd clearly bought Streeter's smoke and mirror logic. And Adamley and Banyon, once flexed for combat, now slumped despondently, having accepted it as well.

Lamp offered his own assessment. "The pamphlet's timing is even more understandable when you consider that the Tennessee sheriff who investigated the murder died recently, leaving his estate to a school founded by Norris's widow. This naturally resurrected suspicion for those who believed his bequest was motivated by conscience."

"This is beginning to make perfect sense," Longbridge said. "It's logical to infer from Crenshaw's bequest that he either knew or suspected Norris hadn't committed the crime. How large was his estate, Greg, do you know?"

He nodded. "My late partner represented the children, who are contesting the will. Regrettably, Morris's murder is also what started this manhunt. Because he supervised their work, he was recruited to help expose their involvement in the Bureau conspiracy. And upon discovering this, as the charges now state, they were forced to kill him. And back to your question: Crenshaw's estate was valued at ten million dollars."

"More fuel to the fires of speculation," Longbridge nodded. "How does a Tennessee sheriff amass that kind of wealth, and why leave it to the widow of a man he executed?"

"Those questions aren't just fuel for gossip," Travis said. "They're quite legitimate, and should be addressed."

"The man's dead, for Christ's sake!" Lamp snapped. "And the bequest to the widow's school doesn't prove anything. As I recall, Morris said the challenge in the will contest was overcoming the notorious worthlessness of Crenshaw's children. His disappointment would've been a natural reason for cutting them out of his estate. And if so, why shouldn't Norris's widow receive his charity?

"Furthermore, assuming Crenshaw's wealth was illegally acquired, it's hardly something he'd put in his memoirs. Nor is it a rare phenomenon, regrettably."

"The point is, there could be any number of explanations," Falkingham said. "Eccentric millionaires make mysterious bequests every day."

Travis's glare chilled him, then Lamp. Liars to the core, and murderers — on the Supreme Court, no less. Yet because of their status, no one was willing to consider the serious charges against them. "Despite your deft dancing around the facts," he said, "we return to my point, which is: that this particular eccentric millionaire left his fortune to the widow of a man he helped execute. And if there could be any number of explanations, certainly one is that Crenshaw felt guilt over sending an innocent man to his death. And having heard nothing which eliminates it, I believe it merits an investigation, just as the fugitives request."

An impasse now lay heavily on the table. And in a democracy, he realized, the majority ruled. But a vote was hardly necessary. Clearly it was he, and the two cowardly Senators, against the others.

"We've covered a lot of ground," Longbridge said. "I believe this is a good point to summarize.

"First, we have a grave charge leveled against our three jurists — one that has found its way into the pamphlet of a fanatical sect, whose avowed mission is the destruction of our government. Needless to say, these Halos are dangerous, as demonstrated by the arsenal seized at their camp and their hate propaganda, clearly intended for dissemination.

"That they were a desperate bunch is further demonstrated by their mass suicide, a tragedy which exposes them as self-obsessed creatures who, unable to have their way, drew as much attention to themselves as possible. Sadly, these fanatics, like the fugitives they rescued, became so enslaved by their muddled prophecy, they were willing to sacrifice everything to its fulfillment. Even human life."

"Your description fits many people," Travis observed. "The problem is, we can never be certain who or where they are. Sometimes we're shocked to discover they are people we trust. People who sit at the same table as we discuss issues affecting national security."

"Sometimes, too," said Longbridge as his eyes hardened, "They're the children of close friends, whom we believe incapable of the violent crimes others commit every day, even when the truth is placed before us. I'm sorry, Travis," he sighed. "If you can't accept it, I find myself unable to get past it."

"With all due respect, sir, the part you can't get past is that men sitting at this table, who know quite well who they are, have not only betrayed your trust, but the nation's, whose interests they've sworn to serve."

An astonished silence fell over the table as Longbridge beheld him, not with shock, but a heavy sadness. "Despite my desire to behave as the Lord expects, I've found myself lacking at least one important virtue that, with prayer, He's mercifully provided. Tolerance, Travis. A virtue that, if we all possessed it, would mean an end to lives sacrificed to violence, and hearts corrupted by hate.

"Among that which I'm bound to tolerate is your aggressive advocacy of the fugitives. But that doesn't mean I must accept what I know to be a lie, conceived not of a pure heart, but a vengeful one.

"Now," he resumed, "I find the following quite clear: the fugitives were rescued by the Halos, and during Corelli's recuperation, the two factions shared their contempt for government, and desire to exact revenge. Proof of this is found in the arsenal, printing press and hate propaganda seized at the Halo camp.

"With motive and means established, let's now consider this pamphlet. First, no one can doubt the Halos' knowledge of the TSU murder case, the rich speculation around it, the incessant protests of Norris's widow, and most recently, the Crenshaw bequest. Secondly, we can assume the Halos and fugitives were well aware the public would gobble up any fresh theory of Miss Sandover's murder. The more sensational, the better. And who'd refute it, so long as it vindicated the martyred Norris and his saintly widow, who'd devoted her life to disabled children?

"Can there be any question then," he said as his eyes locked on Travis, "that had we not seized this pamphlet, and had it gotten into the public's hands, within hours the Tennessee mountains would have been crawling with reporters? We would've had a circus on our hands, precisely what our enemies intended. This administration, the Supreme Court — indeed, every government institution — would have been placed on public trial. Our noble mission, to prove that a government not just of men, but those guided by the Lord's wisdom and inspired by His divine purpose, is the best government — pure and incorruptible — would have been irrevocably damaged, if not destroyed.

"More than a circus," he continued, "we'd have been faced with a national crisis, not to mention a painful travesty for Greg, Thomas, Chase and their families."

A decisive silence fell over the table as he turned to Adamley and Banyon. "I know you gentlemen take vigorous exception to my Christian views. You've made no secret of that. But politics aside, I invited you here because I felt it best to get the matter out on the table, and then work towards a solution together. I don't view this as a partisan issue. It's not just a threat to my administration, but to the integrity of government as a whole. Given this, how do you plan to deal with the situation on Capitol Hill?"

Adamley scowled. Politicians never considered a problem partisan when it was directed at them. Of course this situation was partisan. Weren't the three jurists Longbridge appointments? Yet his earlier inspiration had evaporated. He'd come to this meeting with such high hopes for Lamp's withdrawal, perhaps even Mann and Falkingham's resignations. But these hopes had disappeared.

At this point, he wasn't sure he had enough to fuel a Senate investigation or even justify reopening the hearings. Perhaps the fantastic claim shouldn't be disclosed at all. Whatever political advantage gained would quickly fade as no evidence emerged to support it. Public sympathy would shift to the falsely accused jurists and the besieged President who'd sponsored them. They'd become the victims while he and Banyon would become the opportunistic accusers. Yet how could they maintain their silence in the face of such a sensational claim?

Turning to an equally burdened Banyon, he spoke for them both. "We'll caucus with party leaders to determine how this sensitive matter should be addressed, and then notify you."

"What's there to caucus about?" asked Longbridge. "I've heard no objection to my assessment of the situation."

"Nevertheless," Banyon replied, "as Marcus said, this is a sensitive matter, with potentially grave repercussions."

"Fine, then," he said. "Caucus all you want. But I want Greg on that court by spring. If you think I'm . . ."

"How did you know they'd go to Florida?"

All eyes shot to Travis, who'd directed the question at Streeter. "What do you mean?" he shrugged.

"I mean, how did you and Larry know that when the fugitives left New York they'd go to Naples, Florida?"

"It was Crenshaw's domicile when he died."

"We know that now, but how did you know then, and connect the fugitives with him? If your theory about the Halo pamphlet is valid, they wouldn't have known about Crenshaw or the murder case, until they'd been rescued."

"But they did know," Lamp argued. "Don't you remember? I said they worked for Mendelsohn, who represented Crenshaw's children in the Naples probate suit. And while we can't say what they knew, one thing's certain — within hours of Morris's death, his Crenshaw files were missing."

"Were they ever found?" Longbridge asked.

"In Corelli's office," he nodded. "Because she was the prime suspect in Morris's murder, we suspected a connection with Crenshaw and alerted the authorities who, I assume, targeted

Naples and Pine County as places the fugitives might go."

Longbridge added, "Then perhaps it was the two of them who conceived this libelous trash, after all."

"It's only libel if a court says so," Travis qualified. "Which leaves trash. And by that, don't you mean 'unworthy of investigation?' "

"You're right," he said. "There'll be no investigation."

"Then there'll be no surrender either, I'm afraid. Which means this meeting has been a complete waste of time."

"No, Travis. If it didn't end the crisis, we at least reached the truth. When that's done, a meeting is never a waste of time. I'll expect everyone here to refrain from further publication of this inflammatory pamphlet."

Adamley would not be intimidated. "Senator Banyon and I will handle this matter in accordance with our legislative duties and consciences, not yours. We're neither accountable to you or to members of your flock. And if the pamphlet's publication . . ." He paused as Travis suddenly started out.

Turning, Longbridge snapped, "I was led to believe a Virginia gentleman excused himself when leaving a meeting."

"Then you've misinterpreted this assemblage," Travis replied. "It's not a meeting, it's a religious service. And if a Virginia gentleman disagrees with the sermon, he neither protests nor excuses himself — he simply leaves quietly, which is what I'm doing."

Longbridge bristled. "Not every factual summary is a sermon."

"No sir, but yours are quite often refrained by trumpets and set against stained glass."

"Travis, a man's views are sharpened by his religious faith, his judgments made sound by his moral conscience. Why should his words conceal their divine inspiration?"

"They shouldn't, sir. But that man should just make sure it is divine inspiration, and not self-interest. The line between the two isn't always clear."

"Then am I to understand that you no longer believe me capable of distinguishing between good and evil?"

Solemnly, Travis gazed at the doorknob in his hand. He didn't belong here. Perhaps he never had. Then wasn't the man he'd served entitled to know why?

"Sir, there is an Evil One whose poisoned whispers have been in our ears all morning, as he's guided us down this road. And as we reach the end of the road, you ask me to confirm his presence? How can you not recognize him for yourself? He's been the driving force behind this operation from the start. The one who's placed this so-called truth."

He paused to inventory the shambles: Longbridge's icy glare, Adamley and Banyon's confusion, the conspirators' fright. Had he brought a cold sweat to their armpits? He hoped so.

"Sir, if you refuse to trumpet the Evil One's achievements, then I will. They read like an obituary: Rogers, Mendelsohn, Swanson, Harvey and his companion, six Halos. And to that list will soon be added the two fugitives. Today's truth destines them not to prosecution, but resting places in the Evil One's growing graveyard. And if you believe otherwise, you're only fooling yourself."

Longbridge looked at him coldly, as he completed his indictment. "And who is this Evil One, in whose filthy hands you have — unwittingly, I believe — placed the instruments of power? Not Satan, Hitler or Stalin, although he perhaps embodies the worst of them all. Seth Harrington is the Evil One of whom I speak."

He slipped out, leaving a terrible silence behind.

Streeter was the first to reach Harrington. "Longbridge buried the pamphlet and issued a gag order on Waddill's charges. After a bit of impassioned Dixie sermonizing, Culpepper left — for good, I'd say, after the way he ridiculed Longbridge. Adamley and Banyon left a minute later."

"Praise the Lord!" he rejoiced. "But can we reasonably expect them to let this die?"

"They'd be fools not to. You just don't attack one-third of the Supreme Court with the unsupportable claim of religious fanatics and desperate fugitives. It's political suicide. And speaking of attacks, Culpepper had some pretty outrageous things to say about you."

Hadn't Moses been vilified by heretics, too? "Culpepper's opinion means nothing as long as the President is unaffected."

"Affected?" Streeter chuckled. "He was furious — not over the charges, but at Culpepper's audacity in making them. He's as good as gone."

The others soon called to echo the welcome news — Larry, Chase, Greg, and the toadish Mann. Finally, the phone grew quiet and he was able to hear his heart's tranquil beating, certainly another sign that the worst was over.

Longbridge's call came later that evening. "Seth, I hope I'm not disturbing you?" he asked.

"Certainly not, Tom. I've been concerned about the First Lady's arthritis. Despite her brave face Sunday, I sensed it bothering her. I've asked the Lord to relieve her pain, because I know she's much too unselfish to petition Him on her own behalf."

"Praise the Lord. Yes, she's much better. At the moment, she's knitting up a storm in front of the TV. Seth, I hate to bother you with my secular problems, but your insight has been invaluable, especially in my critical appointments. And if we're to establish a government deserving of the Lord's grace, our leaders must be the purest of heart. If they're not, we risk collapse of the entire house."

"And hasn't the Lord blessed us with these righteous people, Tom? Isn't Lamp the last one needed to complete our house?"

Patiently, he listened to yet another version of the White House meeting, and then offered the message Longbridge needed to hear. "Certainly this pamphlet is just what you've described: hate propaganda. Chase, Thomas, Greg, rapists? Murderers? I can't imagine anything more preposterous. And if it were true, neither Larry nor Thomas would cover it up. They'd have no reason to, but more importantly, their consciences wouldn't allow it. As I'd tell our television audience . . ."

"No, no," Longbridge sighed. "There's no need for a pulpit confirmation. You've told me all I need to hear."

"I must say I'm surprised by Culpepper's violent reaction."

"As am I," Longbridge confessed. "Travis has misplaced his loyalties, and will have to live with the consequences. Unless he offers it beforehand, I plan to ask for his resignation in the morning. Had I listened to you, I wouldn't be faced with the problem now."

"Please, Tom, don't torture yourself. After all, Culpepper is just one rotten apple. Surely we can find a good one to replace him. And when the time's right, offer the olive branch, like the good Christians we are."

Solemn seconds passed as he drank in this wisdom. "Truly Seth, you're the one to whom we must turn in this dark hour. Praise the Lord."

Chapman called an hour later. "That fourth tractor-trailer has been located north of Moorhead, Minnesota. Apparently the driver left his scheduled route in an effort to outwit the storm. While we were watching 10 and I-94, he was traveling some uncharted back roads.

"Things went well until he skidded into a monster snow drift. With his radio dead, he hiked back to the nearest farmhouse. Our team arrived to discover the trailer's doors had been tampered with. We found a crowbar that we assume Waddill used to force an entry. Also, one of the two is apparently ill. Some bloody vomit was found inside the trailer."

"So where did they slip off the truck?" he asked.

"Elk's Crossing. It's sixty miles northwest of the truck stop, where we assume they jumped on."

"They certainly didn't get far in all this time."

"The snow's shut down the entire region," Chapman explained. "No one's traveling unless it's absolutely necessary. Anyway, one report places Waddill in the Elk's Crossing Pharmacy buying, among other things, anti-nausea medicine and tampons. The woman who waited on him said he looked fine, so we assume Corelli's the sick one." He laughed, "First a broken leg, then the flu. Now it seems the little lady has her period.

"The second report came from an Elk's Crossing resident named Gully, who suspects trespassers of occupying a storage shed on his farm. The Minnesota Patrol has dispatched units to the scene, with instructions not to advance until our agents arrive. This could be it, sir."

Leopold reported in minutes later. "I'm on my way to Elk's Crossing. You wouldn't believe the driving conditions, sir. It'll be spring before this snow melts."

He'd just hung up when the phone rang yet again. "They were definitely there," Chapman confirmed. "More bloody vomit was found in Gully's shed. Also a rubber pod from one of Corelli's crutches."

"You idiot!" he exploded. "Don't tell me about vomit and crutch pods. Or tampons and menstrual cycles. Just explain how one man, saddled with a sick, crippled woman, can walk away from an army of police in two feet of snow and not leave a trace!"

"We're checking. Somebody must have seen them. Elk's Crossing is no more than a blink of the eye. Gully's place is on the edge of town, just across from the Highlands."

"The Highlands?"

"A truck stop."

CHAPTER THIRTY-ONE

★

Marty Kennesaw couldn't believe his luck. Just an hour ago, he'd been sitting at the kitchen window, his morning coffee cooling at his elbow. Gloomily, he'd stared at the cold, gray lake, contemplating another miserable day in Northwood, another bitter Wisconsin winter. Number forty-one.

Life had been passing him by without a single prospect, unless handyman qualified for such a thing. He'd learned his trade as a kid, keeping the Kennesaw Inn in rentable condition. He'd become so capable, in fact, that his parents had been glad to keep him around, instead of packing him off to Minnesota State. And he hadn't known any better. He'd had free room and board, a decent wage and use of the pickup when he wasn't buying supplies for the Inn. Poor Dutch, his older brother, had been in college studying his butt off. And why? To spend his life behind some desk? He'd had much better plans. Specifically, taking over the inn when his parents retired, then building more cabins, filling them with eager guests and, in the process, getting very rich.

Things hadn't quite worked out as planned. Back then, the Inn's business had been at its peak, with Route 2 being the primary road west from Chicago, Milwaukee and Green Bay. And there'd been plenty of tourist attractions, with Lake Superior and the Ottawa National Forest nearby. His parents had been raking it in. His father drove a big Buick, and his mother shopped in Duluth's fancy stores. They'd belonged to the country club and eaten dinner out three nights a week at Jillian's Steakhouse. The inn had seemed like a cash machine that ran itself and in his sunny dreams, one that would belong to him some day.

But a few weeks before construction was to begin on the inn's five new cabins, plans were announced for I-94. Paul Kennesaw, seeing the handwriting on the wall, had quickly shelved his own expansion plans. Then I-35 had opened. Routes 2 and 51, that had once brought the guests in droves, were suddenly obsolete.

The inn's occupancy rate was cut in half. To save money, his mother released the staff and assumed the daily chores herself, while his father worried over the books, as if the solution lay somewhere in the numbers.

Large hotel chains soon found opportunity on the scenic lakeshore, and with their vast resources and more efficient operations, were able to offer lower rates than the smaller independents. Again, the inn's occupancy dropped. And Paul Kennesaw finally found the answer in his numbers, although not the one he'd hoped for. He'd made the discovery the night his wife found him slumped over his books, the victim of a massive heart attack.

Poor Emma had never recovered and a stroke took her own life a year later. And Marty, at age thirty, was left alone to contend with an empty inn, mounting bills and worse, no prospects for a dreamer without skills or education.

Forced to find work, he drifted from one contractor to the next, each growing tired of his arguments with foremen who were paid more, but knew less. Finally, he'd ended up doing things his way as a self-employed handyman — not nearly as lucrative as he'd once thought. But maybe now that he and Dutch were warming up after a decade of silence, his brother would help him start his own contracting business.

Dutch made six figures as a St. Paul ad executive, lived in an expensive high-rise and had babes drooling over him. Fortunately, as Marty had just learned, he'd broken up with the one invited on the cruise, and with the fare paid, there'd been no reason not to ask his brother to tag along. Now instead of bitter cold Wisconsin, Marty would spend Christmas basking in the warm Caribbean sun.

Returning to pack, Marty quickly inventoried: underwear, flip-flops, shirts, slacks and swim trunks. Dutch probably had a dozen pair of Jantzens and matching terrycloth robes. Some decent sandals might be nice, too, and one of those wide-brimmed straw hats. He'd never score with the babes unless he looked right. Hopefully, there'd be time to shop in Miami before the ship left.

When he was packed, he hauled his suitcase out to the Trooper. His flight from Duluth was at noon, and with the road conditions it'd take twice as long to reach the airport.

As he hurried back to the inn, a tractor-trailer groaned away from Lacey's Truck Stop below the ridge. Trucks and local heaps were all that used Route 51 anymore. No one knew that better than a Kennesaw.

He stopped and contemplated the ten cabins overlooking Lake Superior. Once handsome and proud, they now drooped from neglect as much as from the heavy mantles of snow, their cock-eyed shutters squinting in the sun. How long had it been since the last rental? Two . . . no, three years now.

Returning to the inn, he went from room to room, checking window latches and door locks. Why he feared burglars, he hadn't a clue. There was nothing here he wouldn't sell for a buck at the Northwood flea market. He couldn't even call it a . . . He froze suddenly at the sight of a tall young man in the front office, his eyes concealed by dark glasses, his strong, even face chapped by the icy wind. His hat was tilted Clint Eastwood style, his coat shabby, boots scuffed. Drifter, Marty concluded. "Can I help you?" he inquired.

"I'd like to rent one of your cabins."

He looked at the man as if he were insane. "We . . . I mean, I haven't rented them out in years. Besides . . ."

"The sign out front says the Kennesaw Inn. Isn't this the place?"

"Well yeah, but . . ."

"How much are they?" The man withdrew his wallet.

His eyes popped at the thick wad of bills. What had the cabin rates been? He couldn't even remember. "Look, I have a plane to catch. There won't be anyone here for two weeks. You'll just have to find another place."

"My car's stranded five miles west," the man explained. "I froze my ass off just walking here."

"You want to call a tow?" He nodded at the phone.

"No, I want a cabin. Why's that so much to ask?"

Marty picked up his drawl - Georgia maybe? "Look, why not call a tow, get your car fixed and go on to Duluth?"

"Look, all I want is a bed, heat and some running water."

His eyes fell again to the wad of cash. *Panama shirts, Jantzen trunks, new sandals.* What difference did it make if he left Eastwood here alone? He couldn't do more than burn the place down.

"Only three cabins are in rentable condition."

The man smiled. "That's not a problem, since I only want one. Now how much?"

"They're oil heated. Hot water, lights . . ."

"How much?" Eastwood repeated.

He glanced at his watch. Precious minutes were slipping away. "How long do you plan on staying?"

"You'll be away two weeks?"

"Yeah," he squinted warily. "So what?"

"I was thinking I could watch the place while you're gone."

He was about to ask why, when Eastwood stuffed the wad of bills in his hand. "Six hundred bucks for the cabin, plus I'll guard the place for nothing."

Fresh visions of a Miami shopping trip swirled in his head as he now gave Eastwood the key. "This opens the office. Get what you need – towels, sheets, whatever. And use the phone if you want. Only no long distance calls. I don't want to come back and find myself stuck with a thousand-dollar phone bill."

"What about the cabin key?"

"Oh yeah." He retrieved #10 from the counter drawer. Starting for the door, he turned, "Hey, you're not related to . . . ah, never mind," and he slipped out.

Related to whom? Tyler wondered, watching the Trooper disappear over the ridge.

Returning outside, he loped after Mayson, who was slumped against a tree, her crutches beside her in the snow. With his stocking cap, Sister Cook Rebecca's coat and scarf, Sister Maid Ruth's sweater, thermal underwear and socks, she was heavily bundled, yet still shivered as much from her fever as from the Arctic chill. Tucking the spittle-stained scarf in her collar, he hoisted her over his shoulder. "Come on," he said as he grabbed her crutches and started off. "There's a warm bed waiting."

Since abandoning the Nova, their world had been one dank trailer after another, brutal cold and constant fear. There'd been no choice but to keep changing trucks. Who knew when the driver might inspect his cargo, check a suspicious noise, hear a report or worse, send one? No wonder Mayson had developed the flu.

She'd barely uttered a word since leaving St. Cloud — the same time the vomiting had started.

The next three days had been an endless hell of truck rides over snow-crusted highways, across Minnesota, then Wisconsin, just to avoid the lurking patrol cars and hovering choppers. They had to keep moving. Stop and they'd surely die.

In the process, he'd become a master burglar. Give him a crow bar or decent knife and there wasn't a truck anywhere he couldn't break into. Not to steal, but survive; another minute, another ride. There'd been no hope beyond that.

Between rides, they'd rested in the woods and abandoned buildings. Once in an Elk's Crossing farm shed, until the hounds had chased them off. They'd slept little in that time. Hopefully this would change at the isolated Kennesaw Inn.

The cabins loomed as he crested the ridge. Number ten, like the others, slumped beneath a mantle of snow, its sagging shutters protesting their heavy burden and years of neglect. Using Mayson's crutches, he brushed away the snow and dense dead vines, then groped for the key. "I'll need to do some pruning before we have company. A little painting, too. The windows, I'll leave to you. I don't do them."

Pushing inside, he scanned the musty room, cluttered with dust-coated furniture and cheap paintings that portrayed the lake and surrounding wilderness. The kitchen was an equal disaster of rot and neglect. "Maybe the back rooms are better," he suggested.

He soon found himself on the threshold of a large bedroom, with full bath, canopied four-poster and stone fireplace. "Now we're talking," he said. He opened the drapes to Lake Superior and its awesome majesty directing the earth north, into the gray horizon.

Careful not to disturb her healing ribs, he laid Mayson across the bed. Her lush, dark hair sprung out as he slipped off the cap, its natural wave relaxed after weeks of growth. He removed the scarf and coat next, then Brother Captain Jeremiah's donated khakis, split to accommodate her cast. Removing the sock, he examined her toes. The circulation was better, the swelling down.

As Tyler settled her into the covers she moaned, then in seconds slept again. And he inhaled deeply, his shoulders instantly relaxing, his strain fading. Seconds drifted as he indulged the small pleasure of her slumber. He hated to see her suffer, even more because she tried to hide it, as if his worry was less tolerable than the pain. Mayson was a good person. Whatever he'd sacrificed for her was well worth the price.

As she slept, he explored their new world, starting with the inn. The ground floor consisted of the front office and supply rooms, and in back, the well-stocked living quarters. The remaining floors were devoted to the guest rooms: empty, orderly, beds crisply made, bathroom towels neatly hung, unopened soap boxes on the counters — all for guests who'd never arrived. Finally, he reached the cluttered attic with its racks of moth-eaten clothes and musty boxes of memories — a ghostly museum of the inn in its heyday.

Back outside, the chill tightened its grip on the gray afternoon. Dipping his hands into his pockets, he continued his exploration along the snowy ridge. He was weary, yet restless, his muscles aching after weeks on the run.

His gaze was drawn north to the frigid lake, where police cutters waited but posed no threat, as long as they didn't attempt a reckless escape to Canada. To the east, the forest hemmed the jagged coast for miles. Beyond was a cold, barren wilderness, a narrow strait and, on the northernmost point, Copper Harbor, where they'd rested briefly before stealing a ride south to Merrill. Or was it Wausau? They'd left few towns untouched in the last days.

Duluth lay to the west; his eyes drifted along the coast. They'd gotten as close as Monegha Falls before heading east again. Snow Peak lay a hundred miles beyond Duluth, a place they had to reach, but never would. At least not while an army of Feds waited for them to try.

Descending the ridge, he glimpsed Lacey's Truck Stop and desolate Route 51 below. How long until a suspicious patrol car crept up the inn's snowy drive?

Night fell, then deepened before Mayson finally woke to her strange new world, where light came from a crackling fire, its shadows swaying on the wall. The soft bed was foreign, too, but quite welcome, as was Tyler's concerned face over her.

"I heated some soup," he said, motioning at the bedside tray.

"I'd rather have a shower. Do we have one?"

He pressed his palm to her forehead. It was still warm, but dry, at least. "I can't believe I broke the thermometer."

"Then you shouldn't have put it in your back pocket. Any fool would know it'd break the second you sat down."

"You're feeling better," he smiled.

"Tyler, where are we?"

"The Kennesaw Inn. It's just above Lacey's Truck Stop, where we last hopped off. Don't you remember?"

"Just you lifting me from the truck, then hobbling up the hill. It's fuzzy after that."

He explained the deal he made with the inn's proprietor. "A Kennesaw who hung around after the place closed, I guess. And he was strapped for cash, obviously."

"How much do we have left?"

"Twenty-five hundred. But I don't think we'll be spending much more."

"Why?"

"Because there's nowhere left to go." He watched her crawl gingerly from the bed. "Where are you going?"

"To take a shower, if it's all right."

"Well it's not. You still have a fever. The shower will have to wait."

"It can't wait! My skin's crawling with vermin from those rancid trailers and rat-infested farm sheds. Can't you hear them?"

"No. Now be polite, and try the soup I made."

Shrugging, she nibbled on a Saltine, then sipped her ginger ale. "There. Maybe I'll feel more like eating after my shower."

"Try the soup. It's tomato."

"So?"

"You don't like it?"

"Why should I? Because I'm Italian?"

"We've done this with pizza, remember?"

"Which you obviously didn't learn from, since you still suffer from your brainless stereotypes. Like all Italians are dark-haired, dark-eyed meatballs who love tomatoes."

"I should've gone with the chicken noodle."

"Yes, you should. And so you'll remember next time: I don't like tomato soup. I've never liked it, and I never will. Is that clear enough?"

"Perfectly," he nodded. "I'll eat the goddamn soup myself and enjoy every spoonful."

"Now?"

"Why not? You've insisted on taking a shower. So take the damn thing."

Hopping after her crutches, she stubbed her toe on the cedar chest. "Shit! " she swore. "Who in their right mind puts a chest in the middle of the floor?"

"You know, it was really peaceful when you were asleep. You're awake five minutes and already bitching about everything under the sun." Tasting the soup, he said with satisfaction, "Excellent!"

She hopped into the bathroom, then quickly returned. "What's the matter now?" he asked.

"You know perfectly well I can't take a shower by myself!"

Thumping back into the bathroom, she slammed the door and, still trembling, gazed at her reflection in the mirror. The flu had left her so weak. Her face was pale and drawn, her eyes, heavy. The only positive was her hair. Weeks of growth had relaxed the waves.

She turned as Tyler entered. Turning on the shower, he cupped his hand under the warming spray. "Come on, let's get this over with."

This had become their ritual since her first shower at Dr. Stanley's clinic. He held her waist as she wriggled out of her clothes. The last shower had been days before in Chicago, and she was embarrassed now, not by her nudity, but her body's neglect. Besides, he never opened his eyes, an honorable practice over which she teased him unmercifully. "See," she said as she tossed her panties to the floor. "I told you there'd be little creatures crawling on my skin. Yuk, just look at them!"

"I don't see anything."

"Honestly, Tyler, we both know you're a Peeping Tom!"

"Mayson, get in the goddamned shower."

"How do you know I've finished undressing unless you're peeking?"

"Mayson, I'm losing patience here."

"You're right though, I have finished. I'm naked as a jaybird. Oh look, my rib bruises are fading. Go on, Tyler, I know you're dying to. And after all the . . ."

"Get in the goddamned shower!"

Instead, she studied her breasts in the mirror. They were small, but well formed. Like apples, she often thought. Why didn't he want to look? "Tyler, are my breasts too small?"

"Mayson, for the last time . . ."

"They are, aren't they?"

Scooping her up, he deposited all but her casted leg in the shower. "Now hurry up."

"Tyler, does Kara have large breasts?"

"I can't hear you," he said while he held her leg securely.

"Are large breasts . . . *Fanculo!*"

"Now what?"

"I dropped the soap."

She always dropped the soap, he thought, groping blindly in the tub. "Here. Now be more careful."

"Tyler, is that what attracted you to Kara? Her breasts?"

"Hardly." He envisioned a bare-chested, six-year-old playing in the James's gentle surf. He'd known Kara long before she had breasts.

Singing cheerfully through her lather and rinse, Mayson then whined, "There's no shampoo!"

"Then rinse off."

"I've already rinsed off. I need to wash my hair. There must be some shampoo somewhere."

"Nope," he said, looking in the cabinet. "Now get out."

"How about the bedroom?"

"You're one huge pain in the ass, you know that?" Irritated, he left on his forage. He returned quickly with a dusty shampoo tube, passing it through the curtain. "Now hurry up!"

When she was done, he took his turn, then joined her by the crackling fire. Her cheeks glowed with fresh color, her casted leg stretched comfortably across the carpet. "You're recovering quickly," he said.

"I have a good doctor. Tyler, I'm sorry about the soup."

"Forget it. Oh, when it's time, your medicine's in the bathroom cabinet, with your . . . the . . ."

"Tampons?"

He nodded. "There's just one box left. Will you need more?"

"No thanks," she smiled. "I'm almost finished."

In his eagerness to go to bed, he crawled in on the wrong side, a mistake she quickly pointed out. "I'm right, you're left. The precedent was established in your apartment, then followed in Naples, and later at Eagle's Nest."

"I can't say I've ever noticed." He rolled over.

"Nor the extra pillow you require," she said as she stuffed it in his gut. Joining him, she shut off the light.

Before long, the fire's last embers popped in the oak-scented darkness. Its lingering presence reassured her, as did the warm bed, and the man she shared it with. But beyond the bed, they shared little. He remained emotionally distant and Kara, the mysterious icon he so jealously guarded, was the reason. She'd broken his heart and Mayson wanted to mend it. Yet neither circumstance mattered. As safe as they might feel at this deserted inn, they'd eventually be captured. Perhaps a raid was underway at this very moment, its patrol cars en route to the Kennesaw. This possibility haunted her as the sheets rustled. "Tyler, are you awake?" she asked.

"I just remembered something. Before leaving, Kennesaw was about to ask if I was related to someone. Then he stopped himself."

"You think he recognized you?"

"I doubt it. He was in too much of a hurry."

"What if he sees your picture on the news and makes the connection?"

"What do you think I'm lying here thinking about?"

"Then should we stay or go?" she asked.

"There's nowhere to go in this weather. We stay — and pray."

"Let me do the praying," she sighed. "As much as you take the Lord's name in vain, I doubt He's inclined to listen with much sympathy to anything you have to say."

"Go to hell."

"Your destination, exactly, until you find a more suitable way to express your anger." She shivered in a darkness growing colder by the minute. "I thought you said this cabin was heated."

"Oil. I'll turn it up in the morning."

"It's almost that now."

"Mayson, I'm not getting up to adjust the heat."

Not yet maybe, but certainly after a few minutes of guilt. "I hope you've noticed my compliance with your stupid gag order."

"Kara. Yes, I've noticed."

"You still haven't explained the reason for it."

"I wasn't aware I was obliged to."

"Is it because she's too painful to discuss?"

"Go to sleep, Mayson."

"If you're still getting over her, I suppose any reminder would be like reopening . . ." The covers flew off her as he suddenly sprung up. "Where are you going?" she demanded.

"To turn up the goddamned heat!"

CHAPTER THIRTY-TWO

★

She slept peacefully in his arms as dawn crept into the win-window. The flu, which had gripped her these last days, was fading quickly and again, she was the pain in the ass he'd grown accustomed to. She was a paradox who became, with time, not simpler but more complex. Her exquisite face, thickly lashed eyes and sensuous mouth became even more beautiful; her capricious moods, if irritating, became even more intriguing. He wrestled with this paradox as the sun finally opened her eyes.

The kiss that followed was as fresh and sweet as all those before it, bridging the time since the last one — before those terrible days of danger, cold and sickness. Her slender arms clung to him with the hunger, not of days, but of a lifetime. And with an equal desire, he imagined the kisses that might have filled those days had she not been ill - kisses that couldn't be responsible for the poison creeping over him now. No, it wasn't kissing over which the germs of hell had crawled, but the dank quarters of endless trailers and abandoned buildings.

He just had time to dash to the toilet and sink to the floor before the vomiting began. Over and over he convulsed, until the stench filled his nostrils and the vileness choked his throat. The world spun painfully.

"Tyler, you're on fire!" Mayson's fingers suddenly pressed against his forehead. Running cold water over a cloth, she swabbed his face and then the vomit-stained toilet. "Men are such babies," she said, filling the cup with Emetrol and holding it under his nose. "Drink this, and let's get back to bed."

He gulped her anti-nausea medicine and the thick, warm liquid soothed his throat; hopefully it would do the same for his stomach.

She noticed the sickly green shadow that had crept over him. He'd get worse before getting better, and the only thing to do was let it pass. "Come on," she said, grabbing his arm and leading him back to bed.

"It's so . . . cold!" His teeth chattered.

She jumped back out to turn up the furnace, returning with an extra blanket. "Tyler, I'm so sorry I gave you this," she said, and she wrapped herself around him. "But don't worry, I'll take as good care of you as you did to me. Now get some sleep."

He did, fitfully, burning one minute, chilled, the next. The Emetrol effects faded and nausea gripped him again. Dashing to the bathroom, he wretched until his gut emptied, and blood flecked his vomit. His head was spinning, and he doubted that he'd make it back next time.

But he did. As did she, hobbling, coaxing, washing his face, giving him more Emetrol. Her tender care was rewarded with his childish whines; her patience, with his curses. "*Amore mio*, you're such a baby. What would you do without me?"

The question echoed through the fog; it was one he couldn't answer, and wouldn't have to. They were trapped like rats on the coast of Lake Superior. It was just a matter of time until they were smoked out. They couldn't count on another miracle. There were no Halos in Wisconsin.

Again, she bathed his feverish skin. "Can you eat yet?" she asked. It was night again, a fire was flickering in the hearth, and the furnace was rumbling. Yet the sheets were like ice. He couldn't get warm — or eat.

"How about a banana?" she asked. "I went up to the inn this afternoon. You were right — the kitchen's fully stocked."

He pulled the covers around his neck. "How can I eat when my stomach won't sit still long enough to digest it?"

"I was so hungry I made a bowl of tuna salad. I even made hard-boiled eggs and added mayonnaise."

"Do you know how disgusting that sounds?"

"Yes, I do." She stroked his hair. "I've been there, bought the T-shirt. Just one banana — it's full of potassium."

"No," he said, rolling away.

Greasy globs of mayonnaise and rancid tuna swirled in his dreams, and again he paid homage to the Toilet God. "There's nothing left in my gut but blood and lining," he moaned.

Still bundled up, her cheeks glowed from the arctic air. "I went back to the inn, and guess what? More Emetrol . . . and this." She lifted a banana from her pocket.

In disgust, he rolled away again. Then he felt guilty; she'd suffered the same agony, without a warm bed. And with far more adversity: a broken leg, bruised ribs, deep snow and icy trailers. Yet she'd never complained. "You're right. I am a baby. I just can't deal with this shit."

"Maybe not," she nodded. "But you can deal with so much more. Like me, for instance." She put his hand to her chest. "Can you feel it?"

"An apple?"

"The vibrations, you dope! When the heart vibrates, it means the songbird is singing." But her eyes became grave. "I turned on the news at the inn. Travis Culpepper resigned."

Meaning their last link to the world had now been severed. With Longbridge alienated, they had neither evidence of the conspiracy nor an audience, if by some miracle, they discovered any evidence.

"We still have Vernon's story," she said, groping for optimism.

"His account is purely circumstantial. Standing alone, it's worthless. What we need is that damn chest."

"So where do we start — Dale Markham?"

"He's the one who turned it over to Morris. But how can we contact him, without risking exposure?"

"Even if we could," she said, "haven't the Feds already pumped him for all he knows? Still, we have to assume they don't have the chest. What makes you think we can find it?"

"Because it's our only hope."

"Then let's give it our best shot. Which means getting you well." She gave him more Emetrol for his nausea, some Tylenol for his fever and, over his whining, a banana. "Now go to sleep," she ordered softly.

It was a restless slumber, in which patrol cars rushed from the darkness in an endless stream. Black choppers, like bats, menaced the sky. Dark-suited Feds, with the same stony glares, marched towards the cabin. He was motionless, when he should be moving; his mind was paralyzed, when it should be calculating. Mayson screamed, yet he couldn't react . . .

Shivering, he woke to the icy sheets and the black wilderness in the window. Then, like a tidal wave, the nausea rushed over him. He streaked to the bathroom.

As he heaved more bloody spittle, she thumped from the darkness like she had each time before. She washed his face and gave him more Emetrol. Slumped over the toilet, he moaned, "Just shoot me, all right?"

"Please, *amore mio*, have patience." She dabbed his mouth. "Now, let's get back to bed."

Getting him situated, she started a fresh fire and returned. "So, little boy." She settled his head in her lap. "Would you like a bedtime story to make it all better?"

"Chapter Two. You promised."

Yes, she had. And if he was entrusted with her life, wasn't he also entitled to know it? Even the parts never told before? His interest had deeply touched her. But now she wanted to know its nature. Did it rest in their friendship? Or had she become his rehabilitation project? His good deed?

"Like Papa had left, Santa did, too," she began. "The moment he was eighteen and no longer subject to Mama's control. We were lucky to see him on Christmas, and those rare occasions when he popped in drunk, boasting about what a big shot he was in the Bertolucci family, and all the money he was making. But did we ever see a dime? Santa was a bum, which made Stephen shine even brighter in my eyes."

"Stephen was a boyfriend?"

"For so long, Stephen was everything." She smiled sadly. "And then nothing. We'll get to him later, all right?"

"Tell me about your other brother."

Idly, she coiled his thick hair around her finger as she drifted back to a world that had never seemed farther away. "Vinny was sweet, but irresponsible. A great-looking guy, but not too much upstairs, if you know what I mean.

"After dropping out of school, he washed dishes at an Upper East Side club, eventually landing a waiter's position. With his looks and charm, he was an instant hit with the ladies, many of whom I suspect he was sleeping with. Vinny wasn't a bad person. He just didn't always think clearly. The little boy in him wanted to please everybody.

"Shortly after his twenty-first birthday, we learned that he'd pleased the wrong woman. He was working at an expensive club in the Hamptons, and she was the wife of a club member who was running for Congress.

"When they were caught in the caddy shack one night, she started screaming and clawing, as if he'd forced her rich buns to the floor. We got a call later, informing us he'd been arrested for rape." She sighed. "We couldn't afford bail, much less a lawyer. Finally the judge appointed one, who met with us at the jail. When Vinny confessed the affair, he said, to our shock, that it didn't matter.

" 'How can the truth not matter?' we asked, to which the lawyer replied, 'Because this woman's husband is a very powerful man who can't be made to look foolish. Especially when he's running an expensive campaign for Congress.'

" 'But the people at the Club!' Vinny cried. 'They'll testify about the affair.'

" 'Don't count on it,' he smirked, as if we were stupid. Then he advised Vinny to plead guilty in exchange for a lenient sentence he was confident could be negotiated.

"When Vinny refused, the case went to trial and, as the lawyer predicted, the people who knew of the affair denied it. Witnesses testified that Vinny had forced himself on the woman that night. Then she swore tearfully to the same lies. By the time he took the stand, the jury had already convicted him. You could see it in their eyes. They took less than an hour to reach a guilty verdict.

"So he was shipped off to Attica to begin serving a thirty-year sentence we knew he wouldn't survive. And he didn't. Three months later, we learned that he'd hanged himself with electrical cord stolen from a supply room. Again, Mama's heart broke. And mine hardened. I was beginning to see the world's darkness and understand its unyielding laws."

"Such as?"

"That truth is reality shaped by powerful men. Ambition and greed drive the system. Love and trust aren't strengths, but weaknesses to exploit by the corrupt, the same as ignorance. Life is a chess game. You're either a king or pawn. There's no in between."

He pondered these observations. Had he experienced what she had, he would have felt the same way. "I'm sorry, Mayson, but I'm also relieved to know these things."

"Then is there a need to hear more?"

"I need to hear it all. How many chapters are left?"

"Two, I suppose – Mama, and Stephen. But they'll have to wait. I want you to sleep now."

What was the expression?

It came to Marty Kennesaw seconds later, as he gazed at the sleek, golden babes sunning in front of him. So close to heaven, yet so much like hell. Heaven was the crystal sky, the tickle of the balmy Caribbean breeze, the gentle glide of the mammoth cruise ship. It was realizing he had ten days left of fine food, Bacardi rum, and making no decisions greater than whether to hang by the pool or in the air-conditioned lounge below.

Hell was sharing this floating leisure palace with bikini-clad babes who bounced across the deck, splashed in the pool, lolled on soft towels . . . being so close to their smooth, coconut oil-scented skin that his mouth watered and his dick hardened with a sweet torture. Being so close, yet so far away. So far, they were unreachable.

He'd spent Eastwood's money on Panama shirts, madras shorts, Jantzen trunks, leather sandals and the fancy shades now resting on his nose. And for what? To be ignored by primo babes, like the two sunning at his feet? Sipping piña coladas, they whispered and giggled, unaware of him even though he'd introduced himself an hour ago.

Gulping his daiquiri, he brooded over his empty horizons and Dutch's infinite ones. The lucky bastard had latched onto Deanna Taylor just minutes after dropping anchor, and days later, was still banging the big-busted redhead, while he hadn't gotten to first base. "Time for another," he said. "How about you, ladies?"

The one with cascading auburn hair turned to swat him away. "No, thank you."

Their conversation returned to its triangular pattern. Boston to New York to D. C. They'd been Radcliffe roommates before "Auburn" had gone to Harvard Law School and the sleek, honey-blond went to New York with her portfolio of pictures. "Auburn" was now a D.C. lawyer and "Blondie" was a fashion model.

They were equally beautiful, with stunning faces and long, angular bodies that, thanks to their dental floss bikinis, left little to the imagination. Glamorous, worldly, and educated, they were a planet away from Northwood. But hadn't this cruise brought them closer, maybe even within reach? "What are you ladies drinking?" he tried again. "Piña coladas, I bet?"

"That's right." Blondie turned to swat him this time.

Without missing a beat, they returned to their triangular excursion. From Radcliffe to the fast-paced worlds of D.C. Law and Fifth Avenue fashion they glided, then giggled, as they landed on some sacred ground shared in their lives — a man of mythical attraction. "If that waitress doesn't return soon, I'll have to mosey down to the lounge. Would you ladies like another round – my treat?"

"That's sweet Monty, but no thanks," Blondie replied.

"Marty," he corrected.

"The lounge is still a great idea," Auburn said. "It's air-conditioned. And they have TV and games. Go on, Marty, we won't mind."

"May just do that if the waitress doesn't show up soon. In the meantime, I'll catch a few more rays. This sun's great, isn't it? Say, I'm from Wisconsin," he said again. "My inn's on Lake Superior. Forty rooms and ten cabins. I'm seriously considering adding a wing on it. Maybe ten more cabins."

Auburn looked nauseated. Blondie pretended not to hear. And he pretended not to notice their lack of interest. "If you ladies ever get out my way, look me up. The Kennesaw Inn. I'll give you free cabins for as long as you want to stay."

Their silence became too heavy to ignore. And he'd run out of lines, anyway. Slumping back, he eavesdropped on their conversation. "If he had to be a criminal, at least it was a notorious one," Blondie mused.

Auburn squinted against the sun. "Are you saying, Kelly, you honestly believe Tyler Waddill's mixed up in a conspiracy to steal FBI records?"

"Listen, Darcy, he may have been ours for a few sweet minutes, but there's a legion of women who can claim the same."

"Your point being?"

"That if he can steal so many women's hearts, why not a few government records?"

"Scoring with women is hardly the same as obstructing justice," Darcy frowned. "Besides, he never misrepresented his intentions. I spent that first night in his Harvard Square apartment because I wanted to."

Kelly had been forced to wait another year for her turn. "The way he looks at you — it's like you're the only woman on the planet. An illusion, you discover, when you're coming out of your trance —after he's slipped off. That's deceitful, and therefore dishonest."

"A non sequitur," Darcy said, shaking her head.

"Please, you promised no legalese on this cruise." Kelly became aware now of the leech's slobbering eyes and turned to him. "Say Marty, the lounge might be a good idea. You're getting a nasty case of sunburn."

"The sun's brutal down here," Darcy added. "Nothing like Michigan."

"Wisconsin," he said. "And this sun ain't nothing."

"Even so," she said as she tossed him a tube of suntan lotion, "I'd rub this on. You'll be sorry if you don't."

"Great!" Kelly whispered. "Now we'll have him all afternoon."

"We would, anyway," she said. "Besides, he's harmless — I think."

"So are flies," Kelly said, watching him smear suntan lotion over his bony, lobster-red torso.

"So you ladies know that fugitive, huh?" he asked.

"Marty, it's not nice to snoop. Don't they teach you things like that in Wisconsin?" reprimanded Kelly.

"It's not snooping when a person talks loud enough for you to hear."

"I believe he has you on a technicality," Darcy smiled. The waitress returned and Darcy ordered two piña coladas and another daiquiri for Marty. "Our friend here's a Minnesota innkeeper," she explained.

"Wisconsin," he corrected again, as the waitress whisked off.

"And thanks for the drink. Darcy, is it?"

"That's right," she nodded, and then introduced Kelly.

He returned to his earlier probe. "So Waddill's hot stuff with the ladies, huh?"

"More like a legend," she said wistfully.

A handsome guy for sure. Marty envisioned his picture on the news and that of his beautiful companion.

Kelly squinted at the bright sun. "So where are they now, Darcy — Minnesota or North Dakota?"

"There or Wisconsin. Maybe they've stayed at Marty's inn."

"I'd definitely remember that pair," he said.

"They're gorgeous, all right," Darcy nodded. "With those stunning cheekbones and huge, dark eyes, Corelli could pass for Audrey Hepburn."

"How about Waddill? Who does he look like?"

"Ryan O'Neal," Kelly glowed. "Only a shade more handsome."

"His hair's a shade darker gold, too," Darcy added. "And his eyes are bluer. I vote for a tall Brad Pitt."

"He's tall?" Marty asked. "The news just shows his face."

"A lean, muscled six-three. Kind of a young Clint Eastwood."

"So you're changing your vote?" Kelly frowned.

Dark gold hair? Marty's brain scratched suddenly. Tall, lean, Clint Eastwood. Could Waddill be his Eastwood? Wisconsin was in the tri-state region the fugitives were believed to be in now. And Eastwood had given him six hundred bucks for cabin #10 without even taking a look. Didn't that show his desperation? "How are they traveling?"

"What difference does it make?" Kelly squinted.

Maybe a lot, he thought, recalling the truck leaving Lacey's. He'd been packing the Trooper. Minutes later, Eastwood had mysteriously appeared at the inn.

"Supposedly, they're jumping trucks like stowaways," Darcy explained.

It was looking more like Eastwood by the second. If only he hadn't been wearing shades. "Does either of you have a picture of Waddill? The one from the news isn't too fresh."

"Sure," Kelly laughed. "Large, framed ones we carry everywhere."

"Actually, I do have one," Darcy said. "It's of me, Tyler and the Chief Justice taken at a big bash on the Potomac."

"When Falkingham arrived by helicopter?" Kelly asked.

She smiled. "He was drunk as a skunk, which Tyler said wasn't unusual. When we greeted him on the Dearing's lawn, someone snapped our picture. Tyler had this silly Safari hat on . . . here, let me show you." She reached for her wallet.

Kelly's eyes lifted as a man approached — a darker, better-looking version of Marty in his red Panama shirt, madras trunks and sandals. "Hey Dutch!" Marty said as he jumped up.

"Ladies," Dutch grinned cockily.

In your dreams, clodhopper, Kelly smiled back.

Darcy, who'd found the picture, beamed, "Hi, I'm Nedda!"

"And I'm Wedda," Kelly chimed. "Cute, huh? Nedda and Wedda. Kind of like Heckle and Jeckle."

Dutch's smile faded as he turned to Marty. "April's feeling better. She wants you to join us this evening."

Marty's heart jumped. April was Deanna's friend who'd been sick ever since leaving Miami —a real knockout with blond hair, dimpled cheeks and big blue eyes.

"You ladies don't mind, do you?" Dutch asked.

"It's a sacrifice, but we'll manage," Kelly replied. "April — what a beautiful name."

Darcy fought the laugh tugging at her face. "Marty, you don't plan to run off without taking our picture, do you?"

"Heck no!" he grinned. Grabbing his Nikon, he shoved it at Dutch, as half-naked Darcy and Kelly sprung up. "Damn if this isn't my lucky day!" he said, wrapping an arm around each. Sick with envy, Dutch began snapping pictures. The memory stick was exhausted before Marty let him stop. Darcy retrieved her wallet. "Marty, do you still want to see Tyler's picture?"

"I guess not." He glanced at Dutch crossing the deck. "Hey, can I bring April around to meet you?"

"We'd be crushed if you didn't," Kelly said.

"Marty!" his brother shouted, "come on!"

"I gotta go," he said, shuffling backwards. Grinning and waving, he scrambled off.

Kelly sighed. "Now that Forrest Gump's gone, what do you want to do?" Flipping through Darcy's pictures, she found the one of her standing between Tyler and Falkingham. Tyler's Safari hat was rakishly angled for the camera. "You're right," she nodded. "With that hat, he's definitely a young Clint Eastwood."

CHAPTER THIRTY-THREE

★

Dawn became morning and Mayson could see that the brutal winter had frozen the wilderness outside. Nothing moved or made a sound, except the occasional wind gusts and the groaning trucks at Lacey's below the ridge.

Yet the quiet hadn't lulled her into a false security. Neither had the news reports, which put them somewhere in a tri-state region that included Minnesota, Wisconsin and North Dakota. Not a minute passed that she didn't expect the sky to thunder with choppers. It would happen sooner or later. It was just a matter of time.

Tyler slept like a rock one minute and squirmed the next, as if comfort was a place that couldn't be found. He should be recovering, but he wasn't — an observation she kept to herself.

Twice, she'd gone to the inn for supplies and to catch the latest news. It was an arduous trip on her crutches. Yet when he woke, she was always there with the next Tylenol dose and hot soup. Although his vomiting had decreased, his fever and weakness remained, a reality that increased both his frustration and her concern.

Her leg's new ache was another unspoken concern. Dr. Stanley had said she'd need weekly evaluation, but that was impossible under the circumstances. Then why tell Tyler, if there was nothing he could do?

Stirring, he shivered despite his feverish sheen. "Why is it . . . so cold?"

Hopping to the bathroom, she returned with a damp cloth to wipe his face and chest. Then drawing the covers around him, she pressed her hand to his forehead. Was it her imagination, or was he getting warmer?

"We need a plan," he said.

"Hush. There's nothing to plan except getting you well."

"But we should be more prepared than we were in . . . Tennessee."

"And how do you prepare for a raid, except to be gone when it occurs? Besides, the news gives us a three-state cushion."

"Cushion, hell!" he grumbled. "A damn cage, since Wisconsin is one of the states."

"So what do you plan to do? Swim Lake Superior with a raging fever? Or hike across the snow-covered wilderness? No, I'll tell you what you're going to do: take your medicine, eat a banana and go back to sleep!"

And he did, much too easily. Putting a fresh log on, she crawled back to wait for the first threatening crack in the quiet wilderness, pray it didn't come and, in lapses of helplessness, surrender to exhaustion.

The gray afternoon deepened, then drifted into darkness. He woke again, his eyes heavier, his moans weaker. Along with the Tylenol, she gave him antibiotics that she'd found on her last trip to the inn, then fed him hot soup and bathed his clammy skin. Would his fever ever break?

"It's taken weeks in the wilderness to find out what a big baby you are," she teased, resettling his head in her lap. "Now go back to sleep, and when . . ." Her stroking finger stopped on the ridge of his jaw as she realized he'd already slipped off.

The scene was familiar: bikini-clad Kara strolling along the shore, her golden braid swaying, eyes peeled for colored glass. Only this part didn't make sense: instead of the bucket, he lugged the tree house jar containing her entire collection.

"Kara, it's too heavy!" he shouted.

Not until he reached her did she finally turn, her stony expression unlike any he'd ever seen, "Didn't you hear me? The jar . . ." Dumbfounded, he watched her start off again. "Kara, come back!" But she refused, forcing him to shout over the breeze, "Kara! Kara . . . !"

Waking to Mayson's pained eyes, he knew instantly that Kara's ghost had slipped out again.

"You're shivering like crazy," she said.

Crawling from the bed, she put another log on, then retrieved the damp cloth, water and medicines. Administering the medicine, she settled his head in her lap and drew the covers up again. Still, his teeth chattered in a hopeless struggle for warmth.

Had Kara ever seen him like this? Washed the spittle from his face? Given him medicine or held him as he slept? No. Kara hadn't done these things — which made her unworthy of him. But wasn't the question not Kara's worthiness, but Mayson's own? "Tyler, is there an us? If so, could you define it?"

"Best . . . friends," his teeth chattered.

"That's it?"

"It's a lot . . . don't you think?"

She sighed. "I don't mean to pry."

"Of course . . . you do."

"Well, I wouldn't have to if you'd express yourself more clearly — and honor your part of the bargain. I've confessed two chapters of my life, and you haven't shared the first word of yours. Personally, I think you're blocking out what you don't want to confront. You need to deal with your feelings."

"And you need to . . . quit asking so many goddamned questions."

Her cheeks reddened. She'd crossed the line, and he'd shoved her back. But he was sick. And hadn't she once drawn the line even farther back? "What would you rather talk about?"

"I don't know," he said. "I'm just tired of feeling green. Or gray."

"At least you've changed colors. Maybe pink will be next."

"I'm sorry for snapping," he apologized. "You can ask questions. Just not so damn many."

"You mean, just not the ones you'd rather avoid."

He soon slipped back into a feverish sleep, and her eyes closed, too, with a prayer: if you dream of her again, please don't let me know.

Again he woke to the chilling darkness, with his clammy skin stuck to the sheets. Every joint in his body ached. Exhausted, he tried to sleep again but couldn't. Fever scorched him when the covers were up, and chilled him when they were down. Infuriated, he finally threw them off and planted himself at the window.

"Tyler, what are you doing?" Mayson asked.

Skin prickling, teeth chattering, he refused to acknowledge her. "Tyler, get back in bed."

"No."

"Then you'll just get sick again, and we'll have to go through all those damn colors. Tyler."

"All right, goddamnit," he said, burrowing back in the covers. "Warm me up, please. I'm so cold."

"What you are is hopeless." Nevertheless, Mayson wrapped herself around him to share her warmth and whatever else he needed. Would the list one day include her?

"If I could just . . . sleep," his teeth chattered.

"You will." She cradled him. "Now just lie still."

"Tell me something. Chapter Three, for example."

"It's no prettier than One and Two." She stroked his face.

"All the more reason I should hear it."

"Don't say you weren't warned," she began. "Let's see . . . I was in my second year at Columbia, and working the library's graveyard shift. One night I came home and Mama wasn't there. She'd just started a job on the waterfront making ship furniture - hard work for a woman, but she didn't complain. It took several calls to discover that she'd fallen from some scaffolding and was in the hospital. According to her crewmates, she was lucky to have escaped with no more than a back injury.

"After her release, she returned to work, against Dr. Hoffman's orders, because she was afraid of losing her job. No one told her she could file for workmen's compensation — at least not until Stephen looked into it."

"Is this Chapter Four: Stephen?"

"The same." She smiled over a man whose memory had once made her skin crawl. "Stephen took Mama to a lawyer and had the claim filed. It didn't take long for Dr. Hoffman to change his diagnosis. Now we learned Mama had arthritis, a degenerative process that had begun long before her fall, which although traumatic, was unrelated to her back condition. Without medical evidence, her claim was denied, and we were left with enormous medical bills. And worse, without her wages, since her condition kept her from returning to the heavy factory work.

"Once again Stephen came through, helping us get welfare and Social Security. He was there when we needed him. I assumed he always would be.

"Mama's back condition worsened, until finally she gave up, languishing in bed or on the living room sofa. The TV blared constantly, but I'm not sure she even watched. Her eyes were usually closed, a sign that she was far away. Sometimes that seemed good, other times not. But wherever her reflections took her, I'm sure Papa was nearby. Life for her stopped after he left, her existence reduced to memories. I shared my dreams, hoping that once I began my law practice and was able to take better care of her, that her mental state would improve.

"Just weeks before I moved into the Lyons, I came home one night to find her slumped in the chair, the TV blaring. It was a nightly scene, but somehow I knew this time was different, that she'd passed quietly from this world into the next. Alone. Something that should never have happened. I buried her that Sunday, taking note of those at the graveside, but also of those who weren't."

Tyler held her, as she cried softly. "But one person was there," he said. "One whose love for your mother was never compromised. Who represented her greatest achievement and proved that she hadn't lived in vain. Whatever her regrets, they were certainly overshadowed by the comfort of knowing that her life's lasting legacy could have no greater value. One very special person who was certainly the focus of her last thoughts. You, Mayson — you preserved for her what all the others would've destroyed."

Tearfully, her eyes lifted. "That's the most beautiful thing anyone's ever said to me."

Kissing her, he enjoyed her sweet sigh, the familiar curl of her leg, her tender stroke of his neck. "Mayson, you've changed so much, it's almost impossible to believe."

"How do you mean?"

"Well, for one thing, you can go minutes now without even one contentious word. You're less suspicious of people. And you sing in the shower. Have I left anything out?"

"A lot," she nodded. "The world looks so different. It's as if I have new eyes. I see stars where before there was infinite black space. The days also have more color than I remember. And there are people, of all things. I see their faces — Lou, Earl, Dr. Stanley and his fidgety nurse, craggy Brother General Isaiah, taciturn Jeremiah, and the kind-hearted Halo women who took care of me. I see them all — the Halos especially. I feel sorrow over their tragedy and regret over my inability to express my gratitude and prove that the life they saved on that mountain was a worthy one. What scares me most is dying just when I've begun to live."

She kissed him, reveling in the awareness that, for the moment at least, he was hers. Each moment spent with him was a life within itself, warm, happy and complete. If only they could be multiplied to include all the moments they had left. Yet weren't they? Weren't they destined to die together, perhaps very soon? "I have faith in God, too," she said after a time. "Or at least the inspiration to seek it. I guess you could say that I've finally seen the light."

"Harrington would be so proud," he smiled.

"I'm afraid we don't believe in the same God."

"Of course not. Yours is spiritual; his is human. He sees it in the mirror every morning when he shaves."

His head in her lap, he slept as her soft soprano drifted into the darkness, a sweet eulogy for her life's three painful chapters that had been closed forever.

Leopold grumbled at the Marlboro pack, but finally opened it and lit the first cigarette. Smoke soon crept up the wall of another cramped motel room — this one in Windy Plains, a little Wisconsin ice hole so obscure it wasn't even on the map.

The minutes crawled by as he puffed. Christmas was just days away. Would he be back in Houston for the special celebration? The long-awaited Renaissance? With a Christian President and a Christian court, wasn't its dawning imminent?

Yes, the Chairman would confirm Lamp in his special holiday sermon to be viewed via satellite by millions around the world. The CMA's Tabernacle Choir would sing in praise as he descended the pulpit to receive the children. First, he'd tell them a Christmas story, and then take each upon his saintly knee as he gave them their presents. Would he be there to share this joyous occasion, or left to watch it on TV in this cramped motel room or another one just like it?

But who said the Lord's work should be performed in a palatial suite? Deprivations were to be expected. Hadn't Jesus been born in a lowly manger?

Fugitive sightings had ended days ago, which meant one thing

— they'd found a suitable hideaway. The chase had become a seek and find. Or rather, search and destroy. But if the strategy had changed, nothing else had. Despite the millions of dollars and man-hours invested, the fugitives remained no closer to capture than they were weeks ago.

Lighting a fresh cigarette, he limped to the window and gazed at another storm that veiled the frigid night. Did it ever stop snowing here?

For days now, Nicholas's army had been in Snow Peak, braced for the fugitives' arrival. But they hadn't come. Still, they had to assume the fugitives would get as close to Snow Peak as possible. Didn't it hold the key to their salvation? If the chest wasn't there, it would at least hold a clue to its location. But why hadn't it been found?

As this was being debated, a new strategy had been implemented to deal with the lengthening crisis. Nicholas had begun a systematic air and ground reconnaissance of the tri-state region, while he positioned his own men in a 100-mile ring around Snow Peak. He'd taken Windy Plains, the westernmost point, and put Frankie in Crookston to the east; George and Barber were at strategic points north and south. Hopefully, the fugitives would be grabbed crossing the line, either by his men or Nicholas's.

Wearily, he reviewed the few facts known about the chest. Crenshaw had placed it in his sister's custody, with instructions not to open it until he directed, or else died. By then, Doreen Markham was afflicted with Alzheimer's and had forgotten the chest, along with everything else.

For forty years, it sat undisturbed in a Snow Peak bank vault until Doreen's son, Dale, had finally stumbled upon it while assembling his mother's assets. Only instead of contacting his uncle's Florida executor, he'd called his cousin, Jasper, Jr., who — after quickly caucusing with his brother and sister — notified Mendelsohn, who was vacationing on the Outer Banks.

Mendelsohn, no doubt salivating, had flown immediately to Snow Peak. There, he'd met Markham, and the two had driven to the bank where the still-sealed chest was turned over. What happened after that remained unclear, except for the bits and pieces picked up from Markham, and records of Mendelsohn's activities.

Together, they established a confusing scenario of travel and phone calls.

After checking with forensic experts on the steps necessary to authenticate the chest, Mendelsohn had instructed his Wall Street broker to establish a confidential Swiss account for the movement of assets (meaning the payoff expected from Lamp), when they met Sunday evening. Unfortunately Lamp had sent a proxy — Leopold — with orders not to negotiate, but to bring a quick end to the negotiation.

Mendelsohn's demise had sparked a frantic search for the chest. Post offices, banks, and storage facilities in every conceivable location had been checked, first in Mendelsohn's name, then every Jew relative and friend. No detail of his life had been overlooked — and still the chest hadn't been found — leaving more questions than answers.

Why had Mendelsohn checked out of his Snow Peak hotel Saturday morning, dropped his car off at the St. Paul airport and boarded a New York flight — only to get off in Chicago and head for Duluth? And why lease another car and proceed across Wisconsin, as far as Copper Harbor?

They'd traced his movements through the car rental and hotel records, gas receipts and witness accounts. They'd also checked storage facilities along his eastern route, but the effort had turned up neither the chest nor answers to his puzzling activities.

Crushing his cigarette out, Leopold grabbed the phone. "Arch, we've had a development," Harrington reported. "It's clear now the Lord is answering our prayers. Three days ago, a Great Lakes truck left Chicago with video equipment destined for northern distribution centers. In Green Bay, the driver developed this horrible flu that's ravaging the Midwest, no doubt the same one that afflicted Corelli. This trucker, however, refused to let it throw him off schedule, and continued west on Route 51. Still, he was forced to stop frequently. Wausau, Merrill, Rhinelander, and . . . what's this?" He squinted at his own scrawl. "North . . ."

"Northwood, sir. It's a small town on Lake Superior."

"Yes, that's it. Anyway, this stubborn trucker made it to Duluth before finally collapsing on the loading dock. The warehouse crew, after getting him in an ambulance, discovered that his trailer lock had been tampered with. They also found blood-speckled vomit. So the fugitives must have been on that truck between Green Bay and Duluth.

"The plan is to seal off this area, then infiltrate it with a large reconnaissance force," he explained. "Streeter assured me every inch of road, earth and sky will be scoured until our vermin are flushed out and taken to the closest sewage dump. You and your men should maintain your present positions. You'll be called when the time's right."

It was a good plan. The distance between Duluth and Stevens Point was two hundred miles — a large chunk of ground, but not for a massive force of Feds, troopers and choppers. And there were only two primary roads, 51 and 2.

"Arch, I truly believe the Lord will answer our prayers soon. Pray for it — for this dark cloud to vanish and the harbinger skies of our Renaissance to brighten the horizon."

"I will, sir. Any word from Capitol Hill?"

"Not a peep. If Adamley and Banyon were going public, they would've done so by now."

"And Culpepper?"

"I assume he's returning to his York estate, but he's no longer a threat."

"And the President's mood?"

"Excellent. I was at the White House for dinner last night. It seems he's interested in creating a new agency devoted to the nation's spiritual welfare, which we feel the court will sanction. If government is permitted to protect the nation's social and economic welfare, why not its spiritual welfare? I believe the court will see this point clearly and give us its blessing.

"But that's just the beginning. As head of the new agency, I'll need to put a program together that incorporates rules defining the moral conduct expected of our citizens, and also form solid partnerships with those legislators who've been the most sympathetic to our mission. The Lord has decreed that we reward them with important roles in our new Christian government. It'll be a wonderful Christmas, Arch. And yes, I'm certain we'll be back in Houston to celebrate it."

CHAPTER THIRTY-FOUR

★

Thunder shattered the darkness. Would the cabin walls collapse? It was no icy gale or furious tornado. No . . . the choppers were back.

Finding Tyler's empty pillow, Mayson sprung from the bed, screaming his name. Grabbing her crutches, she thumped down the hall, swinging first into the kitchen, then the living room. Where was . . .? Her eyes shot up to the quaking ceiling — the choppers were directly overhead.

She went down the hall and peered out the drapes. Three police cutters were moored offshore. Thumping across the room, she scanned the inn's empty drive. "Go away!" she screamed at the maddening thunder.

Hobbling to the bathroom, she sunk into the tub. Tyler had rescued her once before. Surely he would again.

It seemed an eternity until the vibrations finally faded, and silence returned to the cabin. Had the choppers left? You could never be sure. Sometimes they flew off, only to swoop back seconds later.

Crawling from the tub, she returned to the window, scanning the drive and the snowy ridge. Tyler, where are you, she thought. Her eyes drifted down the hall. Would the door open this time? Hadn't he promised that if it didn't, she'd know something was wrong and that instead of waiting, she should go through it herself and find him?

She slipped on her socks and boot and grabbed her coat and scarf from the closet. Starting out, she caught her reflection in the mirror. The crutches dug into the armpits of her shabby coat, dark brown curls fringing her tattered cap.

She opened the door and started up the slope, her eyes scanning for choppers in the frigid sky. Like daggers, the icy air slashed her bruised ribs as she covered the deep snow in robot-like motion — right crutch down, left crutch down, swing the body.

Reaching the inn, she thumped into the office shouting Tyler's name and then headed back to the living quarters. She hobbled from room to room and then started up the stairs. Right crutch, left crutch over narrow steps. Breathless, she reached the second floor and thumped past the vacant rooms. Arms burning, leg throbbing, she climbed to the third floor. The leg pain was constant now, but she hadn't told Tyler. Calling his name as she hobbled down the hall, she climbed to the next floor.

Reaching the attic minutes later, she collapsed into the corner chair. She surveyed the dust-coated boxes and racks of moth-eaten clothes and soon found herself digging through the inn's memorabilia. She leafed through news clippings and postcards and finally came to the family pictures. The Kennesaws, she assumed — Mrs., a plump, plain woman; Mr., a large man with moustache and stern dark eyes; and the two boys, scrub-faced and grinning.

The Corellis had once been a family picture, too. But now there were only voices. Fathers leave their little girls . . . Brothers disappoint and abandon . . . Friends take your trust . . . Songbirds slip off in the night. Only miracles can bring them back.

Was Tyler that miracle? Hadn't he returned her to a world she'd once abandoned? Persuaded her to trust, when she thought she never would again? Yes, he was. Then please, her tears crinkled the attic quiet like delicate glass. Please . . . Her eyes lifted as the first vibrations reached the walls and again, the sky thundered.

Pulling herself up, she waited for the floor to settle, then quickly descended the stairs. Had the tri-state region suddenly been cut to two? One, maybe? The smaller the area, the more frequent the reconnaissance missions over the same ground. Their ground.

Finally reaching the kitchen, she scanned the wilderness outside — the northern ridge, the vast gray lake beyond, the coastal ports to the west, the dense forest to the east. Her gaze settled finally on the inn's storage shed, its flapping canvas roof, and the stacked firewood beneath. A dozen or more logs lay scattered in the snow, with colorful patches among them — colors that didn't fit. Blue, tan, gold . . . "Tyler!" she screamed, hurrying outside and then quickly freezing at the sky's sudden tremble. Horrified, she watched three black bats emerge from the northern clouds. One glided east and another west, with the third maintaining a steady course towards the inn. She glanced at Tyler, and quickly thumped back inside.

The kitchen's walls trembled, glass rattling in the cupboards as she dashed for the window. The chopper was directly overhead — had they seen Tyler among the logs? She cringed as his hat scooted across the snow. Did they see it? Holding her breath, she waited.

Finally, the thunder faded as the chopper resumed its southern course. Thumping back out, she found him sprawled beneath the logs. She struggled to roll them away, then knelt to examine him. Blood had clotted around a gash in his temple. How long had he been out here? And more critically, how could she get him back inside before the choppers returned? The same way the small girl did what she had to, a voice whispered.

Mr. Cellini, I need more overtime.

You're working sixty hours a week now. That's more than your Mama likes.

She likes worrying about money even less. The warehouse stock is piling up. It should be moved out to the shelves.

No, Mayson Angelina. You can't lift those heavy boxes.

Yes, I can. I'll show you.

When his sons hadn't moved them by Monday, she begged again.

Please, Mr. Cellini, let me move the boxes, and save Frank and Sal's wages. The delivery truck will come soon, and there won't be room for the shipment.

Okay, he'd finally relented. But don't tell your Mama.

She'd moved them all, just as she'd move Tyler now.

Leaning on her crutches, she grabbed his hand and tugged. Then again, and again. Finally, the snow scraped beneath him. Encouraged, she tugged until his deadened body had been moved ten feet across the snow. She rested and then tugged another ten feet. Her breath quickened, the icy air slicing her ribs until the pain finally caused her to collapse in the snow. Gasping, she sat up and checked his pulse, rubbing her gloves' warmth into his face. Hold on, *amore mio*, we're almost home. Pulling herself all the way up, she grabbed his hand and continued the arduous journey. Slowly, but steadily, she drew closer, her eyes fixed on the gray sky.

When she finally reached the cabin, she pulled him inside. It took several minutes before the pain faded and she could take a decent breath. Then, stripping off his wet clothes, she wrapped him in blankets and rolled him onto the mattress by the fire. As he thawed out, she dressed and bandaged his temple.

A feverish glow returned to his face. How much today's disaster had worsened his condition, only time would tell.

The coastline shimmered in the blazing sun and the heavy jar felt like lead in his arms. "I can't carry it any further," he shouted to Kara, who strolled ahead in the gentle surf.

Turning, she frowned. "Then you shouldn't have brought it — or followed me here. I explained it all in the tree house that afternoon. Now please go back and do what you promised."

His head throbbed suddenly. Why was it so hot? "But Kara, the jar's too heavy. And I . . ."

"I have to go," she said fading away.

"Kara, come back! Kara . . .!"

The heat intensified, melting the scene away. Cool, fragrant fingers brushed his face, and Mayson's soft voice confirmed his safety. "How do you feel?" she asked.

"Like Jerry Quarry after the Ali fight," he said, discovering his bandaged temple.

"That's some gash. I cleaned it, but it needs stitching. Do you remember what happened?"

"The avalanche of logs? Yeah, I remember."

"The choppers paid us three visits while you were in those logs. You shouldn't have gone to the inn in your condition."

"We needed firewood," he sighed. "I must've been in a daze. By the time I reached the shed, I could hardly stand up. Otherwise, I would've known better than to grab the logs from the middle of the stack. The last thing I remember is the wall collapsing. How the hell did you get me back here?"

"Very slowly."

A silence settled over them as they gazed at the fire. Kara's memory remained heavy, but unspoken, between them. "This inn's supposed to be vacant," he said. "With choppers visiting, we have to keep it looking that way. That means no more fires."

"Then let's enjoy this last one," she said.

He started to rise, then caught himself. "Where's my underwear?"

"Drying in the bathroom, with the rest of your clothes."

"I assume you peeped."

"After so many conquests, I felt sure you'd had it bronzed."

"Go to hell," he said. Wrapped in his toga, he rose to go to the window. "At least this latest snow will cover our tracks."

"Either way," she shrugged, "it's just a matter of time until the inn is searched."

"How much time depends on where we were last spotted."

Meaning they had two choices. Leave, or wait to be caught when the operation finally reached the inn. But where could they go, with snow piling on snow and the arctic air hovering at zero? "Tyler, I hate Kara for what she did to you."

"Mayson, you don't know what you're talking about."

"Then it's your fault." As he ducked into the bathroom, she said, "Your clothes aren't dry yet."

"They're close enough," he replied, slipping into his shorts.

Wriggling out of her split-seam pants, Mayson tossed them to the floor. "I'm sick of these baggy things! With icy air blowing through them, what good are they?"

As he took his medicine, she slipped into the blankets. "Tyler, you won't get better until you start acting sensibly."

"Look who's talking." His head throbbed, his feverish skin crawling against a chill that the blankets were useless against. "Just shoot me, all right?"

"I would, except I'm afraid I'd get so bored alone in this cabin, I couldn't stand it."

"Thanks a lot."

"I'm just joking." She kissed him. "I'd be lost without you."

"Me, too," he confessed.

"Well, that's something you don't have to worry about." Her slender leg slipped inside his. "I'll be here as long as you want me." Had Kara made the same promise? "Tyler, you're trapped in a past you either can't, or won't, leave behind."

The fire brought a glow to her large, dark eyes. Had he ever known anyone with her insight?

"What are you smiling about?" she asked.

"How well you know me."

"And how well is that?"

"Better than anyone else."

"Tyler, the past can't hurt us. But you've got to be willing to share it."

Sharing meant letting go. Voicing what *had been* confirmed that it was no longer. And he wasn't ready to reduce Kara to a memory. She was much too alive inside him.

A sharp silence settled over the cabin, soothed by the fire's soft flicker. It was certain to end with her next words. Wasn't it this anticipation that made the silence, if strained, also alive? Then wasn't there something he could share with her in return?

"I've always had this fascination with clowns – once I got used to their cap guns, anyway. They make people laugh, not with punch lines, but with perfectly timed antics. If the timing's off, the whole performance suffers."

"Clowns fascinate me, too," she confessed. "Not so much by their ability to make me laugh, but by how well they hide themselves behind their circus paint and silly clothes. 'Who is this clown?' I find myself wondering. What drove him to seek refuge behind the circus mask? Is he secretly crying at the same moment he's making the rest of the world laugh? I've wondered this about clowns, but more recently, Tyler, about you."

As the fire quietly died and the night drifted, he revealed his childhood dream. The one inspired by Uncle Frank's Thanksgiving tales. "That first moment inside RFK stadium — the noise, the crowd, the field sparkling like glass — it took my breath away. The players were like gladiators preparing for battle and by game time, the stadium was rocking. I told myself, 'I have to do this!'"

"And you did," she said. "You were sensational. I wish so much that I'd seen you play." Had Kara? Would he admit it if she had? "I used to dream of being in Giants Stadium for the opening kickoff, with the world suddenly reduced to the field and its fate decided by the two armies lined up for battle."

"A great childhood fantasy," he smiled.

"A great grownup fantasy, you mean. My childhood fantasy

took place in my cousin Maria's tree house. I spent many afternoons imagining myself a queen — the streets below, my empire. The people, my loyal subjects." She sighed. "I wanted a tree house so badly. Did you have one?"

His eyes became distant. "We could see the whole world from up there. Where it began at the Castlewood oak, and where it ended — south, with the rolling meadows; west, where the forest hemmed the crystal sky; and north, where the James drifted into the horizon. We didn't care that Columbus had proclaimed it round or that Magellan had circled it. This was our world, discovered one summer afternoon."

"Who is 'we?' A childhood friend?"

He nodded, and with that the book closed, the story having just begun.

Dawn returned to the window. Anxiously, she gazed at the gray sky. When would the choppers return? They would, she was certain of that. Again and again, until they found what they were looking for.

Fear shadowed every minute. But at least there was a glimmer of light. Tyler's . . . She froze as his fingers crept inside her shirt, then slowly climbed the tender flesh of her ribs. No, he wasn't . . . Yes, he was. He was claiming her naked breast . . .

"How do they feel?" he asked.

"They?"

"Your ribs. Are they still sore?"

"No . . . yes . . . I mean, a little. Only that's not a rib you're holding."

"I feel like a confused shopper in the produce section. What have I stumbled upon here – an apple or pear?"

"Then you're saying I'm a fruit?"

"The sweetest," he replied.

Minutes drifted. "Your hand's still on my breast."

"Is that a problem?"

"No, just a happy bulletin." Her eyes closed.

Time had become as meaningless as the gray world outside. Huddled in the blankets, she was oblivious to all but the warmth created by their bodies, and the thoughts of a bright future she'd never know. "Tyler, I can't wait for a Redskins game. Can we drink beer and eat hot dogs?"

"As many as we want."

"And will we have good seats?"

"Fifty-yard line," he replied.

"*Madonna mia!* I'll learn all the players. We won't even need a program. You do plan on taking me to more than one game?"

"If you behave," he said.

"And if the Skins are in the Super Bowl?"

"What makes you think they will be?"

"Because Todd Hansen is the franchise quarterback they envisioned, and their defense is vastly improved."

Were there any Redskins players she didn't already know? "If Hansen gets the Skins to New Orleans, we'll go."

"Except the Super Bowl's in Phoenix this year. Tyler, tell me about the oyster roast."

"You really are a pain in the ass, aren't you?" His gaze fixed on the rafters, he described the annual event: oysters in every possible form eaten on the riverbank, followed by the Club's dance.

"Did you go every year?" She idly twirled his chest hair.

"The first twenty," he replied.

Meaning he'd missed the last seven - because of his split with Kara? "I'll go to the oyster roast with you, only I've never eaten oysters. Does it matter?"

"Not unless someone finds out."

"Let's see now," she inventoried. "A Redskins game, the Barnum and Bailey, an oyster roast, Disney World . . . and Sea World, of course."

"I don't recall Sea World as part of the package."

"Tyler, let's say that by some miracle we survive and do all these things. How will it work, with you at Castlewood and me in New York?"

"Distance won't be a problem."

"I don't have to live in New York. I could move closer."

"Let's get out of Wisconsin first," he said.

"Tyler, you hate New York. Will you really visit me?"

"Yes, but you'll visit me more. In fact, you'll enjoy a nice, long rest at Castlewood before going home."

"And what will your parents say about having a young Italian woman from a poor Brooklyn neighborhood as a guest in their home?" she asked. "I don't have anything resembling a pedigree."

"And you think one will be required?"

"Honestly," she sighed. "You can't just pretend I'm not different. The moment I walk through the door, my accent will send shock waves not heard since Sherman's cannons. And if I make it to the dinner table, I'll be totally clueless over which fork and spoon goes with which bowl and plate."

"Then we'll just have to feed you in the kitchen. At least until you've had the proper training."

"You're making a joke and it's not funny. It's terrifying to imagine what they'll think of me."

"I see your point," he agreed. "But they'll notice how beautiful you are right away. There's no way to hide it, unless we change your hair again and find another pair of hideous glasses. And it'll take just a minute for them to discover what a pain in the ass you are."

Her slender body was like tense cord in his arms. But wasn't her anxiety pointless? There'd be no Redskins games, Disney World or oyster roasts. She wouldn't return to New York, nor he to Castlewood. They'd probably die right here on the coast of Lake Superior.

"Don't worry," he said. "You'll be well received at Castlewood, whether or not you've eaten an oyster or know which fork to use. They'll love your accent and you'll love Castlewood."

She envisioned the breathtaking river mansion she'd created in her mind, then filled with uniformed servants, antique furniture, glass chandeliers, silver trays and gilded paintings. She hadn't sketched Kara, but should she? Did Kara live near Castlewood? Was Tyler forced to see her at their fancy country club with her husband and the children he'd once dreamed would be his? The sight would be agonizing.

"You're so quiet," he said. "What's the matter?"

"I can't be quiet unless something's the matter?"

"No. So what is it?"

"Nothing," she replied. "Now hush."

He began counting the seconds until . . . "Tyler?"

Eighteen, he smiled to himself. "Yes?"

"All those times you saw *My Fair Lady*, you were with Kara? And the piano recitals; they were hers, too?"

"Yes."

"Oh." Had there been words to follow, she would've certainly choked on them. But he allowed no time anyway, lifting her chin and kissing her with such tenderness it was impossible to doubt the depth of his feelings, which flowed through her like sweet honey.

CHAPTER THIRTY-FIVE

★

Thunder shattered the darkness, and once again Tyler was missing. Springing up, Mayson knocked over the table, sending clutter flying everywhere. Directly overhead, the chopper's thunder shook the walls; they'd discovered the hideout. Then, just as her heart stopped with this reality, the chopper streaked away. She pulled on her pants and seeing her misting breath, hobbled out to check the thermostat - forty-two degrees and falling.

Opening the cabin door, she anxiously scanned the inn's grounds. The last storm had covered their . . . Her eyes lifted suddenly as the chopper returned! Slamming the door, she thumped back to the bedroom as two patrol cars glided up to the inn. A trooper and a Fed emerged from each as the chopper touched down. Climbing out, two Feds joined the group and they quickly descended the slope.

A white-haired trooper unlocked the first cabin and the group disappeared inside. Why did he have a key? Had Kennesaw contacted him?

They soon reappeared; two Feds, their collars braced against the wind, started towards the next cabin. They were going to search them all.

Frozen at the window, Mayson watched them enter the second cabin. Minutes crawled by until they emerged, the others greeting them with shaking heads and fingers that pointed at the smooth, trackless snow. Yes *gavonnes*, listen to your lazy comrades - there are no tracks, she thought to herself. No fugitives unless they have wings instead of feet. Unconvinced, the stubborn Feds started for the third cabin.

The sky darkened, the chill deepening as they completed their search and moved on. Nearby, the others remained huddled, each icy gust forcing them to hunch their shoulders and dip their chins into their coats. Clearly, their patience was fading. Emerging from the fourth cabin, the Feds were met by ridiculing cackles, yet they moved on. Why won't you listen, she thought, as she watched them enter the next cabin. We're not here!

She waited anxiously at the window as they completed their search and again moved on. Her leg throbbed more by the minute. Something was terribly wrong, she realized, as the young trooper climbed the slope. Ducking into his unit, he stuffed something into his coat and returned. Soon a whiskey bottle was being passed from one gloved hand to the next.

It was a merrier band that greeted the Feds as they moved on to the next cabin. Was Tyler watching this tragic comedy from an inn window? Or was he . . .? Tears she'd been fighting now slipped down her frozen cheeks. The group's taunting laughter rose, and the empty whiskey bottle was tossed into the snow as the Feds moved on to the eighth cabin, then, minutes later, the ninth. Pausing on cabin nine's stoop, they glanced over at ten, eyes darting from snow to window to door. Did they see Tyler's tracks? Heart pounding, Mayson waited until finally they entered the cabin.

Sinking to the floor, she shut her eyes against her leg's deepening throb. They'd be coming for her soon. She'd die alone in this icy hell, a dark reality that settled over her minutes later as cabin nine's door opened and the Feds' boots crunched again on the snowy ridge, their voices reaching her: "Nicholas said search every inch of space between Stevens Point and Duluth, and that's what we're doing," a voice said. "Someone's bound to get lucky sooner or later."

"I hope it's sooner," the other Fed grumbled. "I'd like to be home by Christmas."

Keys jingled as they passed the window above her. Terrified, her eyes shot to the end of the hall as she waited for the door's creak. Instead, the silence was broken not by a creak, but by a siren suddenly screaming over the ridge. The Feds, voices agitated, boots crunching, returned past the window. "Look at that damn fool flying over the ice; let's pray it's a fugitive report."

Mayson cautiously peered out to see the men huddled around a flustered female trooper who'd just arrived. Her mouth twisted furiously, her arms slashing the air as she answered a dozen questions at once. Had the Russians invaded Northwood?

Two Feds returned to the chopper and quickly thundered

away in it as the other pair squealed off in the closest unit. The female trooper, joined by her white-haired companion, followed in her car as the young trooper climbed into the last unit. Its engine roared, then quickly died. Cranking again, he stubbornly persisted until it flooded. In a rage, he jumped out to kick snow and tires before dropping back behind the wheel.

Now what? Didn't the unit have a radio? Or would he just sit there until the others returned? The wilderness silence deepened, the sky blackened and the chill sunk deeper into her bones as she waited. Sinking with despair to the icy floor, Mayson envisioned a roaring fire, a snifter of brandy and Tyler's embrace. A Castlewood Christmas, cinnamon scenting the halls, the air dancing with carols, the grand rooms filled with joyful people who welcomed her as she drifted through on his arm . . . An engine's roar suddenly jerked her back from her daydream. Rising, she watched a patrol car approach, its headlights aglow in the darkness. Reaching the inn, its doors flew open and silhouetted figures passed through the lights. The unit's engine was quickly resurrected. Relief surrendered to confusion, however, as the party left with the young trooper remaining behind.

Wrapping herself in a blanket, Mayson remained at the window. Minutes crept by, each heavy with the same questions: Why was the trooper still here? If Tyler was alive, wouldn't he have returned by now? Did he lie injured somewhere waiting, like she waited?

A long hour passed and still the wilderness didn't deliver him. The patrol car remained, dark and still, in the drive. Should she go find Tyler, she wondered? How far could she get in her condition? Stubbornly she remained at the window, huddled in her blanket as the silence grew heavier. Her numb fingers clasped the drape. Tyler, please come back, she wished. Tears returned to her eyes.

The night deepened, as did the cabin's chill. The window frosted, obscuring her vision. Each minute became a struggle with her throbbing leg. If she survived, would it be as an amputee? She sank to the floor again, certain it was for the last time. Hadn't their fate been determined long before this moment? No one eluded the police forever. Sooner or later everyone's luck ran out. Tonight was their turn.

Car doors opened in the distance. Were they finally coming for her? It no longer seemed to matter.

Step, fill the track, smooth the snow; then again and again. Tyler raced against time and the choppers, which could light up the sky any second.

Reaching the cabin just before dawn, he rushed down the hall, stopping at the sight of her huddled in blankets beneath the window. Picking her up, he laid her gently across the bed. Her face was pale and her lips were parched. Slipping off the sock, he grimaced at her swollen toes.

Mayson's eyes opened and she sprang up to embrace him. "Tyler! I thought you were dead! They were at the door . . . then the siren screeched and they scrambled off - except the one. But then they came back. I knew . . . I mean, I thought . . ." Tears rushed out as she clutched him tightly.

"It's all right," he said as he held her. "They're gone."

"But what sent them away?" she asked.

"The trucker's call, I guess."

"What trucker?"

"The one out on 94," he answered. "How long have your toes been swollen?"

Were they? She could hardly feel them. *Madonna mia,* they were! "I . . . don't know."

"Does your leg hurt?" he asked. When she nodded, he said, "I need to know, Mayson."

"Were you at the inn last night?" she asked.

"Of course."

"Then you should've left a note."

"I did." Spotting it beside the overturned table, he snatched it up.

Reading it, she realized that once more, she'd doubted him. Again he'd come through.

"The furnace died," he said. "It's out of oil. We'll move up to the inn tonight when the choppers can't spot us."

"What if our friends return?" she asked.

"They won't; not for a while anyway."

"How do you know?" Her eyes narrowed. "And about the

trucker's call? Who did he talk to? And what did he say to make those men take off?"

"He called the Northwood Sheriff's Office to report leaving Lacey's an hour earlier. Only he didn't detect the strange rattle until reaching the 94 junction."

"The strange rattle?"

"One suspicious enough that he pulled over to check it out. That's when he spotted the fugitives. Going back to check the trailer, he caught them fleeing into the woods; a man and a woman in their mid-to-late twenties. The woman was on crutches and thumping as fast as she could - a darn pretty thing, too. Then he found the crowbar used to break into the trailer, most likely at Lacey's, his last stop. They'd jumped on there and when he stopped again, bailed out to avoid detection. They fled west, which by the way, is in the opposite direction of Northwood."

"And also the Kennesaw," she added. "Did this trucker happen to identify himself?"

"Barney Bodelski. The last name he had to spell twice. He was about to give the carrier's name when the line went dead."

"And did this create suspicion?"

"Hell no, the dispatcher was much too pumped. Twice during the call, she tried reaching the sheriff but couldn't because he was out here searching the inn, with Deputy Ichabod and the Feds. No doubt that was her who barreled up the drive last night. If she'd arrived a second later, they would've found you."

"But they didn't, Tyler. That call saved my life."

"I should've thought of it sooner. I felt so helpless watching those pricks move from cabin to cabin. If something had happened . . ."

"It didn't." She kissed him gratefully, then wrinkled her nose. "Have you been drinking?"

"I found a couple six packs in Kennesaw's refrigerator."

"You drank twelve beers!" she exclaimed.

"I was up there a long time," he shrugged defensively. "How does your leg feel now?"

"Do you plan on asking me that every five minutes?"

"I need to know, Mayson."

Not because he could relieve her pain but insisted on sharing it, she fully appreciated. "So besides guzzling beer, how else did you kill time up there?"

"I made some calls to Snow Peak with that cell phone I bought in Wausau, hoping to pick up a few scraps about Dale Markham."

Wrapping herself in the blanket, she crawled up beside him. "I hope you disguised your voice?"

"Dick Jessup, from Dallas," he drawled Texas-style.

"Longbridge country; how poetic," she smiled. "Who did you call?"

"The Chamber of Commerce. A woman there gave me the information I needed to move my business to Snow Peak. You know, cars, trucks, anything on wheels."

"But each one you touch breaks down."

"She didn't know that. I gave her a phony address to send brochures and took down all the names and numbers of doctors, lawyers, real estate and insurance agents she'd give me."

"Don't tell me you called them all?"

"I didn't have to. I hit the Snow Peak Insurance Agency halfway through the list. It's amazing what you can learn by asking the most basic insurance questions, especially if you get the town gossip."

"The town gossip works at the insurance agency?"

He nodded. "You remember that Chatty Cathy doll? That's her. One question and she starts rambling. I figured if she rambled long enough, something useful might stumble out."

"And did it?" Mayson asked.

"Well, we now know that Markham owns the agency, and that he's attending a property and casualty underwriter's convention in St. Paul. I haven't been able to reach him yet at his hotel."

"What makes you think he'll talk to you? And haven't the Feds already asked the same questions?"

"I know they've asked questions," he replied. "Just not the right ones."

"But you will." She looked at him skeptically. "So what else did Chatty Cathy say?"

"That Markham bought the agency from his boss's estate four years ago, and that it currently has five agents, including him; all are close friends, as was the previous owner. Big fishermen, too.

Each spring and fall they take a week off and drive up to Copper Harbor, where they rent the same cabin and fish from the same boat they began with twenty years ago. Chatty says they do as much drinking and poker-playing as fishing. His kudos took up a good quarter-hour. He wasn't just the best insurance man around, but the best golfer, fisherman, etc. Apparently Markham and the other agents thought so, too. When he died, they renamed their boat in his honor; they even kept the lease at the Copper Harbor Marina in his name."

She vaguely sensed a connection to be made suddenly - the fishing pact or something else? As he finished, she fell back against the pillow. "Let's take a nice, long nap."

Kicking off his boots, he joined her in the blankets. "I found some pain pills in Kennesaw's medicine cabinet and a bottle of decent bourbon in the pantry."

"I see." She stroked his jaw. "So then after the beer, you plan on spending the rest of our odyssey snockered?"

"That's not a bad idea, but I was thinking about your leg."

"It doesn't hurt that much," she said.

He knew better, and also knew the likelihood of it getting worse. "We'll leave for the inn at dark."

"How much time do you think Barney's lead has bought us?"

"A day or two," he replied. "And the search area has shrunk dramatically. His call puts us between Northwood and the 94 junction. Imagine a thousand cops concentrated into a twenty square mile area and you've grasped our situation."

"Won't they try to confirm where the call came from?" she asked.

"I'm sure. Let's just hope they exhaust Barney's lead first."

As the gray morning drifted, they fell into a weary silence, the wilderness asleep outside. But for how long, he wondered, his nose settling in her perfume-scented hair? L'Air du Temps — he'd never imagined enjoying its fragrance again.

"You can kiss me if you want," she smiled lazily.

He studied her face instead. More than beautiful, it was perfect, just like her slender body that molded perfectly to his. It terrified him suddenly to imagine the world without her.

Their kiss was a deep one that carried them beyond the

threatening clutches of the cold, gray world outside. Breathlessly she clung to him. "If you want, I thought, well . . . you might want to go shopping."

He smiled. "For apples and pears, I suppose?"

"Whatever you're in the mood for," she smiled seductively as their eager lips met again.

Not a chance. He held the reins on all but his hungering fingers, which slipped beneath her shirt to envelop her soft breast. The nipple hardened instantly and he imagined its sweetness, his lips brushing over it. His fingers then slid slowly down her spine and inside her panties, clutching her delicate buttocks, their soft swells suiting him perfectly. Forcefully she moved against him, her fingers urgently scraping his back. He'd struck a passionate chord, lifting her to a plateau of pleasure she'd never known. The cabin was like ice and yet she was melting, a furnace burning out of . . . She shriveled suddenly as he broke their last kiss.

Gazing into her bruised eyes, he sighed, "Don't you think I want the same thing?"

"Obviously not," she said, and turned away.

"Mayson, you're the most important person in my life."

"Because Kara has chosen not to be?" she asked.

"It has nothing to do with choice."

"Then what?" she persisted.

"Fate maybe," he sighed in frustration. "I don't know."

"Tyler, people determine their own fate."

"Not always."

"Then I don't understand."

"Neither do I, so let's change the subject."

Instead they slipped back into their gloomy reflections, the world outside a million miles away, quiet and lifeless, the same as the hump they formed in the blankets.

He envisioned Castlewood's giant Christmas tree, fully dressed, lights glittering, presents piled beneath, a holiday beacon that could be seen for miles out on the James. Christmas morning would arrive with Schuyler's potent eggnog and carols on the stereo. They'd manage a gentle buzz while opening presents, then lose it over Hunter Leigh's huge breakfast.

Her bruised feelings fading, Mayson stroked his nose. "What

are you thinking about?"

"Christmas," he smiled wistfully.

"I was thinking of best friends," she said. "The person you share everything with, who colors and defines your world, makes you smile, laugh and sing, angers you sometimes but makes you happy more. To lose that person must be the most horrible thing in the world."

Wasn't this the book he could write, if he wasn't so desperate to forget? Wouldn't it contain all those deep feelings he'd never shared with anyone? "At first you deny the loss," he said. His fingers crawled restlessly over Mayson's breast, cradling it as a child would his blanket. "There's too much of that person inside you for you to comprehend they're gone. And it's much easier to believe they aren't. But you can only deny reality for so long. Sooner or later you need to face it.

"You're bewildered initially. Fate has singled you out, but no one can tell you why, and finally you quit asking. You're left empty inside, but not for long. Soon you fill with rage, so much that you want to strike out at everything in your path. You look for someone to blame, but there's no one. Finally, your rage fades away. Emptiness returns and a dark shadow like death settles over you; and then you know."

Her eyes were now wide, intense. "Know what, Tyler?"

"That you've sunk into a place between life and death. There's pain, but at the same time no feeling at all. You see, hear and move, but without purpose or direction. You're *in* the world but not *part* of it. The worst thing is knowing you're trapped, unless you can somehow crawl your way out." He smiled mournfully at her. "I bet you didn't bargain for Kafka."

"Your description's so vivid . . . it's like you've actually been to this place yourself," she marveled.

"You must've felt the same emotional deadness when your father left."

Which was why she hated to think he'd experienced it, too. "Does Kara know about this place?"

It had been her greatest fear; that he'd find it and be unable to return. "I couldn't tell her."

"You mean you were afraid to. I understand perfectly."

"No, Mayson, you don't."

"I hate her, Tyler. I'm sorry, but I do."

"You can't hate her."

"And why not?" She frowned as he sprung up and started out. "Tyler, come back here!"

At the end of the hall, he turned into the kitchen. Stopping at the window, his furious eyes could've melted the snow outside. Then as his anger faded, he sat at the table burdened by all he'd been unable to leave behind. He was hopeless. Soon he'd be dead. *Wrong*, a voice refrained. *You died six years ago.*

Kara had been an inseparable part of him, the one who made his world a wonderful place. Then suddenly she'd been gone. Her absence was a cold, dark, empty place that hurt too much to inhabit; and so he'd left. Only Mayson could lure him back with the promise of a new life. Didn't she already exist on the edge of every thought? Wasn't it her voice dancing upon his heart now? But the music always stopped. Did he want to find himself once again humming alone in the darkness? Did he want to search for Mayson as he'd searched for Kara — around every corner, in every room? Did he want to hear her whisper, see her fleeting shadow, long after she was gone?

Mayson stood quietly in the doorway as his eyes shut to tears. She'd put too much pressure on him, insisted on knowing his private pain when he wasn't ready to share it. She'd been selfish and this was the result. "Tyler, I'm so sorry," she said. "I've asked questions you're not ready to answer."

"There's nothing to be sorry about," he replied. "Just forget it, all right?"

"I owe you far too much to do that," she said, shaking her head. "You befriended me when I neither wanted nor deserved a friend. You climbed over my rage to help me. When I needed you, you were there. And I plan to be there for you, with comfort and support, not questions. If you've been to that terrible place you described, I'll see that you never return. I promise you that."

He nodded. "I may hold you to it one day."

She prayed more than anything that he would. "Let's get back in bed. I have something to tell you."

"What?" he asked.

"Chapter Four."

Once under the covers, she curled up like a contented cat inside his arm. "I was sixteen when I met Stephen. He was twenty-two, a sales rep for a distributor of men's toiletries, and Cellini's was in his territory. He'd drop by each week to inventory his products, put up displays and talk with Mr. Cellini. Then without fail, he'd track me down wherever I happened to be — sweeping the aisles, stocking shelves or helping in the warehouse. Sometimes I'd be eating lunch and we'd talk a long time. He seemed to know exactly how I felt. It was very important to me to be understood."

Idly twirling Tyler's chest hair, Mayson described a world that had never seemed farther away. "Sitting on a warehouse crate, Stephen would reassure me the world wasn't nearly as dark as I believed. That all men weren't like Papa and Santa; that some were good and that I must learn to trust again. *And what about you, Stephen?* I asked myself. *Are you one of the good ones?* I looked for cracks in his armor but found none.

"His own father had been a hopeless alcoholic. The last time Stephen saw him, he was dying of liver disease in one of those crowded welfare wards at Bellevue. Watching him cry over his wasted life, Stephen vowed never to waste his own. He went to college, earned a business degree and then started with the distributorship. He soon earned his own territory and was promoted to district sales manager. He didn't drink or smoke, and he stayed home nights to save his money. He was determined to have his own business one day."

"And you believed all this?" Tyler asked.

"I believed everything Stephen said. He hit all the right buttons. Mama adored him. And at some point, I guess, his good looks hit me. He was blond, blue-eyed, soft-spoken, a strange sight in my Italian neighborhood. Anyway, our attraction for each other was growing. We held hands often, and we went to the movies and the park on Sunday afternoons.

"When I was eighteen, we created the scandal of the decade by attending my senior prom together. But Mama approved and I was officially a woman. Stephen was twenty-six, a dreamboat in his tux that night. The other girls were sick with envy as we danced beneath the glowing lanterns.

"I started Columbia that fall, a hectic time with a full course load and two jobs. And Mama wasn't doing well. One minute she cried over Papa, the next Santa, then Vinny. Stephen was such a good sport, waiting every Tuesday and Thursday night when my shift ended at the 'Flop Shop.' I washed dishes, waited tables and was exhausted by the end. But the instant he took me in his arms, my exhaustion vanished.

"We'd either stroll to our favorite coffee shop or go for pizza in his car. He'd fuss over my raw hands after hours of washing dishes, then say how proud he was of me. *You're not just the world's most beautiful girl, but also the toughest!* he'd boast."

"And he was right on both counts," Tyler rejoined.

"The two greatest compliments I've ever received." She glowed.

"His and mine?"

"No, 'beautiful' and 'tough,' just now when you made them compliments. But I never thought of myself as tough. I just did what I had to. And I never cared about being beautiful – until now, anyway."

His fingers slid down her spine. "Are you saying the Old Spice salesman didn't inspire one ounce of vanity?"

"So we've given him a nickname? The 'Old Spice salesman' - I suppose it's appropriate."

"And my question?" he asked.

"We'll get to that, just be patient. Anyway, Stephen had an apartment on the West Side. His brother, Paul, came by sometimes but there were rarely other visitors. We enjoyed our privacy. My schedule allowed us so little time together. I looked forward to our long, carefree Sundays — the strolls in the park, romantic dinners, old movies and Chianti, snuggling in the dark."

"That's when you started . . . ?'"

"Be patient, I said." She playfully smacked his arm.

"At least tell me if we're getting close."

"All right, we're getting close!" Gratefully her eyes closed as his fingers again slipped down her spine. "Tyler, I wish so much that I'd known you back then."

"Finish your story," his said as his nose settled in her hair.

"Where was I?" she asked thoughtfully.

"You and the Old Spice salesman were about to do it."

"No, we weren't. We were about to cook dinner and watch TV - every Giants game, of course. Stephen didn't care for football, but he'd sit there patiently as I absorbed every detail." She smiled, "I bet you've never known a girl who knew so much about football?"

Just one, he thought, but finally it seemed there was another.

"Anyway, I thought it perfectly natural to surrender my virginity to the man I planned to marry," she confessed. "Stephen had waited five years for me to grow up. I couldn't ask him to wait any longer."

"And . . .?" Tyler nudged her. "How was it?"

"Well if I didn't sizzle with passion or collapse in his arms like in one of those old movies . . ."

"That bad, huh?"

"No, you dope! And the second time was better. There were six times altogether."

"Why not a seventh?"

"Because I found out . . . everything." Her eyes gleamed with an old bitterness. "We'd just returned to his apartment one Tuesday evening when he announced we wouldn't be spending Christmas together. His mother was taking the family to Vermont to visit a dying aunt. I accepted this because I trusted him, although I wasn't happy about it. Anyway, when I hung my coat in the hall closet, I found a jewelry box, and being the nosy person I am, I couldn't resist a peek."

"An engagement ring?"

"The most beautiful diamond necklace I'd ever seen," she exclaimed. "My fingers trembled just holding it. And I knew Stephen must be the most wonderful man on earth. He was also coming down the hall; I was lucky to get the box back on the shelf before he turned the corner."

"Did he give it to you that night?"

"No, but I felt sure he would that Thursday, on our last date before his trip. It was a dreadful night." She shivered. "An unexpected storm had dropped a foot of snow on the ground. When I got home, I found his message saying he'd gotten stranded on his return from a Connecticut business meeting and wouldn't be able to make our date.

"He sounded so depressed. I knew he must be looking forward to giving me his big surprise, so I thought, 'Why not surprise him?' When he returned, instead of a dark, empty apartment, wouldn't it be nice to find that adorable Corelli girl waiting with a warm dinner? So after taking care of Mama, I rushed out to shop then returned to shower and dress. By eight, I was in a cab headed for the West Side. Not until reaching his apartment did I realize I'd overlooked one minor detail."

"What?" he asked.

"His apartment key," she laughed. "There I stood in my best dress, hair coifed, arms loaded with groceries and no way to get inside. However, at that moment, a neighbor appeared and seeing me standing there like a fool, tried to free me — not of my heavy bags but my apparent misconception. He said that Mr. Ford lived there all right, but not Stephen - his brother, Paul. He said Stephen lived out in Long Island. Naturally I assured him he was the one mistaken. He then assured me just as emphatically that he wasn't.

"A lump crept up my throat as I asked where in Long Island Stephen lived. He went to his apartment for the address and to call me a cab. In minutes, I was on my way to Long Island wondering if it was actually possible that Stephen had lied to me about where he lived, and if so, why?

"Finally the cab turned down a street with handsome, snow-mantled houses, lights glowing in the windows, like stepping into a Norman Rockwell painting. As we reached the house, I was in a daze and stupidly sent the cab away. Grabbing my bags, I went up to knock. Tiny voices began squealing, feet pattered and the door opened to four pajama-clad children. Grinning at my bags, the oldest asked if they were Christmas presents. Certain now that I had the wrong house, I smiled at the large pile of packages beneath the twinkling tree.

"As I turned to leave, a plump woman with a sweet, almond face suddenly appeared. Starting to explain the intrusion, my eyes fell to her dazzling necklace—my necklace; I knew then I had the right house.

"When she asked who I was looking for, I bit back my tears to say the Smiths, of all people. Stephen finally appeared, freezing at the sight of me. I was equally shocked, of course, because I realized that everything he'd ever said, done, represented - all that I'd believed about him - was a lie. *He* was a lie." She shook her head with bitter irony. "All the years I'd invested in him . . . in one minute, he'd destroyed it all.

"When his wife said she didn't know the Smiths, he explained that they lived in the next block. I declined his offer to drive me, given that I contemplated his immediate castration. So in a daze I left, walking for blocks until I reached a store, where I dumped my bags and called a cab."

"Did you ever see him again?"

"One night after the holidays I returned from work to find him waiting in front of our building. He said he wanted to explain. I said there was nothing to explain. He then begged me to forgive five years of lies. I said he must be crazy to think I might. He asked how I could be so unforgiving. I asked how he could be such a bastard. He said he'd told his wife about us and then moved out of their home. This meant he'd also lost his job, since his father-in-law owned the company. I calmly replied that he wasn't just a bastard, but a very stupid one and advised him to crawl back to his wife and beg *her* forgiveness, not mine, since I had no intention of ever seeing him again.

" 'But I've sacrificed my family for you!' he protested.

" 'People don't sacrifice families,' I said. 'They love them.'

"He then dropped to his knees and began wailing like a wounded animal. It was horrible," she sighed. "Not just the disgrace, but seeing Stephen as he really was. Not the man of the world, but this sniveling creature groveling at my feet, tears springing from his eyes as he begged me not to leave. It was so embarrassing, so pathetic. And deciding it was much too cold to waste another second on him, I went inside. I never saw or heard from him again."

Tyler studied her solemnly. Did he need another word to understand her mistrust of the world? Her father, Santa and finally Stephen; each in his turn had failed her. Why should she assume he wouldn't also? "Mayson, I'm sorry for all you've suffered and for not having done more to understand."

She smiled. "Tyler, you've done far more to understand than I could've ever hoped. So now having suffered my miserable story, how do you feel – better or hopelessly depressed?"

Chapter Four's telling had been to distract him from his pain. "Better." His gaze drifted to the darkened window. Were their pursuers drawing near in the wilderness outside? "We should leave for the inn soon."

"Can't we sleep a while first?" she sighed. "I'm so comfortable."

Sleep came quickly for him but not for her, as she watched the night deepen in the window. His conversation with Chatty Cathy scratched again at her brain. What was the connection she was trying to make? Again she laid out the details – Markham and the other insurance agents, five living, one dead; the Copper Harbor fishing trips; the marina storage facility. Did the pieces make a picture or did she just want them to?

He woke to the choppers' thunder — and Mayson at the window, seemingly oblivious, her eyes frozen on the wilderness outside. "What's the matter?" he asked.

She'd finally made the connection. Morris's interrupted vacation, his flight to Minnesota to meet Dale Markham, their shared passion for fishing — it was easy to imagine.

Morris: You called just when the blues were biting.

Markham: Oh yeah? Well let me tell you about our last catch at Copper Harbor . . .

Morris: Your own boat, kept right there at the marina?

Markham: It's safe and the storage unit's only opened twice a year; once in the spring, once in the fall.

Morris: You pay rent fifty weeks out of the year and the boat just sits there?

Markham: Yeah, but we split it five ways. And the lease isn't even in our names. We kept it in our buddy's name; the one who died.

Morris: No kidding? So everyone has a key?

Markham: Lock combination. It's also written down in a secret place if we forget. No one else has access.

Morris: Unless they discover the combination. Where do you keep it anyway?

Markham, ignorant of Morris's intentions, must have told him or been tricked into it. Morris had then gone to Copper Harbor, via Duluth, that Saturday. "Tyler, the man who owned the Snow Peak Insurance Agency before Markham," she asked. "The one in whose name the boat's stored at the Copper Harbor Marina - what is it? Did Chatty Cathy say?"

Gazing at the scrap of paper in her hand, the one recovered from Morris's apartment, his eyes widened. A shiver rushed up his spine. "Hunter," he answered. His name was Robert Hunter."

CHAPTER THIRTY-SIX

★

Harrington had returned to Houston to complete arrangements for the historic Christmas celebration, now just days away. The Tower of Faith had been buzzing not just over Christmas, but the emerging Renaissance, which would establish him as the spiritual leader of a New World Order. Longbridge's call had come in the midst of his preparations. "Seth, I know you're especially busy this time of year but I'd appreciate your return to D.C.," he said. "There's an urgent matter I need to discuss. Can you come?"

How did you say no to the President of the United States, a close friend no less, whose cooperation was vital to the mission?

Seconds after hanging up, Harrington's heart lurched and in crippling pain he'd sunk to the floor, there offering his simple prayer: *Please heal me, Lord, so I may continue Your divine work, upon which the souls of so many rest.*

There'd been no pain since that desperate prayer, nor would there be, he was convinced, as he waited to discover the urgent matter that had brought him to the Oval Office on this bitterly cold afternoon.

"Two months of costly operations, yet the fugitives remain at large," Longbridge began. "That they're young professionals with otherwise spotless records — one on crutches, the other a wealthy Virginia baron — only adds to a public persona unhealthy for this administration. It's surely fueled Adamley's recent rumblings about a Senate investigation and these new appeals from public interest groups stirred up by Travis Culpepper and Schuyler Waddill. These groups are funded by conservative Americans who put me in office and who have to vote for me again, if I'm to remain in office. They believe, as I do, that this fugitive crisis has gone on long enough, and they don't see it ending unless I intervene."

"Intervene how?" Harrington asked.

"By issuing a statement guaranteeing the fugitives' safety if they surrender and assuring them due process in their criminal prosecutions."

"But haven't Thomas and Larry already done that? And how can you guarantee the safety of two dangerous fugitives? You have no control over what they might do. They say they want to surrender, but don't you think they'd prefer freedom if given the chance? Who can predict what desperate stunt they might pull, like taking a hostage or killing someone?"

Across the desk, Longbridge brooded over these observations. Surrender was a delicate process and would have to be meticulously planned. Still as Seth pointed out, something could go wrong. He couldn't control the events that might follow or guarantee the results. "You're right," he nodded. "I can't make the statement. So then what should I do?"

"Why do anything? Assuming you still have faith in Larry and Thomas, they'll soon capture the fugitives and bring this crisis to an end."

Longbridge frowned. "That's what I keep hearing. But how long do I wait before admitting these are empty promises they can't fulfill?"

"Then you have lost faith in them."

"No, but I'm clearly losing patience. We need to close this chapter soon."

"Certainly the Lord will see them through it. We must keep our faith, Tom — in Him and those who do His work. You do still believe Thomas and Larry are the Lord's servants?"

Longbridge studied his friend thoughtfully. Since the Green River tragedy, rumors of conspiracy had run rampant. If there was no cover up, the critics argued, why hadn't an investigation been ordered? Wasn't Green River as suspect as Waco? And what about those serious charges against the three Supreme Court Justices, the impeachment advocates shouted.

Did he believe the rumors? Was he prepared to admit that men he'd entrusted with enforcement of the nation's laws were possibly criminals themselves? Criminals of the worst kind: those who exploited the nation's trust to advance their own illegal enterprises. Until he was sure this was the case, it wouldn't just be irresponsible, but suicidal to hint at his suspicion. "Of course I believe Thomas and Larry are committed to the Lord, Seth. If I've led you to think otherwise, I apologize."

"Then what will you do, Tom?"

His eyes hardened with resolve as if addressing the nation. "This operation has been entrusted to the proper authorities and executed in accordance with federal law. As President, I've seen that the men responsible are qualified and of unimpeachable character. I've let them do their jobs, yet also demanded frequent reports. Further, I've kept the nation informed and reassured the people of my faith in the men in charge. Unless you suggest any changes I'll incorporate this message into an afternoon statement. Beyond that, I'll do nothing except pray, of course, for a swift end to this nightmare."

Walking Harrington to the door, he expressed his deepest regret over the fugitive crisis. "Travis Culpepper has contributed so much to my administration. It's difficult to lose someone of his caliber."

"Doing what's right is never easy," Harrington reassured him. "The Lord said there'd be sacrifices and, so it seems, He was right as usual."

Longbridge nodded. "I must say, He's seen fit to provide me with a wonderful friend and adviser who's not just molded me into a successful politician, but guided me safely over treacherous roads."

"I've done no more than the Lord has asked," Harrington shrugged modestly. "If accolades are due, they're His alone."

Longbridge studied him solemnly now. "I gather the excitement of the special Christmas celebration has put some additional stress on you. You haven't seemed yourself lately. No medical problems, I hope?"

This unexpected probe startled Harrington. Speculation over his health could threaten his position in the administration. "I'm fine," he smiled convincingly. "My last checkup couldn't have been better. As you say, it must be the excitement."

Hours later, he summarized the meeting for the group gathered in the Lakeland study. "I'm glad he listens to you," Streeter sighed. "I can't imagine anything worse than his personal guarantee of the fugitives' safety, especially since we've planned their swift executions. With Green River no longer an option, they'll take place at the site of capture, or as close as circumstances permit."

"What about this latest report on their location?" Harrington asked.

"We haven't yet confirmed the trucker's identity, but his information is consistent with what we already know," Chapman explained. "The Northwood Sheriff's dispatcher who received his call tried to determine his identity but experienced problems with the connection. We've discovered, however, through available satellite detection that the call, from an untraceable cell phone, was made within a forty mile range west of Lacey's Truck Stop, where the trucker believes they jumped on; it's a supposition made more credible when you consider a rundown inn is also nearby. A place called the Kennesaw."

"Why did the trucker call the Northwood Sheriff?" Harrington asked.

"Because Northwood was his last stop," Chapman replied.

"Yes, but he'd covered up to forty miles since that stop. What made him think the Northwood Sheriff would have jurisdiction?"

"He's a trucker, not a lawyer," Streeter said. "What difference does it make what he thought?"

"Possibly a lot," Falkingham mused. "Especially since the fugitives weren't found where he claims they jumped off; and neither his identity nor the specific origin of his call have been confirmed. How do we even know he was a trucker? Possibly he was more interested in the Northwood Sheriff's activities than in reporting the fugitives' location. Does anyone know what the Sheriff was doing when the call came in?"

Chapman glanced at his notes. "The dispatcher, who was unable to make radio contact, located the Sheriff a quarter-hour later engaged in a search with our people."

"A search of what?" Harrington asked.

He suddenly looked ill. "A small inn, west of Northwood on Route 51 . . . the Kennesaw."

"Tyler made that call!" Falkingham snapped. "I bet he was sweating bullets inside that inn and knew he had to get your boys to bite on a fast one. He must've gotten a good laugh when they scrambled off like rabbits."

Harrington suddenly felt sick, too. "Find out where that call was made," he turned to Chapman. "And search that inn immediately. If we've fumbled the ball again, at least tell me we've reduced the search area?"

"It's been redrawn based on this latest report," Streeter confirmed. "Northwood is the new axis, with a forty mile radius, about one-tenth the size we were working before. One thing's certain: the fugitives are inside this area with a concentrated force of six hundred men, two hundred patrol cars and a fleet of choppers. Checkpoints have been established at every junction. No vehicle can get through without proper ID. We also plan to search every building and question every person inside the zone. This time, the fugitives will be caught."

Harrington wasn't interested in his worthless assurances, but with assuring that no detail was overlooked. "Is Lake Superior in this new zone, and have you considered it in your strategy?"

"Northwood's on its coast," Chapman replied. "Police cutters have already sealed it off."

"Why haven't the fugitives contacted the Markhams?" Lamp addressed another concern.

"They must assume the family's phones are bugged," Chapman replied. "Still, they're certain to make contact at some point. What other choice do they have?"

"What's the situation in Snow Peak anyway?" Mann asked.

"Quiet for now. Markham's in St. Paul until Friday."

"How do we know the fugitives haven't contacted him there?"

"They'd obviously disguise their voices," Streeter said. "Maybe they just haven't been identified on the tapes yet. We've bugged every phone within a hundred miles of Markham, and Nicholas is screening every call."

Falkingham lit his last Dunhill, crunching the empty pack in the ashtray. "After our public guarantees, Longbridge will go ballistic when they're not taken alive."

"I've made him aware this is a real possibility," Harrington said. "As desperate killers, their actions can't be predicted, much less controlled. And just because they've convinced people they want to surrender doesn't mean they won't resort to violence when the time comes. I'm referring to the shootout that'll take place." He glanced at his watch. "What else, gentlemen? It's getting late."

When no one responded, he adjourned the meeting. As the three justices left, he and Streeter waited for Chapman to call Snow Peak. He found them at the front door, minutes later. "Nicholas is confirming the origin of the trucker's call and reviewing recent phone conversations from Markham's home and insurance agency. If there's anything suspicious, we'll know in the morning."

Hours later, the phone rattled the darkness. "Good news," Chapman reported.

"At this hour, it better be."

Streeter chimed in, "Larry, in his typical fashion, has understated the developments."

Both dummies on the line together - the news must be special indeed, which Chapman now confirmed. "We've determined that the trucker's call and the one to the insurance agency originated from the same cell phone. The caller claimed to be moving his business from Dallas to Snow Peak. When the secretary said Markham was out of town, he wasn't interested in talking to anyone else. But he had plenty of questions, making it clear he was on a fishing expedition."

Harrington now sprung up in bed. "Are you saying Waddill was the caller?"

"A report just received confirms it," Streeter replied. "The captain of a Caribbean cruise ship has a passenger on board named Martin Kennesaw, who owns the inn we discussed earlier. Kennesaw's identified Waddill from a photo shown him by an ex-girlfriend on the same cruise. He stated that he rented Waddill a cabin the same morning he left and didn't think anymore about it until meeting up with the ex-girlfriend."

Chapman added, "The inn's being secured and the state boys withdrawn, so we can dispose of the fugitives the moment Nicholas and Leopold arrive. If they attempt a last-minute escape, it would logically be in the direction of the eastern forest, where our guys are now concentrating."

Harrington glowed. Everything was falling into place; certainly the Lord was responsible.

Streeter offered another promising possibility. "Whether or not Waddill realizes it, his call to the agency may have uncovered the nugget we overlooked."

"What do you mean?" Harrington asked.

"During his conversation with Markham's secretary, it came out that the agents go fishing twice a year at Copper Harbor. Their boat is stored at the marina there, something previously unconfirmed."

"Why is that?"

"Because the lease isn't in the agents' names we checked. It remains in the previous owner's name, the one who died four years ago. Robert Hunter. Our agents are en route to Copper Harbor now to search the storage unit. We'll know soon if it holds the chest."

Chapman laughed. "It makes perfect sense, doesn't it?" he said. The Jew flies to Minnesota, lamenting all the blues he's missing on the Outer Banks. Later, while trading fishing tales with Markham, he learns about the storage unit at Copper Harbor."

"One leased to a dead man," Streeter added. "And also the travel records suggest one he almost certainly visited for the purpose of dumping his treasure chest."

"That must be it!" Harrington rejoiced. "We've searched every other conceivable place!" Would the next hours see the fugitives finally captured and the chest recovered? "Call me the instant you get word."

Hanging up, he gazed joyfully out the window. What a wonderful Christmas it would be! What a grand era they were marching into! With the Lord's blessing, he would soon lead the flock to salvation. And faithfully they'd follow and love him, as they loved the Lord.

He pondered this as the next thunderbolt struck.

CHAPTER THIRTY-SEVEN

★

At the boarding call, the young man fell in line with the others booked on Midwestern Flight #247. Presenting his ticket, he hustled along the bridge. A smiling stewardess welcomed him aboard, "No overcoat or briefcase? You must've left that meeting in a hurry."

"I had to get out of town before they read the fine print," he winked.

"That drawl," she asked her handsome passenger in the charcoal suit. "What is it?"

"Pure Virginian." He teased his friends that he hadn't lived in Georgia long enough to have it tarnished. Claiming his window seat, he gazed out to see baggage being loaded and equipment checked. Was this a wild goose chase? He'd asked himself this when he left Atlanta and now again, hours later, at O'Hare. This last leg of the journey hopefully would get him closer to an answer.

The cabin noise soon faded and the mammoth jet climbed into the northern sky. His thoughts returned to the circumstances that had so quickly sent him flying off to Minnesota, instead of driving to Virginia for the holidays. The call to his Atlanta real estate office that morning as he wrapped up a dozen pressing matters before leaving for Virginia had changed everything. "We have a live one on the line," his secretary had said, her head poking through the door.

"I'm running late. Give it to Betty."

"He insists on speaking with you."

"Who is he?" he'd looked up to ask.

"Dick Jessup. He's moving his car business here from Dallas and needs a new house."

This was a layup he'd normally jump at, one that promised a fat commission if Jessup was like most Texans. Only he couldn't have picked a worse time.

"Good morning," he grabbed the phone. "I understand you're

moving your business and need a new home."

"That's right," Jessup drawled. "And I don't have time to waste with a bunch of *negotiatin'*."

"I understand. And I have the perfect agent for you. I'd handle it myself but . . ."

"Let me put it plainly," Jessup interrupted. "I hear you're the best real estate man in Atlanta. And I have this rule, you see, of *dealin'* only with the best; cars, homes, whatever. When money's on the line, it don't make sense to go to anyone else. Say for example, you're the quarterback in a football game. The score's tied, time's running out and you're twenty yards from pay dirt. You call a pass play; a hitch and slant, let's say. Who do you go to? The receiver who gives you the best chance of scoring, right? Well the same logic applies . . ."

Matt froze as the Texan's meaning sunk in. "I . . . see your point and may have a new listing you'd be interested in. It looks like South Fork, if you remember the show 'Dallas.' I'm heading there now in fact. Could you call me in twenty minutes?"

"Sure. You got that number handy?"

Relaying it, he hung up and started out. "South Fork?" the secretary followed. "Which listing are you talking about?"

"The Bergin's place," he replied.

"But it doesn't look anything like South Fork."

"Jessup doesn't know that," he said, throwing on his coat. "Besides, I promised Ned Bergin I'd check on his place before leaving town. This way I can kill two birds with one stone." Heading for the door, he turned back and said, "Ask Betty to dig through our listings for the closest thing to South Fork - oh, and Merry Christmas."

Twenty minutes later, Matt stared at the kitchen phone in the Bergin's recently abandoned North Atlanta home, happy he'd remembered Ned hadn't cut off the service. Where else could he have safely taken the call? He quickly grabbed the phone now as it began ringing. "Hello?"

"So you still remember the old hitch and slant?"

Matt laughed. "I'd be damn stupid not to, considering how many times I bailed you out with it."

"Bailed me out? All you had to do was shake some lead-footed safety long enough for me to stuff the ball in your gut."

"Waddill to Culpepper," Matt smiled. "That connection won a bushel of games for the Academy."

"And a state championship, don't forget."

A patrol car suddenly passed the window, snapping him out of his trance. "Goddamnit Tyler, we've been worried sick about you! It's about time you called."

"I wouldn't have risked it if the situation wasn't life or death."

"Then you had no choice. And by the way, that Texas drawl was pretty good."

Tyler sighed heavily. "Man, I really fucked up Travis's career."

"Tyler, you didn't fuck up anything," Matt snapped. "Dad's happy to be out of the Longbridge administration and I know Mom is. So tell me about Corelli? Is she nice?"

"A royal pain in the ass," Tyler laughed. "So how's Kelly? And those two little farts? I guess you have big Christmas plans."

Ones that might change, Matt sensed. "We're going to York - this afternoon, as a matter of fact."

"I see . . . Well, that's great."

"Tyler, our plans can be changed. That's what this call is about, isn't it? Don't bullshit me, man. If you need help, ask for it."

"Matt, it's not like that. I just . . . What I mean . . ."

"Will you shut the fuck up and tell me what I need to do?" Grabbing a leftover listing, he jotted notes as Tyler finally relented and explained the plan. He'd been right. The York trip was screwed. But if the plan worked, it could be the best Christmas they'd had in a long time.

"Matt, you've got nothing to gain by sticking your nose into this," Tyler said. "It could be a complete waste of time, and if caught you'll be lucky to get prison. The odds favor a swiftly executed death sentence."

"I could also be a national hero," he said, slipping the notes in his jacket. "All I can say is you'd make a shitty real estate broker. But even you can't talk me out of this."

"I'd do it myself but there's just no way to move," Tyler said. "Cops are everywhere, the snow just gets deeper and deeper and Mayson's getting worse by the minute. If I don't get her to a hospital soon . . ."

"She'll die," Matt filled in the silence. "Then she's different. Like..."

"I'm not sure, Matt. I mean, I don't have time to think about it right now. So does my plan sound feasible? I'll understand perfectly if Kelly vetoes it. Any wife in her right mind would."

"She won't. Now, can I tell your family we've talked?"

"Sure. But we can't again."

"No big deal. If I hit the jackpot, you'll know. Now take good care of Mayson. We both know she'd want you to."

"Who?" Tyler asked.

"Kara, of course," he said, hanging up.

Minutes later, Matt pulled into the driveway of his handsome Colonial home. Kelly quickly emerged to greet him, with Little Bets and Trip trailing behind. "You always manage to arrive just in time." She nodded at the Land Cruiser, crammed with luggage and Christmas presents. Her smile faded as she detected his anxiety. "Matt, what's wrong?"

Turning away from the children, he revealed the morning's startling developments. "Tyler said he'd understand if you vetoed the plan," he told her. But veto or not, his hard eyes explained that he was determined to help. And in the same predicament, there was no question Tyler would do the same. Reluctantly, Kelly nodded her consent.

"You'll do fine on the road," he said. "Eight hours, tops."

Her eyes locked gravely with his. "Matt, please be careful."

After seeing them off, he drove to the airport and caught a flight to O'Hare, then a second one which had just touched down on Duluth's frozen tarmac.

Bracing against the cold, he left the terminal minutes later in search of his rental car. Soon he was creeping east over Duluth's icy roads, a map beside him. The stranded vehicles he passed were grim reminders of what could happen if he got too cute. Patrol car sightings increased as well, as he left the city and burrowed deeper into the wilderness.

The first roadblock he encountered was just west of Northwood. Creeping with the traffic, he watched a fleet of choppers simultaneously patrolling the night sky. How many cops did it take to catch two lawyers, anyway, he wondered as the line crept past Lacey's Truck Stop. One vehicle after another was released. Soon he was able to observe the troopers as they snapped up driver's licenses and stuck flashlights into the faces of helpless travelers. Their motions were brisk, their expressions hard. Was their mission to capture the fugitives or execute them? Need he look any farther than the Halos' mass *suicide* at Green River?

Did Longbridge know the true nature of the men around him? Was he blinded to their conspiracy, or its central figure? Travis believed Longbridge, if pathetically naive, was without question an honorable man. Incorruptible.

A jeep was released and a Lexus waved forward. Following it, he watched another chopper streak across the sky. Again he thought of Longbridge's refusal to guarantee the fugitives' safety and his repeated votes of confidence in Chapman and Streeter, a confidence Matt didn't share.

As the Lexus rolled on, the trooper waved Matt forward. "Your license and registration, please," the trooper asked. Quickly the doors flew open. Flashlights scanned the interior and brisk hands searched the floor and seats, as he passed his documents to the trooper. "You're headed for Copper Harbor?" asked a trooper as he studied the map beside him.

"I'm looking at property there." Matt offered his broker's license. "To develop, if the price is right." The trooper at the window was now joined by a Fed, who studied Matt's documents carefully before returning them. "Why does a Georgia broker travel all the way to Wisconsin to buy real estate?"

"I'm not particular about where my profits come from," Matt smiled.

The Fed clearly wasn't amused as he flashed his badge. "I'm Agent Dilman. Let's see those keys. We need to inspect your trunk"

Giving him the keys, Matt waited anxiously as the trunk was searched. Dilman returned to the window. "You always travel across the country without a suitcase or overcoat?"

"I'm going home tomorrow. Is that a big deal?"

Dilman studied him closely as angry horns began blasting. Matt turned to see the lengthening string of lights. "Sir, I'd be grateful if you let me pass. These people are getting impatient."

Culpepper, Dilman groped. Not Georgia, but . . .

"Fred!" Agent Kirby now loped over. "The traffic's really piling up. What you got?"

Unable to make the connection, he waved Matt on. "Nothing, Jim, nothing at all," he replied.

Nevertheless, Culpepper remained on Dilman's mind as the night sky suddenly exploded with choppers. He watched a dozen or more converge on Northwood as Kirby rushed over to grab him. "We just got orders! Come on!"

"What the hell's going on?" Dilman asked.

"You remember the trucker's call that sent us scrambling from the Kennesaw? We just found out where it came from."

"Where?"

"The Kennesaw; Waddill made it. Nicholas just arrived in Northwood for an emergency briefing."

As they squealed off seconds later, Dilman asked, "What do you know about the plan?"

Kirby shrugged. "Clear the State guys out, then stage the shoot-out. The rest is just details."

"It'll take place at the Kennesaw," Dilman predicted. "The .38s will be fired and placed next to the bodies. There's not much else for Nicholas to plan."

Kirby glanced at him as they reached the Sheriff's Office. "You mean Leopold, don't you?"

Dilman laughed. It didn't take a genius to figure out who was actually calling the shots.

As they crossed the lot, Kirby relayed the rest of the report. "Franklin and Benoit were sent to Copper Harbor an hour ago. I wonder what's so damn important up there, if the fugitives are here in Northwood?"

Dilman stopped abruptly as he suddenly made the connection. "That's it!"

"What the hell are you raving about?" Kirby shrugged.

"Travis Culpepper. I bet he has a son Waddill's age. A kid named Culpepper passed through our checkpoint earlier, claiming to be a Georgia broker looking for property."

"So what?"

"Christ, Jim, who the hell flies across the country to look at real estate without baggage or overcoat!"

"Do you know where he was going?" Kirby asked.

He nodded gravely. "Copper Harbor."

Matt reached the Copper Harbor Marina at one a.m. Its long cinderblock building had been abandoned for the night, the windows secured — except for the one rattling in the breeze. So where were the boat storage units?

Crawling from the car, he hurried across the empty lot, then down to the docks. The icy breeze sliced through him. If only he'd remembered his damned coat.

He finally spotted the framed storage units beyond the last pier and reaching them, moved quickly down the first alley, then up the next, until coming to Unit #36. The door's plate provided the lessee's name: R. Hunter. This was it.

The chilling breeze rattled down the dark alley as he groped for the scrawled equation - a lock combination, phone number or something else? Did the storage unit hold a secret that would rock a nation, or just rob the fishing boat of a few insurance geeks, he wondered as he turned the dial in obedience to the numbers. The lock didn't respond. Had he written down the wrong numbers? He tried again, and again it refused to cooperate. What should he do now? Find a goddamned hammer and break it open? Again he tried the combination. This time the lock clicked.

Lifting the door, he switched on the light and surveyed the unit. It was ten feet wide and twenty deep, plenty big for the Boston Whaler it housed. Deck chairs, rope, buckets and rags cluttered the floor.

His scanning eyes snagged on the dry sink in the corner, a box of folded canvas sitting on top. Going over, he inspected the sink's interior cabinet and quickly moved on to the wall racks, which held a hodgepodge of fishing gear and accessories. Turning next to the boat, he lifted the tarp and climbed inside, carefully examining every compartment from bow to stern. Scowling, he crawled out. He was missing something; he could feel it.

Again his gaze stopped on the dry sink. What was he missing?

Yes, it suddenly jolted him. The boxed canvas was oddly folded and crookedly shaped - as if packaging a large, rectangular object. Quickly, he stripped the canvas away, shivering at his discovery — a rusted metal chest, its seal sliced. Carefully he opened it to examine the contents – large manila envelopes and brittle, plastic evidence bags labeled *Pine County Sheriff's Department. May 5th, 1954.*

Shocked seconds passed as he absorbed the monumental dimensions of his discovery - a chest, the forty-year-old contents of which promised to shake the very foundation of the United States government and save Tyler's and Mayson's lives, but also bring a quick end to his own, unless it got into the right hands. Putting the items back, he carried the chest outside, then secured the unit and returned down the alley.

Arms aching, he reached the parking lot a few minutes later and locked the chest in the trunk. Opening the car door to leave, he froze as headlights suddenly broke the darkness. A patrol car reached him, the trooper parking and climbing out as a Fed emerged from the passenger side. "Is that your car?" the trooper asked.

"My rental, yeah," he nodded.

"I'll need to see the lease, along with your license."

Heart pounding, he handed over the documents. The trooper studied them carefully, then gave them to the Fed. "You're a long way from home, Mr. Culpepper. What's the nature of your business up here?"

"Real estate development. I met with some people earlier to discuss a project, only I didn't expect to be this late."

"Where are you going now?" the Fed asked.

"To my hotel in Duluth."

The Fed's face relaxed as he returned the documents. Sliding into the driver's seat, Matt cranked the engine. It clicked unresponsively. Pumping the gas, he tried again. Again it clicked. *Shit, not now!* he thought.

"It's the cold," the trooper nodded. "You got jumper cables?"

"All rentals have them," said the Fed, who started for the trunk.

Desperately Matt tried the engine again. Sputtering, it finally chugged to life. "I guess it's the cold, like you said," he shrugged with a heavy relief. As they stepped back, he crept from the ice-patched lot.

Crawling over the slippery roads, he tensed each time the tires spun. Copper Harbor was an eerie, desolate place, a ghost town submerged in deep snow and with few phones, he discovered. Travis had been expecting his call hours ago and it was beginning to appear he'd have to risk using his cell phone.

Reaching the highway, he turned west towards the bridge. One patrol car, then a second and third, passed east in the direction of Copper Harbor. A fourth zipped by as he finally spotted a service station, a coveted phone booth in its darkened corner. As he turned into the icy lot, his tires suddenly spun, angling the car into the station's wrecker. The collision hurled him against the door.

His head spun painfully as he crawled from the floor. Warm blood trickled down his neck. Groping for tissues in his jacket pocket, he pressed them to his burning temple. Then turning the key, he groaned at the familiar click. Pumping the gas, he tried again and again. *Now what*, he thought, as he crawled out to inspect the damage. Then he remembered the call he had to make. As he hurried for the phone booth, choppers suddenly lit the western sky. A dozen or more, they converged on the same point. Northwood? Had something happened? Slipping into the booth, he quickly placed his call.

Ten, eleven, twelve . . . Tyler counted the choppers as they crossed the night sky, all headed for Northwood. What had brought them? Had Matt reached Copper Harbor? Had the lock combination proved to be their salvation — just too late to save them?

He turned at Mayson's soft moans. Her leg had gotten worse since moving up to the inn. After settling her in this second floor room, he'd returned to cover his tracks, then spent the next hours nursing her and waiting. Kennesaw's liquor cabinet had been quickly cleaned out as he plied her with bourbon and vodka for the pain. She'd languished in a drunken stupor as the pain faded, then tossed and moaned as it returned. The codeine pills had smoothed out the cycle, but only two were left.

As the choppers landed, his vigilant gaze returned to the empty sky. Had they discovered the origin of his calls? Was a raid being planned? His eyes closed with the collapsing situation. With choppers in Northwood, police cutters in the lake and a massive land force closing in, wasn't the chase finally over?

As Mayson's moans grew more urgent, he went to the bathroom for water, then gave her the last codeine pills. "They know we're here. We have to leave."

She shook her head in protest. She was so confused, in so much pain. The chilling darkness, the running, hiding, spending every second either cheating death or battling pain that only got worse... she couldn't take another minute. As she began crying, he held her tightly. "Mayson, we can't give up. Not when there's a chance."

"What chance?" she cried. "Even if Matt finds the chest, it won't be in time to save us."

It wasn't the tears, but her eyes' jaggedness and the tightness of her mouth that sent shivers through him. Her pain was brutal, but getting worse. "We can't waste another second. They'll be here soon," he said. He began slipping her socks on, then the boot. Bundling her in coat, cap, and gloves, he retrieved a blanket from Kennesaw's quarters. "All right, let's get out of here."

Wrapping her in the blanket, he lifted her over his shoulder and descended the back stairs. Pushing out the door, he hurried past the storage shed and started across the ridge on what would very likely be the last leg of their journey.

Travis Culpepper stood at the York mansion's bedroom window as the Land Cruiser glided up the lane. His smile quickly faded as his daughter-in-law parked and climbed out with the children. Where was Matt? He dropped the curtain and hurried downstairs where Betsy waited in the entrance hall. As Kelly came through the door, her urgent eyes quickly found him. "Tyler called this morning and asked Matt to help him find some mysterious chest."

"Where does he think it is?" Travis asked.

"Copper Harbor, Wisconsin. He believes it's hidden in a marina storage facility. Matt flew up there this afternoon."

Travis detected the fear in her eyes. "He'll be fine," he said. "And he's done the right thing."

"I know," she nodded. "But I'm so frightened."

"We all are," Betsy refrained, although in full agreement with the action taken.

"What happens next?" Travis asked.

"Matt will call at midnight with a report," Kelly explained. "If he's late, he said not to worry."

"Doesn't he know our phones are almost certainly bugged?" Travis said. "And if you didn't notice, there's a Federal agent posted near the entrance to our estate."

"He won't call here," Kelly said. She revealed the rest of the plan.

At eleven that evening, Travis left the mansion in his Mercedes. Passing through the stone archway, headlights quickly appeared in his mirror, sticking to him as he covered the dark, winding lane. Soon the forest surrendered to his club's darkened fairways, tennis courts and riding stables. Matt had been smart to realize this trip wasn't unusual. He often swam his laps at night; just not quite this late.

Reaching the Tudor clubhouse, he grabbed his gym bag and started across the lot, waving cheerfully as the tailing lights appeared. *In your face*; isn't that what the kids said these days? He hurried downstairs to the men's locker room. Usually a place where stress was released, tonight the quiet chamber trembled with enough to shake the walls. He sat at the card table, not to play his beloved gin, but to wait in anxious vigil over the phone.

Midnight passed quietly. At one, he called the mansion to report he'd heard nothing. At two, Kelly called to confirm he still hadn't. Three slipped by in a sharpening silence. Surely the Fed remained outside, his suspicion rising. Had he somehow managed to establish surveillance of the locker room, too?

His weary eyes glued to the phone, Travis drifted back in time ... Matt's Academy years; the long-awaited driver's license. He'd seen enough of his son's boat piloting to know their world would never be the same again. While his friend, Tyler, had also been a hellion, the ubiquitous Kara had kept him in check. But Matt, not blessed with such a tempering influence, had destined his parents to camp by the phone on weekends until he returned safely from his whirl of social engagements. Countless times his curfew had passed as they waited first for his call, then the police and finally, God forbid, the hospital. But always his headlights had broken the darkness. Would their fears also prove unfounded on this cold, dark night? Four o'clock arrived. Damn it Matt, where the hell . . . He lunged for the suddenly ringing phone.

"Dad, I'm sorry to be so late."

Travis sighed heavily with relief. "Matt, where are you?" he asked.

"Copper Harbor. My rental car just died. But I see some lights up the road that may be a motel. When we hang up, I'll check it out."

"You can't wait for a patrol car?"

"Dad, this place is crawling with patrol cars. They're probably looking for me by now. Either way, I can't risk being spotted." He paused. "Dad, I have the chest. It was hidden in that storage unit just as Tyler said. I examined it long enough to confirm it proves who murdered that girl forty years ago."

Travis quietly absorbed this stunning news. "And who is the murderer?"

"*Murderers.* Three, all sitting on the United States Supreme Court. So what do we do now?"

"I have a friend in Washington who's rather sore at me for the moment, but not enough he can't be trusted. I'll contact him immediately. And you, son, head directly for that motel."

A once-whispered admonition now played in his mind as he hung up: *Memorize the number, Travis, because I can't have it found some day on a scrap in your wallet by some robber, good deed-doer, or your sweet wife, Betsy. And don't use it unless you're absolutely convinced we have a national emergency.*

I'll most certainly never have to, sir.

Maybe not. But if the time comes, don't pussyfoot around. Make the call. And when it comes, I'll know before you tell me that we have a national crisis on our hands.

Do we ever, he thought, as he dialed the number.

CHAPTER THIRTY-EIGHT

★

Harrington was much too euphoric to sleep after Streeter's call. This was the moment of triumph; his and the Lord's. Dressed and standing at the study window, he noted the time: 5:30 a.m. Thursday, December 21. It must be remembered and later documented.

The phone rang. "Culpepper's son has been spotted in Copper Harbor," Chapman reported. "Apparently he flew into Duluth last night."

"Larry, we can't permit this last-minute threat to destroy the mission. I want him apprehended now! Has the marina storage facility been searched?"

"No chest was found," Chapman replied. "We just got word."

"Are you telling me young Culpepper beat us to it?" Harrington growled.

"Sir, we're not even sure it was there."

"Of course it was, and now the fugitives have it. I want it recovered, Larry!" Slamming the phone down, he stormed to the window. Was there no end to this nightmare?

Minutes passed as he finally calmed enough to envision Houston's serried skyline and the Tower of Faith rising above it, with the worship hall decorated for the Christmas Eve service. A desperate nation hungered for his wisdom and his guiding hand to rescue it from the chains of its sinful bondage.

Praise the Lord and His earthly partner, Seth Harrington.

Matt trudged through the trees rimming the dark, icy highway. Could Travis find a way to rescue them, or was the situation too desperate? Time was the variable. If they could survive long enough, there was a chance. He shuddered against another icy gust. The numbness in his hands and feet had deepened. He needed shelter and he needed it soon.

Another patrol car zipped by in the direction of Copper Harbor, then inexplicably screeched its brakes and, sliding over the icy road, returned west. As it entered the service station where another unit waited, he finally understood. Together the troopers and Feds began a search of his abandoned rental car.

Continuing towards the lights, he spotted the small motel with its bungalows situated around a courtyard. The sign flashed *Harborside* and beneath, the greeting he'd hoped for: Vacancy. Rushing forward, he quickly froze as two patrol cars pulled into the lot. The men jumped out and hurried into the office. He easily imagined their inquiry: *Have you seen a white male in his late twenties, six feet, dark hair and eyes? A dumb Georgia shit with no overcoat, gloves or boots?*

Seconds later they came out, went back to their cars and continued towards the bridge. Matt's desperate gaze returned to the bungalows. Could he reach them without being spotted? Creeping closer, his heart sank. They had neither rear doors nor windows. And with the lit courtyard, it was too risky to enter through the front. Lifting the chest, he started once again through the trees.

Without destination, his spirit soon faded. His Gucci loafers, not designed for hikes through the Wisconsin snow, were soaked. His feet, like his hands, were losing feeling fast. Each step became torture as the chill's grip deepened, snow fluttering once again from the dark sky. He couldn't go on much longer.

Once Chapman's office atop the FBI's headquarters, the elegant enclave had become in recent weeks, a cluttered command post where plotted maps covered the walls, files rose daily on the furniture and trash accumulated on the Persian rugs. From here, he and Streeter had directed the fugitive operation. Hardly embarrassed, they were proud of the growing mess, which demonstrated clearly that no one was working any harder to end the crisis. Buried in the shambles, they now listened anxiously to the latest report from Northwood.

"Every building between here and Copper Harbor has been searched," Nicholas said. "Culpepper should be found momentarily, most likely dead of hypothermia if he's been out in the cold all night."

"If that was the case," Streeter muttered, "you would've found him by now."

Chapman asked, "Pete, if the area between his car and the bridge has been scoured, where else could he be?"

"We're not absolutely sure he's heading towards the bridge. He could be moving in any direction. And with several hours' head start, there's a lot of ground to cover."

"Have you checked all the motels along the highway?"

"Yes," Nicholas replied. "Beginning with the Harborside, the one closest to his abandoned car."

"How large is your force in Copper Harbor?"

"A hundred men and three choppers - it's all we can spare until the Northwood operation has been concluded."

"What's the latest at the Kennesaw?" Chapman asked.

"The snow tracks indicate the fugitives headed for the eastern forest as expected. Further, given that there's only one set of tracks, Waddill must be carrying Corelli, and she's bound to get heavy in knee-deep snow. They can't have gotten far."

Streeter grumbled, "The fact remains the operation has been underway for two hours now and they haven't been captured. And if they make it to that forest, who knows how long it'll take to find them? How far is it from the inn?"

"A mile and a half," Nicholas replied.

"Then they're already there! Goddamnit Pete, how could you let this happen?"

"Sir, really, how long can a bunch of trees protect them against a wind chill of twenty below?"

After weeks of Nicholas's arrogance, Streeter had endured all he could. "Listen to me, Pete. There'll be no more excuses and weather reports. We want the fugitives, and we want them now!" Hanging up, he said, "I'm sorry, Larry. I know he's your man, but he's also the most arrogant sonofabitch I've ever known."

Nodding, Chapman grabbed the flashing phone. It was Jim Ketchfield, the agent in charge of the Culpepper surveillance in Virginia, who reported: "Our distinguished subject just left Langley Air Force Base in a chopper headed for Dulles. Whatever the plan, it must've been conceived during his all-night workout at that posh club of his."

Chapman was alarmed. "We'll need a team at Dulles when he

arrives. His activities have been suspicious enough to haul him in for questioning. If he refuses to disclose his mission, at least we'll prevent his participation in it."

"I'll take care of it, sir. In fact, Dan Weston . . . Hold on. I have one coming in."

Chapman's stomach churned as he reported the developments to Streeter. "You know what this means, don't you?" Streeter groaned. "Culpepper's son found the chest. Travis intends to plead again for Longbridge's intervention. Only this time, he has the firepower to support his case."

"Not yet, Thomas. If his son has the chest, he's either dead from hypothermia or else busy keeping himself from ending up that way. Either way, we'll recover the chest before Travis gets his hands on it."

Ketchfield returned to the line. "Sorry to keep you holding, but I just received a report from Dan Weston out at Dulles. He said that when he arrived, someone was already there to meet Culpepper's chopper."

Chapman's heart pounded. "Who?"

"The President, sir."

Streeter watched the blood drain from Chapman's face. "What the hell's going on?" He turned on the speaker as Ketchfield explained, "Air Force One will fly the men to Duluth the minute young Culpepper arrives. From there we assume they'll proceed to Northwood. What should we do, sir?"

Chapman gaped at an equally desperate Streeter. "Tell Weston to stay at Dulles until they leave. Resume your surveillance at the Culpepper mansion and report any suspicious developments immediately."

Pale and trembling, he hung up. "We have to call Harrington. If anyone can intercept Longbridge, it's . . . ." He stopped as the phone flashed again. Grabbing it, he switched on the speaker. "Yes?"

"Longbridge has ordered an immediate suspension of the operation," a shattered Nicholas reported. "He, Culpepper and God knows who else are en route from Dulles. Further, he warned that if any harm came to the fugitives or Culpepper's son, he'd hold every agent on site responsible."

Chapman sunk deeper behind his cluttered desk. "This means he suspects our involvement in the cover up."

"Still," Nicholas insisted, "he can't confirm his suspicions unless he gets the chest."

Streeter frowned. "You don't plan to disregard his order?"

"Why not?" Nicholas asked. "I'm dead anyway if the chest is recovered. You know the scenario, sir: One agent cuts a deal, then another. Soon we're all falling like dominos."

"I say the hell with Longbridge's order," Chapman said. "Our only hope is to dispose of the fugitives, Culpepper's son and that damned chest."

Streeter's desperate eyes found the window. "We're going down. Not even Harrington can save us this time."

"Don't talk like that," Chapman snapped. "There's no proof of our part in this conspiracy."

"Not yet maybe, but there will be soon. It's time to run."

"Leave now?" he asked, incredulous. "There must be another option."

"He's right," Nicholas said. "If I weren't trapped here in Northwood, I'd do the same thing."

Chapman watched Streeter grab the phone. "Harrington?"

"Screw Harrington!" yelled Streeter as he dialed a number. "He's the one who got us into this mess. Let him fend . . . Custer!" he barked into the phone. "Get my car ready. I'm going to Dulles." He frowned at the hesitating silence. "Custer, did you hear me?"

A strange voice now came on the line, "I'm sorry, Mr. Streeter, but your flight's been cancelled." In the same instant, three National Guardsmen marched crisply into the office.

"What's the meaning of this?!" Streeter demanded.

"What the hell's going on?" Nicholas chimed.

"I'm Guard Captain Rimstead," the ranking officer announced sharply into the phone. "And you're . . . ?"

Outta here, The line clicked.

Flanked by his subordinates, Rimstead studied the two men submerged in their bunker of files and sophisticated electronic devices. "The President's ordered me to assume your custody until the urgent matter in Wisconsin has been resolved."

"If you're referring to the fugitive operation," Streeter

snapped, "that resolution should occur momentarily, with their capture on the southern coast of Lake Superior."

"I've been instructed not to discuss the matter with you," Rimstead replied. His gaze fell to the phone in his hand. "I'm sorry your flight was cancelled. Perhaps you'd care to disclose your destination?"

"Wisconsin naturally, to assure the operation's proper conclusion."

"You needn't worry. The President has made the trip himself. Although I must say," he said as he studied their grim faces, "neither of you seems relieved by the news. Now let's move, gentlemen."

CHAPTER THIRTY-NINE

★

Tyler carried Mayson over his shoulder, using her crutch to swiftly cross the snow-covered ridge. Speed, more than deception, was their ally now. It was critical to reach the eastern forest, both to avoid detection and to shield them from the gale force wind ripping through his flu-weakened body. Forced to stop finally, he looked up into the dark sky. The choppers could return any second to find them exposed on the ridge. Taking a deep breath, he stabbed the crutch back in the snow and started off again.

Searchlights soon scanned the dark ridge. As he froze, Mayson muttered inside the blanket, "What's wrong?"

"The party just started at the inn."

They covered another quarter-mile before choppers appeared over the ridge. Rushing for the closest trees, he moved again once they thundered past. Finally reaching the forest, he stopped to calculate. They could continue east without leaving the trees, while also remaining near the lake. But did its proximity really offer an advantage? Yes, he decided, forging ahead.

The forest soon challenged him, too, not just with deep snow but sharp rocks that couldn't be seen until his boots hit them. Finally a twisted ankle forced him to stop. "Are you all right?" Mayson asked.

"Hell no, I twisted my damn ankle," he answered. Grimacing, he resumed his eastern course. When would searchlights break the darkness? Their presence here was no secret. As they covered another mile, Mayson groaned again inside the blanket. "Sick..."

Stopping, he asked, "Do you have to vomit?"

"Already...did."

He dropped beneath a tree and pushing back the blanket, studied her face in the moonlight. It was ghostly pale, her eyes glazed. Wiping the spittle from her mouth, he asked, "Are the last pills still working?"

"Yes," she lied. "How's your ankle?"

"It hurts like hell." Rising gingerly, he hoisted her back over his shoulder. "I'll do my best to keep the bouncing down."

The icy wind died down as they plunged deeper into the forest. Scanning the darkness, he froze as searchlights now filtered through the southern trees. He turned as other lights shimmered in the west. "They're sealing us off," he said.

"Then drop me . . . and run," she replied, squirming.

"Goddamnit Mayson, we've been through this before." His grip on her tightened. "Now be still!"

The searchlights quickly grew in both number and density, breaking the eastern darkness as well. It was time to make a decision. "Tyler . . . let me down,!" Mayson said again.

"Shut up and let me think!" Escape by land was now impossible; their only hope was to the north, where the cutters maintained a quiet offshore vigil. Between was the rocky coast; if it was too dangerous for their pursuers' assault, what were its prospects as a refuge?

Twinkling choppers appeared over the lake . . . seven, eight, nine, he counted. Reaching the coast, they splintered like a meteorite, streaking off in different directions. He made his decision: north, to the rocky coast.

He soon found himself in a game of cat and mouse, hopping from tree to tree to avoid the scanning lights. Each time they brushed past, he moved. Each time they returned, he kissed the closest tree, then waited for the next precious second of darkness.

Finally, he reached the forest's edge. As the next chopper streaked past, he broke furiously across the snow, reaching the precipice before the next approached. With no trees in its path, the icy gale blew fiercely, Lake Superior roaring below. Lifting the blanket, he found Mayson's eyes shut tightly against the pain. "At least we know what it takes to shut you up," he smiled. "Just a compound fracture of the tibia."

"I'll be . . . all right," she smiled faintly.

"I know. He kissed her and prayed to God she would be. Hoisting her back over his shoulder, he tossed the crutch away. It'd be useless on the slippery rocks. "Hold on tight," he said, and he began the dangerous descent, cautiously inching down the rocks. One miscue could hurl them to a quick death a hundred feet below. Still, the unseen ice patches were unavoidable, each spinning him into the jagged rocks.

Reaching the first parapet, he lifted the blanket to find Mayson's eyes still closed, not tightly as before but relaxed. She slept soundly as he resumed his treacherous descent, slowed not just by ice but the returning choppers. Timing the lapses in their procession, he moved as one glided past, then squirmed back into the crags as the next approached. The tedious journey ended on a parapet offering both dense brush and a scalloped basin in the rocks. Piled snow could also be put to excellent use. And to descend further would bring them within range of the cutters' lights.

Setting Mayson down, he assessed the situation. The lights overhead had intensified, meaning the search party was drawing close. Would they try the same reckless descent or let the choppers smoke them out? Darkness was fading quickly over the lake as he tucked Mayson inside the basin, then swiftly gathered the earth's gifts — snow, brush and stone — molding them into an inconspicuous canopy. He then joined her in a hibernation he prayed was undetectable by the human eye.

Dawn found Harrington immersed in another anxious vigil. The bags under his eyes had grown heavier with the passing hours as he sat in the study's shadows. The call would come any second. The crisis would end. He'd interpreted the signs and received the Lord's assurances.

His gaze went to the quiet phone and then, as he'd done each quarter-hour, he went to the window. Lights were beginning to glow in . . . He lunged for the ringing phone.

"The inn's been searched," Leopold reported. "No question the fugitives were there."

"Then they haven't been captured?" he asked.

"No sir. They skipped out before we arrived and headed for the eastern forest, which Nicholas is sealing off now. With choppers on the ridge and cutters in the lake, they should be picked up soon."

Always soon; would 'now' ever arrive? "And Culpepper's son; is there anything new to report?"

"No sir, but he'll be scraped up, too; this morning, guaranteed."

"Then as Moses led the Jews from Egyptian bondage, I shall deliver our mighty nation from its bondage of sin."

"Praise the Lord, sir."

"Yes Arch, praise Him, the One who's chosen me for this great mission. And I shall honor Him by leading the flock to Salvation. You don't deny this, do you?"

"Of course not, sir." The Chairman was obviously unraveling. The brutal stress was affecting everyone; he watched Nicholas rant at his subordinates across the hall, throw a message to the floor and stalk to the window. What had sent him off? "Sir, something's up. I better check it out."

"The fugitives have been captured!" Harrington rejoiced. "Yes Arch, go confirm it!"

Beaming, he hung up and returned to the window, his attention drawn to a gray sedan parked down the street; a military vehicle, National Guard. Lakeland had a neighbor in the Guard? If so he was at least a colonel to afford this neighborhood and his own driver; he spotted the man behind the wheel.

Lights now glowed in more of the handsome townhouses. When would Arch call back? Had Chapman and Streeter received the news? He tried reaching them at their Command Center. One ring rolled into the next. He tried their cell phones and then their home, before hanging up. Worry crept over him as he fumbled through his indexed phone numbers. How did they always manage to get out of . . . He grabbed the ringing phone - news at last!

His anticipation died quickly as Sonja's timid voice crept over the line. "I'm sorry, Mr. Harrington, but something has come up. I won't be in this morning."

What did she mean be in? She lived upstairs for Heaven's sake! He demanded an explanation.

"I'm sorry, sir, but that's all I'm permitted to say."

"What do you mean *permitted*?," he yelled. "Sonja . . . !" As the line clicked, he slammed the phone down and returned to the window. What the devil was going on? His gaze sharpened on the Guard car still parked down the street. The Colonel hadn't come out yet. His driver must be furious by now.

Turning the TV on, he returned to his phone numbers, first trying the trio at the Supreme Court, then on their cells and finally at their homes. By the time he got Maddy Falkingham's recorded drawl, his pink forehead glistened with desperation. "Chase, call me as soon . . ." The line clicked.

"Mr. Marsden?" a voice asked.

"No, Maddy, it's Seth Harrington. I was . . ."

"Mr. Harrington, I don't mean to appear rude, but we need to keep this line open. Hale Marsden should be calling from Charleston any minute."

"Hale Marsden?" he asked.

"The best criminal lawyer in South Carolina, Chase assures me. And he better be."

Criminal lawyer? "Maddy, it's really important that I speak with Chase."

"Sir, he's in no frame of mind to discuss anything and won't be until Mr. Marsden assures us he can deal with this terrible hoax. Now, if you want . . . Oh, good Lord!" she gasped. "It doesn't take those reporters long to get wind of something, does it? That man in our drive . . . Chase!"

"Reporters?" he snapped. "Maddy, what's wrong?"

"Please, we could be missing Mr. Marsden's . . . Chase, stay away from that door!"

As the line went dead, a bewildered Harrington hung up and returned to the window. Criminal lawyers, reporters — what the devil was going on? Why hadn't Chapman and Streeter called? And Arch — hadn't he confirmed the fugitives' capture? Again his restless eyes stopped on the Guard car down the street. With the rising sun, he saw the driver's companion.

"These shocking developments in the fugitive operation . . ." Glancing at the TV, Harrington saw the notoriously cool, silver-haired anchorman Lyle Darden visibly shaken as he reported, "White House sources have confirmed that Attorney General Streeter and FBI Director Chapman were taken into National Guard custody this morning pending the outcome of the fugitive operation, which GNN has learned, is quickly coming to a head in Northwood, Wisconsin. Further," Darden scanned his papers, "it's reported that Justices Falkingham, Mann and the recently nominated Lamp, have been placed under house arrest . . ."

His horrified eyes clutched the screen as Darden concluded,

"While admitting these developments, the White House will say little about the circumstances behind them. Nevertheless, it confirms that a statement will be forthcoming later in the day."

In a rage, Harrington returned to the window. How dare Longbridge undermine his authority! Did he believe he was more powerful than the Lord? Stinging with betrayal, he spotted a second Guard car on the street. No Guardsman lived in this neighborhood; these cars were here to watch him like some common criminal. Vengeance trampled over reason as he marched into the glorious fog. Longbridge must be punished to insure this never happened again. He needed a plan. Go to this foolish President, the Lord whispered. On his way out, he grabbed the ringing phone. It was a weary Leopold. "You just caught me, Arch. I'm on my way to the White House."

"I take it then you haven't heard?"

"Yes, yes, I've heard. That's the reason for my visit. We must punish Longbridge for his betrayal."

"We sir?" Leopold asked.

"The Lord and I; we're partners now. I'd planned on announcing it at the Christmas Eve service. I trust you'll keep it to yourself until then?"

"You have my word, sir."

"Well, Arch, I suppose We should get to the White House now and make an appropriate example of Longbridge."

"Sir, Longbridge isn't there. He's here in Northwood, along with Culpepper and a dozen National Guard units. Nicholas openly disregarded his cease order and will likely pay for this stupidity with a long prison sentence. He's in custody now. I was a bit smarter and slipped away while I could . . . Sparks are really flying. I just received a note from Agent Stevens, whose place on Chapman's payroll hasn't yet been discovered. But it will soon. When guys at the top start falling, it's usually too late for those below to find cover . . . Hold on, sir," he read Stevens's note, revealing that there was as much happening in Washington as in Northwood.

"Sir, in case you've missed your housekeeper, the Guard picked her up this morning. She's given a statement confirming the Georgetown meetings these past months. Apparently all this time you assumed she was upstairs minding her own business, she was taking minutes, thoroughly enough to convince Longbridge that a conspiracy existed and establish you as its central figure."

"Arch, this is grievous news!"

"To say the least, sir, and I'm afraid it gets worse." He glanced again at Stevens's note. "A Charleston lawyer has made some disturbing inquiries. His name is Marsh. Or is it . . ."

"Marsden," Harrington corrected. "She thought I was him."

"Who sir?" Leopold asked.

"Maddy, of course."

Of course. Leopold lamented Harrington's obvious madness. "Marsden is a criminal lawyer Falkingham retained to negotiate a deal. He must assume being the first to squeal will earn him immunity from prosecution. That's just like Falkingham, isn't it - gutting everyone else to save his own skin."

"Nothing can save him, Arch. He's already been judged and will be punished severely."

"But sir, you don't understand . . ." Ah, what was the use? He'd become God and perhaps had been all along. Leopold gazed mournfully at the crowd choking Main Street with the news that Longbridge was in Northwood. *Lord, forgive my wickedness,* he prayed.

"Arch, are you still there? The chest must be recovered; there's no other way to save the mission!"

"The mission's dead, sir," he sighed. "And finding the chest won't resurrect it. It'll just reveal that forty years ago an innocent man was executed for a murder three men, now sitting on the Supreme Court, were able to buy their way out of. And with this revelation will come our conspiracy to cover it up. The witnesses will be plenty — the housekeeper, Falkingham and others. Perhaps even me, if I can find the courage. It's over, sir; that's the grim bottom line."

"Arch, Judas was banished for his betrayal. Longbridge will be for his. Must you force me now to cast you out as well?"

"I cast myself out, sir."

"Our mission will survive without you, Arch. What the Lord smiles upon can never be destroyed."

"He's not smiling now, sir. If your eyes weren't so clouded by madness you could see it."

"Arch, I'm sorry we won't be together on the glorious march. I'm destined for greatness."

"You're destined for prison, sir."

"Preposterous! The Lord won't allow it. I'm with Him now."

"Then drop to your unrighteous knees and beg forgiveness for all you've done to defile His name."

Trembling with fury, Harrington slammed the phone down, his eyes glowing strangely as sight faded. The familiar study, the mission's nerve center these last weeks, was suddenly beyond his reach, replaced by a dense fog he interpreted confidently as the Cloud of Heaven. Wasn't it the Lord's whisper brushing his ear now, sweet and reassuring, even if the words were incomprehensible? The confusion would pass soon, along with the crisis and then with the lifting fog, he'd lead the flock . . .

"To repeat this latest development," Lyle Darden's voice marched gravely into the haze. "Greg Lamp, the recently confirmed Supreme Court Justice, has been found dead in his McLean home, the victim of an apparent suicide . . ."

Greg dead? No Darden, you're mistaken, Harrington thought. *Greg's needed in his new role. Shall I correct him, Lord, or is that Your province? I'm not yet clear on the rules of order. Indeed very little is clear, if I might be candid. Should We not sweep away this dense fog? Replace it with some golden light and perhaps a few harps? I've always envisioned them. And some fresh air, Lord.* He tugged at his collar. *It's so . . . difficult to breathe.* He wobbled to the window on legs that suddenly seemed encased in concrete. Sweat sprouted on his forehead as he discovered the third Guard car on the street. Yet this growing humiliation was the least of his concerns now. He needed air!

With trembling fingers, he ripped furiously at his shirt collar. Buttons popped off and still he couldn't breathe. The first jolt threw him against the window; the second one dropped him to the floor. *No more tests, Lord!* he pleaded as he squirmed helplessly. *If the others have forsaken You, have I not remained . . .* The third jolt swept the air from his chest. Furiously he clawed harder, then deeper as the fourth and fifth struck in quick succession. By the sixth, his frantic fingers had drawn streaks of blood from his flaccid, white skin. *Air . . . air . . .* his desperation screamed!

As the seventh jolt shuddered through him, his fingers slipped away from his bleeding chest and he flopped on the floor like a hooked fish. His eyes, no longer maddened, rolled back in his head. *Then I'm not to be rescued this time, Lord?* The eighth jolt struck and still he flopped. His eyes fluttered, his face twisting as the waves rocked through him; there was a purplish pall on his skin from the lack of oxygen.

How deceitful You are! he raged even as life slipped away. *To seduce me into Your service, only to wait until life's final seconds to show Your true colors; to forsake me as I writhe in helpless agony. If I'm to die, then let my last cry be one of vengeance - your vile name that I spit back like the vomit of my shame. Not the Lord, but You, Satan . . . !* The curse slipped off Harrington's lips as he died.

CHAPTER FORTY

★

Lieutenant Dean Burrows followed his companion, Lieutenant Tim Fielder, out of Craver's grocery on Route 51. They'd been summoned to Copper Harbor an hour earlier with their unit. There, the CO had briefed them on their critical mission. "The President's counting on us. Let's not disappoint him," he warned.

Burrows dropped behind the Jeep's wheel as Fielder climbed in beside him. "If Culpepper's out here, at least I'll be able to see him now. The cobwebs are finally lifting."

"They should," Fielder smiled. "That's your third cup of coffee. Your gut must be lined with lead."

Burrows glanced across the highway where men from another unit, their rifles flexed, crept over the snow-crusted wilderness. Matthew Culpepper wasn't the enemy, the CO had explained, but they couldn't be sure he understood that. So they had to be prepared for whatever his fear might throw their way.

Impatiently, Burrows wondered how long it could take fifteen Guard units to find one frostbitten Georgian in this tiny ice-hole? Yet the large force of Feds and Wisconsin troopers, their choppers working through the night, hadn't been able to. And what connection did Culpepper have to the fugitives, anyway? The CO had failed to address this question before sending them out. "What's left?" He glanced at Fielder, who was studying the map.

"Another couple hours, I'd say. That small craft shop just ahead is our next stop."

Burrows smiled. "It's only six-fifteen. That craft shop isn't open yet."

Fielder shrugged. "Then we'll just inspect the outside, check it off our list and keep moving."

Finishing his third cup, Burrows scanned the wilderness again. Jurnigan's, where the rental car had been abandoned, was a quarter-mile east; the Harborside about twice that. Although Culpepper hadn't been at the motel, it seemed logical that he was nearby. He couldn't have gotten far on foot, and if the CO was right, he was also lugging a heavy chest. Starting the engine, his eyes dusted the landscape one last time. "If I was..."

"What's the matter?" Fielder asked as he watched him suddenly frown.

He nodded at the snow tracks leading to the grocery's dumpster. "How do you explain those?"

Fielder shrugged. "Craver took the trash out?"

"There'd be another set leading back to the building. And if you'll notice," he nodded. "They don't begin there, anyway. They come out of the trees. Whoever came down to the dumpster is still here."

A lump crept up Fielder's throat as he grabbed his rifle and followed Burrows over to the dumpster.

"All right, come on out!" Burrows ordered. "Hands first and very slowly!" Rifles aimed, they waited, but the dumpster lid didn't move. "Look, you have to come out. We're not going anywhere."

Another minute crept by. "What now?" Fielder whispered.

More information, he decided. "I'm Lieutenant Burrows, and this here is Lieutenant Fielder. We're National Guard officers ordered to Copper Harbor to apprehend a subject named Matthew Culpepper. If you're him, you should know the President is in Northwood waiting to speak with you."

Another minute passed. Fielder said, "He's not coming out."

Still, Burrows tried one last time to draw the subject out peacefully. "Look, I have no idea why those Federal agents are looking for you. But if you are Culpepper, we've just been instructed to take you to the President and your father, who's with him."

Slowly, the lid opened and a young man emerged, his blanched, bloodless face frozen beyond expression. Seeing their rifles, his hands rose quickly.

"Are you Matthew Culpepper?" Burrows asked.

When he nodded, they dropped their rifles and came over to help him out of the dumpster.

"Can you... give me a hand... with something?" Matt's teeth chattered fiercely. Sinking back inside the dumpster, he quickly popped back up with the heavy chest.

The next minutes passed in a fog as Matt was given hot coffee and flown to Northwood with his precious cargo. Travis's call was received en route. "Son, how are you?" he asked.

Glancing down at the gray lake rushing past, he shouted over the chopper's thunder, "Cold! Any word yet on Tyler and Mayson?"

"No, but there should be soon. Listen son, take care of that chest."

"That's a big ten-four!"

"Ten-four my butt!" Travis snorted. "Just get it back here."

Minutes later, the chopper arrived at the Northwood Sheriff's Office. Waiting Guardsmen held the crowd back as Matt, clutching the chest, was escorted inside and taken by elevator to the top floor, where a dozen Feds waited to sweep him down to the large, corner office. A relieved Travis rushed forward to embrace him. "Damnit son, you scared the hell out of me!" he said.

"What else is new?" Matt winked at the solemn faces around him. "Still no word on Tyler and Mayson?"

President Longbridge, towering like Abe Lincoln above his advisers, fielded the question. "The last report has them in the forest just east of here. We should locate them soon." Smiling wearily, he came forward to shake Matt's hand. "We're all deeply grateful for the courage you've shown. Now let's put that chest on the table and see what we're dealing with."

As the others gathered around, Longbridge found his stocky aide. "Garrison, why don't you take down my description of the items? I'll have to report our discovery to the nation later this afternoon, and I have no intention of examining this shameful chest again."

As Garrison dropped at the table, his eyes focused not on the chest but the tall, grim-faced man looming over it. Travis, standing nearby, now fully understood and appreciated that no President before Thomas Longbridge had possessed a stronger obedience to justice or been more deeply burdened by a nation's tragedy. If committing an error in judgment by trusting men like Harrington and his disciples, Longbridge also had the courage to admit it and accept responsibility for the consequences that followed. He'd poignantly demonstrated this in the last few hours.

Seconds after leaving Dulles, he'd emptied Air Force One's cabin and began his painful confession. "Travis, my grief is deepened by the stance I took against you in that meeting. You came to me bearing the hard truth, just as I'd always asked of you, and yet to preserve my reputation for sound judgment, I shut my eyes." He'd smiled ruefully. "*Sound judgment.* If only I'd known how little there was to protect."

"Sir, you're being much too hard on yourself," Travis had replied. "You'll recall it was five against three at that meeting. You can't fault yourself for going with the majority. After all, this is a democracy."

"Poppycock!" Longbridge had rejoined. "That majority was composed of evil-minded men - the same ones responsible for this mess we're forced to clean up now. What happened at that meeting had nothing to do with democracy. It was a test of conscience and I'm afraid I failed miserably."

After the last difficult weeks, Travis had suddenly found himself in the role of alter-conscience for the President of the United States. "Sir," he said, "you had no reason to believe the men you placed on the court, each with exemplary records, were also murderers. Were you to suspect it because my friend's son or I said so? Wasn't it more reasonable to believe your Attorney General and FBI Director, who said it wasn't so?"

"No, Travis, my choice wasn't reasonable at all," Longbridge replied. "Whatever your motive, you wouldn't have been at that meeting to place your honor on the table unless convinced you were right. I knew it then, as I do now. But driven by self-interest, I allowed myself to be seduced by the story that served it most effectively - a clever cover up of an ancient crime that brings us now to Lake Superior on this cold morning."

"Brings us because you acted with such swift resolution," Travis pointed out. "The measures taken in the last hours are both warranted and appropriate. But they're also aggressive, even reckless some might say, given that they're based on unproven accusations."

Longbridge had sighed heavily. "Whatever inconvenience my measures cause are nothing compared to the punishment these men will face once their crimes have been exposed."

"How can you be certain they will be, sir? Just because you've suspended the operation doesn't mean those young people are out of danger. I assure you, this Agent Nicholas fears that chest far more than any punishment he might face for violating your order."

"Matt will be found with the chest and safely returned to his family," Longbridge vowed.

"Which warms me, sir, but hardly relieves my fear; and the chest's significance, despite Matt's assurances, hasn't been confirmed."

Longbridge frowned. "Travis, why must you dance around that blasted chest as if either of us questioned its ugly truth? I don't need a sugar-coated analysis; I need a friend. And perhaps some divine inspiration if the Lord sees fit, to get me through what I'm certain will be the toughest day of my Presidency."

Few words had been exchanged after that as they landed at the Duluth airport and were flown by chopper to Northwood.

Within minutes of arriving, President Longbridge had taken over the County building's top floor and, learning of Nicholas's flagrant disregard of the cease order, immediately placed him and four subordinates in custody. And while Nicholas had proven unyielding to the following interrogation, the others had not. By the time news of Matt's rescue was received, ten more agents had been placed in custody and there seemed little doubt that others would be, as well.

The minutes before Matt's arrival had brought two dramatic developments - the first in a call from a Charleston lawyer named Marsden; the second, from Captain Rimstead in D. C. Hanging up with Rimstead, a devastated Longbridge had pulled Travis into the adjoining conference room. "I'm glad our burden has been lightened by Matt's rescue, because the one I share with you now is the heaviest imaginable," he said. "Seth Harrington has masterminded this conspiracy right under my nose. It's caused the slaughter of numerous people for whom I'm equally accountable - a catastrophic blow that, spread over a lifetime, would challenge any man's conscience. Yet it's clear that I'm to receive its full force on this one tragic day."

"Sir," Travis replied, "you've been ignorant of this conspiracy from the beginning; and you were ignorant through no fault of your own. By hiding their activities, the conspirators not only prove your innocence but also their belief that you'd never condone them."

The President studied him sadly. "Believe me, Travis, your words resonate sweetly in my ears. But the fact remains that I put these men in their powerful positions. I cloaked them with the authority they needed to conduct their criminal enterprise. This makes me just as guilty."

"Of what, sir?" Travis asked. "Trusting the same man that half this country's citizens donate their savings to every Sunday? How can people possibly fault you?"

Longbridge's aide, Garrison, had then rushed in to report Matt's arrival.

"So what will you do?" Travis asked.

Longbridge studied him solemnly. "Let's first see the chest's contents, shall we?"

A grave silence settled over the room as Longbridge removed the chest's first article: a large gray envelope. Inside were brittle, yellowed documents, which he carefully examined. "These are student records taken from Tennessee State University's archives. Collectively, they establish that three young men graced the TSU campus as first-year law students during the fall term of 1953 and spring term of 1954. Namely, Gregory Reynolds Lamp of Westchester, New York; Chase Beaufort Falkingham of Charleston, South Carolina; and Thomas Cartwright Mann of Des Moines, Iowa.

"Please note," he nodded at his frantically writing scribe, "that the young men did not complete the spring term, but left the university abruptly before their final exams."

Opening a second envelope, he examined the documents inside. "We have here financial records documenting the transfers of large sums of money over a twenty-year period, totaling several million dollars beginning in May 1954 and ending in June 1974. May 1954 is, of course, the same month Miss Sandover was murdered. The payments, in identical sums, come from three accounts: the first, with Gliebman and Sons, is registered to Ronald L. Lamp,

Westchester, New York; the second, First Capital Investments of Des Moines, Iowa, to Carson B. Mann; and the third, New York Trust Company, to Charles Moss Falkingham, III, of Charleston, South Carolina. And not to leave you in suspense, all payments found their way into the same Wall Street account owned by Jasper T. Crenshaw." Slipping the records back in the envelope, he glanced at his busy aide. "Do you need anything repeated?"

"I believe I have it all," Garrison said as he jotted furiously.

"Then you're a master scribe, indeed." Longbridge now removed a package from the chest. Inside was a rumpled white shirt, which he held up for inspection. Forty years had left it brittle but preserved the apparent bloodstains on the collar. He squinted at the pocket's blue-stitched monogram, "GRL. Or should I say, Gregory Reynolds Lamp."

"Sir, there's an envelope with it," Matt added.

"Oh yes." Longbridge grabbed it, then read the memo inside, typed under the logo of the Pine County Sheriff's Department: " *'May 4, 1954: Enclosed, one white oxford shirt bearing the monogram GRL and apparent bloodstains on the collar; discovered this a.m. in trash bin behind the Boone Ridge Apartments. Suspect, Gregory Reynolds Lamp leases Apartment #4, with suspects Mann and Falkingham. Lab analysis ordered.'* The author's initials JTC belong to Jasper T. Crenshaw, I feel safe in saying."

Travis detected Longbridge's hand trembling as he struggled to return the memo to the envelope. "Sir, there's no reason you need to conduct this exercise yourself," he offered. "I'd be happy to inventory the remaining items."

Longbridge smiled as he answered, "I admit this isn't one of my more enjoyable duties. However, when I took the oath of office, I swore to execute them all, good and bad, and that's precisely what I intend to do."

"Sir, responsibilities aren't just good and bad. They can also be delegated."

"Travis, I can't ask a subordinate to do something I'm not comfortable with myself. And if ever there was a task to illustrate my point, it's this one. Now please, enough of your kindness."

Longbridge was both humiliated and exhausted by his ordeal. Yet its revelations were still unfolding, and if he was tired now, how much more would he be later when facing the nation he'd so miserably failed? All his grievous mistakes had been spawned while under the spell of a demonic Rasputin whose judgment he'd allowed to replace his own. If this was the explanation, it certainly wasn't the excuse. There could be none. As President of the United States, he'd committed an unpardonable blunder; he'd be fully accountable to the nation and then ask for nothing more than his dear wife's embrace.

Rummaging through the chest, he pulled out a small box containing dirt, several brittle cigarette butts and another memo, which he now read for the record: " *'May 7, 1954: Exhibit discovered last p.m. at the Sandover exhumation site which, as reflected in the primary report, is within fifty feet of the TSU maintenance shed. The Exhibit consists of five cigarette butts with unusual black-and-gold-ringed filters identified this a.m. as one Dunhill, an imported brand not sold in this County. Two witnesses, whose statements have been obtained, establish the brand as that smoked by the suspect, Falkingham.'*

"I knew I'd seen those strange cigarettes," Longbridge said sadly. "In the nervous fingers of our chain-smoking Chief Justice."

Removing another large envelope, he impatiently tore the seal. Minutes crept by as he appraised the documents inside. At the table, Garrison used this time to flip through his accumulation of notes.

Finally Longbridge was ready with his next assessment. "We have here the purloined clinic records of a first year law student, admitted for treatment of lacerations around the right eye claimed to have been sustained when falling into a thorn bush while hiking the day before. The time of admission is 7:45 a.m., May 5, 1954, the student's name, Gregory R. Lamp." Pausing at the sudden rumble, he observed mournfully, "If nothing else, we now at least know how our newest Justice acquired those half-moon scars around his eye.

"However if he deceived the TSU clinic, he didn't fool the late sheriff." Longbridge flipped to the next document. "The Pine County Coroner, Dr. Harold Stone, who we can assume was on Crenshaw's payroll, reports that blood samples taken from the victim's fingernails match perfectly those from Lamp's shirt, which he was wearing the night of the murder. Miss Sandover must've clawed his face in a futile effort to save her life."

Briskly he summarized the next records, consisting of statements given by Wallace Vernon and George Elroy, two TSU employees who'd worked with Norris. Describing him as a hard worker and devoted family man, each claimed to have seen Miss Sandover leave Luke's Tavern on the night of the murder, accompanied by three white males identified as both TSU students and regular Tavern patrons. Elroy also stated he spotted them again later parked on an isolated mountain road. "This man knew enough that Crenshaw felt compelled to buy his silence," Longbridge mused.

Reviewing the next records, he set them quietly on the table. "For Garrison's sake, as well as our own, these are simply identified as the signed murder confessions of three understandably terrified law students who found themselves cornered by a crafty Tennessee sheriff."

He opened the last envelope, which contained a letter dated July 5, 1954, addressed to Doreen Crenshaw Markham, Route 6, Snow Peak, Minnesota. "The sheriff's sister," he explained, as he began reading the letter for his audience:

" *Dear Doddy,*

As the person I trusted most in this world, I've delivered this chest into your safe hands and pray with my admittedly unworthy soul it won't prove a heavier burden than you can bear. I have faith you'll honor my instructions, expressed moments ago in our call. Because of this, you won't discover the chest's contents until after what I hope proves a long, fulfilling life. And since you're now reading this, you know that I'm gone and the time has come to deliver the chest to the Tennessee governor, whoever that man happens to be. That being said, here's my confession, Doddy, no doubt already ringing in your ears - if you've examined the chest which represents both my salvation in this life and, if the Good Book is right, my burning torment in the next.

  That girl's murder has made me Pine County's richest man, and when I'm done maybe Tennessee's. Millions, I'm talking about, that'll triple if that New York investment banker knows half what he claims. Because of that wealth, I've been able to leave you a large bequest for assuming the chest's burden. I just executed my new will yesterday and can't imagine ever needing another one, unless some day the guilt over that nigger starts rubbing at my craw. That ain't likely, however.

His name's Edgar Norris, the one to be tried for the white girl's murder over at the university; and if I could prevent his suffering, I would. I ain't never intentionally hurt a soul, Doddy, but sometimes it can't be helped. There must be a killer to convict just as there's a victim to bury. And folks at the university is convinced he done it anyway. A dozen witnesses swear he forced his attentions on the girl. And the dumb nigger ain't got no alibi. Claims he was fishing by 'hisself' the night of the murder. I reckon he ain't smart enough to have his coon friends swear to it.

We dug the girl up behind the maintenance shed where he works. Prosecutor Arlen even thinks he can prove she was put in the ground by the nigger's own shovel. With such accommodating circumstances, and the dollars invested to keep a few mouths shut, I've handed Arlen a dandy case.

I'll end this epistle by mentioning them three boys who, after a good drilling, admitted killing the girl. And their rich daddies, I learned after a few discreet calls, were quite willing to meet my stiff terms for their freedom. At the same time, however, I figger where there's wealth, there's power to go with it - power them boys' daddies wouldn't hesitate to use, considering their desperation. And yet despite all them payments, I still have the one thing they want most badly — that damn chest. And they have no assurances I won't use it. Nothing, that is, except my powerful greed. Yet they also know that if they don't meet my demands, their boys'll go to prison, maybe even the chair. So they'll pay: the Falkinghams, Lamps and Manns, and be reminded with each payment that if they had the chest, there wouldn't be another one.

Knowing the risks, Doddy, I did what every smart businessman does. I took out an insurance policy that'll surely bring me peace of mind in the years ahead. First, I told them families that the chest was in a place they'd never find. Second, that as long as I remained free of misfortune, the chest would remain where it is and that nobody'd be the worse for it. How things shaked out, I said, was entirely up to them. Lord willing, things'll work out just fine. But either way, I want to express my appreciation now and pray that my estate bequest fairly compensates you for carrying the burden of this chest. I pray also that you'll forgive me for whatever terrible sins you think I've committed.

My fingers are cramping so I best get to the point, which is this: the time's come to cash in my insurance policy and turn the chest over to the

Tennessee governor. Then let the chips fall where they may. I promised them boys' families only that their money would buy freedom equal to my life and no matter when or how it ended, they were on their own after that. That time's come, Doddy."

Gravely, Longbridge now looked up. "This hellish tale's author affectionately pens himself *Your loving brother, Jasper Crenshaw.* I suppose we should at least be grateful that Doddy, institutionalized with Alzheimer's, has been spared the pain of her brother's confession."

He returned the letter and the other items to the chest. "The Special Prosecutor I appoint will find the chest in the precise condition we did. I hope he has a stronger stomach." He smiled at his weary scribe. "Garrison, I trust you've captured the gist of my lengthy inventory?"

"Yes sir," the aide answered, nodding over his notes.

"Good. Then after a short break, put it into a coherent form for my afternoon address to the nation."

"Will we broadcast from here?" Garrison asked. "If so, arrangements must be made."

"We'll broadcast from Washington. I'd like the comfort of familiar surroundings."

"Are we shooting for a specific time, sir?"

"I can't leave until the fugitives are rescued. I will, however, the moment they are. Wisconsin winters are much too cold for my delicate Texas bones."

"I'll alert the crew," Garrison said, then grabbed the flashing phone. His face quickly paled. "I see. No, it's best I tell him."

An agent near the door now took a courier's message and gave it to Longbridge, who read it quickly. "Weather conditions have delayed efforts to locate the fugitives, but Guard units are now out in full force. It shouldn't be much longer."

Grim-faced, Garrison reported, "Sir, Greg Lamp has committed suicide. Apparently he just went into his study and put a gun to his head."

Travis watched Longbridge slump with the blow. Had there been a darker day for any President?

"I'm afraid that's not all, sir," Garrison continued. "Seth Harrington's body was just discovered in the Lakeland home.

A heart attack, presumably." He grabbed the phone now as it flashed again. "I see . . . No, there's no reason to bring him here. Take him where he wants to go . . . Yes I'm sure you've done everything possible. And please convey our deepest concerns."

Hanging up, Garrison explained, "The fugitives have been rescued. Waddill appears in excellent shape, but Corelli . . ." He grimly nodded at the conference room. "Let's discuss it in there."

CHAPTER FORTY-ONE

★

Mayson's fever had climbed through the night. She slept one minute, mumbled incoherently the next. Meanwhile, their protective canopy had been reduced to rubble by the choppers' random machine gun fire that had begun at dawn. But if the shredded canopy no longer took the bite from the icy wind, at least it hid them from the choppers. But for how much longer? The spraying bullets were certain to reach them sooner or later.

Their chilled, cramped quarters had become unbearable, the parapet's jags digging into his bones. Movement was impossible, except for occasional glimpses at the hovering choppers that were never absent from the sky for very long.

The gray morning had by now fully emerged over the lake. Cradled in his arm, Mayson squirmed again for space that didn't exist. Her flushed face crumpling with tears, she muttered, "Afraid..."

"Afraid of what, Mayson?" he asked. "What are you afraid of?"

"Please... don't leave!"

He kissed her damp cheek. "No, I won't leave."

His soft singing soon drifted into the desperate silence. *"Non dimenticar means don't forget you are..."* As one verse rolled into the next, she began to calm down. Soon the world beyond their rocky parapet vanished, and he drifted into a wordless void, where thoughts were felt more than defined, sensed more than shaped, one blending into the next.

As the silence deepened, he slipped farther into this welcome void, but not so deep that a voice didn't reach him. *Don't be seduced... the world's often the most quiet before the storm.* If one was promised, its first winds arrived as gentle whispers above the rocks. Were their pursuers about to try a dangerous descent?

As he waited, their muttering was drowned out by the sky's rising thunder. Quickly, the rocks clattered with gunfire. The first chopper reached them, its thundering breath sweeping away bits of the canopy, its gunfire chewing into the rocks. As it moved on, the second arrived to shred more of the canopy, and splatter hot shells into the parapet.

Mayson's eyes had yet to flutter in protest against this latest assault. He brushed the debris from her face and hair, wondering when they would react again. He had just seconds to wonder as the next chopper approached. Through slits in the shredded canopy, he watched it splatter the rocks, without logic or mercy, as it glided along the coast. As the next one drew within range, it stopped suddenly and streaked away. The others quickly followed as he watched them vanish into the northern sky. What was going on? Had they run out of ammo?

His eyes lifted to the rustle above, then returned to the lake where the cutters had also begun to retreat. *Hang on*, he thought as he kissed her burning forehead. *Maybe God has a miracle for us, after all.* The clouds drifted quietly as he began to believe that the rocks had been assaulted for the last time. Was it possible that Longbridge wasn't part of the conspiracy? That he had the character, once confronted with the evidence, to admit that the men he'd placed in power were cold-blooded killers? Yet the sky remained quiet. Maybe, just maybe . . . Then the sky again trembled and, forming a shield over Mayson, Tyler waited for the next assault. But it didn't come. Peering out, he watched four choppers emerge from the northern clouds. Not black but green ones, forming a gliding procession along the coast. What did this mean? Four green choppers that didn't spit fire or pummel the rocks? Slowly he realized they were being rescued.

Clawing at the rubble, he lifted himself above the parapet and waved furiously. "Over here!" he shouted. The closest chopper turned and started towards him. Quickly, the others followed.

A harness was lowered as the canopy's last bits swirled at his feet. Dropping into the basin, he threaded Mayson into the harness, then himself. As the cable was lowered, he attached it to the harness, then offered a thumbs up. Slowly they began rising into the chilled morning sky.

Fatigue-clad Guardsmen swarmed as the chopper touched down on the precipice minutes later. Struggling with the harness, Tyler found himself surrounded by them. "Here sir, let me help," one said, and quickly took over.

"Move back!" A shout arose, as medics pushed through with a stretcher and lifted a wilted Mayson from the cockpit.

As Tyler climbed out, a small, wiry officer pushed forward. "Welcome home, son. I'm Colonel Morefield."

A second officer, tall and silver-haired, appeared next. "I'm Dr. Waters," he introduced himself, then glanced at the medic bent over Mayson. "Sergeant?"

"I'm not getting much of a pulse, sir. And her fever's off the chart."

Waters knelt to examine her. "Captain Vincent!" he yelled. His eyes searched for a man in the crowd. "Get your rig ready; we have to move!"

"A chopper?" Morefield asked, puzzled. "The ambulance can have her . . ."

"There's no time for that. Sergeant, alert Duluth Memorial that we're on our way."

Mayson's feverish muttering had stopped, her face, stone-like, as the stretcher was lifted. "How long will it take to get to Duluth?" Tyler asked.

"A half hour," Waters replied. "But you're not going, I'm afraid. There's no room on the chopper. I'll get you a report as soon as possible."

"Our orders are to take you to Northwood, anyway," Morefield explained. "The President's most anxious to see you."

Tyler watched the medics' swift, capable motions as they placed Mayson in the chopper. The last thing she needed now was a power struggle to delay her medical treatment. "Go ahead," he said. "I'll catch my own ride."

He watched the chopper streak west across the gray sky. She'd be frightened to wake and not find him. Then there'd be hell to pay. It wouldn't be pretty.

The troops buzzed restlessly as Morefield placed a call on his field phone. "I have a most urgent report for the President," he explained. "Oh . . . Well, of course, Mr. Garrison, I can tell you just as well. I'm happy to report the fugitives have been rescued. Mr. Waddill, who is with me now, appears in excellent shape. Miss Corelli's condition, however, is critical. She's been flown to

Duluth for emergency treatment. Because of this, Mr. Waddill wants to skip the Northwood meeting and fly there, too. Naturally this is out of the question since . . . Yes, of course; immediately. And thank you, Mr. Garrison," he nodded emphatically. "The moment we hear. You have my word."

Tyler watched him hang up. "So what's the verdict?" he asked.

"That was the President's aide. He said that since your safety has been confirmed, we should skip the Northwood meeting and fly you directly to Duluth."

"He's one damn fine President," Tyler said. "Hell, I might even vote for him next time."

Minutes later, he strapped himself into the cockpit and watched the snow-glazed earth quickly sink beneath him. Soon, the coastline rushed past as he contemplated the ominous possibilities waiting in Duluth. Turning to the pilot, he shouted, "How much farther?"

The man's shaded eyes turned from the glass. "Ten minutes, tops. Don't worry," he smiled. "I'll set you on that hospital just like a butterfly." His fluttering hand simulated the landing.

"Were you part of the rescue effort?" Tyler asked.

"The standby craft. Lannie Benson," he said as he offered his hand.

"You're a helluva pilot, Lannie. Captain, I bet?"

"Lieutenant. And you're a chopper expert?"

"The way I've been ducking them lately, I feel like one."

A large, granite cluster soon rose out the window. *Duluth.* His stomach knotted. "Hold on to your shorts!" Lannie shouted as the chopper swooped, shimmied, then fluttered onto the hospital roof, where three administrators waited. Crawling out, Tyler shook Lannie's hand. "Thanks for everything, man," he said.

"No sweat. And listen; Corelli will be fine. She wouldn't have made it this far, unless she was tough as nails." Offering a crisp salute, he streaked back across the sky.

The next minutes were a blur of disjointed voices and endless gray halls. "Miss Corelli's condition stabilized quickly," a female administrator named Darcy explained. "Dr. Waters's IVs are working."

"There aren't many infections resistant to those new antibiotics," Jerry, a tall male administrator added as they turned into the next hall.

"Powerful stuff," echoed Bruce, a shorter, heavier male.

"The bottom line," Darcy said, "is that she has responded well to treatment and her fever is under control. Dr. Claiborne wouldn't have operated, otherwise."

"Then Mayson's in surgery?" he asked.

"Correct," Bruce nodded, as they boarded the elevator.

"What type of infection does she have?"

"Staph . . . and possibly gangrene," Bruce replied.

Darcy frowned. "Gangrene wasn't part of Dr. Claiborne's diagnosis."

The very word shivered Tyler's spine. "What exactly did he say about gangrene?" he asked.

"She," Darcy corrected. "Aggie's head of our Orthopedic Surgery Department. And she only said gangrene was a *suspicion*."

"Which means very little," Jerry added as they exited the elevator and started down another hall. "Gangrene is always a suspicion in cases like this."

"Like what?"

"High fever, swelling, skin discoloration."

"Wouldn't gangrene mean an amputation?" Tyler asked.

"Possibly," Bruce said.

"But not necessarily," Jerry pointed out.

Darcy was the first to reach the window at the end of the hall. "Oh no!" she cried.

Tyler saw the mob scene below — TV vans, camera crews and a curious crowd that had taken over the hospital parking lot. "How'd they pick up our scent so quickly?"

"Because they're wolves!" she snapped. "The President's aide requested that no statements be made until the White House briefing later today. That includes you, obviously."

"I have no intention of talking to those bastards. How long does Dr. Claiborne expect the surgery to take?"

"She didn't say. But it's already been an hour."

Tyler's stomach churned. Was Mayson's leg being amputated

at this very moment?

"Miss Corelli's been assigned this corner room," Bruce said. "Why not settle in until she returns? We'll see that Dr. Claiborne speaks with you as soon as possible."

"Our procedures naturally require some paperwork," Darcy added. "Does Miss Corelli have any family we should contact?"

"Whatever's needed, I'll take care of personally."

With his guarantee sufficient, they left as he watched the chaos grow below. Then, wearily, he drifted into the empty room, collapsing in the chair. Mayson's surgery was into its second hour. Would she return minus a leg? How would that affect his feelings? It wouldn't. He'd welcome her in any condition except one. He couldn't have her dead.

His dreams soon swept him off to a place with rolling meadows and tall oaks where the James lapped gently to shore and the sky was silky blue, like the robes of heaven. Castlewood, the land of his childhood — happy, beautiful and enduring. Yet how fragile it had proven to be when just one piece was ripped away, and the rest came tumbling down. What remained had been a dark, frightening place, where ghosts haunted the days as much as the nights. And unable to . . . His eyes flew open when he remembered the call.

Jumping up, Tyler grabbed the phone and quickly dialed. Schuyler answered on the second ring. "Dad, it's me. We were rescued this morning," he said.

"Thank God!" Schuyler gasped. "Travis called. And we've followed the reports. But not until hearing your voice . . . Hell, the point is, you're safe, just like I told your mother and sister you would be. So what's Mayson's situation?"

"I expect her back from surgery any minute."

"Well, let us know the moment you hear. Oh, and two things before I forget: Travis and Matt are stopping by the hospital. Honestly son, we're at a loss over how to thank them."

"We'll find a way, Dad. Good friends always do. Now what's the other thing?"

"Jock's preparing the J.R. Eagle for a five p.m. departure. We should arrive in Duluth by eight."

"Dad . . ."

"All right, Hunter Leigh . . . Yes, he's fine!"

"Dad, please . . ."

"Listen son, I've got a real tug-of-war going here with the phone. Your mother . . ."

"Dad, wait. Mayson won't be up to company after the surgery. I appreciate your willingness to come, but it's just not a good time."

"I see. All right, then. I'll explain it to the family."

"But do you understand?"

"I'm beginning to, I think."

A lump crept up his throat. "Dad, I'm ready to come home. I think I have been for a while. Just let me do it my way. After the surgery, when Mayson's well enough to travel." He remembered something else now. "Dad, can you give me Peter Hamilton's number?"

Puzzled, Schuyler asked, "You've just been rescued and the first thing you want to do is call your broker?"

"I have to repay a small debt."

"How small?"

"Five-hundred thousand should take care of it."

Giving him Hamilton's number, Schuyler added, "Son, I know we're rich, but half a million dollars isn't peanuts."

"No," he said, envisioning Lauren's smile. "It's a horse farm."

"Sweetheart!" Hunter Leigh shrilled. "Why has it taken you so long to call?" In rapid-fire succession, her questions demanded every detail about Mayson and her relationship with Tyler. She wore down finally with regrets over the postponed reunion.

"Assuming the surgery goes well, Mother, we'll be home by Christmas," he promised. "I can't wait to see Castlewood." The line deepened with her longest silence of record, until he was forced to ask, "Mother, are you still there?"

"I was just thinking what a switch this is, you wanting to come home."

"Things have changed."

"You've changed, Sweetheart. I can hear it in your voice. I think I love Mayson already . . ."

"Tiles, I can't believe it!" Stafford shrieked. "But did I hear right? We're not flying to Duluth?"

THE LONGBRIDGE DECISION

"Not today. Mayson's in surgery."

After Stafford came Parker, then Bo and Anne Randolph. His patience wore thinner with each handoff. When he could finally hang up, his anxious eyes returned to the empty bed. The surgery was now into its third hour. Had something gone wrong? He inquired at the nurses' station, but received only sympathetic smiles and assurances he'd know as soon as they knew.

Returning to the room, the air seemed thinner, the walls, grayer, than when he'd left. Time crawled as he gazed helplessly at frigid, snow-mantled Duluth outside. Mayson remained in surgery, with one leg or . . . Turning as the floor squeaked, he found a small woman in green hospital fatigues. Her soft face was delicately featured, dark curls fringing her surgical cap. "Dr. Claiborne?" Tyler asked.

"Mr. Waddill?" she answered. When Tyler nodded, she said, "The surgery went well. Miss Corelli should be out of recovery any minute."

Relief rushed over him. "Then she . . . I mean you didn't have to . . ."

"No," she smiled. "We didn't amputate her leg. A displaced pin was responsible for the staph infection. We simply removed the infected tissue, then inserted a new pin, which I assure you will do just fine. Still, she'll need to be followed closely to insure a satisfactory healing process. Compound fractures are bad enough, but when complications occur, recovery often becomes a lengthy ordeal that doesn't end when the cast comes off."

"I know it's premature, but I want to get Mayson home for Christmas, if this doesn't conflict with your experienced medical opinion."

"That experienced medical opinion will require some details first."

"Such as?"

"Where home is. When you'll leave. How you'll be traveling. Who'll be treating her. Little things like that."

"The James River Eagle will fly us to my family's Virginia home on Saturday."

"What's a James River Eagle?"

"My family's jet."

"Oh yes, how stupid of me," she smiled. "Naturally you'd have your own jet. And resident orthopedic surgeon, I suppose."

"Not resident exactly. Moss lives in Surry."

"Moss?"

"Dr. Moss Sternfield. He'll treat Mayson — and quite capably, too, if he knows what's good for him."

"Then you find intimidation an effective means for insuring a doctor's satisfactory performance?"

He shrugged. "I wouldn't call possession of an embarrassing childhood secret intimidation, exactly."

She smiled. "I suppose I shouldn't ask what this secret is. But I do need to know if Moss is an orthopedic surgeon."

"Board certified. With his own clinic in Surry."

She studied him thoughtfully, then nodded. "All right. I'll release Miss Corelli Saturday morning, if the following conditions are met: First, I'm convinced she's well enough to travel. Second, I receive confirmation of Dr. Sternfield's qualifications. Third, he accepts her as a patient. And fourth, she continues to be in your care during treatment. If you're agreeable, I suppose we have a deal."

"We do indeed." He kissed her hand gratefully. "One that leaves me forever in your debt."

"Don't be silly," she mumbled, her cheeks glowing red as she drifted backwards from the room. "You really should be more careful with that smile of yours. Hasn't anyone told you?"

"What? That it's dangerous?"

"Lethal," she said as she whisked off.

A heavily sedated Mayson was soon wheeled in. Transferring her to the bed, the two orderlies left the nurse to hook up the IVs and monitor. Before leaving, she instructed him on use of the emergency call device.

"And the monitor?" he nodded. "What does it measure?"

"Her vital signs. And don't worry about waking her. She'll sleep like a baby, at least until the medication wears off. When it does, just buzz me like I showed you."

"She'll want a shampoo in the morning," Tyler said. "L'Oreal. She won't put anything else in her hair. And a conditioner, too."

He smiled. "Some things you don't forget after being cooped up with a person for two months."

And some, because you care so much, she thought. "The L'Oreal won't be a problem." She replied. "Can I have a cot brought in for you?"

"The chair's fine," he said. "But thanks, Ginny."

As she left, he pressed his palm to Mayson's forehead. It was warm, but no longer burning. His eyes then trailed the powerful antibiotic along the snaking IV into her arm. He imagined it flowing through her veins, killing the last vestiges of an infection that hours ago had imprisoned her inside her restless nightmares.

A knock soon came at the door. As Travis and Matt entered, he rose, grinning, to meet them. Tall and rangy, each possessed the Culpeppers' gray-blue eyes and poker faces, their age difference defined by Travis's extra baggage and silver hair.

Travis's concern faded with a quick inspection. Other than the strain around his eyes and a haggard appearance that could be fixed with fresh clothes and a good night's sleep, the boy seemed as fit as a fiddle. "Damnit, son, don't ever do anything crazy like that again, unless you want a few strokes on your conscience," he scolded.

"Thanks for saving my reckless life, sir" Tyler said, embracing him warmly. "I'll try living it a little safer from now on."

Travis watched him quickly wrap Matt in a big bear hug. "Have you talked to your parents yet?"

He nodded. "They appreciated your call, as I do."

Travis smiled. "It was refreshing to hear that sparkle in Hunter Leigh's voice again."

"So where's my reward?" Matt asked. "I assume it's something big, seeing as I've risked my priceless ass to save your worthless one."

"Free legal work for your real estate agency."

"You don't practice in Georgia, bonehead."

"I said free, dickweed — nothing about who'd be doing it."

"Well, how about doing something for the human race," he said, his nose wrinkling. "Like washing off that stench you carried in from the woods?"

"I admit I need a shower," Tyler nodded. "But don't pretend I smell half as bad as you did that first summer at Camp Warwick. Christ, Matt, you didn't change your underwear for two weeks!"

"I have one better," Travis laughed. "Ask him where he spent last night."

"Where?" Tyler pounced.

"In some goddamned stinking trash bin," Matt growled. "Why? To save your ungrateful ass."

Travis beamed. They'd been going at each other like this forever. Until that dark November morning when the passion had died in Tyler's eyes. And now it was back, he realized, as his gaze settled on the young woman in the bed. If it wasn't Kara Randolph, wasn't Mayson perhaps the only one who could take her place?

Matt now saw her as well. "Damn, she's beautiful!" he said.

Indeed, Travis studied her closely. Held captive by a web of medical tubes, she nevertheless slept peacefully, her casted leg like a camel's hump beneath the sheets. Her face was delicate, her skin smooth, the hue of a pink rose, her fluffed hair, a rich brown, and he imagined her eyes just as dark, or darker. More than beautiful, she was breathtaking.

"Who's that actress?" Matt asked. "Mom would know."

"Audrey Hepburn," Travis said. And indeed, the resemblance was amazing.

Matt said, "Mayson's like . . ."

"Kara?" Tyler smiled. "Hell, no. They're as different as night and day."

Maybe, Matt thought as his eyes connected with Travis's. But if Tyler's new glow was any indication, in one way they were identical: each woman possessed the rare potion capable of restoring life to his fragile soul.

From Mayson, their conversation drifted to Christmas, fond reflections, then finally, the morning's developments. Matt sighed. "Watching Longbridge sort through that chest made me sorry to have been the one to find it. There was such deep pain in his voice as he inventoried the contents, as if each item represented a shovel-full of dirt that wasn't just burying those judges, but his Presidency, as well."

Travis checked his watch. "It's time for Longbridge's broadcast. Can we?" He nodded at the overhead TV.

"She's sleeping like a log," Tyler said. He turned it to GNN as anchorman Lyle Darden and Forest Steinman, a popular political analyst, engaged in last-minute speculation over the Longbridge address. "Lamp shot himself?" he gasped.

"And Harrington died of a heart attack," Matt added.

"Falkingham's already pressing for a deal," Travis explained. "Singing about all he knows might just be enough to keep him out of prison."

The broadcast shifted to the Oval Office, where a somber Longbridge sat at his desk. Pale and shaken, his eyes were nevertheless clear, his voice resolute, as he began, "My fellow Americans, it is with a heavy heart that I come to you this afternoon. Much of what I have to say you've no doubt heard by now. But as your President, it's my duty to confirm these developments, and explain how they'll be addressed by your government."

He reported the astonishing events that had begun early that morning. No details were spared, nor the depth of his indignation and sense of responsibility.

Three Supreme Court appointments — two, now targets of a criminal investigation, the third having taken his own life that morning. Two other appointments — the FBI Director and Attorney General, targets of the same investigation. Five appointments. Five disastrous errors of judgement.

Solemnly, he moved on to the sixth, an unofficial appointment, yet also the most disastrous, for out of it had flowed the others. It was an appointment made years ago when he was an aspiring Texas Governor. Mentor some called it; others, Adviser, Friend. And the man so honored who, had he not died that morning, would've become a target of the same investigation as the others? Seth Harrington.

The victims' names were recited next, the last one most shocking of all. Chief Justice Rogers, not a drowning victim, but a murder victim. Murdered, not to conceal an ancient crime, but to advance the religious fantasies of a madman.

What a black day for the CMA, he lamented. For the victims and their families. For Mayson Corelli and Tyler Waddill, who'd spent the past weeks as fugitives. The innocent hunted by the guilty, not in pursuit of justice, but its shameful cover up. And finally, what a black day for a nation committed to truth, honor, and justice — ideals betrayed by this tragic experience. Indeed, was there a soul anywhere who had escaped the shadows of this abomination? He paused as his eyes began to fill.

Here it comes, Travis thought.

"At six p.m.," Longbridge resumed, "I will resign my office as President and relinquish my duties to Vice President Bentley, who was notified of my decision just before this broadcast. While expressing both shock and regret, the Vice President has nevertheless pledged his full commitment to the responsibilities I leave behind. I pray that you give him the same unwavering support you've given me. I only wish that I'd better met your expectations. I now humbly apologize, and thank you again for the privilege of serving as your President. God bless you."

In a respectful silence, the camera slipped out of the Oval Office. Matt switched off the TV. "I don't see anything noble about a good man taking the rap for so many rotten ones," he observed.

"But they're his rotten ones," Travis replied. "They were from the moment he endorsed them to the American people. Unwittingly or not, he staked his Presidency on their character. When they fell, how could he not fall also?

"But that's just the political explanation. For Longbridge, resignation was more an ethical decision than anything. He's lost confidence in his ability to lead and, being the man he is, couldn't ask of the American people something he no longer feels himself."

"What'll he do now?" Tyler asked.

"Enjoy life a lot more, I'm sure. His fondest reflections are of life on his Galveston ranch. I expect he'll return as soon as possible." Out the window, Duluth's gray sky had deepened. The afternoon was slipping away. "We should get to the airport. I expect that Guard crew is getting a little impatient. Will you be all right?"

Tyler nodded. "Go home, Travis."

Matt smiled. "Damn if that isn't just like you, to drag our asses up to this arctic wonderland, then boot us out after one lousy hour."

"Then stay, dickweed. Maybe we can arrange a medal ceremony

or dedicate a hospital wing in your honor."

He turned to Travis. "I think the ungrateful bastard actually wants us to leave. What do you think, Dad?"

"That I'd forgotten how annoying you two can be."

Tyler accompanied them out to the elevator. "Don't leave York until we return. I want you to meet Mayson. And I want to see Kelly and those two little farts. Is that clear?"

"As the Wisconsin ice," Matt said as the door closed.

Evening's shadows slipped into night. Gray Duluth became black Duluth. Sitting by the bed, he took comfort in the quiet darkness and his drifting thoughts, and when the thoughts finally slipped off, so did he.

Then the sheets rustled. Her urgent sigh broke the darkness. Instantly, he was over her, his fingers brushing her neck. "We made it, Mayson. Can you believe it?"

Not immediately. It took another minute of stroking fingers and soothing whispers for the message to sink in. They were safe. But how? "Where . . . are we?" she asked.

"Duluth Memorial." He summarized all that she'd missed, including the chest's recovery, the Guard's intervention, and Longbridge's resignation.

Bentley, President? Her head spun. Lamp and Harrington dead? The others, going to prison? *Madonna mia*, how could so much happen in one day?

He smiled. "You know what the most intriguing thing about all this is?" he asked. "We finally know how Lamp got those scars around his eye."

She envisioned a young Mary Sandover, clawing at Lamp's face in a desperate attempt to save her life. How horrible those last seconds must've been!

He detailed the chest's contents, including Lamp's bloodstained shirt, Falkingham's Dunhill butts, the financial records and Crenshaw's letter to his sister. "And me?" she asked. "Why am I here?"

"You've had surgery on your leg."

Surgery, yes. She remembered the terrible pain. Her fear of gangrene. But now she felt . . . nothing at all. "Tyler, my leg! I can't feel it!"

"Only because of an ungodly amount of morphine," he said, holding up the IV. "If you want, we can trade places for a while."

"That's not funny."

"The cast will come off in eight weeks. The time will fly."

"Oh sure! Just like the last eight weeks!"

"Maybe you'd rather they'd amputated the leg?"

Her petulance faded as the day's developments sunk in. Their ordeal was over. There'd be no more running, hiding, desperate escapes across the frigid wilderness, thundering choppers and chilling rides in monster trucks. Fear would no longer haunt every minute. But wouldn't the new hope that brought them together vanish, too? And what about the future? How was it to be shaped? They had to face those questions. But not now — she was much too tired.

As Mayson's eyes closed, Tyler smiled above her, his thoughts a refrain to the quiet darkness. *Sleep, he thought, as long as it takes to recover your beautiful spirit: stubborn, but fragile; impetuous, but gentle; and always passionate.*

Why did her soul run deeply with virtue when she'd found so little of it in her world? Where had she found her strong character? Was there no end to her contradictions? They all seemed to merge in him. Because in them, he found symmetry, harmony — a perfection that existed nowhere else. Which made him what? Perhaps the greatest contradiction of all. "Goodnight," he said, kissing her gently.

CHAPTER FORTY-TWO

★

Her fingers slipped idly through his hair as he slept hunched over the bed. Was it too much to hope that one day she, and not Kara, would bring richness to his life?

His dream moments ago — what had he meant? *Kara, it's too heavy...* What was too heavy?

His eyes soon opened to find her sitting against the pillows. "How do you feel?" he asked.

"Better." She watched him rise to stretch at the window. He'd showered, shaved, and managed a new outfit: gray sweater, white oxford and jeans. "Where'd you get the new duds?"

"Darcy, one of the staff administrators, bought them."

"Her job description includes buying your clothes?"

"When I can't go shopping myself," he said, retrieving two bags from the closet.

"What's in there?" she asked.

"Your new clothes. You didn't think I'd have her buy mine without getting yours, too, did you?" He emptied one bag on the bed: a navy sweater, white blouse, khakis, socks and loafers.

"Darcy's certainly thorough," she agreed, nodding at the khakis that were already split to accommodate her cast.

He removed lingerie and a red ski jacket from the second bag. Dazzled, she studied everything. He smiled. "I believe this is where an expression of gratitude is offered."

"Thank you."

"I was thinking more about a kiss . . . or several."

"But I thought you didn't like counting . . ." She stopped as he lifted her face for a kiss. As it ended, she sighed, "You know it's different now. We're no longer fugitives."

"Is that important?"

"I don't know." Her eyes caught his. "Is it?"

"I hate it when you do this."

"What?"

"Make up some obscure question and pretend I'm the only one

who can answer it."

"Well, you must admit it's different now."

"What's different?" He shrugged. "You're still the same pain in the ass you were before."

"I don't mean that. I mean we've returned to the world, where people have choices over their lives. Where Tyler no longer must spend his time protecting Mayson."

Arms folded, Tyler gazed out at gray, snow-leaden Duluth. "So are you saying I should leave?"

Didn't he realize she was trying to make this easier for him? How long would he stay now that the danger was over? Until her leg healed? Then what? A few obligatory calls for progress reports? Or would he fulfill his promises of Disney World and Redskins games?

"All I'm saying, Tyler, is that I can take care of myself now, which means you're free to do what you want and when you want, without worrying about me."

He watched her pick nervously at her gown. "I remember leaving the firm some evenings. I'd spot you eating supper through the glass of Giordani's, or dashing from that Chinese place with your takeout bag — always alone. And like everyone else, I found myself wondering, why does such a bright, beautiful woman eat alone, when any guy at the firm would jump at the chance to buy her dinner?"

"It was no mystery," she replied. "I didn't want dinner with any guy at the firm. Just one. But he never asked me."

"Would you have gone?"

"We'll never know, I guess. That woman no longer exists. But you obviously have your doubts. Why?"

"Because I sensed her pushing me away just now."

"That was me, reminding you that you're a free man."

"Mayson, what are you afraid of?"

"I'm not afraid of anything!" she yelled. What a lie; she was terrified.

"The Culpeppers stopped by yesterday. They saved our lives, and yet I haven't the slightest idea how to repay them."

She studied him pensively. "I've wrestled with the same question for a long time now."

"And what did you come up with?"

"That after saying thank you, there's really nothing left but to live your life in a way that proves you're grateful for the second chance."

They turned as Ginny breezed in. "I couldn't leave my shift without checking on our lovely patient here," she said to Mayson, sitting against the pillows. "Ummm, ummm! What a good night's sleep'll do."

Mayson smiled. "It's nice finally to meet the person who's taking such good care of me."

"Well now, that's our job. But it's still nice of you to say." Checking the IVs, she glanced at Tyler. "I thought you said she was tough. A real pussycat, this one."

"Will Dr. Claiborne be in this morning?" he asked.

"Already has. I guess she didn't want to wake you. Aggie said the leg looks great." Her eyes fell to the clothes spread across the bed. "What have we here?"

"Darcy bought them," Mayson said. "What do you think?"

"Well," she said as she peered at the labels, "they're better than that gown you're wearing."

"That's a safe answer," Tyler smiled.

"I think they're nice," Mayson nodded. "I just can't imagine when I'll be able to wear them."

"Oh, I'm sure Tyler will get you into them soon enough."

"I doubt that," she scoffed. "He's much more interested in getting me out of my clothes."

As Ginny laughed, Tyler felt compelled to add, "She's teasing, of course."

Plopping a thermometer into Mayson's mouth, Ginny lifted her wrist for a pulse reading. Mayson made a silly face over the inconvenience. Ginny laughed. And Tyler smiled, not in amusement but awe, as he tried to remember the woman with the cold, dark eyes, the beautiful but expressionless face, who spoke only out of necessity or irritation. Was she really gone?

"Ninety-nine." Ginny squinted at the thermometer. "Now, that's real progress. How about some breakfast?"

"Wonderful, I'm starving!"

The breakfast cart soon arrived, and a tray was placed before

Mayson. She sipped her juice and then attacked a poached egg. "Umm, delicious!"

"Delicious?" Tyler grimaced with disgust. "It looks awful."

"And you think grits are appetizing? So Ginny, tell me about your family. Are you married?"

"You better believe it," she nodded. "And don't think Tim Watson doesn't appreciate what a lucky man he is."

Mayson's questions continued, until the family picture was complete. In addition to husband Tim, there were two children, Tim, Jr. and Dottie, both married and living in Duluth, and seven grandchildren, with the eighth due in April. "Holidays are wild with that noisy herd," Ginny laughed.

"What does Tim do for a living?" Mayson asked.

"He's a foreman on the docks. It's hard work, but the pay's great."

"And did Tim, Jr. follow in his father's footsteps?"

"Heck no. Timmy's been dodging manual labor ever since he was born. He's a life insurance agent."

Tyler smiled. "I knew there must be a reason someone chose that line of work."

"And Dottie?" Mayson asked.

"Full-time housewife and mother." She glanced at Mayson's empty plate. "I declare, you get me going on my family, and I lose all track of time." Lifting the tray, she winked at Tyler. "Yep, you've got a real sweetie here."

"Have a great Christmas!" Mayson called as Ginny left.

Tyler studied her in awe. "That was some performance. If we weren't leaving, I expect you'd soon have every doctor, nurse and orderly eating out of your hand."

"Leaving?" Mayson frowned. "When?"

"Tomorrow. I've already cleared it with Dr. Claiborne."

"But not with me. I'm the one who just had surgery."

He'd assumed she would be thrilled. "You're leaving. It's settled."

"To the contrary. It's not settled, and I'm not leaving." She wasn't ready to deal with her new freedom and its limitless options. And until she was, the hospital was much safer than the frightening world beyond. "Tyler, I'm not your responsibility."

"No, you're my friend. And I thought I was yours."

Folding her arms, she retorted, "For the sake of argument, let's say I was crazy enough to leave tomorrow . . . who would provide my medical care?"

"Moss Sternfield, an orthopedic friend of mine."

"Have you talked to him about this? Maybe he doesn't want to treat me. And maybe I don't want him to."

"You'd rather spend Christmas in the hospital?"

"It's just three days away," she fretted. "People are already traveling. I bet you can't even get a flight."

"The flight won't be a problem."

"Then you've already made reservations?"

"Are you afraid my family won't like you – is that it?"

"Of course not. I just can't believe you made all these arrangements without consulting me."

"You've been indisposed. Have you forgotten?"

"I'm *still* indisposed, you dope! But if I wasn't, for the sake of argument, when would we leave?"

"I'm not sure."

"How can you not be sure? You just said you'd made flight reservations."

"I mean that our departure time depends on how long it takes to get to the airport. That's not a routine question, given that the media has laid siege to the hospital."

She stared at him, convinced that one of them was insane. "Flight times, Tyler, aren't determined on the basis of when the passengers are ready to leave. Are you saying that if the media ambushed us on the way to the airport tomorrow, the plane would simply wait until we arrived?"

"Well, Jock certainly wouldn't leave without us . . . It's the silverware thing, isn't it? Fork or spoon?"

"How many times do I have to say it: I'm not afraid . . . Jock? You know the pilot's name?"

"I'd be dumb as hell if I didn't."

"Why? I mean whoever knows their pilot's name? Next, I guess you'll tell me the plane has a name, too."

"If not the forks and spoons, then what? Your accent? The pedigree thing?"

"That's it. I'm not going!"

"Yes, you are. And the jet's name is the James River Eagle. Only we call it J.R. for short. Like the guy on Dallas, remember?"

Her head was swimming with the fragments of too many conversations. "Now what are you yammering about?"

"You asked the plane's name. Now, what are you afraid of?"

"Listen carefully, Tyler, because I'll say it just once. I'm not afraid of your silverware, my pedigree-less ancestry, my accent, your family, your dogs, or anything else."

"There's just one. Church."

"Stop doing that!" she shrieked.

"What?"

"Changing the subject every time I say something."

"You're the one who brought up my dog."

"You have a dog named Church?"

"A golden retriever. Schuyler and I used to take him hunting on Sunday mornings. Only Church liked chasing squirrels more than retrieving. Not that we gave him much to chase – a dove every now and then, an occasional buck. But we always had fun." He glowed with deep affection. "Damn, I miss that dog."

Yes, she could see that. She loved Church already. "How did he get his name?"

"Sunday mornings are when most people go to church, Hunter Leigh was forever reminding us. 'But go ahead and hunt,' she'd say. 'We'll pray for you at St. Vincent's. Maybe God will understand. And then again, maybe He won't.' I guess naming my dog Church was a way of letting her know she wouldn't dampen our fun." His eyes dimmed. "We haven't hunted much lately. I guess that's bothered Church. But I couldn't help losing that passion you need to crawl from the covers on a freezing November morning and shoot the first thing that moves."

"That passion," she asked. "Do you think you'll ever get it back?"

"I think I already have. Only Church is too old to go with me now. He turned thirteen in September. The squirrels would just laugh to see him creaking through the woods. I couldn't have him embarrassed that way. I love him too much."

And he loves you, she thought. *And so do I. Please Tyler, love me me back.*

"You'll meet Church tomorrow," he said now. "He has white whiskers. And his joints creak. But . . ."

It hit her suddenly. Not Church, but the other thing he was saying. "The J.R. Eagle is your family's plane. That's why we don't need reservations — and Jock's your pilot!"

"Amazing," he confirmed. "So with all that established, and your discharge cleared, that leaves only your fear standing between us and the morning flight." If it wasn't the silverware, the pedigree, the accent, or this foreign world, Castlewood, what was it? Did the subject of Kara still weigh heavily on her mind?

Expectantly, her eyes lifted, ready for his next word, his next expression. In that instant, the world became for him as clear as it had ever been.

CHAPTER FORTY-THREE

★

It wasn't easy, slipping away in broad daylight with the media watching. Yet it was managed nonetheless. At nine a.m., an ambulance left the ER. Minutes later, a second one left.

At 9:14, the first one pulled into the North Lakes Nursing Home, a routine stop. When the second arrived at 9:18, a blue Explorer crept up to conceal the patients, as they shed their hospital gowns and slipped in back. Then quietly it left, and a block later squealed off for the airport. At 9:58, the J. R. Eagle hit the runway and climbed quickly into the southern sky. Inside the plush cabin, Mayson slept against Tyler's shoulder. His own eyes closed as he thought to himself, *a brilliant plan, Darcy. Thank you.*

Tyler didn't wake until the Eagle's first thump, as its claws flexed for landing. Out the window, he saw the sparkling James, the sprawling shipyard to the east, and finally — after weeks of absence — the blessed sun filtering through the clouds.

Mayson's eyes opened with the Eagle's next thump. "Tyler, I'm scared."

"You're beautiful," he smiled.

"I'm serious."

"So am I. And there's no reason to be afraid."

"Don't say that when my heart's pounding in my ears."

He studied her with growing frustration. Makeup highlighted her exquisite facial angles, mascara enhancing her thickly lashed eyes, widened now by an unreasonable fright. In the last day, she'd made friends of Nurse Ginny, Dr. Claiborne, Darcy Norton and taciturn Jock Barnes. Was there any doubt she'd soon forge a much deeper relationship with the Waddill clan? Why couldn't she understand that?

With a final shudder, the Eagle landed and glided towards the hangar. "Listen," he said, brushing back her hair. "For the last time: there's nothing to fear."

"Right! I'm sure they won't even notice my accent."

"A dozen noisy Virginians will drown it out. Now relax."

"Relax!" she worried. "How can I possibly relax? You haven't even told me what to call your family?"

"In Virginia, it's customary to address people by their names."

She was about to blister him in Italian, when tall, rugged Jock Barnes appeared in the cabin doorway. "I'm sorry, ma'am, if I shook you up. Conditions were a bit rough this morning."

"It wasn't bad, Jock. In fact, I didn't even notice."

"That's because you were asleep," Tyler said.

"That accent," Jock said, squinting. "Brooklyn?"

Anxiously, she nodded. "Too sharp?"

"Shucks no, ma'am. Here, let me give you a hand."

As they disembarked, she found the limo parked near the hangar, and the two men standing out front. "Dad's the white guy," said Tyler, taking her arm.

Her breath left her now, as she thumped along beside him. She wanted it all, yet not even a slice was promised. Neither Tyler's words nor his actions assured her of anything more than a nice long rest. Would she stay a week? A month? And as what? Friend, lover or co-author of a book describing their misadventure?

Davis, the chauffeur, reached her first, his broad face grinning and large hand extended. "Welcome to Virginia, Mayson. Real pleased to meet you."

Schuyler came next, with a big bear hug — one that Mayson gamely returned. His tall, lean body was Tyler's, just like his angular jaw that, in the human equation, translated into handsome. His blond, white-streaked hair, if longer, would also form Tyler's windswept tangles. His eyes, a paler blue, hinted at some deep emotion she couldn't fathom. "Mayson," they said, brightening. "Let's go home."

"Schuyler, would you look at this?" Davis held up their small travel bag. "Gone two months, and this is all they have to show for it?"

As Tyler helped her into the limo, she whispered, "Did you hear that? Mr. Davis called your father 'Schuyler.' "

"Not Mr. Davis — Davis Thadley. And my father's Schuyler Waddill. Names. That quirky Virginia custom, remember?"

The next minutes brought further understanding as they left

the airport and started east along the Peninsula. The front glass down, she listened to the light chatter and easy laughter, as driver and passenger moved from current events to local gossip. Davis wasn't a chauffeur, Schuyler, not an employer. They were simply friends, and one happened to be very rich.

As they crept between the lights on Warwick Boulevard, she saw Tyler and the Old Dame's mopper in Schuyler and Davis. Tyler, and the blind girl who operated the newsstand. Tyler and whoever happened to be in his path — rich or poor, worldly or illiterate. For him and his father, people were just people. There were no classes, just good ones and pains in the asses. Yet even though she'd come to know him so well, there remained a sacred piece still locked away —Kara, this woman she didn't know, yet to whom her fate seemed oddly bound.

She slipped from her reflections as they started across the James River, the jagged coastline emerging in the window. Towering steel beams and enormous ships dominated the eastern horizon for miles. "Is that . . .?"

"Waddill Shipbuilding," Tyler nodded.

"The entire coastline?"

Schuyler stretched his arm across the seat. "Mayson," he said, "you need an awful lot of space to build those giant carriers the Navy likes so much and to repair those fatboy tankers that keep the oil moving." He smiled at her awestruck eyes. "I'd love to give you a tour, once you're off those darn crutches."

"That would be wonderful," she answered. But would she be here that long? Tyler's pensive eyes didn't hold the answer. They'd been fixed on the window ever since leaving the airport.

Crossing the bridge, they continued north. Soon, the traffic thinned and civilization faded away. Turning into a private lane, it seemed like they'd left the world entirely. The sun slipped behind the tall oaks, then returned with the next meadow. The James had vanished, yet its soothing presence remained on her shoulders. Wherever the trip ended, she sensed it would be waiting like a loving mother.

They were gliding into the bosom of a pastoral paradise that existed only in fairytales. Where kings and queens held court and handsome princes kissed beautiful princesses. "I understand now why it's called Castlewood. It's so beautiful!" she marveled.

"Wait until you see the house," Davis said.

"Does it look like a castle?"

"Eighteen bedrooms," he said. "I'd say that qualifies, wouldn't you?"

Eighteen bedrooms — *Madonna mia!*

"Now, now," Schuyler said. "Mayson, you have to understand that Davis tends to exaggerate. If you're not careful, he'll have you believing we're the Rockefellers of the South. And there're only sixteen bedrooms."

"I exaggerate?" Davis huffed. "Who brags his golf handicap is ten when anyone at the Club will tell you it's sixteen?"

"It was ten at one time," he insisted with a smile. "Anyway, Josie, the pretty little gal who runs Castlewood with her Mama, has fixed up one of those bedrooms especially for you, Mayson. I hope you'll be comfortable."

"I'm sure I will be, thank you."

"Do you play golf?" he asked.

"No sir," she replied, amazed he'd ask such a question. He was so warm and unassuming.

"Would you like to learn?" Davis asked. "After the cast comes off. We can teach her, can't we, Schuyler?"

"We'll have to. It's for sure, Tyler won't. You can't get him anywhere near a golf course. How about it, Mayson?"

"That would be great!"

They soon encountered three young equestriennes crossing the lush meadow on their handsome steeds. When Davis honked, they waved. "Who are they?" she asked.

"The Randolphs," Schuyler replied. "Our families have lived side by side for more generations than I can count. The Culpeppers did, too, until Travis and Betsy got uppity and bought that fancy place over in York. Blair Randolph is Tyler's godmother; Austin, his godfather. And Hunter Leigh and I are godparents . . .well, we were," his voice dropped into a canyon.

"Godparents to one of the Randolph children?" she asked.

"That's right. And those little girls are their grandchildren."

"Wow!" Tyler suddenly came out of his shell. "I'd forgotten how rich the colors are. The trees, the grass, the sky — everything seems so much brighter."

Schuyler's eyes filled as he studied his son. "I know exactly what you mean," he agreed.

Then please explain it to me, Mayson wanted to scream.

As they reached the brick-column entrance, she read its simple brass plate: Castlewood. Enraptured, she scooped up every detail as they glided up the evergreen-rimmed lane. She was entering a dream world, and wanted to remember it all later.

The enormous colonial mansion soon loomed above the trees, its white-pillared portico and latticed windows dressed in garlands of holly and spruce. *"Madonna mia!"* she gasped. "It really is a castle!"

As they crested the knoll, people flowed joyously into the drive, an ancient golden retriever creaking along the edge of the chaos.

"Just be yourself, and the rest will take care of itself," Tyler said as he kissed her and the welcome party converged on the limo. "It'll all make sense, I promise."

Would it explain his mysterious silence on the drive, and Schuyler's misty eyes?

Helping her out, Tyler vanished into the crowd of family. Quickly, she was scooped up and hugged. It was a warm, smothering introduction, and if she didn't yet know a single person, she now knew them all. She knew Castlewood as the safe, happy place of dreams and the handsome prince who dwelled here, as a promise — only not hers. She wasn't part of this world and never would be. She knew this just as she'd known the magnificent James would be waiting at the journey's end.

"It's breathtaking, isn't it?"

She turned to find Tyler's mother gazing at the placid river. "I lost sight of it when we crossed the bridge, but never the sense that it was close, as if it was following us," Mayson answered.

"That's because it was," Hunter Leigh laughed. "Once you turn off the highway, it runs with the lane, right up here to the house." Her soft, blue eyes gleamed. "I've lived on its banks my entire life, and yet its beauty still grabs me. I hope it always will."

"I hope so, too," Mayson said. Already she was drawn to Hunter Leigh's warmth and sincerity.

"Mayson, I love your accent." Stafford appeared now, a female version of Tyler, with the same gold hair, precise features and river-blue eyes.

"I was afraid you might need ear muffs."

"Your accent's rather refreshing, like spice on grits," Hunter Leigh smiled.

"Mayson, do you eat grits?" Stafford asked.

"Once, when Tyler ordered them at a business breakfast. I thought they were terrible."

"At last! Another soul with my tastebuds."

"Grits were a morning requirement when Lavinia was here," Hunter Leigh explained. "And she made the best I've ever tasted. She was a wonderful cook. A wonderful person."

"Then she died?"

"Three years ago," Hunter Leigh nodded.

"When Tiles and I were growing up," Stafford said, "'Lavinny wouldn't let us up from the breakfast table until we'd finished our grits. But the instant she turned her back, I'd dump mine in his bowl."

The others strolled into view along the riverbank. Church crept faithfully behind Tyler, impervious to the noisy children around him. "My son never strays far from the water," Hunter Leigh smiled. "And old Church, never too far from him."

"He wants to start hunting again," Mayson revealed.

"I knew it!" Stafford beamed.

What? That Tyler had a sudden urge to stalk prey?

"That sparkle in his eyes," Hunter Leigh sighed. "Then you noticed it, too? I was afraid to say anything." Her eyes watered as she followed her son across the bank. "I haven't seen such a spring in his step for so long — his tenth birthday, do you remember?"

"The Sunfish," Stafford agreed.

"He was too young for it, Mayson. But he could swim like a fish. And he was cautious around water."

"Cautious with his precious cargo," Stafford laughed. "And as I recall, the Sunfish was a joint birthday present, anyway."

Hunter Leigh nodded. "Born hours apart, they practically breathed the same air from the moment they left the hospital.

'Little shadows,' Travis called them . . . Oh Good Lord!" she burst as Tyler scooped Church up and began dancing across the riverbank. "I haven't seen that silly doggie trot in years!"

"Tiles gets him so dizzy!" Stafford laughed.

Tyler and his father soon fell behind the others to solemnly confer. The conversation ended with their embrace, and Tyler's deep grin. Mayson had never seen him so happy. If only she could be part of it!

"Would someone please tell me what that was all about?" Hunter Leigh asked, then noticed the sudden cloud over Mayson's eyes. "Here we are rambling on, and I bet you're dying to get off those crutches. It's too cold to be on this riverbank, anyway. Let's go inside."

They entered the side hall, where the air was warm and cinnamon-laced, and alive with Christmas music. Slipping into the kitchen to arrange for pecan pie and coffee, Hunter Leigh returned to lead them down to the study. Mayson's first glimpse of the giant Christmas tree with its glittering lights and ornaments took her breath away. "A holiday beacon they say can be seen for miles on the river," Stafford explained.

In awe, Mayson's gaze drifted over the extravagant piles of presents, holiday bric-a-brac, pine-laced windows and stone hearth, where a cozy fire flickered. Inspecting the presents, she was astonished to find her name on several. "I'm sorry I don't have any for you," she confessed.

"You've given us far more than we could've hoped for," Hunter Leigh said, glowing.

She had? How? By tagging along with Tyler to Castlewood? Like a magnet, her eyes returned to the giant tree. Never had she seen so many ornaments — sparkling balls . . . gleaming gold and silver charms . . . embroidered hand-carved figurines.

"You'll find every Barnum and Bailey animal brought to Norfolk," Hunter Leigh explained. "Tyler adored the circus."

Especially the clowns. She noted their absence, and knew at least one present she would've given him, had there been time.

She studied the footballs next, each one inscribed with a team and year. "And this?" she lifted a gold charm. "His first car?"

"Second," Hunter Leigh replied.

"Here's the first." Stafford held up another. "An XKE. Matt Culpepper got a Corvette the same Christmas. They used to race on some now infamous country road."

"Fortunately, they grew out of it," Hunter Leigh sighed.

"Grew out of it?" Stafford laughed. "Tiles totaled the XKE in one of those hellacious Saturday night races. Poor Kara didn't know if he'd crawl from the crumpled metal or have to be cut out."

"After a rather tense summer," Hunter Leigh added, "Schuyler convinced himself that our son's racing days were over, and sent him off to college with a new car and some firm fatherly advice."

Mayson's attention was drawn to the gold figurine of a girl playing the piano. Kara. She didn't need to read the inscription to know what it said.

Hunter Leigh saw her suddenly tear-filled eyes, "Are you all right, dear?" she asked.

She nodded. "A little tired, I guess."

"Good Lord, I'd almost forgotten your surgery! How about a nap? You must be exhausted."

Dead was more like it. Tyler's apartment had been a shrine to Kara. She'd been his childhood friend, lover, everything – and always would be. The revelation settled over her now like a black cloud.

"That nap sounds good," she said, as her fingers slipped off the piano figurine. Would he check on her? They were no longer fugitives. This was Castlewood, where the old rules didn't apply and the new ones were yet to be established.

Stafford studied her strangely. "Tiles did tell you about Kara Randolph, didn't he?"

"Of course," Mayson replied. Masking her disappointment, she recited everything she remembered from Schuyler's commentary. "He also told me the Randolph estate adjoins Castlewood and that your families are very close, which makes it only natural that he and Kara would be, too." She turned to Hunter Leigh, "You and Schuyler are Kara's godparents. And the Randolphs are Tyler's, right?"

Hunter Leigh nodded, ready to dispense with the sudden stress choking the air. "I'm sorry Tyler bored you with all that family history. Come on, we'll show you to your room."

She led them down to a suite on the mansion's west corner.

"I'm sure I'll be quite comfortable," Mayson said as she peered inside at the bright, handsome furnishings.

"Nap as long as you like," Hunter Leigh said. "Supper isn't for awhile."

"You'll tell Tyler I'm resting?"

"Of course, dear."

As they left, she caught Hunter Leigh's fading voice. "Audrey Hepburn, yes — I knew it was an actress."

Leaning on her crutches, Mayson gazed out at Castlewood's manicured grounds, boxwood-lined walks , latticed gardens, the lush meadow and the forest beyond. It was like a beautifully painted landscape in a Manhattan gallery.

Enraptured, her eyes settled on the ancient oak rising above the knoll. A tree house was tucked into its sprawling branches looking, she imagined, just as it had when Tyler had first climbed inside. Holding this image, she drifted off, then was quickly jerked back, finding a pretty, ebony face poking through the door.

"I wanted to make sure you had everything you needed," Josie explained.

"Yes, thank you. Have you seen Tyler?"

"Hunter Leigh told him you were napping, so he just grabbed a wreath off the window and left. But don't worry," she smiled. "He'll be back for supper."

A wreath? "Do you know where he went?"

"Same place he always goes. Randolph Estates, to pay his respects to Kara."

Pay his respects. What an odd way to describe groveling after a woman. "I guess you know Kara broke his heart."

Josie shrugged. "That's one way of putting it, I guess. Only she didn't mean to."

How could a person break another's heart without meaning to? She watched Josie slip out. Wistfully, her gaze returned to the tree house in the ancient oak. Love him, Kara. He deserves it so much. She was too tired to fight any longer.

Instead, she prayed, *Lord, I've worked so hard to do what's right, and not become a burden. I don't want to start now. I just want to rest and be warm. I've been so cold.* Was He listening? Faithfully, she continued, *I love him so much, Lord. I want to take care of him and have him take care of me. To know, as my eyes close at night, that he'll be there when they open again in the morning. I want to share my life with him, and share his. The good and . . .* She turned at the creaking door.

"I knocked, but I guess you didn't hear." It was Stafford. "Mayson, has anyone ever told you that you look like Audrey Hepburn?"

"A few people," she answered. Stafford and her brother were so much alike — easy, warm, likeable. "You and Tyler have the same smile, the same sparkle in your eyes." Stafford wore solemn expressions like stiff Sunday dresses — only when required. After that, she slipped back into her smile like it was a pair of comfortable sneakers.

"Tiles's sparkle disappeared for a long time," Stafford said. "But it's back now. I saw it the instant he arrived . . . Mayson, when you said Tiles had told you about Kara, I thought, 'Well, if he's ever confided in anyone, it's only natural it would be you.' He's always been so private about her, treating her like a precious, yet fragile piece of himself that might break in someone else's hands."

"A piece of him did break," Mayson said. "Kara — this one you call precious and fragile – broke his heart into so many pieces that it can't be fixed. And the reason he doesn't share her is because of the enormous pain he still feels. Tyler isn't one to burden others with his suffering. He'd much rather help people with their problems and forget his own."

Stafford realized now she'd had it backwards. After weeks together, Mayson knew everything about Tiles except Kara. Mayson was the one person capable of forcing him to finally lay Kara to rest. "You obviously understand my brother very well," Stafford said.

"At this point, he's all I understand," Mayson sighed. "Everyone else here has me spinning like a top."

Indeed, Stafford studied her doe-like eyes; they were intense, but uncomprehending. "Mayson, do you love my brother?"

She was surprised by the blunt question. What could be less

relevant than her feelings for Tyler? Then why not confess them?

"At first, I did my best to deny my feelings, terrified of believing anyone like him really existed. Life had taught me many bitter lessons. And yet my heart was prepared to challenge each one."

"What kind of lessons?" Stafford asked.

"That peace doesn't exist. That people can't be trusted. But can he? And how am I to know?"

"And what did you discover?"

"That Tyler can be trusted not just with the truth, but with my very life. I can place it in his hands, and I know he'll protect it. When the door closes behind him, I know it'll open again. I've discovered all this in each moment I've spent with him. Time merely deepens my trust."

"And does all this translate into love?"

"Far more than I could ever explain."

"Try," Stafford coaxed, confident she'd do a splendid job.

"Love is so elusive," Mayson began, her eyes drifting to the window. "Yet, when you find it like that rare flower in the forest, and the petals unfold, so does its mystery. In one miraculous moment, you understand everything."

"What, Mayson?"

"That peace in this violent world is attainable, that anger and fear are curable conditions. That happiness isn't a fool's fantasy, but something within reach. Even more amazing, that a person is happiest when caring most about another's happiness. And if I was convinced that Kara could provide it, I'd choke on my disappointment and walk away. Please, Stafford," her begged. "Tell me what's going on."

"It's time someone did. Come on, let's go for a drive."

Rising on her crutches, Mayson followed her out. Hunter Leigh met them in the side hall. "Where are you two going?"

Stafford dug into her handbag for the keys. "We've decided Mayson needs fresh air more than a nap."

"More confused than tired?" Hunter Leigh asked.

"Never more," Mayson nodded. Slipping into her jacket, she followed Stafford out to the drive, where they encountered Schuyler, Parker, the children and Church resting nearby. Her stomach knotted at their lack of curiosity, as Stafford announced their plans. Did they already know about this drive?

Schuyler stopped them as they reached the Pathfinder. "Travis called to say GNN has reported another suicide. Leopold. Does that name ring a bell, Mayson?"

Not a bell, a nightmare, she thought, envisioning the dark giant. They'd stumbled upon Leopold at the grocery store. Tyler had escaped, but could've just as easily been caught. There'd been so many moments like that — so many grocery stores, trucks, cold, dreary places that she just wanted to forget.

"The police found him in a Chicago motel with a bullet in his head," Schuyler explained. "He left a note apologizing for his crimes, the worst being his association with Harrington."

He sensed her reluctance, like Tyler's, to discuss the last weeks, which was fine by him. The story could come out in its own time. What mattered was that Tyler and Mayson were here. She was the piece missing these last six years. He knew by the air's new buzz and the sky's brightness on a chilling, gray afternoon. He knew because Castlewood had suddenly returned to life. "What are you doing?" he asked as he watched Stafford help Church into the Pathfinder.

"He's never been on this drive either," she replied. "If a mystery's to be solved, I don't see why he can't be included."

Nor did he. "Just be back for supper."

Kissing Parker good-bye, Stafford started down the drive. "Mayson, you must understand that when Tiles and Kara opened their eyes to this world, the first thing they saw was each other. Not by design, but because their mothers, who happened to be best friends, had gotten pregnant at the same time. They were born in the same delivery room, just hours apart.

"After that, they were together whenever Blair and Hunter Leigh were — which was constantly in those days. They shared baby bottles, toys, everything . . . They shared life," she turned solemnly. "That's what I'm trying to explain."

Crossing the first bridge, she continued, "Not long after they were born, our parents began taking vacations together. Consequently, whatever the discovery — the beach, Disney World — Tiles and Kara made it together. Not surprisingly, they took their first steps and spoke their first words within hours of each other. They smiled, laughed — even breathed in chorus. No one ever told them it wasn't supposed to be that way.

"Hunter Leigh and Blair thought it so cute to come home from parties and find them curled up asleep on the nursery floor, their toys scattered around them. They predicted that one day their babies would get married and eternally bond the two families. Schuyler and Austin swore, however, that they'd eventually grow sick of each other."

Mayson braced as they bounced over another bridge. The sun had been lost in the deepening afternoon. Nor had they seen the first car. Where were they going, besides farther away from civilization?

"The tree house was either a blessing or a curse," Stafford said. "Whichever, after its inaugural climb, no one questioned again the permanency of their bond. If life's a journey, they decided at six years old to take it together . . . And they did." Her eyes filled with tears.

"Until Kara broke his heart, you mean."

"No, Mayson, Kara didn't break his heart. Just be patient. We're almost there."

"Where?"

"I'm getting to that. Anyway, the tree house wasn't really a curse. It's a dream come true for most six-year-olds, right? And they graced it with their childhood years. It really defined them, I think, because all that they became in life was conceived there – Tiles's football, Kara's piano."

Stafford smiled. "Blair would say Kara couldn't eat the day of an academy football game — butterflies. You'd have thought she, not Tiles, was the team's quarterback. And because she'd memorized the game plan, it was difficult to believe that she wasn't. She loved football because Tiles did, and because they were so tightly bonded, she never truly grasped that they were different people.

"And it was the same for him. He had no appreciation for music. He refused to take piano lessons and laughed at every boy who did. Yet when Kara took an interest, the piano suddenly became the greatest thing since sliced bread." She smiled once more. "If I told you he got stage fright just sitting in the front row at Kara's recitals, would you believe me?"

They turned into a private lane, like Castlewood, featuring a handsome column entrance. Randolph Estates. Mayson's stomach lurched at the plate's inscription. The stone mansion rose above the trees. Kara's house! But just before reaching it, they turned onto another lane that burrowed deeper into the forest.

"Kara was many things to Tiles, but one thing very special," Stafford said. "It was the foundation upon which their relationship was built. Sadly, it's also what has made her absence so painful. Kara was Tiles's best friend. The greatest compliment he could give anyone."

Parking behind a black Range Rover, she watched Mayson's eyes flit nervously over the landscape. "So how about it? Is there finally a successor to Kara's title?"

So what if she was Tyler's best friend? Now that he was home, wouldn't he try to put the crown back on Kara's head? "Is that his?" she asked, nodding at the Range Rover.

"Yes," Stafford answered. She slipped out to help Church down. The old dog seemed to shed half his years as he trotted crisply into the woods. "Come on," she coaxed Mayson.

Her stomach turned again. Did she have a choice? Crawling out, she thumped after them. "Is Kara here, too?"

"In a manner of speaking."

She had no time to ponder this mystery, as Stafford started into the woods, Church creaking behind. The gravel path presented her with difficulty on her crutches. Stafford stopped to play with Church until she caught up. "Is this a private park?" she asked Stafford.

"Just follow me, all right?" As Mayson glanced at an equally clueless Church, Stafford started off again. "Obviously, I'm telling you all this for a reason – specifically, so that you'll understand everything when we arrive. Tiles, if he'd been thinking clearly, would've explained it before."

"He and Kara were in love. Then Kara broke his heart. What else is there to understand?"

"Quite a lot, I'd say. Tiles, if I understand correctly, wasn't initially involved in the murder case, but plunged into it voluntarily to rescue you. Why, Mayson? Certainly you've asked yourself the same question?"

Indeed. "He knew I'd been wrongly accused, and was much too noble to stand by as my life was destroyed," replied Mayson.

"So noble that he abandoned his own life just to help you?"

"He hated New York and was leaving anyway."

"And going where?" Stafford frowned. "Florida, Tennessee . . . Wisconsin?"

"All right!" she snapped. "I get your point!"

"No Mayson, I don't think you do."

"*Madonna mia*, Stafford. He still dreams of Kara."

"And when he does, who's beside him?"

"Me — as if he had a choice."

"My point exactly. Before Wisconsin, Tennessee and Naples . . . before getting himself into the murder case, he did have a choice. You, Mayson. You were his choice."

The trees now surrendered to gray sky as they reached the end of the path. Would they be stumbling upon the starry-eyed lovers? Mayson's heart out-thumped her crutches.

"Travis used to say Tiles and Kara never left each other's shadow," Stafford said. "The day they did, he said, the sun would burn up the earth and we'd all die. Obviously, it didn't happen that way." A branch in her fingers, she held Mayson mysteriously. "Kara was being taken away, without choice or consideration of her feelings. She must've been terrified, and yet her greatest fear was how Tiles would be affected. Her love was unselfish, without conditions, just as his was for her. It was one that could've endured an eternity, and yet it ended so quickly, without reason — just deep pain."

"That pain still exists," Mayson replied. "And if it's without reason, it's not without an explanation. One which you and everyone else, seem to forget. Kara abandoned Tyler, which proves to me, at least, that she didn't care."

"Oh, Mayson, you're so very wrong," Stafford said, shaking her head. "Kara couldn't have cared more. And she didn't abandon Tiles. Given a choice, she wouldn't have gone anywhere."

"Well, she's certainly had a choice at some point in the last six years. But she hasn't returned . . . or has she?"

As Church groaned impatiently, Stafford fluffed his coat.

"Hold on, boy, just a second," she said to the dog. "Mayson, it's as impossible for Kara to return as it was for her to stay."

"Impossible?" Mayson huffed. "Where is she? Paris? Tahiti? Or some other remote corner of the earth, where planes don't fly and phones don't exist?"

Stafford smiled at her delicate hands, clenching the crutches, as an angry tremble worked through her. Whatever the emotion, Mayson never failed to express it passionately. "I can see that you and Kara are entirely different creatures, yet your love for my brother is the same."

"No Stafford, I love him far more. Only he loves her and he always will. I can't change that. And if you brought me here to prove it, you've succeeded."

"I didn't bring you here to prove anything, Mayson. I just wanted you to understand that Kara never wanted anything more than my brother's happiness. In spite of what happened six years ago, Tiles was always her first concern. To know what she was facing, and yet to place his welfare above everything else — there could be no greater proof of her love than that."

"And what does her absence prove? Don't smother me with her attributes or offer excuses for her behavior. I'm sick of them. Just tell me where she is."

Calmly, Stafford pulled the branch back to permit a full view of the cemetery. "Over there."

"Oh . . .!" Mayson's breath left her as she found Tyler standing over a grave, the wreath he'd brought resting against the gray headstone. *Madonna mia!* How long had he been standing there, so still, his solemn eyes fixed on Kara's grave? Oh, *amore mio*, why didn't you tell me?

Tired of waiting, Church began the slow journey across the cemetery. Stafford cried as she recalled how he'd once run after Tiles and chased squirrels through the woods. And how Kara had been waiting when they returned.

"You'll get just one more lesson from me," she said as she turned to a speechless Mayson. "But take it to heart. No one would be more at peace now than Kara to know that for the first time since she's been gone, Tiles is happy. Only you could bring him back, Mayson. We knew it the instant he got out of the car.

That sparkle had returned to his eyes. And his smile . . ." Her face cracked and tears spilled as she embraced Mayson. "Thank you. Thank you for bringing my brother home."

Across the cemetery, Church reached Tyler, and sensing the solemn moment, dropped respectfully on his hindquarters to study the grave. A few seconds later, Tyler saw him. Turning, his eyes connected with Mayson's.

Starting across the cemetery, she thumped faster as she drew near. Reaching him, the crutches fell away as she threw herself into his arms. Church barked joyfully at their feet.

"Atta boy! You tell 'em!" Stafford laughed tearfully as she started back through the woods.

"I should've told you before," Tyler sighed.

"Yes, you should have," Mayson agreed.

"I've had this dream recently. I was lugging a jar up the beach, but it was too heavy, so I yelled at Kara to say I couldn't carry it any further. She said I should turn back. I got mad and told her to take it. But she wouldn't – until that night in the hospital. She took it, and then I understood."

"Understood what?"

"That I'd finally escaped that place between life and death. Lauren told me before I left New York that I was in love. I said she was crazy, but I realize now she was right. I must've been from the beginning."

She had the sense of floating suddenly. "The beginning?"

"That Monday morning in the library, when Lamp reported Morris's murder. Our eyes connected, and yours revealed the first emotion I'd ever seen – fear, so genuine that it shook me. Whether or not you realized it, you were reaching out. And I just needed that first glimmer of humanity. Only I was too stubborn to admit it. Then when I did, I felt guilty, as if I was betraying Kara."

A deep sadness filled Mayson's eyes. "Tyler, I'm so sorry for those terrible things I said. Kara was obviously a wonderful person. She loved you very much."

"I loved her just as much," he said. "So much, that when she died, I couldn't let go. I knew I'd never feel the same, something that time just seemed to confirm. It was pretty awful for a while, but then I realized . . ."

"What Tyler?"

Pushing back emotion, he said, "That I wasn't saving you, but myself. I realized that running for my life was nothing compared to running from my pain. With you I had direction, and after six years I knew I'd finally made it home."

"To Castlewood, you mean?"

"No, Mayson, to you. You're my home. I'm saying that I love you, and I want to spend the rest of my life with you. Will you marry me?"

Her mouth fell open, fresh tears glistening in her eyes, as she struggled to absorb this miracle.

Grabbing his handkerchief, he dabbed her cheeks. "I swear, you cry at the blink of an eye. So do I get an answer or not?"

She nodded tearfully. "Of course I'll marry you, Tyler."

"Mayson, I don't want you to cry anymore," he said, taking her back into his arms. "I want you to sing."

She was — more joyfully than she'd ever dreamed possible. If only Rosa were alive to celebrate this moment. "Tyler, I love you so much!" she said.

"I was thinking about tomorrow," he said, as his chin dropped in her hair. "It'd be nice to sleep in the same bed on Christmas Eve. I know it's awful to admit, but I miss your toes digging into my legs."

"Tomorrow's fine, if you're sure today's definitely out."

"I doubt Schuyler can get Reverend Motley out to Castlewood this evening."

"You told him on the riverbank, didn't you?" she asked.

"Just that I planned to ask. I wasn't crazy enough to predict your answer."

"Why not?" She stroked his jaw with a well-worn intimacy. "You knew it'd be Yes."

"Like hell. Must you always mess with my face that way?"

"Surely Kara had at least one silly habit?"

"Well," he smiled, "she did occasionally play piggly wiggly with my fingers. And she collected colored glass, the kind that washes up in the surf. She'd comb the beach for hours, scooping up every piece she could find."

"Tyler, I'll do everything in my power to make you happy. But there's one thing I can't do — I can't be Kara."

"I don't want you to be. Kara's finally what she should've been six years ago — a precious memory . . . Hey," he grinned suddenly. "The Super Bowl's next month! Want to go?

"The Redskins won't be in it."

"Neither will the Giants."

She marveled at his deep smile. She'd never seen him so happy. "Tyler, I'll never let you down."

"Just be happy, Mayson, that's all I want."

"I couldn't be happier than I am now."

They started back across the cemetery, she thumping, Church creaking, and he, the anchor in the middle. "I have some Christmas shopping to do," he said. "Would you like to go to the mall? We can get you one of those motorized wheelchairs."

"Sure." Her eyes lifted seductively. "I guess this means we finally get to do it, huh?"

"Then you're offering more than apples and buns?"

"I have been since Tennessee."

"We should call the Adkins and wish them a Merry Christmas."

"Not until after we do it."

"I knew it'd be coming soon," he said, wincing.

"What?"

"Your first order."

"Want my second?" She nodded at Church, creeping beside them. "Get him a little brother."

"I'd planned to. Church can keep you company while Schuyler and I take the pup over to Gobblepatch."

"What in the world is Gobblepatch?"

"Where we hunt." He sighed. "I can't wait to get back in the woods. You should see the new hunting jacket I got Schuyler."

"Is it nice?"

"Oh, yeah . . ."

★

The New York Times, Coke, American Express, Visa, Exxon, Diners Club, Leave It To Beaver, Andy Griffith, Deputy Barney, Sheriff Andy, Ford Taurus, Big Mac, Juicy Fruit, The Great Escape, Larry King Live, Oprah, Honda Prelude, Cadillac, Lincoln Town Car, Ford Explorer, Ford Escort, Forrest Gump, Snickers, Volvo, Disney World, The Sound of Music, Mary Poppins, Molson, War and Peace, Gone With the Wind, Non Dimenticar, L'Air du Temps, iPod, Rhett Butler, Porsche 911, Fritos, Jeep, Indy, Jawbreakers, Jordan Almonds, My Fair Lady, The Good, the Bad and the Ugly, Butch Cassidy and the Sundance Kid, Bullitt, Super Bowl, Washington Redskins, Dallas Cowboys, Barnum and Bailey Circus, Father Knows Best, Volkswagen Beetle, Castor Oil, Ford Pinto, Robes of Vengeance, Jack Daniels, Kirby, The Beverly Hillbillies, Granny, Dunhill, The Three Stooges, Perry Mason, Gilligan's Island, Ozzie and Harriet, Ford Mustang, Nova, VW Beetle, Chevy Cavalier, Suzuki Trooper, Saltine, Emetrol, Bacardi, Jantzen, Heckle and Jeckle, Nikon, Chatty Cathy, Old Spice, Dallas, Mercedes-Benz, Gucci, and Range Rover are all trademarks, registered or unregistered, of their respective trademark holders.

★